D0640878

100
Menacing Little
MURDER
STORIES

100
Menacing Little
MURDER
STORIES

SELECTED BY
Robert Weinberg,
Stefan Dziemianowicz,
& Martin H. Greenberg

BARNES
&NOBLE
BOOKS
NEW YORK

Copyright © 1998 by Robert Weinberg,
Stefan Dziemianowicz, and Tekno-Books

The acknowledgments appearing on pages 591-96 constitute
an extension of this copyright page.

This edition published by Barnes & Noble, Inc.,
by arrangement with Tekno-Books.

All rights reserved. No part of this book may be used or
reproduced in any manner whatsoever without the written
permission of the Publisher.

1998 Barnes & Noble Books

Text design by Sabrina Bowers

ISBN 0-7607-0854-1

Printed and bound in the United States of America

98 99 00 01 02 03 M 9 8 7 6 5 4 3 2 1

BVG

Table of Contents

Introduction

MURDER, which is a frustration of the individual, and hence a frustration of the race, may have, and in fact has, a good deal of sociological implication. But it has been going on too long for it to be news." When Raymond Chandler made this observation in his famous essay "The Simple Art of Murder," he was being perhaps too dismissive of his subject. The popularity of his own tales of private detective Philip Marlowe, and the tradition of crime fiction they helped to shape, are eloquent testimony to our abiding fascination with murder and murderers.

The murder story is one of the most enduring genres of literature. Its distinguished lineage extends back to the events recorded in the biblical tale of Cain and Abel, which depicts murder as the first crime against humanity. Long before this story was recorded, murder was a staple of drama and catalyzed the plots of countless Greek tragedies. The myths and legends of virtually every culture feature at least one story in which murder serves to highlight a moral or a basic truth integral to our understanding of the individual and society.

Reading between the lines of Chandler's remarks, we can conclude that tales of murder compel our attention because they say something essential about humanity. Murder represents the ultimate taboo, the worst transgression of the social contract and the divine will. Ironically, murder is the easiest crime to commit. All it takes is a strong impulse and weak empathy. Anyone is capable of murder, and the founders of western civilization seemed to understand this when they stigmatized murder not only as a crime but a sin. "Thou shalt not kill," says the fifth commandment, indicting by its fundamental proscription a potential in all of us.

So why do we *enjoy* murder stories? The answer can be found in the stories collected here. Murder often brings out the best in a writer's imagination precisely because it is the worst of crimes. It represents an extreme of human behavior, after which *anything* is possible. A world in which murder occurs is one in which the most crucial boundaries have been violated and the darkest possibilities admitted. Murder invites a response that is its complete opposite: an expression of the noblest virtues to solve the crime and reestablish order. Between these opposite poles of human nature, there is a vast terrain whose many palisades and canyons writers have only begun to explore.

100 Menacing Little Murder Stories provides a road map to that wild and largely uncharted territory. The murders featured in these stories occur in settings ranging from the sunlit heartland to the grimy city and even to dimensions beyond our own. The perpetrators run the gamut of social position, from the idle rich to the ordinary man, woman, and child. Impulse killers, contract killers, and serial killers are just a few of the personalities profiled. The variety of techniques the killers employ is a tribute to criminal ingenuity: the crude blunt object, the sophisticated surgical excision, the blatant bomb, the insidious poison, the stealthy approach from behind, and the unconcealed full-frontal assault. The killers' motives range from a simple delight in death to justifiable homicide. Some get away with murder—but not all. In many of the selections, there's a punishment to fit the crime and a sleuth whose objectives are as ambitious, methodical, and ruthless as his quarry's.

The stories you are about to read span more than a century—a mere drop in the bucket as the history of murder goes, but a fair representation of the murder story at its best. We can't guarantee that these stories will bring you any closer to understanding the sociology of murder or the psychology of the murderer.

But we do think you'll have a good time reading them.

—Stefan Dziemianowicz
New York, 1998

40 Detectives Later

Henry Slesar

I WASN'T FLATTERED when Munro Dean walked into my office. I'd been hearing about Dean since '49, when I was still a hotel dick for the Statler chain. He'd taken his case to every private investigator east of Chicago. Half of them had turned him down. The others had strung him along for a few days of expense money, and then sent him off with a shrug and a promise to "keep the file active."

I kept him waiting outside for a couple of minutes, while I worried a hangnail on my thumb. Then I invited him in.

He walked like it was a struggle, and there wasn't enough flesh on his frame to excite a starving buzzard. The skin was molded to his face so that you had a pretty good idea of what kind of a skull his head would make. It wasn't easy to look Munro Dean in the eyes.

"Have a seat," I said, with professional briskness. "Seems to me I've heard your name before, Mr. Dean."

"Probably," he answered. "Were you ever with the police, Mr. Tyree?"

"Not exactly. But I've got a lot of friends on the force. It was something about your wife, wasn't it?"

"Yes. It happened in 1948, October. In Rahway, New Jersey. A man—killed her. A slim, dark man, with bushy black hair. I came home from work and saw him running out the back door. The police never caught him."

"I see. And you're still interested in finding this man."

He laughed abruptly, but without a change of expression. "Interested? Yes, I'm interested. I've been looking for him since it happened. You know that, Mr. Tyree. All you——people know that."

"Mm." I drew up a pad and poised a pencil over it. "Well, suppose we go into some detail. Have the police—"

"They've closed their books on the case. But I haven't, Mr. Tyree. I've never given up. I've had at least forty private detectives looking for him. None have helped. Some of them"—his face clouded—"have taken advantage of me."

1

It was time to clear things up.

"Look, Mr. Dean. Guys like me are in the business for money. Only some of us take the long view. Some of us figure a real unhappy client is a bad advertisement. If I don't think I can help you, I'll hand you your hat."

I was talking too loud, and I knew it. But Munro Dean was like some gaunt symbol of failure, a patsy for the Fates. You either rubbed your hands gleefully and picked his pocket, or you got sore and shouted at him.

"You can help me," he said finally.

"What makes you so sure? Nobody else could."

"But you can. Because I've found the man."

I dropped the pencil. "Well. So what can I do now, Mr. Dean? Why not call in the police?"

"Because they'd pay no attention. Too much time has passed. They've lost interest."

"Nuts."

"It's true. I can't really prove this is the man. For one thing, he's changed. He's lost his hair. He's fatter. He's older. But he's the man."

"What makes you so sure?"

"Because I am." His eyes, two burned-out lumps of coal, suddenly glowed. "That face is engraved, here." He tapped his forehead. "It's funny, you know that? All those experts, all those years. Nobody could find him. And just by chance, I see him at a lunch counter—"

"It happens," I said curtly. "Don't forget, Mr. Dean, your description wasn't much help. Maybe you're the only one who could have spotted this man."

"Perhaps. But now I need help, Mr. Tyree."

"What do you want me to do?"

"I want you to act as go-between for this man and myself. I want you to arrange a little meeting."

"What for?"

"What do you suppose?"

I stood up. "Look, pal. The last time I set up a target was at Fort Dix. I'm not interested in that kind of work."

"Please. I just want to talk to this man. I want to make sure."

"It could be dangerous, you know. If he is your wife's killer, and if he knows you are—"

"That's where you can help. Arrange the meeting, but don't let him find out my name."

I took my seat again and sighed. It was an off-beat assignment, but the only one that had crossed my battered desk in two weeks. Beggars don't get many choices, and the rent on my cubicle of a LaSalle Street office was looming like the National Debt.

"Okay," I said. "Let's have the story."

The lunch counter wasn't what I'd expected. I cruised by it in a cab around eleven-thirty the next day, looking for the kind of a grease-pit you'd expect to find on the corner of a city street. But this was a new-style hash joint, with concealed lighting and Muzak and wait-resses with black-chiffon blouses.

I strolled in around five of noon and slipped into a booth. According to Munro Dean, my pigeon fed himself regularly at twelve-fifteen in this modernistic eatery. That gave me a chance to get well into a meal by the time he arrived.

The food wasn't any great improvement on Joe's Place. I chewed on the leathery fringe of a fried egg, and kept my eyes on the door-way.

At twelve-fifteen, a burly gent with a pink scalp and red face sauntered in, holding a tabloid under his arm. His complexion looked like a bad case of soil erosion, and his beady eyes were shrewd and old. This was my boy.

I watched him hunt up a seat at the counter, and tried to place him in my mental rogue's gallery. Nothing clicked.

He spread his bulk on a stool, clipped out an order to the hard blonde in the black blouse, and fanned out the newspaper. All through his meal, he never took his eyes from the page. I thought of taking the direct approach, but decided that he was too suspicious a type. Instead, I waited until he was through and followed him outside.

We took a bus together, the pigeon and I. Throughout the ride I kept thinking up approaches and rejecting them just as fast. This was no easy trick, cozying up to a knowing character like this one. I had to play it by ear, until the method of operation made itself plain.

The bus swung into Michigan Boulevard, and the guy started for the doors. I didn't take any chances; he looked like he'd been tailed before. I got off one stop before he did, and followed the bus on foot until he hopped off.

When I saw his destination, the method I needed was clear. It was one of those glass-fronted record shops—not a fancy LP joint, but a dusty storehouse piled high with ancient 78's. My pigeon had hidden depths. He was a record collector, and this was one language I knew.

I waited a few minutes before entering the shop. Then I browsed around a stack of discs until I found something interesting.

"Pardon me," I said as I walked up to him. "Can you tell me the price of this?"

"Huh? Oh, you got me wrong, Mac. I'm a customer myself."

I laughed. "Sorry," I said, and started to turn away. Then I performed a double-take and ogled the record in his hand. "Hey—old Whiteman band, huh? Think Bix is on it?"

"I dunno." He looked at me curiously. "I was wonderin' the same thing."

"Had some good luck with Bix lately," I said. "Found some of his old Goldkette stuff in a store on State Street. Found an old Fletcher Henderson on Vocalion, too—"

"Yeah? No kidding?"

I had him hooked. His mouth became unhinged, giving me a lovely view of a lot of bad teeth. And there was interest on his face. "You must use radar, pal," he said. "I get nothin' but the junk."

"Just a matter of luck," I said smugly. Then I frowned, unhappily. "Trouble is, I gotta dump my collection. I'm leaving town the end of the month, and I'll be on the road a lot. Can't lug all those records with me. Think a joint like this would give me any kind of a price?"

His eyes bugged. "Hell," he said. "They'd only give you peanuts, Mac. You ought to sell to a private collector."

"Sounds great. Only who?"

A smile spread across his ugly map, and I had that numb, contented feeling you get when you know a problem is solved.

In another ten minutes, we were splitting a bottle of beer in the tavern across the street and talking labels. He was calling me Bill and I was calling him Otto. By the time we broke up, we had an appointment all set up in the Hotel Bayshore for eight-thirty that night. Only Otto was in for a different kind of serenade from the one he expected . . .

Back at the office, I put in a call to the Bayshore and spoke to Munro Dean. I told him the good news, but he cut me short, asking me to drop over. I growled about it, but remembered who was paying the bills.

I found him in shirtsleeves in Room 305, keeping company with a bottle of bourbon.

"It's all set, huh?" he said, squeezing his hands around the glass. "He's coming, right?"

"He's coming. To look at some records." I explained the details of the ruse, but Dean didn't seem interested. He kept staring into the glass, his lips white.

"It's been so long," he whispered. "So many years . . ."

"And so many dollars," I said. "This search of yours hasn't been cheap, Mr. Dean."

"No," he answered hollowly. "It's cost thousands. Hiring all those men . . ."

I headed for the door. "Well, if you need anything else—"

"I do!"

"What?"

He put his glass on the floor and went to the red-leather suitcase on the bed. He fumbled at the straps, and his hands were shaking as he snapped open the locks. But they were steady when they came out with the V-shaped parcel in brown paper. Even before he got the wraps all the way off, I knew it was a .32 automatic.

"Good idea," I said approvingly. "You'll need the protection, Mr. Dean."

"No." He came towards me. "This is for you."

"What?"

"Take it. I—I don't know anything about guns. They frighten me."

"What do you want me to do with it?"

He looked at the floor. "I want you to do it for me. I thought I could do it myself, but I can't. After all these years—I can't."

He shoved the weapon at me, but I wouldn't touch it.

"Look, Mr. Dean," I said. "You better let the cops handle our friend Otto. If you can prove he's your wife's murderer—"

"Don't lecture me!" he said hoarsely. "I'm offering you a deal. This man killed the most important thing in my life. I'll give you three thousand dollars to avenge me!"

That stopped me cold. "Three grand?"

"Yes! And there won't be any risk. Not when the story comes out. It'll be self-defense. After all, I hired you to protect me. And when this man threatens my life . . . Don't you see?"

"Yeah. I see all right. Only I can't buy it, Mr. Dean. Not even at your price."

He snatched the gun back angrily. "All right! If that's the way you want it."

"And I'd think twice about doing it yourself, Mr. Dean. The law's pretty definite about murder—no matter what the reason."

He took a wallet from the jacket draped over a chair and slowly counted out my fee.

"Here you are, Mr. Tyree. Thank you."

I opened the door. "You sure that's all?"

"Positive." I closed the door.

I got back to the office around five-thirty and typed out a report on the case, leaving out my speculations about what might happen in Room 305 at the Bayshore that night. I figured that part was none of my business.

I dropped the folder into the file and frowned at the skimpy number of reports in the cabinet. I wasn't getting rich at this business, and I began to wonder if hotel sleuthing wasn't such a bad dodge after all.

I dropped into the chair behind my desk and chewed thoughtfully on the hangnail. Behind me, the sun was making a last splash, and the blood-red color reflected in my window started me thinking about Dean and his long hunt for the killer of his wife. I supposed that I should feel sorry for Dean. But for some reason, I was feeling sympathy for the heavy-set bald guy named Otto who would be knocking on the door of Dean's hotel room in a couple of hours. It had been a crummy way to earn my rent money, setting him up for ambush. No matter how good the cause, I felt like some kind of pimp.

Around seven o'clock, I dropped into the chophouse down the street. Nothing on the menu stirred my appetite, so I ordered a couple of coffees and sipped them in silence for an hour.

Then I went for a walk. I didn't think about my destination, until I got within viewing distance of the cheap neon sign that said HOTEL BAYSHORE, TRANSIENTS.

I set up a minor stake-out across the street, suddenly hoping that the pigeon wouldn't show.

But he did. At twenty-five past eight, the burly gent with the fondness for old jazz records came striding down the street. He headed straight for the hotel doorway.

I smoked another cigarette while I tried to make up my mind. Then I dropped the butt to the street, stomped on it and headed for the Bayshore.

I took the elevator to the third floor, strolled down the empty hallway to Room 305. It was awfully quiet behind the door. I put my ear to it, listening for sounds.

For another minute—nothing.

Then—*bam!*

Without thinking, I hit the door like a fullback. It crashed open, and somebody yelled. At the same time, a lamp spun crazily off an end table, the shade rolling at my feet, the naked bulb setting up a glare in the small room that fell revealingly on the frightened face of Munro Dean.

He was crouching against the wall, still in shirtsleeves, with the .32 in his white-knuckled hand. He was blubbering, and his eyes were on the burly man on the carpet. Otto wasn't dead, but he was flopping like a fish, and muttering a hoarse monologue of foul words. His hand was trying to get inside his jacket, and there wasn't any doubt about what he was after.

Munro's arm straightened out again, and I yelled at him not to shoot. He wasn't listening, so I made a flying leap over the wounded man and batted the gun out of Munro's hand. That broke him up; he slipped down against the wall and covered his face with both hands. I got the gun in time to cover the man on the floor.

"Outa the way!" he shrieked, his revolver half out of his jacket. "I'll kill the son-of-a-bitch—"

"Hold it!" I leveled the .32. "Don't draw!"

He didn't listen to me. He had the revolver out. Behind me, Dean was making noises like a sick calf.

"You're not hurt bad, pal," I said to Otto. "Looks like a leg wound. Don't make things any worse."

"Get outa the way!"

Instinct told me to shoot now and avoid trouble, but I couldn't do it. The next thing I knew, Dean was on my back, clutching me like a log in a rough sea, blubbering at me to protect him. The revolver barked, and chewed out a splinter in the wall behind us. Dean grabbed for the .32 in my hand, yelling for me to fire. I tried to shake him off, but he was obsessed. In the struggle, he got spun around and Otto's next bullet caught him. I didn't mean to set Dean up that way, but I caught a look in his eyes, when he went to the floor, that was accusing.

I had no choice now. I squeezed the trigger and saw blood spurt from the burly gent's wounded hand. He moaned as the gun dropped from his hand, then he fell forward on the carpet, his face contorted with pain.

I looked at Dean. The bullet had caught him in the abdomen, and there was no doubt that he was through. I went over to Otto.

"Can you talk?" I asked him.

He nodded his head.

"You know this guy?" I said. "You recognize him?"

"Yeah, Rahway, 1948 . . ."

"You killed his wife, didn't you?"

600 W

Basil Wells

J IM CATHER SHIVERED again despite the thick brown warmth of his overcoat. He was standing on the frost-whitened platform of planking that permitted access to the lower gears of the huge old, overshot waterwheel. Water spurted thinly through holes in the rimmed metal buckets of the wheel. And below the wheel a constant soft splash of falling drops sounded from the dark waters of the mill race.

The great shaft of the wheel, held securely by ungainly, but well-babbitted journals, ended in a gear that in turn meshed with a huge wooden-cogged gear. And upon the teeth of the gears there was a sticky red substance that shone wetly in the dusty light of the naked bulb overhead.

"He *could* have slipped and fallen across them," admitted the owner of the grist mill reluctantly, "but after nine years at the same job . . ." He frowned thoughtfully.

"Looked like he was trying to oil the machinery," said the lanky farmer whose grist waited upstairs on the mill floor. He shook his head. "Poor Pauline," he said. "She's gonna take this hard. They was twins, you know."

Jim Cather nodded absentmindedly. "I'd forgot you married his sister," he said. "Jeff Bryan was the best man I had, Arch, and I'd planned to give him a party this weekend."

"Too bad he didn't quit last week," said Arch Nelson sourly. "This mill's a regular death trap."

Cather choked back an angry retort. He leaned out over the small gear to peer more closely at the oil slot in the oversized journal. His eyes narrowed as he looked down below the shaft and the gear at the upset quart metal measure the dying man must have dropped there as the meshing gears caught his head and right arm.

Carefully he extended his arm and with his finger stirred at the thin mixture of fresh greenish oil in the oil slot of the journal. When he turned around his forehead was deeply furrowed. He wiped the oil from his hand on an old scrap of belting.

"We're calling the sheriff," he said to the lanky farmer and to broad-faced slow-witted Milo Parker who stood at the top of the dust-whitened steps on the main mill's level. Parker's face remained as impassive as before but Arch Nelson turned a startled reddish stubbled face.

"Wh—whaddya mean?" he demanded. "Think maybe he was made 'way with, Jim? Killed on purpose?"

"Afraid so," admitted Cather. "Let's go up to the office. No use freezing down here."

The office was a small barren room with a half dozen battered old chairs and board-topped nail kegs closing in around the rusty pot-bellied warmth of the stove. In one corner, behind the black wooden counter, perched Hilton Scott, the mill's manager, toying nervously with a well-chewed green pencil. Cather frowned as his foot bumped a sticky black oil measure beside the stove leg.

Milo Parker opened the stove door and tossed half a bucket of corn cobs into the fire. "Cold," he said, and grinned in a puzzled half-hearted fashion.

"Think back, Milo," said Cather abruptly, "to just before you turned up the gate to start the wheel. Did you hear anything?"

"Nope," said the man, and now the normally ruddy color was oozing back into his putty-colored face. "I hollered, like I always do. Nobody answered so I figured she was all clear. I raised the gate and the water hit the wheel. Then I see the red on the cogs of the big wheel and I stopped it."

"Only by that time," sneered Scott, his yellowed false teeth worrying the tobacco in his right cheek, "Jeff was dead."

Milo Parker's pale blue eyes squinted at his employer curiously.

9

"Maybe you're thinking I started up the wheel on purpose," he grumbled. "I didn't. Had no reason to hate Jeff. But he had."

Parker's head jerked in the general direction of the foreman. Scott jumped off his stool, swore, choked on his chew, and started toward the broad-faced man.

"Sit down," said Cather mildly, his brown eyes amused in a remote sort of way, "and let's get to the bottom of this . . . Murder's a serious business you know." He turned to face Parker. "Spill it," he offered.

"Hilt's been short weighting some of the customers." Milo Parker's face darkened stubbornly. "A few pounds here and a few more there. Been making mistakes on change, too. Jeff jumped him about it again yesterday."

"That's no reason for killing a man." Cather eyed his foreman thoughtfully.

Parker's thick jaw quivered. "Jeff threatened telling you. Said he was quitting Saturday anyhow. Had nothing to lose."

"You going to swallow that lie?" broke in Hilton Scott with an angry snort. His stained pink moustache bobbed like a wind-blown cork. "Milo and Jeff was always squabbling. Had to part them a dozen times this last few months."

Arch Nelson deliberately tamped coarse buckskin-colored tobacco into his old pipe. His long narrow face lengthened.

"Jeff told m'wife about him and Milo always wrangling," he said, "but he carried the idea that usually it was just chewing matches." His narrow gaze swung to Hilton Scott. "Jeff always said that Hilt was kind of close in his dealing. Maybe he was scraping off more cream than Jeff thought.

"I always checked over Hilt's figures before I paid him," he finished, holding the flame of a match over the blackened bowl. He puffed out a miniature blue cloud. "Caught a lot of mistakes."

The mill's manager snorted and turned to his employer. "Before he paid!" he gritted. "Jeff had to lend him the money lots of times before I let him take a grist home. Arch is sore because I didn't give him the whole mill for nothing!"

"I'm finding out a few things," said Cather wryly. "Maybe I'd better spend the next few weeks here. The other three outfits can run themselves I guess." His stubby capable fingers knotted into fists.

"Always been proud of the Cather record for fair dealing," he went on, "and I intend to keep it that way."

"Fine," applauded the lanky farmer, his pipe spouting quick bursts of smoke. "I can tell you plenty things wrong. You been losing plenty customers, Jim."

"If you used some of those ideas around home," growled Hilton Scott, "maybe you wouldn't have lost your farm, Arch." He paused to shoot a jet of amber fluid at a sawdust-filled wooden bucket. "I bet you run through the stock and tools your daddy-in-law left you in less than a year."

Milo Parker closed his mouth abruptly. A car had pulled up outside the office door. He peered out through the window at the two overcoated men, both of them tall and clean shaven, who were crossing the loading platform toward the office.

"Sheriff made a quick trip," he said. "You didn't phone more than ten minutes ago, Jim." He went back to his nail keg seat. "Got that reporter fellow, Herrick, with him too."

The door opened. Cather went to meet the lawman and his companion. Their voices were hushed. The reporter stamped the snow from his feet.

"Who do you think they'll arrest?" Milo Parker asked. Neither of the other men answered. He frowned. "Wonder why Jim is so sure Jeff was killed."

"Been wondering that myself," said Hilton Scott as his jaws worked mechanically at the chewing tobacco in his cheek. "Looked like an accident to me."

Then the sheriff and Cather were with them. Cather's cold brown eyes raked them. Finally his gaze halted at the red-stubbled face of the deadman's brother-in-law. An uneasy silence gripped the bare little office.

"There's your man," accused Cather calmly. "He's the only possible suspect!"

Arch Nelson stepped backward into the hot iron belly of the stove. He screeched with the sudden pain and his pipe jounced up from the floor, tobacco flying. He started as though to run but the cold steel of the bracelets snapping about his wrists seemed to drain all the life from his lanky frame.

The sheriff was puzzled. He had looked over the scene of the crime and checked it with the story that Arch Nelson had seemed so eager to babble out. The feel of those handcuffs about his bony wrists had broken down the farmer's resistance completely, but that did not explain how Cather had suspected him.

"Wasn't a lucky guess was it, Jim?" he inquired. "I see how you figured he would have motive enough. Jeff wasn't married and Nelson's wife would be his heir. Nelson figured he'd get the farm Jeff inherited from his father, as well as the stock and tools that had been his wife's share of the estate.

"But knowing he had a motive didn't tell you that Nelson was the man who knocked Jeff Bryan unconscious and dropped his head across the gear he was oiling."

Cather smiled thinly. "He wasn't oiling the waterwheel journal, Sheriff," he said. "That was light oil in that quart measure Arch Nelson upset so carefully below the gears. And Nelson made his mistake when he filled the oil slot with that light oil.

"You see that quart measure of black oil beside the stove? That's 600W. Only place we use it is on the waterwheel journals. In cold weather it's like tar—can't be poured without being heated.

"That's how I knew neither Milo Parker nor Hilton Scott were responsible for Jeff's death. They would never have used anything but a heavy oil. That left Nelson."

Action

David J. Schow

D. W. STEPPED OUT. The door had been opened for him. The county sheriff was huge, bristle-cropped, with mean piggy eyes. He had just slugged D. W. with his baton. The bailiff was bigger—6'6", all starched blouse, body armor and attitude. Both packed 9mm autos. Hardly a cop in LA would shame image with a revolver anymore. They had been easily legalized. A snip of red tape. Bang.

D. W. stepped into the light.

The judge's nameplate soberly proclaimed HER HONOR FRANCES MCCLANAHAN. D.W. caught her eye and smiled a matinee idol smile. She was robed, sexless, a turkey neck above all-business wire-rims in gold. Brown hair, chopped short, graying more with each verdict. Dying a little every day.

Cops with auto pistols. Lady judges. Things had changed.

"Action."

D. W. had whispered the magic word to himself. *Lights, camera . . .*

All his life, more than anything, D. W. had aspired to be a good actor. Since he was nine. Before that it was paleontologist, then paramedic. Actors knew what to say. A quip for every crisis. They could pretent to be paleontologists and paramedics and get paid for it. Actors got girls effortlessly. D. W. presumed actresses could get guys with equal casualness. But they were all called actors now, both sexes. More progress.

Actors knew how to hit their marks and pick up their cues. Actors were in the public eye. *People* Magazine. *Entertainment Tonight.*

D. W. saw lights, cameras, an audience. He was conducted to a seat next to his defense attorney, Rupert the Lawyer. D. W. took short steps because of the ankle cuffs.

"Howdy, Rupert."

"Reino," said Rupert, giving a discreet thumbs-up. Rupert was wearing his gray pinstripe today. Rupert had known the TV people and news crews would be in attendance. Rupert owned twelve lawyer uniforms and D. W. knew them all. Tomorrow, if there were cameras again, Rupert would brush off his black three-piece.

Several yellow index cards lay face-down at Rupert's spot. Last-minute notes and updates. As he sat, he flashed his killer smile for the cameras. The audience rumble stirred up. Magic.

Her Honor Frances McClanahan called for order.

The prosecution had set up its charts for Blackwood Avenue. That was one reason the media had poked up their snouts. Coffin was present at the enemy desk; that was two. Gardner Coffin was the masthead go-getter for Coffin, Boles, Thatcher, Grimes and Halliday, P.P.C. His firm had undertaken the successful imprisonment of seven of LA County's more notorious mass murderers and serial killers, including the Jigsaw Ripper fiasco.

That had been before D. W.'s time.

He flipped up the top card, handcuff links clinking. All the cards were in Rupert's post-Harvard scrawl.

Rumors of hung jury #2. Appeals.

Another reason for the news folks. Next:

Blanchard's evidence ruled contradictory.

Remove enough lugs and the wheel falls off and the car won't go no more. Blanchard's key testimony had sprung a leak. Three:

Coffin to step in personally.

Oh well. D. W. would follow script regardless. If his accusers pulled bigger guns, it might signify a panicked fortification of an already wobbly case. Public opinion would shift if there were the slightest whiff of wrongful arrest.

The judge droned. D. W. checked out the spectators. A redhaired woman in the second row was mopping tears and fighting to keep a stiff upper. That would be the mother of Number Five, Ruth Ann Fowler.

Who had been abducted from Blackwood Avenue.

Ruth Ann Fowler's corpse was not discovered until May 11th, dumped off Mulholland Drive to cook in the spring sun for four days after her murder. She had been tripped over by a sitcom writer chasing a lost Porsche hubcap downhill. She had been naked except for the tennis ball duct-taped into her mouth. She had evacuated fluids but bloated with bacterial gas. Her wrists were tightly bound with coathanger wire. She had been cut with a scalpel, long incisions from armpits to wrists, plus similar cuts from the inside thigh to the ankle on each leg. A pathologist testified that the same scalpel had been used to remove her lips and labia. Semen tracks were identified in her throat, her anus, and on the flathead screwdriver they pulled out of her. The obvious C.O.D. was massive hemorrhage. The coathanger marks indicated that she had lived for at least four hours after being bound. Ruth Ann Fowler had been 14, a nail biter. She had many more friends at school after she died, when the TV cameras showed up to provide human interest at 4,5,6 and 11.

D. W. turned to his public long enough for lenses to zoom in on the three sixes tattooed on his forehead. He shot his smile at Ruth Ann Fowler's mother. "I love you," he said. "Baby, I need you so bad."

Chaos.

Two days later, Ruth Ann Fowler's mother wept in the courtroom as Rupert the Lawyer's prediction of a hung jury came shockingly to pass. The cameras ate up her breakdown.

"I want you. I *need* you."

Ruth Ann had been Number Five. Five out of eleven. Other mommies and daddies present erupted in rage or grief. They could do little about D. W. because another bailiff had scanned them all with a metal detector prior to entry.

Two cameramen cranked in contrary directions and cracked lenses. D. W. laughed—a shrill, fluting giggle that was one of the trademarks of Reino Salazar, the Meat Man.

Another day, another trial, a new jury. D. W. hit the #1 slot on the news consistently. He was more exciting than the freeway snipers or the gang hits.

They shot him being hustled from the courtroom. They freeze-framed a shot emphasizing the 666 on his forehead. He looked as lethal as a cobra, as compelling as a TV star.

He had an interview at five.

The setup was a tad grotesque.

D. W. had been looking forward to fucking with Mario Escovar's head. Mario was the top-rated news anchor on LA's #1 independent station. His producer had decided to hurl in Tracy Whitmore at the last minute. Tracy was darkhaired, with a weird frost job and a pretty dead-ahead set of legs. It was an angle—woman quizzes sex killer—and much better showbiz. Mario Escovar would have asked penetrating questions. Multi-leveled. Tracy would lean into frame, representing an entire sex against whom this maniac was destructively devoted, and try to probe *why* for her viewers. In post, editors could insert shots of her leaning, crinkling her surgically perfect brow, pursing her lips and nodding importantly as though she actually comprehended. They put her on a barstool to mold her calves and had a keylight especially for her legs.

Grotesque.

D. W. sat shadowed by bars in his interview cell. Dark killer versus the shed light of prime-time reportage. There was a good nine feet of dead space between his bars and her stool. You never knew; nobody really wanted to see Tracy get snatched while tape was running. Nobody except maybe her producer and Mario Escovar. And the audience that would make the show a ratings giant.

Still, this was a matter of serial killer decorum.

"So, Reino . . . is it true your mother abused you as a child? Hit you? Made you wear a dress?"

Why I Hate Women 101A. Jesus.

"You honestly believe that you've done nothing wrong, that you haven't hurt anyone, Reino?"

First-name familiarity with each interrogative. That clumsy have-you-stopped-beating-your-wife entrapment. Christ, what a tyro!

"Ms Whitmore." He consciously drew out the *mizzz*. Tape ground away, loop upon loop of three-quarter-inch gold grade, capturing everything. "Are you attempting to help the media convict me for something I did not do?"

That rattled her leash.

"How do you feel about being imprisoned, then, if you're . . . innocent?"

No first name now. That tiny pause before she said *innocent*. She did not believe Reino Salazar was innocent. Time to shake her up and give the viewers what they wanted.

"Not thirteen," he said. Sly.

"I beg your pardon?"

"Only eleven. Not thirteen. An error. Thirteen is a perfect number, you know."

Eagerly, as if programmed, she asked him why. And he told her. From that moment, he owned their exchange. He played her the way gangbangers play ghetto blasters. In minutes her skin was acrawl and she could not meet his eyes directly.

"Who's your buddy? Satan's your buddy." He had almost forgotten to pitch in the devil reference. "Satan's your pal."

According to censors in the know, an upturned thumb, plus index and pinky fingers, signifies denial of the Holy Trinity, as well as the infamous triple-six.

D. W. looked the camera in the eye. It did not turn away from him.

Cut.

Seated around the conference table in the judge's quarters were Her Honor Frances McClanahan, Rupert the Lawyer, Gardner Coffin and a crony, and Edward Truex, to whom D. W. referred affectionately as Emerald Ed. D. W. was escorted in by a quartet of armed bulldog guards, chains and cuffs aplenty.

"Are you positive you don't need at least one of us to stay in here with you, Your Honor?" It was the sheriff's deputy with the piggy eyes, like shiny glass beads, the one who had nightsticked D. W. He did not approve of this due process shit.

"I think these men should be adequate to the task if the prisoner does anything untoward," said Judge Frances. The sheriff left without a Milk Bone.

Once the sheriff was gone, D. W. said, "That motherfucker hit me in the stomach with his baton."

Her Honor went bloodless. "Did he speak to you?"

"He said, and I quote, 'I'm waitin for ya, rapist scumbag. I'll cut off your *cojones.*' Then he struck me. Twice." D. W. nailed the judge with a glare. "Muzzle that asshole, Frances, and I do mean *now.*"

Emerald Ed spoke up. "My client is not supposed to be subjected to physical abuse. This has occurred more than once. I think it's time to discuss a little extra compensation."

There was no one responsible enough to deserve scorn, so Ed helped D. W. out of his restraints and brought him a club soda with lime.

"D. W., what can I say? I'm sorry." Frances frowned.

D. W. waved it to insignificance. "Didn't see it coming, is all. Let's get it on."

"The hung jury got you the fever pitch you asked for," said Coffin, a fortyish man who looked like a graduate of aftershave commercials. "Time to drop the blade and let 'em see a little blood."

"Especially since you'll be the executioner," said Rupert the Lawyer. "You bag the glory of nailing the Meat Man in court."

Nobody needed to remind Rupert that Coffin's media-hog image was precisely the reason he had been hired.

"Think the copycats will come through for us?" Emerald Ed was musing again.

"Be nice if they capped some poor shmuck inside one of the original hit zones." Coffin fired up a cigarillo, one of his many eccentric trademarks. "Maybe Blackwood Avenue. Did you *see* that lady in court?"

Judge McClanahan nodded. Mrs. Fowler's had been a stellar collapse, fraught with raw sympathy and parental anguish. Emmy material. They'd gotten it for free. On all channels, all timeslots, D. W.'s grinning mug had almost been crowded out by those choice-cut closeups of that red and weeping face.

"We need to turn that into an advantage," said Rupert.

"Rupert, I think that shot will mold public opinion the way we want *without* some foggy reliance on a copycat," said Judge McClanahan.

17

"Unless you farm out the copycat job to take advantage of the news." It was D. W.'s first commentary.

"We're not in the business of taking human life." They all turned to the judge when she spoke; they all saw there was no room to wiggle on this particular issue.

Emerald Ed was quick to crack the tension. "Besides, D. W.'s contract expressly forbids violation of his exclusivity." He could quote whole clauses from his eidetic memory, and beyond his banker's soul lurked an instinct for blood that would shame a tiger shark. "No add-ons. D. W.'s the star."

"Just a notion," Coffin said defensively. He had forgotten it had been Ed who raised the idea of the copycat hit in the first place.

Ed was talented, no lie.

Judge McClanahan rose magisterially. "All right, gentlemen. We proceed with the new jury. Cull the primary list." Jurors for the first two abortive passes had been carefully selected to hamstring the trial, and they had come through like the TV-mesmerized nincompoops they were. "Third try, we pitch a no-hitter. So, D. W., it looks like your contract with us will be satisfactorily discharged in, oh, approximately—"

"Say six months," said Coffin. Rupert the Lawyer nodded approval. Just enough time to make the docket shenanigans appear authentically rigorous.

Her Honor addressed prosecuting and defense counsels respectively. "Pool your notes. Let's give them a good show."

"Yes *ma'am*," Rupert said happily. He gathered up the chain restraints from the table and untangled them. "Time to keep the public safe from you," he said to D. W.

"What about that sheriff?" D. W. could confer with Emerald Ed later; find out what was on tap for their next gig.

Judge McClanahan nodded. "When D. W.'s gone, walk that officer in here. He strikes my prisoner again, I'll cornhole him a wind-tunnel."

"That guy'd probably enjoy it," said Coffin.

D. W. smiled and willingly extended his hands toward the waiting cuffs. He was a trouper.

That night, he watched himself on the news. Rather, the rerun of the news in the wee hours. He videotaped each broadcast onto a scrapbook cassette. He squinted at his own closeup. He contemplated the tears of Ruth Ann Fowler's mother, and reassured himself that he was a force for good in the world.

Somewhere out there in the bad old LA smogscape, the genuine Meat Man was probably face-down in a landfill, chopped apart by a gang shotgun. Gone underground. Blown town. Schizzed out. Working a new identity as a mushroom picker upstate.

It did not matter.

What mattered was that the bad old LA TV-watching public felt security due to the capture of the Meat Man, a gruesome killer of white urban females. What mattered was that they were confident that their police forces and judicial machinery actually functioned for the good of the people. They could sleep at night, knowing the Meat Man was max-locked.

D. W. removed his nose, his chin cleft, and tilted out his brown contacts. He shampooed his hair from black to auburn, with streaks of gray. He washed the three sixes off his forehead.

His jail togs were bagged; he'd done the right thing and changed in Rupert's car. That was why Rupert's car had black mirror windows.

He showered, almost to scalding, and irrigated away his assumed persona. His role.

Towelling his hair, he heard the news video playing back, talking about Reino Salazar and all the bad things he had done to women in Los Angeles. He had turned off the VCR before showering.

There was a burglar watching D. W.'s television. He had helped himself to a bottled beer from D. W.'s fridge. As D. W. entered, the intruder kept his eyes mostly on the screen, and his short-barrel .357 mostly on D. W.'s crotch.

"Don't bother to tell me, man—I already know this is a security building."

The guy wore glasses and had mangey, scouring-pad patches of beard bristle. Teeth too big for his head, horsey and uneven. His eyebrows had tried to grow together. Acne pits and big, oily pores. He looked as though he had mugged some Brentwood yupster and wrestled in a trash dumpster for his clothes. And won.

"What . . . are you doing here?" D. W. was off-guard and out-of-character. He was still dripping. His penis tried to telescope up to hide between his lungs.

"Sit on down," the burglar said. "Check out the news. Man,

there's murderers everywhere out there tonight. You're safe in this place. You're smart, am I right?''

D. W. sat where the gun told him to.

"Whackos from hell." The burglar chuckled; stayed conversational. He indicated the Meat Man playback. "Now, this home, check him out. He fucks them, he cuts them up, he kills them, and everybody tries to figure out why.''

D. W. felt he should stand tough despite his nudity, wetness, and lack of a suitable equalizer. The shocked yet resilient urban dweller. Reasonable in the face of crisis. "I don't have much money. But you're welcome to what there is. I don't want any—"

"Will you *relax?*" D. W. was overridden. "Let me talk for a minute. You want a beer?''

Thousands of responses scrolled in D. W.'s head. "No."

"Okay, so shut up and don't interrupt. Check it out." Onscreen, the Meat Man glowered at his accusers. "Man, I love it when he gives, like, the devil-stare, you know?''

"I've already seen it."

Ruth Ann Fowler's mother came unhinged. Tight shot, intimate. In D. W.'s head, Reino Salazar was wondering what this thug would look like with a screwdriver jammed up his fundament.

"Okay, so you *know,* man."

"Know what?"

"That's entertainment! The devil made him do it! Whoa, look out, heavy metal made him do it! Porno, handguns, Bud Lite and the Texas Chainsaw Massacre made him do it. Poor dude's just a victim of our Constitution, am I right?''

As the tape winked to static, the burglar launched from his seat with such viper speed that D. W. could only track his wake. By the time D. W. registered the foam and spilled beer on the throw rug, the burglar was pressed right into his face, one hand preventing a block, the other aiming the gun. D. W. was shaking. When the burglar touched his chin—gently—D. W. opened his mouth. He kept it open as he felt the .357's front sight bump past his teeth.

"Let me educate you, amigo," the man said in college-lecture tones. "The only way to know, is to do it for real." He inclined his head back toward the snowy TV. "Those donkey-butts, they don't know. I know. I can see right through you, man. But that's okay. Are you scared? Nod your head."

His mouth full of gun, D. W. nodded. Gently.

"You think you're gonna die now, right? That's okay, too. Listen:

The money in your wallet? I already got it. I already got the cash from the phony peanut butter jar in the kitchen. What, is that supposed to fool me? Don't ever offer a crazy person *anything*. He'll take what he wants anyway. Don't negotiate. You paying attention? Scared people, they always try to parley. You still scared?"

He cocked the hammer of the pistol. D. W. felt it all the way to the base of his spine. Sweat had rinsed away his shower.

"Okay, good. Listen to me: This guy Reino Salazar, they say is the Meat Man, you know what I think? I think they're gonna nail him with this new jury. Put his ass away, max-lock, everybody relaxes. The cops get raises, the Suits get re-elected, everybody's smiling, right? Am I right? Answer me or you're gonna die."

There was no play to make. D. W. nodded.

"Good."

The burglar snapped the trigger. He sprang back from D. W. No gunshot. D. W. was still tasting metal and feeling the impact on his teeth and fearing the bright light as his heart thuddingly urged him to have a coronary. He bleated and thrashed spastically on the couch . . . until he finally understood that he was still alive.

The burglar cocked the hammer again. "Okay, okay, calm down, it was a crummy trick, okay? Next chamber up is for real, just so you don't get Western. People watch too much TV; they think they can be heroes, am I right?"

All D. W.'s moisture was outside his body. His tongue was an emery board, his mouth, a dry well. He managed one line: "What do you want from me?"

"I don't want nothing from you, man. I love you. I *need* you. What you did for me—no price. I just want to tell you that I thank you from right here." He thumped his fist against his chest. Then he moved behind D. W.

Behind the couch, he hovered close enough for D. W. to feel the .357 teasing his earlobe. His whisper was the sound of ghost relatives, calling in favors.

"Okay, listen to me: You're all messed up now, so what I need you to do is go take another shower, all right? You wash up. I'll take another beer, and that's all I'll take, other than the cash, which I genuinely need. I'll rewind your little archive tape, and when you come out, I'll be history. Like I was never here, am I right?"

D. W., certain a bullet was next, closed his eyes. He wanted to weep but didn't have the juice for tears. He just couldn't summon up Reino Salazar while this guy was in the room.

"Always remember: I love you, man. Who's your pal, right? But this is important: To *know* it, you've gotta *do* it. The rest is all horseshit and circuses. Go take your shower."

Take Two.

D. W. padded into the living room after an invigorating hot-and-cold. He replayed the video and watched one commentator after another talk gravely of the Meat Man and all the bad things he had done to women in Los Angeles.

D. W.'s video editing needed polish.

Reino Salazar was old news. All that awaited the Meat Man was an ironclad conviction, a unanimous verdict. Tracy Whitmore would write a paperback with a lurid cover, emphasizing Reino's 666.

Past that guy on TV that gave the public their safe little chills, there was no Meat Man. D. W.'s nighttime visitor had murdered the Meat Man long ago.

Who's your buddy?

D. W. got his robe and whipped up a brandy espresso. It was time to smoke one of the six Havana cigars he permitted himself annually. Beyond the high windows of his security building, the people of Los Angeles watched TV and got murdered, among their other normal pursuits.

He reran the tape and watched it again, with the attitude of a student winnowing data. He assessed each of the news anchors, each personality.

Nah, too easy, he thought.

After contemplation, he pulled down a phone book, and picked a name and address at random.

All the Angles

Basil Wells

DUNN'S MIND must have wandered for a moment, but now his senses were keenly alert. He had not realized it was evening; darkness was near.

On the sparsely-grassed level of soil before him, his relaxed red-haired knuckles filled half his vision. Just to the left of them, he knew, lay the long-barreled revolver with which he had shot Paul Ebbins. And he was lying here above the fallen man, alert for any possibility of the guard's shamming death until the arrival of reinforcements.

He scowled as he tried to recall what he had done, and what he must tell them; for the moment, Lee Dunn could not distinguish the truth of what had happened from the carefully calculated webwork of half-truths and lies.

He cursed at the sharp jut of stone, or sun-baked clay, that gouged into his ribs and attempted to wriggle away; it was useless. The shift in position brought his body into contact with yet another fragment of unseen and yet-more painful rock.

"I was worried about Fred," he would tell the other guards on the Marvin estate when they arrived. *"What with this strike at Metalcraft and the ill-feeling of his employees—well, I just couldn't stand doing nothing."*

He'd pause there and his throat would seem to choke up with emotion while he looked down at the frail twisted old body of Frederick Marvin. And there would be blood on the grass of the valley below this grassy ledge where he sprawled, waiting. There would be the tiny black hole left by a rifle bullet in the gnarled old manufacturer's forehead, too.

"So I rode over the path above the Rocks up there." Dunn could sense the smooth glibness with which his words would flow. *"I knew Fred and his wife would be riding along the valley soon, and I planned to join them."*

His lips twisted as he recalled abruptly the care with which he had wormed his way down among the rocks until he could see the bridle path clearly in the wooded valley below. And there, too, he had an unobstructed view of the sheltered ledge where Paul Ebbins sat on guard, an open green thermos bottle smoking at his elbow.

Ebbins was using field glasses to study the broken slope of the Rocks. Below him, the electrified barrier about the Marvin estate crossed the valley, its twelve-foot mesh of galvanized wire barring legitimate passage, but from this vantage point an attack was possible.

And the strike was already more than three hundred days old.

"Frankly," Lee Dunn would say, "I was worried about the trustworthiness of Ebbins. With the reduction of Metalcraft's guard force he was laid off. His brother had lost his car and the home he was buying, and his father had to mortgage his own property to live. All this because of the strike."

He would shake his head sadly at this, and his voice would drop lower—as though reluctant to tell of the horror of the moments just passed.

Of course he had known of Ebbins' plight, and he'd been the one to suggest to Frederick Marvin that the unemployed plant guard might be put to good use policing the outer rim of Marvin's thousand acre wooded estate. Only he'd cautioned Marvin about mentioning his, Dunn's name, suggesting that the strikers might assume he was weakening by showing concern about Ebbins' relatives.

For five years, Lee Dunn had been manager of Metalcraft Incorporated, and year by year old Frederick Marvin had yielded more authority. Today he was taking over *all* that authority—and Velma Marvin, his employer's youngish wife as well!

He'd come to that decision two years before—a few months before his wife was killed by an armed bandit's chance bullet while he struggled with the killer for the weapon. His lips twisted faintly. Her death had been very convenient—she'd been asking too many questions about securities he was supposed to have purchased.

Sudden sweat stood out on his forehead as the painful pressure under his ribs shot fresh agony through his body. He *would* have to pick the roughest patch of ground on the slope!

Why didn't those guards hurry? Surely they'd heard the exchange of shots; they'd find him above Ebbins' station on the slope, and beside the dead guard would be the rifle that had killed old Frederick Marvin. Even without a word from his lips they could see what had happened.

Dunn's eyes blurred momentarily as he tried to shift his cramped body, and when they cleared again he saw the scuffed brown shoes and the square-toed black shoes of two men planted firmly on the sparsely grassed level before him.

He was conscious of the distant roar of their excited voices, and commanded his legs and arms to push him up to face them. And, unbelieving, he twitched not a muscle!

And then, beyond the toed-out twin pair of shoes, he caught the velvety brown of a rifle's wooden stock—the gun that should have been lying beside Paul Ebbins' stiffening fingers!

A voiceless scream tore up from his lungs and convulsed stomach and burst from his contorted lips like a pent-up gust of breath. For now he knew what had really happened when that deadly rifle had slammed out its murderous missile of metal.

Across a great wavering void of silence Dunn heard the thready pipings of men's voices. He strained his failing hearing.

The softer, slow-spoken whisper demanded, "How'd you suspicion him, Paul? Why'd he want to kill pore ol' Mr. Marvin?"

That would be Glenn Balca, another of the plant guards, laid off when the strike first started. And Paul—that would be Paul Ebbins! He felt his ragged breathing rattle out hideously.

"I expect it was the way his wife was killed," Ebbins' crisper voice replied, distantly. "I couldn't help wondering if Mr. Dunn hadn't planned the whole affair to dispose of her. And his killing the man he'd hired made him a hero.

"Probably gave the poor guy a fiver to stage a fake holdup."

Ebbins was wrong; the muddy brain of the prone man denied his words. It had been forty dollars.

There were the softer, Southern tones of Balca: "So you smelled th' same kinda trouble here, Paul? Reckoned maybe Dunn was fixin' to saddle you with the Boss' killin'?"

"Not exactly," denied Ebbins. "I wasn't sure what sort of deviltry Dunn was up to getting me this job. But I did know he disliked me—almost as much as I despised him."

"So that's why you cut me in—splittin' yore wages like you done—so's I'd keep yore back covered!"

"Uh huh." The thinning filament of sound was almost inaudible to Dunn's echoing eardrums. "And it paid off; you downed him just as he was shooting at the Boss.

"I figure he'd have got me next, tossed down the rifle, and played hero again. Funny how a killer always follows the same pattern."

Sluggishly Dunn's thoughts mulled over what he had heard. He'd not considered the possibility of a second watcher on the slope; he thought he'd covered all the angles, but . . . well, now he must get to work on a new plan, one that would implicate both men!

Lee Dunn was not conscious of the fading of the pain in his chest, or the swift darkness that swallowed his vision—even as the last of his blood reddened the grass. His brain was busy.

This time he would consider *all* the angles . . .

All-Star Team

Jon L. Breen

I HAVE RESENTED TELEPHONES the whole of my natural life. After umpiring an eighteen-inning game at New Hopton Stadium, getting back to the hotel at 1:30 A.M. with a day game scheduled for the next afternoon, finally dropping off to sleep a little after 2:00, and then hearing that obscene ringing in my ears, I especially resent telephones.

With commendable restraint, I grab the phone off its cradle and say "Hello." Just "Hello."

"Ed Gorgon?" says the voice on the other end.

Do I admit it? Probably some disgruntled fan wants to chastise me for that call at third base he thinks I blew in the bottom of the sixteenth. I didn't blow it, by the way. Oh, I've blown a few, but not that one.

"Yeah, this is Ed Gorgon."

"This is Rojas."

"Good to hear from you, Sarge, but you've picked better times to call. What's up?"

"Sorry to wake you, Ed, but you and I have to talk a little baseball."

"I'd talk about murder at this time of night, that being my hobby, but baseball is my profession and I'm off duty."

"Professionals are never off duty. Don't you think I'd like to be home in bed? We'll talk murder, too, but first baseball. What do you think of this all-star team?"

I fall back groaning on the bed, letting the receiver fall gently against my ear. If this is going to be a discussion of the comparative skills of Eddie Murray and Wally Joyner, I'm going to sleep through it.

"Abbott at first base, Best at second, Dilnot at third, Kott at short, DePuy in right, Adey in center, Fox in left, Adimov pitching, Elms catching. Horst is the designated hitter. Coors and Fry are warming up in the bullpen. Jopp, DeGhoort, and Hill are available for pinch-hitting duty."

I feel like I've just walked into *Alice in Wonderland.* Has Sergeant Rojas, a normally level-headed and competent member of New Hopton's police force, been drinking? Is he playing some kind of game with me? Drawing a deep breath, I decide to play it straight.

"Not much of an all-star team. Most of those guys I never heard of. Nelly Fox was a second baseman, not a left fielder, or was it Jimmy Foxx with two x's? Jim Kaat was a pitcher, not a shortstop, though he about fielded well enough . . ."

"It's K-o-t-t. Spelled differently. So these aren't real players?"

"They don't ring many bells with me. Who did you say the first baseman was?"

"Abbott."

"No, Who's on first, What's on second . . ."

"Ed, this is serious."

"Well, if it's so damned serious, quit playing games and tell me what it's all about. You said something about murder."

"I was hoping you could tell me what all those players had in common."

"Oblivion. Come on, Sarge, I don't work without the facts."

I've played into his hands. Now instead of being angry at getting woken in the middle of the night, I'm begging him for details.

"A man named Clarence Fortune, partner in a large corporate law firm, was found murdered in his office at about nine o'clock last night. Actually, we can pinpoint it at exactly 8:53, because a cleaning woman heard the murder take place. She was sweeping out an adjacent office and heard Fortune talking to a visitor. She says he said something like, 'You could make my all-star team. Here, look.' She didn't hear the other person speak, but she did hear a shot and somebody running out of the office.

27

"She was scared out of her wits and sort of stood there frozen for a couple of minutes, though she had presence of mind enough to note the time. Finally, she got up the courage to go around to Fortune's office and found him dead. She called us at once.

"We were able to determine from the watchman on duty that no one had left the building since the murder, so we could narrow our range of suspects to three other people who were working late on Fortune's floor. One was Mabel Hollister, a secretary in Fortune's firm who was working in an office down the hall."

"Did she hear the shot?"

"She says not. The offices are fairly soundproof and she says she was typing all the time. Actually, the only reason the cleaning woman could hear the shot was that the wall between her and Fortune's office was a temporary partition.

"Now the other two were Wilbur Chow, an importer of Asian art who was also working late—he thinks he heard the shot but says he's used to unexpected noises in the city and thought nothing of it—and Gilbert Formby, a tax accountant, very nervous and edgy guy. He says he didn't hear the shot either."

"Funny time for him to be working overtime. It's long past April 15. What about the weapon? Did you find it?"

"Yeah, dropped in the wastebasket of the office. Very clever. No prints, of course, and the killer must have been pretty confident the gun couldn't be traced to him. Or her."

"Any connection between Fortune and the three others?"

"Well, they all knew him. Mabel Hollister used to go out with him, but they'd broken it off some months ago. She said she couldn't stand his game-playing."

"Did she mean that figuratively or literally?"

"Maybe both, but for sure literally. He loved puzzles and word games and all that stuff. She had it up to here. Formby had done some work for Fortune's firm in the past, and Chow had sold him some Chinese art. No apparent motives, but we'll keep digging. We can handle the ballistics and the doorbell ringing, though, Ed. I called you because of the baseball angle."

"This all-star team . . ."

"Yeah. At the time of his death, he was making out lineups for this all-star team of his. Mabel Hollister said he was always making up imaginary teams of guys who were all under six feet or whose names all started with Y or who came from Connecticut or whose

28

names were kinds of food. Things like that. Only he always used real players' names. But this team he was working on when he was killed didn't seem to use real players. And we couldn't figure out what all the names had in common. And what the killer's name might have had in common with them."

I have a sudden glimmering in the back of my mind. A theory is taking shape.

"So you were lucky I was in town—your baseball consultant, huh? I don't think you have to know a baseball from a volleyball to figure this one out, though. What did you say the cleaning woman's name was?"

"I don't think I did. But it's Clarice Singleton."

"Uh-huh. And give me those names again from the top. Abbott was on first . . ."

"Yeah, no Costello."

"Costello couldn't make this team. And Best was on second. Yeah, that checks. Give me a spelling on all of these."

He runs them down. The one that has me worried is Adimov. "That's not Adamov?"

"No, it's A-d-i . . ."

"Good, good." I finish the list and look it over carefully, looking for a loophole, inviting Rojas to do the same. After a couple of minutes, I say, "Now do you see what they have in common?"

"No."

"I suggest you take a long look at Mr. Wilbur Chow. He killed Fortune. How did I know that?"

"I don't know."

"Third base!"

"Ed, quit kidding around."

"You wake me up in the middle of the night to figure out a puzzle any school kid should be able to do. I have the right to a little fun. Look at the names again, Sarge. What do they all have in common? Nationality? No. Number of letters? No. Association with some special field of endeavor? No. But look closely at the names, at the letters in the names. It's as simple as A, B, C."

After a slight pause, Rojas says, "Oh, geez . . ."

"You mean you finally got it?"

"Yeah."

"And did you have to know anything about baseball?"

"Not a damn thing."

29

"And are you going to arrest Wilbur Chow?"

Rojas laughs. "Not just yet. I don't think we can convict a guy of murder just because the letters in his name are in alphabetical order."

Art Is Anything You Can Get Away With

Stefan Jackson

MARTIN COLE LIT A CIGARETTE, drew in tight and hard on the butt. He tossed the lighter back on his desk, it bounced off a couple of photos. Pictures of a fat, dead and skinned man. The corpse had a name: Eddie Jacobs. Age: 39. Residence: 385 Roseland Drive, Phoenix, Arizona. His wife had reported him missing about twenty-six weeks ago. He was found ten days ago in Elmont Park by some kids playing frisbee. Single shot to the head. (9mm. Barrel had to be kissing the temple.) His torso and back were skinned. M.E.'s report suggested that those skinned areas had recently been tattooed. And most exuberantly, as far as Dr. Thomas was concerned. Eddie's wife swears he didn't have any tattoos. The couple had five kids, safe bet she knew her husband's flesh. Eddie used to sell cars at Peabody Dodge. He was a good salesman.

Martin hit the butt again. Let the cigarette dangle from his lips. He studied the photos and M.E.'s report on Elyana Stevens. 27. Working mother, divorced. Blonde, athletic; played third base for the Blue Angels. A local women's softball team. She had also been french-kissed by the same 9mm. A Luger. And she too had been skinned; legs, torso, back and buttocks. Strong indications that those areas had been recently tattooed. Her four year old son doesn't remember Mommy having tatts. Neither does anyone else.

Martin took the cigarette from his lips, set it in the ashtray. He glanced at all the photos and reports on his desk. Seven bodies in all. Kissed by the same Luger, tattooed and skinned. And that's where their connections ended. There were seven tattoo parlors in Phoenix. He had talked to over twenty tattoo artists and scored more "canvases," that is, people who have (wear?) tattoos. Martin couldn't really get a grip on this scene. A lot of the art was indeed fascinating to behold, but it was permanent. Always, you wore it everywhere, doing everything. Never faded away. Martin didn't like that. And he had learned something from an elderly canvas. In Japan, people have clauses in their wills to be skinned when they die. And their families honor the request. The tattooed skin is well cared for, and sometimes sold, if the family has come upon hard times.

Martin softly shook his head, pressed the butt out. Some cultures, strange.

But he wondered if that was what he was dealing with. Was somebody selling the skinned art? This was his project for the now; dive into the art scene.

Martin rubbed his eyes, yawned. He looked around the office; watched his co-workers move about. Languid, quick, sleepy, determined, angry, tired. (Why did we get into law enforcement?)

Martin stood up, pulled his coat off his chair. Started walking. He left his desk in disarray. No one would notice.

Phoenix wasn't that strange when it came to art. The galleries were common fare; their curators all looked down on tattoos. Fine art for the military, prison inmates and drug addicts. He got the indication that the Orient was the only region that had any respect for the art form. Well, maybe L.A.

It took Martin a few days to get on the underground track. Violent, sexual, fearless and blatant. Interesting patrons, good information but no solid leads. In fact, Martin believed that he may have given some people a new religion. One punk wondered aloud if your skin would grow back. And if not, you could always get a lot of little tatts, skin and frame them. Kinda make a collage. That'd be cool.

Martin was skimming through *Interview, BAM, Rocket, Pump* and about a dozen other L.A. and N.Y. based art and trade periodicals. Checking for new, avant-garde artists. Who's making wave or flavor of the month. He might have to do some travelling. Art shows in Cincinnati and Miami really have the locals up in arms. Something new was happening in Seattle. Nothing to do with tattoos but all kinds of people gravitate to view the controversial. Just to get a taste of it. Martin could meet someone interesting.

A manila folder was slapped down hard on Martin's desk, its

contents loosely spilled out. Martin looked up from the magazine and into the ice green eyes of Peter Bines. Racist. With a badge and a gun.

"Got 'nother one for ya, *Super Nigger*." Bines was stern and tight-lipped. "Learnin' anything from those prissy magazines. Ain't filled with nuthin' but freaks and faggots. Artist . . . shit."

Martin stared into a pair of hard orbs. Thought about putting a bullet right between them.

"Ya know, we can handle a case like this. Don't need no federal help. Especially not from some affirmative action monkey."

"This whole district seems to have a problem with race. Did you know you were under investigation for racism? And I'm gonna personally behead you in court." Martin held his nerves in check. "Get the fuck outta my face," he said, low and firm.

Bines sighed, smiled. Adjusted his hat, gunbelt. Posture.

"Do your job boy. Do it right—then get the fuck outta our town. I'm tired of lookin' at you."

"Then commit suicide . . . BOY!"

The looks could've melted steel. Anger so hot, it blistered the soul. Could almost bring tears to your eyes.

Bines, still smiling softly, gently spun on his heels, slowly walked away. He didn't seem to have any outward support. He didn't get a high five from anyone. But the office was alive and aware. Martin sighed, his stomach tight and surging. He knew what he was walking into—he just couldn't believe they were so damn smug about it. How high up does this shit run? And is that why no indictments have been handed down yet?

Fuck it. Focus. Your job; your speciality. Finding murderers who get too damn happy. Martin lit a cigarette, drew in tight and hard on the butt.

He looked at the new evidence. Couldn't believe the luck. The corpse had an unfinished tattoo on his back. Martin checked the ballistics memo: same 9mm kiss. He was getting sloppy.

Martin studied the more detailed photos. The tattoo was outlined in dark ink. It was a jungle waterfall scene. The water appeared at the top of the right shoulder then abruptly dropped straight down the spine, exploding into the wading pool at the top of the buttocks, then streamed down the left cheek and faded off onto the left rear thigh. The tattoo was painted in spots; vivid, brilliant colors. The work looked fine to Martin but then he wasn't the artist. Obviously, he wasn't happy with it, or else he wouldn't have thrown it away.

Martin decided to drop by the morgue and get a better look at the corpse. The body was found about seven hours ago, behind Peterson High School. The body, David Meeks, was reported missing three months ago. He was 24, slight mental retardation. His mother had sent him to the store to get groceries. An easy task that David had done for years.

Martin rose up from behind his desk. He thought about David Meeks, then about Bines. Wondered why the wrong people were always being taken out.

Martin walked into *Live Studio,* a tattoo shop in South Phoenix. Seven people were waiting in the lounge, looking at the hundreds of designs on the wall and watching the three artists work with flesh and ink. Three women were amongst those waiting, two of them were alone. All three were pretty. Martin wondered why they wanted to disfigure such lovely flesh. The first pure and sweetest of arts.

The artists all made eye contact with Martin, they gave him a slight nod or wink. He had talked to all of them at one time or another. No one seemed nervous about him being there. He leaned on the hardwood railing. Watched Pat Simms put an Iron Cross on a young skinhead's beefy bicep. The boy gave Martin his hardest stare.

It was beautiful to see that shit in youth. Fucking lovely.

"How you doin' Pat?" asked Martin. He lit a cigarette, offered Pat one.

"Same-ol-same-ol." He took the offered smoke. The fingers of his rubber glove were stained black. Martin lit Pat's cigarette as James Brown pumped through the Infinities.

"All art has a style, think you can I.D. one for me?" asked Martin. He pulled a photo from his coat pocket. The pictures didn't really show the body. The lab boys had altered the photo so that the tattoo was more than ninety percent of the picture but still displayed the entire waterfall scene. He waved the photo at Pat.

Pat displayed his hands. Martin realized, ink. He showed Pat the shot. The punk also got an eyeful.

"Doesn't look familiar but it's fuckin' good work. Damn good!" Pat turned. "Yo, Eddie, check this man out!"

Martin walked over to Eddie Tuscatrado. The small, wiry Mexican stared the photo down.

"Fuckin' tough. Who did it?" he asked.

Martin smiled. "I was hoping you could tell me."

"Sorry man. Maybe Shel can help you." Pat pointed at the back wall. "We got a studio in the back. Shel is doin' a guy's back right now. Step over the chain, knock on that door over there."

Martin did as he was instructed. He heard the idle talk behind him. Apparently the word was out. Everyone knew what he was looking for: some freak with a passion for tatts. It seemed to make patrons of the scene uncomfortable; they were eager to help. For as Martin often made the point, stressed it in fact; what if the guy gets tired of doing the tatts himself. Decides to go hunting for finished art. No one wants to be skinned. Like an animal.

Martin walked into the brightly-lit studio. It was small but well ventilated. All the supplies were also kept here. Shel was standing over a male body. The body was laying face down on a well padded hospital gurney. The body only had on a pair of shorts and sandals. Martin edged closer . . .

"How you doin' mate?" asked Shel. He was tall, thin, shoulder-length ash-grey hair. Six earrings in total.

"How you doin', Shel? What are you doin'?"

Shel just smiled, stepped back a pace. Martin got a full view. The tattoo covered the man's back. It was a dragon locked in mortal combat with a winged panther. They were fighting in the sky.

"Chris, meet, ah . . ." Shel paused.

"Martin Cole."

"Sorry mate, I'm not that good with names."

"That's alright. Nice work. How long has this taken and how long before you're finished?"

"Mr. Quiz, eh. O.K. mate. It took one four-hour session just to outline the scene. I'm doin' some detailin' now, I'll start colorin' soon. I figure, about three, maybe four three-hour sessions." Shel shrugged his shoulders.

"Chris, how do you feel? I mean, what goes on in your head?" asked Martin. He stepped around to the head of the gurney.

"Well, me and Shel do a lot of talking. I can see him work, check out the mirrors." Chris pointed to the wall. Martin knelt down. Three mirrors twisted at the right angles gave Chris a limited but clear view of his back.

"So you guys just bullshit as Shel gets artistic. Hmmm." Martin stood up. Looked Chris over. He was covered with tatts. Legs, arms . . . "Is your stomach or chest printed?"

"Not yet, but I got time."

Martin just nodded. Thought about the cigarette he left out in the lounge. He wanted to light another one, then beat the urge down. He pulled the photo out of his pocket, showed it to Shel.

"Whoa! That's some work, mate. You want me to tell you who did it? . . . I can't. I don't know anyone that works like this. This is the ol' style. You know, about twenty different sized needles and that thin, hard ink. This wasn't done with one of these guns." Shel handed a tattoo gun to Martin. The gun was small, fit comfortably in the palm. Its needles were tiny and numerous. It sounded like an electric shaver; that dull drone. He handed the gun back to Shel.

Martin sighed. "So, this style is alien to the scene?"

"Western culture, most definitely. I can't even guarantee that its still practiced much over in the Orient. It takes too damn long. Very tedious. You've got a serious artist on your hands. If he worked every day, ten plus hours a day, that outline had to take at least seven, eight weeks. I could do it in about three four-hour sessions."

"Why do you always clock like that? Three four-hour sessions."

"Because most people can't take much more. The process can be uncomfortable. Mind you, I didn't say painful. Although, it does have its moments, but hey . . ." Shel smiled and lightly shrugged his shoulders.

"Yeah, it kinda gets tough when the coloring begins," said Chris.

Martin showed Chris the picture.

"Awesome. This is a tattoo? Incredible." Chris studied the photo, ran his fingers over the picture. "I tell ya, this looks a lot like Peabo," he said at length, very softly.

"Who?" asked Martin and Shel, in unison.

"Peabo. He's a Haitian artist, about seventy years old. Modern impressionist. He hit the scene around '46–'47. He's quite well known." Chris was more sure of himself.

"So you're sayin' this looks like the style of a famous artist? Actual oil and canvas kinda guy?" Martin asked.

"Yep," replied Chris. "I teach art at Saddleback Community College. Come by anytime during the week. I'll educate you on Peabo. We can also go over tattoo art. It's got a rich history, you know. Just ask for Chris Syned. Room A-318."

Chris handed the photo back to Martin. Martin took it, wrote

Chris's name, room number, and the name of the school on the back of it. Then put it back in his coat pocket.

"Thank you, you both have been a tremendous help. Chris, I'll see you tomorrow. Gentlemen, good night."

"Same to you too, mate." Shel slipped on a pair of rubber gloves.

"I'll be waiting for you then. I should be free around one. I've only got two morning classes tomorrow."

"Count on me then," replied Martin. And he walked out the door.

"Any help?" asked Pat. The skinhead was gone. One of the girls, a redhead, was seated before Pat. Pat was rubbing salve on her virgin, right shoulder blade.

"Yeah, I just got another education. Gotta love this job. I'm outta here. Take care."

"You too," said Pat.

Martin walked out of the shop. Hit the streets. He took his windbreaker off, draped it over his arm. The night was warm and dry. It felt good.

You can learn a lot in school. Especially when the teacher is really high on the subject and the student is more than willing to learn.

To both Chris's and Martin's amazement, the waterfall tattoo was an exact copy of a Peabo original; circa 1932. It had been a charcoal relief. Very immature. Then again, Peabo was just starting out.

Martin checked into Peabo. Haitian national who owned property in New York, Los Angeles and north of Phoenix. A lot of well-to-do people have winter retreats in Phoenix. But not many spend summers down here.

Martin drove to Peabo's house. It was in Sunnyvale. Nice area. Clean and wealthy.

He pulled into Peabo's driveway. Parked, got out of the Ford Taurus. Checked out the neighborhood. It was quiet. One could get away with murder here. Hell, one can get away with murder anywhere, he's proven that fact many a time.

Martin spoke into a small recorder. Logged the time and scene.

He walked up to the front door. Knocked.

No answer. So he knocked again. He didn't see a doorbell in sight.

No answer. Two-fifteen in the afternoon. Bright, warm day. Martin sighed, scratched his chest. Then he pulled out a small, hard, thin wire. Jimmied the lock. Walked inside.

The house was cool, almost cold. It was clean, well lit and smartly decorated. Ready for a party or a wake; depending on your mindset. Martin quietly drifted around. He looked at the art; paintings and sculptures, tapestries and painted china.

Martin gave the stairs a quick eye, decided to give the ground floors a clean sweep. He thought about the garage.

In the kitchen, Martin heard the muffled gunshot. Just one report. (One shot to the temple. One lead kiss.) Martin pulled out his service piece. A Colt .45. A classic; strong and true. Direct and as lethal as the Lord's will. It felt good in Martin's hand. He paced slowly toward the garage door.

He pulled out his tape recorder, noted the event.

Martin wondered how a respected, seventy-four year old man got this twisted. And how long has it been going on? Before Phoenix, Martin had encountered only four other similar cases. All in the Utah, Colorado areas. And those incidents happened over four years ago. Did Peabo just go mad? Came to believe that Phoenix had the best flesh around? Flesh that would do more than just accent and compliment his work? Was this the flesh that was bringing his work to life?

Martin snapped himself out of the trance. Those moments scared the hell out of him. The mind link. Psyche mating. He wanted to spit.

Martin gripped the gun with his right hand, opened the garage door with his left.

Peabo had his back to Martin and he was standing under a large studio light. The garage was dark and roomy, it looked like Peabo was under a street lamp. A body laid still on a makeshift bench/bed. The arms and legs were stiffly tied to the legs of the bench. Martin could see from his position that there was nerve-splitting stress on the victim's skin. It was so taut, you could split it with a butterknife. The gun, the 9mm, was on the work table at Peabo's right. Peabo seemed to be just standing there.

Martin eased in. The door softly shut on its own.

Peabo reached out, his old and stiff fingers pushed aside a multitude of stainless steel needles; dirty with paint and blood. Peabo grabbed a straight razor. Moved back toward the body.

"Put the razor down, Peabo. Put it down ole man!"

Peabo turned around. His eyes were old and under a lot of strain. He couldn't see Martin.

"I said, put . . . the . . . razor . . . down. Stay still and don't make me shoot you."

Peabo stood still. Razor in hand. He was squinting quite hard.

"What is this?" the old man said softly.

Martin came into the light. About three feet from the old man. Gun out and pointed at Peabo's small, taut chest.

"F.B.I. You're under arrest."

Peabo saw Martin, understood. He sighed, lowered the razor. He looked at Martin, not really angry, not really guilty. But sad that he wasn't going to be able to finish the work.

"Put the razor down, please." Martin didn't ease his position. But for a second, out of the corner of his eye, he saw blood trickle from the bullet hole on the left of the victim's head. (The right side of his head was splashed on the bench and was dripping onto the concrete floor.) Then Martin smelled the blood, paints, and the tinny taste of urine. He exhaled, a long, slow breath.

Peabo just stood there. He looked at the victim's back. His art.

Peabo looked back at Martin. His eyes pleaded to be allowed to start, to finish. To remove the skin, set the art free.

"For the last time, put the blade DOWN!"

Peabo started to cry. In time, the razor slipped from his hand and fell to the floor.

Martin had logged six weeks vacation time. He was punching that ticket.

Peabo had already exhibited fifteen pieces of the skinned tattoos. A gallery in New York had the work. A court order kept them from continuing to publicly display the art. The order is being fought in court. But, currently, the gallery is complying with the order. Everybody who has anything to do with art is screaming censorship. (Have they forgotten, or does it matter, how the art was produced?)

The families of the victims, once forensics had determined who the flesh (art) belonged to, wanted nothing to do with the skins. Although one family is suing the gallery for back revenue generated from the exhibit. Other families will probably follow suit.

But none of that matters to Martin. He's on vacation. Trying to find fish in some lake in upstate New York.

Aunt Dolly

Ardath Mayhar

OUTSIDE the tightly closed window, the ivy leaves were beating against the small panes in the first real storm of winter. Even though the house was tight, the windows closely fitted, Dorothy shivered, feeling that the heavy draperies, only half drawn as yet in the last light, should be billowing in the fury of the wind.

Snug in her rose-shaded room, safe in the bed in which she had been born, Dorothy should have been content, but in the last month that had been lost to her. The hearty old woman who had broken wild horses, reared her three great-nephews to adulthood, if not to responsibility, and managed the horse farm she had built up from the tatty farm her father left her seemed lost in the past.

Now she was an invalid, wrapped in plush blankets, confined to this room that had never fitted her personality. The pale rose blankets, the deep rose velvet of the draperies, the charming flower pattern of the sheets, those were matters that had appealed to her mother.

Dolly was a farmer, a horse breeder, a tough-minded, tough-bodied creature who had never been ill in all her sixty-seven years. This terrible thing that had happened to her frightened her for the first time she could recall.

A small stroke—what nonsense! You stroked a cat or the nose of a horse. This was more like a blow, aimed not only at her mind but at everything she had ever stood for. Aimed, worst of all, at the independence she cherished above anything else.

There came a stir in the hallway outside her door. A timid tap told her that Cynthia, her third nephew's wife, stood outside with a cup of chocolate and the afternoon paper.

Dolly sighed. "Come on in," she grunted. "And close those damned drapes. That wind wants to come right through the glass, it seems like, and at my age I don't need that for a bedfellow."

Cyn set the tray just so, its legs straddling Dolly's lap, and moved to tug at the velvet rope that shut out the chill pewter of the evening. The delicacy of her motions, the finicky precision of everything she did grated on the old woman's nerves like diamond on glass. She suspected that in private Cynthia was far less ladylike than she appeared now.

"Do sit down!" she commanded. "And don't fiddle! I like my room messy. Makes me feel at home."

She stirred the marshmallow into the steaming cup of chocolate and took a tentative sip. Ah! The warmth relaxed her a bit, and she settled back against the piled pillows behind her, holding down her irritation at the frills edging the cases.

"Tell me about the mare—did Mr. Winlow find out what ails her? She's too valuable to risk, let me tell you, and if we need another vet we've got to get one. Winlow isn't bad, but he's an old fogey in a lot of ways."

"Oh, Auntie, don't worry yourself about the horses. Jerry is taking the most splendid care of everything . . ."

"Don't give me that! Jerry never took splendid care of anything but himself, and that includes taking care of you. He's checking out every salable item on the place with an eye toward sneaking it out to a pawnshop is more like it. He'll rob his brothers, if they're not careful." She watched the young woman closely, but Cynthia had learned to hide her feelings when Dolly went on a tear.

Rather disappointed, Dolly drank down the chocolate and poured another cup from the rosebud-sprigged pot. That was Haviland that she had bought to please her mother, once there was money for that sort of nonsense.

She wondered if any of the pieces had been sold, downstairs, by her rapacious kinsman. The stuff was worth a mint, the antiques-dealer had told her when she made the purchase.

She always rolled her food and drink around her tongue, these days, trying them for any odd taste. She wouldn't put it past Jerry and his nasty-nice wife to try poisoning her. Then they'd have a free run at everything while Ed and Charlie traveled the long miles from England and Africa to protect their interests.

Cynthia turned even paler than usual, but she held her peace. The old saying, "Wouldn't say boo to a goose" applied nicely to her, Dolly thought.

"Winlow," she said again, her tone stern. "Tell!"

"The mare was only bloated. He tended to it and gave her something to help. Jerry says he thinks she'll be fine tomorrow." The words came out slowly, precisely enunciated, spent grudgingly as if they were dollars instead of breath.

"Good." Dolly finished the cup, placed the thin china in its saucer with a decisive clink, and motioned toward the door. "Now go and do whatever it is you find to do all day and all night. I'd as soon talk to a parrot!"

When the door closed behind the thin behind and the sharp elbows of her great-niece-by-marriage, Dolly sighed. She had tried. She truly had!

But those boys were a handful, and no matter how she worked them and taught them and made them toe the mark, they kept breaking out whenever she wasn't expecting it. If she'd had a husband it might have helped. A man would have understood them better.

But as it was, she was a better man than any of the three, and they all knew it. They all resented it, too, which was why Ed had gone to London as soon as his paper had an assignment there. Charlie had taken himself off to Botswana or some such godforsaken place to write a book.

Jerry had been closest, and that only because the chemical firm for which he was a sales rep was based on the west coast. They gave him leave and here he was, complete with baggage and wife, who was also a pretty fair baggage herself.

She listened sharply as the crisp steps descended the uncarpeted stair. The kitchen door gave its usual definitive thunk as it closed, and she smiled. Time to practice walking again.

She didn't intend to be a bed-ridden invalid for the rest of her years, that was certain. But every time she suggested that Jerry help her stand and walk he fussed and worried and all but said that he wanted her flat on her back.

There was no way she was going to put up with that, and his refusal was motivation enough to drive her to secret exercises that by now had strengthened her legs considerably.

"How is the old . . . darling!" Jerry asked, as Cynthia entered the kitchen. "Bitchy as ever?"

She sighed, her thin face pinched. "I think she's a lot stronger than she was. It wouldn't surprise me if she got out of that bed one day and went back to running the farm."

Her husband turned pale. "That's impossible. At her age, with a stroke . . ."

"It was a minor one, with no permanent damage," Dr. Armworth said. "Sixty-seven is not old. Not any more. I warned

41

you to take your time and be certain, but no, you had to sell those two fillies when you had that offer from the breeder in Kentucky. If she takes hold again, you're going to have to buy them back, whatever it costs, and you know we haven't a dime between us."

She glared at him. "We could both go to jail, Jerry, if she gets back to normal."

The man dropped into the rockingchair behind the long table where the family had always eaten informal meals. His sallow face was still pale, and his dark hair drooped dispiritedly over his forehead.

"When Ed and Charlie come, the fat's going to be in the fire. You thought she was a lot worse off than she was, or you never would have risked going ahead with those sales. Now what do we do?"

"We think," he said, putting his head into his hands.

"Think!" she muttered, clanging pans together as she started supper. "With what, I'd like to know?"

"I can't get that money back. Arnie will turn his bruisers loose on me if I don't get another fifteen thousand within the next two weeks. The boys will be here next week, as well. I've just got to sell the gray stallion and use that to clear my account."

She turned on him, red spots glowing in her cheeks. "That's my Jerry—just keep going ahead, even when you know you're going to fall over a cliff in the dark. The old woman's going to get *well*, you fool!"

"Maybe . . . not." He looked up from the rocker, a gleam dawning in his eyes. "Maybe not. Armworth is a lot like the vet—he doesn't keep up with the times, and he all but said that someone her age was likely to pop off at any time. He won't be surprised if she does, and he'll sign her death certificate without any question."

She in her turn, went pale. She turned back to stir the pot on the stove, into which she had been slicing carrots, turnips, potatoes, and cold roast with vicious precision.

Back turned, she said, "You mean to kill her?"

"No, no. Not strangle or anything violent. There's some stuff they prescribe for her that should do it. Just give her her regular dose and put a double-sized one in her supper. She's supposed to have it in her system anyway, and Armworth will never think to do an autopsy."

Cynthia's skinny shoulders sagged suddenly. It was the only

way, and she knew it as well as Jerry did. She didn't like the old biddy, anyway.

Jerry rose and went upstairs. She knew he was visiting the bath that connected their bedroom with that of Aunt Dolly. There was a new vial of medication there, along with a few tablets in the old one.

Like it or not, they were about to become murderers.

Dolly heard the heavy steps coming up the stairs. She had gained a lot of mobility in the past couple of days, and she managed a pretty fair sprint back into bed before they reached the top and came down the hall. To her relief, Jerry went into the bathroom, instead of looking in on her.

She picked up a mystery novel and turned a page, staring at the lines without reading them. She had, she felt, to pretend to be a coddled old lady, helpless, weak, unable to get about. Some instinct told her that her life might depend on it.

Water ran. The toilet flushed. There was a tap on her door, and she glanced about to make sure everything was normal before responding. Her slippers, shed in her flight back to the bed, lay in the middle of the floor. She reached for the cane she used in going to the bathroom and raked them close beside the bed.

"Come in," she said, in her most unoffending voice.

"Cyn's making her special stew tonight," he said. "You'll like it a lot, I think. Should be ready about six-thirty. How are you getting on, auntie?"

"As well as can be expected," she said, her tone dry. "I'm not twenty, Jerry, but I seem to be holding up pretty well, considering." She felt a sudden pang, recalling the thin, tanned little boy who had brought his troubles to her.

He had been the youngest of the three, hit hard by the loss of both parents to a virus infection while they were abroad. He had seemed wary of everyone, as if fearing that they, too, might go away and never return.

She sighed. "That's nice. I like a good stew. But I'm tired now, and I think I'll take a little nap before suppertime."

He nodded and crept out, looking entirely too satisfied with himself. She knew him too well to believe that such a look could possibly be innocent.

When his steps had died away in the distance, she waited. Usually he walked around the place before supper, and when that was something that could be left to simmer Cynthia went along. Perhaps the cold wind would keep them inside, but she hoped they might at least check on the animals in the barn some three hundred yards from the house.

When she had heard nothing from the lower floor for fifteen minutes, Dorothy swung her feet to the floor, slid them into her slippers, and rose unsteadily. The cane propped her nicely, as she donned her robe and headed for the closet.

This was a very old house, and rooms, stairs, even the floors had been altered time and again, over the years. There had been a back stair, once, and her closet was the head of it, using the space between the inner and outer walls to make a walk-in space.

The steps were still there, leading down into blackness and emerging in the back entryway as a deep supply cupboard beside the kitchen door. The well was narrow enough to allow her to brace one hand against the wall while bracing the cane on the other side, securing her slow downward steps.

She paused from time to time, resting, listening for any sound from the kitchen, now just on the other side of the partition. But no hint of movement came to her ears other than the slap of wind-blown shrubbery against the outer wall.

Then her descending foot found no further steps. She was in the cupboard, her right shoulder brushing the shelves stacked with preserves and canned goods, some of them years old. She opened the door a crack and peered into the hallway, finding that after the darkness on the stair even this dim passage was visible.

Nobody.

She crept along the hall and into the kitchen, finding one light burning over the stove and the stewpot simmering obediently, its contents smelling delicious. She was tempted to take a taste before doing what she came to do, but she pushed the impulse away.

She took a vial, salvaged from her stash of medications for healing—and killing—animals, from the pocket of her robe and dumped its contents into the stew, stirring it vigorously with the spoon conveniently placed in the flower-shaped holder. When the last hint of oily liquid was gone, she turned away and made her painful trek back up into her room.

When she dropped into bed again she was genuinely exhausted. Jerry, checking on her before bringing her supper, found himself wondering if he needed to trouble himself to doctor her food, but he knew it was better to be safe.

"She doesn't look good at all," he said with great satisfaction, as he helped Cynthia dish up the stew into rose-sprigged Haviland bowls. He piled crackers on the plate under the bowl, and his wife added a salad to the tray as he assembled his aunt's supper, complete with special seasoning.

Dorothy had to be helped into a sitting position, and he almost felt a qualm, remembering all the times she had nursed him through childhood illnesses. But he placed the tray across her lap, folded the napkin over her chest, and asked if she needed anything else.

"No, no, I'm quite all right. You go and eat your supper. I'll manage by myself. And when I'm done I'll set the tray on the table, here. This does smell good . . ." she inhaled greedily, and he smiled as he closed her door behind him.

Cynthia was waiting for him. She was very persnickety in many ways, he had to admit, but she was an excellent cook. They dug into their meal with good appetite, his enjoyment augmented by relief at the solution of his immediate problem.

Dolly set the tray aside on the bedside table, the stew untouched. That was bad—she had to get rid of it, and the best way was to flush it, if she could make it that far.

She didn't want to risk the Haviland, her footing being as unsteady as it was, so she dumped the stew into the emesis basis kept in the drawer and carried it cautiously into the bathroom. The stew went down without leaving untidy fragments in the bowl, and she rinsed out the basin and set it in the bathroom cabinet before turning toward her room again.

The cane hit a slick spot on the tiled floor and skidded. Dorothy flung out both hands to catch herself as she went forward toward the tub, but even before she hit the hard edge she felt that familiar blackness engulfing her again.

Dr. Winlow rapped on the door. "Miss Pelling? Mr. Danvers? Is anyone there?"

He rapped his heel irritably against the flagstone walk as he waited. Surely, so early in the morning, there would be someone stirring. He had taken the trouble to check again on that mare, and here they were lying slug-abed, neglecting their work.

He rapped again. "It's the vet! Come on, now, I'm a busy man."

He touched the knob and it turned. They hadn't locked the door last night? That was odd, in these days of vandalism and pilfering.

He pushed and went into the wide, inviting hall at the front of the house. Lights were on at its other end, in the kitchen, and he went that way, calling at intervals.

The Danverses were there, all right, convulsed, soiled, and quite dead beside the cold remnants of their meal. On the stove a scum of scorched stew smoked nastily on the low-set burner. There was an odd tang there, even amid the smell of burning.

He turned to find the phone, which he knew was in the hall. Then it occurred to him that the old lady might be upstairs, helpless, hungry, wondering what had happened. He called the sheriff and Dr. Armworth; then he climbed wearily up the dark walnut stair, clinging to the banister and feeling very old and tired.

There was a line of light below Dorothy's door. He tapped softly. "Miss Pelling? Miss Pelling? It's Dr. Winlow."

There was no reply, and he turned the knob and thrust his grizzled head into the room. The covers were tumbled back, but the bed was empty. The door into the bath was, however, open.

He felt something tighten in his throat. He stepped to the door and tapped again. "Do you need help, Miss Pelling?"

Still there was no sound.

He flipped the switch and light blazed from the old-fashioned white ceramic tiles. Dorothy lay sprawled, face down, against the tub, her cane caught beneath her hips, her legs at ungainly angles.

Dead? He touched her wrist, found it cool but not with the chill of death. She was alive, he thought.

Catching her as gently as he could manage in the cramped space, he turned her onto her back, straightening her limbs and pulling her nightgown down over her knees. Her face was drawn down on the left side, the eyes wide, staring up into his, trying, he could feel, to convey something to him.

But this stroke was a major one, unlike the earlier. This time Dorothy Pelling would never ask the question or say the words that burned on her frozen lips.

The Backslider

John Metcalfe

T HE MAN WAS NOW only a couple of miles from the house whither he was bound, and by the time he reached it day would just have broken.

Trudging along the frost-gripped winter lanes, he hardly felt the soreness of his feet or the pain and dizziness that sometimes shot across his head. He rather liked this dizziness and numbness at his brain, when he realised it at all. It helped the illusion that he was walking upon air, suspended somehow between the frozen road and the faint greyness of the sky.

The moon had set about an hour ago, and above him he could just make out the lumpish clouds, floating in a sick and giddy welter. There must be a wind up there to make them swim like that. Their edges were beginning to take on a dirty reddish gleam, the colour of rust.

The man was called John Hawthorne, but now, as he approached the village and the house that lay beyond it, he remembered that he used to have another name. He had been born in that village, gone to school there, and afterwards worked for a time at the house, Caudle End. That was five years ago.

As the thought of Caudle End visited his mind he shot his hand uneasily into his pocket and halted for a moment in his tramp. It was all right. His fingers closed an instant upon what they sought, and with a half-sigh of relief he plodded on again.

Hedges, vague and shadowy, filed past him. Sometimes they slid across and pricked him with their thorns and when he had disengaged himself with a weary oath, he found that the side of the road had changed and he was being pricked again. When this had happened twice or thrice, he realised that he must be walking crookedly, and sat down for a moment's rest. Then he rose and staggered on once more.

As he passed through the village it was just light enough for him to see his breath, puffing out about him in a cloud. Here and there a candle or a lamp shone yellow through a cottage window. Near the church he found, with the tramp's instinct, a crust of bread and a forsaken apple-core. He began to gnaw them ravenously, but loathed them suddenly and let them fall.

The trees were showing out now against the windy greyness of the east, and before long he could distinguish the sky-line of the bitter fields. By the time he had topped the slight rise beyond the village, the cat-ice in the ruts of the lane was salmon-tinted, and a quarter of an hour after that, as he turned a corner and entered upon his final mile of road, the wind dropped all at once, and in the distance a long, low-lying group of buildings stood out a stark and utter black before a blood-red glow.

Daylight—and Caudle End!

In front of him, somewhere in the middle distance of the lane, was a gate opening into a field. He had walked perhaps for a minute before he noticed it, but after that it filled his consciousness absurdly.

For one thing, it showed him how slowly he must be progressing, for although he tried to quicken his pace, the gate seemed to slide away before him and he could not catch it up. He recognised within himself a furtive gladness at its behaviour. Until the moment when he passed it there would be no need for that final bracing and tautening of his weary frame, that last spurring and driving of himself which he dreaded more even than the act for which it was to be the preparation.

After interminable hours he saw there was a figure seated on the gate, and by its skirt he made it out to be a girl or woman.

John Hawthorne smiled, though he knew it was a smile of weakness.

He was thinking that when he got up to her the girl would almost certainly speak to him. He would have to answer her, and that might reasonably delay him a little. It would be funny, too, to stand there talking to her, and she without ever an idea of the thing he carried in his pocket.

He wondered what she would say. In any case, and whoever she was, she could not possibly recognise him. He reminded himself that it would never do for her to recognise him. Recognition in that village and so close to Caudle End would mean taunts and bitter words, perhaps even blows and hounding and pursuit. Old Debb was in the cottage near at hand and might set the dogs on him as once before. And he would be too weak to run. . . .

The words the girl would say to him were gathering an immense importance in his mind. For a moment he even dallied with a thought he knew to be unworthy. Perhaps, if she spoke gently, as the girls of that country-side of his knew how, if she did not scorn his rags and his unshaven face, if she had blue eyes to smile at him, he might never go on to Caudle End at all, might even leave the score unsettled and never find a use for those half-dozen inches of cold and gleaming metal about which his fingers closed so often.

Just for a second he gave one great gasp of utter joy, but then his features fell and hardened back into their mask of steeled resolve. Again the dire weariness descended on him. It was no good. He could not cheat himself. The relief for which he yearned could never come by leaving debts unpaid. After walking forty miles. . . .

"Georgie Davis!"

He had come opposite the gate before he knew and she had called him by his name. That name too! After all, he had been recognised. Fear leapt in his eyes and already he had started to run. . . .

"Georgie Davis!"

The voice was gentle.

In another, or in him at another time, the peculiar, almost tone-less quality of that very gentleness might have produced a different effect. As it was he heard only the softness and beguilement. It seemed that a miracle had come to him. Stopping in his half attempt to run he turned upon her slowly and then burst into tears.

"Come here, Georgie Davis. Tell me why you're crying."

He approached her with hesitation, for it was now light and he was ashamed of his tattered clothes and of his three days' beard.

He found himself speaking:

"I've walked so far. More'n forty mile."

She had pale and rather hollow cheeks and a mass of flaxen hair bound loosely with a green ribbon. She wore only a thin print dress as she sat on the gate in the chilly morning air, yet she did not seem to feel the cold. Her eyes, he could see through his tears, were wide and light and butcher-blue, but, owing to some trick of shadow or accident of posture, he could not fully catch their glance.

He repeated presently with an almost maudlin self-pity:

"More'n forty mile. It's a long tramp."

"Yes, it's a long way. Where are you going, Georgie?"

Suspicion seized him, and he answered her question by another.

"How do you know my name?"

She remained silent a long time, plucking with one hand at the ribbon in her hair, and then replied:

"I remember everybody. I knew you when you were here long ago. I remember all about everyone."

She smiled at him, and something in the monotonous sweetness of that smile distressed him. With a pang he began to wonder whether after all the miracle had not played him false and abandoned him halfway. Once again he was confronted with the horror of his journey's end, and realised, with a dull twinge of shame and self-contempt, how all along those forty weary miles he had been hoping and praying for something that might take the power of vengeance from his hands and render his design impossible. Perhaps he had hoped too much. A voice sang drumming in his ears: "Can't turn back now, can't turn back. . . ." Meanwhile the moments slipped away and he stood there faltering and undecided. Despite the bitter cold the sweat gathered on his brow.

Unconsciously he had moved nearer to the gate on which she sat, and with a sudden start felt her arm against his side and her hand within his pocket.

He leaped back, glaring. Fury possessed him. He had clapped his own hand instantly outside the place where hers had been, and though, through his jacket, he was relieved to feel the same hard, familiar outline, his anger did not leave him.

Then he saw that the girl in her startled shrinking from his violent movement had lost her balance on the gate and was falling backwards. She seemed to fall for an eternity of time, and as he watched his rage evaporated. At last she struck the ground with a soft thud and lay for a few seconds in an awkward, tumbled heap. She picked herself up presently and stood, looking at him fixedly. She did not seem to have hurt herself, for on her face the smile still lingered.

Fright had replaced his fury. She had not succeeded in her attempt to rob him, but at any rate she knew now what his pocket held. She was smiling because she was going back over the hill to get old Debb to set the dogs upon him. He turned to flee.

Then he heard her calling him: "Georgie Davis, Georgie Davis!" and looked back.

Her smile had vanished and her face streamed with tears. "My ribbon," she said. "My ribbon. In your coat."

He thrust his hand within his tattered jacket. For a moment he felt only the cold steel of the revolver, but then his fingers touched something soft and silky, and with a little, wondering cry he pulled out the broad green band that the girl had taken from her hair and stuffed inside his pocket.

He understood it all now, and his heart dissolved in penitence and ruth. A memory of his schooldays visited his mind and brought hot tears springing to his eyes. In that old time the boys had exchanged love-tokens with their sweethearts—perhaps a penknife or a whistle on the one side, and on the other a ribbon or a lock of hair. The poignant recollection unmanned him utterly and he sobbed in fitful, stormy bursts.

"Georgie!" she called again, "Georgie!"

In the bitter morning air and across the gate—that Gate now so stupendous with its weight of symbolism and significance—they kissed, and in the pulsing warmth and glow of that caress the dire purpose that had lain like ice about his heart melted and swam and was no more. . . . The unbelievable had happened. Miracle was accomplished.

She held him long and hard. Her kisses, ravenous and burning, fled about his face with a fiery rapidity of motion that almost resembled the hungry nuzzling of a horse. Her breath and her red, tireless lips seemed to lap him at every point like flame and incense. He had never been kissed like that before. . . .

Then he drew back. Perhaps for a second, even in his joy, some faint misgiving crossed his brain, but it faded instantly. She was a wonderful girl and it was natural her embraces should be wonderful as well. His only regret was that he was too weak and tired to return her kiss for kiss.

Out over the hill voices became audible. They were calling to someone: "Nancy, Nancy. . . ."

The girl started away from the gate and backed slowly into the field.

"I'll have to go," she said in hurried, frightened tones. "They'll find me if I don't. Good-bye, Georgie. But I'll come back soon."

For a fleeting instant her face, as it caught the morning light, was turned towards him in farewell, and for the first time he met the expression in the eyes. His own glance somehow shrank and fell before that stare, and when, a second later, he raised his head to look at her, she had already vanished.

And then, opportunely, he happened, almost directly afterwards, upon the travelling coffee-stall.

He had walked for a few paces—on air indeed, yet painfully and with many a stumble because of his still-present physical distress—away from the gate where the girl had left him when, round a hidden turning of the lane it clattered suddenly into his view—a long barrow upon wheels with a polished copper urn steaming at its rear and in front of that a great cyclinder of tin from which arose into the frosty air the smell of fried potatoes.

Miracle had come to him it was true, yet in the meantime his stomach was empty and his throat dry. The memory of some few odd halfpence in his pocket struck his mind with the force of a revelation, and presently he was gulping down delicious draughts and cramming his mouth with hot and savoury crisps.

The old fellow who served him gave him a shivering "Good-morning" and was surprised when his customer after returning the salutation subsided into immoderate bursts of laughter.

When the coffee-stall and its proprietor had trundled off towards the village, Davis, sitting down beneath a hedge, began to shout and sing. His soul was shouting too, and his body warmed now to a generous, tingling glow by the hot food and drink.

Nightmare had lifted its last shadows from about him. Near the side of the road lay a heap of building-stones, and the coating of frost upon them, as it moistened and melted and began to run, caught a rosy radiance like the radiance that filled his heart. In this moment of deliverance and joy all that had gone before, his hatred and his ancient grudge, his year-long nursed desire for revenge, the arduous forging of the final bitter purpose in the smoky caverns of his mind, the destitution that had made him desperate and careless of the results of what he planned, the weary tramp of forty miles—all save the sudden and bewildering transport of the reaction from misery to bliss, fell from him as the forgotten terrors of some fevered dream. Tears of utter relief and thankfulness coursed down his cheeks.

And for his self-respect he was able to tell himself that it was by something that the girl had been or done that this miracle was wrought.

He sat under the hedge a few minutes longer, and then decided he would get a shave. He still had three-halfpence in his pocket, and now that this scheme had been abandoned it did not matter much where he was seen. As for that he had already passed the time of day with the owner of the coffee-stall. If he went on to the next village it was unlikely that anyone would recognise him and taunt him with what had happened five years back. Then, after his shave, he would return and see the girl again. . . .

Sitting in the barber's chair half an hour later he remembered the ribbon and drew it from his pocket. He held it out between finger and thumb and chuckled with a foolish exultation at the chaff of the man who lathered him. As his hand returned the token to its place he felt the revolver and frowned. He would have to get rid of that before he went much further.

He left the shop and ambled back at ease. He washed his swollen feet in a brook and felt much better. To some extent he was now rested and refreshed. He was able to think.

His mind reverted to the girl and to her kisses. He was stronger now and could kiss as passionately as she. He longed to do so.

He began, curiously, to look back upon those few minutes at the gate with incredulity and a sort of glamorous tenderness as upon something that might have happened very long ago but certainly would never come again.

He wished she had not been called away like that. He would have liked to give her some inkling of what he had intended and tell her how she had saved him from himself. He would have struck a figure so. Then they might have walked and talked together. This word "together" gathered about itself a desolating and sentimental sweetness hardly to be borne. And he had been violent with her— with her whose kisses had delivered him. She had even fallen over the gate. How cruel life had been!

Then he remembered the name that had been called to her across the fields—Nancy. He repeated it, slowly and many times, seeking in his brain for some buried hint of memory, some association or forgotten incident that it might recall.

Who was she? The question, now that his faculties were quickened by the hot drink and the food, faced him starkly, as it had not done before. Who, after all, was this girl who had recognised him in spite of his shabby clothes and bristling chin, and had remembered too that old, foolish, sweet tradition of love-making at school? For a moment an image haunted his mind and then faded as he sought to grasp it. Suddenly he frowned.

Glancing up just then he found that in his abstraction he had already passed the gate. The girl was nowhere to be seen. About a hundred yards ahead of him he noticed that the coffee-stall had halted at the corner of a lane. The old man was seated by its side, intent upon his breakfast. Perhaps the girl had come and gone again and he could say which way she had taken. At any rate, decided Davis, he would ask.

He hurried forward, stopped and spoke; he asked the ancient if he had seen her; explained that he had expected to meet her; went on, as the old fellow remained silent, to describe her as well as he could; even, in a strange and growing apprehension, showed the strand of dark green ribbon; ceased finally and waited with a beating heart for the reply.

It was then, as he waited, that the winter morning countryside grew dark about him, that the encircling sky-line of the fields changed to a bitter, blackening ring, that the very heavens above him curdled and hardened to a dire, frowning arch. For at last he had seen the reason for the long-continued silence. The old man before him was shaking, shaking with a repressed and voiceless laughter that caused his dirty beard to wag and pressed tears of merriment from his rheumy eyes.

Presently the paroxysm abated and it was possible to catch the words that wheezed and tickled in his throat: "Nancy Clegg . . . Nancy. . . . Nancy Clegg. . . ."

With an oath the other sprang upon him and shook him till at last the laughing ceased and his question could be heard.

"What about her? Tell me, what about her?"

Presently the withered lips began to move and Davis bent his head to listen.

When at length he raised it he was laughing too, and, a whole minute later, the old man, as he looked up from the breakfast he had calmly recommenced, noted with a mild surprise that his companion was still convulsed by a dry and shattering mirth.

It was not far from the coffee-stall to Caudle End, and Davis, though a little delayed by those constant bursts of laughter, had made short work of the mile or so of field and barren scrub.

Just as half-past eight sounded from the clock above the stables he came upon a man, morning pipe alight, strolling round a corner of the coach-house.

It was the man he had walked so far to see, and he was just turning in to breakfast.

The first shot shattered the pipe and the second whistled through a shoulder. The third was a miss, but the fourth ripped a tear in the jacket and the next found the heart.

As his enemy fell forward dead upon his face Davis noted the time and smiled. It could be little more than an hour and a half since he parted from Nancy Clegg. Well, his backsliding for which she was responsible had been of short duration.

Becoming aware of shouts and cries, he ran. There was good cover under a high wall and then along a deep and frost-bound ditch. He came out at last by the side of a hedge, panting, but on the whole well satisfied. Then, looking up, he frowned.

A little way ahead he saw someone in a print dress. As she neared him he was presently able to distinguish the monotonous sweetness of the smile upon her face.

She came up to him and stopped with her arms stretched out towards him. Her silly, wheedling voice began: "Georgie Davis. . . ."

Then, as the sound of thudding footsteps and hardly stifled shouting rose louder on his ears from behind the screening hedge, he remembered he had one shot left in his revolver.

It entered somewhere above her right breast. She stumbled and then fell backwards.

Just before his pursuers burst upon him and surrounded him Davis had time to notice the expression that still lingered on the mad girl's upturned face.

A look of half-surprised disgust crossed his own. Even without that old man's information he might have known her for the village idiot. She was still smiling.

Blank . . .

Harlan Ellison

DRIVER HALL was an impressive pastel blue building in the center of the city. Akisimov had no difficulty finding its spirally-rising towers, even though the sykops were close behind, but once within sight of the structure, he found himself lost.

How could he do it?

No Driver would intentionally help a criminal escape, yet a Driver was his only possible chance of freedom.

Akisimov's bleak, hard features sagged in fright as he sensed the tentative probes of the sykops in his mind. They had found the flower girl, and they were circling in on him, getting his thoughts pinpointed. *Why* had that stupid urchin wandered across his path? It had been a clean escape, till he had run out of the mouth of that alley, and stumbled into her. *Why* had she clung to him? He hadn't *wanted* to burn her down . . . he was only trying to get away from the sykops.

Akisimov cast about hungrily with his eyes. There had to be some way, some device to corner a Driver. Then he spotted the service entrance to the Hall. It was a dark hole in the side of the building, and he sprinted across the street, in a dead run for it. He made the comparative safety of the entrance without being openly noticed, and crouched down to wait. Wildly, he pulled the defective mesh cap tighter about his ears. It was the only thing standing between him and capture by the sykops, poor thing that it was. Had it been a standard make, not a lousy rogue cheapie model, it would have blanked him effectively, but as it was, it was the best he had.

With unfamiliar phrases he prayed to some unknown God to let the mind-blanking cap work well enough. Well enough to keep the sykops off him till he could kidnap a Driver.

Rike Akisimov had been sentenced to Io penal colony for a thousand years. The jurymech knew such a sentence bordered on the ridiculous; even with the current trends in geriatrics, *no* man could live past three hundred. The body tissue, the very fiber, just wouldn't stand up to it.

But in token hatred for this most vile of criminals, the placid and faceless jurymech had said: "We, the beings of the Solarite, sentence you, Rike Amadeus Akisimov, to the penal colony on Io for a period of one thousand years."

Then, as the jury room buzzed with wonder, the machine added, "We find in your deeds such a revulsion, such a loathing, that we feel even *this* sentence is too light. Rike Amadeus Akisimov, we find in you no identification with humanity, but only a resemblance to some odious beast of the jungle. You are a carrion-feeder, Akisimov; you are a jackal and a hyena and a vulture, and we pray your kind is never again discovered in the universe.

"We cannot even say, 'God have mercy on your soul,' for we are certain you have no soul!"

The jury room had been stunned into silence. For an implacable, emotionless jurymech to spew forth such violent feelings, was unprecedented. Everyone knew the decision-tapes were fed in by humans, but no one, absolutely *no one,* could have fed in those epithets.

Even a machine had been shocked by the magnitude of Akisimov's crimes. For they were more than crimes against society. They were crimes against God and Man.

They had taken him away, preparing to lead him in the ferry-flit designed to convey prisoners from court to the spaceport, when he had struck. By some remarkable strength of his wrists—born of terror and desperation—he had snapped the elasticords, clubbed his guards and broken into the crowds clogging the strips, carrying with him a sykop blaster.

In a few minutes he was lost to the psioid lawmen, had ripped a mind-blanking mesh cap from a pedestrian's head, and was on his way to the one escape route left.

To the Hall and the psioids known as Drivers.

She came out of the building, and Akisimov recognized her at once as a senior grade Driver. She was a tall girl, tanned and beautifully-proportioned, walking with the easy, off-the-toes stride of the experienced spaceman. She wore the mind's eye and jet tube insignia of her class-psi on her left breast, and she seemed totally unconcerned as Akisimov stepped out of the service entrance, shoved the blaster in her ribs, and snarled, "I've got nothing but death behind me, sister. The name is Akisimov . . ." The girl turned a scrutinizing stare on him as he said his name; the Akisimov case had been publicized; madness such as his could not be kept quiet; she knew who he was, ". . . so you better call a flit, and do it quick."

She smiled at him almost benignly, and raised her hand lazily in a gesture that brought a flit scurrying down from the idling level.

"The spaceport," Akisimov whispered to her, when they were inside and rising. The girl repeated the order to the flitman.

In half an hour they were at the spaceport. The criminal softly warned the psioid about any sudden moves, and hustled the girl from the flit, making her pay the flitman. They got past the port guards by the Driver showing her I.D. bracelet.

Once inside, Akisimov dragged the girl out of sight behind a blast bunker and snapped quickly, "You have a clearance, or do I have to hijack a ship?"

The girl stared blankly at him, smiling calmly and enigmatically.

He jabbed the blaster hard into her side, causing her to wince, and repeated viciously, "I *said,* you got a clearance? And you damned well better answer me or so help me God I'll burn away the top of your head!"

"I have a clearance," she said, adding solemnly, "you don't want to do this."

He laughed roughly, gripped her arm tightly. She ground her lips together as his fingers closed about the skin, and he replied, "They got me on a thousand yearer to Io, lady. So I want to do any goddam thing that'll get me out of here. Now what ship are you assigned to snap?"

She seemed to shrug her shoulders in finality, having made a token gesture, and answered, "I'm snap on the *Lady Knoxmaster,* in pit eighty-four."

"Then let's go," he finished, and dragged her off across the field.

"You don't want to do this," she said again, softly. He was deaf to her warning.

When the invership took off, straight up without clearance coordinates and at full power, the Port Central went crazy, sending up signals, demanding recognition info, demanding this, demanding the other. But the *Lady Knoxmaster* was already heading out toward snap-point.

Akisimov, gloating, threw in the switch and knew the telemetering cameras were on him. "Goodbye, you asses! Goodbye, from Rike Akisimov! Stupid! You thought I'd spend a thousand years on Io? There are better things for me in the universe!"

He flicked off, to let them call the sykops, so the law would know he had bested them. "Yeah, there isn't anything worse than a life term on Io," he murmured, watching the planet fall away in the viewplates.

"You're wrong, Akisimov," the girl murmured, very, very softly.

Immediately the sykops and the SpaceCom sent up ships to apprehend the violator, but it was obvious the ship had enough start momentum to reach snap-out—if a Driver was on board—before they could reach it. Their single hope was that Akisimov had no Driver aboard, then they could catch him in a straight run.

On board the *Lady Knoxmaster,* Akisimov studied the calm-faced psioid girl in the other accelocouch.

Drivers were the most valuable, and yet the simplest-talented, of all the types of psionically equipped peoples in the field. Their one capacity was to warp a ship from normal space into that not-space that allowed interstellar travel; into inverspace.

Though the ship went through—set to snap-out by an automatic function of the Driver's psi faculty—the Driver did not. That was the reason they were always in-suit and ready for the snap. Since *they* did not snap when the ship did, they were left hanging in space, where they were picked up immediately after by a doggie vessel assigned to each takeoff.

But this time there was no doggie, and there was no suit, and Akisimov wanted the girl dead in any event. He might have made some slip, might have mumbled something about where "out there" he was heading. But whether he had or had not, dead witnesses were the only safe witnesses.

"Snap the ship," he snarled at her, aiming the blaster.

"I'm unsuited," she replied.

"Snap, damn your lousy psi hide! Snap damn you, and pray the cops on our trail will get to you before you conk out. What is it, seven seconds you can survive in space? Ten? Whatever it is, it's more of a chance than if I burn your head off!" He indicated with a sweep of his slim hand the console port where the bips that were sykop ships were narrowing up at them.

"You don't want to do this," the girl tried again.

Akisimov blasted. The gun leaped in his palm, and the stench of burned-away flesh filled the cabin. The girl stared dumbly at the cauterized stump that had been her left arm. A scream started to her mouth, but he silenced her with the point of the blaster.

She nodded acquiescence.

She snapped. Though she could not explain what was going on in her mind, she knew what she was doing, and she concentrated to do it this time . . . though just a bit differently . . . just a bit specially. She drew down her brows and concentrated, and . . .

blank . . .

The ship was gone, she was in space, whirling, senseless, as the bulk of a ship loomed around her, hauling her in.

She was safe. She would live. With one arm.

As the charcoal-caped sykops dragged her in, lay her in a mesh webbing, they could not contain their anxiety.

"Akisimov? Gone?"

They read her thoughts, so the girl said nothing. She nodded slowly, the pain in her stump shooting up to drive needles into the base of her brain. She moaned, then said, "He didn't get away. He thought the worst was a term on Io; he's wrong; he's being punished."

They stared at her, as her thoughts swirled unreadably. They stared unknowingly, wondering, but damning their own inefficiency. Akisimov had gotten away.

They were wrong.

blank . . .

The ship popped into inverspace.

blank . . .

The ship popped out . . .

In the center of a white-hot dwarf star. The sun burned the ship to molten slag, and Akisimov died horribly, flamingly, charringly, agonizingly, burningly as the slag vaporized.

Just at the instant of death . . .

blank . . .

The ship popped into inverspace.

blank . . .

The ship popped out . . .

In the center of a white-hot dwarf star. The sun burned the ship to molten slag, and Akisimov died horribly, flamingly, charringly, agonizingly, burningly as the slag vaporized.

Just at the instant of death . . .

blank . . .

The ship popped into inverspace.

blank . . .

The ship popped out . . .

Over and over and over again, till the ends of Time, till Eternity was a remote forgotten nothing, till death had no meaning, and life was something for humanity. The Driver had exacted her revenge. She had set the ship in a möebius whirl, in and out and in and out and in again from inverspace to out, right at that instant of blanking, right at that instant of death, so that Forever would be spent by Rike Amadeus Akisimov in one horrible way—ten billion times one thousand years. One horrible way, forever and ever and ever.

Dying, dying, dying. Over and over and over again, without end to torment, without end to horror.

blank . . .

Bless Us O Lord

Ed Gorman

I USUALLY THINK of Midwestern Thanksgivings as cold, snowy days. But as we gathered around the table this afternoon, my parents and my wife, Laura, and our two children, Rob and Kate, I noticed that the blue sky and sunlight in the window looked more like an April day than one in late November.

"Would you like to say grace today?" my mother said to four-year-old Kate.

Kate of the coppery hair and slow secretive smile nodded and started in immediately. She got the usual number of words wrong and everybody smiled the usual number of times and then the meal began.

Dad is a retired steelworker. I remember, as a boy, watching fascinated as he'd quickly work his way through a plate heaped with turkey, sweet potatoes, dressing, cranberry sauce and two big chunks of the honey wheat bread Mom always makes for Thanksgiving and Christmas. And then go right back for seconds of everything and eat all that up right away, too.

He's sixty-seven now and probably thirty pounds over what he should be and his eyesight is fading and the only exercise he gets is taking out the garbage once a day—but he hasn't, unfortunately, lost that steelworker's appetite.

Mom on the other hand, thin as she was in her wedding pictures, eats a small helping of everything and then announces, in a sort of official way, "I'm stuffed."

"So how goes the lawyer business?" Dad asked after everybody had finished passing everything around.

Dad never tires of reminding everybody that his youngest son did something very few young men in our working-class neighborhood did—went on to become a lawyer, and a reasonably successful one, too, with downtown quarters in one of the shiny new office buildings right on the river, and two BMWs in the family, even if one of them is fourteen years old.

"Pretty well, I guess," I said.

Laura smiled and laid her fingers gently on my wrist. "Someday this son of yours has to start speaking up for himself. He's doing very well. In fact, Bill Grier—one of the three partners—told your son here that within two years he'll be asked to be a partner, too."

"Did you hear that, Margaret?" Dad said to Mom.

"I heard," she said, grinning because Dad was grinning.

Dad's folks were Czechs. His father and mother landed in a ship in Galveston and trekked all the way up to Michigan on the whispered rumor of steel mill work. Dad was the first one in his family to learn English well. So I understood his pride in me.

Laura patted me again and went back to her food. I felt one of those odd gleeful moments that married people get when they realize, every once in a while, that they're more in love with their mates now than they were even back when things were all backseat passion and spring flowers.

Of course, back then, I'd been a little nervous about bringing Laura around the house. Mom and Dad are very nice people, you understand, but Laura's father is a very wealthy investment banker and I wasn't sure how she'd respond to the icons and mores of the working class—you know, the lurid and oversweet paintings of Jesus in the living room and the big booming excitement Dad brings to his pro wrestling matches on the tube.

But she did just fine. She fell in love with my mom right away and if she was at first a little intimidated by the hard Slav passions of my father, she was still able to see the decent and gentle man abiding in his heart.

As I thought of all this, I looked around the table and felt almost tearful. God, I loved these people, they gave my life meaning and worth and dignity, every single one of them.

And then Mom said it, as I knew she inevitably would. "It's a little funny without Davey here, isn't it?"

Laura glanced across the table at me then quickly went back to her cranberry sauce.

Dad touched Mom's hand right away and said, "Now, Mom, Davey would want us to enjoy ourselves and you know it."

Mom was already starting to cry. She got up from the table and whispered, "Excuse me," and left the dining room for the tiny bathroom off the kitchen.

Dad put his fork down and said, "She'll be all right in a minute or two."

"I know," I said.

My six-year-old son, Rob, said, "Is Gramma sad about Uncle Davey, Grandpa?"

And Dad, looking pretty sad himself, nodded and said, "Yes, she is, honey. Now you go ahead and finish your meal."

Rob didn't need much urging to do that.

A minute later, Mom was back at the table. "Sorry," she said.

Laura leaned over and kissed Mom on the cheek.

We went back to eating our Thanksgiving meal.

Davey was my younger brother. Five years younger. He was everything I was not—socially poised, talented in the arts, a heart-breaker with the ladies. I was plodding, unimaginative and no Robert Redford, believe me.

I had only one advantage over Davey. I never became a heroin addict. This happened sometime during his twenty-first year, back at the time the last strident chords of all those sixties protest guitars could be heard fading into the dusk.

He never recovered from this addiction. I don't know if you've ever known any family that's gone through addiction but in some ways the person who suffers least is the person who is addicted. He or she can hide behind the drugs or the alcohol. He doesn't have to watch himself slowly die, nor watch his loved ones die right along with him, or watch them go through their meager life savings trying to help him.

Davey was a heroin addict for fourteen years. During that time he was arrested a total of sixteen times, served three long stretches in county jail (he avoided prison only because I called in a few favors), went through six different drug rehab programs, got into two car accidents—one that nearly killed him, one that nearly killed a six-year-old girl—and went through two marriages and countless clamorous relationships, usually with women who were also heroin addicts (a certain primness keeps me from calling my brother a "junkie," I suppose).

And most of the time, despite the marriages, despite the relationships, despite the occasional rehab programs, he stayed at home with my folks.

Those happy retirement years they'd long dreamed of never came because Davey gave them no rest. One night a strange and exotic creature came to the front door and informed Dad that if Davey didn't pay him the drug money he owed him in the next twenty-four hours, Davey would be a dead man. Another night Davey pounded another man nearly to death on the front lawn.

Too many times, Dad had to go down to the city jail late at night to bail Davey out. Too many times, Mom had to go to the doctor to get increased dosages of tranquilizers and sleeping pills.

Davey was six months shy of age forty and it appeared that given his steely Czech constitution, he was going to live a lot longer—not forgo the heroin, you understand—live maybe another full decade, a full decade of watching him grind Mom and Dad down with all his hopeless grief.

Then a few months ago, early September, a hotel clerk found him in this shabby room frequently used as a "shooting gallery." He was dead. He'd overdosed.

Mom and Dad were still working through the shock.

"Is there pink ice cream, Grandma?" Kate asked.

Grandma smiled at me. Baskin-Robbins has a bubble-gum-flavored ice cream and Mom has made it Kate's special treat whenever she visits.

"There's plenty of pink ice cream," Grandma said. "Especially for good girls like you."

And right then, seeing Kate and my mother beaming at each other, I knew I'd done the right thing sneaking up to the hotel room where Davey sometimes went with other junkies, and then giving him another shot when he was still in delirium and blind ecstasy from the first. He was still my brother, lying there dying before me, but I was doing my whole family a favor. I wanted Mom and Dad to have a few good years anyway.

"Hey, Mr. Counselor," Dad said, getting my attention again. "Looks like you could use some more turkey."

I laughed and patted my burgeoning little middle-class belly. "Correction," I said. "I could use a lot more turkey."

The Blind Spot

Saki

Y OU'VE JUST COME BACK from Adelaide's funeral, haven't you?" said Sir Lulworth to his nephew; "I suppose it was very like most other funerals?"

"I'll tell you all about it at lunch," said Egbert.

"You'll do nothing of the sort. It wouldn't be respectful either to your great-aunt's memory or to the lunch. We begin with Spanish olives, then a borsch, then more olives and a bird of some kind, and a rather enticing Rhenish wine, not at all expensive as wines go in this country, but still quite laudable in its way. Now there's absolutely nothing in that menu that harmonizes in the least with the subject of your great-aunt Adelaide or her funeral. She was a charming woman, and quite as intelligent as she had any need to be, but somehow she always reminded me of an English cook's idea of a Madras curry."

"She used to say you were frivolous," said Egbert. Something in his tone suggested that he rather endorsed the verdict.

"I believe I once considerably scandalized her by declaring that clear soup was a more important factor in life than a clear conscience. She had very little sense of proportion. By the way, she made you her principal heir, didn't she?"

"Yes," said Egbert, "and executor as well. It's in that connection that I particularly want to speak to you."

"Business is not my strong point at any time," said Sir Lulworth, "and certainly not when we're on the immediate threshold of lunch."

"It isn't exactly business," explained Egbert, as he followed his uncle into the dining-room. "It's something rather serious. Very serious."

"Then we can't possibly speak about it now," said Sir Lulworth; "no one could talk seriously, during a borsch. A beautifully constructed borsch, such as you are going to experience presently, ought not only to banish conversation but almost to annihilate thought. Later on, when we arrive at the second stage of olives, I shall be quite ready to discuss that new book on Borrow, or, if you prefer it, the present situation in the Grand Duchy of Luxemburg. But I absolutely decline to talk anything approaching business till we have finished with the bird."

For the greater part of the meal Egbert sat in an abstracted silence, the silence of a man whose mind is focussed on one topic. When the coffee stage had been reached he launched himself suddenly athwart his uncle's reminiscences of the Court of Luxemburg.

"I think I told you that great-aunt Adelaide had made me her executor. There wasn't very much to be done in the way of legal matters, but I had to go through her papers."

"That would be a fairly heavy task in itself. I should imagine there were reams of family letters."

"Stacks of them, and most of them highly uninteresting. There was one packet, however, which I thought might repay a careful perusal. It was a bundle of correspondence from her brother Peter."

"The Canon of tragic memory," said Lulworth.

"Exactly, of tragic memory, as you say; a tragedy that has never been fathomed."

"Probably the simplest explanation was the correct one," said Sir Lulworth; "he slipped on the stone staircase and fractured his skull in falling."

Egbert shook his head. "The medical evidence all went to prove that the blow on the head was struck by some one coming up behind him. A wound caused by violent contact with the steps could not possibly have been inflicted at that angle of the skull. They experimented with a dummy figure falling in every conceivable position."

"But the motive?" exclaimed Sir Lulworth; "no one had any interest in doing away with him, and the number of people who destroy Canons of the Established Church for the mere fun of killing must be extremely limited. Of course there are individuals of weak mental balance who do that sort of thing, but they seldom conceal their handiwork; they are more generally inclined to parade it."

"His cook was under suspicion," said Egbert shortly.

"I know he was," said Sir Lulworth, "simply because he was about the only person on the premises at the time of the tragedy. But could anything be sillier than trying to fasten a charge of murder on to Sebastien? He had nothing to gain, in fact, a good deal to lose, from the death of his employer. The Canon was paying him quite as good wages as I was able to offer him when I took him over into my service. I have since raised them to something a little more in accordance with his real worth, but at the time he was glad to find a new place without troubling about an increase of wages. People were fighting rather shy of him, and he had no friends in this country. No; if any one in the world was interested in the prolonged life and unimpaired digestion of the Canon it would certainly be Sebastien."

"People don't always weigh the consequences of their rash acts," said Egbert, "otherwise there would be very few murders committed. Sebastien is a man of hot temper."

"He is a southerner," admitted Sir Lulworth; "to be geographically exact I believe he hails from the French slopes of the Pyrenees. I took that into consideration when he nearly killed the gardener's boy the other day for bringing him a spurious substitute for sorrel. One must always make allowances for origin and locality and early environment; 'Tell me your longitude and I'll know what latitude to allow you,' is my motto."

"There, you see," said Egbert, "he nearly killed the gardener's boy."

"My dear Egbert, between nearly killing a gardener's boy and altogether killing a Canon there is a wide difference. No doubt you have often felt a temporary desire to kill a gardener's boy; you have never given way to it, and I respect you for your self-control. But I don't suppose you have ever wanted to kill an octogenarian Canon. Besides, as far as we know, there had never been any quarrel or disagreement between the two men. The evidence at the inquest brought that out very clearly."

"Ah!" said Egbert, with the air of a man coming at last into a deferred inheritance of conversational importance, "that is precisely what I want to speak to you about."

He pushed away his coffee cup and drew a pocket-book from his inner breast-pocket. From the depths of the pocket-book he produced an envelope, and from the envelope he extracted a letter, closely written in a small, neat handwriting.

"One of the Canon's numerous letters to Aunt Adelaide," he explained, "written a few days before his death. Her memory was already failing when she received it, and I dare say she forgot the contents as soon as she had read it; otherwise, in the light of what subsequently happened, we should have heard something of this letter before now. If it had been produced at the inquest I fancy it would have made some difference in the course of affairs. The evidence, as you remarked just now, choked off suspicion against Sebastien by disclosing an utter absence of anything that could be considered a motive or provocation for the crime, if crime there was."

"Oh, read the letter," said Sir Lulworth impatiently.

"It's a long rambling affair, like most of his letters in his later years," said Egbert. "I'll read the part that bears immediately on the mystery.

" 'I very much fear I shall have to get rid of Sebastien. He cooks divinely, but he has the temper of a fiend or an anthropoid ape, and I am really in bodily fear of him. We had a dispute the other day as to the correct sort of lunch to be served on Ash Wednesday, and I got so irritated and annoyed at his conceit and obstinacy that at last I threw a cupful of coffee in his face and called him at the same time an impudent jackanapes. Very little of the coffee went actually in his face, but I have never seen a human being show such deplorable lack of self-control. I laughed at the threat of killing me that he spluttered out in his rage, and thought the whole thing would blow over, but I have several times since caught him scowling and muttering in a highly unpleasant fashion, and lately I have fancied that he was dogging my footsteps about the grounds, particularly when I walk of an evening in the Italian Garden.'

"It was on the steps in the Italian Garden that the body was found," commented Egbert, and resumed reading.

" 'I dare say the danger is imaginary; but I shall feel more at ease when he has quitted my service.' "

Egbert paused for a moment at the conclusion of the extract; then, as his uncle made no remark, he added: "If lack of motive was the only factor that saved Sebastien from prosecution I fancy this letter will put a different complexion on matters."

"Have you shown it to any one else?" asked Sir Lulworth, reaching out his hand for the incriminating piece of paper.

"No," said Egbert, handing it across the table, "I thought I would tell you about it first. Heavens, what are you doing?"

Egbert's voice rose almost to a scream. Sir Lulworth had flung the paper well and truly into the glowing centre of the grate. The small, neat handwriting shrivelled into black flaky nothingness.

"What on earth did you do that for?" gasped Egbert. "That letter was our one piece of evidence to connect Sebastien with the crime."

"That is why I destroyed it," said Sir Lulworth.

"But why should you want to shield him?" cried Egbert; "the man is a common murderer."

"A common murderer, possibly, but a very uncommon cook."

Boomerang

Hugh B. Cave

I DON'T EXPLAIN this story. It goes nowhere, it offers nothing, it has no beginning except in the thickness of a drunken man's tongue, and if it has an end I was not there to see it. Yet it troubles me and it will trouble you.

To begin with there were three of us in a place then called Kemal Sel's, which is in Sandakan on the northeast coast of Borneo, distant about seven days by steam from Singapore. The hour was near two in the afternoon and Sel's was an oven. The rain outside tumbled down from the hills, over the sandstone cliffs of Bahalla, in a deluge.

We were Kuyper, the cutch man, Matheson, the steamboat agent, and myself, Wilkes, of the B.N.B. Company.

"I ran into a queer one," Kuyper said.

He was home today from two weeks inland by river, by *prahu*, among the Kayan's of the upriver *kampongs* where still, despite trade and religion, the savages are children. He was home and glad to be home, and glad it was safe to drink again. He liked his rum. His belly was a barrel.

"I never did learn the fellow's name," he said. "We'll call him Smith. He—"

I said, "Wait." The fellow at the corner table was getting up. Was coming over.

He'd been there when we arrived, sitting in the gloom of his own thoughts. A white man but an odd one, bushy as a Hindu, his breed and age hidden by his beard. A derelict, perhaps, but that's a hard name. Few whites in Borneo are derelicts pure and simple. Drinking gets some; fever, homesickness, heat and rain and monotony get others.

He came over and nodded to us and said, "I've been working up nerve enough to ask to join you. Shouldn't, of course, but company's damned scarce and I'm fed up, being alone. Mind?"

You don't say no. Whites are whites, even with beards and sick eyes. I leaned back and pulled up a chair for him. We ordered drinks.

"This yarn of yours, Kuyper?" Matheson prompted.

Kuyper fished a pouch from his pocket—a new one, I noticed—and packed his pipe. "We'll call him Smith. I got the tale in a *kampong* deep in Kayan country. Diamonds up there, you know—small ones, not worth much, but plenty of them. Smith had his heart set on getting some."

You either liked Kuyper or you didn't. Most didn't, but it made no difference to him; he was big, important, he liked himself enough to make up for the dislike of others. I've called him a cutch man but that's leaving a lot unsaid. He'd come to Sandakan years ago as owner-captain of a freighter. He'd holed up, sold his ship and gone to work on a spirit farm, then bullied himself into a cutch concession and was rich now. And usually drunk.

He traveled a lot and told ugly stories. This was apt to be one of them.

"I was up there, you know, looking over the territory with an eye for raw materials." He drained his glass and blew smoke into it, grinning. The bushy man sipped slowly and eyed him.

"This fellow Smith wanted diamonds. He'd heard there were plenty in this particular *kampong*—place run by an old *kapala* named Makali. He was right, there was a fortune, but he was too late. Fellow named Phipps was there ahead of him. Young chap, honest trader—the stupid, plodding type. Smith, of course, was a bad one. Like me."

He laughed alone. Matheson glanced my way and raised an eyelid, which was safe enough then because Kuyper was too drunk to notice. The stranger smoked and sat and said nothing, but his eyes belonged in the yellow head of a *krait*.

"This fellow Phipps had been there a week," Kuyper said, "and the Kayans liked him. It was up to Smith, of course, to pay respects. Common decency. But Smith heard about the diamonds, heard that young Phipps had bought the whole mess, and he put his brains to work. You chaps ever see a *lansat* pod, the poison kind?"

"Seen the fruit," Matheson said. "Tastes like a plum."

"Not the kind I mean," said Kuyper, his grin ugly. "Comes from a dwarf variety found in that region. It's a pod, about the size and shape of a lima bean but fragile. Powders in your hand when dry. Deadly poisonous. Worst poison I know. Well . . . Smith had some that he'd picked and dried and was intending to bring back to—that is, to take back with him. He planted them in Phipps' tent."

It was going to be that kind of story. You could see it in Kuyper's ugly grin, in his red-flecked eyes. And not because he was drunk, either. Drunk or sober his idea of humor was always the same.

I signaled the Hainan waiter, but the bearded man was ahead of me. He said, "Mine, this time," and pushed himself up. He was long-legged as a mantis and walked with a limp.

He brought the drinks himself and sat down again, and there was a lull while Kuyper rolled his glass in his beefy hands to warm it. A finger tapped my shoulder and I turned to frown into the withered Javanese face of Kemal Sel.

"Mister Wilkes," Sel said. "I like to ask you question, please. Private."

I was an old customer. I walked with him to the far end of the room, where he held out a wrinkled hand in which something glittered.

"That man—he don't tell me his name—he give me this to pay for drinks. He say it worth money. I take it, but I don't know. I never see him before. Maybe he cheat me."

I looked at the stone and suppressed an urge to turn and stare at the bearded man. I thought, "It's damned queer, his coming to our table like that, not naming himself." The stone was a small uncut diamond. You don't find them on the coast.

When I sat down again Kuyper was saying, "Well, this chap Smith went to old Makali, the *kapala*, with a cock-and-bull story that was sheer genius. He told Makali that Phipps was bad medicine. Phipps was the wickedest *bliam*—that's a witch-doctor, you know—that ever lived. Most likely Phipps was planning to put a curse on the whole *kampong* and destroy it, and it might be a good idea to investigate. You can make those simple natives believe anything, you know."

The bearded man said, "Can you?"

"You can if you're as smart as Smith was," Kuyper retorted.

"Well, the Kayans got Phipps out of his tent on a ruse and turned his stuff inside out. Of course they found the poison pods. That settled it."

"They—killed him?"

"Not in so many words, no. Wouldn't dare, with Divisional Forest Officers dropping in every so often. No . . . they just drove him out. Stripped him to his boots and trousers, hung the pouch of *lansat* pods around his neck and sent him packing."

Matheson shuddered. The bearded man stared over the top of his glass and his breath made bubbles in the rum and his eyes smouldered.

I said, "He had no chance, of course. The jungle, the flies, fever, snakes, starvation . . ." and when Kuyper laughed I added, "Smith got the diamonds?"

"Bought them for a song. Smart man, that Smith."

Matheson said, "A dangerous game. Perhaps he underestimated the chances of this fellow Phipps."

"Eh?"

"With luck, Phipps might have reached some friendly *kampong.*"

Kuyper drained his glass and blew a loud laugh to the ceiling. "Alone, unarmed, with nothing to eat but dried poison pods, he might have licked the jungle? Don't make me laugh!"

"There's a thing called justice, Kuyper," I said, "that sometimes gives a man strength to carry on."

He shook his head, scowling now. "More than likely he ate the *lansat* pods to cut short his misery. Sensible thing to do, at any rate. One would be enough."

There was a pause.

The bearded man said, "I think not. I think he would have saved them."

"Eh? Why?"

"For Smith," he said and stood up.

He gave me the creeps, that fellow, and I was glad to see him go. I finished my drink and looked at my watch and said to Matheson, "Well?" To Kuyper I said, "Sorry to run off, but there's work to be—" and then I was silent, staring.

Something was wrong with the man. His square face was the color of goat's milk and smeared with perspiration. He sat like wood, staring at an object the bushy fellow had left lying there on the table.

It was a tobacco pouch, an old one. I reached for it and my glance fell on Kuyper's glass.

Something more than rum had been in that glass. A little brown thing, only half dissolved, shaped like a lima bean, clung to the bottom of it.

Clean Slate

H. Wolff Salz

E D TOLAN WAITED in a dark doorway across the street from the dimly lighted tavern. The brim of his gray felt hat was pulled low over his eyes and the collar of his overcoat covered the lower part of his face. His gloved hands were buried deep in the overcoat pockets. His right hand gripped a .38 automatic.

When Leroy Mannix finally emerged from the tavern, Ed straightened and his muscles tensed. There was another man with Mannix, someone he had evidently met at the bar. The other man was short and thin, a little guy who couldn't have been much over five feet tall. They talked for a moment and then separated, the little guy moving with a limp in one direction, Mannix walking briskly away in the opposite direction.

Ed crossed the street diagonally, following Mannix. He stayed ten yards behind the other's tall, lean figure. The street was deserted. The warehouses and factories on both sides were dark. Mannix was apparently absorbed in his own thoughts. He seemed unaware that he was followed.

When Mannix neared the mouth of an alley, Ed quickened his pace. Mannix turned suddenly, evidently aware for the first time of the clicking footsteps behind him. His myopic eyes squinted at Ed's approaching figure uncertainly, then opened wide in astonishment as he finally recognized Ed.

"What—what are you doing around here, Tolan?" he blurted.

"I've been following you."

In the wan glow of a distant street light, Mannix's tired face seemed to turn gray.

"Why?" he demanded in a cracked voice.

Ed moved to within inches of Mannix. His right hand emerged part way from his pocket, enough to reveal the automatic cupped in his big, gloved hand. "Does this give you the answer?"

Mannix started violently, his eyes moving in horror from the exposed automatic to Ed's grim face. "Listen, Tolan—it won't do you any good! Killing me won't—"

"Shut up!" Ed snarled. "I'll do the talking!"

Mannix's eyes darted wildly up and down the dark street. His breath caught in a sob as he saw they were alone.

"I'll let Judy get the divorce!" he gasped. "Listen, you don't have to kill me! I'll let her have the divorce, Tolan!"

"It's too late now, Mannix. The last time I asked you to give Judy her freedom, you laughed at me! It's my turn to laugh! You think I'd believe what you say now, when you're facing this automatic!"

"I swear it, Tolan! Let me go and I won't stand in your way!"

"No, you won't stand in my way—"

Ed's finger released the automatic's safety catch. A moment later, a cone of orange-yellow flame spurted from the muzzle. The report in the midnight stillness was like the crack of a bullwhip. A small black circle appeared suddenly between Mannix's eyes, above the bride of his nose. He crumpled soundlessly to the sidewalk.

Ed pocketed the automatic and knelt over the inert figure. Calmly he probed the dead man's pockets, found the wallet. He straightened and darted into the alley as he heard startled shouts from the doorway of the tavern halfway down the block.

Less than five minutes later, when he reached his parked car four blocks away, he paused in the darkness, extracted the few bills he found in Mannix's wallet, and tossed the empty billfold into the gutter. Probably, the cops would put the motive down as robbery. It was that kind of neighborhood.

A smile of satisfaction touched his lips as he drove away. Even if the cops didn't believe the motive had been robbery, there would still be no reason to link him with the murder. Other than Judy Mannix, there was now no one on earth beside himself who knew he and Mannix had even been acquainted.

He and Judy had been careful. Mannix would never have guessed a thing if Ed hadn't gone to his house one evening, introduced himself and flatly demanded that he let Judy divorce him. Mannix had refused to believe Judy no longer loved him, had laughed in Ed's face. Even Judy's demands had failed to move him.

Ed fought down the urge to drive straight to Judy, tell her that Mannix no longer stood in their way, to hold her in his arms, press her close. But that would have to wait. Now, more than ever, they would have to be careful.

Later, in two or three months, there would be time enough for the full ecstasy of her warm lips, and the heady fragrance of her soft blonde hair.

He was humming a lilting tune under his breath as he opened his apartment door. He shut the door, flicked the light switch. His breath caught in his throat as he stared wide-eyed at the thin little man who sat in a chair facing the door. The little man smiled, stood up. His coat was unbuttoned, exposing a blue-striped shirt. There was a gun in his hand.

"Greetings, pal."

"Who are you?" Ed demanded in a stunned-voice.

"A pal sent me."

"You—you must be in the wrong apartment."

"Naw, you're Ed Tolan, all right. Mannix described you to a T."

"Mannix!"

"Yeah, a friend of yours. He thinks a lot of you. Thinks your life is worth as much as five C's. Can you imagine that! Five C's, cash on the barrelhead for a punk like you! Usually, I do a pushover job like this for two or three C's."

Ed's mouth was suddenly dry. His tongue felt thick, hairy. "Listen," he whispered hoarsely, "Mannix is dead!"

The little man grinned wisely.

"You'll have to dig up a better angle, pal."

"It's the truth! I swear it!"

"He must have died awful quick," the little guy retorted, still grinning, "because I just been with him not an hour ago. He told me about you—and I don't like rats like you. Me, I believe in shooting straight where dolls are concerned. Yeah, it'd almost be a pleasure to knock you off for free."

The little guy backed towards the open window. Beyond him and the softly billowing curtains, Ed could see the rail of the fire escape. He saw the tightening of the little guy's fingers around his gun.

"Wait!" Ed called hoarsely. "Don't——"

There was a red flash. Something hot tore into his chest. The room spun as Ed teetered on his heels, sank to the floor. Through a red fog of pain he saw the little guy put one foot over the window sill, sit there a moment. He saw the little guy aim his gun again, deliberately, calmly.

Somehow, Ed found his automatic in his hand. He lifted his leaden arm, slowly, with his last ebbing ounce of strength. He aimed it at the little guy's head. Through a blur, he saw the little guy's eyes widen in surprise, but only momentarily. Then there was the reverberating thunder of rapid gunfire. Ed pulled the trigger of his automatic as darkness closed over him.

The little gunman sat astride the window sill for a stunned moment. A circle of red spread slowly over his striped shirt. His head bowed forward and he stared down at the widening crimson spot on his chest with dull, unbelieving eyes. Then slowly, he tilted forward into the room again, flat on his face, and lay motionless. Above him, the organdy curtains billowed softly into the room.

Close Calls

John Lutz

S HE WASN'T SUPPOSED to die. She had no life insurance, no liquid assets to speak of, no really solid reason to be dead. Yet there she lay, looking, Graham Hopper thought, rather smug about the whole thing. It was so like her.

And here was Graham, now a widower—middle-aged and getting older by the minute—with little cash, very dim prospects, and a voracious mortgage payment. The future seemed an abyss.

His wife Adelle had done this to him—Adelle, along with Martin Marwood. It was their fault that Graham was about to attend a funeral that should never be taking place.

It was one of the most miserable affairs Graham had ever endured. The preacher was garrulous. A chilling light rain fell throughout and the mourners were forced to stand about the grave in a virtual swamp. It took Graham hours to shake his depression.

Then he went directly to see Martin Marwood at Close Calls, Incorporated.

Close Calls was on the sixteenth floor of the Belmont Building downtown. Ostensibly it was a telephone-solicitation company that did seasonal work, but Graham knew better. Close Calls had been very discreetly recommended to him three months ago by a very close friend. Some friend!

At the sixteenth floor, Graham stepped from the nervous elevator and walked down a long gray hall lined with office doors. From behind some of the doors came the rhythmic clatter of electric typewriters. Near the end of the hall Graham saw the wood door with its frosted glass panel on which was lettered CLOSE CALLS, INC. WE COMMUNICATE. Graham cursed under his breath as he entered.

There was no one in the small plainly furnished anteroom. Graham pressed a button as directed by a hand-printed sign, a buzzer sounded, and after a moment Marwood himself opened the door to his inner office and peered out.

Marwood was a small man, neatly if flashily dressed in a muted plaid blue suit that must have been tailor-made. He had a professionally cheerful blunt-featured face, a receding hairline, and deepset electric dark eyes. "Hey," he said, grinning as if nothing were wrong, "Mr. Hopper."

"You bet your business," Graham said.

Marwood appeared puzzled. "I don't follow."

"You muffed it," Graham said with controlled anger. "You killed my wife as dead as the Edsel."

"Oh, that," Marwood said. "Come into the office and we'll talk about it."

He led the way into his large office, plainly furnished as if for efficiency like the anteroom. No high overhead here, the office seemed to say—more for your dollar. Marwood sat behind a cluttered steel desk and motioned Graham toward a high-backed padded chair nearby. Graham shook his head and remained standing. The faded green walls of the office were restful, their framed dimestore prints perfectly aligned. A window air-conditioner emitted a soothing hum. Graham refused to be soothed.

"Now what's this about your wife?" Marwood asked, making a neat pink tent with his fingers.

"My wife is dead."

Marwood appeared perplexed, and then his potatoish features expressed comprehension. "Say, that's right, Graham—may I call you Graham?—I remember reading the operative's report yesterday. Your wife stepped directly into the path of a speeding car. A hit-and-run, I'm afraid."

Graham felt the room becoming warmer. "But the car was supposed to barely miss her," he said in exasperation. "That's the service Close Calls is supposed to render. Adelle was to be badly shaken so she'd think hard about dying and transfer some of her assets into my name and take out a large life insurance policy. As it stands, I can't touch the business, and Adelle had no insurance. You've reduced me to poverty."

"Hey, Graham, I'm sorry." Marwood began to doodle with a gold pen on a small writing pad. Graham saw that he was sketching intricate little mazes. "But you're not exactly poverty-stricken," Marwood said. "In cases like these, Close Calls does refund half the fee."

"Half?"

"That's five-thousand dollars, Graham. Nothing to scorn."

"But nothing to what I've lost!" Graham almost shouted. "Lost because of your incompetence!"

"Don't say incompetence," Marwood implored in a hurt tone. "Ninety-nine percent of our clients are more than satisfied. You are unfortunately one of the other one percent. Hey, nothing is perfect. I assure you I feel as badly about your wife as you do."

"But you profited from her death. I lost."

"Consider the squirrel," Marwood said.

Graham was dumbfounded. "Squirrel?"

"Yes. Have you ever noticed what happens when a squirrel runs out into the street and finds itself in the path of an oncoming car? The squirrel freezes, Graham, then usually it runs away from the car. But occasionally it darts directly beneath the car's wheels. It's a reflex action, a sort of death wish. Well, people are sometimes like squirrels. People are unpredictable. That's what happened, Graham. Your wife froze, then ran the wrong way, directly into the path of the car that was supposed to barely miss her. There are off days in this business when things like that happen, which is the reason we have certain built-in safeguards."

"Safeguards?"

"Sure, Graham. Like recordings of all conversations that take place in this office. I mean, hey, let's be candid, guy, you can't very well go to the police. You're implicated, guilty of second-degree murder." Marwood was sketching rows of barred windows on the pad.

Graham sighed deeply, and stood in the center of the office with his hands in his pockets. "I'm not a stupid man, Marwood. I've taken all this into consideration."

Marwood touched the point of the gold pen to his chin. "Have you?"

"We're both guilty of murder. And you have a profitable business to lose. I'd say the police are out of this entirely."

Marwood smiled and began to doodle again, crossing out the bars on the windows. "I'm glad you realize that, Graham."

"And I understand what you mean about one accident occurring out of a hundred successful close calls. That's inevitable."

Marwood's smile stretched even wider. "It's nice to know you've been listening to me."

"And you can keep my entire fee, for all I care. In my position—which is bankruptcy—the money would simply be devoured by my creditors anyway."

"Vultures," Marwood agreed, but a glint of uneasiness had kindled in his dark eyes.

"All that's left for me, really," Graham said, "is revenge. Or, to be more specific, poetic justice."

Marwood had stopped smiling, but he was still confident. "You should know, Graham, that upon my death certain records will immediately be brought to light. It's another necessary safeguard."

Graham shrugged. "Oh, I'm prepared to place my fate in the hands of chance—both of our fates, in fact."

Marwood began to doodle frantically. "I don't follow."

"One time out of a hundred," Graham reiterated, "something goes wrong. But is it going to be the first time, or the hundredth?"

"There's no way to know," Marwood said, deftly marking out a neat pattern of question marks.

Graham removed the gun from his pocket.

Marwood glanced up just in time to see the flash of the muzzle. He was too stunned to scream as the gun roared and the bullet went snapping past his right ear with a sound like a cracking whip. He lifted a hand to his head incredulously, turned, and stared, horrified at the ugly bullet hole in the green plaster behind his desk. If he had happened to incline his head to the right a fraction of an inch at the moment of the shot . . .

"One," Graham said simply, replacing the gun in his pocket. "Think about the next ninety-nine. Consider the squirrel."

He walked to the door and opened it, then, before leaving, he turned.

"Take care," he said to Marwood.

The Cobblestones of Saratoga Street

Avram Davidson

C OBBLESTONES TO GO," said the headline. Miss Louisa lifted her eyebrows, lifted her quizzing-glass (probably the last one in actual use anywhere in the world), read the article, passed it to her sister. Miss Augusta read it without eyeglass or change of countenance, and handed it back.

"They shan't," she said.

They glanced at a faded photograph in a silver frame on the mantelpiece, then at each other. Miss Louisa placed the newspaper next to the pewter chocolate-pot, tinkled a tiny bell. After a moment a white-haired colored man entered the room.

"Carruthers," said Miss Augusta, "you may clear away breakfast."

"Well, *I* think it is outrageous," Betty Linkhorn snapped.

"My dear," her grandfather said mildly, "you can't stop progress." He sipped his tea.

"Progress my eye! This is the only decently paved street in the whole town—you know that, don't you, Papa? Just because it's cobblestone and not concrete—or macadam—or—"

"My dear," said Edward Linkhorn, "*I* remember when several of the streets were still paved with wood. I remember it quite particularly because, in defiance of my father's orders, I went barefoot one fine summer's day and got a splinter in my heel. My mother took it out with a needle and my father thrashed me . . . Besides, don't you find the cobblestones difficult to manage in high-heeled shoes?"

Betty smiled—not sweetly. "I don't find them difficult at all. Mrs. Harris does—but, then, if *she'd* been thrashed for going bare-

80

foot . . . Come on, Papa," she said while her grandfather maintained a diplomatic silence, "admit it—if Mrs. Harris hadn't sprained her ankle, if her husband wasn't a paving contractor, if his partner wasn't C. B. Smith, the state chairman of the party that's had the city, county *and* state sewn up for twenty years—"

Mr. Linkhorn spread honey on a small piece of toast. " 'If wishes were horses, beggars would ride—' "

"Well, what's wrong with that?"

" '—and all mankind be consumed with pride.' My dear, I will see what I can do."

His Honor was interviewing the press. "Awright, what's next? New terlets in the jail, right? Awright, if them bums and smokies wouldn't of committed no crimes they wouldn't be in no jail, right? Awright, what's next? Cobblestones? *Cobblestones?* Damn it, *again* this business with the cobblestones! You'd think they were diamonds or sumphin'. Aw*right.* Well, om, look, except for Saratoga Street, the last cobblestones inna city were tore up when I was a *boy,* for Pete's sake. Allathem people there, they're living in the past, yaknowwhatimean? Allathem gas lamps in frunna the houses, huh? Hitching posts and carriage blocks, for Pete's sake's! Whadda they think we're living inna horse-and-buggy age? *Awright,* they got that park with a fence around it, private property, okay. But the streets belong to the City, see? Somebody breaks a leg on them cobblestones, they can *sue* the City, right? So—*cobblestones?* Up they come, anats all there is to it. Awright, what's next?"

His comments appeared in the newspaper (the publisher of which knew what side his Legal Advertisements were buttered on) in highly polished form. *I yield to no one in my respect for tradition and history, but the cobblestoned paving of Saratoga Street is simply too dangerous to be endured. The cobblestones will be replaced by a smooth, efficient surface more in keeping with the needs of the times.*

As the Mayor put it, "What's next?"

Next was a series of protests by the local, county, and state historical societies, all of which protests were buried in two-or-three-line items in the back of the newspaper. But (as the publisher put it, "After all, C.B., business is business. And, besides, it won't make any difference in the long run, anyway.") the Saratoga Street Association reprinted them in a full-page advertisement headed PROTECT OUR HERITAGE, and public interest began to pick up.

It was stimulated by the interest shown in the metropolitan papers, all of which circulated locally. BLUEBLOODS MAN THE BARRI-CADES, said one. 20TH CENTURY CATCHES UP WITH SARATOGA STREET, said another. BELOVED COBBLESTONES DOOMED, HISTORICAL SARATOGA STREET PREPARES TO SAY FAREWELL, lamented a third. And so it went.

And it also went like this: *To the Editor, Sir, I wish to point out an error in the letter which claimed that the cobblestones were laid down in 1836. True, the houses in Saratoga Street were mostly built in that year, but like many local streets it was not paved at all until late in the '90s. So the cobblestones are not as old as some people think.*

And it went like this, too:

Mr. Edward Linkhorn: Would you gentlemen care for anything else to drink?

Reporter: Very good whiskey.

Photographer: Very good.

Linkhorn: We are very gratified that a national picture magazine is giving us so much attention.

Reporter: Well, *you* know—human interest story. Not much soda, Sam.

Photographer: Say Mr. Linkhorn, can I ask you a question?

Linkhorn: Certainly.

Photographer: Well, I notice that on all the houses—in all the windows, I mean—they got these signs, *Save Saratoga Street Cobblestones.* All but one house. How come? They *against* the stones?

Reporter: Say, that's right, Mr. Linkhorn. How come—?

Linkhorn: Well, gentlemen, that house, number 25, belongs to the Misses de Gray.

Reporter: de Gray? de Gray?

Linkhorn: Their father was General de Gray of Civil War fame. His statue is in de Gray Square. We also have a de Gray Avenue.

Reporter: His *daughters* are still living? What are they like?

Linkhorn: I have never had the privilege of meeting them.

Miss Adelaide Tallman's family was every bit as good as any of those who lived on Saratoga Street; the Tallmans had simply never *cared* to live on Saratoga Street, that was all. The Tallman estate had been one of the sights of the city, but nothing remained of it now except the name *Jabez Tallman* on real estate maps used in searching land titles, and the old mansion itself—much modified now, and converted into a funeral parlor. Miss Tallman herself lived in a nursing home. Excitement was rare in her life, and she had no intention of passing up any bit of attention which came her way.

"I knew the de Gray girls well," she told the lady from the news syndicate. This was a big fib; she had never laid eyes on them in her life—but who was to know? She had *heard* enough about them to talk as if she had, and if the de Gray girls didn't like it, let them come and tell her so. Snobby people, the de Grays, always were. What if her father, Mr. Tallman, *had* hired a substitute during the Rebellion? *Hmph.*

"Oh, they were the most beautiful things! Louisa was the older, she was blonde. Augusta's hair was brown. They always had plenty of beaux—not that I didn't have my share of them too, mind you," she added, looking sharply at the newspaper lady, as if daring her to deny it. "But nobody was ever good enough for *them.* There was one young man, his name was Horace White, and—oh, he was the *hand*somest thing! I danced with him myself," she said complacently, "at the Victory Ball after the Spanish War. He had gone away to be an officer in the Navy, and he was just the most handsome thing in his uniform that you ever saw. But *he* wasn't good enough for them, either. He went away after that—went out west to Chicago or some such place—and no one ever heard from him again. Jimmy Taylor courted Augusta, and Rupert Roberts—no, Rupert was sweet on Louisa, yes, but—"

The newspaper lady asked when Miss Tallman had last seen the de Gray sisters.

Oh, said Miss Tallman vaguely, many years ago. *Many* years ago . . . (Had she really danced with anybody at the Victory Ball? Was she still wearing her hair down then? Perhaps she was thinking of the Junior Cotillion. Oh, well, who was to know?)

"About 1905," she said firmly, crossing her fingers under her blanket. "But, you see, nobody was *good* enough for them. And so, by and by, they stopped seeing *anybody.* And that's the way it was."

That was not quite the way it was. They saw Carruthers.

Carruthers left the house on Sunday mornings only—to attend at the A.M.E. Zion Church. Sunday evenings he played the harmonium while Miss Louisa and Miss Augusta sang hymns. All food was delivered and Carruthers received it either at the basement door or the rear door. The Saratoga Street Association took care of the maintenance of the outside of the house, of course; all Carruthers had to do there was sweep the walk and polish the brass.

It must not be thought that because his employers were recluses, Carruthers was one, too; or because they did not choose to communicate with the outside world, he did not choose to do so, either. If while engaged in his chores, he saw people he knew, he would greet them. He was, in fact, the first person to greet Mrs. Henry Harris when she moved into Saratoga Street.

"Why, hel-lo, Henrietta," he said. "What in the world are *you* doing here?"

Mrs. Harris did not seem to appreciate this attention.

Carruthers read the papers, too.

"What do they want to bother them old stones for?" he asked himself. "They been here long as I can remember."

The question continued to pose itself. One morning he went so far as to tap the Cobblestones story in the newspaper with his finger and raise his eyebrows inquiringly.

Miss Augusta answered him. "They won't," she said.

Miss Louisa frowned. "Is all this conversation necessary?"

Carruthers went back downstairs. "That sure relieves my mind," he said to himself.

"The newspapers seem to be paying more attention to the de Gray sisters than to the cobblestones," Betty Linkhorn said.

"Well," her grandfather observed, "People *are* more important than cobblestones. Still," he went on, *"House of Mystery* seems to be pitching it a little stronger than is necessary. They just want to be left alone, that's all. And I rather incline to doubt that General M. M. de Gray won the Civil War all by himself, as these articles imply."

Betty, reading further, said, *"Hmmm.* Papa, except for that poor old Miss Tallman, there doesn't seem to be anyone alive—outside of their butler—who has ever *seen* them, even." She giggled. "Do you suppose that maybe they could be *dead?* For years and *years?* And old Carruthers has them covered with wax and just dusts them every day with a feather mop?"

Mr. Linkhorn said he doubted it.

Comparisons with the Collier brothers were inevitable, and newsreel and television cameras were standing by in readiness for—well, no one knew just what. And the time for the repaving of Saratoga Street grew steadily nearer. An injuction was obtained; it expired. And then there seemed nothing more that could be done.

"It is claimed that removal would greatly upset and disturb the residents of Saratoga Street, many of whom are said to be elderly," observed the judge, denying an order of further stay; "but it is significant that the two oldest inhabitants, the daughters of General M. M. de Gray, the Hero of Chickasaw Bend, have expressed no objection whatsoever."

Betty wept. "Well, why *haven't* they?" she demanded. "Don't they realize that this is the beginning of the end for Saratogo Street? First the cobblestones, then the flagstone sidewalks, then the hitching posts and carriage blocks—then they'll tear up the common for a parking lot and knock down the three houses at the end to make it a through street. Can't you *ask* them—?"

Her grandfather spread his hands. "They never had a telephone," he said. "And to the best of my knowledge—although I've written—they haven't answered a letter for more than forty years. No, my dear, I'm afraid it's hopeless."

Said His Honor: "Nope, no change in plans. T'morra morning at eight A.M. sharp, the cobblestones *go*. Awright, what's next?"

At eight that morning a light snow was falling. At eight that morning a crowd had gathered. Saratoga Street was only one block long. At its closed end it was only the width of three houses set in their little gardens; then it widened so as to embrace the small park—"common"—then narrowed again.

The newsreel and television cameras were at work, and several announcers described, into their microphones, the arrival of the Department of Public Works trucks at the corner of Saratoga and Trenton Streets, loaded with workmen and air hammers and pickaxes, at exactly eight o'clock.

At exactly one minute after eight the front door of number 25 Saratoga Street, at the northwest corner, swung open. The interviewers and cameramen were, for a moment, intent on the rather embarrassed crew foreman, and did not at first observe the opening of the door. Then someone shouted, *"Look!"* And then everyone noticed.

First came Carruthers, very erect, carrying a number of items which were at first not identifiable. The crowd parted for him as if he had been Moses, and the crowd, the Red Sea. First he unrolled an old, but still noticeably red, carpet. Next he unfolded and set up two campstools. Then he waited.

Out the door came Miss Louisa de Gray, followed by Miss Augusta. They moved into the now absolutly silent crowd without a word; and without a word they seated themselves on the campstools—Miss Louisa facing south, Miss Augusta facing north.

Carruthers proceeded to unfurl two banners and stood—at

parade rest, so to speak—with one in each hand. The snowy wind blew out their folds, revealing them to be a United States flag with thirty-six stars and the banner of the Army of the Tennessee.

And while at least fifty million people watched raptly at their television sets, Miss Louisa drew her father's saber from its scabbard and placed it across her knees; and Miss Augusta, taking up her father's musket, proceeded to load it with powder and ball and drove the charge down with a ramrod.

After a while the workmen debated what they ought do. Failing to have specific instructions suitable to the new situation, they built a fire in an ashcan, and stood around it, warming their hands.

The first telegram came from the Ladies of the G.A.R.; the second, from the United Daughters of the Confederacy. Both, curiously enough, without mutual consultation, threatened a protest march on the City Hall. In short and rapid succession followed indignant messages from the Senior Citizens' Congress, the Sons of Union Veterans, the American Legion, the B'nai Brith, the Ancient Order of Hibernians, the D.A.R., the N.A.A.C.P., the Society of the War of 1812, the V.F.W., the Ancient and Accepted Scottish Rite, and the Blue Star Mothers. After that it became difficult to keep track.

The snow drifted down upon them, but neither lady, nor Carruthers, moved a thirty-second of an inch.

At twenty-seven minutes after nine the Mayor's personal representative arrived on the scene—his ability to speak publicly without a script had long been regarded by the Mayor himself as something akin to sorcery.

"I have here," the personal representative declared loudly, holding up a paper, "a statement from His Honor announcing his intention to summon a special meeting of the Council for the sole purpose of turning Saratoga Street into a private street, title to be vested in the Saratoga Street Association. *Then*—" The crowd cheered, and the personal representative held up his hands for silence. "*Then,* in the event of anyone sustaining injuries because of cobblestones, the City won't be responsible."

There were scattered boos and hisses. The representative smiled broadly, expressed the Municipality's respect for Tradition, and urged the Misses de Gray to get back into their house, please, before they both caught cold.

Neither moved. The Mayor's personal representative had not

reached his position of eminence for nothing. He turned to the D.P.W. crew. "Okay, boys—no work for you here. Back to the garage. In fact," he added, "take the day off!"

The crew cheered, the crowd cheered, the trucks rolled away. Miss Louisa sheathed her sword, Miss Augusta unloaded her musket by the simple expedient of firing it into the air, the Mayor's representative ducked (and was immortalized in that act by twenty cameras). The Misses de Gray then stood up. Reporters crowded in, and were ignored as if they had never been born.

Miss Louisa, carrying her sword like an admiral as the two sisters made their way back to the house, observed Betty and her grandfather in the throng. "Your features look familiar," she said. "Do they not, Augusta?"

"Indeed," said Miss Augusta. "I think he must be Willie Linkhorn's little boy—are you?" Mr. Linkhorn, who was seventy, nodded; for the moment he could think of nothing to say. "Then you had better come inside. The girl may come, too. Go home, good people," she said, pausing at the door and addressing the crowd, "and be sure to drink a quantity of hot rum and tea with nutmeg on it."

The door closed on ringing cheers from the populace.

"Carruthers, please mull us all some port," Miss Louisa directed. "I would have advised the same outside, but I am not sure the common people would *care* to drink port. Boy," she said, to the gray-haired Mr. Linkhorn, "would you care to know why we have broken a seclusion of sixty years and engaged in a public demonstration so foreign to our natures?"

He blinked. "Why . . . I suppose it was your attachment to the traditions of Saratoga Street, exemplified by the cobble—"

"Stuff!" said Miss Augusta. "We don't give a hoot for the traditions of Saratoga Street. And as for the cobblestones, those dreadful noisy things, I could wish them all at the bottom of the sea!"

"Then—"

The sisters waved to a faded photograph in a silver frame on the mantelpiece. It showed a young man with a curling mustache, clad in an old-fashioned uniform. "Horace White," they said, in unison.

"He courted us," the elder said. "He never would say which he preferred. I refused Rupert Roberts for him, I gave up Morey Stone. My sister sent Jimmy Taylor away, and William Snow as well.

When Horace went off to the Spanish War he gave us that picture. He said he would make his choice when he returned. We waited."

Carruthers returned with the hot wine, and withdrew.

The younger sister took up the tale. "When he returned," she said, "we asked him whom his choice had fallen on. He smiled and said he'd changed his mind. He no longer wished to wed either of us, he said. The street had been prepared for cobblestone paving, the earth was still tolerably soft. We buried him there, ten paces from the gas lamp and fifteen from the water hydrant. And there he lies to this day, underneath those dreadful noisy cobblestones. I could forgive, perhaps, on my deathbed, his insult to myself—but his insult to my dear sister, that I can *never* forgive."

Miss Louisa echoed, "His insult to *me* I could perhaps forgive, on my deathbed, but his insult to my dear sister—that I could *never* forgive."

She poured four glasses of the steaming wine.

"Then—" said Mr. Linkhorn, "you mean—"

"I do. I pinioned him by the arms and my sister Louisa shot him through his black and faithless heart with Father's musket. Father was a heavy sleeper, and never heard a thing."

Betty swallowed. "Gol-*ly.*"

"I trust no word of this will ever reach other ears. The embarrassment would be severe . . . A scoundrel, yes, was Horace White," said Miss Augusta, "but—and I confess it to you—I fear I love him still."

Miss Louisa said, "And I. And I."

They raised their glasses. "To Horace White!"

Mr. Linkhorn, much as he felt the need, barely touched his drink; but the ladies drained theirs to the stem, all three of them.

Come Clean

Donald Wandrei

NOTHING IN THE WORLD sounded more attractive than a good hot shower. He was tired and dusty and full of aches that lurked under the crust that now covered him. As he peeled his clothing off and tossed it aside, he half expected the various pieces to stand around as though he was still inside of them.

At seven o'clock in the evening, Iron Tooth Taylor made a terrifying spectacle. His eyes stood out like two white saucers in a black face. That was where the goggles had protected him in the final race at the State Fair dirt track. He'd got his odd nickname the time he'd cracked up a couple of years back and sailed through the air with his teeth bared in startled surprise. He landed that way on top of the fence railing, and a lucky photographer got a picture before he somersaulted on. The mourners came tearing over but he picked himself up and grinned at them. Somebody said, "Cripes, the guy's got iron teeth and they must of riveted his neck on."

The recollection brought a grin to his face as he tore his shirt off. He wasn't bad looking, what could be seen of him. He had the kind of lean, wiry build that seems peculiar to pilots and race-track speed demons.

He made a kind of hand to mouth living out of his nomad's life, which was traveling around the country from one meet to another. He had a sideline that was always good for a few dollars when his luck was down. He could do magic with ropes and whips. He could flick a cigarette out of a man's mouth at twenty feet with the curling tip of a bullwhip accompanied by a *crack* as sharp as a gunshot. He could make a rope tie itself into knots, and spin a noose that traveled upward from the ground and over his head and away from him in a manner that fascinated people. Strangely, he couldn't lasso anything if his life depended on it. He never figured out the why of it. He didn't care enough. It was just sideline stuff.

He stretched and looked around with a sense of coming home after a long absence. He'd only been in town a few days. Often he didn't see the apartment for weeks or months at a time. It wasn't much to look at—a couple of big, old-fashioned rooms on the tenth floor of a twelve-story residential apartment hotel that must have been a sensation in the Nineties. Now it was half empty, and quietly dying in the dismal way that buildings do. He kept it because the rent was cheap and he needed a place to store his accumulated tokens, trophies, programs, and magazine files.

He went into the bathroom and started adjusting the water taps. It was always a risky venture in these old buildings. Just as you got in, under a comfortable temperature, the shower was apt to change into scalding steam that took your skin right off, and then as you made a frantic grab for the controls, it turned to pure ice water that congealed and paralyzed what was left of you.

He hung up his bathrobe after the shower was flowing at the right temperature. He walked to the tub and got one leg over.

The telephone started to ring. He froze with exasperation, and came as close as any man could to scowling from head to foot. He waited for the ringing to stop, but it didn't. A full minute passed. Finally he stalked out leaving wet right foot-prints in his wake. He grabbed the phone.

"Western Union," trilled a voice. "A telegram for Mr. Iron Tooth Taylor."

"Read it," Iron Tooth said. She giggled. "Yes sir. It reads, 'Congratulations on winning race, lend me fifty, thanks. Signed, Chuck.' "

He banged the receiver and hiked back to his shower. That was a hell of a note, touching a guy when he was trying his damnedest to get clean. Get clean, he thought ruefully. Sure, cleaned out of pocket as well as skin. Maybe he'd send Chuck the fifty, maybe he wouldn't. He wouldn't know till he had that shower.

He got the same leg back into the tub, under the pleasantly spraying water. It felt good.

A muffled thumping came from the floor above. He waited a few seconds for the hammering to stop. It didn't. He'd heard it a couple of times before, but paid no attention. He might have ignored it again except that a piece of plaster smacked down, barely missing him. A little cloud of dust puffed up.

There wasn't much use taking a shower if you had to step out into dust and falling plaster. The thumping continued. Another piece of plaster fell down. He eyed the ceiling wrathfully, stalked out, and tried to get the management on the phone.

He waited for at least a minute, while the thumping went on, and pieces of plaster detached themselves from the ceiling. The management didn't respond. The phone remained dead for all his jiggling of the hook.

He tramped back to the bathroom to get his robe. The pounding increased and a shower of plaster landed on his robe. Wearily he wrapped it around him, and went out to the hall.

An elderly lady looked at his face and robe and made clucking noises as she tottered to her room in a state of collapse. He did look appalling.

He took the emergency stairs three at a time. By the door to suite 1115, he listened, heard the muffled thumping, and rang the room bell.

After a while the door opened an inch on a chain lock and a curiously light blue eye with a piece of white eyebrow above it, a tuft of white chin whiskers below it, looked out. The inch of mouth said, "You need a bath, sir."

Taylor nearly choked with rage. "What the hell's going on here? Plaster's falling down. Stop that racket or—"

"Or?" said the voice briskly.

"Or else take that chain off and I'll fight it out to a finish right now."

A door opened down the hall. A shifty-eyed, gaunt-featured man popped his head into the hall. "Hey, you guys, go scrap somewhere else. Let a guy sleep." He popped his head out of sight.

White Hair said, "It will be over in just a few minutes. I suggest, sir, that you take a bath. You need it. Do you good." The door shut.

Boiling inwardly, Taylor strode back to his room. His bare feet made faint little thumps on the uncarpeted stairs.

Inside, he grabbed the phone and jiggled the hook. The desk clerk answered almost instantly this time. Iron Tooth said, "Outside," and a few moments later, "Police Headquarters? Send a radio car or something to room 1115, The Hillview. Yeah, hell of a racket." Then annoyance boiled over in him. He'd get the cops up here to stop it! "Sounds like a guy getting killed," he said angrily in the exaggeration of fury. "Who—me? My name's Taylor, in the apartment below, 1015."

He hung up, strode to the bathroom, and looked bitterly at the nuggets of plaster still sifting down. The shower ran merrily on, and for all the good it did him, it might as well have been in the wilds of Tibet. He'd get caked with plaster in that shower. The thumping overhead continued for a few moments, then ended abruptly. There was a short silence, then a heavier thud than before. The sounds ceased. Granules of plaster kept dribbling from the ceiling.

He wandered out to the living-room, poured himself a slug of whiskey, and gulped it down. He had a worse case of jitters than he'd had at the race tracks. Sprawled out in an easy chair, he lit a cigarette and inhaled to take the burn off his throat. Probably he ought to tell the management. They'd let him use a shower in some other apartment, but he didn't think he would. He liked his own place where he knew where everything was. On the other hand, it would take time, hours at least, to fix the ceiling.

Iron Tooth smoked the cigarette down to the stub and stamped it out. The hall door suddenly opened and closed on a little man. His wizened monkey-face full of sober wrinkles. He had an automatic in one hand, and carried a big stuffed briefcase in the other.

Taylor cursed wearily, "Get the hell out of here."

"Don't move," the stranger said with easy command. He locked the door. "You're Iron Tooth Taylor, aren't you? That's fine. That's just dandy. I bet it was you who called the cops."

"Righto," said Taylor. "The pounding got under my skin. So did the plaster, almost. Wave that cannon some other way. I don't like it."

"You will," the little fellow said easily. "I'm beginning to see my way clear now. Turn around."

"Go peddle your fish in somebody else's place," Taylor suggested.

"You're a sight with all that plaster on you. You're really a sight," said the stranger, his trigger finger tightening. "You'll be a different kind of sight and a nasty one in about a minute. Then I'll have two dead men on my conscience. Move!"

"Look here, I'm only trying to take a shower," Taylor began, and stopped. Two dead men! Good Lord, he'd just got through making a sarcastic remark to the police about a killing.

"Turn around!" snapped the little man.

Taylor faced the wall, his head whirling. He heard metallic sounds. The voice continued, "You see, I'm in a jam. I killed a man a couple of minutes ago. You guessed it—Schweck, the white-haired fool, trying to hold out on me." He said it in the same casual, indifferent way that people do when they mention, "Nice weather we're having," offhand, like that. "When you came up complaining about the noise old Schweck didn't know yet I was going to kill him."

"That so?" Iron Tooth said politely.

The stranger said, "I've just cut your telephone wire. We don't want to be disturbed, do we? I cut the line in the apartment above, too.

"I feel sorry for you, I certainly do, but I guess there isn't much we can do about that, now, is there? Schweck and I had a—a difference of opinion. I expected to get away without interference, but you spoiled that with your bright idea of calling the cops. Not intentionally, of course, but effectively, just the same. I was coming around the corner when the elevator stopped and a cop galloped out. He didn't see me. I ducked back too fast. I came down the emergency stairs. There's a window I looked out of. Do you know what I saw?"

He sounded as if he was playing a game, unhurried, and sure of the consequence. Taylor, face still to the wall, didn't answer. The little man went on, "I saw a radio car down there. The second cop is lounging outside, watching the entrance. It looks bad for me, but I don't give up that easily. Oh no."

A couple of *clunks* and a *thunk* came from behind Taylor. The voice said softly, gently, "I'm making you a couple of presents."

A loud, peremptory knocking shook the entrance door. The little man whispered, "You can turn around now. The key's on the table. You'd better open up before they break in. I'll be in the bathroom. Don't warn the cops. I've got another gun."

Taylor saw what he meant. He had taken the clip from the automatic and tossed both pieces of the gun on the table. Beside them he left a thin package that he removed from the briefcase.

"Remember, don't warn them. And I'd advise you not to try to put the clip back in. It's empty."

The bathroom door closed upon the little killer.

The knocking became thunderous. Taylor snatched the key and ran to the main entrance. He jerked the door open. "Listen, there's a nut in the bathroom claims he killed a guy—"

A cop in uniform, big, stony-faced, thrust Iron Tooth back with a shove that sent him sprawling in a chair. The cop held a .45 that looked like a big Bertha. "Quit kiddin' me," he stated flatly. "And quit stallin'." He turned the key with his free hand and kept it clutched in a thick fist. "Come clean. Why'd you do it?" He added as an afterthought, "Say, you need a bath."

Taylor had cold anger in his voice. "I'm telling you there's a guy, a nut the squirrels missed, in there who—"

The cop jeered. "Don't pull that old gag. You done nothin' but pull old ones. Why'd you kill Schweck?"

"I didn't! I'm trying to tell you—"

The cop butted in, "Skip it. A guy down the hall upstairs saw you and Schweck tearin' at each other's throats fifteen minutes back. Says Schweck slammed the door on you. So you barged down here and got a gun and went up and shot him. Then you called the cops. Old stuff," he said disgustedly. "Don't you know you know us cops always check up first on the guy that reports a murder?" He looked around.

"Look, you even been takin' the gun apart!"

Taylor said savagely, "I never even touched the damn thing! You won't find a single lousy finger-print of mine on it—"

"So you cleaned it off already," said the cop. "That won't help you much."

"The guy that killed Schweck wore gloves! He's still wearing 'em! My God, officer, you can't let him get away! He isn't twenty feet from you!"

"Sure," said the cop amiably. "I know it. Get some duds on and we'll scram." He picked up the flat package and tore a strip off the brown wrapping. "Nice plates, these. The Feds been lookin' for 'em for years. Schweck sure was a wiz of an engraver. They got him for passin' the queer and sent him up but they never found these. Schweck got out, oh, two-three years ago, and they kept tabs on him, but nothin' happened, so finally they lost him last year.

"Nice set-up. You pass the queer around the country at races and such. No reason for anybody to get suspicious. And while you were gone, Schweck pounded away on his hand-press, turning out new tens or twenties. Nobody was disturbed. Naturally, with nobody home here. . . . Whadja do with the latest queer?"

Taylor's nostrils flared. "It's all there, in the bathroom."

"Now you're talkin'. Wait'll I get Mike, my side kick." He walked to the window, raised it, and blew the police whistle. He waited an instant, then looked satisfied. Not once did he completely take his gaze off Taylor.

A muffled crash came from the bathroom. The cop scowled. "What was that?"

"Plaster, and I hope it knocked the rat that framed me out cold."

"Still play-actin', hey?" The cop waved him to one side of the bathroom door. He had bravery, at least, of a blunt, unheeding kind. He flung the door open and glanced in. A loud report instantly blasted through the steady spray of running water. The cop made a queer jerk backward, then pitched forward.

Taylor sprang to his side. He didn't see the wizened-faced little stranger until he spoke.

"Don't," the stranger said. His face peered down from a hole two feet square in the ceiling above the space between the bathtub rear and the wall. A second automatic nestled in his hands.

The cop was folded over the rim of the tub. In a spasmodic gesture, the key flipped from his fist and slid down the drain vent. Now Iron Tooth was locked in his apartment with a dead cop. The cop's pistol lay under the shower, and the spray wet his head, running red from the hole that had replaced his left eye. He made no sound as he died. The shower flowed on, hissing, maddeningly monotonous, while a red line trickled down the middle of the tub.

"Too bad," said the little man sorrowfully, still peering from the hole in the ceiling. "You're in a hell of a fix. I guess you'll fry. You know what cops do to cop-killers. Did you think I chose your apartment just because I happened to be passing by? Don't be silly. Schweck and I took this place when we learned you were below us. You'd seldom or never hear the hand-press. We even cut through the floorboards, down to the lath and plaster of your ceiling. All that plaster fell on you because I was busy getting the stuff out. If the Feds caught up with us, we'd have a chance to drop down there and lam before they broke the door up here.

"Only it worked in reverse. I stood on the edge of your tub and poked the ceiling with a curtain rod. The cut section fell. I slung my briefcase up, jumped, and here I am. You tell the cops all about it. They'll convict you on possession of the plates and the gun."

Taylor had a hollow feeling that the little man was right. If he could keep the wrinkled, crafty face there a little longer . . . how long would it take the second cop to reach the tenth floor?

He snapped, "The automatic you left down here couldn't have killed the cop."

The stranger clucked. "That won't stop them. Oh, my, no. They'll say you threw a second gat away. They'll look for it. They won't find it. But that won't matter. They'll claim it went down a chimney. Or hit a sewer grating and dropped through. Or landed in an ashcan and got carried away to a city dump. I'm afraid you're sunk. You have the gun that killed Schweck. You have the plates that he made. You were seen quarreling with him.

"And don't try to follow me up here. I left the door unlocked before. I was in a hurry. I still am, but this time I'll lock it so you can't get out. Bye-bye."

The wizened face vanished.

Taylor stood in moody thought. He couldn't get out of his apartment. The key lay tantalizingly below his fingertips in the bathtub drain. He couldn't swing through the apartment above. Schweck's killer would close that apartment's exit with another key. The telephone wires were cut. He couldn't reach a fire escape except through the hall which he couldn't get to.

He turned and sprinted from the bathroom.

The hall door shook with sudden pounding.

He fished the coils of his rope act from a closet, looped the noose around a bedpost, and flung the rest through a window as the pounding continued.

He climbed over the sill and went down, his bathrobe flapping. He passed a window where a man was staring casually out, cocktail in hand. The man's eyes boggled and the cocktail glass shattered. Taylor was getting fed up with having people look at him as though he was something escaped from a nightmare.

The rope burned his hands. He hadn't figured the distance to the ground. He didn't know if the rope would reach all the way, but he didn't have time to worry about it. The second floor slid by and so did the end of the rope. He dropped eight feet to the sidewalk.

A pretty young girl walking to taxi giggled. "What is it—a scavenger hunt?"

He ducked past her to the building entrance. The little man strolled out, jaunty, the briefcase under one arm, his other hand in a side pocket. Taylor dove. The pocket twitched and flame scorched his chest. He bowled the killer over. The briefcase dropped with a thud.

Pint-Size was dynamite. He bounced up, caught Taylor's waist, and heaved. He actually threw the race driver. He was yanking at the automatic when Taylor, dazed, rolled to the briefcase. The killer jumped for it. Taylor reached up and clutched an ankle. The wizened man dove headlong and hit the cement with his forehead.

The hand in his pocket automatically pulled the trigger. The bullet fanned Taylor's knees. . . .

Five minutes later, the second cop said, "That's Benny, Benny the Beaut. Race-track tipster. He just got out of the stir a few months ago after a swindling rap. Nope, he's never been tied up with Schweck before. They must of met in prison, and Schweck waited till Benny got out before taking his plates out of hiding. Benny gets around a lot. He'd be a good one to pass the queer. Looks like he got piggish and killed Schweck to take all. Chances are he'd of gone clean, too. We had no reason to tie him in with Schweck—hey, what's the rush?"

Taylor said, "There must be some place a guy can take a bath in peace. I'm going down in the basement. If you want me, try the laundry room. They've got some swell big tubs there."

A Considerable Murder

Barry Pain

MR. ALBERT TRUSTWORTH MACKINDER, having made much money in the City of London, retired to a house by the sea at Helmstone. He was at this time a widower of fifty-eight and he was accompanied by his only daughter, Elsa, a pretty child of sixteen. Mr. Mackinder was satisfactory to the local society and was not displeased with it himself. But he had had many ideas in his life, and the idea which possessed him most strongly at present was that he was interested in the onward march of science. For this reason he interested himself deeply in Dr. Bruce Perthwell. Dr. Perthwell attended Miss Mackinder once and Mr. Mackinder twice—on all three occasions for colds. When Dr. Perthwell recommended that they should stay in bed, feed light, and take the medicine which he would send up to the house, results had been satisfactory on each occasion. But this did not impress Mr. Mackinder nearly so much as the way in which Dr. Perthwell spoke of the mysteries and magic of science. Dr. Perthwell was a clean-shaven man, grey-haired, with an authoritative face and a very convincing manner.

Mr. Mackinder liked him and asked him to dinner frequently, for though Mr. Mackinder knew that it was too late in life for him to take up any really serious study of science, he was quite glad to have such scientific facts as Dr. Perthwell might be disposed to let drop, duly prepared and seasoned to suit the appetite of the elderly. In this way Mr. Mackinder learnt what was, roughly speaking, the velocity of light, and, if he happened to require Vitamin C, in what articles of diet he would do best to search for it. This was all very good for Mr. Mackinder and kept him up in his belief that the world was an interesting place.

Now it happened that Elsa Mackinder invited to stay with her a friend to whom she had been long attached, Miss Jessie Palkinshaw, of the same age as herself and destined for the nursing profession. On the night of her arrival Mr. Mackinder, to square the table, invited Dr. Perthwell to join them at dinner, which he did. Dr. Perthwell got, perhaps, a little tired of preaching extreme moderation and temperance all day, and liked to relax a little in the evening. Mr. Mackinder's dinners were good. His cellar was good. There was no intolerable excess, but Mr. Mackinder and his guest generally, as is sometimes said, did themselves fairly well. It was after the two ladies had retired to the drawing-room that Mr. Mackinder refilled Dr. Perthwell's glass with '96 and addressed himself to a subject which had been somewhat in his mind that day.

"You know, Doctor, I was reading that murder case in the papers this morning. It puzzles me. Why do those poison people always bungle it? Why do they choose poison such as arsenic which can so easily be traced?"

Dr. Perthwell fixed his meditative eyes on the ceiling.

"I should say it is principally from ignorance. No doctor, of course, would make such a blunder. But not even every doctor, not by a long way, knows what is actually possible.

"And what is actually possible?" asked Mr. Mackinder eagerly.

"Well," said Dr. Perthwell, "there are two drugs which can be procured at any chemist's without any formalities, and neither of them is in the least degree injurious. But if you mix, say, a quarter of a teaspoonful of one with a quarter of a teaspoonful of the other and give that in a glass of water to any person, in less than an hour that person will be dead. And no post-mortem, no examination of any kind will ever find the slightest trace of poison in the body."

"Amazing," said Mr. Mackinder. "Perfectly amazing. That is really so?"

"It is."

"I suppose I shouldn't ask it," said Mr. Mackinder, "but could you tell me what the names of these two drugs are?"

"Undoubtedly I could," said the doctor, "but—"

Mr. Mackinder refilled the doctor's glass.

"After all," said Dr. Perthwell, "you are a student of science. You are no ordinary layman. I have no doubt that your interest is quite legitimate. Would you be willing to swear to me on your word of honour that you have no intention of murdering anybody, and that if I give you these names you will keep them strictly to yourself?"

"Certainly," said Mr. Mackinder. "I am at peace with the world, and have no desire to injure anybody whatever—let alone murder them."

Dr. Perthwell went to the door of the dining-room, opened it, closed it again, and returned to his seat.

"You will pardon me, Mr. Mackinder. I had to be quite certain that I could not be overheard."

He gave the names of the two drugs and Mr. Mackinder wrote them down in his note-book. He put each name down on a different page and the two pages were at some distance apart. Mr. Mackinder was cunning.

On the following day Mr. Mackinder purchased, without question or suspicion being roused, one ounce of each of these drugs, at two different chemists'. He was surprised at the vast amount he got for sixpence. He had enough to murder the entire neighbourhood if he had had any spite against it.

He was a methodical man. He took two large sheets of white paper and cut them into small squares. Into each square he put a quarter of a teaspoon of the first drug and folded it into a neat packet. He then took two sheets of blue paper and did the same thing with the other drug, being perhaps inspired with the classical example of the Seidlitz powder. There was still some of each drug remaining, and this he destroyed in the fire. He placed the packets neatly in a cardboard cigarette-box and put the box in a large desk which in theory he always kept locked, and quite frequently did.

He had now the means at hand to destroy forty-eight people. He positively tingled with power. If the worst came to the worst—and at present there was no worst and it was not coming to anything—he felt that he could deal with it.

And the years went on. It happened that once Elsa asked her father:

"What are all those funny little papers in the cigarette-box in your writing-desk? I noticed them to-day when I went there to get stamps. By the way, you don't keep as many stamps as you used to."

"Well," said Mr. Mackinder, "as regards the papers in the box, I think I may tell you about them because they are of extraordinary interest. But so far as I remember, I am to some extent restricted. You would have to promise me that you would tell nobody what I am going to tell you."

"Of course," said Elsa.

Mr. Mackinder then told his daughter precisely what Dr. Perthwell had told him.

And the years still went on and Miss Jessie Palkinshaw became a fully qualified nurse and went in for private work. And then came the letter from Robert Filminster.

Mr. Mackinder knew Mr. Filminster, whose age was at this time verging on the nineties, quite well. He knew that Mr. Filminster had been a friend of his father's and had, in fact, financed him over various crises before the business came to a position of steady security. He had been assured by Mr. Filminster that the greater part of his property would go to Mr. Mackinder for life and to his daughter after him.

Mr. Filminster's letter was simply pathetic. He said that he knew he was on the verge of death. The end of the lease of his house was up and he had been unable, even by a most extravagant offer, to obtain just two or three weeks' prolongation. He felt that he could not go into an hotel, for that would kill him painfully and at once. He knew that he asked much, but would Mr. Mackinder consent to put him up, together with his nurse, Jessie Palkinshaw, until the end came?

Mr. Mackinder felt that he could not do otherwise than accept. His daughter Elsa agreed with him. She was also glad of this coincidence which brought Jessie Palkinshaw back into her life. Questioned, Mr. Mackinder could say very little about Mr. Filminster.

He remembered him as a very quiet and scholarly old gentleman. He reproached himself that they had not met more frequently in recent years.

So Mr. Filminster was accepted and arrived in his own expensive car with his nurse by his side. He seemed somewhat wearied with the journey and glad to get to bed. Not till he was safely asleep did Jessie Palkinshaw descend to talk things over with the eager Elsa Mackinder. They both rejoiced at the renewal of their rapturous friendship. Miss Palkinshaw looked like a saint of wonderful serenity in her nurse's uniform. Elsa, with her shingled hair, felt worldly and common in comparison.

"Tell me now, darling," said Elsa. "What kind of a man is this Mr. Filminster?"

"I think," said Nurse Palkinshaw, "that you are likely to have trouble with him. It cannot be for long, however, because his own doctor assured me that he could not last for more than a week, and there was even some question whether he would not die in the car coming down here. But Mr. Filminster does not like doctors and cannot be expected to do everything they say."

"But what kind of man is he?"

"He's more than one kind of man. The first week I was with him he was always very patient and nice and behaved himself. He can do it still if he wants to do it. He was all right when he arrived here to-day, for instance. Otherwise he has become so eccentric and wild—no doubt owing to his disease—that sometimes it is very, very difficult to put up with him. Of course, a nurse who is any good must be prepared to put up with absolutely anything. I was sent to him by a doctor who is well disposed towards me and has plenty of work to give. I don't want to lose my market. Whatever Mr. Filminster does or does not do I shall hang on until the lid's screwed down. When he is in one of his bad moods he uses the most terrific language you ever heard."

"Blasphemous?"

"That of course. Only yesterday in three words he implied that my soul was lost, that I had the haemorrhagic diathesis, and that I was of illegitimate birth. But that's not all, by a long way. He often uses language which is—well, physiological."

"But they have physiological language in books, don't they?"

"There are two kinds of physiological language. His is the other. I advise you to keep out of his way as much as possible."

"Oh, but I do want to help," said Elsa. "I don't want you to be worked to death. If you can put up with things, I must make up my mind to put up with them too."

"Well," said the nurse, "he's not perhaps been quite so bad lately. He's had a good deal of pain and that always keeps him quiet. I don't think he's actually broken a measuring-glass for three days."

"I suppose the poor old man can't hold them properly."

"That's not it. He throws them, you know. He throws pretty well everything. He says it's the only form of exercise that he's got now. We buy our measuring-glasses by the dozen, and they don't last long. Every now and then he gets a fit of wonderful activity and would go out into the street if he were allowed to have any clothes in his room. But he isn't. Of course, I have to use a good deal of tact. As a matter of fact I could pick the old chap up and carry him. But if he used any great effort that might bring on the end suddenly. No, I shouldn't describe it as a soft case—not easy, by any means."

At dinner that night Mr. Mackinder heard much of the story and was calmly philosophical.

"We must make up our minds to be patient," he said. "It is a question of a few days only. Surely we can put up with that. Tomorrow Dr. Perthwell will be in to see him. No doubt he will be able to tell us something."

On the next morning at breakfast Nurse looked a little worn. Mr. Mackinder asked kindly how her patient was getting on.

"If anything he seems a little stronger. He had one of his fits of activity, but he's safely asleep again now. He's started porridge-sloshing again."

"Started which?" asked Mr. Mackinder.

"Porridge-sloshing is what he calls it. He always will have porridge for breakfast, and the doctors say he is to have anything he likes. Some days he will eat it and some days he won't. It's when he won't that he starts this porridge-sloshing. He fills the spoon full with porridge, holds the end of the handle in one hand, and with a finger of the other draws back the tip of the spoon and suddenly lets go. He can send it quite a considerable distance that way. He generally aims at the different pictures in the room, but he's got me with it two or three times. It always seems to amuse him. Of course, it makes a good deal of work clearing up afterwards."

"Naturally," said Mr. Mackinder. "I should hate to be unkind, but I think I must just ask Perthwell if he doesn't think the poor old chap had better be put into a—one of those institutions where those old chaps are put, you know."

But Dr. Perthwell gave no support to these hopes.

"My dear Mackinder," he said, "I could not possibly certify this Mr. Filminster. He is eccentric, no doubt, and his temperament is much altered by his illness, as any medical man would expect. But he has no delusions and he is not dangerous to anybody. Even if he were I should advise you to let him remain. So far as I can see, in three days he must be dead. You do not want to stuff him into an asylum just for those last three days of his life."

"Certainly not," said Mr. Mackinder. "I had not realized that the end was so near. Three days, I think you said."

"I may be wrong, but from my observations to-day I should think three days would be the limit."

But Mr. Filminster had no great belief in doctors. He lived on for another two months, and by that time the nerves of Mr. Mackinder, his daughter Elsa, and Nurse Palkinshaw were frazzled and pulped. Most of the work fell on them. The butler had already left on the grounds that he had been engaged for a private house and not for Bedlam. And Mr. Mackinder did not care to risk losing any other of the upper servants. He and his daughter and the nurse saw it through, relieving one another at intervals. All Dr. Perthwell could say was that he had never seen such a case before. He had never met with such extraordinary vitality. Any ordinary man must have been dead long before.

Mr. Mackinder, his daughter and the nurse used no hypocrisy. They longed for Mr. Filminster's death. As a concession to decency they said it would be a blessed release for all concerned.

After luncheon Nurse Palkinshaw and Elsa Mackinder were taking two hours off duty for the preservation of their health and sanity. The nurse had had a fit of hysterics of brief duration just before luncheon. Mr. Mackinder remained on duty. From his study he could easily hear Mr. Filminster's bell if he struck it. However, Mr. Filminster was now asleep and Mr. Mackinder hoped that, as usual, there would be nothing for him to do. Requiring a postcard, he opened his desk, and he left it open. And then he heard the whir of the bell on the table by Mr. Filminster's bedside. Almost immediately it was repeated. Mr. Mackinder hurried upstairs.

He had hardly got inside the door when a slipper, thrown with considerable force, struck him in the face, the heel of the slipper barking his nose.

"Why don't you pay attention?" said Mr. Filminster. "I want a whisky-and-soda. The doctors said I could have anything I liked, didn't they? When you're on duty you're jolly well on duty, and don't you forget it another time or I might hop out of bed and twist your blessed nose."

(The more salient and picturesque adjectives have been omitted or substitutes have been provided.)

"That is hardly the way to speak to me," said Mr. Mackinder. "And you've caused the bridge of my nose to bleed. However, I will bring you what you require."

Mr. Mackinder went downstairs with blue murder in his heart. He remembered the open desk and the cigarette-box with the papers in it. Without hesitation he took a glass and emptied into it a white powder and a blue powder. In this he poured whisky and subsequently soda-water. Mr. Filminster took the contents of the glass in one draught, told Mr. Mackinder where he could go, and then flung the glass after him, but fortunately missed. In two minutes more Mr. Filminster was asleep again.

Downstairs, Mr. Mackinder wrestled with his agonized conscience. But as he summed up the question he could not see that he had done much harm. There was not a day when Mr. Filminster did not beg them to give him something to put an end to it all. There was the best medical opinion that he could only live for a few hours now. The man was simply killing his daughter Elsa and Nurse Palkinshaw and they were both absolute wrecks. On the whole Mr. Mackinder decided he had acted wisely. He then put a small strip of pink plaster across the bridge of his nose.

He waited impatiently for the return of his daughter and the nurse about an hour later. In reply to their inquiries he said that he had taken up a whisky-and-soda to Mr. Filminster and this was all there had been for him to do.

He waited for them to go upstairs and to come down quickly announcing that Filminster was dead.

They did not come down quickly. When they appeared in the drawing-room Elsa rang for tea quite casually and Nurse Palkinshaw said that Mr. Filminster seemed stronger but was not in a good temper.

Mr. Mackinder reflected. Those drugs had been in his desk for some time. Possibly they had now lost their efficacy. He was in reality not sorry to think so.

On the following morning, as Mr. Mackinder sat at his early breakfast at eight o'clock, Nurse Palkinshaw entered the room.

"Mr. Filminster is dead," she said. "He seems to have passed away in his sleep. I have telephoned to Dr. Perthwell. But that is not all. I was tried beyond human endurance. I have a confession to make to you."

She made it.

"What am I to do?" she cried despairingly.

"Nothing whatever at present," said Mr. Mackinder. "Leave things entirely in my hands. I will tell you more after the funeral."

And then, after the nurse had gone out, Elsa entered. She helped herself to a poached egg and a cup of China tea and then burst into tears and said she must confess all. Her father heard the confession and gave his instructions.

"At present," he said, "say nothing to anybody. After the funeral we must decide what is the right and moral thing to do."

Dr. Perthwell had not the least hesitation in giving a certificate that the death was due to natural causes, and in due course the funeral took place. Afterwards, by appointment, Dr. Perthwell attended Mr. Mackinder at his house.

"I think," said Mr. Mackinder, "by your certificate you attribute poor Filminster's death to his illness."

"Of course I did. It was the truth. Why not?"

"I have your promise of secrecy? I am speaking, so to say, under the seal of the professional?"

"Yes, yes."

"Well, I may tell you that Filminster was murdered."

"Murdered?"

"Yes. What is more, he was murdered three times."

"Three times?"

"Yes, and not only that. He also committed suicide."

"I think you'd better give me the details of this extraordinary story."

Mr. Mackinder then narrated how he himself had murdered Filminster. He showed that his motives were the best possible and said nothing about the abrasion on his nose.

"And then," Mr. Mackinder continued, "my daughter and the nurse came back. My daughter is absolutely devoted to Jessie Palkinshaw. She heard the language that Mr. Filminster was using to his nurse and felt absolutely unable to endure it. Unluckily, my desk was still wide open on the study table. She emptied one of each of the powders into the tea which was being taken up to him."

"Go on," said Dr. Perthwell. "He was murdered three times, you say."

"And also committed suicide. I think the nurse did what she did in a fit of temporary insanity caused by the awful overstrain. In the evening she took up to his room the cigarette-box containing the poisons and put the powders into his last whisky-and-soda. I cannot understand it, but she left that box on the table by his bedside. There was also there a jug of water and a glass. In the morning she found that the glass had been used and one of the white papers and one of the blue lay on the table. He had taken his own life."

"I don't think so," said Dr. Perthwell cheerily. "What's all this about white and blue papers?"

"Surely you remember that you once told me that there were two drugs—you gave me the name of them—which were innocuous in themselves but would be fatal in one hour if mixed together?"

"Well," said Dr. Perthwell, "you rather tempted me, you know. You did like to have a sensational story, didn't you? As a matter of fact, those drugs are both of them, singly or in conjunction, absolutely harmless. Had it been otherwise, you can't suppose that any conscientious medical man would have told you the facts?"

"Why not?"

"You promised me absolute secrecy, you know."

"Yes," said Mr. Mackinder. "I think there was something said. As a matter of fact, I told nobody but my own daughter, and the supposed poisons were very frequently kept locked up."

"Then how did the nurse know about it?"

"Well, the nurse is one of my daughter's most intimate friends and she promised Elsa that it shouldn't go any further."

The doctor yawned.

"I see," he said. "Well, I must be getting on. I shouldn't let it worry me if I were you. I don't suppose any one of the three was completely sane at the time."

That afternoon, I regret to say, Mr. Mackinder, his daughter and the nurse went to the Pictures.

Counterplot

Francis M. Nevins, Jr.

THE WEEKEND ICE STORM made the motel cleaning women late for work on Monday morning. The woman assigned to the rooms at the end of the west wing gave a ritual tap on the door of 114, then used her passkey and stepped in. When she saw what lay on the green shag carpet she shrieked and went careening down the corridor in terror. The Cody police arrived ten minutes later. When the fingerprint report came back from F.B.I. headquarters the next day, they knew a part of the story. The rest they never learned, and would not have believed if someone had told them.

She followed instructions precisely. The Northwest jet touched down at Billings just before 5:00 P.M. on Friday, and by 5:30 she had rented a car from the Budget booth near the baggage-claim area. As the sun dropped over the awesomely close mountaintops she was crossing the Montana border into Wyoming. The two-lane blacktop rose and fell and wound among the magnificent mountains like a scenic railway, bringing her to the edge of Cody around 8:00.

She'd been told there would be a reservation for her at the Great Western Motel in the name of Ann Chambers. There was. She checked in, unpacked the two smaller suitcases, left the large gray Samsonite case at the back of the room closet, locked. Then she bathed, changed to a blue jumpsuit, turned on the TV, and settled in to wait. Until Monday morning if necessary. Those were the instructions.

Friday passed, and Saturday, and Sunday. She heard the harsh sound of frozen rain falling on the streets, the screech of brakes, the dull whine of car motors refusing to start. The storm didn't affect her. She stayed in the room, watching local television and reading a pile of paperback romances she had brought with her. Three times a day she would stride down the corridor to the coffee shop for a hasty meal. The only other customers were a handful of pickup-truck cowboys who kept their outsized Stetsons on as they ate flamboyantly. None of them could be the man she was waiting for. She wondered if the storm would keep him from coming.

At 10:00 P.M. on Sunday, while she was sitting on the bed bundled in blankets, boredly watching a local TV newscast, a quick triple knock sounded on her door. She sprang up, smoothed the bedcovers, undid the chain bolt, and opened two inches. "Yes?"

"Software man." The words were exactly what she expected.

"Hardware's here," she replied as instructed, and cautiously drew back the door to let him in. He was heavy-set and rugged-looking, about 40, wearing a three-quarter-length tan suede jacket with sheepskin collar. When he took off his mitten cap she saw he was partially bald. He threw his jacket on the bed and inspected her.

"You sure ain't Frank Bolish," he said. "So who are you?"

"Arlene Carver. One of Frank's assistants." She held out her hand to him and took a chance. "If you read his columns you've probably seen my name mentioned. I do investigative work for him."

"Never read his columns," the man grunted. "I don't think newspapermen should be allowed to attack public officials the way Bolish does. Prove who you are." His accent was heavily Western, almost like Gary Cooper's but too soft and whispery as if he had a sore throat. Taking small steps, she backed toward the formica-topped round table at the room's far end where her oversized handbag lay.

"Hold it right there," the man ordered. "I'll find your ID myself." He strode long-legged across the room, passing her cautiously, reached for the bag, and shook its contents out on the bed.

"There's no gun," she told him, trying to control the irritation she was beginning to feel, "and the money's not there either. Do you think I'm a fool?"

He pawed through her alligator wallet, studying the array of plastic cards in their window envelopes. "Okay, so your name's Arlene Carver and you live in Bethesda, Maryland. That's close enough to Washington all right, but what tells me you're with Bolish?"

"How do I know you're Paxton?" she demanded. "I was told he was a skinny guy with thick gray hair. You're two hundred pounds and could use a toupee."

"I never claimed I was Paxton." He tugged a bulging pigskin wallet from his hip pocket and passed her a business card. "Ted

Gorman, from Cheyenne. Private investigator. Paxton got cold feet Friday, hired me to drive up to Cody and make the delivery for him." He took a long careful breath. "He said either Bolish himself or his chief assistant Marty Lanning would pick it up."

"Frank has to be on a TV show tomorrow morning and Marty's down with flu," she said.

He gazed coldly at her. She knew he was trying to decide if she was genuine or an impostor. "Come *on*, man!" she told him impatiently. "I knew the stupid password and I knew what Paxton looks like. Give me the damn videotape!"

"Not yet." He perched himself on the round table and pointed a finger at her. "If you're with Bolish you'll know what's supposed to be on the tape. Tell me."

"The way Frank said Paxton described it over the phone," she answered slowly, "it's a videocassette made with a hidden camera at Vito Carbone's condo in Miami Beach. It shows Senator Vega taking a $100,000 payoff from Carbone and agreeing to sponsor some amendments to the Federal Criminal Code that the Mob wants." She paused and looked at him.

"More," he demanded.

"The videocassette was made for Angelo Generoso," she went on. "His family and the Carbones have been in an undeclared war for years. Paxton was the low-level torpedo the Generosos sent to Carbone's pad to dismantle the equipment and bring back the cassettes when it was all over. Only Paxton found out what was on that one tape, saw a chance to get rich, and disappeared with the thing instead. He'd grown up in rural Wyoming, so he came back out here to hole up till the heat died down. Then he phoned Frank in Washington and offered him the cassette for $25,000."

"Okay." The bald man nodded slightly. "That's the same story Paxton tells. You got the money?"

"Yes. You have the cassette?"

"Hold still a minute." He strode across the room and out into the corridor, leaving the door slightly ajar. She watched him enter the alcove down the hall that held the soft-drink machine. There was the sound of a lid being lifted, then the rumble of ice cubes being displaced. He re-entered the room rubbing the moist white protective jacket of the cassette against his shirt. "Ice machine didn't do it any harm," he said. "Let's see the money."

She bent over the bureau, pulled out the bottom drawer, and removed the Gideon Bible. Then she shook the Bible out over the bed. Twenty-five $1000 bills fluttered down from the pages onto the rumpled blanket. She picked them up and arranged them in a neat stack but did not hold them out to him.

"They could be counterfeit," the bald man muttered.

"Oh, for God's sake! This is throwaway money for Frank Bolish. Now give me the damn cassette!"

Hesitantly he placed it on the blanket beside the bills, then perched on the edge of the formica again, while she rebolted the chain lock. She then dragged the large gray Samsonite suitcase out of the closet, lifted it to the bed, and unlocked it. She took out the videocassette player, set it down on the bureau top, and used a tiny screwdriver to connect its wires with certain wires of the room television. When the player was ready she flipped the ON switch, took the cassette out of its protective jacket, and inserted it into the machine. Then she depressed the PLAY button and turned on the TV to watch the images from the cassette.

The tape ran for about twelve minutes. Its technical quality was poor, which was natural considering the secrecy in which it was made. It showed a quiet conference between two men in shirt-sleeves. The older she recognized—Vito, lion of the Carbones. The younger—tall, slender, hypnotic-voiced—certainly looked like Senator Vega. The hidden camera caught the quick transfer of an envelope, the counting of the money, the careful repetition of what the senator must do in return for the gift.

She hit the STOP button before the scene had ended. "I don't like it," she said. "There's something staged-looking about that pay-off. One of them's an actor, maybe both of them." She chewed her underlip nervously and turned her back for a second to switch off the TV.

When she faced him again, he was holding a small .25 aimed at her middle.

"You took a gamble and lost, lady," the bald man said. "It happens I do read Bolish's column every day, and I got a real good memory for names. He's never mentioned you in any of his material. Now, who the hell are you!"

She took another long deep breath to gain time. "All right," she told him then. "I—guess I gave myself away with what I said about that tape. My name is Arlene Carver but I don't work for Bolish. I'm a troubleshooter for Senator Vega. We heard rumors about a plot to smear him with a phony videotape, and then when Paxton offered the tape to Bolish one of Bolish's staff leaked the story to us.

My partner managed to sidetrack the man Bolish sent out to make the pickup and I came on in his place. Look, what do you and Paxton care who pays you? The tape's a phony, but the media could crucify the senator with it, so we're willing to pay to keep it under wraps."

"Sure it's a phony. All you true believers who think Jorge Vega can pull together that good old Sixties coalition of the Hispanics and the blacks and the feminists and the Indians and the kids, you'll all swear till you're blue in the face the tape's a phony so your boy can become President in '84. Only if the tape gets out, it's Vega's finish, and you know it."

"It's no use talking politics with you," she said icily. "Take the money and leave this room, right now."

"Not quite yet." He waggled the .25 at her lazily. "You see, I still don't know who you are, lady, but I surely know who you're not. You don't work for Jorge Vega. *But I do.*"

Consternation flushed her face, and she jerked back as though he had struck her.

"Paxton didn't just make one long-distance call to Washington about that cassette," the man explained. "He offered it to Vega for the same price he wanted from Bolish. I'm a Wyoming boy, so the senator took me off my other work on his staff and asked me to get the tape from Paxton. I did. Didn't use money, just muscle. But then I decided to keep Paxton's date with Bolish, hoping I could find out what Bolish planned to print about the senator. Now, you're not with Bolish and you're not with Vega, so before I get angry and ask you the hard way, you tell me who you are and what your game is."

He took two slow steps toward her, his fingers tightening on the .25 as he moved.

"Put that toy away," she told him calmly, "before you find yourself in deep trouble." She reached inside her blouse with careful motions, pulled out a hinged leather cardholder, opened it, and held it out so he could see the gold shield and identification.

"Oh, hell," he mumbled, and gently set down the gun on the dresser top. "Why didn't you say you were F.B.I.?"

"Well, your loyalties weren't exactly displayed on a billboard," she told him. "The Bureau heard rumors about that cassette too, and my job was to run them down. A woman on Bolish's staff leaked it to the Bureau when Paxton made him the offer. I told the truth when I said my partner intercepted Bolish's messenger and I came on in his place. Another two minutes and I would have been reading you your rights. Depending on whether that tape is real or a phony, either Vega's going to be charged with taking a bribe or some big bananas in the Mob are going to face extortion charges. I don't think you broke any Federal laws by hijacking the cassette from Paxton, but I'll keep the tape from this point on."

"I'm not so sure of that." He grinned at her, reached down to his oversized cowboy belt buckle, and disconnected it from its leather strap. From the interior of the hollow buckle he extracted a leather cardholder of his own and flipped it at her. "Damndest thing I've seen in fifteen years with the Bureau." he laughed. "Two agents playing cat and mouse with each other like this. Yeah, I've been working the case from the other side. Picked up Paxton in Laramie on Friday night and decided to keep his appointment with Bolish's messenger on the off chance I'd get something we could use against Bolish. He's written a lot of columns the Bureau doesn't appreciate."

"Nice job," she said. "You fooled me all the way. I never would have guessed you were with the Bureau." She came toward him slowly, almost seductively, until she was two steps from the corner of the dresser that held his gun.

She leaped for the .25 at the same moment his hands leaped for her throat.

Late the next morning, when she entered to clean Room 114, the cleaning woman found the two intertwined bodies—the man shot with a .25 at point-blank range, the woman strangled to death. The police quickly determined what had happened but had no idea why they had killed each other, nor could they make sense of the inordinate number of artifacts of identity found in the room, all of them turning out to be spurious.

The F.B.I. report on the two sets of fingerprints, however, proved to be helpful. The man was identified as a pistolero for the Carbone organized-crime family and the woman as an enforcer for the more progressive and affirmative-action-oriented Generosos.

The Creek, It Done Riz

Ardath Mayhar

ONLY THE LORD KNOWS why I ever took the old road that day, particularly since the water was out all over the map from the big rains. I could have stuck a dozen times, coming across the bottom lands. It's a wonder in this world that none of the rickety little bridges were washed out—or that one of them didn't go out with me halfway across. Still, Pa's old 1939 Plymouth could mighty nearly swim, and we always took it out when we were going way down into the boondocks.

The whole thing was a lot of foolishness, anyway. I didn't get a degree from Texas A&M in order to go paddling around in the river-bottom in the middle of a flood to count hogs. But try telling the boss that. He sits in his air-conditioned office, thinking up dumb schemes, and never knows if it rains or shines. And he can come up with some of the gosh-awfulest ideas. A hog census! Now I ask you. How he thought that knowing where every hog in the county was located would help him sell his damn feed, I don't know.

Anyway, there I was in the river bottom in a car twice as old as I was, sloshing down a road that wasn't much more than a lane, when I could see it, which wasn't often. The wet sweetgum saplings were bent way down and slapping across the windshield. I was crawling along, cussing some, when I saw something out in the woods.

I crept on until I could feel gravel under the wheels; then I stopped. I could have sworn I saw an old man sitting on a stump. I stuck my feet into the rubber boots I had learned to take along with me, being as most hog-pens can't be said to do shoes any good at all. Then I got out and started off into a thicket. And sure enough, there was a grizzly-headed old cuss, soaked to the bone, dripping water of his nose and his eyebrows. He never acted as if he saw me, just muttered to himself as if that's what he'd been doing for quite a while.

When I got close enough to hear, I stood there for a minute, admiring his style. You don't hear cussing like that anymore, with real feeling and meaning to it. And he was cussing the weather, which deserved everything he gave it and then some. But it was wet as all get-out, and finally I went up and touched him on the shoulder.

"Sir, I beg your pardon," I said, "but would you like a ride someplace? Out of the wet?"

He gave a jerk and looked up at me for a minute, sizing me up. Then he gave me a couple of cusses, too.

I shook my head admiringly. "It's a privilege to listen to a man who can handle the language the way you do," I said. "Even my Pa, and he's no slouch, can't touch you. But it does look like you're set to catch your death of cold, if you sit out here much longer."

Then he squinched up his eyes and looked me over, real carefully. "You look to be a Jenkins," he said, when he had gone from top to bottom. "Got that Jenkins jaw. Any kin to Ralph Jenkins?"

"That's my Pa," I said. It's the darndest thing . . . anyplace I go, people spot me for Pa's son right off. Even if they never laid eyes on me before.

He grunted and shifted on the stump. "Tell you, Son," he said, "I ain't got no place to go that you can take me to in no car. But bein' as you're Ralph's boy, why you might help me out a little bit."

Now that's where I should've said goodbye and been off to count hogs. But Pa raised us all to be polite and helpful to old folks, and I can't seem to break the habit. When an old geezer looks at you kind of slant-eyed, with his head cocked on one side like he's figuring out how far he can con you, it's time to take off. Not me, though. No brains, that's me.

So pretty soon I found myself slogging down a pig-trail through the woods, looking sharp for cotton-mouth moccasins and stump-holes. He kept talking all the time, as if he was scared I'd change my mind and leave him. Nothing he said made me anxious to keep on.

"I've got a kind of boat a little piece further on, tied up along Eel Creek. If it's still there, we can take it and get up to my house. The house ain't washed away; it's just the damn creek's done riz so I can't get to the yard. With a strong young fellow like you to help me with the boat, I kin make it." He paused, and panted a while. I could see that he wasn't in too good shape.

I turned around and said, "Why Pa could put you up until the water goes down. He'd be glad to. Why don't you just go back to the car with me, and I'll take you straight on in and have you dry in no time at all."

He started shaking his head before I was done. Then he looked all around, really careful, as if anybody but a couple of fools would have been out in the woods with the river out of its banks.

"I guess I ought to tell you, Son, seein' as how you're helpin' me and all. I've got my life's savings buried in that yard. If the river backs the creek up too high, it'll likely wash it right away. It's all I've got to stand me through my old age. I just got to get back there and get it out before the water comes up any more."

Well, he did sound pitiful. I couldn't help but wonder why he didn't dig up his money before he left, but I guessed that you might be forgetful at his age. So we went on, and the water was mighty near the tops of my boots before we came to his boat. Then I saw why he called it a kind of a boat. The bailing bucket was the only thing that didn't have a hole in it. A good, sound log would have been a lot safer to try to travel on.

"You sure you want to risk that thing?" I asked him.

"It's a sight better than it looks," he answered. "I been fishing in that boat for twenty years and never drowned yet."

I never was one to believe in miracles, but maybe such things happen, or else he was an uncommonly solid ghost. But I was pledged to help him, so I bailed out the water that was sloshing around in the bottom of the thing and heaved it out into the creek. I stood there and watched the little wiggles of water come through the holes and start moving down the sides.

He got right in and started bailing. "Reason I had to have help," he said, "is somebody has to bail while the other one rows. I always borrow one of Rupe Miller's kids to do the bailing, when I go fishing, but they left when the water got high. Get in, Boy. Let's get moving. That water's not going to wait on us."

So I said a prayer, which would have pleased Ma, and got in. Then I didn't have time to pray. That water was wild as a yearling colt. It took everything I could do to keep the boat from taking off in ten directions at once.

I fought with the paddle to fend us off floating logs and brush-piles. I guess I came nearer to poling it along than paddling. In the middle of all that, it came to me. . . . I didn't know his name. I twisted my head round and yelled, "Hey, Mister, what's your name?"

He looked up from his bucket, kind of startled. "Why, I'm Abe Willitts. I thought everybody in the county knowed of old Abe."

Then I really started to sweat. Everybody knew about Abe Willitts, sure enough. When I was little, Ma'd hush me up with, "Crazy Abe'll get you, if you don't be good." When his wife died, all the women looked at each other and said, "He finally killed her. I knew he would, one day." And nobody could prove them wrong, because she was buried by the time he got around to letting anybody know she was dead.

Even Pa, who wouldn't hear a bad word about anyone, had to be still when that hunter disappeared. He'd told his wife that he was going to bird-hunt down in the bottoms, and he'd intended to get Abe and his setter to help him find the birds. Nobody ever saw nor heard from him again. They looked, too. All over the place, with dogs and men. Abe claimed he never got there at all, and nobody could prove different.

So here I was in a leaky boat in the middle of a flood with a crazy man. A hog census looked mightly calm and peaceful, when I thought about it. Still, I hadn't time to worry over much, just then. Working that crazy piece of junk around the bends in the creek took all my energy. By the time we came in sight of the house, I was done in, sure enough.

Abe jumped out onto the bank, only it was the yard fence, the bank being a hundred yards behind us in the middle of the flood, and tied his rope to a fencepost. "Here we are, Boy. You just wait right here, and I'll go round and dig up my savings and be right back." His eyes slid round at me and didn't look quite sane.

"I'm too tired to move, Sir," I said. "You just get your stuff, and I'll rest. It'll take all we both can do to get us back up that creek."

Soon as he was gone around the house, I slid out of the boat and eased up the slope. It took a while, and once he looked out around the corner of the porch to see if I was still in the boat. Luckily, I'd propped up the bucket so it looked like a head leaning against the edge, and he didn't go down to check. I stayed hidden in the bushes for a while to let my heart quit thumping, then I went on.

When I peeped around the porch, he was digging hard. You could hear his shovel going "Shloop! Shloop!" in the mud, because the water had got around to that side of the house, too. He was in an almighty hurry. I scootched down and watched. I don't quite know why, but I just had to know what it was he was in such a hurry and a sweat about. He had to be living on Social Security, just like Pa and everybody else their age. I figured he couldn't have saved up enough to amount to anything.

When a shovelful of mud came out of that hole with something dark and solid on it, I perked up. It was a hunting jacket, as I could tell after it lay there a while and the rain washed off the mud. The kind with a bag in back for shot birds and shell-pockets across the front. Then Abe's hand came up with a shotgun in it and laid it on the ground.

I didn't wait to see more. All of a sudden, I figured I'd better be back at the boat—or further still—when Abe came around the corner of that house. I made it a lot quicker than I'd come and leaned back in the boat as if I'd been dozing. Then I got to thinking.

Whatever he was getting out of that hole, he'd likely send down the flood. Maybe he'd feel safe then. Maybe not. . . . The more I thought about going back up that creek with him bailing behind me, the less I liked the notion. I had a little money in my pocket. Probably about what that hunter had had. And nobody knew where I was or what I was doing.

I eased out into the bushes and crept along until I found a likely log. It was half afloat, already, so I goosed it out into the current and held onto a stub of branch, with my head close under the side so it could't be seen. That log and I whirled and twirled and twiddled down the creek with the rest of the stuff floating there until we lodged way down on Bobcat Ridge. I guess Abe never did know what happened to me.

He must've tried to make it back in that boat, all by himself. We'll never know, though. They didn't look for *him* as hard as they did for that hunter.

Crime Wave in Pinhole

Julie Smith

DOGGONEDEST THING COME in the mail yesterday—a letter of commendation from the Miami Police Department, thankin' me for solvin' a murder case. Me, Harry January, Pinhole, Mississippi's chief of police and sole officer of the law! I figured my brethren on the Bay of Biscayne had taken leave of their senses.

But I got to studyin' on the thing a while and I looked up the date I was supposed to've perpetrated this triumph and the whole thing come back to me. Blamed if I *didn't* solve a murder for them peckerwoods—it just wasn't no big thing at the time.

It happened the day Mrs. Flossie Chestnut come in, cryin' and takin' on cause her boy Johnny'd been kidnapped. Least that was her suspicion, but I knew that young'un pretty well and in my opinion there wasn't no kidnapper in Mississippi brave enough for such a undertakin'. Bein' as it was my duty, however, I took down a report of the incident, since he *could've* got hit by a car or fell down somebody's well or somethin'.

Mrs. Flossie said she hadn't seen a sign of him since three o'clock the day before when she caught him ridin' his pony standin' up. Naturally she told him he oughtn' to do it 'cause he could break his neck and it probably wasn't too easy on the pony neither. Then she emphasized her point by the administration of a sound hidin' and left him repentin' in the barn.

She wasn't hardly worried when he didn't show up for supper, on account of that was one of his favorite tricks when he was sulkin'. Seems his practice was to sneak in after ever'body else'd gone to sleep, raid the icebox, and go to bed without takin' a bath. Then he'd come down to breakfast just like nothin' ever happened. Only he didn't that mornin' and Mrs. Flossie had ascertained his bed hadn't been slept in.

I told Mrs. Flossie he would likely be home in time for lunch and sent her on back to her ranch-style home with heated swimmin' pool and green-house full of orchids. Come to think about it, her and her old man were 'bout the only folks in town had enough cash to warrant holdin' their offspring for ransom, but I still couldn't believe it. Some say Pinhole got its name cause it ain't no bigger'n one, and the fact is we just don't have much crime here in the country. I spend most of my mornin's playin' gin rummy with Joshua Clow, who is retired from the dry-goods business, and Mrs. Flossie had already played merry heck with my schedule.

But there wasn't no sense grumblin' about it. I broadcast a missin' juvenile report on the police radio and commenced to contemplatin' what to do next. Seemed like the best thing was to wait till after lunch, see if the little varmint turned up, and, if he didn't, get up a search party. It was goin' to ruin my day pretty thorough, but I didn't see no help for it.

'Long about that time, the blessed phone rang. It was young Judy Scarborough, down at the motel, claimin' she had gone and caught a live criminal without my assistance and feelin' mighty pleased with herself. Seems she had noticed that a Mr. Leroy Livingston, who had just checked in at her establishment, had a different handwritin' when he registered than was on the credit card he used to pay in advance. Young Judy called the credit company soon as her guest went off to his room and learned the Mr. Livingston who owned the card was in his sixties, whereas her Mr. Livingston wasn't a day over twenty-five.

It sounded like she had a genuine thief on her hands, so I went on over and took him into custody. Sure enough, his driver's license and other papers plainly indicated he was James Williamson of Little Rock, Arkansas. Among his possessions he had a employee identification card for Mr. Leroy Livingston of the same town from a department store where Mr. Livingston apparently carried out janitorial chores.

So I locked up Mr. Williamson and got on the telephone to tell Mr. Livingston we had found his missin' credit card. His boss said he was on vacation and give me the number of his sister, with whom he made his home. I called Miss Livingston to give her the glad tidin's, and she said her lovin' brother was in Surfside, Florida. Said he was visitin' with a friend of his youth, a Catholic priest whose name she couldn't quite recollect, 'cept she knew he was of Italian descent.

By this time I was runnin' up quite a little phone bill for the taxpayers of Pinhole, but I can't never stand not to finish what I start. So I called my brother police in Surfside, Florida, meanwhile motionin' for Mrs. Annie Johnson to please set down, as she was just come into the station. Surfside's finest tells me there is a Father Fugazi at Holy Name Church, and I jot down the number for future reference.

"What can I do for you, Annie?" I says then, and Mrs. Annie gets so agitated I thought I was goin' to have to round up some smellin' salts. Well, sir, soon's I got her calmed down, it was like a instant replay of that mornin's colloquy with Mrs. Flossie Chestnut. Seems her boy Jimmy has disappeared under much the same circumstances as young Johnny Chestnut. She punished him the day before for somethin' he was doin' and hadn't laid eyes on him since. Just to make some conversation and get her mind off what might'a happened I says, casual like, "Mind if I ax you what kind'a misbehavior you caught him at?" And she turns every color in a Mississippi sunset.

But she sees it's her duty to cooperate with the law and she does. "I caught him makin' up his face," she says.

"Beg pardon?"

"He was experimentin' with my cosmetics," she says this time, very tight-lipped and dignified, and I begin to see why she is upset. But I figure it's my duty to be reassurin'.

"Well, now," says I, "I reckon it was just a childish prank—not that it didn't bear a lickin' for wastin' perfectly good face paint— but I don't 'spect it's nothin' to be embarrassed about. Now you run along home and see if he don't come home to lunch."

Sweat has begun to pour off me by this time as I realize I got two honest-to-Pete missin' juveniles and a live credit-card thief on my hands. Spite of myself, my mind starts wanderin' to the kind of trouble these young'uns could've got theirselves into, and it ain't pretty.

I broadcast another missin' juvenile report and start thinkin' again. Bein' as it was a Saturday I knew it wouldn't do no good callin' up the school to see if they was in attendance. But what I could do, I could call up Liza Smith, who's been principal for two generations and knows ever'thing about every kid in Pinhole.

She tells me Jimmy and Johnny is best friends and gives me two examples of where they like to play. Lord knows how she knew 'em. One is a old abandoned culvert 'bout two miles out of town and the other is a giant oak tree on ol' man Fisher's land, big enough to climb in but no good for buildin' a treehouse, on account of the boys have to trespass just to play there. Which is enough in itself to make Fisher get out his shotgun.

It was time to go home for lunch and my wife Helen is the best cook in Mississippi. But I didn't have no appetite. I called her and told her so. Then I took me a ride out to the culvert and afterwards to ol' man Fisher's place. No Jimmy and no Johnny in neither location.

So's I wouldn't have to think too much about the problem I got, I called up Father Fugazi in Surfside. He says, yes indeed, he had lunch with his ol' friend Leroy Livingston three days ago and made a date with him to go on a auto trip to DeLand the very next day. But Livingston never showed up. Father Fugazi never suspected nothin', he just got his feelin's hurt. But in the frame of mind I was in, I commenced to suspect foul play.

Now I got somethin' else to worry about, and I don't need Frannie Mendenhall, the town busybody and resident old maid, bustlin' her ample frame through my door, which she does about then. Doggone if Frannie ain't been hearin' noises again in the vacant house next door. Since this happens reg'lar every six months, I'm inclined to pay it no mind, but Frannie says the noises was different this time—kinda like voices, only more shrill. I tell Frannie I'll investigate later, but nothin' will do but what I have to do it right then.

Me and Frannie go over to that vacant house and I climb in the window I always do, but this time it's different from before. Because right away I find somethin' hadn't oughta be there—a blue windbreaker 'bout the right size for a eight-year-old, which is what Jimmy and Johnny both are. I ask Frannie if those noises coulda been kids' voices and she says didn't sound like it but it could be. I ask her if he heard any grown-ups' voices as well. She says she ain't sure. So I deduce that either Jimmy or Johnny or both has spent the night in the vacant house, either in the company of a kidnapper or not.

I got back to the station and call the Chestnuts and the Johnsons. Ain't neither Jimmy nor Johnny been home to lunch, but ain't no ransom notes arrived either. Oh, yeah, and Johnny's favorite jacket's a blue windbreaker. And sure enough, it ain't in his closet.

No sooner have I hung up the phone than my office is a reg'lar behive of activity again. Three ladies from the Baptist church have arrived, in as big a huff as I have noticed anybody in all month. Turns out half the goods they was about to offer at a church bake sale that very afternoon have mysteriously disappeared and they are demandin' instant justice. There ain't no question crime has come to the country. I say I will launch an immediate investigation and I hustle those pillars of the community out of my office.

Course I had my suspicions 'bout who the thieves were—and I bet you can guess which young rascals I had in mind—but that still didn't get me no forrader with findin' 'em.

I made up my mind to take a walk around the block in search of inspiration, but first I called the Dade County, Florida, sheriff's office—which is in charge of Surfside, which is a suburb of Miami. I asked if they had any unidentified bodies turn up in the last few days and they acted like they thought I was touched, but said they'd check.

I walked the half block up to the square, said hello to the reg'lars sittin' on the benches there, and passed a telephone pole with some sorta advertisement illegally posted on it. I was halfway around the square without a idea in my head when all of a sudden it come to me—the meanin' of that poster on the telephone pole. It said the circus was comin' to town.

I doubled back and gave it a closer squint. It said there was gone to be a big time under the big top on October 19, which was that very Saturday. But the date had been pasted over, like on menus when they hike up the prices and paste the new ones over the old ones. I peeled the pasted-over date off and saw that the original one was October 18, which was the day before. Course I don't know when that date's been changed, but it gives me a idea. I figure long as them circus folks ain't changed their minds again, they oughta be pitchin' tents on the fairgrounds right about then.

It ain't but five minutes before I'm out there makin' inquiries, which prove fruitful in the extreme. Come to find out, two young gentlemen 'bout eight years of age have come 'round seekin' careers amid the sawdust and the greasepaint not half an hour before. They had been politely turned down and sent to pat the ponies, which is what I find 'em doin'.

In case you're wonderin', as were the Chestnuts and the Johnsons, it wasn't nothin' at all to study out once I seen that poster. I thought back to one young'un ridin' his pony standin' up and another one tryin' on his mama's pancake and I couldn't help concludin' that Johnny and Jimmy had aspirations to gainful employment, as a trick rider and a clown respectively.

Then I see that the date of the engagement has been changed and I figure the boys didn't catch onto that development till they had done run away from home and found nothin' at the fairgrounds 'cept a sign advisin' 'em accordingly. Course they could hardly go home, bein' as their pride had been sorely injured by the lickin's they had recently undergone, so they just hid out overnight in the vacant house, stole baked goods from the Baptist ladies to keep theirselves alive, and hared off to join the circus soon's it showed up.

That's all there was to it.

All's well that ends well, I says to the Chestnuts and the Johnsons, 'cept for one little detail—them kids, says I, is going to have to make restitution for them cakes and cookies they helped theirselves to. And I'm proud to say that come the next bake sale them two eight-year-olds got out in the kitchen and rattled them pots and pans till they had produced some merchandise them Baptist ladies was mighty tickled to offer for purchase.

Meanwhile, I went back to the station and found the phone ringin' dang near off the hook. It was none other than the Miami Police Department sayin' they had gotten a mighty interestin' call from the sheriff's office. Seems the body of a man in his sixties had floated up on the eighteenth hole of a golf course on the shore of Biscayne Bay three days previous and they was handlin' the case. So far's they knew, they said, it was John Doe with a crushed skull, and could I shed any further light?

I told 'em I reckoned Father Fugazi in Surfside most likely could tell 'em their John Doe was Leroy Livingston of Little Rock, Arkansas, and that I had a pretty good idea who robbed and murdered him.

Then I hung up and had me a heart-to-heart with Mr. James Williamson, credit-card thief and guest of the people of Pinhole. He crumbled like cold bacon in no time a-tall, and waxed pure eloquent on the subject of his own cold-blooded attack on a helpless senior citizen.

I called them Miami police back and said to send for him quick, 'cause Pinhole didn't have no use in the world for him. So I guess there ain't no doubt I solved a murder in Miami. I just didn't hardly notice it.

Crowbait

Everett M. Webber

THE CLOCK in the hotel lounge said 7:30 as Gillespie came from his apartment house across the street for his breakfast. He needed to hurry for he had a long way to drive—and as a matter of fact he could eat very quickly this morning, for his appetite was none too good.

Walking toward the coffee room, he eyed himself in one of the tall mirrors of the lounge—a comfortably plump man, taller than average, and well enough fitted by his ready-made suit. He had an air of respectability, but was a little shabby, too. After all, his shoes were cracked and the suit should have been discarded last year.

Well, good shoes and good suits, they would come now. Not too swiftly, because that would rouse suspicion. But one of these times he could announce the inheritance of some money from an imaginary and far-distant relative, or put out the story that he had had a fortunate price for some land over in his home state which he had never hoped to unload on anyone, or something like that. Then things would come plenty fast. You could do a lot with twenty-eight thousand dollars. His years of ambulance chasing and fee splitting over third rate cases would be over. They would be over as soon as he had his meeting with Barnett and pulled the trigger of the .22 automatic which was now spoiling the hang of his coat.

Then he could have a real car instead of the thing he drove. He could buy a home, have a wife and open a fine office which would attract moneyed clients and let him build a real career. . . . He sat down and ordered coffee and toast.

As he ate, he flattered himself that he was no fool. He had been a lawyer long enough to know that sometimes innocent men were punished instead of guilty ones, and also that guilty ones got caught when they had every reason not to expect it. He knew a few other maxims, such as that crime does not pay, that murder will out, and that if you can protect your reputation, that is even more important than protecting your honor.

No, he was not fool enough to think that he was any smarter or any luckier than a lot of other guys who quietly and cleverly bumped someone off and then got caught. So he was not going to be quiet and clever. He was going to bring Barnett's body back with him and say: "The fool was going to kill me, so I shot him." And what could they say about that? After all, Barnett was a thief and a criminal. Right now he was lugging around the twenty-eight thousand he had stolen from the fraternal insurance society of which he was treasurer. Conceivably, he might add murder to robbery.

But just to make assurance doubly sure, Gillespie was going to do the job across the state line where they had no capital punishment—where the worst they could do to him at all would be to give him a life term from which he would be free in three or four years on parole. With any luck at all he could beat the case entirely if he should be arrested. It was worth the risk. A few months in the pen for the twenty-eight thousand. It was well worth it.

The trip was a long one and his tires were not very good. It was five in the afternoon when he turned off the gravel highway into the little woodland road where he was to meet Barnett. Men and boys and even women had been in the corn fields for miles shooting the crows that were pulling up the newly sprouted stalks, and now he saw a man in a little patch, with a shotgun waiting to get one of the ebony birds to hang up to scare the others away.

Old man Grady, he guessed. Some of the Grady tribe used to live on this place. This was the country where Gillespie and Barnett were raised, and they both knew these hills with their cedar brakes, blackjack thickets, crow rookeries and old deserted farmsteads along the creeks and rivers. Knew them like they knew the palms of their own hands.

That was why it had been so easy yesterday to tell Barnett where to meet him. For all he knew someone was listening in on his line, hoping to get a lead on the man and the money he had stolen. But all he had to say was, "Meet me at that old cabin at the head of Monkey Run." No one would know where that was.

He hadn't been back here since he was a kid—long enough ago that he doubted anyone's knowing him if he should be seen. And if they should it would make no difference because he wasn't going to try to conceal his crime. He was only going to conceal the fact that it was a crime. Up to the point of the killing, the trip was a perfectly legitimate one. After all, a lawyer had a right to go see a client to try to get him to give himself up to the law! That was a well-established principle.

The blackjacks were taller now, as he went down a steep hill, and the cedars thicker. Before long it would be dark back in here. Crows winged swiftly ahead of him, giving him raucous greeting. A whippoorwill was already tuning up, and from some black brake a screech owl whickered. Yet, overhead, above the forest, it was quite light.

Gillespie came to the old cabin a little sooner than he was expecting to. The yard was grown up in sassafras and sumac and cedar sprouts. The porches had rotted off the house, and the grey clapboards sagged in.

Gillespie sat a moment looking at it. Then, feeling the gun in his pocket again, he got out and raised the hood and pretended to be fiddling with the engine in case anyone might be watching. Then he stepped over the old rail fence and walked down to the spring in the cabin yard and washed his hands.

Now he heard a low voice: "Everything's okay. Come on in."

Barnett. He sounded mighty relieved—and about as nervous as Gillespie felt.

Shaking the water off his hands, Gillespie went up to the cabin and onto the old framework of the porch. Through the doorway he could see Barnett in a corner of the shadowy room. Now the man came forward and offered his hand, as if glad to see someone he knew. He had grown a short, dark beard in the four months he had been gone. But nowhere could Gillespie see the sign of any money. He figured there would be a sizable bulk because a thief tried to get his money in small bills for easy passing.

Without preamble, Barnett said, "Well, what did the prosecutor say?"

What the P. A. had said was very explosive: "Tell the so and so we'll make no bargains. We'll get him sooner or later and hang his hide on the barn door!"

But it hardly suited Gillespie's purpose to tell Barnett that—not when he didn't even know where the money was. The lighting of a bird on the ragged roof startled him. Another crow. It sounded as if it were laughing at him as it loudly answered a friend off across the branch.

He growled an oath at the thing, and then judiciously he said, "Well, if I were in your shoes I'd think things looked pretty rosy. I told Henry that you said you had spent less than a thousand of the money, and that you had enough property to make that up. He said he would recommend that you get a suspended sentence and be put on five years' probation, since it looks like you've learned your lesson."

Barnett seemed to think that over. He was a wizened little man, looking far older than Gillespie, the lawyer flattered himself, though they were of the same age. Barnett sighed.

And finally he asked, "Will his recommendation be followed?"

"Well," Gillespie said, "I won't lie to you. I imagine you'll get a year in jail in spite of everything, and that you'll have to serve thirty to sixty days of it before they parole you. On the other hand, you may not do a day."

Barnett shook his head. "What a fool I was! I haven't had an easy minute since I took it . . . Well, tell them I'll be in tomorrow."

"What's the matter with tonight?" Gillespie asked. "We could drive a while and then get some sleep and still make it before noon tomorrow—"

"I'll have to get the money," Barnett told him. "I don't keep it in my pocket."

Gillespie sensed then that the man did not trust him. That he had foreseen how it would be so easy to get himself killed—Gillespie smiled, controlling his irritation and disappointment. "Well, then," he remarked casually, "I'll see you when you get there."

Barnett nodded and sat on an old tomato crate as if very tired. "I hate it, the long trip you've had," he said. "I didn't see why we couldn't have settled everything with another phone call, after you'd had time to talk to the prosecutor."

"You wouldn't see that for the same reason you couldn't see what a dope you were to get hooked into this in the first place," Gillespie told him with friendly callousness. "I don't like to do any talking into a phone that wouldn't sound good if ever I had it played back to me on a record."

Barnett smiled faintly as if to say, "Who'd bother to tap the wires of a shyster like you?" Gillespie winced under the look and became steadier in his purpose.

But all Barnett said aloud was, "Well—I'll be seeing you."

Gillespie nodded, and, as if on afterthought, he asked, "Where's your car?"

"Hidden in a cedar brake. Take care of yourself."

* * *

A quarter of a mile up the road, Gillespie stopped his car and ran back. It might be anywhere along here, as thick as the cedars were, that the car was hidden. The limbs, often fifteen feet long, grew thickly on the gnarled trunks clear to the ground and you might pass within a few steps of a car or man either without seeing him.

Gillespie cocked his head, listening, as he hid in the brush within sight of the cabin. Barnett would likely give him time to get well away before starting his own car. But he hadn't started it yet, not unless it were a mighty long way from here—farther away than he would have had time to go. Gillespie froze at the thought. Why, the dirty scoundrel might have left it miles from here! He—

Off to the right, he heard a considerable cawing and fussing of the crows. On a hunch, he stepped into the clear of the cabin yard, and now he could see the birds flushing up from the timber over in that direction. Swiftly he ran to the spring branch and there in the damp dirt he saw where Barnett had crossed, going that way. At least, there were shoeprints there—small and pointed. Not the heavy plow shoes of a farmer.

There was sort of a trail—an old wagon road grown up in brush—through the woods here, he remembered now. In a moment he had found it, and as he ran he still saw a footprint occasionally where the dead leaves were blown clear of the ground. This was a regular crow heaven here in the blackjacks, and now the birds flew up again, the ones which had settled after Barnett's passing.

Gillespie felt the fatness of his body and the flabbiness of his muscles as he ran through the deepening twilight. He hadn't exerted himself like this in years. His mouth had that taste in it like the taste of salty, blood-tinged saliva. The taste that is there before the second wind comes, while the lungs are still burning and the heart trying to break out of the chest. Sweat stung his eyes but he kept on, for Barnett had a long start on him. Half a mile, maybe, for he had driven a quarter and walked another quarter back, and then lost some time finding the trail.

He broke his stride as he came to a straight piece of road and saw his quarry a couple of hundred yards ahead. Barnett was carrying a little black bag, and now he whirled, staring at Gillespie. He made an instinctive movement to conceal the bag behind him, and then he seemed to decide on matter-of-factness instead.

Gillespie dropped to a walk. Trying to get enough air into his constricted lungs to talk, he wheezed, "I forgot—to tell you—"

He wobbled on up to Barnett who stood regarding him uncertainly. Then he jerked out his pistol and as Barnett dodged away he fired and the bullet struck the man in the left temple.

He stood there looking at the man on the ground. This was a hell of a note. Three quarters of a mile from his car, and no way of getting the car down here without chopping out the heavy brush in the road. He could carry the body, but a hundred and fifty pounds—that would get mighty heavy.

On sudden thought, Gillespie knelt and felt over him to see if he did have a gun, and he was relieved to feel the hard outline of one in a shoulder holster. Then he reached for the little black bag, but before he could open it a business-like voice drawled, "Mister, we call this murder here."

Gillespie whirled, coming to his feet with the bag. Ten steps away was a hard-bitten man in blue shirt and bib overalls. A rifle in his hands. The muzzle was pointed ominously.

The man spat and said, "I seen the whole thing, mister. Don't try to pick up your pistol—"

Gillespie wheezed, "He was looking for me to kill me. I—"

Taking a long chance, he dived into the cedar brake. The rifle cracked, but the old man got no second shot. In the dark forest, Gillespie crashed on and on. But noise made nothing to shoot at. He zigzagged, seeking the easiest footing. He would circle. Reach his car. He heard the man shout, "Come back here, you fool—"

And then all was silence except for the sound of his running on the dead leaves and over the dead limbs that had fallen, and the sound of the crows.

Sweating, he snapped the bag open and a great relief filled him as he saw that the bundles of money were really here. But with the testimony of that old man—unless the fellow's mouth could be shut—he might get sent up. And now that there was a chance of prison, he suddenly had no stomach for it.

No. No, all he could do was go back home. Put up his story to the prosecutor and turn in the money.

He looked upward, straining and twisting his neck, and the crows mocked at him. Then he saw a little cylinder, like a tomato can, hanging in a tree. And then another, and another, and— The trees were full of them. Thousands of them! He stared in wonder— and then he knew. The crow rookery was going to be bombed! Straining his eyes, he could see the wire running from bomb to bomb in the trees. Millions of death-dealing missiles would fly everywhere, lacing the air and riddling the birds and stripping the leaves from the trees. It was at roosting time that they did it. That was what the old man was up there for—keeping any chance hunter from going down into the danger zone.

With a sucking moan, Gillespie looked about for shelter, but there was none. His only hope was to get into the open. He ran on. And now ahead he did see the cleared space of a field, and he ran faster, for at any second—He saw men out there. He didn't want to meet them, but there was no time to turn aside and try to get out of the forest elsewhere, for one was squating at a box with a plunger on top.

He opened his mouth to yell at them, but the pitiful little squeak he made hardly reached his own ears.

He heard a man yell, "Okay, blow it up!"

In the dimness he saw the man at the box shove the plunger down.

Damp Sheets

H. Russell Wakefield

EXACTLY HOW MUCH are you overdrawn, Robert?'
'Oh, I don't know; quite a bit.'
'That's so like you! Now, you've got to tell me.'
'Oh, about eight hundred.'
'Eight hundred! And how do you propose to work that off?'
'Well, I can't see any way at the moment.'
'Would Uncle Samuel help you?'
'I don't like to ask him.'
'Because he knows you're a born fool about money, and might alter his will?'
'If you like to put it in that typically courteous way.'
'How old is he? I always forget.'
'Seventy-five or six.'
'Is he strong?'
'No, his chest's groggy, but he takes very good care of himself.'
'Why not ask him to stay—he's never been here—and make a fuss of the old thing, and see if you can't get something out of him? We can't go on like this. Are you still betting?'

'Well, I've been doing better lately.'

'How much did you lose last month?'

'Look here, Agatha, I'm sick of your abuse and nagging!'

'Will you write and ask your uncle to stay?'

'Oh, all right.'

This amiable little domestic dialogue took place between Robert Stacey and his spouse, Agatha Henrietta Stacey, in the morning-room of Cardew House, near Hallocks, Sussex. It was characteristic of many such, for Robert was improvident and feeble, and Agatha despised him and was strong. When—and why—she had married him he had been a comparatively rich man, with a delightful little estate and great prospects. He still possessed the estate—mortgaged to the hilt—and the prospects—but his decadent financial condition has just been revealed. He had frittered his money away in conventionally fatuous ways. By a fatuous belief in his racing judgment, by a fatuous confidence in fundamentally unsound commercial ventures, by fatuous personal extravagance. He owned one of those long, dog-like faces sometimes described as 'aristocratic,' a back-parting, a clumsy body, and stupid, loutish hands. He was forty years of age.

His prospects would be realised on the death of his uncle, Samuel—already referred to—who was leaving him £150,000 and Framley Court, in Surrey, an ugly old house, but large, lavishly furnished, and very comfortable. Uncle Samuel knew nothing of his nephew's financial incompetence and straits, and his ignorance of them was just about the only tribute to Robert's intelligence that it had ever been possible to pay. The dispelling of that ignorance would have had disastrous consequences, for Uncle Samuel was very proud of the fortune he had made, and would have regarded the prospect of its improvident dispersal with an absolute lack of enthusiasm. And there was already the complication that the old man disliked Agatha. In that he was of the vast majority. Robert had married her for her looks in a vague 'time I settled down' mood. She was neither 'pretty' nor a 'beauty,' but she outpointed the majority of those who were. Her small, slanting, green eyes, which seemed always to be observing with extreme intensity, set in a face pallid but exquisitely shaped, inevitably seized and held attention. Her other features suggested strength, her red hair temperament; but those glittering, little restless eyes suggested at times frigid malignity and always insatiable egoism. Her body, of which she took the greatest care, was small, slim, but very strong. She neither smoked nor drank, but she never stopped thinking. She had married solely for money, and she had learned bitterly to blame herself for her bad judgment in choosing Robert, for he had had many prosperous rivals. She was just thirty-two.

Robert at first tried to keep his financial collapse from her, but her wits were far too keen for this, and when cross-examined ruthlessly he had collapsed. Since then he had meekly done as he was told, save for a few feeble and ineffectual revolts.

Agatha had one vulnerable spot—her daughter Elizabeth, for whom she showed a savage feline affection; when she kissed her it was as if a panther was licking her cub. She was disliked by her neighbours for her arrogance, but they feared her tongue. She was the daughter of a Polish actress and an Englishman in business at Warsaw. They had both died many years before, leaving her with £200 a year. Besides that she had nothing.

After the pleasant dialogue already related she went to her bureau and began to write, while Robert turned over in his mind the project of this invitation to his uncle to which he had pledged himself. There were difficulties—the old man's dislike of Agatha, his set ways and hypochondriacal tendencies. Then, was it wise to give him a hint of his precarious financial state? Probably not, but he'd got to get money somehow and soon, for the bank had politely intimated that they would prefer not to increase his overdraft. But he had to get some ready money.

'Look here, Agatha,' he said at length, 'there are certain difficulties about asking Uncle Samuel here.'

'One,' she replied, 'is the fact that he loathes me. Well, I can assure you I'll butter up the old fool. He's interested in pictures, isn't he?'

'Yes.'

'Well, tell him we'll ask Sir Arthur Welby to meet him.'

'Who's he?'

'He's a famous critic. I met him at the Gilbeys'.'

'But will he come?'

'Oh yes. He pretended to tell me about painting, but he gave me several languishing glances and put his hand on my knee while praising my appearance. He compared me with some woman in a picture, and said he tremendously looked forward to seeing me again. Oh yes, he'll come when he's called! He's staying with the Gilbeys for another month. Come over here and write down what I tell you.'

Robert did so, and once again his cringing detestation of the tyrant who dominated him was combined with a gruding but deep respect for that bully's brains. It was just the letter, he knew, which might persuade Uncle Samuel to pay them a visit.

And it was so, for three days later he wrote accepting. He would arrive in his car about 5.30 on Friday, January 4th, and stay till Monday. It was clear that the prospect of meeting Sir Arthur had done the trick. He added a list of things he would require—Vichy water, Ryvita bread, and other fussy commodities. He even indicated the number of blankets he wanted on his bed.

Robert scraped together enough cash to ensure his adequate but not lavish entertainment. The atmosphere Agatha wished him to create was that of essential stability but temporary embarrassment; of an economy—not really necessary, but prudently advisable—till the stock he had bought—a purely fictitious purchase, needless to say—had completed its rise and his broker advised him to sell. This mythical holding was in a certain Talking Machine concern then having a frenetic boom.

It gave Agatha a peculiar pleasure thus to plan a coherent, rather complex, deception, but it was an exasperating labour to make Robert word-perfect in it. She'd have forced her way to success, using, breaking, exploiting, fooling other men, and women too!

Sir Arthur accepted an invitation to dine on Saturday—with a gallant postscript. Uncle Samuel arrived precisely at 5.30 on Friday. He was a fussy, frail, sharp-witted and tongued little fellow. He greeted Agatha rather over-politely, but turned quickly away from her. To Robert he was slightly condescendingly affable. He said he was tired by his journey and would lie down until it was time to dress. He appeared highly gratified that he was to meet Sir Arthur on the morrow.

Agatha had told Robert not to open the subject of his finances until she gave the word. She acted perfectly during dinner, seeming deferential and most anxious to please, fond of Robert, a contented, settled, married woman. Uncle Samuel glanced at her sharply once or twice, as if not quite sure; but after some excellent light sherry, the better part of a bottle of estimable champagne, and two glasses of port, he became mellow and loquacious. He was, however, no believer in late hours for a man of his age, and stated that he always retired at 10.30 unless there was some important cause for his staying up late—the company of Sir Arthur would certainly be such a cause. So at 10.15 Agatha went up to his room to see that his fire was all right, and that the Vichy was by his bed-side. She remained there for about eight minutes, during which period she kept the door locked.

Punctually at 10.30 Uncle Samuel went to bed. Next morning he had his breakfast in bed and did not appear downstairs till eleven o'clock. He hadn't slept very well and thought he had caught a slight chill. He was testy, nervous, and looked very fragile. But the prospect of meeting Sir Arthur neutralised his concern about his health, and he was more vivacious and even-tempered after luncheon. He took a short drive in the afternoon, and then went to his room to get into their proper order the photographs of his treasured pictures at Framley, and to catalogue the list of questions he wished to put to Sir Arthur concerning them.

He greeted the great man with effusion, and during dinner insistently claimed his attention. The famous art critic did his best to appear vastly interested in Uncle Samuel's pictures. They were, for the most part, attributed to minor Flemish masters, but their authenticity was highly dubious. Sir Arthur would gladly have preferred to pay *sotto voce* and semi-senile compliments to his hostess, whose personality stirred up within him feelings which he had hoped had deserted him for ever. Agatha was at first utterly bored with all this pernickety high-brow chat, but one thing Sir Arthur said caught her attention. 'The desire to make money is at the root of all artistic endeavour. The rest is humbug!' He didn't quite mean it, but he was getting weary of Uncle Samuel's infatuation for his second-rate stuff, and how fascinated he was by Agatha's little animal green eyes! Later on he made another pronouncement: 'The old should make way for the young. And, furthermore, the old should not become critics when their creative impulse is moribund. When they have said all they have to say in paint let them keep silence, and not attempt to imprison the young and vital in the stocks of their senility.' And his right knee touched Agatha's left. She had never doubted the truth of either of these propositions, but it amused her to hear this old fool subscribing to them. 'Everyone is the same,' she thought; 'money's everything, and the old must pay or go.' She became bland, sensuous, and light-hearted, and slyly tapped Sir Arthur's right knee with her left.

Robert hardly spoke a word, for he had nothing to contribute to the discussion, and he was thinking about Monday morning and the absolute necessity for cashing another cheque. He ate and drank and occasionally smoothed his back-parting. After Sir Arthur had left, Uncle Samuel stayed up for a little while longer, Agatha seizing the opportunity to run up and see that her guest was provided with everything he wanted. She remained eight minutes and kept the door locked.

'When shall I say anything?' asked Robert, after his guest had gone up to bed.

'Possibly to-morrow evening. I'll let you know,' replied Agatha. About eight o'clock the next morning a maid came to Agatha's room to say that Mr. Walton complained of feeling ill and would like to see her. She dressed quickly and went to his room.

'My chill has developed, Agatha,' he said querulously. 'I cannot control my shivering, and I am convinced I have a temperature. Do you know, I'm certain my sheets have been damp on both nights.'

'Oh no, Uncle Samuel; I saw they were aired myself. Let me look at your hot-water bottle.' She put her hand in the bed and drew it out. 'Yes,' she said, 'it's been leaking—it's all wet round the top and wants a new washer. What a pity you did not let us lend you one of ours!'

'It's never leaked before,' said Uncle Samuel.

'I'll go and get you another. Do you think you ought to see the doctor?'

'I *must* have him,' replied Uncle Samuel nervously and irritably. 'Chills are terribly dangerous to those with chests as weak as mine. Send for him at once, please.'

'I'll ring him up immediately.'

However, she didn't quite keep her word, for she went first to Robert's room and said, 'The old man's ill.'

'Ill! What's the matter with him?' asked Robert, a certain excitement in his voice.

'He says he has a bad chill. I'm going to ring up Dr. Prichard.'

'We owe him twenty pounds.'

'Well, he'll have to come, and the old man can pay the bill.'

The doctor was unable to say anything definite about his patient's condition. 'His temperature is just over a hundred degrees, and I have detected what may be the beginning of mischief in the right lung, but it is too early to say yet.'

However, after he returned in the evening his uncertainty ended. 'He's in for an attack of pneumonia, which must be a very serious thing indeed for a man of his age and medical history. He'll have to have day and night nurses, and I'll go and arrange about them at once.'

When he had gone, Agatha and Robert exchanged glances. 'Perhaps there'll be no need for me to say anything,' suggested the latter, inadequately concealing the trend of his thoughts.

'When you're with him you'd better act better than that,' replied Agatha contemptuously. 'He's got plenty of time to make another will.'

Uncle Samuel might just, but only just, have had time, for he became unconscious on the evening following, and made but little fight. On Tuesday evening Agatha relieved the day nurse for a time. She sat by the fire reading *Vogue,* and planning a second trousseau. Uncle Samuel had not been conscious for twenty-four hours. Suddenly, hearing a rustle from the bed, she glanced towards it. Uncle Samuel was sitting up and staring at her. ('How ghastly he looks!' she thought.) He continued to stare for a moment or two, and then he said, in a horrible, harsh whisper, 'Agatha, my sheets *were* damp.' And then he fell back and died.

Two months later Agatha and Robert went into residence at Framley Court. Robert was in so exuberant a psychic state that he made the most fulsome promises concerning his future rectitude, and promised to limit his personal expenditure to an agreed sum.

Agatha was in her element, for she was a born manager and chatelaine. For a time she was almost tolerant of Robert, and a feeble imitation of matrimonial harmony was established. However, a fortnight after their arrival at Framley she was given cause to suspect that she had not finished with Uncle Samuel. She was sitting writing in her boudoir about six o'clock when slowly and insidiously she found herself losing the thread of what she wanted to say. Her head was muddled. She put down her pen and glanced behind her, and then she gripped the sides of the desk, for Uncle Samuel was standing in the doorway and staring at her. She looked away and then looked again, and he had gone.

'Simply an illusion,' she half decided.

But on the next evening, when she was strolling in the garden at dusk, she became aware of a figure standing motionless some distance away across the flowerbeds. The light was dim, but she had no doubt as to who it was. She turned and walked back to the house. The next day she again detected this curious echo of Uncle Samuel watching her from the end of the passage near her bedroom. Agatha had never known such an experience before, but her courage was absolute, and she determined to defy and, as far as possible, disregard this hallucination. No one else in the house seemed to share it. One thing she could never succeed in doing, and that was to stare back. She made the attempt, but her eyes always fell.

She and Robert had decided to give a large weekend party to their friends to celebrate their good fortune. On the Tuesday before the guests were to assemble, Agatha decided to make an inspection of the resources of her linen-room, which might be severely taxed. She went up there after dinner. It was on the top floor next to the laundry-room in which one of the maids was at work. . . . The figure she knew so well came in just behind her.

Presently the maid in the laundry-room heard a slight thud. She looked up, but for a few minutes went on with her work, and then she decided to see if anything had happened in the linen-room. She opened the door and peeped in. A look of amazement came over her face, and she bent down and lifted something; then she screamed.

The Coroner always considered it one of the most inexplicable cases into which he had ever inquired. As he pointed out at the inquest, the sheets, wrapped in paper and resting on their shelves some feet from the ground, had apparently slid from their receptacles, knocked Mrs. Stacey down, and then, as it were, billowed out over her head, so stifling her. He could not see how this could possibly have happened. He closely cross-examined the maid who had first found the body, but her tale never varied.

'But there's one thing, sir,' she added, 'p'raps I should have said—them sheets was all damp.'

'What difference does that make!' said the Coroner testily.

The Dark Hour

Morris Hershman

THE DINNER DISHES had been cleared away at last, but Anne Castle wasn't sighing with relief when she sat down in the soft chair.

She had reached a self-conscious state of life, in some ways, and took pleasure in doing extra work after her husband had got back from the job. Perhaps she wanted to show that she wasn't wasting time while he earned money for the family. It was a silly habit in some ways, she supposed, but middle-aged women were all like that.

She reached for her son's sweater on top of the sewing kit. Having arranged the lamplight so that it fell on her lap, Anna was finally easing the proper thread color through the needle's eye when her son suddenly put on the television set so loudly in the next room that in sheer surprise she pinked herself.

The near-silence lasted until she was ready to turn over the sweater and saw the last crosswise thread diagonally across the pattern she had created at the back of the garment. When an interruption did come, its source was totally unexpected.

Sam suddenly said, "Get me a drink."

Anna looked up, startled. Her husband was sitting in the soft chair with the longer base that was diagonally opposite her.

Sam Castle was a man of dark features in a smooth, unlined face. He had a temper, heaven knew, but Anna appreciated the fact that he did his best to keep it down.

He wasn't angry now, but he was upset enough to break a habit of long-standing. He never took more than one drink in a twenty-four hour stretch, and his hiding the fact from prospective clients and other people was part of the folklore, as he liked to call it, among his managerial colleagues over at Midland Insurance.

"What's wrong, dear?" Anna asked, almost lightly. "Is the world in worse shape than you thought?"

"Just get me the drink and don't ask questions." He closed his eyes heavily. "It's taken twenty years to happen. Twenty years."

His use of the number made her sit up straight and then hurry to do what he wanted. Every New Year's Eve since they had known each other he would say to her quietly, just after midnight, "Well, it's been two years," or "three years," adding one number every New Year's Eve. He never mentioned it from one New Year's Eve to the next, though, which was a blessing.

Anna prepared gin and tonic for him at the sideboard and brought it over. He drained it quickly, but Anna noticed that his eyes didn't leave the opened newspaper he had been reading so casually up to a moment ago.

"What can have gone wrong after all that time?" she asked, getting out the words carefully.

"The police have caught somebody and say that he did that thing."

He started to tell more, but she glanced pointedly over toward the closed door of the room, where Jerry was watching television.

"Let's go upstairs and talk," she said urgently. "Please."

"All right."

She had hoped that they'd go quietly and not catch their son's attention, but her hopes were dashed by the creaking steps. Jerry called out and she hesitated and said that everything was fine. She never would understand how their son could hear them with the television going and his mind on his school work. The younger generation's tolerance of noise and their capacity to work in spite of it were simply beyond her.

They walked up more slowly, though. Never before had she seen Sam's back stooped over slightly, but that was the way she saw it now. She made a point of walking upright.

Not until they reached the bedroom did she realize that she had carried the sweater and needle and thread and thimble upstairs with her. She put them down slowly, as if letting part of the life drain out of her body.

"What did happen, dear?" Anna asked slowly. "According to the newspapers, I mean."

Sam Castle sat down on the bed and clasped his hands tautly. "The police caught a burglar for assault as well as for burglary. He was wearing a sharp-edged expensive ring that didn't jibe with his cheap outfit. The inscription had been filed off that ring, but police scientists brought it back with acids and found that the ring belonged to—Alfred Mettay."

She hadn't heard that name from his lips since the night before they had become engaged, when he had insisted on telling her that

139

he had once killed a man in self-defense and never been accused of it. He didn't give her any other details about the killing, but pointed out that she'd have to decide whether or not to marry him after what she now knew. Anna had never been sorry about her decision.

"This man, this burglar," Anna began carefully. "Has he been charged by the police for that crime?"

"He certainly has," Sam said grimly. "That's why something has got to be done about it."

"But from what you say, dear, the police have got evidence against him for other crimes, too."

"Not murders, but for assaults with deadly weapons."

"In that case," she said, immensely relieved, "the murder charge makes no real difference, because there isn't any death penalty in this state and the man is bound to be put away for a long time."

"If the real killer comes forward to tell the truth about the Mettay case it might show a reasonable doubt in his favor for the other crimes."

Anna said, "You'll destroy yourself and me and our son."

She looked down if only to help get her ideas together. What had started out as an average night was going to end with her having to fight for her home and family, for everything important to her.

"There's no reason in the world for you to practically have to commit suicide." She might have been talking to the furniture for all he seemed to have heard. "You've been honest and respectable, and you shouldn't have to destroy yourself because you once did something to a man in self-defense."

"I killed a man," he said patiently. "I didn't 'do something' to him. He didn't 'pass away', either. He died violently because I choked him to death with these hands and ran out."

Sam picked up the phone.

"I want the nearest police precinct," he said, adding patiently to the operator's question, "No, it's not an emergency. My phone number is—"

But Anna had pressed the phone bar downwards, breaking the connection. She faced her husband from the other end of the night table, leaning forward.

"At least talk it over with Berry before you go to the police, Sam. Do that much for me and Jerry, at least."

Donald Berry had handled a negligence action for them a few

years ago, collecting a handsome amount for them from the township because Jerry had broken an arm. He was a pleasant man and a sympathetic listener.

"He's not a criminal lawyer," Sam said, shaking his head fiercely. "That's what I need."

"Ask him to recommend one and then talk it over. Please."

He finally agreed to do it. Berry recommended a fellow named Norman Jesperson. Anna was half hoping that a night ride to the criminal lawyer's office would help bring back a sense of proportion, but Jesperson said he'd come out to see them instead. He turned out to be a thick-bodied man who dressed neatly and talked in a deep but well-controlled voice.

"Before we go any further I suggest you give me a check and I'll let you have a receipt," the criminal lawyer said. He flushed at sight of Sam's twisted grin, then added, "It establishes a lawyer-client relationship so I won't have to repeat what you tell me."

Sam wrote out the check. Jesperson examined it only casually before putting it into his pocket.

"Newspapers aren't the best news source in this world," the lawyer said after he'd heard a guarded version of Sam's story, not much more than he had ever told his wife. "Here's how we'll handle it, Mr. Castle. I'll look into the case tomorrow and give you a report in the afternoon. That ought to be all right."

Sam Castle had to give in. He spent a restless night, of course, and so did Anna. In the morning she made him promise to phone as soon as he heard from the lawyer. She couldn't help adding that she was sure everything would be all right, and she wished she hadn't noticed the pitying look that her husband directed at her as a result.

Anna forgot to call Rose Markell, with whom she was supposed to have lunch that afternoon. A worried Rose called her instead and it took time to get her off the phone. She prepared dinner with only half her attention, if that much, coiled on a spring while waiting for the phone. But she found herself hardly able to move when the phone did ring at about half-past two.

It wasn't her husband, but his secretary. Miss Lamb sounded worried.

"I don't think Mr. Castle is feeling very good," Miss Lamb said. "He doesn't want to see a doctor because I asked him and he said no. He didn't want me to call you, either, but maybe you should come over here. Make believe it's casual, that you just happen to be in the city, if you know what I mean."

"Doesn't feel well?" It was something else going wrong that she hadn't expected. "What happened?"

"Well, a little while ago he got a phone call and he told me not to take any more calls for him. He just sits and stares in front of him."

A phone call? From the lawyer? "I'll be there as quickly as I can."

Having got dressed, she remembered to write a note for Jerry and leave it on the kitchen table. It took forty minutes with delays before her car took her to the city. Miss Lamb was typing furiously in her cubicle at the Midland offices when Anna got there, out of breath, and started past her.

"You can't go in there right now, I'm afraid," the secretary said, surprisingly. "Your husband is talking to somebody and left orders that he wasn't to be disturbed."

"What's the name of the person he's talking to?"

Miss Lamb had to look it up. "Jes-per-son. Mr. Jesperson. He's the same one called a while ago, just before Mr. Castle started to look real sick."

"I'm going in."

Both men looked up startled as Anna opened the office door, but Jesperson finally greeted her with a nod. As for her husband, his smooth and unlined face was strained and white. Sam looked away at sight of her.

"What happened?" Anna Castle asked.

"The police have just dropped the other cases against that burglar," Jesperson said easily. "They claim there's no substantial evidence. The only case against him now is the one with some circumstantial factors. The Mettay murder."

Anna was furious rather than numbed. Her first thought, surprisingly, was that she wished the lawyer would work only from his own office. When she talked to him again, she couldn't help sounding angry.

"What are you going to do about it?"

"I'm making arrangements for your husband to talk to the police officer in charge of the investigation," Jesperson said. "I'll be with him all the time."

She started to say that it didn't seem as if he would be doing much, but Jesperson was on the phone, speaking briefly to a police lieutenant named O'Keefe. He made an appointment in an hour's time, although Anna gestured to him frantically to put it off for as long as possible.

"He'll be leaving the office soon," Jesperson said to her when he hung up. "The quicker we know where we stand on this, the better for all of us."

Sam left the office first, telling Miss Lamb that he wasn't sure when he'd return. His back was stooped once again. Anna walked behind him and automatically got into the car at his side. He and Jesperson glanced at each other, probably trying to decide what to do about her.

"You'll wait in the car for us when we get there," Sam said.

He would probably never drive again, he told himself.

Police headquarters was gray looking and large. A desk sergeant in a wide anteroom led them—Anna had stubbornly joined the men as soon as they stepped inside—to a small office. There were only two visitor chairs, so Anna stood. She warned herself not to let out a cry no matter what she heard, not to talk at all as long as her husband was in this room.

Frank O'Keefe, the police lieutenant, was a dapper man with probing eyes. Rather than subjecting Sam to an instant grilling, as Anna had more than half expected, he looked only at Jesperson. The lawyer's presence made everybody else in the room unimportant, or so it seemed.

"As I told you over the phone," Jesperson began, "my client wants to give you some information about the Mettay murder."

"After twenty years." O'Keefe's voice was deep, and he slurred his words. "Would this be a confession?"

Sam wasn't able to answer. O'Keefe must have taken Sam's agreement for granted. He nodded and leaned back comfortably.

"Self-defense, wasn't it?" he asked.

Before Jesperson could talk, Sam said, "He started to punch me in the face and I went for his throat. He pulled out a knife and I— well, you know."

"There was a knife in Alfred Mettay's right hand when he was found." O'Keefe scratched his jaw with a thumbnail.

"I've got a scar from that knife on my left hip."

He looked at Anna for confirmation and she caught herself nodding. She had never known that the scar related to the murder, not having heard details of the crime until now.

"Your blood type is AB, I suppose. Traces were found on the

knife tip. Unfortunately, the man we arrested has got blood of a different type, as we've found out after tests. We've been getting ready to let him go."

Anna covered her mouth with a shaking palm. Sam said nothing, but suddenly shaded his eyes with a hand.

"With the help of your testimony, though," O'Keefe added almost casually, "we can hold on to him and go ahead with the prosecution, Mr. Castle."

"I don't understand that," Sam said carefully, "if the blood type doesn't fit."

"It becomes obvious what really happened," O'Keefe murmured. "There was a fight between you and Alfred Mettay. He punched you in the face and then drew a knife. You choked him, left him on the floor and ran. Our suspect is a burglar with a previous record of assaults. He broke into the apartment, saw Mettay unconscious and started helping himself to some goodies. Maybe when he grabbed for Mettay's sharp-edged gold ring the man started to become conscious again. There was a fight, with Mettay in a weakened condition. Our man was then able to finish the job you started."

"How can you be sure?" Sam asked weakly.

"The burglar is thin and five feet one inch tall," O'Keefe said comfortably. "No jury will ever believe that he took the ring off a six foot bruiser like Mettay unless Mettay was already in a weakened condition."

Sam shut his eyes. "I see. Yes, I do see now. If I had come forward twenty years ago, I might not have had to go through all the hell that has just about wrung me dry since then."

"You'll have to testify at the trial, of course," O'Keefe said, "but the D.A. will see your case my way, I'm sure. There won't be any prison for you, Mr. Castle. Thanks for coming in, and keep yourself available."

On the way out they said so long to Jesperson and got in to Sam's car for the trip back to the office. City traffic was slow and awkward, this time. At a stop for a light, he turned to her.

"Things will be better now," he said.

She smiled back at him, but hoped it wouldn't occur to the lieutenant back there that the burglar might have been the first one to come into the victim's apartment at that fatal time after all, hitting Mettay from behind and then grabbing for the loot. Twenty years had passed since then and the burglar had committed many other crimes, so he didn't remember what had actually happened. Sam had encountered a weakened Mettay immediately afterwards, so that Sam had killed Mettay after all.

Anna Castle hoped that her feelings didn't show as she looked at her husband's smooth, unlined face which couldn't ever have been punched by a man wearing a sharp-edged ring.

But, like Sam himself until a few moments back, she'd be on pins and needles for a long, long time to come. Sam had disclosed his secret to a public official, but a secret of sorts had been transferred to Anna's shoulders as well. She could keep it tensely and hopefully, but in a darker world than she had ever known.

The Dead Woman

David H. Keller

HE WAS FOUND in the room with his wife, slightly confused, a trifle bewildered, but otherwise, apparently normal. He made no effort to conceal his conduct any more than he did to take the knife from his hand and the pieces from the trunk.

Fortunately, the Inspector was an officer of more than usual intelligence, and there was no effort made to give the third degree or even to secure a written confession. Perhaps the police department felt it was too plain a case. At least, it was handled intelligently and in a most scientific manner. The man was well fed, carefully bedded, and the next morning, after being bathed and shaved, was taken to see a psychiatrist.

The specialist in mental diseases had the man comfortably seated. Knowing he smoked he offered a cigar, which was accepted. Then, in a quiet, pleasant atmosphere, he made one statement and asked one question.

"I am sure, Mr. Thompson, that you had an excellent reason for acting as you did the other day. I wish you would tell me all about it."

The man looked at the psychiatrist. "Will you believe me if I tell you?"

"I will accept every part of your story with the idea that you are convinced that you are telling the truth."

"That is all I want," whispered Thompson. "If everyone I talked to in the past had done that, if they had even tried to check up on my story, perhaps this would not have happened. But they always thought I was the sick one, and no one was willing to accept my statement about the worms.

"I suppose I was happily married. At least, as much so as most men are. You know there's a good deal of conflict between the sexes, and there were a few differences of opinion between Mrs. Thompson and myself. But not enough to cause serious difficulty. Will you remember that? That we did not quarrel very much?

"About a year ago my wife's health gave me considerable thought. She started to fail. If you are a married man, Doctor, you know there is always that anxiety about the wife's health. You become accustomed to living with a woman, having her do things for you, go to places with you and you think about how life would be if she should sicken and die. Perhaps the fact that you are uneasy about the future makes you exaggerate the importance of her symptoms.

"At any rate, she became sick, a nasty cough and a loss in weight. I spoke to her about it and even bought a bottle of Beef, Iron and Wine at the drug store and made her take it. She did so to please me, but she never would admit that she was sick. Said it was fashionable to be thin and that the cough was just nervousness.

"She would not go and see a doctor. When I spoke to her mother about it, the old lady just laughed at me, and said if I tried to make Lizzie happier, she would soon get fat. In fact, none of our family or our friends seemed to feel there was anything wrong with Mrs. Thompson; so I stopped talking about it. Of course, it was not easy on me, the way she coughed at night, and her staying awake so much. I work hard in the daytime and it is not easy on the nerves to lose a lot of sleep. At last I was forced to ask her to let me sleep in the spare bedroom.

"Even that did not help much. I could hear her cough and, when she did fall asleep, I would have to tiptoe into her room and see if she was all right. Her coughing bothered me so much, but when she didn't cough, it worried me more because I thought something had happened to her.

"One night the thing I was afraid of happened. She had a hard spell of coughing and then she stopped. It was quiet in the house. I could hear the clock on the landing tick, and a mouse gnawing wood in the attic. I thought I could even hear my own heart beat, but there wasn't a sound of any kind from the other bedroom.

"When I went in and turned on the light, I just knew it was all over. Of course, I was not sure. A bookkeeper is not supposed to be an expert in such matters; so, I telephoned for our doctor. On the way to the phone I wondered just what I should say, for he had always insisted that my wife was in grand health. So I simply told him that Mrs. Thompson was not looking well and would he come over? Just like that I told him, and tried to keep my voice steady.

"It was about an hour before he came; guess he had stopped to shave. He went into the bedroom, but I hesitated at the doorway. He spent some time listening to her heart and feeling her pulse and then he straightened up and asked me, 'She is fine. Just fast asleep. What did you think was wrong?'

"That surprised me so much that all I could do was to stammer something about not hearing her cough anymore. He laughed at me as he hit me on the shoulder.

" 'You worry too much about her, Mr. Thompson.'

"Right there my difficulty started. There was a doctor who was supposed to know his business and he said there was nothing wrong with my wife and there I was, just a bookkeeper, and I knew what was the matter. What was I to do? Tell him he was wrong? Send for another physician?

"It was growing light by that time, so I went down to the kitchen and started the coffee. Often did that, and later on fried some eggs and bacon. Then I shaved and made ready to go to the office. But before I went I sat down a while by my wife's bed. Rather bothered but had to keep telling myself that the doctor knew better than I did.

"Before leaving the house I telephoned to my mother-in-law. Just told her that Lizzie wasn't feeling well and would she come over and spend the day? She could get me at the office any time she called. Then I left the house. It felt better out in the sunshine and, after working a few hours over the books, I almost laughed at myself for being so foolish.

"No telephone calls from the old lady. I arrived home at six and found the house lighted as usual. My wife and mother-in-law were waiting for me in the parlor and told me supper was ready. Naturally I was surprised to see my wife out of bed, but I tried to act naturally. At the supper table I watched her, just as carefully as I could without making the two of them suspicious of me. Mrs. Thompson ate about as she always did, just picked and minced at her food, but I thought when she swallowed that the food went down with a jerk, and there was a peculiar stiffness when she moved. But her mother didn't seem to think there was anything wrong, at least she didn't make any comment. Even when I went with her to the front door to say goodnight, she never said a word to show she thought her daughter was in any way unusual or peculiar.

"I started to wash the dishes after that. Often washed the dishes at night while my wife sat in the front parlor watching the people go up and down past the house. After the kitchen was tidy, I lit a cigar and went into the parlor and started a little conversation, but Mrs. Thompson never talked back. In fact, I don't believe she ever talked to me after that, though I'm positive she talked to others.

"When the cigar was smoked I just said goodnight and went to bed. Later on I could hear her moving around in her room; then all was quiet, so she must have gone to bed. She didn't cough any more. I congratulated myself on that one thing because the coughing had kept me awake a good deal. During the night I lit a candle and, shading it with my hand, tiptoed in to see her. She had her eyes open, but they were rolled back so that all you could see was the whites, and she wasn't breathing. At least, I couldn't tell that she was breathing and when I held a mirror in front of her mouth there was no vapor on it.

"The next day was just the same. My mother-in-law came and spent the day. I came home at night and ate supper with them and washed the dishes. The water was hot and it was a pleasure to make them clean. Perhaps I took longer than usual at it because I didn't fancy the idea of going into the front parlor where my wife was sitting, looking out of the window.

"But I went in, tonight without the usual cigar. I wanted to use my nose. It seemed there was a peculiar odor in the house, like flowers that had been put in a vase of water and then forgotten, for many days. Perhaps you know the odor, Doctor, a heavy one, like lilies of the valley in a small closed room. It was especially strong in the parlor where Mrs. Thompson was sitting, and it seemed to come from her. I had to light my cigar after a while and, by and by, I said goodnight, and went to bed. She never spoke to me, in fact she didn't seem to pay any attention to me.

"About two that morning I took the candle and went in to look at her. Her eyelids were open and her eyeballs rolled just like they had been the night before, but now her jaw was dropped and her cheeks sunken. I just couldn't do anything but telephone for a doctor, and this time I picked out a total stranger, just picked his name out of the telephone book haphazardly.

"What good did it do? None at all. He came; he examined Mrs. Thompson very carefully and he simply said that he didn't see anything wrong with her, and then, down in the front hall, he turned on me and asked me just why I had sent for him and what I thought was the matter with her? Of course, I just couldn't tell him the truth, with his being a doctor and I being just a bookkeeper. If he thought Mrs. Thompson was well, what was there for me to say?

"My mother-in-law went to the mountains the next day for the summer, and that left us alone. Breakfast as usual and to the office and not a word all day from the house. When I came back at night the house was lit and supper was on the table and the wife at her end as usual and the food served and on the plates. She ate, but her movements were slower, and when she swallowed, you could see the food go down by jerks, and her eyes were sunken into the sockets and seemed shiny and—well, like the eyes of a fish in the stalls.

"There were flowers on the table, but the smell was something different, it was sweeter, and when I took a deep breath it was just hard for me to go on eating the pork chops and potatoes. You see it was summertime and warm, and in spite of the screens, there was a fly or two in the house, and when I saw one walking around on her lip and she was not making any effort to brush it off, I just couldn't keep on eating. I had to go and start washing the dishes. Perhaps you can understand how I felt, Doctor. Things looked rather odd by that time.

"The next day I phoned the office that I wouldn't be there and I sent for a taxi and took Mrs. Thompson to a first-class specialist. He must have been good, because he charged me twenty-five dollars just for the office call. I went in first and told him exactly what I was afraid of. I didn't mince my words, and then we had my wife in. He examined her, even her blood, and all the satisfaction I got was that she seemed a trifle anaemic, but that I had better take a nerve tonic and a vacation or I would be sick.

"Things looked rather twisted after that. Either I was right and everybody else wrong, or everybody else was right and I was just about as wrong mentally as a man could be. But I had to believe my senses. A man just has to believe what he sees and hears and feels, and when I thought over that office visit, and my wife smiling and the doctor sticking her finger for the blood to examine it, it seemed impossible. Anaemic! Why! That was a simple word to describe her condition.

"That night the flies were worse than usual. I went to the corner store and bought fly spray and used it in her bedroom, but they kept coming in, the big blue ones, you know. Seemed as though they just had to come in and I couldn't keep them off her face. At last, in desperation, I covered her head up with a towel and went to sleep. I had to work; the interest on the mortgage was due and the man wanted something on the principal. It was a good house and all I had in the world to show for twenty years of hard work keeping books.

"The next day was just like all the other days had been, except I made more mistakes with the books and my boss spoke to me about it. And when I arrived home supper wasn't ready, though Mrs. Thompson was in the parlor and the lights were on. The heavy odor was worse than usual, and there were a lot of flies. You could hear them buzz and strike against the electric lights. I got my own supper, but I couldn't eat much, thinking of her in the parlor and the flies settling on her open mouth and pinched nose.

"She just sat there that night in the parlor until I went to her and took her arm to lead her up the stairs. She was cold, and on each cheek there was a heavy purple blotch forming. Once she was in her room, she seemed to move around; so I left her alone and when I went into her room later on she was in bed and rather peaceful. It had been a hard week for me. I sat down by her bed and tried to think, but the more I thought the worse things seemed. The night was hot and the flies kept buzzing. Just thinking of the past and how we used to go to the movies together and laugh and sometimes come near crying, and how we used to bluff about the fact that perhaps it was just as well we didn't have a child as long as we had each other, knowing all the time that she was eating her heart out for longing to be a mother and blaming me for her loneliness. The thinking was too much for me, so I thought I might as well smoke another cigar and go to bed and try to keep better books the next day and hold my job—and then I saw the little worm crawl out.

"Right then and there I knew that something had to be done. It didn't make any difference what the doctors or her mother said, something had to be done and I was the one who had to do it.

"I telephoned for an undertaker and met him downstairs.

" 'It will be a private funeral,' I told him, 'and no publicity. I think after you are through you will have no trouble obtaining a physician's certificate.'

"He went upstairs. In about five minutes he came down again.

" 'I must have gone into the wrong room,' he said.

" 'The second storey front bedroom,' I replied.

" 'But the woman there is not dead,' he blurted.

"I paid him for his trouble and shut the door in his face. Was I helpless? Doctor, you have to believe me. I was at the end of my rope. I had tried every way I knew and there wasn't anything left to do. No one believed me. No one agreed with me. It seemed more and more as though everyone thought I was insane.

"It was impossible to keep her in the house any longer. My health was giving way. Working all day at figures that were going wrong all the time and coming back night after night and cooking my supper and sleeping in a room next to the thing that had been my wife. What with the smell of lilies of the valley and the buzz of flies and the constant dread in my mind of how things would be the next day and the next week, and the mortgage due, I had to do something.

"And it seemed to me that she wanted me to. It seemed that she recognized that things were not right, that she was entitled to a different kind of ending. I tried to put myself in her place and I knew what I would want done with me if things were reversed.

"So I brought the trunk up from the cellar. We had used that trunk on our wedding trip and every summer since on our vacations, and I thought that she would be more at peace in that trunk than in a new one. But when I had the trunk by her bed, I saw at once that it was too small unless I used a knife.

"That seemed to be the proper thing to do, and I was sure that it wouldn't hurt her. For days she had been past hurting. I told her I was sorry, but it just had to be done, and if people had just believed me things could have been arranged in a nicer way.

"Then I started.

"Things were confused after that.

"I seem to remember a scream and blood spurting, and the next thing there were a lot of people in the house and they arrested me.

"And that is the peculiar part of it all, Doctor. Perhaps you don't know it, but I am accused of murdering my wife. Now I've told you all about it, Doctor, and I just want to ask you one question. If you had been in my place day after day, and night after night, what would you have done, Doctor? What would any man have done who loved his wife?"

Deadhead Coming Down

Margaret Maron

FUNNY THING about this CB craze—all these years we trucking men've been going along doing our job, just making a living as best we could, and people in cars didn't pay us much mind after everything got four-laned because they didn't get caught behind us so much going uphill, so they quit cursing us for being on the roads we was paying taxes for too and sort of ignored us for a few years.

Then those big camper vans started messing around with CB radios, tuning in on us, and first thing you know even VWs are running up and down the cloverleafs cluttering up the air with garbage and all of a sudden there's songs about us, calling us culture heroes and exotic knights of the road.

What a crock of bull.

There's not one damn thing exotic about driving a eighteen-wheeler. Next to standing on a assembly line and screwing Bolt A into Hole C like my no-'count brother-in-law, driving a truck's got to be the dullest way under God's red sun to make a living. 'Specially if it's just up and down the eastern seaboard like me.

Maybe it's different driving cross-country, but I work for this outfit—Eastline Truckers—and brother, they're just that: contract trucking up and down the coastal states. Peaches from Georgia, grapefruit from northern Florida, yams and blueberries from the Carolinas—whatever's in season, we haul it. I-95 to the Delaware Memorial Bridge, up the Jersey Turnpike, across the river and right over to Hunt's Point.

Fruit basket going up, deadhead coming down and if you think that's not boring, think again. Once you're on I-95, it's the same road from Florida to New Jersey. You could pick up a mile stretch in Georgia and stick it down somewhere in Maryland and nobody'd notice the difference. Same motels, same gas stations, same billboards.

There's laws put out by those Keep America Pretty people to try to keep billboards off the interstates, but I'm of two minds about them. You can get awful tired of trees and fields and cows with nothing to break 'em up, but then again, reading the same sign over and over four or five times a week's a real drag, too.

Even those Burma Shave signs they used to have when I was driving with Lucky. We'd laugh our heads off every time they put up new ones, but you can't laugh at the same things more'n once or twice, so we'd make up our own poems. Raunchy ones and funnier'n hell some of 'em.

Those were the good old days, a couple of years after the war. WW Two. I was a hick kid just out of the tobacco fields and Lucky seemed older'n Moses, though now I look back, I reckon he was only about thirty-five. His real name was Henry Driver, but everybody naturally called him Lucky because he got away with things nobody else ever could. During the blackouts, he once drove a load of TNT across the Great Smokies with no headlights. All them twisty mountain roads and just a three-quarter moon. I'd like to see these bragging hotshots around today try that!

Back then it took a real man to truck 'cause them rigs would fight you. Just like horses they were. They knew when you couldn't handle 'em. Today—hellfire! Everything's so automatic and hydraulic, even a ninety-pound woman can do it.

Guess I shouldn't knock it though. I'll be able to keep driving these creampuffs till I'm seventy. Not like Lucky. Hardly a dent and then his luck ran out on a stretch of 301 in Virginia. A blowout near a bridge and the wheel must've got away from him.

Twelve years ago that was and the company'd quit doubling us before that, but I still miss him. Things were never dull driving with Lucky. We was a lot alike. He used to tell me things he never told anybody else. Not just the things a man brags about when he's drinking and slinging bull, but other stuff.

I remember once we were laying over in Philly, him going, me coming down, and he says, "Guess what I saw me today coming through Baltimore? A red-tailed hawk. Right smack in the middle of town!"

Can you feature a tough guy like him getting all excited about seeing a back country bird in town? And telling another guy about it? Well, that's the way it was with me and him.

I was thinking about Lucky last week coming down, and wishing I had him to talk to again. 95 was wall-to-wall vacation traffic. I thumbed my CB and it was full of ratchet jaws trying to sound like they knew what the hell they were saying. It was "Good buddy" this and "Smokey" that and *10–4* on the side, so I cut right out again.

I'd just passed this Hot Shoppe sign when the road commenced to unwind in my head like a moving picture show. I knew that next would come a Howard Johnson and a Holiday Inn and then a white barn and a meadow full of black cows and then a Texaco sign and every single mile all the way back home. I just couldn't take it no more and pulled off at the next cloverleaf.

"For every mile of thruway, there's ten miles on either side going the same way," Lucky used to say and, like him, I've got this skinny map stuck up over my windshield across the whole width of the cab with I-95 snaking right down the middle. Whenever that old snake gets to crawling under my skin, I look for a side road heading south. There's little X's scattered all up and down my map to keep track of which roads I'd been on before. I hadn't never been through this particular stretch, so I had my choice.

Twenty minutes off the interstate's a whole different country. The road I finally picked was only two lanes, but wide enough so I wouldn't crowd anybody. Not that there was much traffic. I almost had the road to myself and I want to tell you it was as pretty as a postcard, with trees and bushes growing right to the ditches and patches of them orangy flowers mixed in.

It was late afternoon, the sun just going down and I was perking up and feeling good about this road. It was the kind Lucky used to look for. Everything perfect.

I was coasting down this little hill and around a curve and suddenly there was a old geezer walking right up the middle of my lane. I hit the brakes and left rubber, but by the time I got her stopped and ran back to where he was laying all crumpled up in orange flowers, I knew he was a sure goner, so I walked back to my rig, broke on Channel 9 and about ten minutes later, there was a black-and-white flashing its blue lights and a ambulance with red ones.

Everybody was awful nice about it. They could see how I'd

braked and swerved across the line. "I tried to miss him," I said, "but he went and jumped the wrong way."

"It wasn't your fault, so don't you worry," said the young cop when I'd followed him into town to fill out his report. "If I warned Mr. Jasper once, I told him a hundred times he was going to get himself killed out walking like that and him half deaf."

The old guy's son-in-law was there by that time and he nodded. "I told Mavis he ought to be in a old folks home where they'd look after him, but he was dead set against it and she wouldn't make him. Poor old Pop! Well, at least he didn't suffer."

The way he said it, I guessed he wasn't going to suffer too much himself over the old man's death.

I was free to go by nine o'clock and as I was leaving, the cop happened to say, "How come you were this far off the interstate?"

I explained about how boring it got every now and then and he sort of laughed and said, "I reckon you won't get bored again any time soon."

"I reckon not," I said, remembering how that old guy had scrambled, the way his eyes had bugged when he knew he couldn't get out of the way.

Just west of 95, I stopped at a Exxon station and while they were filling me up, I reached up over the windshield and made another little X on my road map. Seventeen X's now. Two more and I'd tie Lucky.

I pulled out onto 95 right in front of a Datsun that had to stomp on those Mickey Mouse brakes to keep from creaming his stupid self. Even at night it was all still the same—same gas stations, same motels, same billboards.

I don't know. Maybe it's different driving cross-country.

Death Double

William F. Nolan

C LAYTON WEBER EASED himself down from the papier mâche mountain and wiped the artificial sweat from his face. "How'd I look?" he asked the director.

"Great," said Victor Raddish. "Even Morell's own mother wouldn't know the difference."

"That's what I like to hear," grinned Weber, seating himself at a makeup table. Thus far, *Courage at Cougar Canyon,* starring "fearless" Claude Morell as the Yellowstone Kid had gone smoothly. Doubling for Morell, Weber had leaped chasms, been tossed from rolling wagons, dived into rivers and otherwise subjected himself to the usual rigors of a movie stuntman. Now, as he removed his makeup, he felt a hand at his shoulder.

"Mr. Morell would like to see you in his dressing room," a studio messenger boy told him.

Inside the small room Weber lit a cigarette and settled back on the brown leather couch. Claude Morell, tall and frowning, stood facing him.

"Weber, you're a nosy, rotten bastard and I ought to have you thrown off the lot and blacklisted with every studio in town."

"Then Linda told you about my call?"

"Of course she did. Your imitation of my voice was quite excellent. Seems you do as well off-camera as on. She was certain that *I* was talking or she never would have—"

"—discussed the abortion," finished Weber, feet propped on the couch.

Morell's eyes hardened. "How much do you want to keep silent?" Morell seated himself at a dressing table and flipped open his checkbook.

"Bribery won't be necessary," smiled Clayton Weber through the spiraling smoke of his cigarette. "I don't intend to spill the beans to Hedda Hopper. The fact that you impregnated the star of our picture and that she is about to have an abortion will never become public knowledge. You can depend on that."

Morell looked confused. "Then . . . I don't—"

"Have you ever heard of the parallel universe theory?"

Morell shook his head, still puzzled.

"It's simply this—that next to our own universe an infinite number of parallel universes exist—countless millions of them—each in many ways identical to this one. Yet the life pattern is different in each. Every variation of living is carried out, with a separate universe for each variation. Do you follow me?"

Obviously, Morell did not.

"Let me cite examples," said Weber. "In one of these parallel universes Lincoln was never assassinated; in another Columbus did *not* discover America, nor did Joe Louis become heavyweight champ. In one universe, America *lost* the First World War . . ."

"But that's ridiculous," Morell said. "Dream stuff."

"Let me approach it from another angle," persisted Weber. "You've heard of Doppelgangers?"

"You mean—*doubles?*"

"Not simply doubles, they are exact duplicates." Weber drew on his cigarette, allowing his words to take effect. "The reason you never see two of them together, for comparison, is that one of them always knows he is a duplicate of the other—and stays out of the other's life. Or enters it wearing a disguise."

"You're talking gibberish," said Claude Morell.

"Bear with me. The true Doppelganger *knows* he is not of this universe—and he chooses to stay away from his duplicate because it is too painful for him to see his own life being lived by another man, to see his wife and children and know they can never be his. So he builds a new life for himself in another part of the world."

"I don't see the point, Weber. What are you telling me?"

Clayton Weber smiled. "You'll see my point soon enough." He continued. "Sometimes a man or woman will simply vanish, wink out, as it were without a trace. Ambrose Bierce, the writer, was one of these. Then there was the crew of the *Marie Celeste* . . . They unknowingly reached a point in time and space that allowed them to step through into a separate world, like and yet totally unlike their own. They became Doppelgangers."

Weber paused, his eyes intent on Morell. *"I'm* one of them," he said. "It happened to me as it happened to them, without any warning. One moment I was happily married with a beautiful wife and a baby girl—the next I found myself in the middle of Los Angeles. Sometimes it's impossible to adjust to this situation. Some of us end up in an institution, claiming we're other people." He smiled again. "And—of course we *are.*"

Morell stood up, replacing the checkbook in his coat. "I don't know what kind of word game you're playing, Weber, but I've had enough of it. You refuse my offer—all right, you're fired. And if a word of this affair with Linda Miller ever hits print I'll not only see that you never work again in the industry, I'll also see that you receive the beating of your life. And I have the connections to guarantee a *thorough* job."

"Do one thing for me, Mr. Morell," asked Weber. "Just hold out your right hand, palm up."

"I don't see—"

"Please."

Morell brought up his hand. Weber raised his own, placing it beside Morell's. "Look at them," he said. "Look at the shape of the thumbs, the lines in the palm, the whorls on each fingertip."

"Good God!" said Claude Morell.

The man who called himself Clayton Weber reached up and began to work on his face. The cheek lines were altered as he withdrew some inner padding, his nose became smaller as he peeled away a thin layer of wax. In a moment the change was complete.

"Incredible," Morell breathed. "That's my face!"

"I had to look enough like you to get this job as your double," Weber told him, "but of course I couldn't look *exactly* like you. Now, however, we are identical." He withdrew the Colt from the hip holster of his western costume and aimed it at Morell.

"No blanks this time," he said.

"But why kill me?" Morell backed to the wall. "Even if all you said is true, why kill me? They'll send you to the gas chamber. You'll die with me!"

"Wrong," grinned Weber. "The death will be listed as a suicide. A note will be found on the dresser in the apartment I rented, stating 'Clayton Weber's' intention to do away with himself, that he felt he'd always be a failure, nothing but a stunt man, while others became stars. It will make excellent sense to the police. I will report that you shot yourself in my presence as we discussed the career you could never have."

"But my face will be the face of Claude Morell, not Clayton Weber!"

"Half of your face will be disposed of by the bullet at such close range. There will be no question of identity. And we're both wearing the same costume."

Morell leaned forward, eyes desperate. "But why? Why?"

"I'm killing you for what you did to my wife," said Weber, holding the gun steady.

"But—I never *met* your wife."

"In your world, this world, Linda Miller was just another number on your sexual hit parade, but in my world she was my wife. In *my* world that baby girl she carries in her body was born, allowed to live. And that's just the way it's going to happen now. If you'd married Linda I would have disappeared, gone to live in another city, left you alone. But you didn't. So, *I'll* marry her—again."

Claude Morell chose that moment to spring for the gun, but the bullet from the big Colt sent his head flying into bright red pieces.

The man who had called himself Clayton Weber placed the smoking weapon in Morell's dead hand.

Desert Pickup

Richard Laymon

ALL *RIGHT!*" He felt lucky about this one. Walking backward along the roadside, he stared at the oncoming car and offered his thumb. Sunlight glared on the windshield. Only at the last moment did he manage to get a look at the driver. A woman. That was that. So much for feeling lucky.

When he saw the brake lights flash on, he figured the woman was slowing down to be safe. When he saw the car stop, he figured this would be the "big tease." He was used to it. The car stops, you run to it, then off it shoots, throwing dust in your face. He wouldn't fall for it this time. He'd walk casually toward the car.

When he saw the backup lights go on, he couldn't believe his luck.

The car rolled backward to him. The woman inside leaned across the front seat and opened the door.

"Can I give you a ride?"

"Sure can." He jumped in and threw his seabag onto the rear

seat. When he closed the door, cold air struck him. It seemed to freeze the sweat on his T-shirt. It felt fine. "I'm mighty glad to see you," he said. "You're a real lifesaver."

"How on earth did you get way out here?" she asked, starting again up the road.

"You wouldn't believe it."

"Go ahead and try me."

He enjoyed her cheerfulness and felt guilty about the slight nervous tremor he heard in her voice. "Well, this fella gives me a lift. Just this side of Blythe. And he's driving along through this . . . this *desert* . . . when suddenly he stops and tells me to get out and take a look at one of the tires. I get out—and off he goes! Tosses my seabag out a ways up the road. Don't know why a fella wants to do something like that. You understand what I mean?"

"I certainly do. These days you don't know who to trust."

"If that ain't the truth."

He looked at her. She wore boots and jeans and a faded blue shirt, but she had class. It was written all over her. The way she talked, the way her skin was tanned just so, the way she wore her hair. Even her figure showed class. Nothing overdone.

"What I don't get," he went on, "is why the fella picked me up in the first place."

"He might have been lonely."

"Then why'd he dump me?"

"Maybe he decided not to trust you. Or maybe he just wanted to be alone again."

"Any way you slice it, it was a rotten thing to do. You understand what I mean?"

"I think so. Where are you headed?"

"Tucson."

"Fine. I'm going in that direction."

"How come you're not on the main highway? What are you doing out here?"

"Well. . . ." She laughed nervously. "What I'm intending to do is not . . . well, not exactly legal."

"Yeah?"

"I'm going to steal cacti."

"What!" He laughed. "Wow! You mean you're out to lift some cactuses?"

"That's what I mean."

"Well, I sure do hope you don't get caught!"

The woman forced a smile. "There *is* a fine."

"Gol-ly."

"A sizable fine."

"Well, I'd be glad to give you a hand."

"I've only got one shovel."

"Yeah. I saw it when I stowed my bag. I was wondering what you had a shovel for." He looked at her, laughing, and felt good that this woman with all her class was going to steal a few plants from the desert. "I've seen a lot of things, you understand. But never a cactus-napper." He laughed at his joke.

She didn't. "You've seen one now," she said.

They remained silent for a while. The young man thought about this classy woman driving down a lonely road in the desert just to swipe cactus, and every now and then he chuckled about it. He wondered why anybody would want such a thing in the first place. Why take the desert home with you? He wanted nothing more than to get away from this desolate place, and for the life of him he couldn't understand a person wanting to take part of it home. He concluded that the woman must be crazy.

"Would you care for some lunch?" the crazy woman asked. She still sounded nervous.

"Sure, I guess so."

"There should be a paper bag on the floor behind you. It has a couple of sandwiches in it, and some beer. Do you like beer?"

"Are you kidding?" He reached over the back of the seat and picked up the bag. The sandwiches smelled good. "Why don't you pull off the road up there?" he suggested. "We can go over by those rocks and have a picnic."

"That sounds like a fine idea." She stopped on a wide shoulder.

"Better take us a bit farther back. We don't wanta park this close to the road. Not if you want me to help you heist some cactus when we get done with lunch."

She glanced at him uneasily, then smiled. "Okay, fine. We'll do just that."

The car bumped forward, weaving around large balls of cactus, crashing through undergrowth. It finally stopped behind a cluster of rocks.

"Do you think they can still see us from the road?" the woman asked. Her voice was shaking.

"I don't think so."

When they opened the doors, heat blasted in on them. They got out, the young man carrying the bag of sandwiches and beer.

He sat down on a large rock. The woman sat beside him.

"I hope you like the sandwiches. They're corned beef with Swiss cheese."

"Sounds good." He handed one of them to her and opened the beer. The cans were only cool, but he decided that cool beer was better than no beer at all. As he picked at the cellophane covering his sandwich, he asked, "Where's your husband?"

"What do you mean?"

He smiled. It had really put her on the spot. "Well, I just happened to see that you aren't wearing a ring, you understand what I mean?"

She looked down at the band of paler skin on her third finger. "We're separated."

"Oh? How come?"

"I found out that he'd been cheating on me."

"On *you?* No kidding! He must have been crazy."

"Not crazy. He just enjoyed hurting people. But I'll tell you something. Cheating on me was the worst mistake he ever made."

They ate in silence for a while, the young man occasionally shaking his head with disbelief. Finally, his head stopped shaking. He decided that maybe he'd cheat too on a grown woman who gets her kicks stealing cactus. Good looks aren't everything. Who wants to live with a crazy woman? He drank off his beer. The last of it was warm and made him shiver.

He went to the car and took the shovel from the floor in back. "You want to come along? Pick out the ones you want and I'll dig them up for you."

He watched her wad up the cellophane and stuff it, along with the empty beer cans, into the paper bag. She put the bag in the car, smiling at him and saying, "Every litter bit hurts." They left the car behind. They walked side by side, the woman glancing about, sometimes crouching to inspect a likely cactus.

"You must think I'm rather strange," she confided, "picking up a hitchhiker like I did. I hope you don't think . . . well, it was criminal of that man to leave you out in the middle of nowhere. But I'm glad I picked you up. For some reason, I feel I can talk to you."

"That's nice. I like to listen. What about this one?" he asked, pointing at a huge prickly cactus.

"Too big. What I want is something smaller."

"This one ought to fit in the trunk."

"I'd rather have a few smaller ones," she insisted. "Besides, there's a kind in the Saguaro National Monument that I want to get. It'll probably be pretty big. I want to save the trunk for that one."

"Anything you say."

They walked farther. Soon, the car was out of sight. The sun felt like a hot, heavy hand pressing down on the young man's head and back.

"How about this one?" he asked, pointing. "It's pretty little."

"Yes. This one is just about perfect."

The woman knelt beside it. Her shirt was dark blue against her perspiring back, and a slight breeze rustled her hair.

This will be a good way to remember her, the young man thought as he crashed the shovel down on her head.

He buried her beside the cactus.

As he drove down the road, he thought about her. She had been a nice woman with obvious class. Crazy, but nice. Her husband must've been a nut to cheat on a good-looking woman like her, unless of course it was because of her craziness.

He thought it nice that she had told him so much about herself. It felt good to be trusted with secrets.

He wondered how far she would have driven him. Not far enough. It was much better having the car to himself. That way he didn't have to worry. And the $36 he found in her purse was a welcome bonus. He'd been afraid, for a moment, that he might find nothing but credit cards. All around, she had been a good find. He felt very lucky.

At least until the car began to move sluggishly. He pulled off the road and got out. "Oh, no," he muttered, seeing the flat rear tire. He leaned back against the side of the car and groaned. The sun beat on his face. He closed his eyes and shook his head, disgusted by the situation and thinking how awful it would be, working on the tire for fifteen minutes under that hot sun.

Then he heard, in the distance, the faint sound of a motor. Opening his eyes, he squinted down the road. A car was approaching. For a moment, he considered thumbing a ride. But that, he decided, would be stupid now that he had a car of his own. He closed his eyes again to wait for the car to pass.

But it didn't pass. It stopped.

He opened his eyes and gasped.

"Afternoon," the stranger called out.

"Howdy, Officer," he said, his heart thudding.

"You got a spare?"

"I think so."

"What do you mean, you think so? You either have a spare or you don't."

"What I meant was, I'm not sure if it's any good. It's been a while since I've had any use for it, you understand?"

"Of course I understand. Guess I'll stick around till we find out. This is rough country. A person can die out here. If the spare's no good, I'll radio for a tow."

"Okay, thanks." He opened the door and took the keys from the ignition.

Everything's okay, he told himself. No reason in the world for this cop to suspect anything.

"Did you go off the road back a ways?"

"No, why?" Even as he asked, he fumbled the keys. They fell to the ground. The other man picked them up.

"Flats around here, they're usually caused by cactus spines. They're murder."

He followed the officer to the rear of the car.

The octagonal key didn't fit the trunk.

"Don't know why those dopes in Detroit don't just make one key that'll fit the doors and trunk both."

"I don't know," the young man said, matching the other's tone of disgust and feeling even more confident.

The round key fit. The trunk popped open.

The officer threw a tarp onto the ground and then leveled his pistol at the young man, who was staring at the body of a middle-aged man who obviously had class.

Dramatic Touch

Donald Wandrei

"C AN'T SEE any number, but this looks like the place," said
Detective Sergeant Patterson. The police car stopped and he
piled out. Detective Cramb followed him.

They gave the street a quick once-over. Tenements, fruit and
vegetable markets, grimy shops and dirty buildings. A few rundown
brownstones. Kids, dozens of them, and fat, greasy women. Not
much difference from the slums of New York's lower East Side, but
the theater district was only a few blocks distant.

"Phooey!" Patterson mouthed his disgust and shoved his way
across the sidewalk, down a short flight of steps to a basement
door.

A shifty little runt with a face like a weasel sprang out like magic
and swung the iron grille open before Patterson could ring.

Patterson slouched in, asked gruffly: "You the guy that phoned
in?"

"Yes."

"What's the trouble?"

"One of my tenants hasn't been seen lately and his door's
locked. Something's wrong."

"What makes you think so?"

"He has groceries sent in every morning. Calls up the night before. To-day's bunch is still stacked in front of his place with a
couple of bottles of milk."

"That all?"

"There's been some phone calls to me from people wanting to
get in touch with him. Wouldn't leave their names, but said he
didn't answer. They asked if anything was wrong, so I called the
cops."

"Uh!" Patterson grunted. "Where's his rooms?"

The "Weasel" led them through a musty basement, ill-lighted
and poorly kept. At the rear was an exit. Two thirds of the way
back, a door stood in the right wall. A little heap of groceries lay in
front of it.

"Got a pass-key?"

"It don't do any good. The door's locked and his key's inside."

Patterson examined the layout. The door looked pretty solid. Above it, at ceiling level, a sooty transom hung ajar. The transom was only six inches deep.

"Any other way to get in?"

"Only the back window and that has iron bars. The shade is down. You can't see in."

Patterson sighed, looked at the transom, decided it would be simpler to work on the door. But first he pounded and called. There was no answer.

He heaved experimentally against the door, without results. He drew his service revolver and pumped it down the jamb, shooting at the latch. Cramb helped him shove. The door screeched, snapped inward, and the two detectives lurched through.

"Where's the light switch?" Patterson called.

The Weasel said: "I'll turn it on." He fumbled to the right of the door, and a click flooded the room with light.

It was a large room, some thirty by twenty feet. Several chairs, a bed, desk, bureau, table, and one overstuffed armchair filled it—all cheap furniture under which fluffs of dust had collected.

The armchair stood in the far corner near the window. A dead man sat there facing them. He was a wizened old codger with a hawk nose and a sallow, wrinkled skin. A hole and a stain above his heart told the tale. The hole was powder-burned.

Patterson went to a phone, called for the medical examiner, then left the dead man for a moment to study the entrances. Cobwebs and dirt covered the window shade. Obviously it had not been rolled up in weeks or months. But he gingerly lifted it inward. The window was locked. Dust and rust proved that it, too, had not been disturbed for a long period. In addition, an iron grille barred it outside. Stale, stuffy air showed the lack of ventilation.

There were no other exits—just the window and the door.

"Hell!" Patterson snorted. "Another suicide."

Cramb wore a queer expression. "Yeah? Well, where's the gun?"

Patterson said: "Look around. It's here somewhere."

They looked. They emptied the pockets of the dead man, searched the chair in which he sat. They went over every foot of the floor, hunted under each object, turned furniture upside down, pulled drawers out. They found a fully loaded automatic tucked away in the writing desk. There was dust in its barrel and on its surface. It had lain there untouched for weeks.

They were still looking when the medical examiner came. Patterson's sureness turned to doubt, then to exasperated determination.

"Dammit, Fred," he swore, "the gun has got to be here!"

But the gun wasn't.

They went to the other room of the suite, a windowless kitchen to their right, which adjoined an equally windowless bathroom. They prowled, poked, dug, got dirtier and angrier. There was no gun.

Cramb saw some cans on a shelf over the sink, but it was the odd levers around them that drew his attention. He took one down, opened it, sniffed the white crystals within. "Snow!" he cried out.

Patterson straightened, ran up, dipped into the other cans. "Snow is right. A good twenty thousand dollars' worth. What're those levers?"

He examined them, found wires running to a floor button near the outside door. He pressed the button, rejoined Cramb, but not quickly enough to see the levers tilt and water gush from the faucet. If the cans had been in place, they would have spilled their contents into the sink and the water would have washed all evidence down the drain, in case of a raid.

Cramb brightened. "This gives us a motive if the guy was murdered. Probably a hophead bumped him off."

Patterson drawled sarcastically: "And left all that stuff here? A whole year's supply? Nuts! Besides, the guy wasn't murdered."

"Then where's the gun?"

Patterson viciously chewed on a cigar, turned to the examiner, and asked: "How long's he been dead?"

"About twenty hours. He must have been shot around three this morning."

"Could he have done it himself?"

"Easily, though a suicide usually aims for the right temple."

"Shot at close range, huh?"

"The gun couldn't have been more than a foot away."

"Would it have been possible for him to be shot somewhere else, say, by the door, and walk back here?"

The doctor looked up, incredulous. "With a bullet in his heart? He couldn't have taken two steps after the shot."

Cramb broke in and explained the circumstances.

The doctor frowned, asked: "And you say there's no gun? It

doesn't sound possible. Doors and windows locked? Then he couldn't have been killed elsewhere and brought here."

Cramb muttered: "I looked at the transom. Even a kid couldn't get through without smashing the chains, and they haven't been tampered with. And if somebody shot through the transom, there wouldn't be powder burns on the vest. What's the answer?"

On the off-chance that the Weasel might somehow have pocketed the missing weapon, though he had been under surveillance all the while since he entered, Patterson whirled on him and growled: "Shell out!"

Cramb frisked him, but he didn't shell out, for the simple reason that he didn't have the gun.

Cramb muttered monotonously: "If he was murdered, the door wouldn't be locked inside. If he committed suicide, the gun would be here. Everything's locked from inside, and there is no gun."

"Shut up!" snapped Patterson irritably. Then he brightened. "I got it! Shot himself and threw the gun over the transom. Somebody picked it up or else it's still kicking around out there." He started off to search the basement corridor.

The doctor looked skeptical. "Not a chance!"

Cramb studied the floor inch by inch. He couldn't find a single blood spot. That made him sure the man had died where he sat. He did find half a dozen short black hairs. The dead man had tobacco-colored hair.

"I'll get the bullet out when I make an autopsy," the doctor promised, gathering together his kit. He left when two men came and removed the body.

"We're gonna look sweet at headquarters when we report this set-up! It has all the appearance of one of those perfect mysteries you read about," Patterson said.

"Apoplexy will get you if you don't watch out," Cramb said. "I gather that you didn't find the gun outside?"

"Nope!" The bigger man whirled on the Weasel. "Who're you—name?"

"Jim Maravano," he said, almost cowering.

"Who's the stiff?"

"Harry Jones."

"Jones, nuts! He's probably on record for peddling dope. Real name's more likely Moscowitz or Polecki. How long's he been here?"

"Three months."

"Know anything about him?"

"N-no."

"The hell you don't! Think of any reason he might want to commit suicide?"

"No."

"Or why any one might want to put him on the spot?"

"No."

"Jones have many callers?"

"Quite a few."

Patterson grunted: "Thought so. Did he go out much?"

"I never saw him after he came. I think he stayed in regular."

"He knew his onions. Did he keep any money or junk around?"

"I don't know."

Cramb wandered over to the little pile of stuff that had been taken from the dead man's pockets and idly flipped through it—notebook of names and numbers; account book in code; bank book. His eyes widened when he glanced inside this. A slip of paper at its back interested him still more. Abruptly he looked around, disappeared into the kitchen, returned five minutes later while Patterson was continuing his effort to dig nuggets out of Maravano.

"You own this dump?"

"Yes."

"Live here?"

"First-floor front."

"Hear any shots early this morning? Or did anybody in the building mention a shot?"

"No."

"Did Jones know anybody in the joint besides you?"

"I couldn't say," Maravano replied testily. "I don't pay much attention to the tenants as long as they keep up the rent."

"Nice, thoughtful landlord!" Patterson jeered. "I bet that isn't the only reason you let 'em alone."

Maravano showed his teeth. "Aw, what's it to ya?"

Cramb said in an offhand manner: "I think I've got it, Patterson."

Patterson swung around, startled. "Got what?"

"The answer." Cramb stared at Maravano a minute, half in study, half in reflection.

The proprietor squirmed, lighted a cigarette with uncertain fingers.

"What sort of people live here—actors, mostly ham?" Cramb snapped.

Maravano jerked. "How'd you know?"

"Guessed. Did any move out today?"

"Not so far as I know."

"Did any move in recently?"

"One, about a week ago."

"Did he pay in advance?"

"For half a week. He said he just got in town and was broke. I told him he could stay only four days, but he got a job and paid a full week ahead."

"What's his name and where's his room?"

"Walter Megrath. Second-floor rear. Room 16."

"Is he an actor, too? Three-a-day variety, maybe?"

Maravano jerked again. "Good guessing, fella! That's what he is. Why?"

"Is he in?"

"Let's see, midnight. The Acme bill stops at eleven. He's either just come in or he will soon. D'you think he done it?"

Cramb shrugged. "I want a talk with him. Lead the way."

Patterson jeered: "Thought you didn't know anything about your tenants?"

Maravano shut up like a clam.

"You riding a hunch?" Patterson asked Cramb.

"No; a pretty sure thing."

A faint light showed through the closed transom of the door to Megrath's room. Following Cramb's instructions, Maravano knocked hard.

"Who is it?" a gruff voice called.

"Maravano."

"Whadda ya want?"

"A couple of guys to see you."

There came a stir within, and suddenly the soft sound of running water.

Cramb tried the door, found it locked, hurled himself against it in unison with Patterson. It crashed in, and Cramb made a dive for the corner washbasin where a man was trying to flood something down the drain. He succeeded, except for a small handful of white crystals that Cramb knocked to the floor.

"What the hell's the idea?" Megrath yelled, whirling around.

He was a squat, powerful man, square of head, heavy-jowled, with inflamed eyes and a straight, thin mouth.

Cramb said gently: "The idea is to come clean while we look around."

"Got a search warrant? No? Then get out!"

Cramb stooped. "Maybe, after I get this evidence off the floor. Keep him covered, Patterson." He drew an envelope from his pocket, scraped the white powder into it.

Things happened before Patterson's gun left its holster.

Megrath caught Cramb, between the shoulder and neck, a terrific kick that sent him sprawling against Maravano, who flopped headfirst. Dazed, through a burst of stars and red mist, Cramb saw the squat man's hand dart to his pocket. Patterson's gun flashed up and the side of Megrath's coat spouted smoke and flame as he shot through the cloth. Patterson spun sideways, sprawled against the wall, leaned there while his service revolver slipped from nerveless fingers. Megrath lunged to the window, went through like a cat as Cramb staggered to his feet.

From somewhere near by burst a shrill, animal chattering.

Maravano squawked: "He'll kill me!"

Patterson said, a strange, puzzled expression in his eyes: "My arm won't move."

Cramb shook his head to clear it of shooting stars and swirling mist, then leaped for the window. Megrath, a racing blur against deeper shadow, tore through an areaway to the building opposite. Cramb steadied, aimed carefully, fired. Megrath somersaulted, and twisted weirdly on the ground.

Cramb went out of the window. Orange flame spat from blackness where the fugitive rolled. A sharp twinge pained the detective's ear. It buzzed as the slug zipped through its lobe. He swung by his hands, dropped eight feet, dived for an empty ash can as flame flared again.

Windows opened, heads popped out. Excited voices rose. Someone shouted for police.

From the room he had left, a gun barked. Megrath quivered, but did not return the fire. He lay very still.

"Naw; he'll pull through to sit in the chair," the ambulance interne promised. "Bullet in his chest and leg. All you got, Patterson, is a broken shoulder, and this guy merely lost a hunk of ear. You're all bum shots."

Cramb drawled to Patterson: "For left-handed shooting, that last wasn't so bad."

"So what?" growled the detective sergeant.

"Citations apiece. Bravery and capture of a dangerous character, for you; solving a tough murder, for me," Cramb answered, diplomatically splitting the honors.

He looked thoughtfully down at the captive. "It was a perfect set-up, and he had to ruin it because he'd been on the stage so long that he needed a dramatic touch.

"He blew in town, broke, wanted snow and couldn't get it on credit. Then he landed the job and bought a little dope. It wasn't enough. He knew that Jones probably kept a good supply on hand as well as plenty of dough for protection, purchases, from sales, and so on.

"His trained-animal act was the answer to a perfect murder. He went to Jones, having what was left of his week's salary, got in, and killed him. He knew the cops would get wise if he stole all the dope, so he took only half of it, enough to last a year, and cleaned out the money. Fifteen thousand goes a long way.

"If he'd wiped the gun, put Jones' finger prints on it, and left it behind, he'd have got away and we'd have had the perfect murder on our hands, checked off as suicide.

"But he didn't. He had to make it melodramatic. He was likely doped at the time and thought it'd be a swell idea to put the cops up a tree, leave us with a hopeless mystery on our hands. So he took the gun, went out, closed the door, leaving the key inside. Then he sent his trained monkey over the transom to turn the key."

Patterson stared at the bright-eyed, chattering, black little creature that Cramb had taken, cage and all, from Megrath's room.

Cramb continued: "As soon as the door wouldn't open, he knew it was locked. He hauled the monkey back on its string and slid up to his place. He didn't try to disappear because he thought he was safe.

"He made one small slip in not taking away the memo telling how much dough was in the safe behind the ice box. At that, he would have done an almost-perfect job if he'd only been kinder and taken care of his mangy monkey. The thing is lousy. When it went through the transom, it scratched for fleas and scratched out just enough hairs to send this ape to the chair."

The Encyclopedia Daniel

Fred Chappell

YESTERDAY COWS and the day before that *clouds,* but today he had skipped all the way to *fish.*

"What about *dreams?"* his mother asked. "What about *dandelions* and *dodo* and *Everest* and *Ethiopia?"*

Danny's reply was guarded. "I'll come back to them. *Fish* is what I've got to write about today. Today is fish day."

"Do you think that's the best way to compose an encyclopedia? You're twelve years old now. That's old enough to be methodical. You were taking your subjects in alphabetical order before. When you were in the *b*'s you didn't go from *baseball* to *xylophone.* Why do you want to jump over to *fish?"*

"I don't know," Danny said, "but today is fish day."

"Well," she said, "you're the encyclopedia-maker. You must know best."

"That's right," he said and his tone was as grave as that of an archbishop settling a point of theology. He rose from his chair at the yellow dinette table. "I have to go think now," he announced.

"All right," his mother said. "Just don't hurt yourself."

Her customary remark irritated Danny. He didn't reply as he tucked two blue spiral notebooks under his arm and headed toward his tiny upstairs bedroom. Going up the steps, he found his answer but it came too late: "It doesn't hurt me to think, not like some people I know."

He closed his door tight, dropped his notebooks on the rickety card table serving for a desk, and flung himself down on the narrow bed. Then he rolled over, cradled his hands behind his head, and watched the ceiling. It was an early May dusk and the headlights of cars played slow shadows above him.

He tried to think about fish but the task was boring. Fish lived dim lives in secret waters and there were many different kinds and he knew only a few of their names. People ate them. People ate a lot of the things Danny wrote about in his encyclopedia: apples, bananas, beans, coconuts. Cows too—Danny had written about eating cows in a way that distressed his mother. "Slaughterhouses!" she exclaimed. "Why write about that? You don't have to put that in." He had explained, with a patient sigh, that everything had to go in. An encyclopedia was about everything in the world. If he left something out, it would be like telling a lie. He wrote what was given him to write.

Yet today he had skipped from cows to fish, leaping over lots of interesting things. He would come back to *daredevil* and *Excalibur, eclipse* and *dentists,* but it wouldn't be the same. His mother was right. It was sloppy, zipping on to *fish;* it was unscientific. He said aloud: "This method is unscientific."

Then another sentence came into his mind. He could not keep it out. It was like trying to hold a door closed against someone bigger and stronger and crazier than you. You pushed hard but he pushed harder, swept you aside and came on in, sweaty and purplefaced and too loud for the little bedroom. This sentence was as audible in his mind as if it had been spoken to him in the dark and lonely midnight: "He tore the living room curtains down and tried to set them on fire."

He sat up on the edge of the bed and gazed out the window above his table. The dusk had thickened and the lights made the houses on Orchard Street look warm and inviting. But that was only illusion. They were not inviting, all full of people who whispered and said ugly things. They lived happy lives, these people, you could tell from the lights in their windows, but you were not to be any part of that. Those lives were as remote and secret as the lives of fish in the depths of the ocean.

He turned on the dinky little lamp with the green shade and sat down in the creaky wooden chair. Dully he opened a notebook and began to read what he had written in his encyclopedia about cars:

> The best kind of car is a Corvette. It is really flash. Lots of kids say they will buy Corvettes when they grow up but I don't think so. You have to be rich. Billy Joe Armistead is not going to be rich, just look at him. Anyway by the time we grow up Corvettes won't be the hot car. The hot car will be something we don't know about yet, maybe it has like an atomic motor.

Danny flipped the page. He had written a great deal about cars; that was his favorite subject. He had learned all about them by looking at magazine photos and articles and talking to the guys in the neighborhood. Corvette, they all said.

He turned through the scribbled pages until he came to a blank one to fill up with the facts about fish. Except that he didn't know any facts. Well, a few maybe—not enough to help. And then while he was looking at the page with its forbiddingly empty lines another sentence sounded in his head so strongly that he reached for the green ballpoint: "Then he vomits a lot of red stuff, yucky smelly red stuff." But he couldn't write and dropped the pen.

The house began to tang with kitchen smells and Danny understood they would have spaghetti for supper; he and his mother chatting at the dinette table. He understood too that he had better write at least a paragraph about fish because it would soon be time to go down. With a heartfelt groan, he began:

Fish have gills so they can breathe water. They are hard to see but fisher men find them anyhow with radar they have. Some fish are real big like whales but most are not as big as people. When the police men come he tries to hit them all and then they put hand cuffs on him and drive off.

Three times he read the last sentence and then slowly and with close deliberate strokes marked out the words one at a time. Then he used his red ballpoint to make black rectangles of the canceled words. Red on green makes black.

He had interpreted the smells correctly. Supper was spaghetti and meatballs with his mother's pungent tomato sauce. She offered him a spoonful of her red wine in water but he preferred his Pepsi. There was a green salad too, with the pasty raw mushrooms he would avoid.

His mother raised her glass in his direction. "So—what is your schedule tomorrow? After school, I mean."

"Baseball practice," Danny said. "I'll be home about five."

"Homework?"

"I don't know. Math, probably. Maybe history."

"How about tonight?"

"None tonight."

"So you can go back to writing 'The Encyclopedia Daniel.' How is *fish* coming along?"

"Not so hot."

"That's because you skipped," she said. "You were going like a house afire when you wrote the entries in order. Now you've lost your rhythm."

"I'll come back," he said. "I'll pick up *doors* and the *Dodgers* and *elephants* and *engines* and *farming* and *falcons*. I'll do *fathers*."

Her eyes went wet and she set her glass down as gently as a snowflake. *"Fathers,"* she said. "That's what you skipped over, isn't it? You didn't want to do that part."

"I don't know. I guess not."

"Maybe you'll be a writer when you grow up," she said. "Then you'll have to write about sad things whether you want to or not."

"No. I'm not going to be a writer. Just my Encyclopedia. When I get it finished I won't need to write any more."

"Maybe I could be a writer." His mother spoke in a murmur—as if she was listening instead of talking. "When I think about your poor father I believe I could write a book."

"No," he said. His tone was imperious. "Everybody says they could write a book but they couldn't. It's real hard, it's real real hard. Harder than anybody thinks."

"Are you going to finish your encyclopedia?"

"I don't know. If I can get past this part. But it's hard."

"Maybe it will be good for you to write it out."

"It makes me scared," he said. "Stuff comes in my mind and I'm scared to write it down."

"Like what? What are you scared to write?"

New sentences came to him then and Danny couldn't look into her face. He stared at his cold spaghetti and recited, "He said he would kill her no matter what and she said he never would, she would kill him first. If that was the only way, she would kill him first."

"Oh Danny," his mother said. "I didn't know you heard us that time. I didn't realize you knew."

"I know everything," he said. "I know everything that has already happened and everything that is going to happen. When you write an encyclopedia you have to know everything."

"But that night was a time when we were both pretty crazy. I wouldn't hurt your father. You understand that. And he's never coming back. They won't let him. You understand that too, don't you?"

"Maybe. Maybe if I write it down I'll understand better."

"Yes," she said. "Why don't you write it all down?"

But it was coming too fast to write down. Already there were new words in his head, words that spoke as sharply as a fire engine siren:

176

"Then in August the father got away and came back to the house. It was late at night and real dark. He didn't come to the front door. He went around back. He was carrying something red in his hand."

Eye-Witness

Wilbur S. Peacock

S O THIS IS THE WAY *it feels to die,* Jason Craig thought sourly, and toppled from the chair. There was no pain, for which he was glad—only the shock waves of deadness rippling through his chest where the .38 slug had smashed. Slowly the blankness spread through his entire body. When the edge of the desk caught and ripped the skin of his right cheek, he felt nothing.

The chair skidded back from the weight of his body, and he went to his knees, sliding a bit, then bending sideways, one limp arm striking the polished floor first, then his shoulder, and finally his head. He lay in the grotesque position of a strangled cat, tobacco still fluttering to the floor, a limp machine rolled cigarette lost in the grip of his clenched right hand.

"You dirty stinking swine!" Jason Craig heard his murderer say, and a polished shoe slammed viciously into his scrawny chest.

Why don't I die? Jason Craig asked himself. *I've got a bullet hole through my chest, and I know that my heart has stopped beating!*

His eyes felt gummy, as they sometimes did after waking from a night's restless sleep and he could not move his eyelids. He stared straight ahead at the man who had fired the deadly shot.

The killer had moved back now, watching for any sign of movement, listening for any outcry in the old house. His young face was hard and cruel, the thin line of mustache accenting the weakness of a petulant mouth. His hair was long, sleek and oiled, and his eyes stared viciously at the body on the floor.

He stepped forward, lowered the revolver, pressed Jason Craig's slack left hand about the butt, marking it with fingerprints, then let the hand and gun fall naturally, the gun bouncing away a foot from the fingers.

Straightening, he stripped rubber gloves from his hands, tucked them into the side pocket of his topcoat. His mouth was a thin line then, and he laughed at the dead face on the floor.

"You look good that way, you old buzzard," he said softly. "I've wanted to see you like that for a long time."

Me the buzzard! Jason Craig thought wryly. *You're the one who's been waiting for me to die, waiting for my money to come to you.*

He knew he was dead, though he could not reconcile himself to that idea. Eighty years he had fought the world, his indomitable will fighting all odds. He would not admit now that this sneaking killer towering over him was the better man.

Stop this thinking like a damned fool, Jason Craig told himself. His gaze was a bit hazy now, and he tried to blink. His lids didn't move. He watched the killer walk toward the door, saw him pause just within the entrance, dark eyes searching the room for any clue he might have left which would trip him up. Satisfied, he stepped outside, the door closing softly behind him.

That's that, Jason Craig told himself. *He'll get the money Bob should have, blow it to hell and gone in no time. He's no good—never was. Why I took him in, I'll never know.*

But he did know. Rance had looked so damnably forlorn behind the fence of the orphanage, so out of place with his serious, intent features. Jason could still see Rance's small compact body hunched against a tree, while he watched the older boys playing softball.

It had been lonely with Sarah gone, the big house creaking with night noises, only the servants for company all day. And Jason Craig liked people about.

That had been ten years ago—before he had found out he had a grandson; but by then he was so wrapped up in Rance he could see little wrong in the boy. Oh, Rance had been mischievous, but all kids were.

Only the last five years had given him a real insight into Rance's character, and he had tightened up on the boy. But he had never fully realized his hate until Rance had lifted the gun three minutes before and squeezed the trigger.

"Change your will, huh!" he had snarled. "Give most of the dough to your damned Bob. I guess not!" Then Rance had shot his foster-father—to kill!

Jason Craig sighed from lungs which did not move, felt awareness sweeping away on black wings. The next he knew something was poking a stethoscope at his chest and saying:

"This man is dead."

Hell, yes, I'm dead, Jason Craig said without words. *You think I sleep like this every night—blood all over my shirt, a hole in me you could drive a truck through?*

His eyes focused. That was strange, for he knew his lids were shut now, closed, as a last gesture, by the doctor. He saw Bob and Rance standing by the door, and a detective nearby.

"You found the body then, Mr. Thomas," the detective said, reading notes from his book, "and immediately phoned the police."

"That's right," Bob Thomas said grimly, his voice strained, mute pain stirring in his eyes. "I came home from the theater, saw the light under the door, stepped in to say good-night. I didn't see grandfather for a moment, but I did notice his hand-machine, tobacco and papers on the desk, so I knew he was still up, rolling his cigarettes. I went to the desk, saw him lying behind it. I phoned the police, right after I made sure he was dead."

He felt sorry for his grandson then, for only a damned fool would think the kid wasn't hurt—deeply hurt—by what he was going through. He wished he could see the detective's face, but the man had his back turned.

Then he *could* see the detective's calm features! *This is a hell of a note! Being dead has given me X-ray eyes; he didn't turn, and yet I see his face,* Jason thought.

He heard Sarah's voice then, calling as though far away in a great, deep tunnel, and he answered peevishly.

"Hush, Sarah, hush! I'll be along presently."

"You're his grandson?" the detective asked.

"Yes, sir! I've been living here about three months, ever since my discharge from the Navy."

"Have any fights with your grandfather?"

"No, sir. Why?"

"Just checking." The detective swung to Rance, eyed him dispassionately for a moment. "You're Rance Craig, the adopted son?"

"Yes!" The intonation was insolent.

"Were you here tonight?"

Rance smirked. "I haven't been here in three weeks. The old man and I didn't see exactly eye to eye." He scowled at the body on the floor. "Why anyone with his money should insist on rolling his own cigarettes, I never could understand. The old buzzard must have—"

Bob hit him then, throwing his right like a rocket, blasting Rance from his feet. He lay silent for a moment, glaring at the standing man, then climbed to his feet. The detective watched interestedly.

"You'll regret that, Thomas," Rance said softly.

"Break it up," the detective said. "You and Mr. Craig didn't exactly hit it off together, then?" he questioned.

"Hell, no!" Rance frowned. "But don't try to switch this thing to murder. Anybody with eyes can see it's suicide."

Rance sneered, lit a cigarette. The detective looked at the two boys for a silent moment.

"My men will be here shortly," he said. "Stick around."

So, you're a detective, Jason Craig thought wrathfully. *You couldn't find fire in Hell's own furnace. Get after Rance—beat in his smile a bit.*

He swore angrily, harshly, making no sound, feeling no pain, feeling nothing.

"I'm sticking," Rance said harshly. "This is all mine now, so I think I'll hang around."

"So!" The detective pursed his lips, glanced up from where he and the doctor had had a few quiet words. "You know what's in the will, then?"

"Yeah!" Rance's voice was triumphant, his eyes grinning at Bob. "He left everything to me."

I shouldn't have given him that last chance, Jason Craig's mind went on, unwilling to lie still like the rest of him.

He watched Rance stride toward the desk, saw him lift the packet of matches to relight his cigarette. He caught the wave of hatred from the man, and his will fought dead vocal cords, striving to make them vibrate, to condemn the killer who stood over him. No sound came. . . .

He stared at the immaculate trousers Rance affected, saw the polished shoe which had kicked him after he had died. *"Give me a chance,"* he begged. *"I haven't been too bad a guy; give me a chance to hook this murderer."*

His hand flopped slightly, as Rance touched it with his shoe in turning away. Then he lay as he had been, watching Rance go again to range himself at Bob's side.

"Let's go downstairs," he said. "I think we could all use a drink." Rance's voice broke the silence, and the detective looked up from where he lifted the revolver with a pencil thrust into the barrel.

"This Mr. Craig's gun?" he asked.

"Yes, sir. He kept it in his desk," Bob answered briefly.

"We'll make nitrate tests, of course," the detective said. "I suppose you know a gun blows exploded powder into the hand of the shooter?"

Jason knew, though, that Rance was safe on that point; nobody had seen him enter or leave the house.

The detective accidentally dropped the gun, and it slid to the feet of Bob and Rance. "Don't touch it," he snapped. "Fingerprints are evidence." He bent forward, lifted the gun again.

That's it! Jason Craig cried, without sound or words. *Now we've got him!*

The detective was straightening, the murder gun in his left hand, his own in his right. He pointed the gun at Rance.

"So you haven't been here in three weeks?" he snapped. "So you and your foster-father didn't get along too well?"

"Look," Rance cried, and the first sheen of terror was in his small eyes, "what's the idea of the gun?"

Shoot him now, Jason Craig thought brutally. *Save the expense of the trial.*

"We'll be taking a walk, Mister Craig," the detective said flatly. "We'll go down to headquarters and talk a bit. Maybe you can tell me then how it is one of Jason Craig's machine-rolled cigarettes got in the cuff of your trousers."

Good, the late Jason Craig thought happily. *He won't last long, not when you bear down.* He wished he could smile at Bob, wish him luck as a doctor in the future. But his rigid features would not move.

He tried to flex the fingers of his right hand, where he had held the cigarette, but they were unfolded now, as dead as the rest of him.

Thanks, he said humbly.

He heard her voice again then, went toward the sound. He moved lightly and easily.

Wait for me, Sarah, he said happily.

Feature Attraction—Murder

Richard W. Bishop

BEN WROTH KNEW that the movies didn't provide the best alibi in the world. That was why he chose them. It wouldn't be too obvious. And with his elaborate precautions, it should be safe enough.

Ben knew that he would have to depend on his alibi to pull him through. He would have to answer questions, he expected that. There were only three of them who knew the combination to the big office safe at Central. Only three of them who knew it would be bursting its doors with real pay dirt tonight.

As Ben purchased his ticket at the Majestic, he wondered which of the other two would be holding the bag. Old Carson would be home in bed. Ben knew that. He always went to bed at nine-thirty as regular as the minutes of the hour. A swell alibi that would be for him.

"What time will the pictures be over?" he asked the ticket seller.

"The vaudeville is on now," she told him. "You should be out at eleven-forty."

She'd remember him now. She'd seen him before. Every Tuesday night for nearly a year. A year's planning. But a hundred grand was a good year's pay.

Secretly Ben hoped that Carson wouldn't be pinned for it. He'd much rather see Green get the works. Green, he figured, had been seeing too much of Marge lately. More than made Ben comfortable. But Marge was going away with Ben as soon as the heat was off.

Not that Marge knew the score; she didn't. She might have been squeamish about it. Ben painted pictures to her of a little chicken farm in the country. An uncle had left it to him, he told her. That was a good one. The more he thought about it the more he wished he'd made it a villa in the south. Oh well, that could be changed.

Ben cupped his cigarette and nodded at the ticket taker. "Good show, Jim?" He had cultivated Jim's friendship for months now. The taker nodded. A little absent-minded, Jim, but he'd do. He'd remember.

Ben slid down the aisle and found a seat near the opened exit door. Even in the dark he could picture the crooked corridor that led to the outside. He drew covertly on his cigarette, still cupped in his hand, so the usher wouldn't see him.

The last actor bowed off the stage and the feature began. Ben knew it by heart. He had sat through the same show a week before in a distant city. He waited until the audience had settled down to enjoy the show. Then he flicked away his cigarette and eased himself out of his seat.

The drive across town was easy. The traffic ban had reduced the number of cars to a minimum. Ben made good time without hurrying. His watch showed that only a half hour had elapsed since he had left the theater.

Ben grinned to himself as he thought of feeble, hard of hearing Trist, the night watchman. What a set-up! Even the black-out regulations were helping his plan.

With black gloves on his hands, Ben let himself into the factory building and, with a different key, into the office. It was as black as pitch but he needed no light. He was on familiar ground. His hand felt and found the circular dial of the huge, old-fashioned safe. A moment later and the same hand lifted out great manila envelopes of currency.

It was as easy as that. Ben carefully locked the office door behind him and soft-shoed his way through the factory corridor.

He was almost at the door when his foot struck something hard and a wastebasket tipped clattering to its side. A side door swung wide, enveloping Ben's form in the shaft of light it poured into the room.

"Who's there?" Trist's silhouette showed in the doorway, a perfect target. Ben was ready for him. He fired only once. Trist crumpled to the floor.

More quickly now, but noiselessly again, Ben slid through the outside door and hurried to his car. He'd have to get back at once, he thought, before the time came for Trist to punch his clock again. Before the alarm.

Driving back across town, Ben lighted another cigarette and turned on the radio. His self-assurance was returning. He could slide through the side door and into the theater without difficulty. Hadn't he practiced it before? The ushers didn't watch the exit door. Its spring lock prevented it from being opened from the outside. Hadn't he a key made for that very purpose? He tossed the manila envelopes into the glove compartment and breathed more freely.

Tomorrow they would ask him where he had been. "At the movies," he'd tell them. He could see their skeptical looks now.

"See anybody you know?"

"Sure." Had he? He should hope to say so. A lot of people. He would give their names. And he would tell them all about the picture too.

It was the kind of alibi that Ben knew would hold. It wasn't a strong, cement-vault alibi that immediately looked suspicious. It was the indisputable, unbreakable alibi that no amount of checking would show to be false. It was the kind of alibi that would let him out and one of the others in.

He was glad Marge had gone out with some friends tonight. Green wouldn't be with her. He chuckled. Perhaps Green had gone to the movies too. Alone. He wondered if Green knew any ticket seller or ticket takers. It didn't make any difference. There was always Carson. Ben flicked his cigarette out of the window and swung his car around the corner toward the theater.

Cold sweat broke out on his forehead. Something had gone wrong! The marquee that had been so brilliantly lighted was black now! Ben was startled, unnerved. He drove by the theater slowly. There was no light from within.

Outside, a few stragglers stood about the door as if watching. They seemed to be talking and they made funny little excited gestures. Ben dared not stop.

He looked at his watch. Eleven o'clock. Time for the regular news broadcast. . . .

A near panic at the Majestic Theater was averted tonight by the quick thinking of the manager, Harvey Spencer. The audience filed out under his direction as the cloth drapes on the east side caught fire and the flames went to the ceiling. The sprinkler system prevented a serious holocaust, but thoroughly drenched the patrons. The fire, which took place shortly after the feature picture had started and was of only a few moments duration, was believed to have been caused by a cigarette dropped by a careless patron who failed to comply with fire regulations. The fire commissioner has ordered an investigation.

Ben swung to his right and toward the turnpike leading out of town. But somehow he knew that out there state troopers would be waiting, hunting for him. . . .

Fin de Siècle

Joyce Carol Oates

DOC JUNIUS was this disgustingly obese old guy eighty-three years old weighing three hundred pounds in a motorized wheelchair up in the Hollywood Hills, that Bobo killed. Wound a cord around his neck and didn't stop squeezing until the struggle was over. We'd gone up to have a talk with Doc 'cause he was giving us trouble in our transactions and him and Bobo got to quarreling, and Doc ordered us to leave—"Go home. Get out. I vanquish you. You are bad dreams *—I exorcise you!"*—shouting like he'd gone crazy. So Bobo quieted him.

Doc's grandniece Mignon was living there at the time, in a guest house that opened onto the pool. She might have heard the noise over the sound of her transistor but didn't investigate. Lifting barbells in the sun, in her swimsuit, hair the color of broom sage blowing wild in the wind. It was a dry scorching wind, late September. Fires up in the foothills and the smell of scorch in the air, not something's-going-to-happen but something already did.

Two, three years we'd been working with Doc through the private mail services then the old bastard says one day on the phone he can't fill our order, he's "retiring from the field," wants out, like it was that easy to break off with *us.* So we drove up. Uninvited but we drove up. "To what do I owe the honor of this visit?" Doc Junius asked in this snotty voice looking us over like we were dirt. *He* was some sort of a freak, so fat his skin looked as if it might not be able to hold him, beady turtle's eyes and fat loose wet lips and big hairy hard-breathing nostrils. Saying, "Nightmare apparitions come to life—acquiring visible form—but what, pray, have you to do with *me?"*

You could see the old guy was high—shot himself up every few hours with a secret concoction of his own. He rolled around in this fancy wheelchair with all the push-buttons, wheezing and snorting and chuckling to himself. What's so funny we asked him you old shit we tried to be reasonable but he laughed at us shaking his head like we really were some kind of ghosts not *there* in any way he had to respect, "—I banish you—vanish you—d'you hear? Out! Out!

Away! At once!" His head was hairless as an eggshell, eyes weird-red, the floor gave way a little beneath him where he rolled. If Fritzie hadn't jumped aside Doc would have run over his foot. *Watch* it damn you Fritzie said but Doc wasn't watching or listening. Too far gone already!

Junius James Huizingo was Doc's full name. Wanted us to know he'd once been a renowned physician an internist by specialty then for no clear reason his patients abandoned him one by one, or died and failed to be replaced. The obituary in the *L.A. Times* would say he'd retired from the practice of medicine in 1967 after a malpractice suit of "scandalous dimensions."

Also that he was survived by only a grandniece, who shared his residence at the time of his death.

Our first meeting face to face old Doc tried to impress us with his hot-shit way of talking. Scrunched in his wheelchair eyeing us one by one like we were all sort of *equal*—the asshole way fancy talkers kid themselves that the language, *talk,* puts us all in the same boat. Saying in this slow wheezy voice like he thought somebody might want to write it down, "This world's a vale of tears but it can be overcome by *transcendence* and *scorn* in equal measure!"

Of the five of us it was Bobo listened hardest. What's *transcendence,* Doc, he asked. *Scorn* never gives me no trouble.

Doc's house was this Spanish-style hacienda place on a dead-end lane, fancy but wrecked-looking like it was abandoned. Weeds growing in the pink-gravel driveway and newspapers and other crap on the lawn that's all weeds too. Doc had a yard boy named Ramon he said but the little spic never showed up. Had a maid named Juanita but *she* never showed up. He had to feed himself which by the size of him he did O.K.—delivery things he could order by telephone, Chinese and Italian takeout. Before his niece came to live with him Doc said he'd been alone in the tunnel that's so long and so black—drawling *soooooo blaaaaack* and bugging out his eyes. If old fuckface wasn't so comical you'd naturally want to put him out of his misery was our common thought.

Still, said Doc, he was disappointed in Mignon over all. A girl so pretty—"She *is* pretty, boys, isn't she?—for so she strikes *me*"—yet so cold, icy-cold, so distant. It's heartrending said Doc. Perverse said Doc. Mignon accepted his hospitality scarcely thanking him as if it was her due. Actually she avoided him. Didn't share—let alone *prepare*—meals. Didn't converse with him except to say *Hello* some-times, *How are you Uncle?* or *Nice day!*

A mysterious young woman Doc went on lowering his voice (though we could see Mignon plain as day out by the pool lifting barbells to the beat of her FM radio—she surely wasn't eavesdrop-ping on *him*)—"Maybe you boys will have more luck making her acquaintance than I have had!" Bodybuilding was Mignon's life plus lying in the sun and sleeping ten, twelve hours a day and swimming in Doc's pool lazy and dreamy lap after lap after lap in the sparkling turquoise water not caring if anybody (for instance old wheezing pop-eyed Uncle) spied on her.

The five of us observed Mignon working out in her tiger-striped bikini. She wasn't ugly like a lot of female bodybuilders but she was solid muscle especially those hard tight perfect muscles in her shoulders and upper arms and her thighs, gleaming like copper. Actually a small woman about five foot three weighing maybe one hundred twenty pounds. Ash-blond hair and pale green eyes lifting out of the face never any smile or look of knowing who you are. That day one of us tried to talk to her saying *Meeg-non*—is that French? like that kind of a special cut of meat? and Mignon stared deadpan not answering like we didn't exist. Like there was just nothing there where we stood.

O.K. bitch we were thinking you're in line.

(Mignon drove a 1983 white Porsche. Old Doc Junius had a 1965 white Caddie never left the garage, the battery'd been dead for fif-teen years. If we took Mignon away with us—some kind of a hos-tage, say—we'd have the Porsche too which was a good deal.)

Doc never invited us into his real house only the wing where he used to see patients. There was a sad stink of dirt and mice and old tobacco smoke, the tables in the waiting room were piled with *Na-tional Geographic, Reader's Digest, Boy's World, Life.* Those days, the five of us wore white: white polyester jackets, trousers, white T-shirts. Doc kept the place dark 'cause the sun gave him migraine he said so we were floating in the shadows grinning at one another like actual ghosts while old Doc babbled away calling us "my boys" and similar crap. He'd mix up Dago with Bobo, Fritzie with Brush, Brush with me, me with Dago which was an insult like he couldn't be troubled to learn our names.

In his inner office Doc kept a clear space around the desk where he could run his wheelchair 'round and 'round he said which aided in his thinking. At his age and in his condition Doc said you do a lot of thinking—that's about all you can do.

The day we had the trouble, Doc met us at the door and didn't want to let us in at first, talking loud and important like somebody on TV this shape like a three-hundred-pound sponge squeezed in a wheelchair. He was sweating globules of pearly lard and what we could see of his skin—his big bald head, his face, his hands—was dippled with liver spots like dirty water. Five months since we'd seen him and he looked older, puffed up under the skin, water-logged. "Who are you? What claim do you have on me? What proof have you that *I* know *you? Why are you here?*" Excited and guilty not meeting our eyes saying, "*Why are you here?*"

So we looked at one another thinking the same thought. Like twins, the five of us.

When we drove up Mignon was swimming in the pool, and when the quarrel got serious she was working with her barbells and weights by the poolside so absorbed she didn't hear what was going on over the blast of her transistor or if she heard didn't care. Doc said he was *not* betraying us he was *not* working with someone else what he *was* was repenting of his ways before it was too late. Benzedrine, Dexedrine, Valium, Librium in such doses—some pharmacist was sure to get suspicious said Doc and we said O.K. Doc but why right now why right *now* and he hadn't any answer to that just repeating he wanted out, stammering and sputtering he was in terror of dying and wanted to repent his ways. Rolling in his wheelchair like a crazy son of a bitch you could feel the heat coming off of and his skin quivered and sagged like it was too thin to hold the fat inside. We looked through the stuff on top of his desk looked through the filing cabinet looking for prescription blanks and Doc said to keep our filthy hands off his things or he'd call the police he'd trip the burglar alarm so loud and crazy there wasn't much else to do but what Bobo did: got behind him and wound a cord around his neck and choked and choked until it was over—which took some time.

All this while Mignon is doing her exercise routine not paying the slightest attention to us. We stuff all the blanks we can find in a valise and some syringes and other doctor's crap and search the house for cash and valuables of which there isn't much, smudging our fingerprints behind us, or trying to. Then we go out to where she is. Hey Mignon we say. Hey sweetheart guess what. Mignon's breathing a little hard lifting a fifty-pound weight over her head her upper lip damp with sweat and her skin gleaming with points of light like stars. Hair still damp falling past her shoulder blades and those greeny-green eyes cold as ice. Sweetheart we say clearing our throats nerved up but sort of like teasing too we got some, y'know, serious talking to do, your uncle and all, but Mignon continues with her workout lifting and counting and not a one of us wants to interfere it's so pleasurable to see, or more than pleasurable. Our five shadows on the ground, watching.

So Mignon finishes the exercise and lays the weight down at her feet with perfect poise. It's startling to see, her in her tiger bikini, sweating and oily and every wisp of white-blond hair on her arms and thighs standing out against the tan, *this is a lady.*

Looks at us for the first actual time, this calm scornful deadpan kind of smile, says, "There's where you're wrong, fellas."

Fixing Mr. Foucher's Fence

Todd Mecklem

WHEN BOB BATY was hired to do odd jobs for the dairyman up the road, he considered himself lucky. Sort of. After all, an eighteen-year-old pothead who lives eight miles from the nearest rat's-ass town doesn't have many prospects for employment. Bob could pretty much set his own hours to work, and Mr. Foucher was such a hick that he probably couldn't tell marijuana-breath from Chanel No. 5. But the main reason Bob was happy was that he knew this would get his mom off his back.

Anyway, it's better than a real job, Bob thought.

To celebrate, he smoked a quarter-gram of black Afghani hash. Precious stuff. He'd been saving it for a special occasion.

Bob had just finished off the hash, and was kicked back on the bed, completely toasted, when there was a knock on his bedroom door.

Bob was stunned. It could only be his mother, and she never bothered him during the afternoon. She knew well enough that she might catch him getting stoned, and she didn't want to deal with it.

They had an understanding. He wouldn't be blatant about it, and she wouldn't give him any shit.

It took Bob a while to get to his feet and navigate to the door.

"Yeah?" To Bob, his voice now sounded rather like a frog's. *Christ, she'll know I'm stoned for sure,* he thought. The door was shimmering as he stared at it.

"Honey?" His mom's voice was high and mousey. She always called him "honey," even in front of his friends, which horrified Bob. "Honey, Mr. Foucher just called. He'd like you to come up today. He has a job he forgot about, wants to get started right away. OK?"

Bob's head reeled. This was *perfect*. Completely fried, ready for an afternoon of relaxation, and *this* happens.

"But I was just—"

For one of the few times in her life Bob's mom interrupted him. "You've been needing a job for a long time. I don't want you to lose this one. I'll tell Mr. Foucher you'll be right up."

The day was hot, the hottest yet that year. Bob was finding his bicycle more difficult to deal with than usual, and it seemed that he was getting more stoned, not less, as time passed. At one point, everything looked like Bob was staring through a fine-meshed screen, and he had to stop his bike and blink his eyes a few times before his vision cleared. He also was having difficulty riding in a straight line, and twice almost rode off into the bushes. Luckily, there was no traffic on the quiet country road, and Bob made it to Mr. Foucher's without any major disasters occurring.

Mr. Foucher was of French descent, but his accent was pure Oregon Country Bumpkin. He was muscular, as most farmers are, but wore a sizable girdle of fat built during a lifetime of eating mostly dairy products. He had never married, and looked to be about sixty years old, though no one knew his exact age. Along with his house Mr. Foucher owned three hundred acres of pasture and forest, fifty or so cows, and two barns. His dairy was a small one, but every morning a milk tanker rumbled up the Cherryville road and loaded up.

When Mr. Foucher saw Bob alighting unsteadily from his bicycle, he smiled broadly. Mr. Foucher was always smiling. *I'll be glad to give your boy a job,* he'd told Bob's mom when she'd called him after Bob refused to. Now Bob was having to face the music. And still the hash was throbbing in his head.

"Hello, Bob," said Mr. Foucher. *Hello fatface,* Bob thought, but he just said "Hi." He immediately regretted using the word, considering how high he actually was. He avoided Mr. Foucher's gaze as much as possible.

"I thought I'd set you to fixing the fence," said Mr. Foucher. His eyes were active, darting back and forth, trying to hold Bob's eyes. "I think you can handle it alone. I've gotta clean out the milking room. You can work as long as you want, then come back here and we'll settle up."

"OK," Bob said. He was fascinated by Mr. Foucher's nose. *The nose is a strange thing,* Bob thought, then caught himself. *Hold it together until you get rid of this pigfucker,* he thought, but he may have mumbled part of it, because Mr. Foucher looked up sharply. Bob froze, but all Mr. Foucher said was: "Come on. I'll show you what you're up against."

Mr. Foucher walked into the weather-grey wooden barn and emerged carrying a green five-gallon bucket full of tools, and a shovel. He led Bob through a gate and across a bare, rock-strewn field. A few dozen scruffy-looking cows lounged at the far end of the field, nibbling at grass stubble and blackberry leaves.

As he followed Mr. Foucher across the field, Bob walked very deliberately, trying not to stumble, and trying to avoid the numerous piles of cowshit that dotted the landscape.

"This fence is twenty years old," Mr. Foucher said, as they continued to walk. He was grinning widely, and the folds of his jowls and chin drew Bob's fascinated attention.

"It's a good fence," Mr. Foucher continued, "but the stakes are gettin' loose, some of 'em."

At last they reached the fence, three strands of rusty barbed wire tacked to split-log posts. The corner post was actually a huge old stump, almost as tall as Bob, and as big around as Mr. Foucher.

"You can leave *this* one," Mr. Foucher said, grinning even more broadly than before, and pounding goodnaturedly on the stump with his fist. Then he explained the job to Bob. Yank out the U-shaped nails that hold the wire to the post. Rock the post until it comes free from the ground. Knock off the rotten wood, dig the hole deeper, replant the thing, and then nail the wire back on. And then do it again. And again. And again.

As Bob looked down the line of fenceposts, the sun suddenly seemed ten degrees hotter.

When Mr. Foucher had finished his lecture on the finer points of fence-fixing, he tromped back across the field to the barn. Bob relaxed a little. His head was buzzing; if anything he felt higher than he had right after he'd smoked the hash. He wanted to sit against the stump and blank out for awhile, but the thought of the sardonic dairyman, who would probably be watching him, kept Bob moving.

Bob touched the first post, just to the right of the stump. It rocked in its socket like a rotten tooth.

May as well get down to it. Bob picked up the claw hammer, put it down again, and pulled on the stiff leather gloves Mr. Foucher had thrown in the bucket. They smelled faintly of cowshit. Then he picked up the hammer again, and, with just a little difficulty, pulled the nails from the post.

Far out, he thought. *I can do this.* Just then a wave of stupefaction swept over him. Everything took on a pinkish tinge.

Must've been something on that hash, Bob thought as he leaned against the stump, trying to regain control of his senses. *Opium, strychnine, something.* He didn't feel queasy, and there was no real pain. He just felt . . . bizarre.

After a minute he felt a little better. Things looked more normal.

Gotta do at least a few of these. Can't quit now. As unmotivated as he was, Bob didn't want to be a complete failure at this job. And he didn't want to face his mom if he went home now.

He took hold of the post and rocked it. He tried to lift it, and succeeded in scraping his arm on the rough wood as the post toppled over. The rotten end of the post broke off in the hole.

Bob rubbed his arm ruefully. *This is bullshit,* he thought, as he picked up the shovel and started digging dirt and wood out of the hole. The third time he put his shovel in, putting his weight on it this time, he came up against something hard.

Damn rock. It didn't feel like a rock though.

Bob worked the shovel beneath the thing. It finally came loose and popped out of the hole, rolling a few feet across the grass.

A human skull.

It was brown, as brown as the dirt that had surrounded it. The skull-cap had been split open by the shovel-blade.

Shit, thought Bob. *Shit shit shit. Can't be a skull it can't be. Gotta be the drug.*

Still the skull sat there, upright, facing him. Bob stared wildly around, trying to test his perceptions, to see if he was hallucinating.

All was quiet. Cows grazed in the distance. Mr. Foucher was nowhere to be seen. And the skull was still there.

Bob was now faced with the reality of the skull. What should he do? Pitch it into the bushes? Bury it again? Show it to Mr. Foucher?

How old did he say this fence was? Bob's hands were shaking. *Gotta be the drug,* he thought again, but he couldn't believe that.

"I'll get rid of the fucker," he said, and the sound of his own voice surprised him. "Put it back where it came from." As he said the words his fear changed, almost instantly, to exhilaration. He wasn't afraid anymore. The novelty of the situation began to appeal to him. He even thought of taking the skull, hiding it in the bushes by the road, and sneaking it home later. But the skull was obviously rotten. Even now, brown water was leaking from it, staining the sun-withered grass.

After staring at the skull for a while, Bob scooped it up, gingerly, with the shovel, and deposited it back in the hole.

He felt good. In control.

He hacked the rotten edges off the bottom of the post with the blade of the shovel. Hefting the post, he guided it back into the hole. The skull collapsed with an indescribably delicious sound.

When the dirt was packed in, Bob nailed the wires to the now rock-firm fencepost. The air seemed to hum with his accomplishment. Sweat dripped from his face, dripped down onto the rotted wood that littered the ground.

The second post was not as loose as the first had been. Bob put his shoulder against it, trying to break it off at ground level, but it wouldn't give. Hugging the post, he lifted and strained, bracing the post with his foot every time he raised it an inch or so. Finally it came free. Almost two feet of post had stood underground, and the hole was smooth, the ground firm. Bob leaned over the hole.

The skull inside had been buried face up. It was whiter than the first.

Bob didn't see much as he ran across the field toward Mr. Foucher's barns. He didn't see the shit he ran through, didn't see the rocks that caught at his feet. The fear was on him. It licked at his back as he ran.

Mr. Foucher was washing out the milking stalls with an old green hose, using his fat thumb to direct the spray. When he saw Bob standing there, trying to breathe, he laid down the hose.

And he smiled. "Back so soon? Are you havin' trouble?"

Bob couldn't speak for a moment. His mouth was as dry as a sun-bleached bone.

"M—Mr. Foucher, I . . . I found something."

"Yes, yes, what did you find?" Mr. Foucher's yellow teeth were all Bob could see for a moment. That idiot grin.

"I found a—a skull," Bob said. He stared at the ground now, at Mr. Foucher's muddy boots.

"Damn!" said Mr. Foucher. "Thought I'd told you." He walked over to the doors of the old barn, and threw them open. Bob followed him, unable to think of anything but those teeth, teeth that stood like a row of rotten fenceposts as Mr. Foucher turned back to face him.

"When you get to the far end of the field," Mr. Foucher said, "there won't be any more skulls. Then you'll have to start laying in fresh ones."

In the barn, between some rusty old plowing implements and a ten-foot pile of hay bales, was a bathtub, the freestanding type, with claw feet. The contents were piled as high as they could be, piled above the rim of the tub.

Clean, white, human skulls.

Mr. Foucher was still grinning.

And Bob felt his lips drawing back into a fine, broad, friendly smile.

Footsteps of Fear

Vincent Starrett

DR. B. EDWARD LOXLEY (jocularly called "Bedward" by the gossip columnists), the wife-murderer for whom hundreds of police had been scouring the city for three weeks, sat quietly at his desk in the great Merchandise Exchange reading his morning mail. The frosted glass door beyond his outer office read simply *William Drayham, Rare Books. Hours by Appointment.* After three weeks of security he was beginning to feel complacent. For three weeks he had not left his hiding place and he had no intention of leaving it immediately, except feet first.

It had all been thought out beforehand. The office had been rented a month before the murder of Lora Loxley, and he had quietly taken possession and begun his new personality buildup as William Drayham. He had been accepted by his neighbors in the sixth floor corridor. The elevator starter was getting to know him. He breakfasted, lunched and dined at the several restaurants in the building, was shaved by a favorite barber, and was—he had every reason to believe—an accepted fixture. His neighbors were inoffensive, unimaginative workers who did not question his identity, and the words *Rare Books* on the door were formidable enough to frighten away casual visitors.

Lora Loxley, murdered by suffocation, had long been buried and even the newspapers were beginning to minimize the sensational story. The feeling was growing that Loxley, himself, also might have been murdered and a desultory search for his body continued when the police had nothing better to occupy them. As his window overlooked the river where, in addition to the normal traffic, police boats occasionally plied, he was enabled to watch their activities with amused appreciation of their effort. He had now spent two lonely Sundays watching the holiday traffic with a pair of binoculars, waiting for any active renewal of police attention. He was on excellent terms with the watchmen in his part of the building, who were accustomed to seeing him around at unlikely hours.

The Merchandise Exchange was a city within a city. It contained everything he needed—restaurants, laundries, barbershops, tobacconists, dentists, news stands, banking facilities, a gymnasium, even a postal station. He was known by name in the restaurants and barbershops. He bought all the newspapers. Occasionally he dictated a letter to a public stenographer, ordering or rejecting books. As William Drayham he had a sufficient banking account downstairs for his immediate needs. The rest of his wealth, in cash, was in Paris with Gloria.

His principal bogies had been watchmen and cleaning women. He had little fear, however, of the cleaning women, a friendly trio who liked candy and who readily agreed to visit his office while he was having a late dinner. His domestic arrangements were simple. He slept on a couch in his inner office, which held also a vault to which he could retire in an emergency. To date there had been no emergency.

Dr. Loxley pushed the mail aside impatiently. Too early perhaps to expect a response to the little ad he was running in a Sunday book supplement. But not too early for the coffee that Miss Marivole Boggs served at all hours. What luck to have found so admirable a creature in the same corridor, and even in the same line. Rare books and antiques went very well together. She had been responsible for a number of his infrequent customers. He glanced at his expensive wristwatch and left William Drayham's rare books behind him without a pang.

M. Boggs, Antiques, as she described herself on the show window of her small shop at the end of the corridor, looked up at his entrance.

"Hello," she said. "I was hoping you would come in."

"I couldn't miss," he said. His brown eyes took in the familiar room, resting for a moment on the suit of antique armor that dominated one corner of the shop and the Spanish chest that was Miss Boggs' pride and joy. "Well, I see nobody has bought either of them yet." It was one of their standing jokes that some day, when the rare book business was better, he would write a check for them himself.

As she poured his coffee she said, "The newspaper stories about that doctor are getting shorter every day. I'm beginning to believe he really *was* murdered."

They often discussed the missing Dr. Loxley, as indeed the whole city was doing. At first it had been Miss Boggs' idea that the "society doctor" had murdered his wife over some glamorous patient who was now living in sin with him somewhere on the Riviera.

Dr. Loxley had thought not. "Too romantic, Boggs. I still think he's in the river or somewhere on his way to the Gulf of Mexico. That scarf they found on the river banks looks like it."

"Anyway, the police seem to have stopped looking," said M. Boggs.

"Anyway, this is good coffee, Boggs. I hope you'll leave me the recipe. Do you still plan to leave this month?"

"At once," she said. "I'm flying to New York tomorrow, if I can get away. I want to be in London for the Exhibition; then on to Paris, Rome, Switzerland, and what have you. I'm enormously relieved that you'll be here to keep an eye on things, Bill. Coffee at all hours, eh?"

"Morning, noon and night," he agreed, rising to leave. Her change of plan had startled him for a moment; but he was quick enough to see an advantage in it for himself. "Never fear, I'll be here waiting for you when you return."

Strolling back to his own shop, humming a jaunty air, he became aware of a man leaving the doorway of the office directly opposite his own. Something about the man's carriage seemed fa-

196

miliar. He was turning toward the elevators and walking fast. In an instant they would meet.

And suddenly Dr. Loxley realized that the man was, indeed, familiar. He was his own brother-in-law, Laurence Bridewell.

His first instinct was to turn and flee, his second to turn back to *M. Boggs, Antiques.* His final decision, made in a split second, was to see the encounter through. His disguise had fooled better men than Larry Bridewell, although none who knew him better. With his neat little beard and moustache gone, and his blue eyes transformed by brown contact lenses, he was another man. After an appalling moment of indecision, he fumbled for a cigarette, realizing that after three weeks of complacent safety, he was about to face a supreme test.

He tried and failed to light the cigarette. . . . Then they were face to face, looking at each other as men do in passing, and the test was over. Or was it? Bridewell continued on his way to the elevators, walking fast, and Loxley stumbled to his own door.

Dared he look back? Had Bridewell turned to look back at *him?* Moving casually, he stole a glance along the corridor. There was no doubt about it—Larry was looking back, too. Perhaps he had merely been troubled by a fancied resemblance. . . .

Dr. Loxley made some difficulty about opening his own door, and just before he closed it, it occurred to him to look at the name on the door of the office from which his brother-in-law had emerged. Actually he knew very well what he would find there: *Jackson & Fortworth, Attorneys at Law.* And below, the significant word *Investigations.*

He tried to take himself in hand and was annoyed to find himself shaking. Experimentally he ventured a little drink to see what it would do for him. It helped considerably. But the whole incident haunted him and gave him a bad night. In the morning, however his fears had vanished. He was his confident self again until, a few hours later, a second incident shook his nerve. Returning from the cigar stand in the lobby he had to pass the De Luxe Dog Salon in one of the street level corridors and paused, as he had often done before, to look in at the windows at the fashionable dogs in process of being barbered, an amusing spectacle. But as he turned away an appalling thing happened.

A well-dressed woman was approaching the salon with a sprightly French poodle on a leash. She looked familiar. God's teeth! She *was* familiar, and so was the dog. She was Mrs. Montgomery Hyde, no less, an old patient. His heart seemed to stop beating. Would she recognize him?

It was the dog that recognized him. With a yelp of joy the poodle jerked the leash from the woman's hand and flung himself rapturously against the doctor's legs.

With an effort Loxley recovered his balance and somehow recovered his poise. It was his worst moment to date. Automatically he disengaged himself from the poodle's embrace and pulled the black ears.

"There, there fellow," he said to the excited animal in a voice that he hoped was not his own. "I beg your pardon, Madam. Your dog appears to have made a mistake."

To his intense relief, Mrs. Montgomery Hyde agreed.

"Do forgive Toto's impulsiveness," she begged, snatching up the leash. "He loves everybody."

Dr. Loxley left the scene in almost a hurry. She had not recognized him! It seemed to him a miracle, but again he was annoyed to find himself shaking. And yet, could it not be a good omen? If Mrs. Hyde and his own brother-in-law had failed to recognize him, what was there to fear? Immediately he began to feel better. But when he had returned to his office William Drayham again treated himself to a stiff drink.

In a moment of alert intelligence he realized that for three weeks he had been too complacent. His meeting with Mrs. Hyde had taught him something that was important to remember. He had almost spoken her name. In his first moment of panic he might well have betrayed himself. If it was important for him not to be recognized, it was equally important that *he* must not recognize someone by accident.

It was clear to him that this cat-and-mouse existence could not go on indefinitely. He must remain in hiding only until it was safe for him to emerge and get out of the country. Then William Drayham would ostentatiously pack his books and remove to New York. After that, the world was wide.

For several days the chastened doctor lived cautiously, visiting *M. Boggs, Antiques* at intervals for coffee and to admire the suit of armor and the Spanish chest, which continued to fascinate him. He had promised Boggs, now on her travels, not to cut the price on either.

Twice, returning from the antique shop, again he had caught a glimpse of his brother-in-law entering the law office of Jackson &

Fortworth, and had hastened to lock himself in his own quarters before Larry could emerge. What the devil did the fellow want with a firm of investigators anyway?

The visit of Jackson, the lawyer, to the bookshop one morning took him by surprise or he might have locked the door.

"I've been intending to look in on you for some time, Mr. Drayham," said the lawyer cordially. "I'm Jackson, just across from you. Rare books have always interested me. Mind if I look around?"

Loxley rose from his chair abruptly, knocking a book from his desk to the floor. An icy fear had entered his heart. Was this *it,* at last, he wondered.

He shook hands effusively. "Glad to know you, Mr. Jackson. Sure, look around. Is there anything I can show you?"

But Jackson was already looking around. When he had finished he strolled to the window. "Nice view of the river you have," he said appreciatively. "My windows all look out on a court." He strolled to the door. "Just wanted to meet you. I'll come in again when I have more time."

"Any time," said Loxley with perfunctory courtesy.

Dr. Loxley sat down at his desk and reached for the lower drawer. Another little drink wouldn't hurt him. What had the fellow really wanted? What had he hoped to find? Or was he really one of the many idiots who collected books?

One thing at last was clear. Any day now he might have to leave the building and the city. If he was suspected, the blow would fall swiftly. At any minute the door might open again, and perhaps Jackson would not be alone. Why not get the hell out of this trap immediately? What was there to stop him? His stock—three hundred volumes of junk bought at a storage house—could be left behind if necessary.

What stopped him was Gloria's cable from Paris: "Trouble here. Phoning Friday night."

This was Thursday. Whatever else, he had to wait for Gloria's call. His hand moved toward the lower drawer, then was withdrawn. Coffee, not whiskey, was what he needed; and after luncheon he spent most of the afternoon with M. Boggs' weird collection of antiques. There, he had a fair view of Jackson's door, and was not himself conspicuous. If Larry Bridewell was among the lawyer's visitors, Loxley did not see him.

Exploring the antique shop he paused, as always to admire its two star exhibits, the almost frightening suit of armor and the massive Spanish chest. In a pinch, either would do as a hiding place—if there were time to hide.

That evening he was startled to find his picture in the paper again. The familiar face of Dr. B. Edward Loxley as he had looked with the neat little beard and moustache before he murdered his wife. It appeared that he had been arrested by an alert Seattle policeman, but had denied his identity.

Dr. Loxley drew a long breath of relief. After all, perhaps he was still safe. But what could Gloria have to say to him that required a call from Paris? Bad news of some kind. Bad for somebody.

In spite of his new fears he hated to leave the building that had been his refuge. It had been his hope to live there indefinitely, undetected; never again to venture into the streets until Dr. Loxley was as forgotten as Dr. Crippen.

Again he slept off his fears and spent an uninterrupted morning with his view and newspapers. He was beginning to feel almost at ease again, indeed, when the insufferable Jackson knocked on his locked door and called a hearty greeting. There was somebody with him. Through the frosted pane the shadowy outline of another man was visible.

"May we come in?" asked the lawyer. "I've got a couple of friends here who want to meet you."

Loxley rose uncertainly to his feet and moved to the door. So it *had* come at last! He had been right about his damned brother-in-law and this sneaking lawyer. This is *it!* And suddenly he knew what he had to do.

He unlocked and threw open the door. "Come in, gentlemen," he said without emotion. "What can I do for you?"

Jackson was beaming. "These are my friends, Sergeants Coughlin and Ripkin, from Headquarters. They hope you will come quietly." He laughed heartily at his own witticism.

"Come in, gentlemen, and sit down." Loxley forced a smile. He seated himself at his desk, stamped and addressed an envelope, and stood up. "I was just going to the mail chute with an important letter. I'll be back in a couple of minutes."

"Sure," said the two cops genially. "Take your time."

Dr. Loxley closed the outer door behind him and almost ran for *M. Boggs, Antiques.* As he locked the antique shop door he was relieved to see the corridor was still empty. They would follow him, of course. Every office in the building would be searched, probably this one first.

It *had* to be the chest!

It stood open as always, and he squeezed down inside—an uncomfortable fit—then lowered the heavy lid until only a thin crack remained for air. Faintly now he could hear footsteps in the corridor. He drew a deep breath and closed the lid.

There was a sharp *click*, then only intense darkness and suffocating silence. . . .

Twenty minutes later Sergeant Ripkin said to his partner, "Wonder what's keeping that guy. We've still got sixty tickets to sell, Pete."

"Oh, leave them with me," said Jackson. "I'll see that you get your money. Drayham's a good fellow."

The two policemen, who had been hoping to dispose of a block of tickets for a benefit ball game, departed leisurely.

The disappearance of William Drayham, a "rare book dealer" in the Merchandise Exchange, attracted less attention than that of Dr. B. Edward Loxley; but for a few days it was a mild sensation.

Returning from Europe, a month later, M. Boggs wondered idly when Bill would drop in for a cup of coffee. He had told her he would be here when she returned.

She puttered happily among her treasures. Some fool, she noted, had automatically locked the chest by closing it. One of these days she'd have to unlock it and raise the lid. . . .

Four-in-Hand

William Relling Jr.

YOU KNOW WHAT I think?" Tony Summers said to me the day we found the strangler's fourth victim. He was slapping the flipper button with his right hand, twisting his backside hard at the same time—Body English—seeing the silver ball ricochet off a lighted bumper, not looking at me as he spoke. "I think we're going at this all wrong."

I was watching the counter on the pinball machine light up his score—he was Player #1—and listening to the machine's buzzing and jangling; not saying anything myself, just waiting for him to talk. Tony was always like that; being his partner for eight months had taught me that whenever he had something important to say, he would always take his time to preface whatever it was. He liked to let you in things his own way at his own pace, and it could get pretty damned annoying sometimes. But that was Tony. Most of the time, when things were good, he was terrific to be around: a crack-up, a real card. But when things weren't so good . . . well, you either lived with the way he was or you didn't.

"We keep thinking whoever's doing these murders doesn't have any motive," he was saying. "But it just occured to me what he's been up to all along."

Suddenly the machine chunked, his points registering a free game.

"How 'bout that, Tony," I said. "You won."

We went from the pinball machine into a booth that was against a wall opposite the front entrance to the dim saloon. It was late in the afternoon, but the saloon was one of those places that's always dark no matter what time of the day or night. We might as well have been in a cave, like a couple of vampire bats hiding from the sun.

Each of us had a bottle of beer before him—for Tony it was already his fifth one, and we'd been in the place not quite an hour. I was only on number two, and my bottle was still half full.

I could tell just by looking at him that whatever he had on his mind, it was weighing him down. Which should've come as no surprise to me, considering what he and I had been going through the past couple of weeks: Trying to catch up with a phantom killer who the media had just the day before taken to calling the "Streetside Strangler."

The first victim was a young woman, a teller at a savings-and-loan downtown; her body had been found in an alley a few blocks from the place where she worked. The second was an older man, a plumber; he'd been left behind the wheel of his own truck, parked on the street in front of his shop. The third was another man, a gas station attendant whose boss found him in a stall in the station's men's room.

The last one had been just this morning—and it was one that struck a little too close to home. She was a computer operator who worked for the police department, and she'd been found in her apartment by her roommate, a stewardess who had just gotten back from an out-of-town assignment. Four victims: two male, two female; three white, one black; ranging in age from nineteen to forty-five. They each lived in different parts of the city, and none of the victims had ever met any of the others, not even a chance encounter. There wasn't a single common thread, nothing to connect the victims to each other. Nothing at all.

Except for the black knit necktie that had been used to strangle each of them.

It was our case. Mine and Tony's.

At four-thirty that afternoon, after we had come from the morgue where we watched the autopsy on Victim #4, our boss, Captain Ramsey, called Tony and me into his office, where he laid into us. Not that we weren't expecting it; it's been nearly three weeks since the first strangling, and the captain was getting antsy because not one lead nor any of the dozen nutcase phone calls confessing to the murders had panned out. We were at a dead end; we knew it and the captain knew it. But he chewed us out anyway, for half an hour.

Tony didn't take it well. As we came out of the captain's office, he steered me by my elbow, out of the homicide squad room, past our desks. Whispering to me, "We gotta get out of here." I knew it wouldn't do any good to argue; in spite of all of the work that we were skipping out on, Tony was in no mood to stick around.

I looked down at my watch. It was after six.

Tony signaled the bartender for another beer, then looked over at me. I drained the rest of my bottle and nodded. He called out to the bartender, "Make it two!" The bartender waved back.

I watched Tony reach into his pocket for a pack of cigarettes, pull one out, tap it on the table, light it and draw in a deep breath of smoke. He exhaled a heavy sigh, then looked over at me again. The corners of his mouth turned up into a thin smile.

"Waiting me out," he said. "You know me pretty good."

The bartender came over with fresh beers and took away our empties. Tony waited until the guy was out of earshot, then lifted his beer and took a long swallow.

I waited.

"We been lookin' for the connection," he said at last. "Tryin' to figure out what our victims got in common, right? It looks like there isn't a thing. Random killings. Different sexes. Different ages. We

x

203

find their bodies in different places, all over town. Where's the connection?"

"You tell me," I said.

He nodded slowly, still not entirely sure that he'd made up his mind whether to do that or not. Then he said in a low voice, "What've we got? A bank teller, a plumber, a kid who works in a gas station, a computer operator. Again, what's the connection?"

I sipped my beer. "It's your theory, pal."

His thin smile reappeared. Then he asked me, out of the blue, "Did you know the last one?" He mentioned the name of the victim we'd found this morning. "Did you ever have to deal with her, ever have her run a record check or anything for you?"

I shook my head no.

"You're lucky," he said. "She was a real cunt, man. I'm talkin' cunt with a capital C. Like it was a major favor to have her do something for you—something that was part of her job anyway, but still she had to give you grief about it." He swallowed the rest of his beer, then gestured to the bartender again. "I can think of a dozen people off the top of my head who'd like to've strangled her. She was that miserable a human being."

"So?"

He frowned, then said, "So think about it. Bank teller, plumber, filling station man. And her." He was looking at me, waiting for an answer.

I shrugged.

"You're not tryin'," he said.

I said impatiently, "Then why don't you tell me—"

Just as the bartender set another bottle in front of Tony. The guy looked at me and I shook my head. He went away.

Tony was watching the bartender move back to the other side of the bar and resume a conversation he'd been having with a pair of young ladies—they looked like secretaries who had just gotten off from work. Still looking at them, Tony said to me, "You ever notice what's really wrong with the way things are today? I mean *really* notice?"

I didn't say anything.

"You go into a supermarket," he said. "You see a kid stacking cereal boxes, you ask him, 'Excuse me, but where do you keep the stewed tomatoes?' 'I don't know' he says, 'ask the manager.' And you say, 'Okay, where's the manager?' And he says, 'He's not here today.' "

Tony stubbed out his cigarette. "Or say you're in a department store. You ever notice how the sales help, they don't find the customers anymore, it's the customers who have to go find the help? You got to look for somebody who's hiding in a corner or a woman who's walking real slow down an aisle or somebody who's trying to stay out of sight behind a counter. Or maybe three or four people together, and they're all laughin' and having' a good time, and you walk up to 'em and say, 'Can somebody help me please?' and what you get is, 'Sorry, we don't work in this section.' "

He had reached into his coat for another cigarette, and seemed to be having trouble remembering which pocket he'd put the pack into. He found the pack at last, but had to put the cigarette to his lips slowly to keep it under control. I took his lighter from him and lit the cigarette, and he nodded thanks. I noticed that his eyes had started to glaze over, and I thought to myself: *That's enough for you m'lad . . .*

"It's a fucking epidemic," he was saying. Then he was leaning over the table, resting his arms. He motioned for me to come closer. I could smell the stale beer and burnt tobacco on his breath.

He said, "What if you got somebody who's had it up to here?" The edge of the hand that was holding the cigarette slashed across his throat. "Somebody who's so sick and tired of being treated like a piece of crap by people who are s'posed to be serving *him.*"

" 'Him'?" I said.

"Or her. Man, woman, doesn't matter. Maybe it's somebody whose job it is to be nice to people all day himself. Maybe another salesman or something, or somebody who runs a complaint department and works damn hard and just sees everybody else getting away with being ignorant slobs all the time. I don't know, maybe somebody who has to spend all day listening to other people's problems . . . like a priest or a shrink or—"

"Or a cop?" I said.

His eyes locked on mine. "Yeah," he said. "Sure. A cop. Why not?"

I saw him looking over to the bartender once more, and I caught his arm as he raised it to signal. "Forget it," I said. "It's time you and I went home—"

"What do you think pushes him over the edge?" he went on, ignoring me. "He goes to the bank 'cause somebody there's screwed up his statement or something. And after he stands in line for half an hour, the teller treats him like it's his fault that on account of their screwing up his deposit he's bounced a couple hundred dollars worth of checks, and it's tough luck, but he's gonna have to pay the ten or twelve or fifteen dollar service charge on each one anyway. That's one. Then say a couple days later, the guy's bathtub backs up and the plumber gives him a hard time about it, like he's the reason why all his pipes are corroded. That's two. Then the guy pulls into a gas station and maybe asks the kid to check under the hood, and the kid says, 'Who me?' 'Yes, you, dammit, it's supposed to be a goddamn *service* station . . .' "

He caught himself when he noticed that everybody in the place was looking in the direction of our table. He had gotten very loud.

"C'mon," I said, pushing myself up. I dropped some money on the table, then bent to help my partner to his feet. "We're getting out of here."

The alley was dark. It was also deserted except for the two of us, and I could make out his lumbering figure ahead of me, staggering as he walked to our car. All the while I was running through my mind what he'd said to me in the saloon.

As well as what he didn't say.

I was thinking to myself: *What is it that you're* really *telling me?* That he could sympathize? Or that maybe he was confessing to me he knew who the killer really was . . . ?

Or what?

I wanted to ask him, very badly.

I considered asking him as I came up from behind while he was fumbling with his keys, trying to open the passenger's side door. But I decided not to as I looped my necktie around his throat. I couldn't risk it, because there were still too many people who needed taking care of.

But I was also remembering what Tony had said that afternoon in the squad room as we were leaving. He'd said, "Let's you and me go tie one on."

I pulled the loop tight, smiling to myself. Thinking: *That Tony, he sure is a card.*

Tie one on. I like that. I like that a lot.

Fresh Thuringer Today

Leo R. Ellis

THE AIR in the dingy delicatessen hung heavy with the mingled odors of spices, vinegar and aged cheeses. Down the narrow room, behind the refrigerated showcase and back against the wall, a white-haired woman sat in a chair. Her tiny body was poised on the edge of the seat, rigid, with her wrinkled hands folded on the black apron in her lap.

The eyes of Mama Geis were fixed straight ahead. They never moved, not even at the high-pitched animal squeal from the back room, or the rapid scurrying sound of the rats.

The building was old—as old as Mama Geis, no doubt—and the back room was a kitchen where the food now on display in the showcase had been prepared. Papa Geis' butcher block, with the worn knives hanging on the side, stood back there in the blackness. So did the meat grinder, and the brick smoke oven where Papa Geis prepared his neighborhood-famous Thuringer. Each Thursday the delicatessen featured this succulent cooked sausage, and tonight a hand-lettered card stood in the window.

FRESH THURINGER TODAY

The back room was silent and the only sound in the store came from the wall clock, whose pendulum swung in a wooden case with a glass door. The hands stood at eight twenty-five, the exact time Mama had left Papa Geis alone in the store just five nights before.

Business had been quiet and Papa Geis had sent her upstairs early. "The health inspector was here today," Papa said. "He complained about the rats in the back room again. I bought some poison and I'll put it out before I close up."

Mama Geis waited upstairs for half an hour, and when she came back down, she found Papa Geis lying just inside the unlocked front door, his head battered in. Mama Geis knew who had killed her husband; she knew it as surely as though the murderer had scrawled his own signature across the wall in his victim's blood.

When Detective Carver arrived on the scene, Mama Geis told him to arrest Dink Totono for the crime.

Had Mama Geis heard any sounds when she was upstairs? Had she looked out of the front window and seen Dink Totono leaving the store? Had the man been seen hanging around that evening?

Mama Geis was forced to shake her head at each of the questions, but she still insisted she knew the murderer. "Dink Totono is a rat," she said. "A week ago last Thursday he came into the store. He demanded Papa pay him ten dollars each week, or something bad would happen to Papa's business."

Detective Carver took out a notebook. "Did your husband pay?" he asked.

"No. Papa said he paid taxes to keep something bad from happening to his business, and for Dink Totono to stay out of the showcase."

Detective Carver wet his pencil tip and looked up. "Huh?" he said.

"It was Thursday," Mama Geis said patiently. "Dink Totono was eating a piece of Thuringer. He took eight more slices without paying when he left."

"I see," Detective Carver said and wrote something in his notebook.

"Dink Totono came back two days later. When Papa refused to pay any money, Dink opened the doors and threw gasoline inside the showcase. It ruined all of our food," Mama Geis said.

The detective wrote this down. "Did you see it happen?" he asked.

"No, I was upstairs. But Papa told me."

"Did he report it to the police?"

Mama Geis shook her head. "Papa went out and talked to the other merchants in the neighborhood. He told them they would have to organize, and if they would refuse to pay, he would be the leader against Dink Totono." She regarded Detective Carver solemnly. "You will arrest Dink Totono now?" she said.

Detective Carver put the notebook into his pocket. "I'm afraid you haven't given me enough evidence so we can hold a man for murder," he said. "I could pick him up for questioning—" He looked at Mama Geis' face. "I'm sorry, Mrs. Geis," he went on, "but so far we don't have any direct evidence. Unless we find somebody who heard Dink Totono threaten your husband's life, or somebody who—"

Mama Geis heard the detective, but his logic was only so many words beating against the emptiness that had engulfed her. She was alone now. Papa was gone—her mate for almost fifty years had been struck down by Dink Totono, yet Detective Carver was asking her to understand why the law must protect his murderer because there was no direct evidence. Mama Geis had evidence in her own mind, because she knew Dink Totono.

Death—even violent death—was no stranger to the neighborhood, so Papa Geis' murder had caused little comment. The funeral service had been brief, with only a few old customers at the mortuary, and Mama Geis had returned to take down the wreath and had opened the store for business.

The clock on the wall struck eight-thirty, and Mama Geis' eyes flickered to the front window of the delicatessen as a couple appeared on the sidewalk outside. The couple paused to read the card in the window and sauntered on.

Mama Geis could remember Dink Totono as a pudgy and somewhat surly youngster of ten. The memory was clear, because every Thursday young Dink Totono would appear to buy his quota of Thuringer. Through gossip, Mama Geis had kept track of Dink Totono's early trouble with the police, and where the other boys had been caught in petty crimes, Dink Totono had always been accused of an act of violence.

Dink Totono might have changed physically—he was now a hulking figure of a man who dressed well. His cockiness had matured into self-assurance, but to Mama Geis he was still the Dink Totono she had always known. He was a creature of habit; he had proved that by heading straight for the pan of Thuringer in the showcase. Dink Totono had always used violence, and Papa Geis had been murdered by a blow over the head.

The hands on the wall clock now held at eight-fifty, ten minutes until closing time. The coroner's report stated Papa Geis had been killed shortly before nine o'clock. Mama Geis' eyes remained fixed on the front window. Dink Totono was bound by habit; he would not let Papa's death keep him from demanding money. Mama Geis was as sure Dink Totono would return tonight as she was that Papa was really gone.

A brief, hurried scamper and the back room was quiet again. Footsteps sounded on the sidewalk, and Mama Geis' eyes darted over to follow a man across the front window. He passed without looking in and disappeared.

A second figure appeared on the sidewalk outside. It paused for a moment before the card in the window and strode on to push the front door open. Dink Totono walked by the bread rack, around the end of the showcase and on back to stand before the chair, where he almost filled the space behind the counter.

"I guess you know why I'm here," he said. "I want the money."

Mama Geis' seamed face remained expressionless as she slid her hand into her apron pocket. Slowly she brought out a tightly crumpled bill and held it up.

Dink Totono took the money, smoothed it out and examined it before he shoved the bill into his pocket. "Ten bucks is right," he said. "Ten bucks each week and don't forget it."

He walked back. He stopped at the end and pulled the showcase door open. Taking most of the Thuringer left in the white enamel pan, he ripped off a length of butcher paper and wrapped up the meat. He took tape from the machine on the counter, sealed the paper and dropped the package into his coat pocket. At the bread rack he took down a loaf and turned. "I'm sorry Papa got knocked off," he said. "Now that I'm back in the neighborhood, I was looking forward to getting his Thuringer again."

When the door closed, the pendulum in the wooden case with the glass door swung monotonously. The tick-tock of the clock made the only sound in the delicatessen as Mama Geis got to her feet and walked down to the end of the showcase. She slid the door open and took out the nearly empty enamel pan. She went on to the front window, where she took out the Thuringer card and tucked it under her arm. She released the spring lock on the door and snapped off the front lights.

A single bulb over the slicing machine remained on, and threw her shadow, tall and irregular, across the opposite wall as she trudged back through the store. When the light in the back room was turned on, a brief scratching sound came from the cartons stacked in the corner, but Mama Geis did not look over.

She placed the enamel pan on the butcher block. Taking one of the worn knives, she began to cut up the remaining Thuringer in the pan.

"Dink Totono came back tonight, Papa," she said as she worked. "I didn't put the card in the window until all of our regular customers had been in."

Mama Geis carried the enamel pan over to the cartons stacked in the corner. Methodically she began to place the poisoned meat along the baseboard. "No sense in wasting what's left of the Thuringer," she said. "The health inspector said he'd be back again about the other rats. But tonight, papa, we got the biggest one of them all."

Hi, Mom!

William F. Nolan

AMONG ITEMS FOUND by police in the apartment of William Charles Kelso, 4200 E. Ivy, Hays City, Kansas:

ITEM: A pair of recently severed human hands. Female. Each fingernail lettered in red nail polish. B-I-L-L-Y (on left hand) K-E-L-S-O (on right hand). Lettering identified as by subject, William Charles Kelso.

ITEM: A baby's plastic rattle, pink. Apparently belonged to subject, W.C.K., when infant.

ITEM: A Sportsman's hunting knife with yellow bone handle, human hair adhering. Bloodstains on blade from victims, various.

ITEM: A photo, undated, of W.C.K. as young boy (five? six?) standing in backyard of unidentified house next to his mother, Mrs. Ella Patrick Kelso. Mother's features (Caucasian) defaced by knife cuts across photo. Word, "SLUT!" written in blue ink by subject at margin of photo, with arrow pointing to Mrs. Kelso.

ITEM: A scrap of what appears to be butcher's wrapping paper, undated. Written (in pencil) on paper by subject:

> *I am a void*
> *I am not part of this planet*
> *There is no Billy Kelso*

ITEM: A snapshot (faded, n.d.) of Mr. and Mrs. Kelso seated on cement steps of apartment house (location unknown) with subject as infant in arms of Ella Kelso. Father is black. Full name: Leonard Edward Kelso. Written (blue ink) in subject's hand:

> *This is only photo I have of my goddam father. The bastard split when I was four. Used to beat up Mom a lot when he was drunk. She's deaf in one ear because of a table fork he stuck in there. I hope he got cancer. Hope it hurt a lot and that he rots.*

ITEM: A typed school report sent to Mrs. Kelso from grade school teacher Catherine Vanne in 1966 when subject was eight years old:

> *Your son Billy is a very difficult child to control in class. He openly rebels against all forms of discipline. On the playground today he attacked a smaller boy with a wooden bat and had to be physically restrained. Billy is aloof, and has made no friends among his classmates. If his behavior does not show a marked improvement over the remainder of this semester he will be expelled.*

Subject added, in blue ink, at bottom of this page:

> *Mom whipped me plenty bad for this with her leather belt. Later, I was real dizzy and started spitting blood. Mom says maybe I've got an ulcer.*

ITEM: A membership card in an organization known to be on Anti-American list by FBI. Card is marked:

> *Cancelled. Non-Caucasian.*

ITEM: A human ear. Female. Found in ziplock bag in subject's refrigerator.

ITEM: A poem, undated. Pencil. In subject's adult hand:

> *Moonlight eating*
> *severed flesh*
> *in dreams*
> *of icy death*

ITEM: A loose news clip from the *Daily Register,* Benford, Illinois, dated July 10, 1968:

CAT MYSTERY SOLVED
Local Boy Admits Killing Felines

In response to a neighbor's phone call, local police entered the home of Mrs. Leonard Kelso, 1222 Vincent Avenue, to discover the decomposed bodies of some two dozen cats listed by owners as missing over the past year. The animals were buried in the dirt in one corner of the Kelso basement. They were headless.

Mrs. Kelso's 10-year-old son, William, told police that he was responsible for slaying these animals, but could not remember what he'd done with the heads.

The boy was taken to Juvenile Hall.

ITEM: A child's sketch (by W.C.K.) done when subject was attending grade school in Benford. In colored crayon, sketch shows a row of downtown office buildings with red-and-yellow tongues of flame coming from the windows. At bottom of this sketch, in child's hand:

FIRE IS NICE

ITEM: An untitled story, written in pencil by W.C.K. (when schoolboy) in blue-lined tablet, n.d.:

Once upon a time there was a littel boy named Billy who had a Daddy that was called a niger who used to hit his Mom before he went far away to another place. Billy was also called a littel niger but his Mom told him he was white like her so he didn't know which he was and he wanted to run away with a circus and get his face painted all colors like a klown's is.

ITEM: A plastic bag found in subject's bedroom, stuffed with human hair, used as pillow.

ITEM: A copy of the Benford High School Yearbook for 1975. On page 79 is a student graduation photo of subject, with description beneath:

"Billy." Independent. Quiet. Not one of the crowd. A nut for boxing. (Don't get him sore at you!) Odd sense of humor. Likes small animals. Ambition: "to be an undertaker." (He's got to be kidding!)

ITEM: A private reel-to-reel tape recording:

TAPE BEGINS

Voice of young woman: What *is* this shit? Are you recording us?

Voice of William Charles Kelso: That's right.

Woman: Well shut it the fuck off! I didn't come here to be put on some fucking tape.

Kelso: Watch your mouth. I don't like to hear a lady talk like that.

Woman: And who says I'm a lady? Okay . . . are you going to shut it off or not?

Kelso: No, I'm not.

Woman: Then I'm splitting. Since we didn't do anything I'll just charge you ten bucks. For coming over.

Kelso: You're not leaving.

Woman: The hell I'm not! I don't dig freaks. Get out of my way, damn you!

(SOUNDS OF STRUGGLE)

Kelso: You're never going to leave me again, Ella.

Woman: (terrified) I'm not Ella? . . . who the fuck is Ella?

Kelso: Time to die, slut! (STRUGGLE INTENSIFIES. SOUND OF BLOWS. A HIGH-PITCHED SCREAM. GASPING. SILENCE.)

TAPE ENDS

ITEM: A pair of initialed white-silk underpants. Initials: E. K. (Thought to have belonged to subject's mother.) Slashed repeatedly with knife.

214

ITEM: Letter, hand-written, dated November 7, 1984, from ex-convict Alvin P. Stegmeyer to subject (then living in Indianapolis):

> *Dear Billy,*
>
> *Hey, old buddy, how are things? You promised to keep in touch when you left the joint. How come I never hear from you? As for me, just like I told you, I am back in K.C. in the plant, working as a meat packer. Job is okay, and I am back with my girl Nancy and get laid regular. You getting any? I hope you are, because a guy needs his pussy! (ha, ha) Why not come out to K.C. and visit an old pal? Have you watched one of those 500 Indy races yet? I hear they are great to see with lots of crashes into the wall. (ha, ha) Well I'd better go. Take it easy, buddy, and let me hear from you.*
>
> Your friend Al
>
> *P.S. Still looking for your Mom? As for me, I never want to set eyes on my old lady ever again. She never done nothing good for me. Or for my sis or brothers either, that's for sure. Maybe because you don't have sisters or brothers your Mom treated you better. Anyway I hope you find her.*
>
> See you, Al

ITEM: A magazine article, torn from a copy of *Psychology Today*, dated October 3, 1985. Titled: "Portrait of a Compulsive Killer," by Anne Franklin. Following a paragraph underlined in red by subject:

> *With each subsequent murder, this type of maladjusted individual compulsively repeats his ongoing pattern of violence. He is unaware of why he must kill since the elements leading up to his acts are usually deep-rooted in childhood and he has no conscious realization of what motivates him.*
>
> *He is satisfied only with the death of his latest victim (usually chosen at random). This pattern remains unbroken until he is either apprehended or commits suicide. (Between killings he may experience severe guilt or remorse for his aberrant behavior, but these periods are not constant.)*

ITEM: A list, scribbled in subject's hand, on sheet of lined notepaper:

> Kill her dog
> Break into her house
> Kill her
> Get momento (maybe her thumbs ???)
> Burn house

ITEM: A scrapbook of news clips (collected by subject) relating to murders ascribed to William Charles Kelso:

> COED FOUND FATALLY STABBED IN
> UNDERGROUND PARKING LOT
>
> MOTHER AND BABY SLAIN IN HOME
>
> TEENAGERS BEATEN TO DEATH
> ON HIGHWAY
>
> PATTERN OF KNIFE MURDERS POINT
> TO SERIAL KILLER

ITEM: A postcard from subject (sent from motel in Jasper, Wyoming) to Kelso's mother in Chicago, dated December 15, 1984. (Card was returned, stamped "Address Unknown"):

> Hi, Mom
> Plenty cold this time of year in Wyoming. In Chicago too I know! The wind sounds like people screaming. How are you? I am pretty good except for the bad dreams that wake me up sometimes at night. You can write me care of the postoffice here in Jasper in case I leave this motel. Working as a frycook at a burger place. I'm doing okay but I need to see you.
>
> Your son,
> Billy

ITEM: A poem, written on back of a large brown mailing envelope in subject's hand, n.d.:

> Teeth of acid
>   tear my flesh.
> Young flowers bleed

and worms of fire
consume me.

ITEM: Final section of a printed transcript from a televised interview with subject. Show, titled "Insights," telecast over KRRO-TV, Missoula, Montana during August of 1988. Interviewer: Dean Hawkins.

HAWKINS: . . . and despite the fact that you warned the psychiatrist that you were still a danger to society and could not function outside prison, the parole board nevertheless released you?

KELSO: They did, yes. The prisons in this country . . . they're very overcrowded and don't care much who they let out on the streets. I kept trying to . . . trying to tell them that I wasn't fit to leave . . . that . . . I didn't want to leave.

HAWKINS: Are you telling us you *like* living in a prison environment?

KELSO: No, I'm not really saying that . . . I . . . well, in a way I guess I do . . . like being in prison better than outside where there's . . . no control.

HAWKINS: What is it you're trying to control?

KELSO: Things I do . . . that I don't like doing.

HAWKINS: Then why do them?

KELSO: Because I *have* to. I don't seem to . . . to be able to have any choice.

HAWKINS: Just what things are you talking about?

KELSO: (mumbles—not audible) . . . can't say them. I don't want to talk about them. I got put in prison for robbing a store to get some food after I lost a job I had. But I never got caught for . . . for doing what bothers me.

HAWKINS: Are you, as of today, a danger to society?

KELSO: Yes . . . I am. That's true.

HAWKINS: What is it you want to do with your life, Billy?

KELSO: Get it stopped. End it. I just . . . think it's better if I'm dead. That would be better for everybody.

HAWKINS: But what about your family? Don't you have people who care about you?

KELSO: I got no brothers or sisters. Pop left us when I was real small, and Mom split when I was ten. Said she . . . couldn't handle me anymore . . . and she put me in a home where I ran away. I looked for her but I could never find her. Now I don't care.

HAWKINS: Maybe she's ill and can't contact you. A mother's love is a strong force.

KELSO: Mom never loved me. She used to . . . to beat me with a belt of hers that had a metal buckle that cut me up pretty bad. I got lots of scars on me from that buckle . . . (Pause) I'd get . . . terrible headaches after she beat me. I just couldn't even think straight. That's when I got a cat from the street and . . .

HAWKINS: And what, Billy?

KELSO: I'm not going to talk about that. I needed to find Mom and tell her . . . about how much she hurt me as a kid. But I guess she doesn't care.

HAWKINS: I see. (Long pause) Why did you volunteer to come here today, Billy?

KELSO: To let people know about how these parole boards let you out of prison when you're not ready to be outside. It's a bad thing for them to do . . . very bad.

HAWKINS: We . . . uh . . . certainly thank you for your honesty. There's no doubt that our overcrowded prison system is in severe need of adjustment . . . Thank you for coming here today to tell your story.

KELSO: I didn't tell a lot of it. I left out the . . . the
           worst parts. I'd really like to be dead now.

NOTE: With regard to the case of William Charles Kelso: Conclusion, computer transcript of signed statement from Ella Patrick Kelso, freely given in presence of Chief of Police
Darren Arnwood and police stenographer Philip Eston, at
police headquarters, Hays City, Kansas. Dated June 21,
1990:

> . . . and when I got here to his apartment I found all this
> blood. Billy was on the couch in his sweatshirt, drinking a
> beer and watching TV. There was blood on his hands and
> all over his pants and shirt and I knew he'd killed somebody
> else. I'd been reading about him and I knew it was my boy,
> Billy, doing all these killings.
>
> He was rotten, like his father. Just no damn good, ever.
> Didn't give me a minute's peace all the time I had him with
> me. I never wanted to be the mother of some freak kid like
> he was. I prayed to the Good Lord to deliver me from such a
> burden. Billy did sick things from the start, and whipping
> him didn't change him any. Just made him meaner. Maybe it
> was his mixed blood. I never should have married no black
> man, that's for sure. One summer Billy set six fires down-
> town, but nobody knew it was him.
>
> I heard he'd been looking for me a long time, and then I
> heard he was here in Kansas working in a bakery. So I
> drove out here to Hays City, to Billy's apartment, and when
> he looked up real surprised to see me, and said "Hi, Mom,"
> I shot him. Six times. In the head and chest. With a boy like
> that you just have to do your duty as a mother. So I did that.
>
> I did my duty.

Hiding Place

Basil Wells

HE SWUNG RIGHT in Terry Square while the light was red with a green arrow below it. He headed east on Sixth.

Traffic was light. A glimpse in the mirror showed no trailing headlights; his breath whooshed out, relieved. One way street, intersecting. He turned left, went up two blocks and turned right on two-way Eighth. No trailing lights . . .

Avoya had seen him, all right. After the argument with McCoyle on the sidestreet—an interesting look into what went on in the numbers racket, Kimmel had been thinking—the snaky little man had lunged at the larger man. Only when his hand came away had Kimmel seen the knife it held.

He had cringed back into the seat of the Lincoln he drove for Orson Chalmers Reed—and Avoya's darting glance caught the movement. The little man had started toward him, and Kimmel, in sudden terror, had sent the big black car roaring eastward across State and up through Terry Square . . .

All thought of his employer, attending a dinner at a sea food restaurant near the public dock, was forgotten in that first wild panic. For he knew that Avoya would have his men try to silence the only witness to the murder—and Avoya must have seen the big car's license plate.

He had a few hours, probably until the middle of the next day, to drop from sight. After the trial—*if* Avoya went to trial—he could emerge from hiding.

Marlon Kimmel was the first to admit that he was no hero.

Out past the airport, he drove to the paved narrow side road that passed through an open metal gate and ended with the buildings and garages of his employer's lakefront estate.

A package of clothing, all the money—especially change—that he owned. Then, back to Presque Isle and the hiding place that his slow-paced mind had decided upon. And he must stop at Drake's service station on the way back for more nickles and dimes—possibly at a few taverns where illegal slot machines yet were operated. The Lincoln he must leave near the sea food place.

Until morning, he could hole up in an all-night movie less than two blocks from his goal . . .

At seven o'clock the rear entrance to Castrite Electric's shop and warehouse was open, and by seven-thirty most of the two hundred employees had arrived. By eight o'clock the rambling old brick block was humming with the activity of the five other firms sharing space with Castrite.

Kimmel had worked at Castrite Electric for a few months, less than a year before he resigned to go to work for the retired doctor; he knew that shortly after eight—with luck—he could go through the receiving dock, up a side runway, and into an echoing loft that served as castings and rod storage.

Were he seen, he could ask to see one of the other employees; there were no guards at Castrite, and he could then vanish into the dusty, unused portions of the old building.

Kimmel was lucky. He passed the time clock, glancing in at the screw machine section briefly, and turned left along a metal-plated alley. Under his rubber soles the corrugated floor plates were silent.

He passed the open door leading down into the brazing room, chancing a quick look to the left. No one in sight. Past the door twenty feet the alley ended in a thick wooden door. He swung it open and was hidden from the main plant as its heavy barrier closed.

Sudden sweat soaked through his shirt, and his knees were weak. For the moment he was safe from Digger Avoya's men.

His mind had already run over the possible hiding places—on this floor and on the floor above and in the third floor loft fronting the main street—and he had decided to hide above the rod and casting storage room until night.

Rough open stairs of dirty wood were placed just inside the long high loft where the mounded metal rods and bars were stored according to size and material. He climbed them. A series of four rooms spread out from a narrow landing, and in one of these unused rooms perhaps two hundred empty nail kegs were stacked.

It was the work of but a few minutes to move enough kegs, and pile old burlap and crumpled cardboard into the opening, so he could lie hidden from view. He crawled inside, re-arranged the concealing kegs, and lay there, almost stupidly relaxed, listening to the rattle and clink of the occasional wheeled flat being pulled along the metal floor plates.

Not until darkness came did he venture from the deserted room above the bar storage loft.

The ebb and flow of roaring screw machines—the only machines yet in operation—came from beyond the thick door. The noise would drown any sound from this side, but an operator might be out in the hall away from them. Kimmel walked carefully.

His mouth was dry. He had not eaten all day, and had tried chewing gum until his stomach rebelled. Now he headed through the long dark rooms where bins, kegs and loaded shelves contained the rough—and sometimes, finished—castings that Castrite Electric manufactured. In the upstairs pattern room—unless it were locked now, and it never had been before—there was a men's room and a drinking fountain.

He stumbled over a hand truck that someone had left in the runway between the bins, and swore silently as he rubbed his bruised shins. Then the light from the street was visible. He could see the steps going upward. The second floor was not locked.

A moment later he was no longer thirsty. There was no electric cooler cabinet but even warm brackish water tasted fine. And here, even as on the first floor, he discovered there were cigarets, candy, and milk vending machines. This was a stroke of luck he had not counted on.

If his nickels and dimes only held out—of course the coke vendor made change for a quarter, too—he could endure several weeks of isolation if necessary.

With four bottles of milk, five candy bars, and two bottles of coke for his rations, Kimmel went on through the racks of wooden and metal patterns to the dust-grimed staircase to the third floor loft.

Up there, a vast sun-blasted, and winter-chilled, area opened. It extended for the full length of the front of the ancient building and was used to store little used machinery, parts, and plastic covers for the Castrite's products. In an ordinary week one—or at the worst—two—trips into the dusty confusion of the third floor were necessary.

Any chance of detection was very slight.

Kimmel, with the aid of the faint light from the street, found his way to an angling section of this great attic where he knew an old mattress, household goods, books, dishes, electric fixtures, and other mysterious boxes were stacked behind the dusty cartons of plastic covers. Here he had no trouble in contriving a sleeping place that defied any casual inspection.

He had food, water, a bed, and time.

Two weeks of inactivity in a loft superheated by a July sun, with nothing to read save a ten-volume set of metallurgical knowledge, a huge set of Biblical picture books, and some copybooks written in pencil. Two weeks of milk, candy bars and coke. Two weeks of waiting for detection—or perhaps, appendicitus to flush him out of his covert. . . . Kimmel could take no more.

After midnight, Kimmel would go down through the dark floors and into the basement shipping room. There he set to work making an opening beneath the elevator cage that brought him out at the base of the cable-tracked ramp to the upper floor. On the third night he was prepared to leave and re-enter without disturbing the burglar alarms. So he had waited.

But all that was over. Tonight, he decided, he would go out, take a bus, and try for a job in Cleveland or further West. Hiding out was sheer stupidity. Distance was the best protection. And Avoya would not have men looking for him—he hoped.

He chanced a shielded sliver of flashlight glow as he walked through the darkened basement. A lot of new equipment was just being received: new desks, filing cabinets, racks, and a couple of tape recorders. Castrite Electric's office force must be expanding, he thought. If he had stuck here and not taken that chauffeuring job . . .

Out through the narrow slot of boards where the brick walls had been trimmed away. Carefully he closed the door-opening he had contrived—he might need this entrance again—and went across the U-shaped area behind Castrite Electric's rear entrance. He headed uptown.

Two blocks up and two blocks to the west brought him to Presque Isle's bus depot. He bought a ticket for Cleveland, bus due to leave in an hour, and bought a *Presque Isle Dispatch* to read while he sat on one of the arm-compartmented benches.

The paper served to shield his face—he did not trust the carefully trimmed rectangle of his new moustache for disguise.

The paper shook. He had reached the second section, the local news. He groaned inwardly; it was a small item but it carried a message that struck hard.

Police were still hunting for Marlon Kimmel, the chauffeur suspected of the murder of his employer, Orson Chalmers Reed! Reed's body, in the half-submerged Lincoln, had been discovered the morning after Kimmel had witnessed McCoyle's stabbing. The car had crashed through flimsy guard rails above Davis Cove and plunged a hundred feet into the lake, but investigation had shown that Reed was already dead when this occurred.

"Great!" Kimmel murmured. A choking wave of heat burned upward within his vitals. He was choking—suffocating; he had to get outside.

The bus terminal's door's closed behind him. Slightly cooler out here. He leaned against the side of the building, saw an officer walking in his direction, as yet uninterested, and Kimmel started off again around the depot's corner.

They'd killed Reed, killed that puffing, red-faced, harmless little man, just because they thought he had witnessed McCoyle's death. Avoya had seen the car, taken down the license number probably, and his men had assumed the driver to be the man who was a witness.

Kimmel felt guilty of the murder—as guilty as though he had sent the old man to his watery tomb. And anger arose now to destroy his fear of Avoya. He knew it was too late to go to the police—until he had some concrete evidence.

He re-entered the terminal and went to a telephone booth. Memory of the office equipment, of the tape recorders, came to him as his brain stirred into unwonted activity. He nodded, and looked for the phone number of Pete Gerris. Gerris was a numbers man—Kimmel had once written "bug" for him—and he was close to Avoya. Someone answered—a man. He was sleepy.

"Pete?"

"Yeah."

"I got something on Avoya and McCoyle that's worth five hundred. I need it to clear out of town."

"Come again?"

"Tell Avoya he got the wrong guy; I saw it. I need five. Get it? Have him meet me down back of Castrite. In an hour."

"Avoya's in jail."

"So what? You or somebody's got some of his dough?"

"Just a . . . Who're you, anyhow?"

"Dillinger maybe." Kimmel snorted harshly. "Or Malenkov."

"I'm afraid I can't."

"Suit yourself, Pete; it's Avoya's neck."

Kimmel hung up. He headed back toward Castrite Electric. He must set up the tape recorders, fix barriers that would slow down any of Avoya's men, and rig the burglar alarm so the police would come in time to rescue him. One advantage he owned was his knowledge of the shipping rooms and the warehouse departments. And he did not think that there would be any gunplay by Avoya's men if they could avoid it.

His usually-dulled wits seemed to have slipped into overdrive. The adrenals, perhaps, spurred on by hatred and fear?

He fairly ran into the areaway behind the factory.

They hadn't shown up yet. Of course it was only three quarters of an hour, but he had a hunch that they would try to arrive first— before the hour. He had no illusions that they might dismiss his call as a prank. Avoya's organization was too thorough for that.

Kimmel was past caring what they might do to him now. By this time they must have linked the call with his former relationship to Reed. They would be out to get Kimmel before the police now.

Just inside the warehouse, he had set up one of the tape recorders. It was running now—picking up the sounds of his impatient movements. Further back in the basement, at a juncture of bins and bolt-filled kegs, the second tape recorder reeled and unreeled. And at his side, well-wrapped in burlap and scraps of old overalls, leaned two short lengths of pipe.

He had no gun; he wished now that he had planned more carefully and procured one, but the pipe should account for at least one man—if his plans went through as scheduled!

Another five minutes. Impatiently he stepped out from the shadow of the skeletonized ramp, up which a wheeled cable car ground during working hours. And stepped back, too quickly.

A policeman was passing the areaway; saw the movement, and came crunching across the cindery way to investigate.

Kimmel felt a pit hollowing out within his vitals. No use trying to explain what he was trying to prove to the policeman. He, Kimmel, was wanted for murder; he was trespassing. He had broken into the tape recorders and used them.

He slipped back through the boards, the wrapped length of pipe in his hand. He heard the policeman's feet come closer, a grunt of satisfaction, and the head and extended gun loomed dimly.

His breath sobbed out as he swung the length of pipe at that vague round blur he identified as the officer's head. He had gone too far to retreat now. He held back on the power of the sweep. A dull thud, and the policeman groaned, struggled, and sagged into the cluttered darkness.

One minute of struggling with the limp body and dragging it to the barricaded stairway that he planned to use for an exit to the first floor. He wondered if he had struck too hard—and then wished he had used more force. The officer was regaining consciousness.

Quickly he roped the big man's arms and legs and took the revolver from its holster. "Better turn me loose, bud." The man's voice was unsteady.

"Sorry. But if things go as they should you'll be free soon. I'm trying to trick the real murderers of Mr. Reed into confessing. And you . . ."

"You're Kimmel!" The words were an angry roar.

"That's right." Kimmel felt the hopelessness of trying to convince this outraged prisoner at that moment. Yet he must try. "It was like this . . ." he began.

Three minutes later he had gagged the spluttering, and unbelieving, police officer, and was waiting at the elevator's sunken outer opening. The other length of pipe was with the bound man.

This time he saw a car wheel slowly past, park, and two men come—separated and alert—toward the back of the building.

It was after two o'clock with a three-quarter moon just riding up over the shabby roofs of the eastern rows of paintless houses.

"In here," he called, backing into the basement.

One of the men kept coming but the other hung back. Probably a third man was waiting in the car too. They both were armed.

"You the guy who phoned?"

That was Pete Gerris. He had heard the voice enough times before to recognize it. High pitched and grating—toneless.

"You know who I am, Pete. Come on and let's talk business."

"No need to hide in there, Kimmel; we'll talk out here."

"Think I'm nuts?" Kimmel laughed. "You know I saw your boss knife his partner. Now I want five hundred to blow town; a bullet would be cheaper."

"You know me better than that," protested Gerris. But he put away his gun and came down under the ramp.

Just inside the elevator shaft, Kimmel halted him. "That's far enough, Pete." The tape recorder was at its best with Gerris in this spot. "I got a shotgun trained on you."

"Don't be a fool. Why would I want to shoot you? I got the money."

"If you'd been smarter," Kimmel gibed, "you wouldn't have Reed's killing to account for. Were you trying to pay him off too?"

"I wasn't in on that, Kimmel. A couple of the boys got trigger-happy; they thought the only way to shut him up was to kill him. It wasn't my idea."

"Avoya's then?"

"Avoya didn't know about it; their own idea. He was picked up too quickly to do anything more than tell them he'd been seen."

"Only they killed the wrong man. My boss was attending a dinner. It was me you were after."

"Not me," protested Gerris, "Virgin and F— doesn't matter who."

"Couldn't be Virgil and Fred Lewes could it?"

"Look, Kimmel, I came here with the five hundred. You take it and leave town until after the trial. You won't want to come back either with that murder rap hanging over you."

Gerris laughed—a short barking sound without humor.

"Here's the money—all fives and tens."

"Leave it on the edge of the shaft."

"You're sure yellow ain't you?" Gerris said.

And then, his movements hard to follow in the darkness, his gun was in his hand and was blasting in the direction of Kimmel's voice.

The two kegs of bronze bolts that sheltered Kimmel took one bullet. He heard Gerris call back to the other man, a man he called Fred—one of the killers of Orson Chalmers Reed, he realized, if his deductions were correct—and he knew that they were going to try for a quick kill and a getaway before police arrived.

Kimmel fired one shot from the police weapon and zigzagged back through the tables and bales of the shipping room to the barricaded stairway. The stairs were of metal and had been recently enclosed with sheets of aluminum. His plan had been to get to the top of the steps and secure the door until the burglar alarm could be tripped to summon aid. That had been *one* of his hastily contrived plans.

Now he set to work with his pocket knife freeing the patrolman and he slipped the heavy revolver into the officer's hand. "Believe me now?" he demanded.

A grim sound that could have been assent, or merely pain, answered him.

"From the upstairs, the receiving dock," Kimmel said, "you could cut off their escape."

"Show me."

They hurried up the steep steps, one lone shot spanging fairly close at hand. The policeman fired back down the stairwell to keep the killers interested and then followed Kimmel to the upper dock. Kimmel eased open a locked window overlooking the rear area.

The third man, whose presence had only been suspected, was now easing the car toward the loading dock. A few feet distant he stopped and sprang out. He edged under the ramp and vanished inside. Kimmel hurried to the burglar alarm.

After that it was confusion and gunshots, with more men in blue arriving and Kimmel's shanghaied officer being congratulated. Two of the gunmen were carried to the ambulance and Gerris was limping as they led him away.

Kimmel's brain was wrapped in unreality. The murder charge was cancelled. Remained only now the unlawful entry, trespass, assaulting an officer—plus a few dozen other charges. He could probably slip out with the crowd and escape—but he wasn't going to.

He was through running away from anything.

High Heels in the Headliner

Wendy Hornsby

E XQUISITE PROSE, charming story. A nice read." Thea tossed the stack of reviews her editor had sent into the file drawer and slammed it shut. The reviews were always the same, exquisite, charming, nice. What she wanted to hear was, "Tough, gritty, compelling, real. Hardest of the hard-boiled."

Thea had honestly tried to break away from writing bestselling fluff. What she wanted more than anything was to be taken seriously as a writer among writers. To do that, she knew she had to achieve tough, gritty, and real. The problem was, her whole damn life was exquisite, charming, nice.

Thea wrote from her own real-life experience, such as it was. One day, when she was about halfway through the first draft of *Lord Rimrock, L.A.P.D.,* a homeless man with one of those grubby cardboard signs—Will Work for Food—jumped out at her from his spot on the median strip up on Pacific Coast Highway. Nearly scared her to death. She used that raw emotion, the fear like a cold dagger in her gut, to write a wonderful scene for Officer Lord Rimrock. But her editor scrapped it because it was out of tone with the rest of the book. Over drawn, the editor said.

Fucking over drawn, Thea muttered and walked up to the corner shop for a bottle of wine to take the edge off her ennui.

In her mind, while she waited in line to pay, she rethought her detective. She chucked Lord Rimrock and replaced him with a Harvard man who preferred the action of big-city police work to law school. He was tall and muscular with a streak of gray at the temple. She was working on a name for him when she noticed that the man behind her in line had a detective's shield hanging on his belt.

She gawked. Here in the flesh was a real detective, her first sighting. He was also a major disappointment. His cheap suit needed pressing, he had a little paunch, and he was sweating. Lord Rimrock never sweated. Harvard men don't sweat.

"Excuse me," she said when he caught her staring.

"Don't worry about it." His world-weary scowl changed to a smarmy smile and she realized that he had mistaken her curiosity for a come on. She went for it.

"What division do you work from?" That much she knew to ask.

"Homicide. Major crimes." *He smiled out of the side of his mouth, not giving up much, not telling her to go away, either. She raised her beautiful eyes to meet his.* No. Beautiful was the wrong tone. Too charming.

"Must be interesting work," Thea said.

"Not very." *She knew he was flattered and played him like a . . .* She'd work out the simile later.

"What you do is interesting to me," she said. "I write mystery novels."

"Oh yeah?" He was intrigued.

"I suppose you're always bothered by writers looking for help with procedural details."

"I never met a writer," he said. "Unless you count asshole reporters."

She laughed, scratching the Harvard man from her thoughts, dumping the gray streak at the temple. This detective had almost no hair at all.

Thea paid for her bottle of Chardonnay. The detective put his six-pack on the counter, brushing her hand in passing. Before she could decide on an exit line, he said, "Have you ever been on a ride-along? You know, go out with the police and observe."

"I never have," she said. "It would be helpful. How does one arrange a ride-along?"

"I don't know anymore." *The gravel in his voice told her he'd seen too much of life.* "Used to do it all the time. Damned liability shit now, though. Department has really pulled back. Too bad. I think what most taxpayers need is a dose of reality. If they saw what we deal with all day, they'd get off our backs."

Thea did actually raise her beautiful eyes to him. "I think the average person is fascinated by what you do. That's why they read mysteries. That's why I write them. I would love to sit down with you some time, talk about your experiences."

"Oh yeah?" He responded by pulling in his paunch. "I just finished up at a crime scene in the neighborhood. I'm on my way home. Maybe you'd like to go for a drink."

"Indeed, I would." Thea gripped the neck of the wine bottle, hesitating before she spoke. "Tell you what. If you take me by the crime scene and show me around, we can go to my place after, have some wine and discuss the details."

Bostitch was his name. He paid for his beer and took her out to his city car, awkward in his eagerness to get on with things.

The crime scene was a good one, an old lady stabbed in her bedroom. Bostitch walked Thea right into the apartment past the forensics people who were still sifting for evidence. He explained how the blood spatter patterns on the walls were like a map of the stabbing, showed her a long arterial spray. *On the carpet where the body was found, she could trace the contours of the woman's head and outstretched arms. Like a snow angel made in blood.*

The victim's family arrived. They had come to look through the house to determine what, if anything, was missing, but all they could do was stand around, numbed by grief. Numbed? Was that it?

Thea walked up to the daughter and said, "How do you feel?"

"Oh, it's awful," the woman sobbed. "Mom was the sweetest woman on earth. Who would do this to her?"

Thea patted the daughter's back, her question still unanswered. How did she feel? Scorched, hollow, riven, shredded, iced in the gut? What?

"Seen enough?" Bostitch asked, taking Thea's arm.

She hadn't seen enough, but she smiled compliantly up into his face. She didn't want him to think she was a ghoul. Or a wimp. To her surprise, she was not bothered by the gore or the smell or any of it. She was the totally objective observer, seeing everything through the eyes of her fictional detective character.

Bostitch showed her the homicide kit he kept in the trunk of his car, mostly forms, rubber gloves, plastic bags. She was more impressed by the name than the contents, but she took a copy of everything for future reference to make him happy.

By the time Bostitch drove her back to her house, Thea's detective had evolved. He was the son of alcoholics, grew up in Wilmington in the shadow of the oil refineries. He would have an ethnic name similar to Bostitch. The sort of man who wouldn't know where Harvard was.

In her exquisite living room, they drank the thirty-dollar Chardonnay. Bostitch told stories, Thea listened. All the time she was smiling or laughing or pretending shock, she was making mental notes. *He sat with his arm draped on the back of the couch, the front of his jacket open, an invitation to come closer. He slugged down the fine cold wine like soda pop. When it was gone, he reached for the warm sixpack he had brought in with him and flipped one open.*

By that point, Bostitch was telling war stories about the old days when he was in uniform. The good old days. He had worked morning watch, the shift from midnight to seven. He liked being on patrol in the middle of the night because everything that went down at oh-dark-thirty had an edge. After work he and his partners would hit the early opening bars. They would get blasted and take women down to a cul-de-sac under the freeway and screw off the booze before they went home. Not beer, he told her. Hard stuff.

"Your girlfriend would meet you?" Thea asked.

"Girlfriend? Shit no. I'd never take a girlfriend down there.

There are certain women who just wet themselves for a cop in uniform. We'd go, they'd show.''

"I can't imagine," Thea said, wide-eyed, her worldly mien slipping. She couldn't imagine it. She had never had casual sex with anyone. Well, just once actually, with an English professor her freshman year. It had been pretty dull stuff and not worth counting.

"What sort of girls were they?" she asked him.

"All kinds. There was one—she was big, I mean big—we'd go pick her up on the way. She'd say, 'I won't do more than ten of you, and I won't take it in the rear.' She was a secretary or something."

"You made that up," Thea said.

"Swear to God," he said.

"I won't believe you unless you show me," Thea said. She knew where in the book she would use this gem, her raggedy old detective joining the young cowboys in uniform for one last blow out with young women. No. He'd have a young female partner and take her there to shock her. A rite of passage for a rookie female detective.

The problem was, Thea still couldn't visualize it, and she had to get it just right. "Take me to this place."

She knew that Bostitch completely misunderstood that she was only interested for research purposes. Explaining this might not have gotten him up off the couch so fast. They stopped for another bottle on the way—a pint of scotch.

It was just dusk when Bostitch pulled up onto the hard-packed dirt of a vacant lot at the end of the cul-de-sac and parked. A small encampment of homeless people scurried away under the freeway when they recognized the city-issue car.

The cul-de-sac was at the end of a street to nowhere, a despoiled landscape of discarded furniture, cars, and humanity. Even weeds couldn't thrive. She thought humanity wouldn't get past the editor— over drawn—but that was the idea. She would find the right word later.

Bostitch skewed around in his seat to face her.

"We used to have bonfires here," he said. "Until the city got froggy about it. Screwed up traffic on the freeway. All the smoke."

"Spoiled your fun?" she said.

"It would take more than that." He smiled out the window. "One night, my partner talked me into coming out here before the shift was over. It wasn't even daylight yet. Some babe promised to meet him. I sat inside here and wrote reports while they did it on the hood. God, I'll never forget it. I'm working away in my seat with this naked white ass pumping against the windshield in front of my face—bump, bump, bump. Funny as hell. Bet that messed up freeway traffic."

Thea laughed, not at his story, but at her own prose version of it.

"You ever get naked on the hood of the car?" she asked. She'd had enough booze to ask it easily. For research.

"I like it inside better," he said.

"In the car?" she asked. She moved closer, *leaning near enough to smell the beer on his breath. During his twenty-five years with the police, he must have had half the women in the city. She wanted to know what they had taught him. What he might teach her.*

She lapped her tongue lightly along the inner curve of his lips. Thea said, with a throaty chuckle, "I won't do more than ten of you. And I won't take it in the rear."

When he took her in his arms he wasn't as rough as she had hoped he would be. She set the pace by the eager, almost violent way she tore loose his tie, ripped open his shirt. His five-o'clock shadow sanded a layer of skin off her chin.

They ended up in the back seat, their clothes as wrinkled and shredded as the crime scene report under them. At the moment of her ecstasy the heel of Thea's shoe thrust up through the velour headliner. She looked at the long tear. *The sound of the rip was like cymbals crashing at the peak of a symphony, except the only music was the rhythmic grunting and groaning from the tangle of bodies in the back seat. She jammed her foot through the hole, bracing it against the hard metal roof of the car to get some leverage to meet his thrusting, giving him a more solid base to bang against.*

Bostitch seemed to stop breathing altogether. His face grew a dangerous red and drew up into an agonized sort of grimace that stretched every sinew in his neck. Thea was beginning to worry that she might have killed him when he finally exhaled.

"Oh Jesus," he moaned. "Oh sweet, sweet Jesus."

She untangled her foot from the torn headliner and wrapped her bare legs around him, trapping him inside her until the pulsing ceased. Maybe not, she thought. Pulsing, throbbing were definitely overused.

After the afterglow, what would she feel? Not shame or anything akin to it. She smiled with pride in her prowess. She had whipped his ass and left him gasping. Thea buried her face against his chest and bit his small, hard nipple.

"You're amazing," he said, still breathing hard.

She said nothing. That moment was definitely not the time to explain that it was her female detective, Ricky, or maybe Marty Tenwolde, who was amazing. Thea herself was far too inhibited to have initiated the wild sex that had left their automobile nest in serious need of repair.

When they had pulled their clothes back together, he said, "Now what?"

"Skid Row," she said. "I've always been afraid to go down there, but I need to see it for the book I'm working on."

"Good reason to be afraid." *The cop spoke with a different voice than the lover, a deep, weary growl that* something or other. "You don't really want to go down there."

"I do, though. With you. You're armed. You're the law. We'll be safe."

She batted her big, beautiful eyes again. Flattery and some purring were enough to sway him. He drove her downtown to Skid Row.

Thea had never seen anything as squalid and depraved. Toothless, stoned hookers running down the middle of the street. Men dry heaving in the gutter. *The smell alone made him wish she hadn't come along. He was embarrassed that she saw the old wino defecate openly on the sidewalk. But she only smiled that wry smile that always made the front of his slacks feel tight.*

There was a six- or seven-person brawl in progress on one corner. Thea loved it when Bostitch merely honked his horn to make them scatter like so many cockroaches.

"Seen enough?" he asked.

"Yes. Thank you."

Bostitch held her hand all the way back to her house.

"Will you come in?" she asked him.

"I'll come in. But don't expect much more out of my sorry old carcass. I haven't been that fired up since . . ."

"I thought for a minute you had died," she said. "I didn't know where to send the body."

"Felt like I was on my way to heaven." He slid a business card with a gold detective's shield from behind his visor and handed it to her. "You ever need anything, page me through the office."

So, he had a wife. A lot of men do. Thea hadn't considered a wife in the equation. She liked it—nice characterization. Bostitch called home from the phone on Thea's desk and told the wife he'd be out late on a case. Maybe all night.

"No wonder you fool around," Thea said when he turned his attention back to her. "It's too easy. Does your wife believe you?"

He shrugged. "She doesn't much bother anymore believing or not believing."

"Good line," Thea said. More than anything, she wanted to turn on her computer and get some of what she had learned on disk before she forgot anything. She had a whole new vocabulary: boot the door meant to kick it down, elwopp was life without possibility of parole, fifty-one-fifty was a mental incompetent. So many things to catalog.

"Where's your favorite place to make love?" she asked him.

"In a bed."

That's where they did it next. At least, that's where they began. Bostitch was stunned, pleased, by the performance Thea coaxed from him. He gave Thea a whole chapter.

All the next week she was his shadow. She stood beside him during the autopsy of the stabbing victim, professional and detached because female detective Marty Tenwolde would be. The top of the old lady's skull made a pop like a champagne cork when the coroner sawed it off, but she wasn't even startled. She was as tough and gritty as any man on the force. She was tender, too. After a long day of detecting, she took the old guy home and screwed him until he begged for mercy. Detective Tenwolde felt . . .

That feeling stuff was the hard part. Tenwolde would feel attached to her old married partner. Be intrigued by him. She couldn't help mothering him a bit, but she could by no stretch describe her feelings as maternal. Love was going too far.

Thea watched Bostitch testify in court one day. A murder case, but not a particularly interesting one. It was a garden-variety family shootout, drunk husband takes off after estranged wife and her boyfriend. Thea added to her new vocabulary, learning that dead bang meant a case with an almost guaranteed conviction.

Bostitch looked sharper than usual and Thea was impressed by his professionalism. Of course, he winked at her when he thought the jury wasn't looking, checked for her reaction whenever he scored a point against the defense attorney. She always smiled back at him, but she was really more interested in the defendant, a pathetic little man who professed profound grief when he took the stand in his defense. He cried. *Without his wife, he was only a shell occupying space in this universe. His wife had defined his existence, made him complete. Killing her had only been a crude way to kill himself.* If he had any style, he would beg for the death sentence and let the state finish the job for him. Thea wondered what it felt like to lose a loved one in such a violent fashion.

Detective Tenwolde cradled her partner's bleeding head in her lap, knowing he was dying. She pressed her face close to his ear and whispered, "My only regret is I'll never be able to fuck you again, big guy. I love your ragged old ass." Needed something, but it was a good farewell line. Tough, gritty, yet tender.

Out in the corridor after court, the deputy district attorney complimented Bostitch's testimony. Thea, holding his hand, felt proud. No, she thought, she felt lustful. *If he had asked her to, for his reward in getting the kid convicted, she would gladly have blown Bostitch right there on the escalator.* Maybe she did love him. Something to think about.

After court, Thea talked Bostitch into taking her to a Hungarian restaurant he had told her about. He had had a run-in with a lunatic there a year or so earlier. Shot the man dead. Thea wanted to see where.

"There's nothing to see." he said as he pulled into the hillside parking lot. "But the food's okay. Mostly goulash. You know, like stew. We might as well eat."

They walked inside with their arms around each other. The owner knew Bostitch and showed them to a quiet booth in a far-back corner. It was very dark.

"I haven't seen Laszlo's brother for four or five months," the owner said, setting big plates of steaming goulash in front of them. He had a slight accent. "He was plenty mad at you, Bostitch, I tell you. Everybody knows Laszlo was a crazy man, always carrying those guns around. What could you do but shoot him? He shot first. I think maybe his brother is a little nuts, too."

"Show me where he died." Thea said, her lips against Bostitch's jug-like ear. He turned his face to her and kissed her.

"Let's eat and get out of here." he said. "We shouldn't have come."

There was a sudden commotion at the door and a big, fiery-eyed man burst in. The first thing Thea noticed was the shotgun he held at his side. The owner rushed up to him, distracted his attention away from Thea's side of the restaurant.

"Shh, Thea." Bostitch, keeping his eyes on the man with the shotgun, pulled his automatic from his belt holster. "That's Laszlo's brother. Someone must have called him, told him I was here. We're going to slip out the back way while they have him distracted."

"But he has a gun. He'll shoot someone."

"No he won't. He's looking for me. Once I'm out of here, they'll calm him down. Let me get out the door, then you follow me. Whatever you do, don't get close to me, and for chrissake stay quiet. Don't attract his attention." Bostitch slipped out of the booth.

She felt *alive. Adrenaline wakened every primitive instinct for survival. Every instinct to protect her man. If the asshole with the gun made so much as a move toward Bostitch, Tenwolde would grind him into dogmeat. Bostitch was only one step from safety when Tenwolde saw the gunman turn and spot him.*

Dogmeat was good. Thea thought. The rest she was still unclear about. That's when she stood up and screamed, "Dont shoot him. I love him."

Bostitch would have made it out the door, but Thea's outburst caused him to look back. That instant's pause was just long enough for the befuddled gunman to find Bostitch in his sights and fire a double-aught load into his abdomen. Bostitch managed to fire off a round of his own. The gunman was dead before he fell.

Thea ran to Bostitch and caught him as he slid to the floor, leaving a wide red smear on the wall.

His head was heavy in her arms.

"Why?" he sighed. His eyes went dull.

Tenwolde watched the light fade form her partner's eyes, felt his last breath escape from his shattered chest. She couldn't let him see her cry; he'd tease her forever. That's when she lost it. Bostitch had used up his forever.

"It's not fair, big guy." she said, smoothing his sparse hair. She felt a hole open in her chest as big as the gaping wound through his. Without him, she was incomplete. "You promised me one more academy-award fuck. You're not going back on your promise, are you?"

He was gone. Still, she held on to him, her cheek against his, his blood on her lips. "I never told you, Bostitch. I love your raggedy old ass."

His Beard Was Long and Very Black

Stewart Toland

PETER DRAIK had gone west to Arizona. Just another stranger standing on the Pullman step, gaze intent, even anxious in the blazing sunshine, then swinging gently down into people's lives. Not many came to Canotee; it had been six years since any bought land. But Peter took the old Wilsey place. Paid cash. That in itself caused talk.

He hired Mrs. Evett as housekeeper—old Mrs. Evett who had minded everybody's business for sixty years. Afterwards it was a local wonder it had taken her so long to get onto Peter Draik. Almost a whole year.

But that was because he'd always kept that particular closet locked.

The Wilsey place had been on the slow road to ruin, the house sagging in a kind of terrible defeat. Rattlesnakes had made paths in the dust and sand upon the floor; no door would close over warping boards. No man in his right sense would have bought the place. Save it was out of town. Alone. Acres and acres, thick with cacti and quartz rocks and scuttling desert creatures. And a drainage ditch sparkling in the sun. Water.

That was what Peter Draik bought. Water and an Arizona sun. What he did first was to plant sweet peas, row upon row. The seeds vined green, and while he waited for the miracle of their blooming he patched up the old house. He worked until it stood straight and proud again. As proud as Peter Draik.

The town thought him strange, peculiar, even distinguished. His back was so straight, in spite of the slight limp that kept him out of the war. His eyes were clear and gentle, with just a touch of sadness, as though they wanted to smile—and couldn't.

Mrs. Evett was remembering that smile as she traded her last bit of gossip over her ration points at the butcher's on that day almost a year after taking service with Mr. Draik. The day that was to be a milestone in her life, in all the lives in Canotee.

Mrs. Evett swished her skirts and her tongue and when she got back to the old Wilsey place that was now the new Draik place, she found the closet door unlocked. And there wasn't a thing inside. For all the mystery about that door there wasn't a thing inside. But wait— On the shelf, way in the dark of the corner so she could only see it by standing on tiptoe, was a small black bag. She snatched at it. This was Peter Draik's secret.

That he had one she held no doubt. A body couldn't cook three meals a day for a man for almost a year without learning more than that he liked his meat well done and plenty of pepper in the sauce.

There were initials on the bag. G.H. And she knew what it was even before she opened it. A doctor's bag.

There were instruments inside and mustiness and a newspaper crisp and noisy to her touch. It was from far away, a little town in New York State she'd never heard of. There was a man's picture on top. Middling aged he was and handsome, laughing so his eyes were almost tight shut. He had a long black beard. Under the picture were words:

DR. GEORGE HEATHTON, WEALTHY PHYSICIAN FEARED MURDERED. HIS BLOODSTAINED CAR HAS BEEN FOUND. NOTHING ELSE. STATEWIDE SEARCH FOR THE PAUPER HE BEFRIENDED WHO HAS DISAPPEARED. A MENTAL PATIENT NAMED P—

There it was torn, just the letter P, and George Heathton. G.H. Mrs. Evett looked quickly at the initials on the bag, then back at the date on the paper. Five days before Peter Draik had hired her. Peter Draik whose name began with the letter P. Five days, and it took around four to get from New York to Arizona. . . .

Peter Draik saw her coming, stiff and quick, justice with the blindfold gone. And in her anger she was blind to her own danger. She held the bag accusingly, and the paper, and looked to the gun he'd always worn. For potting rattlesnakes he'd said. Indeed!

"You killed him! You killed the man that owned this bag. That's why you're here. You're not an honest farmer nor yet no lunger. You're hiding because you killed him!"

The man just shrugged and smiled, "Yes, I killed him." He went on working with his sweet peas.

He was still there when she got back with the cops. He stood and watched them come through his new green fields and he was glad. It was time. Time and enough. Eight months was too long for a man to lie dead. Murdered.

The police licked their jowls like hungry wolves and Peter Draik didn't keep anything from them. Why bother? The bag did belong to Dr. Heathton. The New York cops had his car, and the bloodstains, and the thin air he'd vanished into, and not in all the months since had they found anything more. Until this bag.

Fingerprints flashed across the continent and Draik's matched some of those found so long ago in the bloody car. He admitted they were his. That much he'd give them. But no more. And he smiled at the handcuffs, at the man getting on the train with him.

"No murder without a corpse. Find the body." That was what he said when he left Canotee.

He said it to all who would listen. Even to Francis Heathton, the murdered man's step-brother. They met in the jail, thick with tobacco and reporters and the lust for drama in men's eyes.

It was Mr. Heathton who did the talking. Hesitant, a bit sadly, he nodded to indicate Peter Draik. "Yes, this is Peter. He was a homeless, no-good when he came to our house six years after the first world war. He had a story to tell. Not many knew, but 'brother' George and I were adopted, unrelated except by the love of the man we learned to call father. It was a very real love, and it was of father that Peter Draik told.

"He had tried to rescue our father from death. The battle of Belleau Woods. He told the story well. We saw and felt every minute of that horror in which men died and some lived. He had father's silver identification tag, with Y.M.C.A. on one side and his number on the other. It had not been hard to get, lying loose in the mud of France, for father's arm had been blown to blood and pulp. The tag was washed clean now. It was something to stare at and feel and to hang thoughtfully from a watch chain.

"After that we kept the stranger, this Peter Draik, year after year in memory of that last day he had shared with Father. A man's last day on earth. It was something to be treasured.

"Then we found he lied.

"That was when my brother George told Peter Draik to go. Told him in threat and wrath. That was the night George's car was found all red and soaked with blood."

Francis Heathton stopped his talking. There was nothing more to say. Silence lay like a thick, black hand over all the staring people in that room. And it was laughing that broke it! Peter Draik's laughing, deep and hearty and strangely contented.

Weeks passed and a million questions and still Peter Draik sat unperturbed in the midst of all the hate.

"No murder without a body."

He always smiled when he said it and the police had come near to breaking his bones, yet they hadn't broken his spirit. There had been no trial, there was no body. He was booked on suspicion merely.

Finally they let him go. It was a beautiful day—a nameless space of time, filled with wide blue sky, and a sun, a living wonder, so warm, so close. That was what Peter thought, standing on the steps of the jail. Almost he had forgotten. The cell window had held such a narrow view, and this was all the world.

By and by he began to walk, slowly at first, pausing by each store window, seeing each thing as though it were new. All of the necessities man had educated himself into needing! In jail one learned a different sort of need. A shirt, a pair of pants, a razor, and a smile now and then.

It was while he was looking at a pink flowered dress that Francis Heathton walked by.

Mr. Heathton stopped short. Stunned. The glistening whiteness that crept up from his neck into the roots of his hair, made him rather terrible to look at. Strange.

He turned and ran, as if already the devil's pitch fork burned deep between his shoulder blades. That was how he came to the jail to tell the story he had so long withheld.

"You had no right to let Peter go! Murder has been done. I can prove it!"

He sobbed the first words and then calmness came, there in the safety of the jail, in the circle of these blue-coated men he had known most all his life.

"I know where the body is." Words trembled, to match the shaking lips. "I saw the murder. I didn't tell before because I wasn't sure who the murderer was. Not at the time. He was just a dim shape that made up a horrible nightmare.

"It was a hot night and I had accompanied my brother on a late call. I'll never forgive myself. I went to sleep, waiting in the back seat. When I awoke, the car had been moved into the country. I looked out and there was my brother lying on the ground, eyes wide and sightless and dead. There was no doubt of it. And the man above him threw a knife away and stooped low and grabbed George's beard—the beard was long and very black—and he pulled him by it, pulled him all down the winding, moon-struck road.

"I followed in the distance, witless with terror. I watched a hole dug beside a large boulder and when the hole was done the killer took a pen knife, slashing at the beard . . . and I turned tail and ran. I'm not proud of that, but my bones had turned to jelly. They had done more than that. They laid in bed for days afterwards beset with fever and delirium."

Francis Heathton twisted and broke the pencil in his hand. Then once again he looked to the listening men.

"Long ago I thought the murderer might be Peter Draik. But I couldn't be sure. And then when he practically confessed, still I wouldn't tell, wouldn't sign a man's death warrant. I thought that, then. For days I've fought with myself, hoping Peter would break. But he hasn't. Now I'm telling, for Peter Draik is free. He will tire of looking in windows, he will remember what I have said of him. He will come to kill me."

Francis Heathton shrugged, licked his lips twice.

"I will show you where the boulder is."

So Peter Draik was sent to the Death House to wait for a certain 15th and midnight. To wonder how many volts there would be. Did a man feel their burning or die first?

The world forgot. Even the jury that convicted him. All save Peter Draik, worrying about his sweet peas in the garden in Co-notee. An old man had come to care for them. A man so old and hungry he didn't mind working for a murderer.

Then the week before the 15th Peter Draik asked the young jailor who brought him his food if he might see the judge who had sentenced him. The judge was kind and fair. He came.

And when he got to the cell door he stood transfixed.

The man inside smiled, and stroked the beard he'd been so many weeks growing. It was short still but very black.

"Come, judge, don't tell me you've forgotten. You've known me since I was little enough to crawl under your fence and steal ap-ples."

"George Heathton! The likeness is amazing!"

"It should be. I am Dr. George Heathton. Though none of you recognized me without my beard. A beard is a strange thing, it so completely molds and masks a face. But then that's why I grew it in the beginning. I looked so ridiculously young when I got out of college, I thought no one would hire me to cure their aches and pains. Remember? Or is it too many years ago. . . ."

The judge was skeptical. "If you are George Heathton why have you masqueraded as Peter Draik? Why did you sit so passively all through your trial? Why wouldn't your own brother know you?"

"But he does. He's known all along who he was sending to the chair." A laugh, grim and sardonic came out of the beard. "I was curious, wondering how far he would go. Now I know. I have only seven days and seven nights to live."

The judge shook the bars in his very vehemence. "You are mad! This can't be so. If it were it would mean Francis Heathton is a fiend!"

"And clever. Don't forget that. Francis is clever."

"Why should he send you to the chair, and if you are George, where is Peter Draik?"

"Dead. Buried under the name of Dr. George. My name. His was the body found beside the boulder. He was the reason I went away to Arizona, the reason I waited eight months and more to find where he lay.

"Come, judge, sit on the cot beside me and let me tell you a bit of the story that hasn't yet been told. You never knew Peter Draik. None of the townspeople did. He was an invalid all the years he lived with us, and never left the comfort of our grounds. If you had known him I wouldn't need to tell you that Peter Draik didn't lie about father. I was never disappointed in Peter. But I was in Francis.

"Francis hated Peter Draik. With each year the hate grew greater. It was because of the affection between Peter and myself, and the money I lavished on Peter. Francis even started counting the mouthfuls Peter ate at the table, to resenting every dime. There was no need, there was money enough for all three, money I earned—for Francis dabbled at painting and made nothing.

"And then one night poor, invalid Peter disappeared. Just like that. Without a trace except for blood all over my car, all over a pair of white ducks stuffed in the laundry. The clothes of Francis.

"There was a terrible argument between us, and the end was nothing. Nothing but blood on Dr. George Heathton's car, and no doctor. Just a vast silence with Francis taking all the estate and living contentedly and the neighbours forgetting to whisper . . . until 'Peter Draik' came from Arizona." The blue eyes smiled.

This last part everyone knows. But there is something that hasn't been told. The little bit before that last, before my car was found, after my argument with Francis.

"I still held the bloodstained trousers, and Francis only laughed. What did they prove? You can't spell murder without a body. He swore an oath and raced wildly into the night and I laid the trousers down and picked up the phone. I'd been very fond of Peter. Maybe I could find a way to spell murder without a body.

"But as I stood there I saw my brother stalking through the trees. That was why he had gone out, to be in the shadows while I was in the light. But there was a moon, and I saw the gun in his hand, and a terrible hate in his face. I laid the receiver back; it would do no good to call the police, we both were bloodstained now, people would say we two had killed together.

"They aren't saying that now, they are saying only one man killed Dr. George. And they are right. But you can't electrocute a man for killing himself. That's what I did, what Dr. George did. I laid the telephone receiver down, picked up my bag and disappeared in the night. I shave my beard and called my Peter Draik and for eight months I waited in Canotee for my nosey housekeeper to find the bag with its so carefully careless and incriminating paper. She was the type to read even in anything; that's why I hired her.

"I was sent home a hunted criminal, and the opportunity was too great for Francis' hating will. That was what I hoped, that in his hate, in his joy at hurting me, he would lead me to the body. It was the only way I'd ever find Peter. Peter Draik's body."

The man with the prison pallor lying thick upon his hands smiled. "I've been waiting ever since the trial, growing this beard, that someone might know me for myself and call me George."

The judge sent for Francis Heathton.

Francis Heathton laughed in their faces. And then he showed them what fools they were, how clever Peter Draik. For it was Peter Draik. He swore it on the bible.

"Yet I can't much blame the man for making this last desperate gamble." Francis Heathton shrugged. "George and Peter were of a near age,"both had blue eyes and black hair, they were of the same build, their fingerprints were jointly all over the car. Peter knew this, and played upon it. They lived so long together, they knew each other's thoughts and habits."

And then for the first time the man in the prison suit lost his composure. He beat upon the table and screamed.

"I am Dr. George! Bring me my bag, and a wound. I will dress it, I will operate. I will prove that I am Dr. George!"

And Francis Heathton laughed, with strange amusement. "You forget, Peter, that we know you are a doctor, too. There are the war records . . . you were in the medical corps. Remember?"

"But the beard! The body found had no beard, no more than normally grows after a man dies. That proves it was Peter Draik."

"It proves that Peter was clever when he cut George's beard off before burying him. I saw you do it, Peter, and you did it just for this. To wriggle out of your own crime."

The listeners, the silent pawns in this game of death, went away, marveling at this brazenness, and another came to shave the beard off the prisoner's face.

A whole morning he sat in his death cell rubbing the smooth shaven skin, then in the afternoon he wrote the governor a letter, quite as calm and strange as Peter himself.

Your Honor:

You probably have read the papers and know my story well. This is to add just a little.

If in your clemency you will go to the records in the soldier's hospital of Montreal, Canada, you will find that Peter Draik laid there for five years after the first world war. There was shrapnel in his lung. They said he would carry it to his grave and bring him an early one. This is why I have been so patient. Perhaps foolish. Men look very much alike behind beards. I'll grant Francis Heathton that, or with the mold in their bones . . . . but if you will again exhume the body found beside the boulder you will find the shrapnel.

Francis didn't know about that. He was never interested in Peter's health. If he heard of it he didn't remember or he would never have disclosed the body with which to railroad me to the chair.

Peter Draik and I had been so similar, I couldn't even claim a specialized knowledge. We were both doctors. Francis could find no loophole, so he sent me down the long road to death. And I took the trip willingly, all this weary way, that Peter Draik's murder might be avenged and he be buried for the last time with all a soldier's honor. Poor Peter, who was so fond of sweet peas.

Sincerely,
George Heathton

There were more letters. Questions—pounding and ceaseless, to break the courage of a Samson. Then they let the man they had known as Peter Draik go back to Arizona where he picked up the threads of his life and his medicine kit and let his beard grow full again. The beard that was long and very black and by which he hadn't been pulled down the winding moonstruck road, except in the fiendish cleverness of his step-brother's mind, Francis Heathton, who died by the will of the State of New York, November 21, 1943 at midnight.

Homesick

Richard T. Chizmar

TIMMY BRADLEY hates his new house.
He hates the slippery, shiny floors and the long, winding hallways and the big fancy rugs. He hates the stupid, ugly paintings on the walls and all the weird looking statues that sit on the furniture. He hates just about everything.

Including the strange way that his father and mother have been acting ever since they moved here. To this house.

He sits alone in his bedroom—lights off, door closed—looking out the window at the darkened city. Crying.

Timmy misses his old house and the way things used to be when they lived there. He misses his friends and Sarah and he even misses his school. But he *especially* misses the way that his father—even though he'd been busy back then, too; after all, his father had been the Governor of Massachusetts for goodness sake—used to take time out to play with him each and every day. That's what they had called it back in those days—"time out." No matter what was going on, his father always found a few minutes to go out for a walk with Timmy or play a card game or watch some television. Sometimes he would even take Timmy along on a short trip when it didn't interfere with school and his mother said it was okay.

None of this happens anymore.

His father is always surrounded by people now. And on those few occasions when he is alone or just with the family, his father is always so quiet and serious. And distant. Nothing at all like the goofball who once danced around Timmy's bedroom with a pair of Jockey shorts on his head or the father who once bounced on his bed so hard that the frame broke and they laid there giggling for what had to be fifteen minutes.

This house has changed him, Timmy thinks.

He moved away from the window. He sits on the edge of his bed and stares at the back of the bedroom door. He is no longer crying.

Timmy knows that his mother is trying to make things better for him. She, too, is much busier now, but *still* she plays with him a lot more often than before and seems intent on kissing him on the cheek at least a hundred times each day. Or at least it feels like a hundred times.

And, of course, once or twice a week she gives him her little speech: "You have to understand, Timmy. Daddy's job was important before, but now he's the President. For the next few years he's going to be very, very busy with real important things. But you'll get used to it here; it's such a beautiful house. It really is . . ."

That is part one of the speech; some days he gets part two; other days, he gets both: ". . . And soon you'll meet new friends and find fun and exciting things to do. You just have to be more patient and remember, we *all* have to make sacrifices. Especially your father. Don't you think he'd rather spend time with us than go to all those stuffy meetings? Of course he would. He misses us too. Just remember, sweetheart, he's the President now, and that's a very big deal . . ."

Timmy almost always comes away from these talks feeling sad and lonely and a little guilty. Jeez. What can you say to all that talk when you're only twelve years old?

Some days—usually on those days when his father smiles at him the way he used to or spends a few extra minutes with him after dinner—Timmy thinks that his mother might be right. That things might turn out okay after all. He thinks this because sometimes if he concentrates long and hard enough, he can remember not being so happy in their old house for those first few weeks after they'd moved in.

Back then, like now, there were so many adjustments to make. All the fancy stuff he wasn't allowed to touch. All the secret service men and the stupid security rules he had to memorize. The stiff, new clothes he had to wear and all the dumb pictures he had to dress up for. And, worst of all, he remembers, all those boring parties he had to go to.

When Timmy thinks back to all those things and how, over time, he'd learned to live with them, he sometimes thinks he is just being a baby. A big, fat crybaby, just like he'd heard his father whisper one night last week when he thought Timmy wasn't listening: "I've *got* to get going now, dear. I'll talk to him later. Besides, he's just being a baby again."

Timmy sits back on his bed and listens to his father call him a baby. *(He's just being a baby again. Being a baby.)* Just thinking about that night hurts his feelings all over again, makes his face red and hot and sweaty. And it also makes him angry.

Who is he to call me a baby, Timmy thinks. *He's* the one who messed everything up. *He's* the one who made us come here in the first place.

Timmy looks up at the picture frame on his dressed at the pretty smiling blond girl in the photo. His stare locks on the wrinkled pink envelope sitting next to it.

Dear Timmy,

I got your letter and the package. Thanks so much; it's sooo beautiful. This letter is so short because I have to eat dinner in a couple of minutes. My mom says I have to stop mooning over you, can you believe that she actually said that, that I was mooning over you. Anyway, she said that I was wrong to promise you that we'd still go steady and she made me go to the dance with Henry Livingston this past weekend. I ended up having a lot of fun. Henry sure can fast dance. Not as much fun as I would have had with you, but what can we do?—you being there and me being stuck back here. Henry asked me to go to the movies with him on Friday and I told him yes. He's a bunch of fun, not like you, but what can we do? So, I guess we're not going steady or anything anymore. My mother's making me show her this letter before I mail it, so she'll know I "broke it off." Sorry. Those are her words, not mine. I miss you, Timmy, and I'll write again soon if my mom lets me. She said she has to think about it. Please write back as soon as you can and don't be mad, okay?

Love, Sarah

P.S. Henry said to say hi and don't be mad at him.

Timmy feels the tears coming and looks away from the picture. But it's too late. He's already crying. Again. Jeez, maybe he is a baby. Maybe his father is right about him after all.

But that doesn't matter now. Timmy no longer cares *what* his father thinks. Besides, he knows this is different than last time. Last time they moved he didn't get sick, he didn't cry, he didn't have nightmares. This time is different, he thinks.

He looks at the bedroom door and wonders what is happening downstairs. He figures it is just a matter of time now. If all goes according to his plan, he'll be back in Massachusetts in time for soccer season. Back holding hands and walking home from school with Sarah. Back playing video games and tag-team and roller-ball with all his friends (except for that back-stabber Henry Livingston).

Timmy looks at the clock on the wall. It is after seven o'clock— Sarah and Henry are probably inside the movie theater by now— and he wonders again why it is still so quiet outside his bedroom.

Just be patient, he thinks. Just like his mother always says, *you have to be more patient, Timmy.* To pass the time, he tried to imagine everything as it happened. Inside his head, he watches himself as he . . .

. . . pours the poison directly into their coffee, careful not to get any on the edge of the cups or on the tray. Then he swirls it around real good with his finger until all the white powder disappears. Finally, he pretends to stretch out on the sofa and read a comic book but he really waits and watches them take their first sips, then tiptoes upstairs to his room.

He looks at the clock again. He can't imagine what's taking so long?

He walks to the window and sits down with his back to the door. He wonders what move Sarah is watching. He thinks of her there in the dark, eating popcorn and sipping soda, Henry's fingers touching her hand. Closing his eyes, he whispers a quick prayer. He asks only that everything goes according to his plan. That soon it will all be over and they will send him home again. Back to Sarah. Back to his friends. Back to his old house.

A few minutes past eight, when he hears the loud, angry voices and the heavy footsteps outside his door, he knows that his prayer has been answered. He is going home.

Hot Justice

Glenn Low

AFTER LINDLEY shot Little John in the back of the head and watched him fall and die, he threw the gun as far as he could. Which was only about fifteen feet.

Not far, but plenty far enough to permit him to skip the gallows.

Anyway, Little John had done such a thorough job of tying him that he had only the use of his hands and wrists.

After he threw away the gun, he worked off Zerl's driving gloves and threw them one at a time toward their owner's corpse. The gloves were leather; if any, their markings would be on the gun. Then he settled his back against the wall of the horse stall to wait.

He had about two hours of waiting ahead of him before the mail carrier would pass out in the road. The barn door was open and Lindley could see when he pulled in and stopped at the mail box. Then he would call to him and the mail carrier would come and cut him loose.

He glanced over at Zerl's feet and saw the satchel with the forty-five thousand dollars in it lying there. All the money Zerl had collected in payment for the coal beneath their three farms! Little John's, Zerl's, and his.

Forty-five thousand in cash! Fifteen thousand of it had been rightfully his, the other two-thirds had belonged, fifty-fifty, to Little John and Zerl. Now it was all his. When the mail carrier came along and cut him loose it was all his.

He glanced at Little John, then quickly turned his eyes elsewhere. Little John's tiny face was turned toward him, blood-streaked, eyes wide, a miserable grin spreading it. The grin was apologetic, as if left as a plea for forgiveness.

"He was glad enough to double-cross Zerl, the little louse," Lindley told himself. "After the agreement was drawn stating the money was to be divided amongst the living in case one of us died, he was mighty glad to hear about my plan. He never stopped to think that the same agreement states that if two of us died the one left living was to have all the money."

Lindley's big, pink face wrinkled in a satisfied grin. He looked at Zerl, lying in the big splotch of sunlight from the barn window. There was nothing revolting about Zerl in death. He lay sprawled on the straw of the barn floor, his face buried in the dry litter, one arm out-flung, the other bent beneath him. His glasses, powerful and thick of lens to suit his weak eyes, were beside him, setting nose-wise on a dry corn cob. His hat stood brim down at the side of his face.

Lindley had told Little John: "You tie me to the stall wall boards, lacing the cords through the cracks. Tie my arms flat to the boards, but leave my hands and wrists free. Tie me so the mail carrier will know I couldn't have tied myself. Then you go home. I'll come after you as soon as I can. It'll be as easy as rolling off a log, and with Zerl dead and out of the deal it'll mean seven thousand five-hundred extra for each of us."

Lindley and Little John had been in the barn when Zerl drove up and parked his car out front. Lindley called to him.

"We're here in the barn."

Zerl waved, then quickly climbed the bank from the road, wading through the snow of the barn-lot.

"How'd it go?" Lindley had asked as Zerl entered the barn. And Little John said: "Did they pay in cash so we can divide it?"

"Yes," Zerl said. He opened the satchel and showed them the money.

Then Lindley shot him, using a gun he'd borrowed from Little John. He'd meant to shoot him from the first, since the three of them pooled the coal acreage beneath their farms, which adjoined, and drawn up the agreement.

Zerl had gone to town that morning to meet the coal company's purchasing agent at the bank. He had power of attorney to act for Little John and Lindley, and now the deal was closed.

It was part of Lindley's plan that Zerl should die slowly, so he shot him in the stomach. Then he and Little John held him until he died.

After Lindley had slipped on Zerl's driving gloves and wiped the gun clean of fingerprints, he sat down on the barn floor with his back to the wall of the horse stall, and Little John tied him.

"Tell me again," Little John said, straightening up from making fast the last knot, "how is it you've planned to tell the sheriff what happened?"

Lindley lied glibly. "All right, I'll tell him Zerl came here after you left. They'll see your tracks in the snow and know you've been here. I'll say he pulled a gun on me and forced me to sit down here, then tied me. I'll tell them that he meant to set fire to the barn, kill me like that, so he could keep my share of the money. But while he was tying my wrist I managed to grab his gun. Then I shot him. See, it's a story that'll stick. It has to stick, because I'll be sitting here tied fast when the mail carrier comes along, and I'll have the gun in my hand."

Lindley knew the story wouldn't satisfy the sheriff. The sheriff would want to know more about Little John's tracks coming to and leaving the barn, he'd want to know why Little John's gun had been used, and he'd go after Little John to find out. And Lindley knew that Little John would never bear up under severe questioning, that he'd crack. That was why, when Little John turned to leave the barn, he shot him in the back of the head and then threw away the gun and the driving gloves.

Besides the play had stood to earn him seven thousand five-hundred dollars.

He had a better tale to tell now, one that would stick. He'd tell the sheriff that Little John and Zerl had planned to murder him by tying him to the horse stall, then setting fire to the barn, but had gotten into an argument and Little John shot Zerl. Zerl, though, had been smart, and when Little John had leaned over him to make sure he was dead he'd snatched the gun and shot Little John. Shot him after Little John had turned and was running from the barn. Afterwards Zerl had died. The location of Zerl's wound would clinch his story.

A gloating expression filled his eyes as he gazed at the satchel lying in the straw. Forty-five thousand dollars! All his! And the getting of it had been as easy as rolling off a log.

He glanced skyward through the barn door, finding the position of the sun. In a few minutes it would be noon, then the mail carrier would be along, and then—

Suddenly the thoughts slipping through his brain stopped. His big nose wrinkled as he lifted his head and sniffed. "Smoke?" he said, speaking aloud, his voice tight. "Smoke—"

Then he saw it, trailing up in a thin wisp from around Zerl's glasses, centering a blue point in the dry straw. Horrified, he watched the smoke lift in a small white finger toward the mow—the mow that contained tons of ripe, dry straw.

A minute later his wildly fascinated eyes saw the first tiny flame leap up. It was a small yellow and purple flame, seeming happy to be alive, thankful to be born, flicking merrily around the strong spectacles lens that had engendered it, that had created it by bringing the sunlight in a small round red spot to the bosom of the dry straw.

. . . When the mail carrier drove up and stopped, the barn was in smoking ruins. The tracks in the snow across the barn-lot showed him that three men had gone into the barn, and that none of them had come out.

Hound of Justice

Thomas A. Hoge

A MIDDAY SUN beat down upon the thin roof of the Homestake Mining Office with broiling intensity. Yet the sallow-faced man seated inside shivered slightly as he turned up the collar of his linen coat.

The sound of a clock clacking off the minutes seemed to fill the heat-parched room like the throb of a tom-tom. The clerk looked at it and bit his lips. It was two minutes to noon. In approximately two minutes he would remove his linen coat, lock up the office and walk out to murder a man.

His gaze shifted to the window. He remained motionless, staring. Suddenly he stiffened. Through the shimmering haze of heat he could see a dark blob against the sunlight. It was the figure of a man walking toward the forest.

The clerk looked at the clock again and checked the time with his wrist-watch. With a nod he removed his coat. Before he closed the drawer he took out an object wrapped in a handkerchief. It was a revolver. He placed it gingerly in his pocket.

Locking the door, he looked about him briefly, then strode off in the direction the other man had taken. He wasn't shivering any more.

When he reached the cool of the forest, the sallow-faced man slowed his pace. He looked at the tangled mass of foliage and cursed softly. Taking a tiny compass from his pocket, he struck out through the brush.

After he had walked for about ten minutes he paused, listening. There was a crackling sound ahead of him. He moved forward several steps. The noise stopped.

"Who's there?" a startled voice called out.

The clerk smiled slightly. "It's me, Sanford. I wanted to see you, Mr. Jargin."

The bushes were separated and a tall, heavy-set man stepped into the clearing. He had a rugged, firm face that contrasted vividly with the pasty features of the other.

"What are you doing here, Sanford?" he demanded. "Never knew you went in for hunting."

"I don't. I came out here to speak to you, sir."

Jargin shrugged impatiently. "I don't see why you have to trail me with some business matter while I'm out hunting. You had all week to do that. Well, out with it, man. What's on your mind?"

"It's nothing to do with business. I wanted to speak to you about your daughter."

The older man's eyes narrowed slightly, but his voice was softer when he answered.

"What did you want to ask me?"

The sallow-faced man spoke slowly, weighing his words.

"As you know," he said, "I was engaged to Marylin for nearly a year. We were both happy then."

The older man nodded. "I know, son. She did care for you. She still does, but—"

"But she's going to marry that fool, Craddock; marry an empty-headed trapper whose only distinction is the fact that he can shoot a tin-can off a post. Is that what you were going to say?"

Jargin walked over and patted the other on the shoulder. "I didn't know you'd take it that way, Sanford," he said, his deep voice sympathetic. "You've got a good mind and a fine future ahead of you. But Marylin—well, she's different. She's an outdoor type and she kind of felt she'd be a good bit happier with a fellow like Craddock. He may not be a business man, but he's a good, honest worker, and I figure he could handle the men in the mine with a little training. But, hell, I'm sorry you took it so hard, lad."

The other took a step back, his voice tense. "So you plan to leave the mine to Marylin, and have this chump Craddock in charge after you die, is that it? And, if I stay here, I'll be working under him?"

Jargin frowned. "Now look here, Sanford, I understand how you feel, but don't carry it too far. What I do with the mine is strictly my business. Whoever I leave in charge now, or after I die, is none of your concern. You're hired to do the bookkeeping and if you don't like the atmosphere, you can go somewhere else. Is that clear?"

Sanford, instead of showing anger began to smile. "Perfectly clear, Mr. Jargin," he murmured. "I only wanted to make sure how things stood."

He pulled the revolver from his pocket and fired two bullets into the other's chest.

The heat of the evening was even more oppressive than it had been during the day. Its torrid breath wafted into the sheriff's office and lay like a pall over the little group seated within.

In the far corner a slim, blonde girl sat weeping softly into her handkerchief. Occasionally she would turn and glance tearfully at the stalwart youth on her right. With clumsy fingers he attempted to pat her shoulder. There was something almost dog-like in Ted Craddock's devotion.

Next to them sat the sallow-faced man called Sanford. His head was bowed in an attitude of grief.

Through the window came the sultry drone of a locust.

The only person in the room whose face seemed untouched by sorrow was the sheriff. Wiping a handkerchief across his florid, sweat-beaded features, he cleared his throat and turned to the others.

"Well, folks, I'm mighty sorry to have to question you so soon after the death, 'specially you, Miss Jargin, but it's got to be cleared up. Let's see. Guess I'll start with you first, if you don't mind. Did your father go hunting pretty regular?"

"Why, yes." There was a puzzled frown on the girl's tear-stained face. "You used to go with him often, didn't you?"

"I know," the sheriff coughed. "I just wanted to keep the record straight. Now that would mean that anyone who knew his habits would have a pretty good idea that on Saturday around noon he'd trek off through the brush, right?"

The girl nodded.

"Fine. Now you, Sanford." He turned to the clerk. "Your office is located so that you could see Mr. Jargin on his way to the woods. Isn't that so?"

Sanford nodded his head in assent.

"All right. Then suppose you tell us what happened today."

The clerk paused a moment, his eyes closed.

"Well about noon I was locking up to go out to lunch. I happened to look out of the window and saw Mr. Jargin walking towards the forest with his gun."

"Was he alone?"

Sanford hesitated. "Well, not exactly. A few minutes after he passed into the brush another man crossed the field in the same direction. He wasn't carrying a rifle. I got the impression he was following Mr. Jargin.

"I didn't think much about it at the time, but when Mr. Jargin didn't return during the afternoon, I began to worry. When night fell I notified you to send a posse out. You know the rest."

"Any idea who this second man was? The one who followed Jargin?"

Sanford looked confused. "Well, if you don't mind, sheriff, I'd rather not answer that. When I saw the man, I thought I recognized him, but I couldn't be sure, the distance was so great. Now, since there is a murder involved, I'd hate to cast unjust suspicion on anyone."

"Well spoken, my lad," said the sheriff. "You may have to talk later on, but for the present we'll skip it. Now then, let's have a look at the gun." Reaching in his desk, he drew out a black wooden box. Inside lay the revolver.

"This is the gun we found next to the body. The bullet checked with those that did the killin'. I took the trouble to trace the serial number, too." His pudgy finger shot out with surprising speed. "It's yours, Craddock!"

"What's that?" The brawny youth leaped to his feet in amazement. "That's impossible! My gun's in my cabin. It's got my initials carved on the butt."

"Got your initials, eh?" The sheriff gingerly removed a strip of green felt from the handle of the revolver. "So it has—T. C. stands for Ted Craddock, don't it?"

"Let me see." The youth stepped forward and stared at the gun. His shoulders sagged as he drew back.

"It's my gun, all right," he said dully. "But I had nothing to do with his murder. I swear it."

"It's ridiculous." The girl stood up, her eyes flashing. "Ted would never do such—such a horrible thing."

"Now, Miss," said the sheriff soothingly, "don't get yourself all riled. I'm only doing what I can to clear this thing up." He turned to Sanford. "Is this the man you thought you saw walking towards the forest this morning?"

The clerk nodded. "Yes. I hated to tell you, because I wasn't sure. But in the light of this evidence, I guess it's my duty to admit it."

"I was nowhere near the woods this morning," said Craddock desperately. "Sanford has mistaken me for someone else, that's all. Anyway, why in God's name would I want to murder the man who has been so decent to me—a man whose daughter I'm going to marry?"

"Because you stand to gain more by murdering him than anyone except one other person," retorted the sheriff. "He's willed everything to his daughter, so if you marry her, that makes you a pretty rich man. There've been killin's for less than that."

Craddock sank back into his chair, his face grey. "I tell you I didn't do it," he muttered brokenly. "Someone must have stolen my gun and left it there so that I'd look like the guilty one."

Sanford cleared his throat. "If you don't mind my interrupting, Sheriff, there might be something in what Craddock says. Now, if someone did use the gun, the fingerprints would be fresher there than Craddock's. Why not make a test?"

The sheriff scratched his chin. "That's a mighty sensible suggestion, Sanford. Only thing is, I never took a leap of stock in fingerprints. Too easy to cover 'em up by wearing gloves. I think I got a better idea. I have a hound bitch out in back that's supposed to be the best tracker in the county. She's plumb uncanny on picking up a scent.

"Now you take this gun here. If Craddock hasn't used it for a couple of days, like he says, his scent is dead. I put it in a box when I brought it back from the woods, so my smell wouldn't make no difference.

"But whoever killed Jargin had that gun in his hand for some time. He might've used gloves, but when a body commits murder,

I'm told his hands sweat considerable, so there'd be enough odor for old Trixie to get it. How about it, Craddock, are you willin' to sit there while she tracks the scent on that gun?"

Craddock nodded promptly. "Certainly. I haven't touched it in over a week."

Sanford frowned. "Just a moment, Sheriff. Isn't this a bit fantastic? How is a dog to show whether Craddock committed this murder or not? It isn't fair to him or the rest of us. Supposing the animal took a fancy to Miss Jargin or myself. Are we to be proven murderers because it runs toward us?"

"Now just hold your horses, young feller. Don't have no fear about that. When Trixie is on a trail, she don't pay no attention to nobody. Now then. Let's see. I'd better sit you further apart so there won't be no confusion in your scents."

He walked over to Sanford and placed a hand on his shoulder. "You just move your seat to the other end of the room, please. You, Craddock, stay where you are. You, Craddock, stay where you are. You sit down at the other end, Miss Jargin. I'll get the dog."

Opening the door he gave a low whistle. There was a bark and a spotted hound loped into the room.

Walking over to his desk, the sheriff picked up the revolver by the snout and held it toward the dog. "Take a good sniff, old girl" he muttered softly.

The animal nuzzled the butt of the revolver.

"Go get it, girl!" The sheriff gave her a push.

With a bark, the animal wheeled and began to sniff about the floor.

A tenseness pervaded the chamber as the group leaned forward and stared at the intent dog. Outside, the drone of the locust seemed to grow deafening.

Oblivious to the attention she was receiving, the hound padded across the room, her nose nearly touching the rug.

Suddenly, she raised her head and sniffed. With a yelp she leaped toward Sanford, pawing at his coat and barking excitedly.

"Well," said the sheriff, "seems like our test wasn't such a flop after all, don't it, Sanford?"

The other leaped to his feet, his sallow face livid. "You crazy fool, you don't think you've proved anything, by that, do you?" He kicked at the dog, but the animal backed away barking shrilly.

"It's enough for a start, Sanford," said the sheriff. "Now that we know who's guilty, it'll be much easier getting what evidence we need. You recollect I said there was one person stood to gain more than Craddock by killing Mr. Jargin. That's you. You were engaged to his daughter once. With Craddock hung for murder you figgered you might win her back and get a fortune in the bargain. It won't be much trouble showing a jury where you stand."

The other stared about him wildly, then snatching a gun from his pocket, began to back towards the open window.

"There won't be any jury," he snarled. "There's a drain pipe outside this window. I'm going to slide down it and get my car. Anyone who tries to stop me will get shot."

He swung one foot over the sill, slowly fanning the room with his gun. As he started to raise the other leg, there was a sharp report from the outside. Sanford's body taunted, then went limp. I swayed once and slid over the sill out of sight. A thud sounded below.

"That was Jackson, my deputy," muttered the sheriff. "Damn good man."

Marylin Jargin grasped Craddock's arm with a shudder. "Then you suspected—"

"Right from the start, Miss," said the sheriff. "For one thing, Craddock here is a crack shot. It ain't like he'd plug a man in the chest, even if he was a killer. He'd have too much pride in his marksmanship for that.

"Then I noticed a hunk of grey clay stuck to the instep of Sandord's shoe. You can find that kind of dirt out in the woods, but not in no office. So I figgered I knew who the guilty man was, but to prove it was somethin' else again."

"Your dog did that for you, eh?" chuckled Craddock leaning over to pat the animal. "I've seen smart trackers, but that beats anything in my experience."

"I guess it does," smiled the sheriff. "No hound could pick a scent that way. I figgered Sanford wouldn't know that, but I was afraid a woodsman like yourself might catch on and give it away."

"What do you mean?"

"Well it was just a little trick of mine. You see, Trixie's crazy about cinnamon candy. I play a little game with her every night. hiding' a hunk and makin' her find it. Just before I brought her in tonight, I rubbed a little cinnamon on the gun."

"But now about Sanford; why would the dog pick him out?" asked Craddock.

The sheriff chuckled. "Remember when I walked over to Sanford, put my hand on his shoulder and asked him to move his chair
so's not to confuse the scents?"

"Yes."

"Well, at the same time I dropped a hunk of cinnamon in his
pocket. Trixie went for it like a homin' pigeon!"

I Could Kill You!

Judith Merril

ACROSS THE PIN-POINTS of light reflected on the dark water,
across from the deeper darkness that was the shore, came
the whispered sibilance of the leaves, murmuring resistance
to the stirring night air. From another canoe—out of sight on the
rippling black lake—came the wailing melody of a mournful banjo.
Leaning back against the thwart, Irene shook loose the heavy
weight of her hair, suffocating on her face and throat in the hot
night.

"Moon trail," Jared said. Irene opened her eyes a little—enough
to follow his to where the line of shimmering light from the moon
danced along the water. But he was not looking out across the lake.
He was watching the flood of light hair, not feeling the coolness
against her neck, as she did; the silver-gold of the moon reflected to
him in challenge when she threw back her head.

Irene laughed, a husky laughter meant to offer acceptance to
admiration. She was used to this; she knew how to do it. Her body
knew how to move; her throat could laugh; she could talk and look
at a man as she should—while inside, always, she lived her own
separate existence.

Now as she laughed to please him, to let Jared know she had
heard his words and understood them, she was thinking, *I hate him.*

She was surprised at the surge of pure emotion that welled up in
her; revulsion was no longer within her power to control, but had
become a thing she felt, lived, and breathed, with her whole body.
It would pass, she knew, and she would be able to go on. She was
Jared's wife, Irene; but just for that moment she was sitting there,
thinking: *He is fat and stupid and I hate him.*

She laughed again, making it sound like a laugh of pleasure as he put down the paddle and lowered himself to the floor of the canoe. *He would kill me if he knew. If he knew how I hate him right now he would kill me.*

It was just a phrase, a way of saying something, but as she thought the words, they came alive, and a thrill of awakening passed through her body. She hated him, and all his desire for her could never move her—but this thought that he might kill *her*, that he might hate her, too—it could move her, if she could believe it.

His hand, reaching for her in the shadow along the floor of the canoe, let her know it was not so. He did not hate her; he had never suspected her own hate. She was his wife. She belonged to him, and he liked to remind her of it. Now he found her leg, stretched bare and brown along the flooring, and he tightened his hand, passionless but firmly possessive, about her ankle.

The strange thing was that the words were alive. Still alive. She wondered for a moment if she had spoken them aloud, they rang so clear in her ears. *I hate him . . . He would kill me.*

"Darling," she murmured, and her voice held promise and caress. His fingers tightened again; the boat rocked as he reached out cautiously, moving his large bulk slowly in the fragile vessel, until he was stretched out, his head in her lap. She let her fingers play idly through his thick hair, waiting for the boat to stop swaying, for the universe to stand still, for her own hatred to drain out of her.

And still the words were alive. She ran her hand down his face, across his neck, felt him shiver at the touch of her fingertips, and thought, *Kill me . . . kill me . . . kill . . . kill!*

She could kill him.

She had never thought of that before . . . not when she was awake. She had dreamed it, but he was so much bigger, stronger, bulwarked by his money, his size, his servants—by all the things that made a man stronger than a woman.

She had never seen before so clearly that she could do it. Now she knew she could, and with the knowledge came purpose. She was Jared's wife; she had lived with him for eight years. Now, surely, she deserved to be Jared's widow, with all that would mean. It would be easy to do.

She looked down, and even in the darkness of late evening, she could see his face, only a little way below. The tight little curls, still damp with hat—the absurdly-vigorous way his hair sprung out of his scalp, as if denying that the mind below it was already dead. The large face, in the last years becoming gross with good living and inactivity. The chin, doubled into the flesh over his collarbone; the heavy sports shirt open at the neck, a few strongly curling black hairs showing above the triangular neckline.

The outline of his body was indistinct, looming large, away from her—and powerless. Jared couldn't swim.

The words in her mind were more alive than ever, but now they went the other way round. *I hate him . . . I can kill him . . . now.* Maybe never again, but now, she could. She could tip the canoe and hold on to him tight, hold on till his own grasp weakened, under the water. She could cling to the canoe for support, and wait till she was sure beyond any last shred of doubt . . . then scream. She could scream and scream; by the time help came, she would be the wealthy widow of Jared, who had drowned by accident.

She moved her hand lightly again through the wiry curls, wondering that he could lie in her lap, with her hand already upon him—not far from where it would hold him, would hold his neck, while she killed him. He would lie like that and never know what she thought. He was stupid and fat and too rich; he did not deserve to live.

"You're very beautiful, Irene." She glanced down again, and saw that he had been looking up at her face. Again she laughed, this time in pure exultation. It was natural enough to him. She loved to be worshipped, to be told of her beauty. He knew that. He repeated, "You're very beautiful; you love me, don't you, Irene?"

"Foolish!" she said lightly, the words coming easily, the lie she had told for years now, and need never tell again, after this night. "Of course, Jared."

"I would know if you didn't," he said. He spoke heavily, as always. Jared did nothing lightly. "I would certainly know, Irene. If you did not love me; if it was only for what I can give you, you . . ." he paused, then went on as heavily, each word weighted with its full content. "You would do better to tell me."

This would be the last time—the last time he would doubt her, the last time she would lie. She bent over him, her hands running down, her fingers cupping his face, dropping around his throat, light and loving. "Foolish darling," she said, and as she bent, she let the boat rock a little.

* * *

She dropped a kiss on his forehead, and the boat rocked again, a little more. This would be easy.

His arm came up to touch her hair, now falling forward over her face, its scented weight hanging close to him. "I know what you feel, my beautiful Irene," Jared said. "I know; of course I know. I am not so foolish."

She sighed a little, smiled into his eyes, let him see the love and trust in hers. She swayed her head, let her hair brush teasing across his face, let the boat rock a little more. *He knew!* He knew only what his fat, stupid mind told him; he knew only what he wished to know.

She lifted her head, and the canoe swayed once more, harder. One quick motion, and it had gone too far. Water pulsed over the side; the world tipped to a crazy angle, the black water changed places with the darkness of the air—and she never forgot to keep her hands tight on his throat.

They bobbed up together, and she kicked out, viciously, reaching with one hand for the side of the canoe, holding to him with the other.

Her free hand found the canoe, grabbed it, and held. The kick pushed him back under. But as her leg shot out, pain tore at her scalp. Her hair—the long moon-gold hair . . . she was going down. Then, still holding to the canoe with one hand, she was shooting past the grin on his face, under water.

She used all her strength to kick back, up against the agony in her scalp, the ripping, impossible pain, where one hand of his held her hair too far below water. But for just a moment she was up again where breath filled her screaming, thirsting lungs. For just long enough to hear him say, "I know, Irene. Everything you think, I know. Always." His big arm, the fat arm, now showed its ridged muscle, the soft hand clenched for life itself around the edge of the canoe. She opened her mouth to scream. Fire pulled at the roots of her hair, and water rushed into her open mouth. She heard the scream, but it was not hers. It was wrong: a man's voice, Jared's deep voice bellowing across the water, "Help!"

Her scalp was on fire, and she saw nothing but the wet blackness. Then merciful cool water came to quench the flaming pain.

Johnny Halloween

Norman Partridge

I SHOULD HAVE never been there.

Number one: I was off duty. Number two: even though I'm the sheriff, I believe in letting my people earn their pay. In other words, I don't follow them around with a big roll of toilet paper waiting to wipe their asses for them, even when it comes to murder cases. And number three: I'm a very sound sleeper—generally speaking, you've got a better chance of finding Elvis Presley alive than you've got of waking me between midnight and six.

But it was Halloween, and the kids next door were having a loud party, and I couldn't sleep. Sure, I could have broken up the party, but I didn't. I'm a good neighbor. I like to hear the sound of kids having fun, even if I think the music we listened to back in the fifties was a lot easier on the ears. So I'm not sour on teenagers, like some cops. Probably has something to do with the fact that Helen and I never had any kids of our own.

It just didn't work out for us, is all. When Helen had the abortion, we were young and stupid and we figured we'd have plenty of chances later on. That wasn't the way it worked out, though. I guess timing is everything. The moment passes, things change, and the life you thought you'd have isn't there when you catch up to it.

What it is, is you get older. You change and you don't even notice it. You think you're making the decisions, but mostly life is making them for you. You're just along for the ride. Reacting, not acting. Most of the time you're just trying to make it through another day.

That's how most cops see it. Like my deputies say: shit happens. And then we come along and clean up the mess.

I guess maybe I do carry around that big roll of toilet paper, after all.

So, anyway, Helen had asked me to get another six-pack and some chips. She does like her Doritos. It was hot, especially for late October, and a few more beers sounded like a good idea. I worry about Helen drinking so much, but it's like the kid thing. We just don't talk about it anymore. What I usually do is drink right along with her, and then I don't feel so bad.

So I was headed up Canyon, fully intending to go to the Ralphs Supermarket on Arroyo, when I observed some suspicious activity at the old liquor store on the corner of Orchard and Canyon (if you want it in *cop-ese*).

Suspicious isn't the word for it. A couple of Mexican girls were coming out of the place. One was balancing a stack of cigarette cartons that was so high she couldn't see over it. The other had a couple of plastic sacks that looked to be filled with liquor bottles.

I pulled into the lot, tires squealing. The girl with the liquor bottles had pretty good instincts, because she dropped them and rabbited. The strong smell of tequila and rum hit me as I jumped out of the truck—a less sober-hearted man would have thought he'd died and gone to heaven. Me, I had other things on my mind.

The girl with the cigarettes hadn't gotten too far. She didn't want to give up her booty. Cartons were slipping and sliding and she looked like a drunken trapeze artist about to take the big dive, but she was holding tough.

Tackling her didn't seem like the best idea, but I sure didn't want to let her work up any steam. I'm not as fast as I used to be. So what I did was I grabbed for her hair, which was long enough to brush her ass when she wasn't running and it wasn't streaming out behind her. I got a good grip first try; her feet went out from under her, she shrieked like a starlet in a horror movie who's about to taste chainsaw, the smokes went flying every which way, and it was just damn lucky for me that she wasn't wearing a wig.

"It wasn't me!" she said, trying to fight. "I didn't do it! It was some guy wearing a mask!"

"Yeah, right. And you've got a receipt for these cigarettes in your back pocket. Sorry . . . got you red-handed, little miss."

I hustled her across the lot, stomping cigarette cartons as I went. That gave me a kick. God, I hate smokers. We went inside the store, and that's when I saw what she'd meant when she said she hadn't done anything.

The kid was no more than twenty, and—like the old saying goes—he'd never see twenty-one. He lay on the floor, a pool of dark blood around the hole in his head.

"We saw the guy who did it," the girl said, eager to please, *real* eager to get my fingers out of her hair. "He cleaned out the register. He was wearing a mask . . ."

Dead eyes stared up at me. My right boot toed the shore of a sea of blood. Already drying, going from red to a hard black on the yellow linoleum. Going down, the clerk had tripped over a stack of newspapers, and they were scattered everywhere. My face was on the front page of every paper, ten or twenty little faces, most of them splattered with blood.

". . . a Halloween mask," she continued. "A pumpkin with a big black grin. We weren't with him. We pulled in after it was over, but we saw him leaving. I think he was driving an El Camino. It was silver, and it had those tires that have the chrome spokes. We were gonna call you before we left, honest. We figured the clerk was already dead, and that we'd just take what we wanted and—"

"Let it lay." I finished it for her, and she had the common decency to keep her mouth shut.

I just stood there for a minute, looking at the dead kid. It was like looking at myself thirty years ago. Like that poem about roads not taken. I almost envied him. Then I couldn't see him anymore—I saw myself at eighteen, so I looked away.

At the papers, at my smiling face.

At the headline: HERO RESCUES BABY FROM WELL.

Some hero. A grinning idiot with blood on his face.

The Mexican girl couldn't wait anymore. She'd run out of common decency and was starting to worry about herself again.

She opened her mouth.

I slapped her before she could say anything stupid.

My fingers striking hard against her tattooed tears.

"The other girl got away," I said. "I'll bet she had the gun. Long black hair, about five-six, maybe a hundred pounds. Maybe a little more . . . it's hard to tell with those baggy jackets they wear. Anyway, she probably tossed the weapon. We'll beat the bushes on Orchard. That can wait until tomorrow, though."

Kat Gonzalez nodded, scribbling furiously. She was one of ten deputies who worked under me, and she was the best of the lot.

"I'm leaving this in your hands, Kat. I mean to tell you, I'm all out." I wanted to take a six-pack from the cooler, but I resisted the temptation. "I'm going home."

Kat stopped me with a hand on my shoulder. "Sheriff . . . Hell, Dutch, I know what happened here when you were a kid. This must feel pretty weird. But don't let it eat at you. Don't—"

I waved her off before she could get started. "I know."

"If you need to talk—"

"Thanks." I said it with my back to her, and the only reason it came out okay was that I was already out the door.

I stomped a few more cigarette cartons getting to my truck, but it didn't make me feel any better. The night air was still heavy with the aroma of tequila and rum, only now it was mixed with other less appealing parking lot odors.

Burnt motor oil. Dirt. Piss.

Even so, it didn't smell bad, and that didn't do me any good.

Because it made me want something a hell of a lot stronger than beer.

I drove to Ralph's and bought the biggest bottle of tequila they had.

I was eighteen years old when I shot my first man.

Well, he wasn't a man, exactly. He was seventeen. And he was my brother.

Willie died on Halloween night in 1959. He was wearing a rubber skull mask that glowed in the dark, and "Endless Sleep" was playing on the radio when I shot him. He'd shown up at the store on the corner of Canyon and Orchard—it was a little mom-and-pop joint back then. With him was another boy, Johnny Halowenski, also wearing a mask.

A pumpkin face with a big black grin.

They showed up on that warm night in 1959 wanting money. The store had been robbed three times in the last two months, each time during my shift. The boss had said I'd lose my job if it happened again. I'd hidden my dad's .38 under the counter, and the two bandits didn't know about it.

Skullface asked for the money. I shot him instead. I didn't kill him, though. Not at first. He had enough spit left in him to come over the counter after me. I had to shoot him two more times before he dropped.

By then Pumpkinface had gotten away. I came out of the store just in time to see his Chevy burning rubber down Orchard, heading for the outskirts of town. There wasn't any question about who he was. No question at all. I got off a couple more shots, but none of them were lucky.

I went inside and peeled off the dead bandit's skull mask. I sat there stroking my brother's hair, hating myself, crying.

Then I got myself together and called the sheriff's office.

When the deputies arrived, I told them about Johnny Halowen-ski. I didn't know what else to do. They recognized the name. L. A. juvie had warned them about him. Johnny had steered clear of trouble since moving to our town, and the deputies had been willing to go along with that and give him a break.

But trouble had caught up with Johnny Halowenski in a big way.

I knew that, and I laid it on. My dad had been a deputy before he got too friendly with the whiskey bottle, and I knew it was important to get things right, to make sure that Halowenski wouldn't be able to get away with anything if the cops caught up to him.

I told the deputies that Halowenski was armed and dangerous.

I told the deputies that Halowenski took off his mask as he climbed into the Chevy, that there could be no mistake about his identity.

Everything I said ended up in the papers. There were headlines from Los Angeles to San Francisco about the Halloween murder/robbery at a liquor store near the border and the ensuing manhunt.

One paper mentioned that the suspect's nickname was Johnny Halloween. After that I never saw it any other way. Almost every year I'd see it a few times. In FBI wanted posters. In cheap magazines that ran stories about unsolved crimes. And, on Halloween, I could always count on it turning up in the local papers.

Johnny Halloween. I leaned back against my brother's granite tombstone and stared up at the night sky, trying to pick out the name in the bright stars above.

Drinking tequila, thinking how I'd never seen that name where I wanted to.

On a tombstone.

I knew he'd show up sooner or later, because we always met in the cemetery after the robberies.

Johnny came across the grass slow and easy, his pistol tucked under his belt, like the last thing in the world he wanted to do was startle me. I tossed him the bottle when he got near enough. "Let's drink it down to the worm," I said.

He didn't take a drink, though. He would have had to lift his mask, and he didn't seem to want to do that, either.

"Miss me?" he asked, laughing, and his laughter was bottled up inside the mask, like it couldn't quite find its way out of him.

"It's been a while," I said. "But not long enough to suit me."

He tossed me a thin bundle of bills. "Here's your cut. It's the usual third. I don't figure you've still got my dough from the last job. If I could collect interest on it, it might amount to something."

I didn't say anything to that. I didn't want to rise to the bait.

"Well, hell . . . it's good to see you too, Dutch. The old town hasn't changed all that much in thirty years. I went by my daddy's house, and damned if he isn't still driving that same old truck. Babyshit brown Ford with tires just as bald as he is. Seventy-five years old and still drives like a bat out of hell, I'll bet. How about your daddy? He still alive?"

I pointed two graves over.

"Yeah, well . . . I bet you didn't shed too many tears. The way he used to beat the hell out of you and Willie, I'm here to tell you. Man could have earned money, throwin' punches like those—"

That hit a nerve. "Just why are you here, Johnny?"

Again, the bottled-up laugh. "Johnny? Hell, that's a kid's name, Dutch. Nobody's called me that in twenty-five years. These days I go by Jack."

"Okay, Jack. I'll stick with the same question, though."

"Man, you're still one cold-hearted son of a bitch. And I thought you'd gone and mellowed. Become a humanitarian. Do you know that your picture made the Mexico City dailies? Sheriff rescues baby from well. That took some kind of big brass *cojones,* I bet."

My face had gone red, and I didn't like it. "There wasn't anything to it," I said. "I found the baby. I'm the sheriff. What was I supposed to do?"

We were both quiet for a moment.

"Look, Johnny—Jack—I'm tired. I don't mind telling you that the years have worn on me, and I don't have much patience anymore. Why don't you start by giving me your gun. I'm going to need it for evidence. I've already got one suspect in custody—nobody will ever connect what happened tonight to you. So you can figure you got your revenge, and you can tell me how much money you want, and we can get on with our lives."

"You know," he said, "I hadn't thought about you for years and years. And then I saw that picture in the paper, and damned if I wasn't surprised that you'd actually gone and become a cop. Man oh man, that idea took some getting used to. So I said to myself, *Jack, now you've just got to go see old Dutch before you die, don't you?*"

He knelt before me, his blue eyes floating in the black triangles of that orange mask. "See, I wanted to thank you," he said. "Going to Mexico was the best thing that ever happened to me. I made some money down there. Had a ball. They got lots of pretty boys down there, and I like 'em young and dark. Slim, too—you know, before all those frijolés and tortillas catch up to 'em. You never knew that about me, did you, Dutch? Your brother did, you know. I had a real hard-on for his young ass, but he only liked pussy. You remember how he liked his pussy? Man, how he used to talk about it. Non-fucking-stop! Truth be told, I think he maybe liked the talkin' better than the doin'. And you so shy and all. Now that was funny. You two takin' your squirts under the same skirt."

"You got a point in here somewhere, or are you just trying to piss me off?"

"Yeah. I got a point, Dutch."

Johnny Halloween took off the pumpkin mask, and suddenly I had the crazy idea that he was wearing Willie's skull mask beneath it. His blue eyes were the same and his wild grin was the same, but the rest of his face was stripped down, as if someone had sucked all the juice out of him.

"It's what you get when you play rough with pretty boys and don't bother to wear a raincoat," he said. "AIDS. The doctors say it ain't even bad yet. I don't want it to get bad, y'see."

I stared at him. I couldn't even blink.

He gave me the gun. "You ready to use it now?"

I shook my head. "I'm sorry," I said, and I was surprised to find that I really meant it.

"Let me help you out, Dutch." That wild grin welded on Death's own face. "See, there's a reason it took me so long to get to the cemetery tonight. I had to swing past your place and talk to Helen. Did a little trick-or-treating and got me some Snickers. Nothing more, nothing less. And when I'd had my fill, I told her everything."

There was nothing I could say . . .

"Now, I want you to do it right the first time, Dutch. Don't drag it out."

. . . so I obliged him.

It took two hours to get things done. First I heaved up as much tequila as I could. Then I drove ten miles into the desert and dumped Johnny Halloween's corpse. Next I headed back to the cemetery, got in Johnny's El Camino, and drove two miles north to a highway rest stop. There were four or five illegals standing around who looked like they had no place to go and no way to get there. I left the windows down and the keys in the ignition and I walked back to the cemetery, hoping for the best.

On the way home I swung down Orchard and tossed Johnny's pistol into some oleander bushes three houses up from the liquor store.

My house was quiet. The lights were out. That was fine with me. I found Helen in the kitchen and untied her. I left the tape over her mouth until I said my piece.

I didn't get through the whole thing, though. Toward the end I ran out of steam. I told her that Johnny and Willie and me had pulled the robberies because we hated being so damn poor. That it seemed easier to take the money than not to take it, with me being the clerk and such a good liar besides. I explained that the Halloween job was going to be my last. That I'd been saving those little scraps of money so we could elope, so our baby wouldn't have to come into the world a bastard.

It hurt me, saying that word. I never have liked it. Just saying it in front of Helen is what made me start to crack.

My voice trembled with rage and I couldn't control it anymore. "Johnny took me over to his house that day," I said. "All the time laughing through that wild grin. He had me peek in the window . . . and I saw Willie on top of you . . . and I saw you smiling. . . ."

I slapped Helen then, just the way I'd slapped the Mexican girl at the liquor store, like she didn't mean anything to me at all.

"I was crazy." I clenched my fists, fighting for control. "You know how I get . . . Everything happened too damn fast. They came to the store that night, and I was still boiling. I planned to kill them both and say I hadn't known it was them because of the masks, but it didn't work out that way. Sure, I shot Willie. But I had to shoot him three times before he died. I wanted to kill Johnny, too, but he got away. So I changed the story I'd planned I hid Willie's skull mask, and I hid the gun and the money, and I said that Willie had been visiting me at the store when a lone bandit came in. That bandit was Johnny Halloween, and he'd done the shooting. And all the time that I was lying, I was praying that the cops wouldn't catch him."

I blew my nose and got control of myself. Helen's eyes were

wide in the dark, and there was a welt on her cheek, and she wasn't moving. "I was young, Helen," I told her. "I didn't know what to do. It didn't seem right—getting married, bringing a baby into the world when I couldn't be sure that I was the father. I wanted everything to be just right, you know? It seemed like a good idea to use the money for an abortion instead of a wedding. I figured we'd just go down to Mexico, get things taken care of. I figured we'd have plenty of time for kids later on."

That's when I ran out of words. I took the tape off of Helen's mouth, but she didn't say anything. She just sat there.

I hadn't said so much to Helen in years.

I handed her the tequila bottle. There was a lot left in it.

Her hands shook as she took it. The clear, clean liquor swirled. The worm did a little dance. I turned away and quit the room, but not fast enough to miss the gentle slosh as she tipped back the bottle.

I knew that worm didn't stand a chance.

I don't know why I went out to the garage. I had to go somewhere, and I guess that's where a lot of men go when they want to be alone.

I shuffled some stuff around in my toolbox. Cleaned up the workbench. Changed the oil in the truck. Knowing that I should get rid of the pumpkin mask, but just puttering around instead.

All the time thinking. Questions spinning around in my head.

Wondering if Helen would talk.

Wondering if I'd really be able to pin the clerk's murder on the Mexican girls. Not only if the charges would stick, but if I had enough left in me to go through with it.

Wondering if my deputies would find Johnny's corpse, or his El Camino, or if he'd left any other surprises for me that I didn't know about.

They were the kind of questions that had been eating at me for thirty years, and I was full up with them.

My breaths were coming hard and fast. I leaned against the workbench, staring down at the pumpkin mask. Didn't even know I was crying until my tears fell on oily rubber.

It took me a while to settle down.

I got a .45 out of my tool chest. The silencer was in another drawer. I cleaned the gun, loaded it, and attached the silencer.

I stared at the door that led to the kitchen, and Helen. Those same old questions started spinning again. I closed my eyes and shut them out.

And suddenly I pictured Johnny Halloween down in Mexico, imagined all the fun he'd had over the years with his pretty boys and his money. Not my kind of fun, sure. But it must have been something.

I guess the other guy's life always seems easier.

Sometimes I think even Willie's life was easier.

I didn't want to start thinking that way with a gun in my hands.

I opened my eyes.

I unwrapped a Snickers bar, opened the garage door. The air held the sweet night like a sponge. The sky was going from black to purple, and soon it would be blue. The world smelled clean and the streets were empty. The chocolate tasted good.

I unscrewed the silencer. Put it and the gun in the glove compartment along with the three hundred and fifteen bucks Johnny Halloween had stolen from the liquor store.

Covered all of it with the pumpkin mask.

I felt a little better, a little safer, just knowing it was there.

Killer Cop

Morris Hershman

P ENNER DIALED the number at his usual speed, not faster, not slower. His heart was beating normally. His eyes hurt a little, pinching at the corners somehow, but that was the only strain.

"Hello? I've just killed my wife. Send a man out here."

The voice on the other end (a desk man whose name he didn't know) said calmly, "Yes, sir, of course. And the name and address, please?"

Like a store clerk asking where to make a delivery! Penner almost smiled.

"Robert Penner, 1218 Locket Drive. I," he paused, "I'm attached to the 30th precinct."

The desk man said only, "We'll have a man right out."

Penner nodded uselessly and hung up. He knew what would happen now. The Signal 32 would be passed to a nearby squad car, and a couple of cops would come right over. He had answered plenty of calls like that.

In his left hand he still carried the nightstick, red-tipped now. The uniform wasn't stained, as he saw, looking down at it in sudden concern.

Outside, softly, a car pulled up. Penner looked thankfully at the door. He hadn't known the tension in him that seemed to dribble out of his body as he heard firm steps up the drive followed by gentle knocking at the door. He opened almost gratefully.

The cop had retreated to one side after knocking, of course, just in case the self-admitted killer was crazy enough to try for another victim; but when Penner stood in the doorway, hands outstretched, the cop loomed up large.

The newcomer asked, surprised, "What the hell are you doing . . . Penner? You?"

"That's right, Fred. Tell your partner to come in, too."

Fred turned and signalled with a hand to the blue uniformed man back of the wheel of the white-and-green police car. It was a cool clear night, and a wafer-thin moon seemed to follow the second cop as he approached quickly.

"What's the story?"

"My wife. Magda. She's dead."

Fred Garfein glanced down at the nightstick. He grew rigid and, oddly enough, the tips of his ears reddened.

"Inside."

Penner looked surprised at the tone of voice, but turned and led the way into the hall. When the door was slammed shut back of him, he turned.

"Keep your gun on him," Garfein told his partner. "Be right back."

Fred Garfein's big boots clumped into the other room, the living room. The other cop, a young guy, drew out his gun and looked Penner up and down for signs of gun-bulges. Finally he nodded and rested his own gun almost negligently in a hand.

Penner ran his tongue over dry lips. "Let's get it over with. I just want to lay down someplace. I'm tired." No reaction. Penner looked at the youngster's firm chin and narrowed eyes. "Your name's Crisp, isn't it? I remember hearing the captain talk about you. Joe Crisp, that's right."

Crisp said nothing, but brought up the gun as Penner ducked a hand to his uniform.

"Just going to prove I'm not carrying my gun." And he added foolishly. "You should've searched me before this."

He sounded angry about it. From the living room came the sound of a phone receiver being set back on its cradle, and heavy steps announced Garfein's return. His eyes were shaded with faint worry. He talked to Crisp.

"It's a mess. Ramsey's coming down in person."

"The captain?" Penner's hands went automatically to his uniform, open at the throat, then he put them down. He had already set down the nightstick on the small table nearby.

"Why can't we get it over with by ourselves? Take me downtown and book me."

Garfein didn't answer, but talked to Crisp, instead.

"Trouble is," he said heavily, "you know the way the newspapers been riding us lately. All cops are sadists, that kind of guck. You can see how this is going to look in the papers: cop bashes in wife's head with his nightstick."

Crisp, eyes always on Robert Penner, nodded slowly. They were light eyes, blue.

Penner was out of it, of course. Whatever the papers said about cops in general, that couldn't be any of his business from now on. He coughed, cleared his throat.

"I'd like a glass of water."

He wasn't thirsty at all, but he knew a grim pleasure in seeing Garfein turn and clump into the kitchen for it.

A faint smile touched his lips when Garfein, coming back, was suddenly attracted by a small table and what lay under its glass covering. The cop stared and moved his lips in a slow count, then looked up almost awed.

"Christ Almighty! I forgot about the citations."

"What's that, Fred?" Crisp asked, gun still up.

"Five citations for bravery here. All of 'em handed out by the captain himself, I remember."

"This is going to make a big stink."

Garfein handed over the water glass, wet on the outside as well, and wiped his hand with a dirty handkerchief. Penner waited for the clouded water to clear before drinking up. His hands were steady.

Garfein talked to Crisp as he moved around, and Crisp answered. Nobody spoke to Penner.

The sound of a television set warmed on in a nearby house, came through to them. A singing commercial. A weather broadcast. Every word was clear.

Garfein drew a deep breath at the sound of a car approaching outside and slowly parking. Crisp ran a forefinger under his collar. Only Penner didn't seem to care, staring into space.

"The captain," Crisp said.

Setting down the drinking glass on a nearby table napkin, so as not to leave a ring, Penner looked up wearily at the door. It opened so quickly that he was caught by surprise all the same. For a second or so, Captain Ramsey was silhouetted against the darkness cut by a slice of moon in the doorway at right of his head. Then he closed the door back of him.

He turned to Garfein. "Where is it?"

"Living room, captain."

Ramsey grunted and walked in; like many heavy men, he walked slowly. Penner felt moisture on the palms of his hands but didn't want to wipe then as it meant drawing young Crisp's gun.

Ramsey came back. He took off his hat and sailed it onto a peg on the clothes tree.

"You son of a gun, Penner, I could kill you!"

Penner was so startled at being spoken to that he drew a loud breath that was almost a whine.

"With my own hands I could kill you!" Instead, Ramsey patted his stomach furiously, then a little more slowly. His voice became more reasonable. "What happened?"

Nobody had asked him yet, but he hadn't expected the question so soon. He shrugged. Ramsay's eyes narrowed in renewed anger. Penner cleared his throat.

"I don't know, Captain, honestly. I got home and Magda, my wife, began to argue with me. You know the way it is between man and wife sometimes, Captain."

Ramsey jerked his bullet head toward the living room. "Not that way."

"Well, she started yelling at me about how I should give up the cops. It seems she's got a brother in the real estate business and he's doing good. She wanted me to go into it, too."

He could hardly remember the argument. He couldn't even re-call Magda's face or voice. He was close to swaying where he stood.

"So you let her have it with the nightstick," Ramsey said softly. "Why?"

"I don't know, Captain. It's just one of those things you do. For years I've had it drilled into me to keep the peace with my night-stick. Keep the peace, keep the peace, there's more law at the end of a nightstick . . . you know the way that goes. And there was Magda yelling at me, screaming in my ears so I couldn't hardly think any more."

"Wait till the newspapers get hold of this." Ramsey took a stiff chair. Again a hand tapped his stomach. "They're after my skin and if they get it, they'll get drunk with power and if the next captain doesn't kiss a reporter's feet they'll go after him, too."

He drew in his breath sharply, as if in pain.

"They want us to stop using nightsticks on the beat. They don't know that nightsticks on cops have prevented God knows how many crimes because a lot of punks know that cops have got 'em. They're even saying cops ought to be off Civil Service because cops are so brutal."

He put up a hand to shade his eyes. Suddenly he smashed the hand down hard on his lap.

"They want to aggravate cops so that morons will have what to read in the papers every morning. That's what they want. And you, Penn, you do a thing like this and you help the newspapers. Some bright reporter's going to win himself an award out of this story, I wouldn't be a bit surprised."

His eyes narrowed as Crisp glanced toward the living room. "I know she's dead, fella," he said softly. "It's been rougher on her."

The television set next door was turned slightly louder to a quiz program. Outside a horn blared. Somebody played chromatic scales on a piano. An ice cream vendor's truck stopped nearby, its pres-ence announced by tinkling bells. Voices of children grew louder, then lower. The television set was lowered in volume; apparently there was a quarrel next door about how loudly it should be turned on.

The normality of it all caught at Penner more than anything else that had happened so far, since he had done it to Magda. He looked around wistfully, eyes lingering on every piece of hall furniture as if he was memorizing its position.

"We take him downtown." Ramsey said heavily. "We fingerprint him, put him on the line-up, maybe the PBA gets him a lawyer—and the papers start to scream for *our* heads."

He rose, hands behind his back. Garfein, wide-eyed, stared at him.

"For all I know," Ramsey said, "this could spark the governor into signing some crazy law to get at every cop in the state. The governor's no friend of ours."

Ramsey fumbled in his pockets for a cigar, drew it out of the cellphone, looked at it sourly and put it away.

"On this man's police force," he said finally, "it's a rough thing to get promoted. You gotta make decisions and, come right down to it, you're as smart as the guys below you and no more."

He would probably never again make such a remark in the presence of two subordinates. Garfein looked embarrassed. Crisp shrugged.

Ramsey paused. "There's a way out of it, one way."

Garfein, who was sweating, said, "Tell us what it is, Captain."

"It means that we'd all be taking a hell of a chance," Ramsey said. "But I want to remind you two again, that we can't afford to let it get in the papers that a hero cop, with five citations for bravery, killed his wife with a nightstick because he got so used to being a hard guy on the beat."

"Sure, Captain, we know," Crisp said, and flushed when Ramsey looked sourly at him.

Ramsey said a little more sharply, "Garfein, get a sheet of paper and bring it here. Then go into the next room. Close the windows and turn down the blinds, then mess up the room, kick the furniture, knock things upside down, throw things on the floor."

Garfein, after a pause, nodded slowly. His eyes looked hurt.

Seeing it, Ramsey said with surprising gentleness, "Give me a better suggestion, Fred, and I'll take it." Garfein looked away. Ramsey nodded firmly. "Hop to it. And when you get finished with the living room, go into the bedroom and do the same thing. You've got gloves with you?"

"Sure thing, Captain."

He stumbled off, first to bring back a clean sheet of lined white paper and a ball point pen, all of which he set down on the small table.

Ramsey looked at Penner. "Sit down there and write out your resignation."

"My resignation?" Penner's hands trembled out of tiredness. He tried to force his mind to think, but nothing happened.

"Listen to me, boy." Ramsey kept his temper. "You are the luckiest son-of-a-gun cop I ever heard of. I'm not going to have a lot of good men loused up when this hits the papers. Instead, I'm going to take your resignation. Garfein will make the house look like burglars came in and while they were at it, they killed your wife. You'll say you came from from a hard day's work and found her dead. *Kapeesh?*"

"Sure, sure."

"Get busy and start writing. You're resigning out of grief. You can't carry on. Put tomorrow's date on it."

Penner sat down on the hard-backed chair and adjusted the paper so that the top-left was inclined to his left. He wrote slowly. Once he looked up to see young Crisp's eyes on him, then on Ramsey.

"Captain, this is all wrong! We can't let ourselves do this."

Penner wrote listlessly. His eyes were half-shut and he paused at the end of every word.

From the next room, Garfein began his job of destruction. The sounds rose in tempo. With each rise, Penner sighed.

"I don't get this." Crisp's jaw was set almost mutinously. Penner saw his fingers stiffen on the gun, and looked away. He wasn't tempted to move or to call out.

Ramsey, who saw everything, had seen this, too. "You're liable to shoot somebody with that brand-new gun of yours, Crisp. How about handing it over to me if you can't do what you're told?"

Crisp walked across the room and handed over the gun with butt foremost. Ramsey sniffed down at it and dropped it into a suit pocket, then swivelled around to Penner.

"Finished?"

Garfein had proceeded to the living room and the wrecking sounds were more faint.

"When we get back downtown," Ramsey told Crisp, "you'll get hold of the desk man who took the message that Penner phoned in. Have him see me. And take Penner's nightstick with you. Wrap it up in newspapers and get rid of it." He put up a hand to his throat and turned to Penner. "I'm thirsty. Get me some water."

"Of course, Captain, Sure." Penner rose and walked tiredly toward the kitchen. Crisp started out to call something, but smothered it. There was a shot and pain seared Penner's back. He turned slowly, and sank to the floor.

Ramsey stood over him, looking down. "Sorry, fella." He raised the gun and fired twice more. Penner was still.

From the living room, Garfein rain in with his usual heavy steps. "Burglars shot a hero cop in the back and beat his wife to death," Ramsey said. He shrugged. "When Penner thought he had a chance to get out with a whole skin, he didn't want it. He wanted things to be finished for him. I tried to arrange it so he wouldn't know when the bullet was coming."

Ramsey glanced down to the resignation Penner had written, folded it and put into a pocket. "I hope I did the right thing. I sure as hell hope so."

"In a way, I'm sorry for him," Crisp said finally. "I guess he'll get a hero's funeral."

"Deserves it," Ramsey snapped. "He was a good cop."

Last Lap

Stan Knowlton

WILBUR SYKES STOPPED on the fifth floor landing and pushed back his hat. He removed his thick-lensed spectacles; with his handkerchief he mopped the beads of perspiration from his broad, low forehead, wiped his weak, watery eyes. Six more flights to go—but it was worth it. He smiled thinly. He'd make the climb any time for half a million bucks.

Wilbur replaced the glasses on his squat, flat-bridged nose, resumed his panting ascent of the winding iron stairs that ran beside the freight elevator from the basement to the top floor. Nearly all the landing lights were out.

"No system," Wilbur muttered disdainfully. But things would be a damned sight different when the property became his. With his eccentric uncle passed along.

Eccentric? Wilbur grinned wryly. Screw-ball was more like it. Any guy was nuts who'd buy the whole damned shebang when the loss of his workroom and makeshift living quarters was threatened by a remodeling of the office building planned by the owners. But, daffy or not, the old boy had been pulling in the dough—and still was. The formula that his uncle was now working on, he'd told him, would net him a cool fifty thousand.

Too bad he'd have to pass that up, but the four or five hundred thousand that he knew his uncle possessed, would do nicely.

Wilbur stopped again. This must be the floor. He turned the latch handle of the metal-sheeted firedoor, pushed it open. One bulb glowed feebly nearby in the hall. He closed the door, checked the faint lettering in it. ELEVENTH. Right.

Except for the dim light near the door and one showing from behind an opaque glassed panel down the corridor, the floor was dark. At midnight there'd be no tenants in the building. The cleaners had gone; no one was there but his uncle and the old watchman; and Wilbur knew that the watchman made his rounds from the basement up. He'd have plenty of time to do his stuff before the old fellow reached this floor.

Wilbur headed for the lighted square of glass, kicked into a pile of rubbish. He swore under his breath. The place certainly had gone to seed! Light bulbs burning out; paint peeling from the walls; plaster cracked and crumbling; rubbish on the floors. What a joint! He noticed, too, that the freight elevator door with its dingy marking, was ajar; and, although he knew that the elevator was in the basement, the safety-gate was raised. Stuck. Wilbur shook his head disgustedly. Well, he'd right such things when he was boss. He closed the door, continued down the hall.

This was going to be a cinch. He'd not even had to bring a weapon; everything was all set for him. His uncle never had made a will, and being the only living relative, all would come to him. Not only the cash, but the building, as well. And he'd soon put that on a paying basis—bring back tenants that his uncle had lost when he'd let it deteriorate.

But he couldn't wait any longer for his uncle to kick off. He had to get out of the red ink; it was up to his nose now. And that little blonde's tastes were damned expensive.

Wilbur reached the door, opened it. The two-inch-squared, three-feet-long piece of timber his uncle used to brace the door since its lock gave out, lay on the floor. His uncle, seated at his desk, was bending over some papers.

"Hi, Uncle," Wilbur greeted him.

His uncle gave him a fleeting look, turned back to his work. "Another touch, I suppose," he growled.

Wilbur picked up the piece of wood, moved slowly toward the desk. His uncle, absorbed with his papers, paid no heed.

Wilbur swung the heavy stick. It struck his uncle's head a glancing blow. With speed and agility that amazed Wilbur, his uncle sprang to his feet, let fly a haymaker. It caught Wilbur on the temple, jarred him to his heels, knocked off his spectacles.

Wilbur swung the stick again, blindly. It landed squarely, this time, with a dull, crunching sound. His uncle crumpled to the floor.

Wilbur groped for his glasses, found the frame. Both lenses were broken. He cursed fluently, scooped up all of the shattered glass that he could find. He put it, with the frame, into his pocket. He stooped over his uncle, felt for a heartbeat. There was none.

Without his glasses, objects were confusingly blurred. He snatched the papers from the desk, stuffed them into his pocket. He yanked open the filing cases, strewed their contents about. The police would think that someone had been after his uncle's new formula. He wiped the handle end of the stick, switched off the light, went out.

The light down the hall was a hazy blob of yellow. He must waste no time; the watchman might be working his rounds differently tonight—might show up right now! He had to lam—and fast! His jittery nerves jumping wildly, he stumbled at a half run toward the firedoor, fumbling along the wall until his trailing fingers found a latch. He stopped, bent over, squinted nearsightedly at the faded letters on the door, made them out, one by one. E-L-E-V—

Wilbur snapped upright, jerked up the latch.

"Okay; eleventh," he mumbled. A flood of relief surged through him; his confidence returned with a rush. "On my last lap now," he chuckled. Wilbur pulled back the door, stepped through. Stepped through the door marked ELEVATOR. . . .

Last of Kin

Jo Bannister

AT THE MENTION of the words "sweet little old lady," everyone who knew her immediately thought of Mrs. Nancy Budgens. Even people who didn't know her got a mind's eye view of someone very *like* Nancy: someone of about seventy with a soft powdery complexion, fluffy peach-white hair, faded but still warm blue eyes, no great height and nothing you could call a waist without setting off a lie detector. They pictured the way she smiled, the blue eyes disappearing in a mass of crinkles pushed up by the apple cheeks, and the way she walked, with a slight roll like a deep-sea sailor. They knew her wardrobe consisted almost entirely of flower-printed cotton dresses.

Asked to speculate further, they would have attributed to this archetypal Little Old Lady a large close-knit family of equally apple-cheeked husband, children, grandchildren and quite possibly great-grandchildren as well. It seemed somehow part of the package, that such a plainly maternal figure should come with all the trimmings.

But in fact Nancy Budgens did not have the perfect family life which would have completed the picture. Mr. Budgens, branch manager of a local bank for twenty years, died at his desk just weeks short of retirement. Their daughter Sandra never married, though she did raise a child. A dull woman, prematurely middle-aged, she seemed content in her undemanding job as an assistant librarian; until one morning she was found hanging from a length of picture cord attached to the specially high shelf for books of a certain artistic nature.

Which reduced the already small family to just two: Nancy and her grandson Trevor. When anyone asked she would put on that brave smile patented by little old ladies and say, "Trevor's all I have left." Then: "And I'm all he has."

This led some of her friends to suppose the relationship closer than in fact it was. Although alone, Sandra Budgens had managed to provide a home and a decent upbringing for her son without recourse to her parents. Young Trevor saw as much of his grandma and granddad as most boys—occasional holidays, birthdays, Christmas—and no more. There was an element of wishful thinking in what Nancy said. Though they were indeed next of kin after Sandra's sad meaningless departure, she and Trevor remained more amiable than close.

For one thing, Trevor wasn't Reliable. As the widow of a bank manager Nancy put a lot of stock in Reliability, which she judged by such things as having a Proper Job and a Nice Home and Nice Friends. Trevor disappointed on every count. He was an actor. He said he was quite a good one and made a decent living. All Nancy knew was that he visited her at times when people with Proper Jobs would be working, and he wore clothes she wouldn't have let Mr. Budgens put in their own dustbin. He shared a run-down Victorian house with several other Thespians of both traditional sexes and one or two others.

In spite of that, he seemed a kind young man. He brought her chocolates on her birthday, and flowers for no particular reason, and phoned her at intervals to check that she was keeping well.

And she was keeping well; but she was aware of the passing of time and the need to make proper provision for her old age. The family home, which had never felt a burden until recently, seemed to be getting bigger, the stairs steeper, the bathroom further down the landing with every month that passed. Once it had been her ambition to die in this house; now that seemed less a hope than a sentence. She thought there must be easier ways for an old lady with a little money to spend her last years.

She asked Trevor round to discuss the situation. He came willingly enough but puzzled, as if she'd asked for his advice on gerbils. All he knew about money was that if you didn't pay what you owed people came after you with pick-axe handles.

"I'm not a wealthy woman," Nancy began coyly. "Your grandfather, God bless him, left me comfortable, but that's getting to be a long time ago. Running this house has eaten into what he left. Then there was the inflation, and the recession . . ." She smiled apologetically.

Trevor glanced around him. It wasn't a big house but it was a considerable asset. He couldn't believe she was desperate enough to be asking him for money. "Grandma, of course I'd help if I could. But—"

But when Trevor said he was successful he meant he could live

284

on what he earned as an actor, and didn't have to work in kitchens when he was "resting." It did not mean he had a numbered account in Switzerland that the Inland Revenue knew nothing about. His mother's estate had boiled down to a few thousand pounds in a building society, which he considered his insurance against destitution if the roles he specialized in—petty criminals, undesirable boyfriends and assorted Shakespearian gravediggers and sword-carriers whose first names were always Second—dried up. His only other assets were an elderly van—his ability to transport scenery had won him several parts—and a fifth share in a house that grew mushrooms.

Oh yes: and an elderly grandmother with a much nicer house of her own and no other relatives.

Nancy patted his hand absently. "Would you, dear? Bless you. But that's not quite what I had in mind.

"You and I are one another's only family, Trevor. When I die what I have will naturally be yours. I've always hoped it would be enough to provide you with a little security.

"But if I do what I have in mind there won't be as much left as I'd like. I'm an old lady now, but I could live another twenty years. And nice residential accommodation doesn't come cheap. I'd have to sell this house and buy an annuity. On the credit side"—Nancy wasn't a bank manager's widow for nothing—"I'd never be a burden to you. On the debit side, there mightn't be much left for *your* old age. Before I burn any boats I'd like to know how you feel about that. Would it be a major blow?"

Trevor had never given it much thought. He knew he was his grandmother's only heir, and anticipated benefiting at some point, but he'd never worked out how much he could expect let alone how to use it. He thought about it now.

She was seventy-one: no great age by today's standards. She was fit, she had no history of illness—she might live to be a hundred. He'd be in his fifties then. There were an awful lot of fifty-year-old actors for whom "resting" had become a permanent state of affairs. Whatever the house was worth, whatever she got for the antiques that furnished it and whatever remained from his grandfather's investments, it would all be gone by then. Even if she didn't live to be a hundred; even if she only lived another ten years, say, which was nothing. Every week she would reduce his expectations by hundreds of pounds.

The mere fact that he wasn't able to brush it off unconsidered, with a gallant smile and a casual "Grandma, it's your money, use it how you want," told Nancy that however well he was doing in his own terms her grandson did not have the kind of financial reserves beside which her own paled to insignificance.

"Oh dear," she said anxiously, reaching for his hand, "it *would*, wouldn't it? You've been counting on it. You're a good boy, you've never asked me for money, even when you couldn't possibly have had enough. And now I'm proposing to spend your inheritance. No, it really won't do—I shall have to think again."

Trevor got a belated grip on his expression and clasped her hand in return. "Don't be silly, Grandma," he said. "It's your money—Granddad made it and he'd want you to use it in your best interests. Spend it and enjoy it. I've some money of my own: not a fortune but enough to see me through the odd sticky patch. Mum left me nearly ten thousand, and I've added a bit to it since I've been working. And hell, I'm only twenty-five: if I can't put together a comfortable stake over the next forty years I should have been a greengrocer instead! Now, tell me about your plans. Is there somewhere you've got your eye on?"

Nancy's face lit up with pleasure. If it was true that Sandra had never fulfilled the highest potential as a daughter, that she and her mother had in fact found it hard to like one another, she had at least raised a son to be proud of. "Trevor, you're a lovely lad." Nancy got up and bustled over to her bureau, coming back with a sheaf of envelopes made of expensively grained paper. "Yes, I have. I've been doing a bit of research, and there's a couple of wonderful places."

She spread the brochures in front of him, pointing out the lifts, the en-suite bathrooms, the extensive gardens with the enthusiasm of a child comparing holiday camps.

"I think Rosedale's the one I shall go for. Look at those *lovely* flowerbeds! And if you pay a little more for a room on this side of the house"—she tapped the illustration with a fingernail—"there's a view of the river. Oh, I did used to love the river when we were younger! I really think it would be worth finding a little more to be able to enjoy it again."

"What's this one?" asked Trevor, holding up a well-thumbed prospectus with a lot of gold-leaf on the cover.

Nancy's voice went schoolgirl breathy. "The Beeches. The Rolls-

Royce of residential provision for the elderly—the sort of place you only get sent to if the family feel really guilty about the way they've treated you. I wish someone had treated *me* that badly! Even by selling this place I couldn't meet the fees at The Beeches." She smiled cheerily. "Still, it's nice to dream."

" 'Course it is, Gran," Trevor said bravely, well aware that her dreams were putting the boot into his. Even if he'd never thought of it in those terms, this house had been his insurance against having to play comic footmen in pantomime in Huddersfield. When it was gone he was on his own. Her news had given him much to think about.

As his had given Nancy. But they parted on the doorstep with their customary brief hug as if all was well.

"You are a *nice* boy, Trevor," his grandmother said again. "I've been quite worried, I don't mind saying. I'm glad we've had this talk."

"There's nothing to worry about," Trevor said firmly. "Like you always say, all we've got is each other. If we don't look out for one another, who else will?"

Normally they met every month or so. But there were practicalities to discuss so there was nothing odd about them going for a drive in Trevor's van just three days later. The inquest heard that it was Trevor's suggestion but that Nancy jumped at the idea.

They drove down to the river and parked where they could just see the roofs of the Rosedale Retirement Home across the municipal playing fields. "It's a nice area," said Trevor.

"Yes, it is pretty," agreed Nancy. "Not that I'll be able to walk this far, but it'll be nice to look at from the bedroom window. That's the advantage with The Beeches, you see." She turned and indicated the butter-coloured stone of a large house surrounded by tree-studded lawns that rolled down to the water's edge a quarter of a mile upstream. "No walking—it's an actual riverside property."

"I'd have thought that was a drawback for a retirement home. Don't the old dears keep sliding in?"

Nancy smiled. "There's a chicken-wire fence to catch them. I don't think they lose many."

Trevor grinned. "You and Granddad had a boat on the river, didn't you?" She nodded. "Mum used to try and make me come out with you sometimes: she said the fresh air would do me good. But I never did like being that close to water."

"I remember," murmured Nancy. "When your granddad tried teaching you to swim you screamed so much he had to give up. Such a pity."

Trevor shrugged. "There are worse handicaps for an actor. The only time it gives me a problem is in *The Tempest.*"

Nancy chuckled. "You must favour your father's side. I can't think how a grandson of mine could *not* love the river. It's *beautiful.*"

A man walking his dog along the far bank saw what happened next. The van doors opened and a young man and an elderly lady got out and strolled along the bank a few feet from the water, a brown torrent swollen by months of rain. As they walked the woman gestured up and down stream as if pointing out items of interest. Then they turned back to the van.

In doing so the old lady lost her footing on the rain-softened bank and fell with a startled squawk first to her knees and then, as she struggled to get up, down the muddy slope into the river. At once the young man threw himself full length on the bank in an effort to reach her. But her hand remained tantalizingly beyond his grasp. After only a brief hesitation he kicked off his shoes and slithered down the muddy bank into the water.

The witness was unable to say quite what followed. Poor Mr. Budgens reached his struggling grandmother and grasped her hand. But then either he lost his footing, or in her panic she unbalanced him, and he disappeared under the rolling flood. He surfaced yards out into the river, here even in normal weather there was depth enough for quite big boats, and yelled and waved his arms over his head until he disappeared again. Twice more he floundered to the surface, further from the bank each time, while the witness watched in helpless horror. After that he did not see him again.

By then help had reached Mrs. Budgens. Strong arms pulled her up the bank, wrapped coats and car-rugs around her, chafed her trembling hands. All she could say was, "Trevor. Where's Trevor? Where's Trevor?"

The inquest was a formality. Death by misadventure, and an eloquent tribute from the coroner for a courageous young man who braved an element he feared deeply in an attempt to rescue a frail old lady. It was the stuff of tabloid headlines, and Nancy Budgens was touched by the kindness paid by so many people who never knew him to poor Trevor's memory.

When it was all done, no one was surprised that Nancy sold her house and used the proceeds to move into residential accommodation. There were a few raised eyebrows that she chose a home so close to the scene of the tragedy. But as she pointed out, she had always loved the river; and in a sort of a way, there was something of Trevor in it now. Perhaps it was odd of her. Bereaved elderly ladies of seventy-one were entitled to be odd.

So she moved into The Beeches. It was worth every penny it cost. With poor Trevor gone there was no one left to consider but herself, so she spent the money with a clear conscience. Together, the proceeds of her house and Trevor's building society bought an annuity that would keep her in the state to which she meant to become accustomed for as long as she lived. It was, after all, what Trevor would have wished.

Trevor had been her last surviving blood-relation, her only heir. And she had been his.

The Last Pin

Howard Wandrei

T HE OLDER BROTHER Emil was the hellion, the brains of the notorious Strobel gang, but he and Ernie Strobel couldn't be considered apart. They complemented each other, much like the butt of a pistol and the hand in which it fits.

The other Strobels were Edna—a wildfire girl who was all arms and legs and whopping black eyes—and the dad. They lived in a frame house on Clinton Avenue below the Western tracks, which cut through our district.

It was nearly noon. The day before it had rained, and the grass was never so green. The neighbor's boy, Johnny Macey, and I were walking barefoot on the boulevard, because the sidewalks stung in the furnace of sunlight. We were taking turns drawing my brother's coaster wagon.

In it were bottles. I had snitched a flour sack from home, and it bulged with medicine bottles in all the shapes and sizes ever manufactured. From the Macey medicine chest had come empties and a few bottles containing driblets. My house likewise. And we had forayed up and down the alleys ransacking rubbish burners. Every bottle in the wagon was spank, and clean; the druggist bought each one on sparkle, paying three cents, a nickel for the stout brown one, fifteen cents for specials. The druggist was a burly, sleepy-eyed man, and he was fair.

Johnny and I had never happened to come down this way before on Clinton. We weren't warned.

The Strobel boys were playing mumblety-peg at the embankment of their parched lawn; there were three more tough kids crouching around. They had a Boy Scout knife to take turns with.

When they saw us coming they quit, and waited. Johnny was pulling the wagon, and he looked back and said they were going to pick on us. I knew they were. I remember how the strength drained out of our legs as we kept on.

"Hi, kids," we said when we got abreast.

"Hi." Only Ernie Strobel answered.

"What you got in that wagon?" Emil asked.

He was the oldest, with a downy black Mandarin mustache on his lip. He wore long pants, and he had thick brown hair which came to points like big, soft camel's hair brushes in front of his ears.

"Just ole medicine bottles," Johnny croaked.

I chimed in deprecatingly. "Yah. We're suppose ta take them down to First Shadlov's." Shadlov had a brother five blocks farther on, and he was Second Shadlov's.

Emil made a sound, and flipped the long-bladed jack knife off the back of his hand into the ground. He stayed up there on the embankment, but the four others came down to surround us.

"Let's see yer bottles," Ernie Strobel said, and pushed me away from the wagon. The sack opened, and some of the contents spilled out and glittered in the sunlight.

Across the street was a hitching post, and the usual block of granite carved with the name of the former owner of the house over there. Ernie pegged a bottle experimentally. It was a good throw, and the bottle made a dandy sound when it exploded, a *pok* and then a splash like water.

The gang fell on the wagon, whooping, and commenced slinging the load of bottles; Johnny and I scuffed desperately, and got in the way sufficiently to make the gang break the rest of the bottles on the sidewalk around the wagon. Whereupon they retreated to the top of the embankment.

Johnny and I started back ingloriously with the wagon, and I heard Emil Strobel say to Ernie, "Well, punk, what did you get out of it?" He was still slinging the big knife into the ground, whipping it down to make the blade go deep.

"Did I tell you to do that?" he demanded. "Huh? All right, I guess you better keep on playing with the rest of the little boys."

He left the knife sticking into the ground and went into the house.

Johnny and I crossed the bridge, and, after bawling a little bit, relapsed into hate and plots of vengeance. We were going to make slingshots and lay for the Strobel gang, and things like that. Both of us had cut our feet on broken glass, but we felt a little important because our dads were so angry about the episode.

Our mothers pooled their butter jars, and when we went down to sell them to the dairy, we cut through Clinton on purpose, with our dads walking along a half-block behind us smoking their cigars. We got more for the butter crocks than we would have for the bottles, but we never collected any more.

I heard my dad saying, "Sure as hell, John, that's where they'll wind up. It's a shame something can't be done."

"What can you do?" Johnny's father asked. "It' s a police matter already, but you know what they say—they're just kids. Just kids, my grandmother! What we need is a police chief with at least a grade-school education."

Ernie Strobel was half a grade ahead of me at school. As I remember it, I was in the A7th when Emil was convicted of murder and sent to prison for life. He had stabbed a man in a quarrel over some dime-a-dance girl. My dad said it was sordid, and told my mother, "When things like that happen, sometimes I'm sorry I belong to the human race."

When he was sentenced, Emil told Judge Munn, "You'll get yours. The rest of them will get theirs, too." He included the jury and probably everyone else handy.

Munn observed, for that, "A recommendation for hard labor will be entered in your commitment papers."

As though Emil's hate had power to kill, his lawyer and the foreman of the jury died within a week of each other. Violently. One had fried toadstools for dinner, and the other shot himself while cleaning the revolver he had bought after Emil threatened him.

Then I met Ernie again at the Hill Club, a gymnasium where Johnny's dad and mine had bought us memberships. Ernie was doing something intricate on the parallel bars when I went in. He recognized me; he came down to the floor without any hurry, and looked as though he wanted to say something. Then his gym shoes squeaked on the floor, and he hiked out into the locker aisles.

He had the damnedest black eyes, and he looked at me as though he hated me. I couldn't figure out why, unless it had to do with those cursed bottles. If I hadn't been there with them, of course, he wouldn't have smashed them and gotten in wrong with his brother.

Some while later Johnny Macey said to me, "Say, you know what? He's got safety pins in his leg."

"Where?"

"Right here."

"You mean pinned right *on?*"

He did, and I told him to "g'wan."

A couple of nights later we were in the pool. The girls had separate classes and wore suits, but the boys went in raw. Johnny and I were at the deep end of the pool under the diving board, and I looked up. Ernie walked out to the end of the board, and when he got set for a dive, I saw them. They were common safety pins, two of them, pinned through the flesh on the inside of his thigh. During the evening Ernie saw me, but acted as though I wasn't there.

There were a couple of bullies around, one named Chuck in my locker aisle. He liked to maul, and the gym master, Goldmark, never interfered. I was getting cuffed around while I was trying to dress, and telling Chuck to cut it out, when Ernie Strobel came into the aisle.

Without any warning he made a pass at Chuck and took him hard across the face with a meaty swat. Not very loud, he said, "Cut that out. That stuff doesn't go around here any more."

Chuck nearly burst, he was so sore. Ernie walked off without giving me a look, and no one down there ever bothered us again.

Ernie was good enough to earn an instructor's job under Goldmark at a small salary. Athletically he was a miracle, all muscle and splendidly proportioned. Eventually it was expected he'd get Goldmark's job. He knew all the gymnastics in the dictionary, and he performed the hard tricks so effortlessly that it was ludicrous. There wasn't any grandstanding about him, either.

One Saturday I looked through the window when he must have thought he was all alone, and he was going up the rope to the two-story ceiling, hand over hand, again and again, as smoothly as a puppet being reeled up at the end of a wire. I wondered if he still had those safety pins in his leg, and why, and why they didn't fester.

Not even Goldmark was his friend. Ernie acted as though he were sufficient unto himself, and his unsmiling expression, with the mouth too wide, the alert black eyes, was somehow hostile. He was a perfect physical specimen doing all that was required of him, carrying out his duties with machine precision.

One day in the pool I noticed that there were three safety pins fastened in his thigh. No mistake about it. One had been added.

My membership in the club was renewed a couple of times, and, in all that while, the only conversation I had with Ernie was hello and so-long. His brother Emil was never mentioned, perhaps forgotten by everyone but Ernie Strobel.

His sister Edna got to be a striking girl, a peach, with something of a reputation with certain characters. Just once I took her out, to a movie. It was a mistake, and I don't know why she accepted my invitation. She acted like a mechanical doll; I didn't kiss her good night, and she didn't expect to be kissed.

Ernie phoned me once about joining up again; I said I couldn't do it because of schoolwork, and he could see it my way.

While I was at the U an item appeared in the news, and then a Sunday feature about Emil Strobel. He was going "over the blue wall," under observation in the prison hospital for transfer to the insane asylum. A member of the Board of Pardons promised that Strobel would never get out, whether from the prison or asylum.

The yarn was that Strobel was bragging to turnkeys and fellow convicts that he was keeping the promise he had made in court, that he was going to "get all of them." He made lunatic claims like being able to transport his mind out of his body and thus was able to prowl at large in the city, and was getting his vengeance, person after person.

When his body was asleep in his cell at night, he gloated, his mind was free to go marauding. He announced that he could sleep with beautiful women if he chose, and that he would continue to kill his enemies one at a time. His less gifted friends suggested that he bump off the lot in one fell swoop, and while he was about it he could do a few favors for his pals.

In a grim way Strobel's chatter was readable, because, since he had been put away, five of the jurors who had brought in a verdict against him, both attorneys, and one of the detectives who had arrested him had died or been killed. At least two of the deaths were murders, unsolved.

Even at the prison—there was the case of the quarry bull living in the town a mile and a quarter away; he commuted by motorcycle until the night he twanged into a wire cable, stretched between two trees, at fifty M.P.H. The writer drew the conclusion that misfortune dogs the heels of persons engaged in prison work.

When I'd graduated from the U, I was job-hunting one afternoon and met Ernie Strobel somewhere. He said curtly, "Have a drink with me."

We picked a speak fronted by a grocery store, and had excellent cold beer at two bits a glass. There was no change in him at all unless his eyes were bigger and blacker, if that were possible, than I had remembered. He was an uncomfortable companion, with a hard stare that was maniacal. Thinking of those safety pins in his legs, I wondered if he was batty like his brother. He wasn't interested in the beer. For a while he held off letting me know what he had on his chest, and when he gave it, I knew he was bats. His lips were thin and he said through his teeth:

"I'm sorry I smashed your bottles."

As though it had happened yesterday! I was shocked.

"For the love of—. Forget it," I said, red in the face. I drank a lot of beer down.

"Then it's all right?"

"Hell, yes! Forget it. That's years ago. We were kids."

"All right. Then we're quits." He got up and went out of the place and out of my acquaintance altogether, leaving me sitting there with my mouth open.

Old Judge Munn, the one who'd sentenced Emil, was set upon one night in his car in the alley behind his house. The murder was executed with such dire dispatch, with a knife, that Mrs. Munn didn't have time to scream. She was in the back seat and the murderer didn't see her. But she saw him, and she didn't faint. . . .

Police visited the house on Clinton Avenue and entered without advertising themselves. They used the back way. Lights were on in the kitchen and the shades were pulled down. Stripped to his shorts, Ernie Strobel was sitting in a kitchen chair. In a neat row down the inside of his left thigh, in flesh that was bruised purple and green, were fastened fourteen safety pins. He was in the act of sticking in the fifteenth.

A terrible battle took place in that kitchen while they tried to arrest him, and, with two men slugging him, he was cleverly shot through the head just one jerk from success in breaking a third policeman's back. When he was so near to finishing his job, it was too bad Ernie never had the satisfaction of sticking in the last pin in the row.

Like Father, Like Son

Richard T. Chizmar

ATHER'S DAY was always a big deal when I was growing up. The old man loved it. Breakfast in bed. (And let me tell you, back in those days, Mom made a ham and egg omelet so big the plate could barely hold it.) Afternoon barbecue in the back yard. Horseshoes. Ball-tossing. Lots of laughter and silly stuff. And then an evening drive downtown for ice cream cones and milkshakes; all four windows rolled down, cool spring air blushing our cheeks; Dad at the wheel, singing along with the radio in that crazy voice of his, big hands swallowing up the steering wheel; Mom, sitting sideways in the passenger seat, rolling her eyes at us, feigning embarrassment.

There were three of us boys—the three stooges, Dad always called us. I was the oldest and most of the responsibilities fell on my shoulders. Come the big weekend, I was in charge of making sure the lawn was mowed, the hedges clipped, and the sidewalk swept. I was the one every year who bought the card down at Finch's Grocery Mart and made sure that Marty and Lawrence signed it. And, most importantly, I was in charge of organizing the gifts. Of course, back when we were kids, our presents were never very expensive or fancy. Usually just something simple we'd each made in school. Individually wrapped and sealed tight with a few yards of shiny scotch tape so as to prolong the official gift opening ceremony after breakfast.

The first gift I can remember making was an ashtray in the shape of a bullfrog. Painted green, of course. Very bright green. The only frog in class with big yellow teeth, too. Dad loved it. Let out a bellow that rattled the bed frame when he pulled it from the box. Shook my tiny hand and told me how proud he was of me. And he was too; you could just tell.

Then there was the year that Marty gave the old man a wooden pipe-holder for his desktop. Sanded and polished and varnished to a fine finish, it was a thing of beauty; it really was. To this day, I think Marty could've had a successful career as a craftsman; it was that nice a job.

Lawrence, who was the youngest and the brightest, was the writer of the family and for a three year period in his early teens, he gave the old man an "original Lawrence Finley book" each Father's Day. Each "book" was composed of five short chapters and each chapter ended with a suspenseful cliff-hanger. They were typed out in dark, clear script on folded construction paper and carefully stapled down the middle. A remarkably-detailed pencil sketch marked the title page of each new volume. The story itself was equally impressive: it featured the old man as an outlaw gun-fighter in the Old West. Strong and brave and with a heart of gold. A wild-west Robin Hood with a six-shooter on his hip and a fast, white horse named Gypsy. Of all the gifts the three of us gave him back when we were kids, I think these stories were the old man's favorite. Not that he ever would've admitted it, of course.

Years later, when all three of us were over at the University and working good part-time jobs, we each saved up and chipped in for something special: a John Deere riding mower. A brand spanking new one with a big red ribbon laced through the steering wheel. We surprised him with it right after breakfast that year, and he flat out couldn't believe his eyes. Neither could we; it was the first time any of us—Mom included—had ever seen the old guy speechless. Makes me smile even now just to think about it. Makes me smile even more when I remember all the times I called home from college and Mom would tell me he couldn't come to the phone right now because he was out cutting the lawn . . . again . . . for the second time that week.

Yes, sir, Father's Day was always a big deal back when I was growing up.

The drive out to Hagerstown Prison takes just under three hours on a good day. I figure the traffic to be a bit heavier than usual this morning, so I leave when it's still dark outside. I ride with the radio off and the heat on; it rained last night and the June air has a nasty little bite to it.

I drive the winding country roads faster than I should, but visiting hours have been extended because of the holiday, and I want to show up a few minutes early to get a head start on the registration forms and to check in the gifts I've brought along with me. In the back seat, I have a big bag of freshly-baked chocolate chip cookies, a stack of brand new paperbacks—westerns, mostly—and a half-dozen pouches of his favorite pipe tobacco.

The road is fairly clear and the trip takes two hours and thirty-five minutes. Plenty of time for a man to think . . . even if he doesn't want to.

When I step out onto the gravel parking lot, the morning sun is shining and the chill has vanished from the air. I can hear birds singing in the trees across the way, and I can't help but wonder what they must sound like to the men locked inside these walls.

There are already a scattered handful of visitors waiting inside the lobby. Mostly young women with pale, dirty, restless children. But a few older couples, too. None of them look up at me when I take off my coat and sit down, but the hush of whispering momentarily fades to silence then picks up again. In all my visits here, I've never once heard anyone speak in a normal tone of voice in this room; only whispers. It's always like this in the waiting room. There's an awkward kind of acceptance here. No one gawks or stares. It's like we're all charter members of the same club—each and every one of us joined together by our love for someone behind these bars and each of us sharing the same white-hot emotions of embarrassment and fear and despair that coming here brings to the surface.

My father has been here for almost three years now. And unless his case is reopened—which is very unlikely—he will remain here until the day he dies. I don't like to think about that, though. I'd rather dream about the day when he might be free again to spend his retirement years back where he belongs—back at the house with me.

But we both know that day will never come. He will never come home again . . . and still the old man claims he has no regrets. Swears he'd do it all over again in a heartbeat. "After all," he tells me, "I was just protecting my family."

*   *   *

Sometimes families just drift apart and it's almost impossible to put a finger on the reason. Age old secrets remain secret. Hidden feelings remain hidden. Sometimes the family was never really that close in the first place, and it simply took the passage of time to bring this sad fact to light.

But you know that's the funny thing. We never drifted apart. We remained close right up to a point and then BOOM—it was over. One day we're a family; the next day we're not. It was almost as if Marty and Lawrence had gotten together behind our backs and planned the whole terrible thing.

After college, Marty went into real estate. He married a fairly snobby woman named Jennifer (not Jenny or Jen, but Jennifer) and moved east to Annapolis and earned a six-figure income selling waterfront property to yuppies. By the time he was thirty-five, he'd had two boys of his own, divorced Jennifer after discovering that she'd been unfaithful with a co-worker, and entered into a second marriage, this time with an older woman who also worked in real estate. I've never met her, but her name is Vicki and she has a very pleasant voice and is downright friendly on the telephone (although I've only spoken with her twice).

Lawrence, who turned out to be not only the brightest, but also the hardest working Finley boy, put his creative skills to profitable use—he went into advertising. He worked a back-breaking schedule and squirreled away his pennies for damn near a decade then opened his own small agency in downtown Baltimore when he was still in his early thirties. Just a handful of years later, he was one of the field's fastest risers, appeared regularly in all the trade magazines, and oversaw an operation of some two dozen employees. Last year (and I read this in the newspaper; we haven't spoken in over five years), he opened a second office—in New York City.

But for all of their successes, it quickly became apparent that Marty and Lawrence had changed. And for the worst. Sure, there were gifts and cards at Christmas and on birthdays, but that was pretty much it. Mom and Dad and I rarely spoke with the two of them—much less saw them—and whenever friends and neighbors asked, our responses were quick, our smiles forced. For a couple of years we kept trying, we honestly did, but our letters went mostly unanswered, our phone calls ignored. The whole situation made Mom and Dad furious. They'd sit around the dining room table, nibbling at their desserts and say, "If they're so ashamed of their small town roots and their small town family, then so be it. Couple of big shots is what they think they are. Good riddance to them." But I could see past their bitterness and resentment. At the end of the day, they were just like me—they were left feeling hurt and confused and abandoned. And it was a miserable feeling, let me tell you. Things like this might happen to other families, but for God's sake not the Finley's.

And so, just like that, we became a family of three.

And, soon after, a family of two.

Mom died in her sleep on Easter weekend 1989, and everyone—including Dad—thought it was a good thing. She'd been suffering something terrible. Lung cancer, if you can believe that. Only fifty-three years old and never smoked a day in her life.

Of course, neither Marty nor Lawrence made it home for the funeral. And if you ask me (and the state police boys *did* ask me in a roundabout way later on), Mom's death coupled with their failure to show up at the service was the final straw. Something inside the old man's mind snapped like a soggy twig and he was never the same again.

Shortly after, he began bringing home the cats. Strays, store-bought; it didn't matter a lick. Sometimes as many as two or three a month. His new family, he called them. The two of us need a family to take care of, he'd say. A family that will stay together and live under the same roof. Just wait and see.

By Christmas later that year, we were living with over twenty cats of various sizes, shapes, and colors. The old man had a name for each and every one of them. And I have to admit, he was right; we were like a family again. He must have felt it, too; he was the happiest I'd seen him in a long time.

Then, just after Easter, right after the first anniversary of Mom's passing, the old man lost it and killed the Benson kid and all hell broke loose.

The drive home takes forever. It's raining again—really coming down now in thick, flapping sheets—and it's all I can do to keep the tires on the road. I change the radio station, try to think of something cheerful, but I can't stop myself from thinking of his eyes. Sparkling with such happiness and love, pleased with my gifts, overjoyed with my presence on his special day. But then, as always, the conversation soon turns and he is asking about his family, and his eyes are transforming into something alien and frightening. Eyes so focused and intense and determined, they belong to someone decades younger; they are the eyes of the stranger who stormed out of the house and chased down the Benson kid that long ago night.

So that's when I take his trembling hand and gently squeeze and tell him what I always tell him: that they are fine. That I am taking good care of them. That his family is safe and sound, and they are all very happy and healthy.

Before I leave he almost breaks my heart when he thanks me with fat tears streaming down his cheeks, and in a quaking voice tells me that I am the man of the family now, that I am the one responsible for their care.

It is after midnight when I pull into the mud-streaked driveway. In the shine of the headlights, I glimpse a blur of black and white fur flash past me and disappear beneath the front porch. For just one moment, I can't decide if I should laugh or cry.

As for me . . . well, I'm still here. I never did leave this town (except for college and, hell, even then, I was back living in my old room ten days after graduation). I never did marry. Never had children. Never made my first million. In fact, you can still find me six days a week working the desk over at Bradshaw County Library and every other Saturday night taking tickets at the movie theater downtown. Not very exciting, I'm afraid.

But, you know, that's okay with me. I turned forty-six a month ago today. I'm finally starting to lose a little ground—going bald on top and a little pudgy on the bottom. Started wearing glasses awhile back too. The kids at the library snicker behind my back once in a while, but they're just being kids; they don't mean anything by it. And, sure, I hear the whispering sometimes, I know the stories they tell—about how old man Finley went off his rocker and strangled little Billy Benson with his bare hands. And all because he'd set one of the old man's cats on fire.

I know they're starting to talk about me, too: about how I'm just as crazy as my old man was. Spending all that time with a house full of stinky old cats. Just like an old blue-haired spinster.

But you know what? I don't mind. Despite everything, I still like this town. I still like my life. There's just something that feels right about it. That's the best way I can explain it. It just feels *right*.

Sure there are nights—usually after drinking too many beers out on the front porch—when I lay awake in bed and stare off into the darkness and wonder what else my life might amount to. I wonder about Marty and Lawrence and why they did what they did. I wonder about Mom and what she would think about all this if she were still alive. And I can't help but wonder about the old man and those haunted eyes of his and that old green bullfrog ashtray and the evening drives for ice cream we used to take back when I was a little kid. But, you know, nothing good ever comes from those thoughts. There are never any easy answers, and those nights are long and lonely and sometimes even a little scary.

But, then, when I awake the next morning and feel the sunlight on my face and smell the coffee in the air and hear the purrs of my family as they gather around my ankles, I have all the answers I'll ever need.

And I'll tell you something else . . . like father, like son. I have no regrets. Not a one.

Listen

Joe R. Lansdale

THE PSYCHIATRIST WORE BLUE, the color of Merguson's mood.
"Mr. . . . uh?" the psychiatrist asked.
"Merguson. Floyd Merguson."
"Sure, Mr. . . ."
"Merguson."
"Right. Come into the office."
It was a sleek office full of sleek black chairs the texture of a lizard's underbelly. The walls were decorated with paintings of explosive color; a metal-drip sculpture resided on the large walnut desk. And there was the couch, of course, just like in the movies. It was a chocolate-brown with throw-pillows at each end. It looked as if you could drift down into it and disappear in its softness.

They sat in chairs, however. The psychiatrist on his side of the desk, Merguson on the client's side.

The psychiatrist was a youngish man with a fine touch of premature white at the temples. He looked every inch the intelligent professional.

"Now," the psychiatrist said, "what exactly is your problem?"

Merguson fiddled his fingers, licked his lips, and looked away. "Come on, now. You came here for help, so let's get started."

"Well," Merguson said cautiously. "No one takes me seriously."

"Tell me about it."

"No one listens to me. I can't take it anymore. Not another moment. I feel like I'm going to explode if I don't get help. Sometimes I just want to yell out, *Listen to me!*"

Merguson leaned forward and said confidentially, "Actually, I think it's a disease. Yeah, I know how that sounds, but I believe it is, and I believe I'm approaching the terminal stage of the illness.

"I got this theory that there are people others don't notice, that they're almost invisible. There's just something genetically wrong with them that causes them to go unnoticed. Like a little clock that ticks inside them, and the closer it gets to the hour hand the more unnoticed these people become.

"I've always had the problem of being shy and introverted—and that's the first sign of the disease. You either shake it early or you don't. If you don't, it just grows like cancer and consumes you. With me the problem gets worse every year, and lately by the moment.

"My wife, she used to tell me it's all in my head, but lately she doesn't bother. But let me start at the first, when I finally decided I was ill, that the illness was getting worse and that it wasn't just in my head, not some sort of complex.

"Just last week I went to the butcher, the butcher I been going to for ten years. We were never chummy, no one has ever been chummy to me but my wife, and she married me for my money. I was at least visible then; I mean you had to go to at least some effort to ignore me, but my God, it's gotten worse . . .

"I'm off the track. I went to the butcher, asked him for some choice cuts of meat. Another man comes in while I'm talking to him and asks for a pound of hamburger. Talks right over me, mind you. What happens? You guessed it. The butcher starts shooting the breeze with the guy, wraps up a pound of hamburger and hands it over to him!

"I ask him about my order and he says, 'Oh, I forgot.' "

Merguson lit a cigarette and held it between unsteady fingers after a long deep puff. "I tell you, he waited on three other people before he finally got to me, and then he got my order wrong, and I must have told him three times, at least.

"It's more than I can stand, Doc. Day after day people not noticing me, and it's getting worse all the time. Yesterday I went to a movie and and I asked for a ticket and it happened. I mean I went out completely, went transparent, invisible. I mean completely. This was the first time. The guy just sits there behind the glass, like he's looking right through me. I asked him for a ticket again. Nothing.

"I was angry, I'll tell you. I just walked right on toward the door. Things had been getting me down bad enough without not being about to take off and go to a movie and relax. I though I'd show him. Just walk right in. Then they'd sell me a ticket.

"No one tried to stop me. No one seemed to know I was there. I didn't bother with the concession stand. No one would have waited on me anyway.

"Well, that was the first time of the complete fadeouts. And I remember when I was leaving the movie, I got this funny idea. I went into the bathroom and looked in the mirror. I swear to you, Doc, on my mother's grave, there wasn't an image in the mirror. I gripped the sink to keep upright, and when I looked up again I was fading in, slowly. Well, I didn't stick around to see my face come into view. I left there and went straight home.

"That afternoon was the corker. My wife, Connie, I know she's been seeing another man. Why not? She can't see me. And when she can I don't have the presence of a one-watt bulb. I came home from the movie and she's all dressed up and talking on the phone.

"I say, 'Who are you talking to?'"

Merguson crushed his cigarette out in the ashtray on the psychiatrist's desk. "Doesn't say doodly squat, Doc. Not a word. I'm mad as hell. I go upstairs and listen on the extension. It's a man, and they're planning a date.

"I broke in over the line and started yelling at them. Guess what? They guy says, 'Do you hear a buzzing or something or other?' 'No,' she says. And they got right on with their plans.

"I was in a homicidal rage. I went downstairs and snatched the phone out of her hand and threw it across the room. I wrecked furniture and busted up some lamps and expensive pottery. Just made a general wreck out of the place.

"She screamed then, Doc. I tell you she screamed good. But then she says the thing that makes me come here. 'Oh God,' she says. 'Ghost! Ghost in this house!'

"That floored me, and I knew I was invisible again. I went upstairs and looked in the bathroom mirror. Sure enough. Nothing there. So I waited until I faded back and I called your secretary. It took me five tries before she finally wrote my name down, gave me an appointment. It was worse than when I tried to get the meat from the butcher. So I hurried right over. I had to get this out. I swear I'm not going crazy, it's a disease, and it's getting worse and worse and worse.

"So what can I do, Doc?" How can I handle this? I know it's not in my head, and I've got to have some advice. Please, Doc. Say something. Tell me what to do. I've never been this desperate in my entire life. I might fade out again and not come back."

The psychiatrist took his hand from his chin where it had been resting. "Wha . . . ? Sorry. I must have dozed. What was it again, Mr. . . . uh?"

Merguson dove across the desk, clawing for the psychiatrist's throat.

Later when the law came and found the psychiatrist strangled and slumped across his desk, his secretary said, "Funny, I don't remember anyone coming in or leaving. Couldn't have come in while I was here. He had an appointment with a Mr. . . . uh." She looked at the appointment book. "A Mr. Merguson. But he never showed."

A Little More Research

Joan Hess

BART BELLICOSE REALIZED *time was running out. In the distance, he could hear the whine of sirens, and he knew the police cars were closing in on him like a swarm of killer bees. He stepped back, then threw his two hundred forty pounds of bulk against the flimsy door. It gave way with a shriek of pain, and Bellicose stumbled into the apartment.*

There on the carpet lay the mortal remains of his client. Even in death, the semi-nude body was as undulating as the ocean, as smooth as the inner petals of a rose. He could see that his client was as dead as the proverbial doornail, one of which had ripped his arms in an angry slash of

"Terry, honey, when are you gonna be finished? I'm getting hungry, and it's almost too late to make reservations."

"I've asked you not to interrupt me. The deadline's tomorrow morning at nine o'clock, for pete's sake, and my editor's about to have an apoplectic fit. I can't concentrate when you come in here every five minutes."

"I'm sorry. It's just that I get all lonesome out there by myself. Maybe it would help if I rubbed your neck. . . ?"

"It would not. I'm on the last chapter and I need to get it done tonight. Please don't interrupt me any more."

"Okay, I'll be a good little guest and wait in the living room. All by myself."

"Thank you so very much. And shut the door, will you?"

grinning blood. It was obvious to anyone who'd ever eyed a fresh corpse that the

"Don't let me disturb you, but how about if I make reservations for later just in case you get done with your story?"

"I'm not going to get done if you don't leave me alone. I told you when you insisted on coming over tonight that I absolutely must have peace and quiet in order to concentrate."

"I happen to be speaking very quietly, my dear Hot Shot Writer."

"You also happen to be standing in the doorway, which means I'm looking at you rather than at the word processor. Go ahead and make reservations any place you want. I really don't care."

"Well, maybe I'll just do that."

It was obvious that . . . It was obviously murder. Bart could see that as he stared at the Bart frowned at the gaping Bart gasped as he spotted the hilt of the dagger protruding from the contoured chest

"Honey, telephone."

"I'm not home. Take a message and I'll call back tomorrow."

* * *

There was something about the dagger that touched a raw nerve. He'd
seen it

"It's your editor, and he sounds real mad."

"Tell him I'm not here, and close the door on your way out."

"But I already told him you were home and working real hard on the story. He says he wants to talk to you right this minute."

"All right, damn it."

before. Sorry, Bart. Back in a minute. Try to remember, huh?

"Yo, Terry baby, how's it going?"

"It was going quite well until you called and interrupted me, Irwin. You do realize every time I'm interrupted I lose my train of thought?"

"Right, right. I wanted to remind you that we go into production tomorrow, with or without the last chapter. The book's gonna look pretty funny with a bunch of blank pages at the end. You promised me this manuscript. We paid a fat advance, and then waited patiently while you missed not one but two deadlines. You're in the catalogue. I've held the production people back till the bitter end, but the bottom line is that's where we are."

"And I'm not in my office finishing the book. *Au contraire,* I'm standing in the kitchen chitchatting with you. Goodbye, Irwin. I'll be in your office at nine o'clock."

"You and Bellicose, I presume."

"At this very moment Bellicose is standing over a body, and he'd like to investigate in the immediate future."

"So you finally got the plot straightened out?"

"Yes, I finally got the plot straightened out. Tomorrow at nine, okay? We can celebrate with Danishes."

"I'll get a dozen of them. Just make sure you show up for the party."

"I'm hanging up now, Irwin. Next time you get lonely, call your ex-wife."

He'd seen the dagger somewhere. Great.

Forget the dagger.

Bart stared at the bullet hole in the forehead. It was a third eye, as unseeing as the deep blue pools he'd

* * *

"Are you off the telephone?"

"No, I had the receiver implanted in my head and I'm listening to the time and weather as we speak. What is it?"

"I was trying to catch you before you started writing again to ask if you think Chinese sounds good. Or Japanese, I suppose, but not squid or tofu or anything creepy like that."

"I don't care. Do you mind? I mean, do you really mind giving me more than three minutes undisturbed?"

"I was just asking. You're acting like you've forgotten about last night. You didn't object to my company then."

"When I get this story done, maybe I'll remember. Please?"

"I'll sit in the living room and be as quiet as a mouse."

Deep blue pools of squid ink. On tofu.

Deadline. Deadline. Deadlineeeeee.

Bart recognized from the size of the wound that the bullet was of a low caliber. Could it have involved the swarthy woman with the mustache who'd come to his office yesterday, the one who'd cried and begged him to help her save her missing dauuuuuu

"What was that, damn it?"

"Don't pay any attention, Terry. I'll clean it up. After all, I don't have anything else to do."

"Clean what up?"

"Don't worry about it. It's no big deal."

"How can you say it was no big deal? It sounded like a friggin' nuclear explosion."

"I don't remember seeing you at Hiroshima. Just go back to work and stop yelling at me like I was some kind of kid or something. I said I'd clean it up."

"Was it the plate glass window?"

"Go back to work."

"The television? My new state-of-the-art television that I have three years to pay on?"

"No, and leave me alone so I can clean it up. I thought you had a deadline tomorrow . . ."

ghter. Bart stared around the room, which looked as if a nuclear bomb had gone off minutes before. The plate glass window was a spiderweb of cracks, and the television, a particularly expensive model with remote, built-in video cassette recorder, quadraphonic stereo, and one hundred thirty-seven channel capacity, was nothing more than a smoldering ruin of useless wires and busted tubes and would still suck up thirty-five more monthly payments.

But Bart warned himself not to dwell on the devastation and bent over the body. The flesh was still warm, and a ribbon of blood flowed from one corner of the mouth, which was twisted into a faint smile of surprise. So the victim had known the perp, Bart decided as he reached into his pocket and took out a pack of

"Did you take my cigarettes?"

"What?"

"I said, did you come into my office and take the pack of cigarettes I keep in the bottom left drawer for emergencies?"

"It was an emergency. I was out."

"Well, so am I. Bring that pack back."

"I smoked all of them this afternoon while I was watching this really great old movie about this debutante that falls in love with her sister's—"

"I'll read the newspaper if I want a review. Go down to the deli and get me another pack. You know I can't write when I'm out of cigarettes."

"No way. It's already late and I'm not about to get myself mugged just because you want a pack of cigarettes. It's your crummy neighborhood, not mine. If you're so desperate, go get them yourself."

Bart realized there was no time for a cigarette, not with the police moving in like a pack of vicious, slobbering wolves. Despite the sense of panic that could be appeased only by a cigarette, by a long deep satisfying lungful of carbon monoxide flavored with nicotine, he reluctantly turned back to the body, keenly aware that the evidence before him would lead to the identity of the murderer.

The clue was there before his eyes. He could almost see it, almost touch it, almost smell it, that acrid redolence of smoldering

"I smell smoke. What the hell's burning?"

"Nothing, Terry."

"Don't give me that. I smell smoke. I smell cigarette smoke, damn it! I thought you said the pack was empty."

"Don't short out your pacemaker over it. There was one cigarette left in the pack, that's all."

"The pack that you stole from my office? Is that the pack we're talking about? I cannot believe you would not only steal the pack from my desk, but then lie and say it was empty while sneaking the last cigarette!"

"If you keep huffing and puffing like that, you're gonna blow the door down. I am sitting in here on the sofa holding my breath so I won't disturb you, and it seems to me you're the one bellowing and snorting and carrying on like a baby who wants a lollipop. It's like you've got some kind of oral fixation or something."

"First you steal my emergency pack, then you—"

"This is very childish. Perhaps you might worry a little less about me and a little more about the deadline tomorrow morning?"

The lingering smoke meant nothing, Bart thought with a snarl. No, the clue, the goddamn clue

No, now he could see what must have happened in the seedy apartment. The jagged corner of yellow paper beside the body was the exact same shade as the scrap he'd found at the nightclub. And that explained it. Yes! Yes!!! It was the link to the woman who'd lost a daughter, and it was the link to the strange fellow in the fedora who'd been following Bart for all those long days while he'd been on the case. It was as if the sun had finally broken the horizon after so many long weeks of arctic winter.

Bart smiled as the police stormed the room, their revolvers aimed at his heart. He knew he could explain

"Terry, I made reservations at that Thai restaurant everybody talks about all the time. We need to leave pretty soon if we're going to get there on time."

"Screw the Thai restaurant."

Bart held up the scrap of paper and said

"They're always packed, and the only reason we got the reservation is because a bunch of Shriners got drunk in the bar and refused to eat."

"Screw the Shriners."

Bart said screw the shriners oh hell come on bart you know who did it and who that fedora dude is and the scrap of yellow paper come on bart bellicose don't forget you can remember you had it a minute ago and it

*was good bart it was good and it was tight and it was right up there with
brilliant and*

  it is gone finito ciao adios arrivederci

"Is everything okay, Terry? You're making an awfully funny noise
in there."

"Don't worry about me. See, here I am in the kitchen and I'm
just fine. As soon as I find a certain something in the drawer, I'm
coming in the living room. Why don't you fix us a nice drink?"

*Bart Bellicose left the police station, trying not to strut as he remem-
bered how deftly he'd wrapped up the case in a pink bow to hand over to
the detectives. They had listened in awe as he'd explained how his client,
an errant husband with a fondness for exotic dancers, had blackmailed
the sultry, smoky-eyed postal carrier who moonlighted at the Turkish
Bizarre. The chump had opened the door to sign the yellow slip for a
registered letter. Now his coffin and the case were closed.*

*There would be another case tomorrow, another chance to outwit the
police. But for the moment, Bart savored this victory. If you wanted a
case solved—and you wanted it solved right—then you called Bart Bellicose, by damn.*

The end.

Yahooooooooooooo

"Yo, Terry, what time is it? Lemme get the light. Jeez, it's after
midnight and I got to face the production guys in the morning."

"Stop at the bakery on your way to work, Irwin. Bart Bellicose
has pulled it off again."

"It's done? You got it done? Lordy, I was sweating in my sleep
for you. I'm not kidding; my pajamas are sticking to my armpits.
All those glitches in the plot, those false starts and stops . . . I
can't believe it."

"I'll admit I was having trouble with it. I just couldn't get a
handle on the corpse sprawled on the living room floor. I couldn't
see him, if you know what I mean. I couldn't touch his body, smell
his blood, analyze his expression of surprise and fear."

"But you figured something out, huh?"

"With a little help from a friend."

"Well, I'm glad to hear it. Hey, I've got a bottle of twelve-year-
old scotch I've been saving for my son's wedding. Now he says he

wants to be a priest. Hop a cab and come on over to celebrate. Bring your friend."

"A fine idea, Irwin, although I'm afraid my friend's not up to a small party. I'll stop at the deli for a pack of cigarettes and be over shortly."

"Then be careful. You may write the hardest boiled private eye series in the industry, but you look more like a genteel lady librarian from Phoenix. Too bad Bart can't come along as your bodyguard. So tell me the truth—how'd you pull it off so quickly?"

"I realized that all I needed to do was a little more research. That's what it took—a little more research."

Locking Up

John Maclay

I WOULDN'T CALL myself a meticulous man; I go two months between haircuts, would rather wear old clothes than new, and often eat my meals in front of the T.V. But I am an orderly man—even my wife says so; my home office may be cluttered with stacks of papers and printouts, yet I know exactly where everything is.

And despite my relaxed days, my intense worknights as a freelance systems analyst, I do have certain routines—or I should say, still have; because many of them are left over from my dozen mistaken years in a nine-to-five job and as a family man/householder only. I go to the post office every day, downtown to the bank once a week, have lunch with an old acquaintance every two, attend a lodge meeting each month, subscribe to the opera. I cut the grass and paint the house in the summer, shovel snow and add antifreeze in the winter. And after all, there's that haircut. So I'm not to be mistaken for that rebel-from-birth, that man or woman who can't fix a car, drive a nail, or even send off the right letter in the right envelope.

I value my relative freedom—but I also need my routines. Because, as I once told my teen-age son, if you bend over backwards to do certain outward things, particularly the unpleasant ones—to take care of them—you'll be even more able to forget them when you go inside yourself, to that place where you really live. As Flaubert said' "Be orderly in your life"—or something like that—"so that you may be violent in your work." And that applied especially well if you live in the city, as I do, where a lack of attention to certain routines can bring real violence into both parts of your existence. Certain routines . . . like locking up.

Every night for the past six years, even since we moved here, I've done the same four things. After my family has gone to bed—and I've counted the numbers off mentally, sometimes even verbally—I've (1) walked out front, checked the street, then come back and triple-locked the front door, (2) checked that all the windows downstairs, and the cellar door, are closed and locked, (3) walked out back, checked the garage, then double-locked the back door, and (4) turned on the Rollins alarm. Only then have I gone upstairs relaxed, ready to work in the midnight quiet, secure in the knowledge that even the outside sounds that do penetrate my far-off mind can mean no harm to me. Every night . . . until last night, when I became aware of a small problem.

It was when I was on the "garage" check, walking through the cool air, taking a moment to look up at the moon. Suddenly, there were the voices—whispering, from beyond the hedge.

". . . There he is."

I thought of stopping, retreating to the house—but the routine, I suppose, was just too strong. So I kept walking, tried the garage door, then turned to go back.

". . . Same thing every night." I heard a chuckle. "So . . . easy. We just wait, grab him, take him inside, kill him—then the silver, the woman . . . all of it's ours."

I guess the voices did bother me—but I had things to do, a computer program to finish for the morning mail. And the police, if I called them, would never come in time. So I just (3a) locked the back door, (4) switched the alarm on . . . and went upstairs to my office.

The program was a good one—one of my best, which, consistent with the masochist's triumph of my chosen profession, kept me up until dawn, at which time I rolled into bed beside my sleeping, unconsciously-grumbling wife. And when I awoke, at eleven in the morning, I felt refreshed. Even the voices, which I dimly remembered as I brushed my teeth, were only details—to be taken care of, in the course of my free-form, resting day, along with more pleasant things: a planned trip downtown, a lunch with an old friend.

So tonight, when I set out once more upon my numbered lock-up routine, there was no problem at all. I went through numbers (1) and (2), then sauntered out to the garage.

The men, the two of them, were even worse than they'd sounded—the absolute dregs of society, like nothing I'd seen even when, by way of diversion, I'd gone "slumming." Cut-off T-shirts, impossibly developed muscles, twisted faces—advancing surreally, pushing through the hedge. And they were laughing.

" 'Same thing every night,' " the taller of them said, leering, extending a huge, filthy hand—

I smiled, turned from the garage door, casually looked up at the moon. Reached into my old jacket.

"Same thing every night," I said quietly—and they laughed again, sure of their horrible conquest over the slow-witted man who stood before them, who could only echo their words. Yet just as surely, my hand closed over the cold metal. "But not same thing"—I continued—"every day!"

"So easy!" I couldn't resist adding, to their unbelieving faces, as I used the Smith and Wesson—*pop, pop*—I'd bought after lunch, then walked calmly into the house to complete numbers (3) and (4) of my routine. And as I climbed to my office, I also couldn't help paraphrasing Flaubert: "Sometimes, to keep the order, to tend to the unpleasant details, you have to be a little bit violent in your life, too." Then, as I sat at my desk, I noted down—as every thinking person should, Chinese proverb-like—what the experience had taught me: "The proof of a good routine is the knowledge of when to break it."

I developed another good program tonight. And now, as I go to bed, I'm leaving a note on my wife's bedside table, asking her to call the police in the morning, explain what happened, and have them remove the bodies in the yard. She, and they, can take care of it—I'll sleep in, and answer questions later. Because, you see, I'm an orderly man—not a meticulous one.

The Longest Pleasure

C. J. Henderson

"Now hatred is by far the longest pleasure,
Men love in haste, but they detest at leisure."
LORD BYRON

THE SUN BEAT DOWN on me without mercy—blazing, tearing the world apart—the hottest sun the world had ever known. I was in the desert, a middle Eastern one, the kind with no plant life—just rolling dunes and vast, unbelievable stretches of dusty grey sand. Survival did not really seem like an option.

The post I had found to lean on was still digging into my back. It hurt no matter how I moved, but I didn't care. It didn't matter. Nothing mattered. Except waiting for Tom.

How we had gotten stranded in the desert alone, without supplies and left to die, none of that was important any more. The heat, the baking, frying dryness that had burned my skin and cracked my tongue . . . that was all that mattered. That and waiting for Tom.

When I had first started to make my way forward out of the desert, I had stopped sweating in less than half an hour. It had only taken my body that long to adjust to the situation . . . to understand that we were lost in a hell of burning glare and blinding pain, and that it was going to take everything we had to get ourselves out alive.

Where Tom was at that point, I didn't know. Or care. For the first time in years I had actually forgotten about him. I had had more important things to worry about. Every step across the drily blowing sand had been a nightmare. Caring about my own neck had shoved the memory of Tom from my mind for the moment.

For the moment.

It took me two days to find my waiting place. Two days struggling across the fiery sands. Across the suffocating forge ever blasting at me—draining me, reducing me, searing and boiling and charring me—stripping me to the most basic components . . . those that kept one foot moving after the other.

Step after step . . . step after step . . . step after step . . . after . . . step . . . after step . . .

Until somehow blind instinct finally dragged me to the dirty wallow and the sickly tangle it supported. What I had found wasn't much. The *oasis,* for lack of a better word, was a hellishly small thing. It had no trees, no lush patch of veld surrounding it. It was a mud hole, no more than two by three, with a scattering of some scrub cactus and tangled weeds and bits of grass and the such around it. So small, in truth, and yet the lie of it as wide as an ocean. That was where I found the rifle.

The pole driven into the ground near it by some unknown traveler gave me something to lean against. The rifle I found at the base of the post gave me something to hold. Something to hold as I leaned in pain and waited for Tom.

I had to wait because I knew he would come. I *knew* he would find the oasis. Say what you wanted about Tom, no matter what you had to admit that he was a survivor. He would survive the desert. "He had to," I thought, as I leaned against the uncomfortable post.

He just had to.

And, he did. I don't know how long it took, but eventually I saw him, on hands and knees, dragging his way across the desert. Coming toward me and the water at my feet. My burnt fingers twitched. Skin cracked as they tightened around the stock of the rifle. Just for fun, I lined Tom up in the sight's cross hairs.

Just for fun.

"Come on," I whispered, throat scratching, head reeling. "Crawl. Crawl, you bastard. Like you made so many *others* crawl."

How many lives *did* you ruin? I wondered. How much *pain* did you cause? Ruthlessly. *Needlessly?*

I gripped the rifle tighter—more determined.

"You're still in my sights, Tom," I thought grimly. But, suddenly it's not so much fun any more.

I kept my bead on him. I wanted to fire so badly I was shaking. Suddenly I didn't care to let him reach the water. Somehow, seeing him crawl toward me—head gleaming in the sunlight . . . such a tempting . . . *perfect* target . . .

One bullet—such an easy shot—a simple pull . . . and it would all . . . *finally* be over.

I could move away from this painful post . . . and make my own thirsty way out of this inferno. Just one . . . easy . . . shot.

But, as I watched Tom drag himself across the broiling dunes, imagining the scraping heat of the sand scrubbing away his skin, as I remembered all he had done, I finally decided against the bullet. With each passing second, I simply watched him strain to pull himself closer. Foot by foot. Until finally, he was before me, inches from the mud hole.

As I lowered the rifle Tom thrust his head under the water. He sputtered and retched, but kept his head in the wallow, gulping it in as deeply as he could. I let him drink undisturbed. Then, after a long moment, he pulled his head up out of the water. Dripping wet, refreshed and arrogant, he smiled at me, his blazing Irish eyes twinkling as he sneered:

"HaaHaaaaaaaaa. You're still a fool. Just like all the others. Weak and stupid—all of you." Shoving his left hand into the water, he splashed it across his head and back and neck.

"That's why I always won," he added. "That's why I always—"

And then, Tom's body froze as sudden, incredible pain exploded within him. Red claws of agony tore through his guts. His eyes went wide, distorting grotesquely. His hands slapped at his neck, blistered fingers digging and rubbing in futile desperation.

"Finally," I thought, as Tom rolled across the sand, dying in pain that seemed all I could have hoped for. Finally, I could step away from the gouging pain of the pole.

I sighed with relief as I pulled my back free from the puncturing horns. The animal skull that had been placed atop the pole to warn desert travelers about the poisonous waters at my feet was an ominous, nasty looking thing. I waited for Tom to see it, waited for recognition of what I had done to him to show in his eyes. The glimmer of realization coincided with a bleating scream that tore itself loose from the center of his tattered soul.

Earlier, when I'd had Tom in the sights of the rifle . . . oh how I'd wanted to pull the trigger. Now I was so glad I hadn't. A bullet would have been too clean.

Too easy.

As I struck out once more across the desert, I whispered,

"Remember me over the next few hours, Tom. As your guts boil and your stomach bleeds. Remember the stupid weakness I showed in letting you gobble down your death."

I hadn't had a drink in three days. But it was worth it. Worth waiting for him to catch up with me. Worth it to see the look on his face . . .

I knew it was quite possible that I wouldn't survive. That perhaps my hate had killed the both of us. At that point, however, it didn't matter. I'd reaped all the pleasure I needed from life at that point. All I could want.

The longest pleasure of all.

The Man Who Was Everywhere

Edward D. Hoch

H E FIRST NOTICED the new man in the neighborhood on a Tuesday evening, on his way home from the station. The man was tall and thin, with a look about him that told Ray Bankcroft he was English. It wasn't anything Ray could put his finger on, the fellow just looked English.

That was all there was to their first encounter, and the second meeting passed just as casually, Friday evening at the station. The fellow was living around Pelham some place, maybe in that new apartment house in the next block.

But it was the following week that Ray began to notice him everywhere. The tall Englishman rode down to New York with Ray on the 8:09, and he was eating a few tables away at Howard Johnson's one noon. But that was the way things were in New York, Ray told himself, where you sometimes ran into the same person every day for a week, as though the laws of probability didn't exist.

It was on the weekend, when Ray and his wife journeyed up to Stamford for a picnic, that he became convinced the Englishman was following him. For there, fifty miles from home, the tall stranger came striding slowly across the rolling hills, pausing now and then to take in the beauty of the place.

"Damn it, Linda," Ray remarked to his wife, "there's that fellow again!"

"What fellow, Ray?"

"That Englishman from our neighborhood. The one I was telling you I see everywhere."

"Oh, is that him?" Linda Bankcroft frowned through the tinted lenses of her sunglasses. "I don't remember ever seeing him before."

"Well, he must be living in that new apartment in the next

block. I'd like to know what the hell he's doing up here, though. Do you think he could be following me?"

"Oh, Ray, don't be silly," Linda laughed. "Why would anyone want to follow you? And to a picnic!"

"I don't know, but it's certainly odd the way he keeps turning up. . . ."

It certainly was odd.

And as the summer passed into September, it grew odder still. Once, twice, three times a week, the mysterious Englishman appeared, always walking, always seemingly oblivious of his surroundings.

Finally, one night on Ray Bankcroft's way home, it suddenly grew to be too much for him.

He walked up to the man and asked, "Are you following me?"

The Englishman looked down his nose with a puzzled frown. "I beg your pardon?"

"Are you following me?" Ray repeated. "I see you everywhere."

"My dear chap, really, you must be mistaken."

"I'm not mistaken. Stop following me!"

But the Englishman only shook his head sadly and walked away. And Ray stood and watched him until he was out of sight. . . .

"Linda, I saw him again today!"

"Who, dear?"

"That damned Englishman! He was in the elevator in my building."

"Are you sure it was the same man?"

"Of course I'm sure! He's everywhere, I tell you! I see him every day now, on the street, on the train, at lunch, and now even in the elevator! It's driving me crazy. I'm certain he's following me. But why?"

"Have you spoken to him?"

"I've spoken to him, cursed at him, threatened him. But it doesn't do any good. He just looks puzzled and walks away. And then the next day there he is again."

"Maybe you should call the police. But I suppose he hasn't really done anything."

"That's just the trouble, Linda. He hasn't done a single thing. It's just that he's always around. The damned thing is driving me crazy."

"What—what are you going to do about it?"

"I'll tell you what I'm going to do! The next time I see him I'm going to grab him and beat the truth out of him. I'll get to the bottom of this. . . ."

The next night, the tall Englishman was back, walking just ahead of him on the train platform. Ray ran toward him, but the Englishman disappeared in the crowd.

Perhaps the whole thing was just a coincidence, and yet . . .

Later that night Ray ran out of cigarettes, and when he left the apartment and headed for the corner drugstore, he knew the tall Englishman would be waiting for him along the route.

And as he came under the pale red glow of the flickering neon, he saw the man, walking slowly across the street from the railroad tracks.

Ray knew that this must be the final encounter.

"Say there!"

The Englishman paused and looked at him distastefully, then turned and walked away from Ray.

"Wait a minute, you! We're going to settle this once and for all!"

But the Englishman kept walking.

Ray cursed and started after him through the darkness. He called out, "Come back here!" But now the Englishman was almost running.

Ray broke into a trot, following him down the narrow street that led along the railroad tracks. "Damn you, come back! I want to talk to you!"

But the Englishman ran on, faster and faster. Finally Ray paused, out of breath.

And ahead, the Englishman had paused too.

Ray could see the gleaming glow of his wristwatch as he raised his hand in a gesture. And Ray saw that he was beckoning him to follow. . . .

Ray broke into a run again.

The Englishman waited only a moment and then he too ran, keeping close to the edge of the railroad wall, where only a few inches separated him from a twenty-foot drop to the tracks below.

In the distance, Ray heard the low whistle of the Stamford Express, tearing through the night.

Ahead, the Englishman rounded a brick wall that jutted out almost to the edge of the embankment. He was out of sight around the corner for a moment, but Ray was now almost upon him. He rounded the wall himself and saw, too late, that the Englishman was waiting for him there.

The man's big hands came at him, and all at once Ray was pushed and falling sideways, over the edge of the railroad wall, clawing helplessly at the air.

And as he hit the tracks, he saw that the Stamford Express was almost upon him, filling all space with its terrible sound. . . .

Some time later, the tall Englishman peered through a cloud of blue cigarette smoke at the graceful figure of Linda Bankcroft and said, "As I remarked at the beginning of all this, my darling, a proper murder is the ultimate game of skill. . . ."

The Marrow of Justice

Hal Ellson

THE COFFIN was a plain one, finished in the shop of Carlos Martinez, without frills, stark naked wood of soft pine. Harsh sunlight splintered off it as the men carried it through the miserable street, treading its dust, stones, and the scattered fire of tangerine peels withering in the heat.

It was a day of flame but, in this land of perpetual sun, not unseasonable. No more than death. The poor in their shacks and crumbling adobes knew its ghastly visits all too frequently. Funerals were commonplace and all of a kind. A plain pine box for the deceased, four men to carry it, and a small group of mourners following.

A vast crowd followed the coffin of Rosa Belmonte, the third young girl in the city to die by violation. Half-starved dogs with their ribs showing, children, toddlers, and beggars amidst the crowd lent it a pseudo air of carnival which was diluted by the somber faces of adults and a muffled silence under which anger awaited eruption.

The police felt it, a news photographer sighted it in his camera. Detective Fiala was aware of the same phenomenon, but unconcerned with the crowd as such. His eyes sought only one man—the murderer who, through guilt or morbid disposition, might be lurking here.

No face riveted his attention till he noticed the limousine, with the crowd breaking around it and the Chief of Police, José Santiago. He was sitting beside his chauffeur, face bloated and dark, tinted glasses concealing incongruous blue eyes that resembled twin stones and reflected the basic nature of the man.

Without the uniform he might be the one I'm looking for, Fiala thought, turning away and moving on with the sullen crowd that refused to acknowledge the naked violence of the sun.

The funeral went off without incident, the police were relieved, Chief Santiago satisfied. His chauffeur returned him to the Municipal building, the location of police headquarters.

As he entered his office with Captain Torres, the phone rang. He picked it up, listened, then dismissed Captain Torres with a wave of his hand. Frowning now, he spoke to his caller, Victor Quevedo, mayor of the city and the one who had "made" him. These two were friends of a sort, but the conversation that ensued between them now was strictly business.

The murder of Rosa Belmonte, with the killer not apprehended, as in both previous murders, had created grave criticism of the police which, in turn, reflected upon Quevedo, exposing him to the machinations of his political enemies. This was the gist of Quevedo's complaint along with his sharp demand that Santiago do something and do it fast.

"Do what?" Santiago said.

"Get the killer before midnight."

Astounded, Santiago hesitated, stuttered inanely, and finally managed to say, "But, Victor—"

Quevedo cut him off sharply. "I am being embarrassed, politically and otherwise," he snapped. "If you wish to continue as Chief of Police, find the killer. Don't, and you're finished."

Sweating profusely, Santiago dropped the phone and sat down. Slowly, with trembling hands, he lit a cigarette and dispersed a cloud of smoke. His thoughts were in chaos, dark face swollen to bursting. Slowly the agitation within him receded. Behind his tinted glasses his cold eyes lit up as a face focused in his mind.

He crushed his cigarette, arose, opened the door, called Captain Torres into the office, and gave him his orders. "Pick up Manuel Domingo for the murder of Rosa Belmonte."

Manuel Domingo's criminal activities were long known to the police—but murder? Captain Torres raised his brows in surprise.

"Are you sure you have the right man?" he asked.

"Are you doubting me, or my source of information?" Santiago wanted to know, asserting both the authority of his office and intimating that the phone call he'd received was the "voice" of a reliable informer.

Captain Torres flushed and retreated to the door. From there he said, "I'll pick up Manuel Domingo personally."

At nine that evening, a black sky threatened the city and the lacy jacarandas stirred to a faint errant wind from the mountains where yellow lightning ignited the empty heavens. Behind the Municipal building four bars faced the plaza, loud voices broke from each of them.

Saturday night was just beginning and musicians lolled on the plaza benches, barefoot boys shined shoes, hawked blood-red and dove-white roses on trays of cardboard, like everyone else, forgetting Rosa Belmonte.

It was on this scene that Captain Torres arrived with three of his men after an intensive and fruitless search of all the usual haunts of the criminal Manuel Domingo.

Captain Torres was convinced that Domingo had fled the city when chance directed his eyes to a bench where two shoeshine boys vied for the privilege of doing the shoes of Detective Fiala.

Granting them each a shoe, Fiala looked up to see the strapping, youthful Captain Torres and his three men confronting him.

The latter were innocuous fellows, Captain Torres an arrogant whelp, but hardly that now. He needed help and Fiala, whom he despised and who despised him, might provide the information he needed so badly.

"I am looking for Manuel Domingo," Torres announced. "Perhaps you know his whereabouts?"

With a derisive smile, Fiala nodded toward a bar directly across the street. "Manuel Domingo is in there. You're picking him up?"

"For the murder of Rosa Belmonte," Captain Torres replied and turned on his heels.

Fiala sat where he was. Half a minute later Manuel Domingo came through the door of the bar across the street, accompanied by Captain Torres and his three men. All five passed through the plaza and entered police headquarters.

Fiala, who had gone off duty early that day, lit a cigarette and shook his head. No matter what, Manuel Domingo's fate was sealed, the murder was solved. Tomorrow the newspapers would be filled with it.

In disgust, Fiala flicked his cigarette to the gutter and noticed the group of men who'd come from the bar across the street. Anger echoed in their voices; word spread quickly around the plaza: Manuel Domingo had been picked up for the murder of Rosa Belmonte. Manuel Domingo . . .

Under the black angry sky a crowd began to converge on police headquarters, but too late to give vent to its feelings, for the brief interrogation of Manuel Domingo was already completed. Guarded by police, he stepped to the sidewalk and was quickly ushered into a waiting car.

Into a second car stepped Chief of Police Santiago and Captain Torres. With an escort of ten motorcyle policemen, both cars roared off toward the scene of the crime, in the desert several miles from the city.

The cavalcade soon reached it, the glaring lights of cars and motorcycles focused on a tall yucca beside the road. At its foot Luis Espina, a gatherer of fiber obtained from a small spiny desert plant, had discovered the body of Rosa Belmonte.

As Manuel Domingo stepped from the car, his face took on a ghastly hue, perhaps because of the lights, perhaps out of fear now that he was at the scene of the crime. Whatever he felt, he said nothing: he appeared dazed.

A sharp command from Captain Torres sent the policemen into a wide semi-circle, with guns drawn to prevent an attempted escape. That done, Captain Torres walked to the edge of the road with Santiago and Manuel Domingo. There, on orders, he took up position, while the prisoner and Santiago proceeded to the foot of the yucca.

Once there, Manuel Domingo, stopped and stood like a soldier ordered to attention. Headlights impaled him in a glaring crossfire. A sheer wall of black enveloped this luminous area. Now the brief interrogation which Santiago had conducted at headquarters continued. He was seen to gesture; his voice in an unintelligible murmur carried only to Captain Torres.

Manuel Domingo turned, spoke for the first time since stepping into the car. He was frightened, the terrible black sky threatened, he did not trust Santiago.

"Get me out of this," he said, "or else."

"Quiet, you fool. This is routine. You've been accused."

"Who accuses me? Name him."

"Shut up and listen."

Manuel Domingo came to attention again. His chest heaved, chin lifted, then suddenly he bolted in an attempt to escape. Calmly Santiago fired from the hip.

Domingo seemed to be running on air. The weight of his body carried him forward, then his legs buckled and he plunged forward to sprawl on the desert floor.

Moments later Santiago stood over him and fired another shot as the others closed in.

The black night enveloped the desolate scene as the cavalcade roared off toward the city. Santiago glanced at the clock on the dashboard and settled back. It was still early, the issue settled. The mayor no longer had reason to be embarrassed.

As Santiago smiled to himself, Captain Torres turned and said, "Officially, we know now that Manuel Domingo was guilty of murdering Rosa Belmonte, but—"

"You don't think he killed the girl?"

"Do you?"

"No."

"Then why did he run?"

"I told him we couldn't protect him from the mob, that if he ran, I'd cover him and let him escape because I knew he was innocent."

"But you shot him down."

Santiago put a cigarette to his lips. "I had no alternative," he answered, flicking his lighter, and the cavalcade moved on toward the lights of the city.

In the early morning the body of the murderer Manuel Domingo, naked but for a white sheet that covered the lower half of his body, lay on a long table beneath a tree in a small plaza near the center of the city for all to see and take warning. Flies came with the heat; the light brought crowds.

All through the day the people of the city filed past the dead man and at dusk he was taken away, mourned by none.

Here the matter would have ended, interred along with Manuel Domingo, but for Detective Fiala, who knew one thing beyond doubt: Domingo hadn't killed the girl. With the murderer still at large, on his own time, Fiala conducted an investigation which quickly proved fruitful. That done, he appeared at the Municipal building, asked to see Mayor Quevedo, and was informed that he was at lunch with several men of importance.

Obtaining the name of the restaurant, Fiala went there, seated himself at a table next to Quevedo's party, bowed, and, in a voice soft enough to elude the ears of the others, said, "If I may have a word. It's a matter of grave important which concerns you."

Such was his manner that Quevedo quickly nodded. When he and his companions finished eating, he contrived an excuse for remaining behind and sat down at Fiala's table.

"Now," he said with some anxiety, "what is this matter of importance which concerns me?"

"I'm afraid it's much too important to discuss here."

"In that case, we'll go to my office."

Fiala nodded and both of them rose and went out the door. A few minutes later they faced each other across Quevedo's ornate hand-carved desk. Quevedo offered a cigarette. Fiala refused it and presented his case, bluntly informing him that the Chief of Police had murdered Rosa Belmonte.

"A very serious charge," Quevedo said, turning pale. "But can you prove it?"

Fiala nodded and described how he'd gone to see Luis Espina, the fiber-gatherer who'd discovered the body of the dead girl. With a series of tactful questions he'd finally gotten the old man to admit that he'd actually witnessed the murder.

"If this is true," Quevedo put in, "Why didn't Espina come forward and say so?"

"He couldn't," Fiala replied, "because at the time of the murder he didn't recognize Santiago. All he knew was that the killer drove off in a blue and white Cadillac. That was significant. I continued to question him and he produced a vivid description of the driver, but not his identity. That came later when I pressed him.

"He then admitted that he'd watched the spectacle last night. The lights drew him from his house, and he saw Santiago gun down Manuel Domingo. That's when he recognized him as the murderer of Rosa Belmonte."

Quevedo nodded and said, "The word of a confused old man. His story won't hold water. Besides, Domingo admitted his guilt at the scene of the crime by attempting to escape."

"Admitted his guilt?" Fiala smiled and shook his head. "That was the one fact I knew from the beginning, that he wasn't guilty. You see, Manuel Domingo couldn't have killed Rosa Belmonte. He wasn't in the city that day. I know. I trailed him to San Rafael with the expectation of catching him in one of his activities, dealing in marijuana.

"He remained at a bar in San Rafael till evening, and his contact never appeared. Perhaps he knew I'd trailed him. At any rate, the deal didn't come off. At nine he headed back to the city. By that time Rosa Belmonte was dead."

At this point Quevedo was convinced of the truth of Fiala's charge, but one thing was unclear. "Why did Santiago pick Domingo for a victim?" he wanted to know.

Fiala smiled again and clarified the point. "One," he said, holding up a finger. "Domingo's reputation was bad; the charge appeared to suit his character. Two: Santiago and Domingo were partners. Domingo controlled the red-light district, with the help of Santiago. They quarreled over money. Santiago claimed that Domingo was holding out on him. He probably was, so Santiago found it doubly convenient to eliminate him."

Quevedo nodded it was all clear now, too clear. He frowned and his face paled. If revealed, Santiago's terrible act would threaten his own position. Frightened, his eyes met Fiala's.

The detective had read his thoughts and understood his predicament. "Of course, Santiago should be brought to justice," he said, "but to arrest him would be embarrassing to you."

Badly shaken, Quevedo nodded, but he was still alert. Fiala's statement implied more than it said.

"What do you suggest?" Quevedo asked.

Fiala moistened his lower lip with his tongue. "Speak to Santiago," he answered. "Give him the facts."

"And if he denies them?"

"If he does, tell him he'll be placed under arrest. After that has taken place—" Here Fiala shrugged. "You cannot guarantee his saftey from the mob. I think he'll understand."

"Understand what?"

"Call him and see."

Quevedo glanced at the phone and hesitated, giving Fiala the opportunity to rise from his chair. "I'm going for coffee. I'll be back," he said, and left Quevedo to deliver his terrible message.

Ten minutes later he returned to the mayor's office. Quevedo was still troubled. He said nothing. Fiala sat and reached for his cigarettes. At that moment the phone rang. Quevedo picked up the instrument, listened briefly, then placed the phone back on its cradle.

"Santiago just shot himself," he announced.

Having foreseen this, Fiala merely shrugged and said, "But of course. He had no alternative."

At this point, Quevedo saw Fiala in a new light. The fellow was devilishly clever and had saved him from his enemies. "I am in your debt," he said.

"Not at all," replied Fiala.

"Ah, but I am," Quevedo insisted. "Besides, I have no Police Chief now. Would you consider the office?"

Fiala grinned and, to the consternation of Quevedo, shook his head.

"But why you?" said Quevedo. "I don't understand. Think of what it means to be Chief of Police."

"In this city," Fiala replied, "it means to have much power, and power corrupts."

"It would corrupt you?" Quevedo asked.

"I'm made of flesh and blood. Perhaps it might, but I doubt it."

"Then why refuse?"

"Because the job doesn't interest me. It's as simple as that," Fiala answered, and rose from his chair to light a cigarette. With that, he walked to the door.

Still puzzled, Quevedo watched him, then said, "But you must want something. What do I owe you?"

His hand on the doorknob, Fiala turned. "Nothing," he answered. "Just be more careful when you pick the new Chief of Police."

Mercy Killing

Dale Clark

I T CAN be cold as hell at two A. M. in June in this state. The
Limited threw its light onto the rails a long ways ahead, and I
picked up my bag with a shiver of relief.

There wasn't a sign of the conductor when I swung aboard so I
gave the porter the ticket and Pullman slip. The Limited was moving again by the time I'd gone the length of the curtained aisle to
the washroom.

This little guy—he was middle-aged—turned from the window.
"What town is this?" he wanted to know.

"Allenburg."

"It isn't very big, huh?"

"Seven thousand."

"Is that a fact? I'd never have guessed it. But it's hard to tell at
night."

I went to the toothwash bowl.

"You live here?" he wanted to know.

I said, *"Uh-huh,"* around my toothbrush.

"Oh. I thought p'raps you were a traveling man." His voice
went on, and I payed no more attention to it than to the click of the
wheels. He was an accountant, he said. And what was my line?

"Electrical engineer," I told him.

He wanted to know how business was, and I said it was as
usual.

I sat down and unlaced a shoe, and then he said: "Excuse me,
brother! I—would you mind—if you didn't turn in just yet?"

That made me really look at him. He was smoking a cigar, and
he'd spilled ashes onto his vest. The vest was wrinkled. His face
was wrinkled, too, and about the same color as the ashes.

He said: "I've got to talk to somebody. The fact is, I'm not making a business trip. I'm going to see my boy. He's dying."

There wasn't anything to say to that, except, "I'm sorry."

"I'll tell you," the little guy said. He shook his head, spilled
more ash onto his vest. "I'll tell you."

* * *

He sat silent a while before he said: "We all have to go some time. The point I am trying to make, and the way I feel about this, is that death isn't extraordinary in any way. When you stop to think about it, a lot of people are going to die tomorrow. I don't know how many, but in the whole world . . . a lot of people. It isn't as if this boy of mine was going through something that never happened before, that didn't have to happen to all of us. The common fate of mankind, if I may say so."

"Maybe he'll pull through. The doctors work wonders nowadays," I said.

The little guy told me, "No," and it was clear he meant this, hadn't any hope of that kind at all.

"Why?" I asked him. "What's the boy's trouble?"

"It happened on the road, a smash-up."

"That's tough."

"It's confused in my mind," he said. "It's really a hard point to explain. Some people think, you know, when a man's time comes. . . . Some really great thinkers have looked on it in that way. I suppose you have got to be more or less of a fatalist to understand it."

"There's a lot to be said for fatalism."

He said: "To an extent, I believe that. If Harry had not gotten into this—it'd be the same, only in a different way. When you think of men going through battles without a scratch, and then maybe stepping on a rusty nail."

"You're right there. I've always had that slant on it. When your time comes, it comes. But on the other hand, nothing can get at a man until it does come."

I didn't really think this, but I could see how he might have to. You've got to believe some things were just in the cards. You could go crazy, otherwise, thinking how they might just as well not happen at all.

He said: "Then there is this angle. You have heard it said, especially about old folks and those who are afflicted with incurable diseases, that death comes as a release."

I told him, "Sure."

"I felt that way when my own father passed on. And my father never suffered as Harry is now."

"Sure."

"From that standpoint," the little guy mused, "there has been discussion on the subject of mercy killings. I don't know what your religious faith may be, and in my own church there is a feeling against that. But there is still an argument."

"Plenty," I said. "Plenty of argument."

His cigar had gone out. He held a match to it and his hand shook.

"I'll tell you," he said. "This is a case where death will be merciful. Very merciful. I don't know as I would make any other choice, if I had to choose."

And all the time I could see that this little guy's heart was breaking.

"When you think of what the rest of life would be," he said. "My boy has always been so active. A great athlete, a great sportsman. And social. It was always parties, dances, always a crowd around him. I don't believe he could ever adjust himself to a life without any of that. Because he could not ever again do so much as go for a walk in the country."

He hadn't got his cigar going after all. He dropped it into the cuspidor.

"I think we'd better say good-night," he told me. "I think I'll go to my berth now."

I could see he didn't want to keep *me* up any longer. He was such a gentle little guy. I thought about this, and him, after I turned in.

I knew he didn't mean a thing he'd said. All the time he would have given anything, his own life, for the boy.

He was still in the washroom when the porter routed me out in the gray dawn. He might have slept a little on the seat in there, but I doubt it. I think he just sat and said those things over to himself.

He didn't look at me while I got into my topcoat. There was a kind of shyness between us.

Only at the last, when he'd put on his own coat, and the train was creeping through the yards, he said: "I want to thank you about last night. You made me feel a lot better."

I told him, "You can't ever tell. It might not be as bad as you think, Mr.—," and that was when I realized he hadn't told me his name.

He said, "Merkle." His face was a ghastly white, scarred with tortured wrinkles. "I'm Harry Merkle's father."

You probably remember the case. Young Merkle was the fellow

who killed his wife with a hammer, and tried to cover up by wrecking a car with her body in it.

The little guy said: "I—I'll see him alive once more. And that's all, except to—claim him." He was all broken up, saying whatever came into his head. "They—you you can't have a Christian burial. Not even a prayer beside the grave. It seems hard—hard." Then he gasped: "Thank you! I'll never forget—I had to talk to somebody—you understand, it's my boy—"

I got him off the train, across the platform, into a cab. "State prison," I told the cabbie. Then I ran down the platform to the warden's car. "Drive like hell!" I said. I was trembling like a leaf. "Beat that cab there!"

I didn't want him to see me going into the place. I knew they wouldn't let him into the chamber.

The reporters were already in there, behind the wire screen. I went past the chair to the wall, and I gave the control wheel a test spin. It'd been tested before, I knew, but I had to be sure. It whined, and the voltage needle climbed. I'd never needed a drink so much in my life. And it seemed ages and eternities before I could decently take one. It's my job, and somebody has to do it, but I'll be damned if I'll ever tackle it drunk.

Moon-Face

Jack London

JOHN CLAVERHOUSE was a moon-faced man. You know the kind, cheekbones wide apart, chin and forehead melting into the cheeks to complete the perfect round, and the nose, broad and pudgy, equidistant from the circumference, flattened against the very centre of the face like a doughball upon the ceiling. Perhaps that is why I hated him, for truly he had become an offence to my eyes, and I believed the earth to be cumbered with his presence. Perhaps my mother may have been superstitious of the moon and looked upon it over the wrong shoulder at the wrong time.

Be that as it may, I hated John Claverhouse. Not that he had done me what society would consider a wrong or an ill turn. Far from it. The evil was of a deeper, subtler sort; so elusive, so intangible, as to defy clear, definite analysis in words. We all experience such things at some period in our lives. For the first time we see a certain individual, one who the very instant before we did not dream existed; and yet, at the first moment of meeting, we say: "I do not like that man." Why do we not like him? Ah, we do not know why; we know only that we do not. We have taken a dislike, that is all. And so I with John Claverhouse.

What right had such a man to be happy? Yet he was an optimist. He was always gleeful and laughing. All things were always all right, curse him! Ah! how it grated on my soul that he should be so happy! Other men could laugh, and it did not bother me. I even used to laugh myself—before I met John Claverhouse.

But his laugh! It irritated me, maddened me, as nothing else under the sun could irritate or madden me. It haunted me, gripped hold of me, and would not let me go. It was a huge, Gargantuan laugh. Waking or sleeping it was always with me, whirring and jarring across my heartstrings like an enormous rasp. At break of day it came whooping across the fields to spoil my pleasant morning revery. Under the aching noonday glare, when the green things drooped and the birds withdrew to the depths of the forest, and all nature drowsed, his great "Ha! ha!" and "Ho! ho!" rose up to the sky and challenged the sun. And at black midnight, from the lonely cross-roads where he turned from town into his own place, came his plaguey cachinnations to rouse me from my sleep and make me writhe and clench my nails into my palms.

I went forth privily in the night-time, and turned his cattle into his fields, and in the morning heard his whooping laugh as he drove them out again. "It is nothing," he said; "the poor, dumb beasties are not to be blamed for straying into fatter pastures."

He had a dog he called "Mars," a big, splendid brute, part deerhound and part blood-hound, and resembling both. Mars was a great delight to him, and they were always together. But I bided my time, and one day, when opportunity was ripe, lured the animal away and settled for him with strychnine and beefsteak. It made positively no impression on John Claverhouse. His laugh was as hearty and frequent as ever, and his face as much like the full moon as it always had been.

Then I set fire to his haystacks and his barn. But the next morning, being Sunday, he went forth blithe and cheerful.

"Where are you going?" I asked him, as he went by the cross-roads.

"Trout," he said, and his face beamed like a full moon. "I just dote on trout."

Was there ever such an impossible man! His whole harvest had gone up in his haystacks and barn. It was uninsured, I knew. And yet, in the face of famine and the rigorous winter, he went out gayly in quest of a mess of trout, forsooth, because he "doted" on them! Had gloom but rested, no matter how lightly, on his brow, or had his bovine countenance grown long and serious and less like the moon, or had he removed that smile but once from off his face, I am sure I could have forgiven him for existing. But no, he grew only more cheerful under misfortune.

I insulted him. He looked at me in slow and smiling surprise.

"I fight you? Why?" he asked slowly. And then he laughed. "You are so funny! Ho! ho! You'll be the death of me! He! he! he! Oh! Ho! ho! ho!"

What would you? It was past endurance. By the blood of Judas, how I hated him! Then there was that name—Claverhouse! What a name! Wasn't it absurd? Claverhouse! Merciful heaven, *why* Claverhouse? Again and again I asked myself that question. I should not have minded Smith, or Brown, or Jones—but *Claverhouse!* I leave it to you. Repeat it to yourself—Claverhouse. Just listen to the ridiculous sound of it—Claverhouse! Should a man live with such a name? I ask of you. "No," you say. And "No" said I.

But I bethought me of his mortgage. What of his crops and barn destroyed, I knew he would be unable to meet it. So I got a shrewd, close-mouthed, tight-fisted money-lender to get the mortgage transferred to him. I did not appear, but through this agent I forced the foreclosure, and but few days (no more, believe me, than the law allowed) were given John Claverhouse to remove his goods and chattels from the premises. Then I strolled down to see how he took it, for he had lived there upward of twenty years. But he met me with his saucer-eyes twinkling, and the light glowing and spreading in his face till it was as a full-risen moon.

"Ha! ha! ha!" he laughed. "The funniest tike, that youngester of mine! Did you ever hear the like? Let me tell you. He was down playing by the edge of the river when a piece of the bank caved in and splashed him. 'O papa!' he cried; 'a great big puddle flewed up and hit me.'"

He stopped and waited for me to join him in his infernal glee.

"I don't see any laugh in it," I said shortly, and I know my face went sour.

He regarded me with wonderment, and then came the damnable light, glowing and spreading, as I have described it, till his face shone soft and warm, like the summer moon, and then the laugh—"Ha! ha! That's funny! You don't see it, eh? He! he! Ho! ho! ho! He doesn't see it! Why, look here. You know a puddle—"

But I turned on my heel and left him. That was the last. I could stand it no longer. The thing must end right there, I thought, curse him! The earth should be quit of him. And as I went over the hill, I could hear his monstrous laugh reverberating against the sky.

Now, I pride myself on doing things neatly, and when I resolved to kill John Claverhouse I had it in mind to do so in such fashion that I should not look back upon it and feel ashamed. I hate bungling, and I hate brutality. To me there is something repugnant in merely striking a man with one's naked fist—faugh! it is sickening! So, to shoot, or stab, or club John Claverhouse (oh, that name!) did not appeal to me. And not only was I impelled to do it neatly and artistically, but also in such manner that not the slightest possible suspicion could be directed against me.

To this end I bent my intellect, and, after a week of profound incubation, I hatched the scheme. Then I set to work. I bought a water spaniel bitch, five months old, and devoted my whole attention to her training. Had any one spied upon me, they would have remarked that this training consisted entirely of one thing—*retrieving.* I taught the dog, which I called "Bellona," to fetch sticks I threw into the water, and not only to fetch, but to fetch at once, without mouthing or playing with them. The point was that she was to stop for nothing, but to deliver the stick in all haste. I made a practice of running away and leaving her to chase me, with the stick in her mouth, till she caught me. She was a bright animal, and took to the game with such eagerness that I was soon content.

After that, at the first casual opportunity, I presented Bellona to John Claverhouse. I knew what I was about, for I was aware of a little weakness of his, and of a little private sinning of which he was regularly and inveterately guilty.

"No," he said, when I placed the end of the rope in his hand. "No, you don't mean it." And his mouth opened wide and he grinned all over his damnable moon-face.

"I—I kind of thought, somehow, you didn't like me," he explained. "Wasn't it funny for me to make such a mistake?" And at the thought he held his sides with laughter.

"What is her name?" he managed to ask between paroxysms.

"Bellona," I said.

"He! he!" he tittered. "What a funny name!"

I gritted my teeth, for his mirth put them on edge, and snapped out between them, "She was the wife of Mars, you know."

Then the light of the full moon began to suffuse his face, until he exploded with: "That was my other dog. Well, I guess she's a widow now. Oh! Ho! ho! E! he! he! Ho!" he whooped after me, and I turned and fled swiftly over the hill.

The week passed by, and on Saturday evening I said to him, "You go away Monday, don't you?"

He nodded his head and grinned.

"Then you won't have another chance to get a mess of those trout you just 'dote' on."

But he did not notice the sneer. "Oh, I don't know," he chuckled. "I'm going up to-morrow to try pretty hard."

Thus was assurance made doubly sure, and I went back to my house hugging myself with rapture.

Early next morning I saw him go by with a dip-net and gunny-sack, and Bellona trotting at his heels. I knew where he was bound, and cut out by the back pasture and climbed through the under-brush to the top of the mountain. Keeping carefully out of sight, I followed the crest along for a couple of miles to a natural amphitheatre in the hills, where the little river raced down out of a gorge and stopped for breath in a large and placid rock-bound pool. That was the spot! I sat down on the croup of the mountain, where I could see all that occurred, and lighted my pipe.

Ere many minutes had passed, John Claverhouse came plodding up the bed of the stream. Bellona was ambling about him, and they were in high feather, her short, snappy barks mingling with his deeper chest-notes. Arrived at the pool, he threw down the dip-net and sack, and drew from his hip-pocket what looked like a large, fat candle. But I knew it to be a stick of "giant"; for such was his method of catching trout. He dynamited them. He attached the fuse by wrapping the "giant" tightly in a piece of cotton. Then he ignited the fuse and tossed the explosive into the pool.

Like a flash, Bellona was into the pool after it. I could have shrieked aloud for joy. Claverhouse yelled at her, but without avail. He pelted her with clods and rocks, but she swam steadily on till she got the stick of "giant" in her mouth, when she whirled about and headed for shore. Then, for the first time, he realized his danger, and started to run. As foreseen and planned by me, she made the bank and took out after him. Oh, I tell you, it was great! As I have said, the pool lay in a sort of amphitheatre. Above and below, the stream could be crossed on stepping-stones. And around and around, up and down and across the stones, raced Claverhouse and Bellona. I could never have believed that such an ungainly man could run so fast. But run he did, Bellona hot-footed after him, and gaining. And then, just as she caught up, he in full stride, and she leaping with nose at his knee, there was a sudden flash, a burst of smoke, a terrific detonation, and where man and dog had been the instant before there was naught to be seen but a big hole in the ground.

"Death from accident while engaged in illegal fishing." That was the verdict of the coroner's jury; and that is why I pride myself on the neat and artistic way in which I finished off John Claverhouse. There was no bungling, no brutality; nothing of which to be ashamed in the whole transaction, as I am sure you will agree. No more does his infernal laugh go echoing among the hills, and no more does his fat moon-face rise up to vex me. My days are peaceful now, and my night's sleep deep.

Murder

Joyce Carol Oates

THE MORNING FOLLOWING the news of the murder the children's uncle went to work as usual at the post office and their parents wouldn't talk about what had happened except to say yes a woman was killed but it's no one we know. The children understood that the woman who'd been killed was a friend of their uncle Dennie's though that wasn't said exactly, or not said in their presence or in their precise earshot. Still, they understood something was wrong, or, if not wrong, not right: the atmosphere in the house wasn't right: and it had to do with Uncle Dennie but it had to do even more with no one acknowledging it had to do with Uncle Dennie and above all—how the children knew this, they could not have said: years later, recollecting, could not begin to say—no one mentioning or even hinting to Uncle Dennie that it had, or had *not,* to do with him. The children were well aware of their parents on the telephone a good deal more than usual, and the telephone ringing a good deal more than usual, but the calls were always made, or taken, discreetly, doors closed and perhaps even locked against the children and none of them—there were two boys and a girl, ages ranging from six to eleven—dared press an ear against the door to eavesdrop. Relatives dropped by the house, seemingly by accident, and a few friends, so the children began to hear things such as how was Dennie taking it and had the police kept him long and were they going to question him further and was there any talk of—and here the voices dropped, the words became inaudible—and the children had to guess it was *was there any talk of him being arrested.* The answer was no not yet. Or the answer was no not so far as we know. Or, *we* don't know—Dennie refuses to talk about it.

The murdered woman, white, had lived in a welfare hotel in what was predominantly a black neighborhood. It was said she'd had four children by four different men and it was a matter of public record that she'd been taken into police custody the previous year for having beaten her two-year-old son so badly he'd had to be hospitalized for six weeks. The charge, subsequently dropped, was aggravated assault, and after the woman's death neighbors told police conflicting stories—yes she'd been guilty of that crime and numerous others against her children which suggested it was only equitable she'd been beaten to death by one or another of her lovers; no she hadn't been guilty of that crime only guilty of shielding the actual criminal who was one or another of her lovers—it was really he who'd beaten the two-year-old one night in a drunken rage and the woman had taken the blame on herself for being a bad mother.

When the woman was found dead early Sunday morning in a weedy rubble-strewn lot near her apartment building no one in the neighborhood or among her acquaintance was surprised—it was going to happen sooner or later—what else can you expect—though a fair number expressed pity, and regret, and even sadness, since in some quarters at least the woman was well liked, admired for what was called her personality, her sense of humor, her guts. At the time of her death she hadn't been living full-time with any specific man but there were several—or more than several—she saw frequently and one of them was Dennis Brewer who worked at the post office and lived with his brother and his brother's family and had acquired a reputation in recent years—though not an official public record—for being "strange." The murdered woman had met Dennis Brewer in a local tavern which was the way she met most of her men friends, according to the testimony of witnesses. She might have been seen in Brewer's company the night of the murder though she might have been seen in the company of two or three other men as well—testimony varied. But no one knew, or wanted to say, which one of the men had killed her: beaten her so badly around the head she hadn't been identified for hours.

The children's uncle Dennie was home from overseas and home from the state university and it looked like home to stay but his family was the kind where personal questions usually weren't asked in order to spare embarrassment. He had gone to the university with the intention of studying art but for some unexplained reason he was back home, and working at the post office, after the first semester: it was said he hadn't even registered in an art course but it wasn't said why and Dennie's own testimony was vague and ambiguous—things hadn't worked out he'd said with a shrug and a tight twist of his mouth as if there was a joke here of some kind but you'd better not laugh. Sometimes Dennie was the shiest most considerate most courteous young man on earth and sometimes, no one could predict when, he was sullen and brooding and "kept to himself" at work, at home, in one or another of the local bars he frequented. Sometimes he drank moderately, sometimes he drank too much. Sometimes he was sweet, sometimes he was mean. He *was* extremely intelligent, overqualified for his job, which was part of his "strangeness."

The children would remember their young uncle as gentle and kindly if occasionally absentminded. When he spoke to them, however, he always spoke carefully and precisely as if words mattered; as if *they* mattered. In this way he wasn't like other adults and they seemed to sense that this meant Dennie wasn't quite right whatever "right" meant.

He was tall and heavyset, muscular in the shoulders and torso, with crimped-looking hair that seemed to lift from his forehead in an expression of vague surprise. A tight look to the mouth which accentuated its smallness and he wore black-rimmed plastic glasses that gave him a sharp focused look as if he were staring, staring really hard, and not always liking what he saw.

The children knew from exchanges overheard between Dennie

and their parents that Dennie worried a good deal about people talking of him behind his back and that these worries were systematically ridiculed by their parents, particularly by their father who was, after all, Dennie's older brother—older by thirteen years— even when the worries might have had some substance in fact: people did talk about Dennie a good deal, and told stories about him, not meant to be malicious but just entertaining, Dennie this and Dennie that and who would have predicted, he'd been well liked in high school, and even a member of the varsity football team, he'd end up like this—the way he seemed to be ending up. Which is to say living in his brother's house as he did aged twenty-nine (in a spare bedroom at the rear the children's mother insisted should be thoroughly cleaned at least every two weeks and if Dennie didn't want to do it *she* would do it to do it and Dennie would be hurt or insulted or angered saying of course *he'd* clean the room *he* was perfectly capable of running a vacuum cleaner but for some reason days would go by and Dennie wouldn't get around to cleaning the room so the children's mother would get upset and the children's father would get involved and words were exchanged and finally in a burst of energy Dennie would clean the room slamming the vacuum cleaner around and talking loudly and angrily to himself and that would be that for a few weeks until the problem reasserted itself) and with no friends male or female he'd dare bring home to meet his family and no prospects for the future. He avoided his old high school friends, for instance. Actually turned away, crossed streets, to avoid saying hello. And if he was cornered in a store he could behave rudely in his haste, you might say his desperation, to get away.

In his brother's house he might have been behaving strangely all along but who could say?—the children, newly aware of their uncle, as so many observers were newly and keenly and nervously aware of him, could see it was "strange" that Uncle Dennie never read the Sunday paper, including the color comics, the way the rest of the family did. He didn't watch television with them, ever: not even weekend football or the World Series. He didn't talk much and was likely to mumble inaudible replies when the children's mother spoke to him. There were times when he kept to his room refusing supper and there were times when he overate, gorged himself at the table making no pretense of listening to the children's parents' conversation just biting and chewing and swallowing, moisture glistening in his eyes. It was said he'd gone without food when he was sick in the army hospital or was he sick from going without food? Those evenings he was at home he'd spend looking through art books from the public library—he took the same ones out again and again since the library's holdings were limited: Van Gogh, Rembrandt, Dürer, Matisse, Picasso—and doing pencil drawings in his sketchbook which he'd tear out and crumple and toss away. (Which was how the children knew about them, finding them in the trash. Uncle Dennie's drawings were quick and careless-seeming and never complete, just parts of heads, bodies, mysterious geometrical figures half human and half machine. The paper was usually badly crumpled as if he'd closed it in his fist.)

The morning after the news of the murder the children's uncle went to work as usual, and the morning after that, and nothing seemed to be changed except, in the house, there was a certain strained atmosphere, and Dennie kept to himself in his room and the children's mother cautioned them not to trouble him without explaining exactly why except to say that something—"something sad"—had happened to him. Telephone calls came for Dennis Brewer from people who wouldn't identify themselves and when the children's mother or father refused to put Dennie on the phone the callers became abusive, used obscene and threatening language. The children's mother became nervous; frightened; began to worry about something happening—and about any of them, particularly the children, being home alone with Dennie in the house. The children's father was annoyed with her saying she didn't really think Dennie'd done it did she?—and she said what about you, what do you think?—and the children, overhearing, understood what was being implied though they weren't altogether certain what was being said. This went on for a week, two weeks. It was true that Dennie had been questioned by police, interrogated was probably the more accurate term, it was true he was a suspect perhaps even a leading suspect though—of course—none of this was official, not in the local newspaper at least, for which, as the children's mother said repeatedly, thank God. The children learned of it to their excitement and dread though they were of course forbidden to say anything about it to their uncle to whom in any case, now, they rarely spoke, though they regarded him—when they had the opportunity—with extreme interest. At school their classmates began asking was their uncle the man who killed that woman? was their uncle going to go to jail? to the electric chair? and they said please mind your own business. But they loved it, those weeks. They'd remember those weeks for a long long time.

Dennie himself never talked about the situation. Never talked about where he went when summoned to police headquarters, or how long he was retained, or what was said to him, or what seemed to be developing. He was quieter than usual but not exceptionally quieter than usual and he never gave any indication (not even to the children's father, as it was afterward disclosed) of what he was going through whatever it was he was going through except some edginess now and then which matched the general household mood. The children's mother was particularly skittish—starting when Dennie entered a room, though she surely knew he was in the house; shrinking involuntarily from him when they passed in the hall. At the same time she made a point of being, in his presence, so warm, friendly, cheerful, solicitous, he was no longer capable of looking her in the face. He carried himself with an air of caution and irony but he was always in control. He did not, for instance, lean his elbows on the dining room table and look at them each in turn to inquire politely did they think he was a murderer—were they curious to know, *was* he the murderer?

Though one night he did ask the children's father—in a voice that was nearly inaudible—Would you like me to move out?—and the children's father said quickly, No, no of course not.

And after a pause: Where would you go, if you did?

And then the murderer was arrested. And confessed. (A local man, a resident too of the welfare hotel.) And though Dennis Brewer was innocent (presumably) people continued to view him with a certain degree of suspicion. It was as if the man had absorbed and been contaminated by evil as freshly laundered white sheets, hung out to dry, might absorb and be contaminated by polluted air. Even the children could not shake off the expectation, or was it the perverse unspoken hope, that their uncle Dennie had done something special—was something special. Though of course they knew better. As everyone knew better.

No one's fault, the children's father was to say, in time. He did not see that it was *his* fault, for instance.

In any case Dennie moved out of the house, with no warning, only a few days after the murderer, the "real" murderer it might be said, was taken into custody. He loaded his car and a U-Haul van and moved across town to a rented room which it was speculated he shared with another person: in some versions a woman very like the slut of a woman who'd been killed, in other versions a man very like Dennie himself. He quit his job at the post office and got a job as a nightwatchman in a factory then after a few weeks quit that job and left town without saying good-bye to anyone and went to live in a city a considerable distance away—or so it was reported: Dennie himself sent no word to his brother, never troubled to call. Isn't that just like him, the children's father said repeatedly—just *like* him. Living under my roof those years and this is the thanks I get—

Two years later at Christmastime the children received a Christmas card from their uncle, postmarked Salt Lake City, Utah. What was Uncle Dennie doing in Utah?—so far away? The card was of a pot-bellied white-whiskered Santa Claus in an utterly conventional pose, a sack of presents over his shoulder, a cheap card sold off a drugstore rack, signed with just the name: *Dennie*. No message, no Christmas wishes, not even an expression of love: just *Dennie*. In a hand that didn't much resemble his but must have been his for whose would it have been otherwise?

Murder Blooms

Charles E. Fritch

I 'M GOING TO kill you," Harry Grissom told the potted plant. He stuck his face close to the golden petals and scowled menacingly. "I'm going to take you in my hands and rip you apart and then flush you down the toilet. What do you think of that?"

If the plant felt menaced, it gave no sign.

Yet it struck back with the means his wife had given it to retaliate.

Harry's nose twitched. His eyes watered. He sneezed.

He quickly retreated to a safe distance, cursing Flora and the bug spray she used to protect her precious flower.

He raised trembling hands. "What I'd *really* like to do, of course," he reminded himself again, "is put these hands around Flora's throat and sque-e-eze . . ." He closed his eyes and clenched his fists and smiled as the pleasant fantasy filled his thoughts.

"What—are—you—doing?"

The shrill female voice startled him.

"I hope," Flora Grissom said sternly, sweeping into the room like some avenging wraith, "you haven't been upsetting Daisy. You know how sensitive she is."

Harry bit back the bitter words that leaped to his lips. A flower, sensitive to cross words? How ridiculous. How utterly absurd!

At one time he had entertained thoughts of having Flora committed as insane because she talked to flowers, but then some crackpot scientist came up with the theory that plants actually prospered when ordinary, sane people had one-way conversations with them, soothed the leafy darlings with soft words lovingly spoken.

Bah!

There was, of course, the other way, the without-a-doubt-permanent way that Hildy had suggested more than once. Hildy was a young, vibrant woman, unlike the scrawny, aging Flora, and Hildy as much as said she wasn't going to wait forever.

"Make it look like an accident," Hildy had said. "Or a surprised burglar. Then you'll have Flora's money—*and me!*"

It sounded good—especially the part about getting Flora's money—the twenty thousand dollars in a savings account in her name only—*and* about having Hildy.

"There, there, Daisy darling," Flora cooed to the plant. "Did the big bad mans scare my little snookums? Don't be afraid, sweetie, mommy's here."

Harry's insides churned. He didn't know if it was the bug spray still infesting his nostrils, the one-way conversation he was listening to or merely that Flora was in the same room with him and he could no longer stomach her.

One thing was certain—he could not go on this way. Divorce or separation was not the answer. He'd have to go back to work then, in order to support himself, and he certainly could not also support Hildy—at least not in the style in which she'd like to be supported. Twenty thousand dollars was not a lot of money, but if it were invested wisely—say on sure things at the track—it could easily grow into a hundred times that amount.

Straightening, Flora fixed her husband with a hawklike stare. "I want you to stay away from Daisy. You've been upsetting her with your harsh words."

"Oh?" Harry said with mock innocence. "Is that what she told you?"

"You're wasting your sarcasm on me, Harry Grissom," she snapped. "My plants are better friends than you've ever been, and you're my husband—in name anyway."

Harry flinched at the barb. His wife's name was Flora, but a more appropriate name would be Cactus. The plants were indeed her friends, but one plant in particular—the yellow-petaled Daisy— had captured her attention and her affection.

She was constantly fussing over the flower, digging carefully into the earth surrounding its roots, measuring in chemicals that would ensure its continued good health, spraying a sickening mist that was supposed to take care of marauding insects.

"Don't bugs have a right to exist, too?" Harry had asked her once.

"In certain places, yes," she had replied, unruffled by his comment.

He couldn't stand the spray, *or* the plant, *or* Flora herself. More than once he had entertained the notion of throttling the plant with his bare hands—oh, Lord, now he was thinking of the plant as a live creature himself—but then Flora would be angry and perhaps angry enough to get rid of him.

She seemed truly to love the flower, more than she ever had her husband. At first, he was grateful for that, because it left him time to pursue other interests—like luscious Hildy, whom he had met one golden afternoon in the unemployment line.

There were places he'd rather be, but Flora insisted the pension from her late husband was barely enough for them and her new husband should institute at least a token search for work, despite his own insistence that no one would hire him because of his bad back.

Trapped in the employment line, Harry had got to talking with the voluptuous blonde. Hildy was a divorcee whose husband had run off with another woman to another country, leaving her with a need to find some suitable means of support.

She invited Harry over to her modest apartment for a drink and a few laughs. Harry didn't mention his bad back, and neither of them noticed anything wrong with it.

There had been many such pleasant interludes, but Hildy was rapidly growing restless.

"I'm going to change my will," Flora said.

The words didn't register right away on Harry's mind. When they did, he couldn't speak for an instant. He managed, hoarsely, "Change your will? In what way?"

She smiled grimly. "Oh, you'll still get the money, don't worry. But I don't like to think that Daisy will be neglected if I pass away suddenly."

"Pass away?" Harry forced a laugh. "What makes you think you're going to pass away—suddenly?"

"I've got a premonition that . . ." She shook her grey head. "Oh well, never mind about that. What I'm going to do is give you all the money—with one provision."

Harry waited, fear icycling his spine.

"You've got to live alone here in this house and take care of Daisy for me," Flora went on. "Daisy must outlive me by at least a year. If she doesn't, the money goes to charity."

Harry began to tremble with anger and frustration. "You—you *can't* do that. I don't know anything about taking care of a plant!"

"Then you'll have to learn, won't you?" she said simply. Her eyes narrowed. "I don't want your girlfriend in this room any more, either."

Harry jerked as though struck a physical blow. *"Wha-a-a-at?"*

Flora smirked. "Thought I didn't know about her, huh? Well, I know everything."

Everything was a lot to know. Harry chewed his lip. He had told Hildy about the plant, of course, and they had laughed at his crazy wife's affection for it. Hildy had this idea about wanting to see the thing, so one day when Flora was visiting the doctor for a checkup, he had brought Hildy to the house and shown her the plant.

Hildy had made obscene remarks strong enough to make the daisy wither, and they both had a big laugh out of the adventure. Daisy, surrounded by her protective mist of perfume, had not been visibly affected by the tirade.

For a dreadful moment, Harry just stood there, not knowing what to do, his eyes searching Flora's thin smirking face. Somehow, she knew about Hildy. He didn't know how she could have learned of it—they had always been so careful—but that didn't matter. What mattered was that she knew. And now she was going to change her will unless he stopped her.

Visions of twenty thousand dollars and Hildy danced before his eyes and then were suddenly obliterated.

"*No!*" he cried, and before he could even think of what he was doing, he had his strong hands around Flora's frail neck, squeezing, squeezing, just as he had practiced in his imagination so many times before.

The woman's scrawny fingers clawed weakly at him. Her eyes bulged. Rasping noises crackled from her throat.

An instant before she expired, Harry realized he was committing murder, but on the heels of this realization came another—it was too late to back down now. He applied extra pressure, and she died and her body went slack like a wilting flower.

For a moment the room was filled with silence broken only by Harry's swift breathing. "I've *killed* her," he told himself finally. "I've actually killed her. I've got to tell Hildy. No, wait. First, I've got to make it look like an accident—or that somebody broke in."

She was obviously strangled, so the accident was ruled out. But an intruder coming in to rob the place, being surprised and having to kill the woman of the house—ah, that was something else.

Harry hurried from one room to another, turning over chairs, pulling out drawers. He took twelve dollars from the cookie jar in the kitchen and broke the jar on the floor, leaving some small change in the debris. Returning to the living room, he broke a pane of glass in one of the windows and unfastened the lock where the top half joined the bottom.

An alibi. He had to have an alibi. He didn't look at Flora's face as he lifted her wrist, set her wrist-watch at a half-hour ahead and then smashed it against the floor, cracking the crystal and stopping the movement.

So far, so good. The time of her death would be established, thanks to the broken watch, at an hour when he would be in the employment office, dutifully looking for work as a loving husband should.

Harry felt elated at how well things were going.

He paused at the door, turned and surveyed the room again to see if he had missed anything. His eyes darted here and there, finally fastened on the yellow-flowered potted plant.

"Might as well kill two flowers with one murder," he chortled.

Eagerly, he crossed the room and, with one sweep of his hand, hurled the plant to the floor. When he left the house, he made sure the front door was ajar.

Harry Grissom was very pleased. A little nervous, perhaps—but after all, this was his first murder, and even though he had come to dislike Flora very much, he did have *some* feelings. But overall, he felt he now had the formerly nasty old world by the proverbial short hairs.

He'd have to suffer through the police investigation and pretend to be grief stricken by Flora's demise, but he was sure he could pull it off. His incentive was twenty thousand dollars and the love of a beautiful woman.

He arrived at the employment office just in time to telephone the police from a pay phone. He said he was a neighbor of the Grissom's who had been walking past the house and had heard all manner of screaming and the noise of things being thrown. Then he hung up, without giving a name.

After which, he marched boldly to a clear window at the counter marked JOBS and raised a terrible fuss about the employment office not being able to get a job for a man who was not only willing but anxious to find one to support him and his wife.

The girl at the counter sent Harry to see a hard-faced man who asked about Harry's back, was delighted to hear it had been magically restored, and who was only too happy to give Harry referrals to three unskilled labor jobs.

When he got home, shouting, *"Flora, great news.* I think I've got a job," the police were there, waiting for him.

"Flora, dead?" Harry sank, stunned, into a chair when he heard the news. "That's impossible. When I left her, she was fine. How did it happen?"

"We thought you might be able to give us details on that, Mr. Grissom."

"*Me?* I think *not.* You see, I was at the employment office. I can prove that—"

The policeman held up his hand to shut off the torrent of words. "Before you go into that, Mr. Grissom, let me read you your rights."

Harry listened, puzzled as the officer told him he had the right to remain silent and so forth. Then he asked, "May I see her?" It would be the natural thing for a husband to ask.

"Certainly." The policeman held the door open for him.

Flora lay stretched out on the floor, as ugly in death as she had been in life, but more agreeable. Beside her lay the remains of the plant he had destroyed, the pot cracked and bleeding dirt over the rug. In that dirt—Harry leaned forward curiously to get a better look—was a small, shiny black object that glistened darkly and a wire terminating in a tiny knobby piece of plastic with holes in it.

"Your wife's plant contained a bug, Mr. Grissom," the officer said.

"That's impossible," Harry said. "Not with all that spray she put on it."

The policeman failed to suppress his smile. "I don't mean that kind of a bug. I mean a *microphone* bug. Apparently she was suspicious of you and wanted to record what you had to say. She did, too. And we might never have found it if the pot hadn't been pushed onto the floor."

"*No!*" Harry cried. He thought of the twenty thousand dollars and of beautiful Hildy, lost and gone from him forever.

"There's an old saying," the policeman said with a wry smile, "that daisies don't tell. Well, here's one that *did!*"

Murder in the Fourth Dimension

Clark Ashton Smith

THE FOLLOWING PAGES are from a note-book that was discovered lying at the foot of an oak tree beside the Lincoln Highway, between Bowman and Auburn. They would have been dismissed immediately as the work of a disordered mind, if it had not been for the unaccountable disappearance, eight days before, of James Buckingham and Edgar Halpin. Experts testified that the handwriting was undoubtedly that of Buckingham. A silver dollar, and a handkerchief marked with Buckingham's initials, were also found not far from the note-book.

Not everyone, perhaps, will believe that my ten years' hatred for Edgar Halpin was the impelling force that drove me to the perfecting of a most unique invention. Only those who have detested and loathed another man with the black fervor of the feeling I had conceived, will understand the patience with which I sought to devise a revenge that should be safe and adequate at the same time. The wrong he had done me was one that must be expiated sooner or later; and nothing short of his death would be sufficient. However, I did not care to hang, not even for a crime that I could regard as nothing more than the mere execution of justice; and, as a lawyer, I knew how difficult, how practically impossible, was the commission of a murder that would leave no betraying evidence. Therefore, I puzzled long and fruitlessly as to the manner in which Halpin should die, before my inspiration came to me.

I had reason enough to hate Edgar Halpin. We had been bosom friends all through our school days and through the first years of our professional life as law-partners. But when Halpin married the one woman I had ever loved with complete devotion, all friendship ceased on my side and was replaced by an ice-like barrier of inexorable enmity. Even the death of Alice, five years after the marriage, made no difference, for I could not forgive the happiness of which I had been deprived—the happiness they had shared during those years, like the thieves they were. I felt that she would have cared for me if it had not been for Halpin—indeed, she and I had been almost engaged before the beginning of his rivalry.

It must not be supposed, however, that I was indiscreet enough to betray my feelings at any time. Halpin was my daily associate in the Auburn law-firm to which we belonged; and I continued to be a most welcome and frequent guest at his home. I doubt if he ever knew that I had cared greatly for Alice: I am secretive and undemonstrative by temperament; and also, I am proud. No one, except Alice herself, ever surmised my suffering; and even she knew nothing of my resentment. Halpin himself trusted me; and nurturing as I did the idea of retaliation at some future time, I took care that he should continue to trust me. I made myself necessary to him in all ways, I helped him when my heart was a cauldron of seething poisons, I spoke words of brotherly affection and clapped him on the back when I would rather have driven a dagger through him. I knew all the tortures and all the nausea of a hypocrite. And day after day, year after year, I made my varying plans for an ultimate revenge.

Apart from my legal studies and duties, during those ten years, I apprised myself of everything available that dealt with the methods of murder. Crimes of passion allured me with a fateful interest, and I read untiringly the records of particular cases. I made a study of weapons and poisons; and as I studied them, I pictured to myself the death of Halpin in every conceivable way. I imagined the deed as being done at all hours of the day and night, in a multitude of places. The only flaw in these dreams was my inability to think of any spot that would assure perfect safety from subsequent detection.

It was my bent toward scientific speculation and experiment that finally gave me the clue I sought. I had long been familiar with the theory that other worlds or dimensions may co-exist in the same space with ours by reason of a different molecular structure and vibrational rate, rendering them intangible for us. One day, when I was indulging in a murderous fantasy, in which for the thousandth time I imagined myself throttling Halpin with my bare hands, it occurred to me that some unseen dimension, if one could only penetrate it, would be the ideal place for the commission of a homicide. All circumstantial evidence, as well as the corpse itself, would be lacking—in other words, one would have a perfect absence of what is known as the *corpus delicti*. The problem of how to obtain entrance to this dimension was of course an unsolved one; but I did not feel that it would necessarily prove insoluble. I set myself immediately to a consideration of the difficulties to be overcome, and the possible ways and means.

There are reasons why I do not care to set forth in this narrative the details of the various experiments to which I was drawn during the next three years. The theory that underlay my tests and researches was a very simple one; but the processes involved were highly intricate. In brief, the premise from which I worked was, that the vibratory rate of objects in the fourth dimension could be artificially established by means of some mechanism, and that things or persons exposed to the influence of the vibration could be transported thereby to this alien realm.

For a long time, all my experiments were condemned to failure, because I was groping among mysterious powers and recondite laws whose motive-principle I had not wholly grasped. I will not even hint at the basic nature of the device which brought about my ultimate success, for I do not want others to follow where I have gone and find themselves in the same dismal predicament. I will say, however, that the desired vibration was attained by condensing ultra-violet rays in a refractive apparatus made of certain very sensitive materials which I will not name.

The resultant power was stored in a kind of battery, and could be emitted from a vibratory disk suspended above an ordinary office chair, exposing everything beneath the disk to the influence of the new vibration. The range of the influence could be closely regulated by means of an insulating attachment. By the use of the apparatus, I finally succeeded in precipitating various articles into the fourth dimension: a dinner-plate, a bust of Dante, a Bible, a French novel and a house-cat, all disappeared from sight and touch in a few instants when the ultra-violet power was turned upon them. I knew that henceforth they were functioning as atomic entities in a world where all things had the same vibratory rate that had been artificially induced by means of my mechanism.

Before venturing into the invisible domain myself, it was of course necessary to have some way of returning. I invented a second battery and a second vibratory disk, through which, by the use of certain infra-red rays, the vibrations of our own world could be established. By turning the force from the disk on the very same spot where the dinner-plate and the other articles had disappeared, I succeeded in recovering all of them. All were absolutely unchanged; and though several months had gone by, the cat had not suffered in any way from its fourth-dimensional incarceration. The infra-red device was portable; and I meant to take it with me on my visit to the new realm in company with Edgar Halpin. I—but not Halpin—would return anon to resume the threads of mundane existence.

My experiments had all been carried on with utter secrecy. To mask their real nature, as well as to provide myself with the needful privacy, I had built a small laboratory in the woods of an uncultivated ranch that I owned, lying midway between Auburn and Bowman. Here I retired at varying intervals when I had the requisite leisure, ostensibly to conduct some chemical experiments of an educative but far from unusual type. I never admitted anyone to the laboratory; and no great amount of curiosity was evinced by friends and acquaintances regarding its contents or the tests I was carrying on. Never did I breathe a syllable to anyone that could indicate the true goal of my researches.

I shall never forget the jubilation I felt when the infra-red device had proven its practicality by retrieving the plate, the bust, the two volumes and the cat. I was so eager for the consummation of my long-delayed revenge, that I did not even consider a preliminary personal trip into the fourth dimension. I had determined that Edgar Halpin must precede me when I went. I did not feel, however, that it would be wise to tell him anything concerning the real nature of my device, or the proposed excursion.

Halpin, at this time, was suffering from recurrent attacks of terrific neuralgia. One day, when he had complained more than usual, I told him under the seal of confidence that I had been working on a vibratory invention for the relief of such maladies and had finally perfected it.

'I'll take you out to the laboratory tonight, and you can try it,' I said. 'It will fix you up in a jiffy: all you'll have to do will be to sit in a chair and let me turn on the current. But don't say anything to anybody.'

'Thanks, old man,' he rejoined. 'I'll certainly be grateful if you can do anything to stop this damnable pain. It feels like electric drills boring through my head all the time.'

I had chosen my time well, for all things were favorable to the maintenance of the secrecy I desired. Halpin lived on the outskirts of the town; and he was alone for the nonce, his housekeeper having gone away on a brief visit to some sick relative. The night was murky and foggy; and I drove to Halpin's house and stopped for him shortly after the dinner hour, when few people were abroad. I do not think anyone saw us when we left the town. I followed a rough and little-used by-road for most of the way to my laboratory, saying that I did not care to meet other cars in the thick fog, if I could avoid it. We passed no one, and I felt that this was a good omen and that everything had combined to further my plan.

Halpin uttered an exclamation of surprise when I turned on the lights in my laboratory.

'I didn't dream you had so much stuff here,' he remarked, peering about with respectful curiosity at the long array of unsuccessful appliances which I had thrown aside in the course of my labors.

I pointed to the chair above which the ultra-violet vibrator was suspended.

'Take a seat, Ed,' I enjoined him. 'We'll soon cure everything that ails you.'

'Sure you aren't going to electrocute me?' he joked, as he obeyed my direction.

A thrill of fierce triumph ran through me like the stimulation of some rare elixir, when he had seated himself. Everything was in my power now, and the moment of recompense for my ten years' humiliation and suffering was at hand. Halpin was so unsuspecting:

the thought of any danger to himself, of any treachery on my part, would have been fantastically incredible to him. Putting my hand beneath my coat, I caressed the hilt of the hunting-knife that I carried.

'All set?' I asked him.

'Sure, Mike. Go ahead and shoot.'

I had found the exact range that would involve all of Halpin's body without affecting the chair itself. Fixing my gaze upon him, I pressed the little knob that turned on the current of vibratory rays. The result was practically instantaneous, for he seemed to melt with a puff of thinning smoke. I could still see his outlines for a moment, and the look of a fantasmal astonishment on his face. And then he was gone—utterly gone.

Perhaps it will be a source of wonderment that, having annihilated Halpin as far as all earthly existence was concerned, I was not content merely to leave him in the unseen, intangible plane to which he had been transposed. Would that I had been content to do so. But the wrong I had suffered was hot and cankerous within me, and I could not bear to think that he still lived, in any form or upon any plane. Nothing but absolute death would suffice to assuage my resentment; and the death must be inflicted by my own hand. It now remained to follow Halpin into that realm which no man had ever visited before, and of whose geographical conditions and characteristics I had formed no idea whatever. I felt sure, however, that I could enter it and return safely, after disposing of my victim. The return of the cat left no apparent room for doubt on that score.

I turned out the lights; and seating myself in the chair with the portable infra-red vibrator in my arms, I switched on the ultra-violet power. The sensation I felt was that of one who falls with nightmare velocity into a great gulf. My ears were deaf with the intolerable thunder of my descent, a frightful sickness overcame me, and I was near to losing all consciousness for a moment, in the black vortex of roaring space and force that seemed to draw me nadir-ward through the ultimate pits.

Then the speed of my fall was gradually retarded, and I came gently down to something that was solid beneath my feet. There was a dim glimmering of light that grew stronger as my eyes accustomed themselves to it, and by this light I saw Halpin standing a few feet away. Behind him were dark, amorphous rocks and the vague outlines of a desolate landscape of low mounds and primordial treeless flats. Even though I had hardly known what to expect,

I was somewhat surprised by the character of the environment in which I found myself. At a guess, I would have said that the fourth dimension would be something more colorous and complex and varied—a land of multifold hues and many-angled forms. However, in its drear and primitive desolation, the place was truly ideal for the commission of the act I had intended.

Halpin came toward me in the doubtful light. There was a dazed and almost idiotic look on his face, and he stuttered a little as he tried to speak.

'W-What h-happened?' he articulated at last.

'Never mind what happened. It isn't a circumstance to what's going to happen now.'

I laid the portable vibrator aside on the ground as I spoke.

The dazed look was still on Halpin's face when I drew the hunting-knife and stabbed him through the body with one clean thrust. In that thrust, all the stifled hatred, all the cankering resentment of ten insufferable years was finally vindicated. He fell in a twisted heap, twitched a little, and lay still. The blood oozed very slowly from his side and formed a puddle. I remember wondering at its slowness, even then, for the oozing seemed to go on through hours and days.

Somehow, as I stood there, I was obsessed by a feeling of utter unreality. No doubt the long strain I had been under, the daily stress of indurate emotions and decade deferred hopes, had left me unable to realize the final consummation of my desire when it came. The whole thing seemed no more than one of the homicidal day-dreams in which I had imagined myself stabbing Halpin to the heart and seeing his hateful body lie before me.

At length, I decided that it was time to effect my return; for surely nothing could be gained by lingering any longer beside Halpin's corpse amid the unutterable dreariness of the fourth-dimensional landscape. I erected the vibrator in a position where its rays could be turned upon myself, and pressed the switch.

I was aware of a sudden vertigo, and felt that I was about to begin another descent into fathomless vortical gulfs. But, though the vertigo persisted, nothing happened, and I found that I was still standing beside the corpse, in the same dismal milieu.

Dumbfoundment and growing consternation crept over me. Apparently, for some unknown reason, the vibrator would not work in the way I had so confidently expected. Perhaps, in these new surroundings, there was some barrier to the full development of the infra-red power. I do not know; but at any rate, there I was, in a truly singular and far from agreeable predicament.

I do not know how long I fooled in a mounting frenzy with the mechanism of the vibrator, in the hope that something had temporarily gone wrong and could be remedied, if the difficulty were only found. However, all my tinkerings were of no avail: the machine was in perfect working-order, but the required force was wanting. I tried the experiment of exposing small articles to the influence of the rays. A silver coin and a handkerchief dissolved and disappeared very slowly, and I felt that they must have regained the levels of mundane existence. But evidently the vibrational force was not strong enough to transport a human being.

Finally I gave it up and threw the vibrator to the ground. In the surge of a violent despair that came upon me, I felt the need of muscular action, of prolonged movement; and I started off at once to explore the weird realm in which I had involuntarily imprisoned myself.

It was an unearthly land—a land such as might have existed before the creation of life. There were undulating blanks of desolation beneath the uniform gray of a heaven without moon or sun or stars or clouds, from which an uncertain and diffused glimmering was cast upon the world beneath. There were no shadows, for the light seemed to emanate from all directions. The soil was a gray dust in places and a gray viscidity of slime in others; and the mounds I have already mentioned were like the backs of prehistoric monsters heaving from the primal ooze. There were no signs of insect or animal life, there were no trees, no herbs, and not even a blade of grass, a patch of moss or lichen, or a trace of algae. Many rocks were strewn chaotically through the desolation; and their forms were such as an idiotic demon might have devised in apeing the handiwork of God. The light was so dim that all things were lost at a little distance; and I could not tell whether the horizon was near or far.

It seems to me that I must have wandered on for several hours, maintaining as direct a course of progression as I could. I had a compass—a thing that I always carry with me; but it refused to function, and I was driven to conclude that there were no magnetic poles in this new world.

Suddenly, as I rounded a pile of the vast amorphous boulders, I came to a human body that lay huddled on the ground, and saw incredulously that it was Halpin. The blood still oozed from the fabric of his coat, and the pool it had formed was no larger than when I had begun my journey.

I felt sure that I had not wandered in a circle, as people are said to do amid unfamiliar surroundings. How, then, could I have returned to the scene of my crime? The problem nearly drove me mad as I pondered it; and I set off with frantic vigor in an opposite direction from the one I had first taken.

For all intents and purposes, the scene through which I now passed was identical with the one that lay on the other side of Halpin's corpse. It was hard to believe that the low mounds, the dreary levels of dust and ooze and the monstrous boulders, were not the same as those among which I had made my former way. As I went, I took out my watch with the idea of timing my progress; but the hands had stopped at the very moment when I had taken my plunge into unknown space from the laboratory; and though I wound it carefully, it refused to run.

After walking an enormous distance, during which, to my surprise, I felt no fatigue whatever, I came once more to the body I had sought to leave. I think that I went really mad then, for a little while.

Now, after a duration of time—or eternity—which I have no means of computing, I am writing this penciled account on the leaves of my note-book. I am writing it beside the corpse of Edgar Halpin, from which I have been unable to flee; for a score of excursions into the dim realms on all sides have ended by bringing me back to it after a certain interval. The corpse is still fresh and the blood has not dried. Apparently, the thing we know as time is well-nigh non-existent in this world, or at any rate is seriously disordered in its action; and most of the normal concomitants of time are likewise absent; and space itself has the property of returning always to the same point. The voluntary movements I have performed might be considered as a sort of time-sequence; but in regard to involuntary things there is little or no time-movement. I experience neither physical weariness or hunger; but the horror of my situation is not to be conveyed in human language; and hell itself can hardly have devised a name for it.

When I have finished writing this narration, I shall precipitate the note-book into the levels of mundane life by means of the infra-red vibrator. Some obscure need of confessing my crime and telling my predicament to others has led me to an act of which I should never have believed myself capable, for I am the most uncommunicative of men by nature. Apart from the satisfying of this need, the composition of my narrative is something to do, it is a temporary reprieve from the desperate madness that will surge upon me soon, and the gray eternal horror of the limbo to which I have doomed myself beside the undecaying body of my victim.

Murder on My Mind

Charles Beckman Jr.

FEAR CAN DRIVE a man to desperate measures. At first, whiskey dulled the nightmare in which John Henry Mascheck lived. But after a while, that wasn't enough. When his ship docked in Far Eastern ports, he sought refuge in opium dens, and there, for a few hours, floated in safe warm clouds, freed temporarily from the grim spectre that haunted his waking and sleeping.

But, back aboard ship, at sea, the horror returned. He would wake up in the night, drenched with sweat, whimpering under the covers, the frightening details of his dream still fresh in his mind—a nightmare in which dark waters closed over his head, dragging him down to deep, silent green depths. . . .

John Henry didn't know the medical name for it. He only knew that drowning held an awesome fear for him, far beyond the normal dread of death.

That fear had lived with him for four years, ever since the night he had been washed over the side in a rough Pacific sea and had been saved only by a miracle. It had become the most important thing in his life. Now, one obsession filled his mind; he was going to drown some day and nothing he could do would prevent it.

It drove him at last to murder.

"First, I need money," he whispered, sitting on the edge of his bunk that night. He had wasted away to a shadow. His eyes were great, dark shadows sunk far back in deep sockets. His face was a grey, lined mask.

As if mocking him, the rough sea lashed the ship's sides. He shuddered and great beads of sweat stood out on his forehead.

Again he looked down at the letter in his shaking fingers. He had read it a hundred times. Its corners were frayed from its being repeatedly taken out of his pocket and folded away again.

It was from his cousin, Alec Mascheck, in Texas, an old bachelor John Henry hadn't seen in years.

"We were like brothers when we were children, here on Papa's farm, John Henry. That's why I am glad that you will inherit this place when I pass away. I have never married and there are no other relatives. The doctor says I have only a month or two. . . ."

The letter had reached Maschek in Shanghai a week ago. It had been mailed two months before that. Alec Mascheck would be dead by now. The farm belonged to him, John Henry.

But you won't get it, the sea mocked him. *You dock in San Francisco next week and all your pay will go to cover gambling debts and you are already signed up for another cruise. You won't get the farm, but I'll get you! I'll suck you down some night. Down where you can't breathe— smothering you. . . .*

"No!" John Henry screamed. His voice reverberated from the steel bulkhead. He lurched to his feet, swaying, soaked with cold sweat. "I won't drown. I'll go to Texas, on a farm. Miles away from water . . . where there's only land. . . ."

He ran up on deck. The wind tore at his hair and the salt spray filmed his face. Off in the darkness, alone, a single passenger clutched the rail, looking out to sea. It was the wealthy Englishman who had flashed his bulging wallet more than once since they left Shanghai. . . .

Seaman John Henry Mascheck moved silently up behind him. His left palm covered the Englishman's mouth while the clutching fingers of his other hand found the man's wallet. Then he heaved his victim over the rail. The Englishman's screams were lost in the darkness of the foaming waters. John Henry visualized the man's struggles down there in the depths that sucked him down, down, smothering him. He shuddered and stumbled back to his bunk.

Three weeks later, John Henry drove through Goliad, Texas. He wore a new suit and sat behind the wheel of a second hand automobile he had bought in San Antonio. There had been enough money in the Englishman's wallet to pay his bus fare from San Francisco to San Antonio and to buy this car. Now he was down to his last five dollars. But that no longer mattered, for he had reached his destination. He gazed around the dusty lane he was now following, a few miles out of Goliad, at the acres of rolling prairie land, stretching as far as the eye could see—dotted with scrubby chaparral, mesquite and clumps of live oak. At the old, moss-covered Spanish mission, "La Bahia," that stood like a sentinel high on a hill, overlooking this countryside.

He was here and he was safe! No more water, no more nightmares. He chuckled deeply, clutching the steering wheel with trembling hands.

He recognized the boundary of the old Mascheck farm. The soil was all rich, fertile loam. It had been planted in cotton when he was a child. Now, waving acres of flax greeted his eyes. A combine stood in a field where it had been threshing seed.

"Good—good," he nodded, wetting his lips. A man could make fine money here. His cousin, Alec, must have planted all these fields before the sickness overtook him.

John Henry drove up to the house. Later, he'd talk with the lawyer in town. First, he wanted to look the place over, see what shape it was in.

He was surprised to find signs of life around the house. Chickens clucked under the creaking windmill in the back yard. Curtains fluttered at open windows. There was the fragrance of cooking in the air.

A moment of panic overtook him. Had Alec Mascheck recovered? Heart thudding, he walked up on the porch of the freshly painted white frame house, rapped on the edge of the screen door.

A woman waddled out of the kitchen. A cheap calico dress hung around her sweating bulk like a sack. She wore anklet socks and frayed bedroom slippers that scuffed the floor as she walked. She was fanning herself with a folded newspaper. A thin white cat wound back and forth between her ankles as she stood there.

"Yeah?" she asked.

"I—" John Henry moistened his lips. "A-Alec Mascheck. Is he here?"

"Dead," she told him. "Died last month. I'm his widder. Whut kin I do fer you?"

"Widow!" The word struck John Henry with stunning force. "But—but he wasn't married. He wrote me that he'd never married. He said there were no next of kin, other than myself!"

She eyed him suspiciously through the screen door. "By the way, you ain't that cousin feller he was always talkin' about? Out to sea, you was?"

"Yes . . . yes. I'm John Henry Mascheck. I'm Alec's legal heir. He wrote me. This place is mine. He wrote and told me—"

She threw her head back, laughed shrilly. "Well, Mister, you missed it by a little. I married Alec after he wrote you that letter. I was nursin' him, an' he seemed t' take a fancy to me toward the end. He wrote you, but I guess th' letter never reached you."

A roar of anguish and rage tore from Mascheck's lips. "Robbed him, you mean, you old fat devil! And robbed me of what is mine. Why he must have been so sick he was out of his mind!"

She retreated two steps. "Now you jest hold on," she warned stridently. "I married him fair and legal. Got th' papers to prove it. You come around here, startin' trouble and I'll phone th' law!"

She reached for the telephone. John Henry drove a weather beaten fist through the screen wire. He unhooked the door, entered the room. The sea was roaring in his ears, mocking him again. *You see, Maschek, you can't get away from me. You don't have a farm after all. You'll have to come back to me. And I'll get you this time!*

"No," John Henry choked. "No!" He reached for the woman.

She squealed once, like a frightened pig. Then his fingers closed around her throat. He held on for a long time after she was dead, to be sure. . . .

He stumbled outside, out in the clean sunshine. He knelt and scooped up a handful of dry earth. Then he began laughing, wildly. "I cheated you," he swore. "By heaven, I cheated you!"

Thank Providence, he hadn't stopped to see the lawyer in Goliad first. He'd driven right out and no one had seen him. He could get back in the car, drive to San Antonio, sell the car and hide for a few weeks or a month. Then he'd come back here to claim the place, acting like he'd just arrived from San Francisco. He'd make it look like a thief had broken into the house, killed the woman. . . .

He hurried back in, ransacked drawers, stuffed some of her cheap jewelry and some cash he found in his pockets. Enough to make the murder appear the work of a thief. Then he walked through the house and out the back door.

He gazed around him, at the miles of farmland that was now his. And he laughed back at the sea. "I beat you! I'm safe at last." There was no water for miles. No more fear of drowning ever to haunt him again. He would be safe here for the rest of his life!

Then he heard voices coming from the field. Hired hands!

If he ran around the house to his car, they'd see him sure . . . and if he stayed here, they'd see him. But they were headed toward the barn. If he could hide for a few minutes, it would be all right.

He looked around frantically. By now they had gotten so near, they'd see him if he tried to get back in the house.

His gaze fell on a trailer with high side boards in the back yard. Almost between him and the approaching men. He ducked, ran toward it bent over. He crawled up one side. It was deep. Ten feet or more. It was filled with flaxseed up to within two feet of the top. The closely-packed seed looked smooth and inviting. He could lie down on that.

He wriggled over the side, rolled to the middle of the surface of seed. And then he felt himself sinking, down . . . down . . .

There was a relentless sucking that grew worse as he floundered. Frantically, he clawed for the sideboards. But he was already down to his armpits. He could not reach the sides! Too late he tried to scream. His mouth was below the surface. He knew a moment of unspeakable terror. The whole nightmare of four years had become a reality! His eyes were filled and his nostrils and mouth and lungs, with the sifting, choking seeds. He was sucked down into blinding smothering depths. . . .

Two of the hands drove a pickup truck out of the barn, backed it to the trailer of flaxseed.

One of the men nodded at the deep load of flaxseed. "Bad business leaving that stuff uncovered like that. I ought to tell the widow. It's just like quicksand. I've seen men fall into a bin of that stuff and drown before you could get to 'em."

The two men got in the truck and started off.

And far on the other side of the world the restless Pacific washed on a sandy beach and the mutter of its surf sounded like a chuckle . . .

A Nice Save

Edward Wellen

MAL SPOTTED WOOLF in the darkness beyond the glassed-in section of the promenade. Mal followed him out onto the deserted after-deck, into the gale-force wind that made the sensible and the queasy take cover.

The deck shoved up and then dropped away underfoot. Woolf was butting through wind buffets right up to the bulwark rail. Mal had to smile; looked as if the guy were going to feed his dinner to the fish.

With alarm, Mal caught on to the stupid bastard's real intent.

Woolf started to climb over the rail, the wind fluffing the surround of his tonsure and flapping his sport shirt.

Mal could reach him in time only with a shout. "Hey! You're forgetting something!"

Woolf's head jerked around. "Who the hell said that?"

Mal, holding the rail along the superstructure, leaned out of shadow. "Me."

"Who the hell are you?"

"A guy who can tell you why you don't want to do it."

"What makes it your business?"

"Look, the wind is tearing our words. Climb back down, and I'll tell you. Don't worry, I won't make a grab."

Mal could almost feel the guy's stare. A toss-up for a long minute, to jump or not to jump.

Then Woolf climbed down off the rail. But he held it, ready to hurdle. "Shit. It would've been all over by now." He sounded somewhere between sore and sullen. "Okay. So tell me why not."

"Because there has to be a body."

He said it so seriously that—after initial surprise—the other laughed.

The laugh died into a thoughtful grunt. "You got something there. If I vanish into salt air, it could take my ever-loving heirs seven years to settle my estate. Not that I couldn't care less. But shit, man, you know how long it took me to nerve myself to the

362

jumping point? I'd have to work up the nerve all over again." He shivered all at once. "Goddammit, let me buy you a drink. I know I sure could use one."

"Likewise."

Woolf let go the rail and skidded downhill to Mal and caught hold beside him. He stuck out his free hand. "The name's . . . Max Schaf." The voice strained but with a politician's rote frank heartiness, the flesh clammy but with a politician's preemptive grip.

"Harry Pace." The name *he* was traveling under.

"Great, Harry."

Mal saw that Woolf failed to make him from the lifeboat drill the *Queen Mab's* first day out. They had the same boat station, and Mal had certainly sized up Woolf at the time, but Woolf's obvious preoccupation had kept Woolf from registering Mal. And in between Woolf had holed up in his cabin, living on room service while he thrashed out whether to stonewall the federal investigation or to spill his guts. Some vacation, the Caribbean cruise his doctor had ordered to avert breakdown and elude the media. Some vacationer, Borough President Al Woolf traveling sans mustache and sans toupee as "Max Schaf."

Woolf looked around. "I guess we go back through the glass section to the stairs."

"Never mind those stairs." Mal steered him to another door. "I found a shortcut. It's a way just the crew uses. It goes straight down all the way to the engine room."

Actually, it didn't go straight down; it corkscrewed. But you could see the shaft had doors so you could get off at the decks along the way.

He ushered Woolf in. "Hold tight and watch your step."

Woolf started down the twisting stairs. "You know, I feel born again." He sounded manic. "I'm glad you happened along when you did."

Mal was busy taking plastic gloves from his pocket and pulling them on. "I'm glad you're glad."

The guy started to look around with a big smile. Mal gave him a hard neck chop and then a shove. Woolf ended in a heap a dozen steps below. Mal swung swiftly down to make sure the guy was dead. The guy was dead.

He had *told* the guy there had to be a body. Mal's client needed

363

to know that Woolf hadn't faked a suicide, needed to know that Woolf wasn't still around in some new identity, needed to be sure that Woolf couldn't still bleat if the feds caught up with him.

Mal's client needed to *know* Woolf was dead.

The Night the Rat Danced

George William Rae

T HE NEWSPAPERS called it "a sordid tragedy." You can put your tag on it; here are the elements: A man with a hole in his head, a rat that danced atop a bar, a lovely woman, and a drunkard who slept through murder. . . .

I took the job in Kelly's because I had to eat. It was a dump on the waterfront. A dim room with crowding tables and a postage stamp-sized dance floor. At one end a thin wall sliced the bar off by itself. That's where I worked, in the bar, four to closing, six nights a week, dishing out rotgut to people who were forever arguing and fighting.

I guess I couldn't have stayed if it weren't for Carmen DeVliss.

Carmen was the one-act floorshow. A ten-minute dance, three times a night. But what a dance. It wasn't the little she wore or what she took off. It was the way she did it. She flowed like music, she worked on you like wine, until the whole place swayed in the semi-darkness and it was as if everybody in the place was dancing to the sobbing of Jimmy Gaylord's sax. That's the way she hit you. The dancer with the child's eyes and the child's face and the woman's body. I loved her; that's why I stayed. I wouldn't have left Kelly's to save my life.

The night the rat danced was a Saturday. He leaped from the floor to the bar, down at the far end, a plump, sleek one, grey as death. He wasn't very big—I'd seen bigger in the waterfront district—but he was fat and sure of himself and entirely unafraid.

A big fellow with a diamond stickpin and a flashy suit noticed the rat first. The man was a newcomer. The night before had been the first time I'd seen him.

"Look!" he said. "A dancing rat!"

The crowd at the bar looked where he pointed. There was the rat on the bar, swaying to the music of Jimmy Gaylord's band. Following the rhythm with his body as he sat up on his hind legs, his long tail switching across the bar behind him.

They crowded around to watch and the rat went right on dancing, his eyes half-closed and glazed as if he were hypnotized. The music speeded up, loud and jarring, and the rat whirled and spun about, claws scratching on the bar.

"He's goin' crazy!" Someone yelled.

But the rat was right with the beat, dancing, spinning, lurching with the music.

I didn't hear the shot. The music was too loud. A woman screamed and pointed. The big man with the diamond stickpin was folding to the floor. The back of his head was a welter of blood.

For a moment we all stood frozen while the man settled to the floor and the rat went on dancing madly to the wild beat of Jimmy Gaylord's band.

I leaned over the bar and looked at the man. Then I looked at the crowd huddled close to the wall away from the body. A drunk named Donatti slept at a table against the wall, his shaggy head pillowed on his arms.

"My God!" someone whispered, and that broke the spell. Women screamed and the crowd headed for the door in a rush. I didn't try to stop them. I'm just a barky, not a cop. I walked around the bar and looked down at the man. He was dead.

Kelly came rushing out of the other room.

"What goes on, Frank?" he asked. Then he saw the body. His face drained of color. His big body trembled. Although he ran a waterfront dive, Kelly hated violence. It made him sick to see blood. "Call the police," he croaked, leaning against the bar. "And give me a double shot."

I called the police and poured two double shots. The bar was entirely deserted except for Kelly and me and the drunk sleeping at the table. With a sick little shock, I noticed the grey rat was still dancing on the end of the bar. . . .

Lieutenant Baker of Homicide was very efficient. He ordered the blinds drawn, questioned the customers in the other room, got their addresses and let them go. Then, the place empty, he came out to the bar where the help stood around in a worried group.

Baker was a chain smoker, jerky in his movements, short and heavily built. He had thin lips that made me feel it'd be tough to have him for an enemy.

"Any of you people know the victim?" Baker asked. His hard brown eyes worked over the musicians, the two cooks, the three waiters, me. They lingered for a long time on the face of Carmen DeVliss and they glinted with strange lights as if he thought he knew her, but wasn't sure.

"Okay," Baker said. "Any of you seen him around here before?" He swung to me. "You seen him?"

"He came in last night for the first time since I've been here," I told him. "That's all I know about him." I don't know why I didn't tell Baker that I'd seen the big man go backstage to Carmen DeVliss' dressing room twice, the night before and that night. I figured if she wanted him to know she would've told him.

Baker went over to the drunk who still slept at the table. He shook him. "Hey, you, wake up!" he yelled. The drunk's head lolled about but he remained asleep. Baker came back to the bar. "Who's he?"

"That's Phil Donatti," Kelly said. "He's a regular. He hasn't been sober since I've known him."

Baker turned to me again. "He drank enough to float the Queen Mary tonight," I said.

"A hell of a lot of good you people are to a murder investigation," Baker said. He took a notebook from his pocket, opened it with clean, blunt fingers.

"Now I'll tell you a few things that might jog your memories." Baker said. "The dead man is Pete King, a cheap hood from New York. He wouldn't be coming in here for nothing. Probably looking for somebody. That mean anything?"

Nobody answered. Baker smirked and went on. Behind him the coroner and several other men worked in quiet boredom, taking pictures, measuring, sorting out the contents of the dead man's pockets.

"King's racket is mainly blackmail. According to the record he wasn't much on pleasure so he must've been here on business." Baker's voice was flat and a little weary. "If any of you are holding anything back you're putting yourself in a tough spot."

Still no answer.

Baker slammed the book shut, shoved it into his pocket and turned his back on us.

"Take that drunk down to Headquarters and sober him up," Baker said to a harness bull at the door. "I want to talk to him when he can make sense."

I happened to be looking at Carmen DeVliss' face when Baker said that. She turned pale and her lips formed the word, "No. . . ." but she didn't say anything aloud.

I knew there was something between Carmen and the drunk, Donatti. I'd seen them together enough. I'd never said anything to her about it because I'd said very little to her anyway. I told you I was in love with her. Well, I guess it was what you call a silent love. To her I was just a barky who worked in the same joint with her. We'd never held any long conversations.

The musicians, cooks and waiters went out when Baker left. Carmen was going to leave, too, but I stopped her.

"Wait a minute," I said. "I'd like to talk to you."

She swung her eyes full at me, and I could see in them what I'd thought might be there. Fear.

"What about?" she asked.

"Look," I said, "I'm with you, kid, but I'd like to know what I'm supposed to say. I know that murdered man went back to see you last night and tonight."

"I figured it was *my* business," she said. "I didn't tell them because I didn't want to get involved."

"That's okay by me. But how about Donatti? You didn't say a word about knowing him, either."

She didn't say anything to that, just caught her bottom lip between two rows of small white teeth and looked at me.

"They'll probably find out about it," I told her. "Why don't you let me help you?"

Her eyes came up to mine. We were standing very close together at the end of the bar. We were alone in the bar.

"Why?" she asked.

What I did then could've been called cheap or beautiful, depending on the way you knew me. I'm just a little guy who got out of the Army with a few battle stars and a kind of humility at being alive. I got kicked around. No decent work. But I never got bitter. I'm not the kind of a man who gets bitter. I can't hate. In war it's an impersonal thing, can you understand that? I couldn't do a cheap thing to somebody I love. I leaned over and kissed her. She knew then why I wanted to help her.

She didn't pull away from the kiss but when it was over she said, "Nobody's ever kissed me like *that*. Be careful, he'll kill you, too."

I said, "Who?" But she was gone and I was alone in the bar and strangely very lonely. Loneliness is common in bars. They bring it in every day and throw it at you but it doesn't touch you until suddenly you are lonely yourself, and then it pounces on you and you hear it whispering from every corner of the room and along the bar where it had daily chewed the hearts of men.

I took off my apron and walked down the bar. There was a scraping scamper and I saw the rat, the plump, death-grey rat that had been dancing while a man died. He was poised on the end of the bar, his glazed eyes aimed at me, his pointed teeth bared, his sharp nose twitching. We looked at each other for a long time and then he whisked off the bar and glided under a table.

Kelly came out of his office then.

"Let's get the hell out of here, Frank," he said, looking around and shivering. I hardly heard him because I suddenly knew something that made the death of the big man with the diamond stickpin easy to understand.

"Go ahead," I said to Kelly. "I'll close up. Guess I'd better clean that mess up in front of the bar."

He shivered again as his eyes struck the bloodstain on the floor.

"Okay, go ahead. I'm getting home to bed." He just about backed out.

I stuck around for about an hour and then I went to my room.

The next morning in a heavy rain I went down to Headquarters.

Lieutenant Baker was in his office, looking like he'd been through a wringer. "We've been sweating Donatti all night," he said wearily, "but we couldn't get anything out of him. He says he was asleep, that he was drunk. That's all he'll say. We'll have to turn him loose."

"I came down to tell you about the rat," I said.

He squinted at me. "What rat?"

"The rat that was dancing on the bar when the big man was killed."

"I heard someone mention that. What about it?"

"Doesn't it seem funny that a rat should be dancing?" I asked. "And just at the time when a man was murdered?"

He lifted his shoulders. "One of those things," he said. I had wanted to tell him what I'd found out but suddenly I decided to let it ride for a while.

"I wonder what was eating Donatti," I mused. "I never saw such a rummy."

Baker was interested now.

"Ever see him with a woman?"

"I saw him with a lot of women," I countered.

"This one would be short and dark," he said. "About a year ago, back in New York, this woman was tried for knocking off her husband. The state said Donatti was the motive but they couldn't make it stick. There was a witness they couldn't locate. After her acquittal she disappeared, and so did Donatti. Maybe she's around. By the looks of things, she knocked her husband off, and she and Donatti ran off together."

It was a nice story but it didn't make a pretty picture in my mind. I went out into the rain feeling lousy.

Carmen lived at a small hotel downtown. I'd heard her mention it once or twice in Kelly's.

She opened the door to my knock almost immediately, as if she'd been waiting for me.

I eased in and closed the door.

"They're going to turn him loose," I said. Over her shoulder I saw the suitcase on the bed, half packed.

She backed against the bed, looking at me as if she'd never seen me before.

"I'm no detective," I said, "but it wasn't hard to figure why the rat danced. *He danced because he was drunk.* Donatti was pouring the booze he was supposed to be drinking into the rathole under the table. I pulled the nest out of there last night; it was soaked with whiskey. I found a gun in there, too, Carmen. That gave me the picture."

Her face was as white as the blouse she wore. She gave a kind of a sob and then took a couple of steps toward me. "It's the wrong picture, Frank," she said. "I don't know how you found out about New York and that trial but you've got the wrong picture."

I took the .38 I'd found in the rathole out of my pocket. "There's only one picture you can make out of this," I said.

With an effort Carmen pulled herself together.

"Yes, that's Phil's gun," she said. "Yes, he did pour some of his drinks down the rathole. But what that adds up to is not what you think. Last night you kissed me, Frank, and you said you meant it. I kissed you back and I meant it, too. If you want to hear what I've got to say, then listen to me before it's too late. . . ."

I put the gun back in my pocket.

"In New York I married a man I'd known one day. I thought I loved him. I was new to that. I found out soon how wrong I was, but by then it was too late. I was married to one of the biggest crooked gambling operators in the city. Phil Donatti worked for him. I could talk to Phil and he understood. There was never any more than that between us. My husband had a partner who hated him and it was this partner who must have killed him. He was the man the state thought they could complete their case with but he was gone. They said I'd killed my husband for Phil Donatti but that wasn't true. The newspapers made a big thing of it and after the trial I thought it best to leave the city. I got the job here and Phil followed me but there still is nothing between us except friendship. . . ."

Someone walloped the door. I stepped aside and Carmen opened the door. It was Jimmy Gaylord, the orchestra leader. He threw the door open and for a minute I was behind it.

"Phil's out," Gaylord said to Carmen. "I was up at Kelly's rehearsing my boys. He came in and talked crazy, said he was going to kill somebody. I rushed over here."

Gaylord's back was to me. I slid out the door, my feet making no noise on the carpet. I had things to do and I had to do them fast.

The cab skidded up to Kelly's a half-hour later and I rammed through the door. The silence of the place wrapped itself around me so suddenly that I stopped just inside and ran my eyes over the dimness and listened for a minute to my heart walloping against my ribs.

I walked through the room with its ghostly white tablecloths. The echoes of my footsteps tramped along with me like those of unseen companions.

He was in there, all right. Up ahead in the darkness his voice whipped. "Stay there. I've got a gun on you."

I stopped, straining my eyes at the dim bulk of his figure.

"You're a sap, Frank," he said. "The telephone call was a dead give-away. I could see that you just wanted to keep me here until you came. Am I right, Frank?"

He came out of the shadows, his face emerging from a white blur until it hung before me, clear and cold and deadly.

"I hate violence," Kelly said, "but it seems to force itself on me. I'll have to kill you, Frank."

"Putty outside and steel inside," I said. "Violence seems to be your forte, Kelly. There was a man in New York, your partner. Then there was a blackmailing hood last night. You took care of them, all right. Then there was a drunken kid named Donatti. . . ."

"What about Donatti? He was around here a short while ago, yelling he was going to kill somebody."

"He was," I said. "He went off the top of the Mercantile Building a half-hour ago."

Kelly laughed a hard little laugh. "Donatti had it coming," he said. "He was trying to help Carmen pin the New York killing on me—and after I'd taken her in and given her a job, the tramp."

"I guess that wraps it up," I said. "You killed the big guy last night because he knew about the murder in New York. Donatti was pouring drinks down the rathole to keep sober so that he could warn the guy, but the temptation was too strong, he got drunk and you went through with it. Is that right, Kelly?"

He wasn't laughing now. "I took a hundred grand away from New York," he said. "I'd kill a lot of guys for a hundred grand—including you. . . ."

He was backing away, his face working. He hated it, what he'd have to see, a lot of blood and more violence. I had nothing to lose. I dived at him. Something sledged my ribs and I slid across the slippery dance floor. I dug in my pocket for the .38. He was throwing shots at me now. Another tugged at my arm. I sat up and shot him in the stomach.

He doubled over the gun, still triggering on an empty cylinder, then he smashed face down on the floor beside me.

I stayed awake long enough to see Carmen come in and then a tall, young beat cop who'd heard the shooting.

In the middle of a kiss I passed out, but there was a lifetime more where that'd come from.

Not Suited for Murder

Stan Knowlton

CYCIL WAUGHTON'S two coins registered with a dull, rattling clang. "On good time, tonight," he genially told the bus driver. He pulled out his watch. "Eleven twenty-three."

"Yeah," the driver answered. "Didn't make many stops this trip."

Cycil stepped off. With a grinding of gears the bus swung from the curb, rolling away, its tail-lights growing smaller in the darkness.

But Cycil was not watching the tail-lights. At a sharp run he already was headed for home. That's for a starter, he told himself. The driver would remember letting him off there at twenty-three minutes past eleven. And it was a twenty-minute walk to his house.

And it was: a good twenty minutes walk to Cycil's house by the road that looped the swampy, wood area between the main highway and the lonely, outskirt section where he lived.

Cycil smiled thinly. "But it's not taking me twenty minutes, *tonight*," he muttered.

He slipped between the bars of the white-painted fence that bordered the side-walk, pushed through the tall dry grass and brush to the edge of the swamp. Gnarled trees, rich in the colorful foliage of early fall, rose crookedly from the soggy soil, leaf-thick vines trailing heavily from their twisted branches.

Cycil turned up his collar, took a flashlight from his pocket, stepped in between the trees. The ground squished moistly beneath his feet. By the light of his torch, dimmed through the blue paper he had pasted over the lens, he picked his way.

He had made the trip once. Several weeks before, when the green leaves were beginning to turn to yellow-orange, he had made it. Carefully, painstakingly he had gone through, mapping out in his mind the quickest way from the highway to his house on the far side. But that was in daylight, and he was dressed for it. Stout, high leather boots, corduroy breeches and canvas hunting jacket.

And the shotgun he had carried backed up his story to Martha: he had been out hoping to flush a partridge in the swampland.

"You're filthy!" had been Martha's reaction. "Get out of those clothes and take a bath!"

And Cycil had. His lips, turned sullen at the thought of his wife, twisted away from his white teeth. But, he swore savagely, he would take no more orders from her!

His marriage for money had not panned out as he had expected. He was still working at his old job; still commuting to and from the city. At first, Martha had driven him to the bus stop in the morning, picked him up there in the evening. But not now. Now, he walked—both ways. And what he wanted, or needed, he paid for from the money he earned—from what of it was left after he had turned over to Martha his share of the household expenses.

And—damn her—Martha's domineering ways. Cycil cursed as the remembrance of them flashed across his mind. Do this, Cycil—Cycil, do that. She ordered him around as she saw fit, planned for him his every move. Each night she laid out his socks, underwear, shirt and tie for the next day, told him which of his three suits he was to wear.

Cycil swore roundly as his foot slipped off a tufted hillock, sank to the knee in the sticky mire. He grasped a tree trunk, worked up his leg. His foot came out of the mud with a sucking plutt!

And what a hell of a fuss Martha had made when he bought that last suit without consulting her. A suit exactly like one he already had. She had said that he was crazy. Crazy! Yeah. He grinned to himself. Crazy—like a fox. He knew why he wanted two suits alike. He had known when he got the second one, months ago.

Cycil plunged on through the bog, his legs soaked to the knees by the muddy water, his clothing torn and disheveled by the clinging brambles and snapping branches. At the edge of the woods near his house, he stopped; by the light of his flash he looked at his watch. Eleven thirty-one. Eight minutes to come through. He had a lee-way of twelve minutes in which to make the phone call, and another five or six to complete his plan—to make it tightly foolproof.

As he had expected, the house was dark. Martha no longer waited up for him on the nights that he was detained at the office. She had made no comment the previous evening when he informed her that he would have to work late the following night, but he had no doubt that she had checked with the firm.

On the lawn in front of the house he wiped some of the mud

and slime from his shoes, removed them. He carried them in his hand up the steps to the veranda. He unlocked the door. Noiselessly he opened it; closed it behind him. Silently, in his stockinged feet, he went to the kitchen, snapped on the light. He left the shoes in the sink, descended the stairs to the cellar. From a beam overhead he took an old-fashioned .32 which he had owned since he was a young fellow. A gun no one, not even Martha, knew he possessed.

Cycil went back to the kitchen. His watch said eleven thirty-five. He had plenty of time. He climbed the carpeted stairs to the second floor, threw the switch to the hall light by Martha's bedroom door. He could hear her measured breathing from inside the room. He opened the door.

The shaded bulb in the hallway threw a diffused light into the bedroom. Cycil could plainly see Martha. She lay huddled under the neat, white bed-clothes, her nightcapped head turned sidewise on the feather pillow. She was sleeping the untroubled sleep of the just.

Cycil spoke sharply. "Martha!"

Martha stirred uneasily. Cycil spoke again. "Martha!"

Martha sat up, stared sleepily at him. Cycil's aim was good. Martha slumped back, a stain of crimson on the white of her nightgown over her breast.

Cycil worked rapidly. He dragged Martha from the bed, laid her on the floor. He disarranged the bedclothing. He kicked askew the rug. He knocked several articles from the dresser—perfumes, powders, a mirror. He overturned a chair. He surveyed with satisfaction the havoc he had wrought. Mute testimony, he figured, of the valiant struggle Martha had made for her life.

For a moment Cycil looked callously down at her. Now, he gloated, he was sitting pretty. Martha never had made a will. Everything would come to him. No more slaving for a paltry salary. No more skimping for this and that. No more being roused from a warm bed on cold mornings. No more commuting back and forth— back and forth—back and forth. How he hated it! And, too—a warmness tingled through him—there was that cute little blonde at the office.

Cycil left the hall light burning, hurried down to the kitchen. Eleven-thirty-nine. In four minutes he must make the phone call. He wiped the gun, held it in his handkerchief-mittened hand. He opened the kitchen door, stepped out on the back piazza. He hurled the gun far into the night. Let them find it. There would be no finger prints on it; it could not be traced to him.

Back in the kitchen, the door again locked, Cycil stripped off his coat, vest, trousers and socks. He wrapped them into a sodden ball, the muddy shoes in the center. He turned on the cellar light, hastened down the steps. Deep under the coal in the bin he buried the soggy bundle. He was panting when he got back to the kitchen. He unlocked a pantry window, raised the sash. He tipped over things on the shelf under the window, spilled them on the floor. He rinsed his hands at the sink, dried them.

Eleven forty-three. He had planned things to the dot! Had he come around by the road from the bus stop, he would have been getting home now.

In his dress shirt, tie, shorts and bare feet, he dialed the operator.

"Emergency!" he barked breathlessly into the receiver. "Get the police!"

"Police station," came back to him after a moment. "Lieutenant—"

"Quick!" Cycil cut him off. "Send the police! My wife's been murdered! I just got home and found her. Some prowler got in through the pantry window and—

"Yes! . . . 43 Lambert Street. . . . Hurry! Hurry!"

Cycil hung up. He had five or six minutes before the police could get there. He darted up the front stairs, flung himself into his bedroom, snapped on the light. He put on fresh socks, another pair of oxfords. He carefully scrutinized himself in the mirror of his dresser. On his mad journey through the wooded swamp his upturned coat collar had protected the shirt and tie. They were no more soiled than from an ordinary day's wear.

Cycil went to the closet, reached into it. Crazy, was he? Crazy to have two suits exactly alike? Yeah. Crazy . . . He reached deeper into the closet. Crazy. Yeah. Like a— He opened the door wider, peered inside. Perplexity shadowed his face. He looked around the room—on the chairs, on the bed.

He rushed to his wife's room, turned on the light. He looked in her closet, on the chairs. He dashed down stairs to the first floor, looked through all the rooms. He stumbled back to his own room. "Where the hell—?" He was sobbing wildly. "Where the hell—?"

Cycil again looked in his closet. Only three empty suit-hangers met his eyes.

"Where the hell—?"

He looked dazedly around the room, saw a paper on the dresser. In his haste he had not noticed it. He snatched it up. His eyes raced over the bold, angular writing—Martha's.

Cycils' flushed face turned ashen. He clutched at the dresser. For a moment he stood rigidly there, staring unseeingly into space.

Then he again read the note. "No, Martha," he whispered. *"No!"*

A third time he read it. Stumbling, incoherently he mouthed the words. " 'Wear the same suit tomorrow, Cycil,' " he mumbled. " 'I sent the other two to the cleaners.' "

Unhurriedly, methodically he tore the missive into tiny shreds, cupped them in his hand. Then Cycil tossed back his head and laughed. Laughed long and loudly. "Yeah," he chortled. " 'Wear the same suit—' "

From a distance came the sound of a siren.

In a gesture of resignation, of utter futility, he threw up his hands, loosed the fistful of tattered paper bits. Slowly, like drifting snowflakes, they sifted down, gently settled on his head, on his shoulders.

Outside, a motor hummed; brakes screeched. Then came running, crunching footsteps on the graveled walk. A thumping on the door.

Old Charlie

Joe R. Lansdale

H I THERE. Catching much?

Well, they're in there. Just got to have the right bait and be patient. You don't mind if I sit down on the bank next to you, do you?

Good, good. Thanks.

Yeah, I like it fine. I never fish with anything but a cane pole. An old-fashioned way of doing things, I guess, but it suits me. I like to sharpen one end a bit, stick that baby in the ground, and wait it out. Maybe find someone like yourself to chat with for a while.

Whee, it's hot. Near sundown, too. You know, every time I'm out fishing in heat like this, I think of Old Charlie.

Huh? No, no. You couldn't really say he was a friend of mine. You see, I met him right on this bank, sort of like I'm meeting you, only he came down and sat beside me.

It was hot, just like today. So damned hot you'd think your nose was going to melt off your face and run down your chin. I was out here trying to catch a bite before sundown, because there's not much I like better than fish, when here comes this old codger with a fishing rig. It was just like he stepped out of nowhere.

Don't let my saying he was old get you to thinking about white hair and withered muscles. This old boy was stout-looking, like maybe he'd done hard labor all his life. Looked, and was built, a whole lot like me, as a matter of fact.

He comes and sits down about where I am now and smiles at me. That was the first time I'd ever seen that kind of smile, sort of strange and satisfied. And it looked wavery, as if it was nothing more than a reflection in the water.

After he got settled, got his gear all worked out, and put his bait on, he cast his line and looked at me with that smile again.

"Catching much?" he asked me.

"No," I say. "Nothing. Haven't had a bite all day."

He smiled that smile. "My name's Charlie. Some folks just call me Old Charlie."

"Ned," I say.

"I sure do love to fish," he says. "I drive out every afternoon, up and down this Sabine River bank, shopping for a fresh place to fish."

"You don't say," I says to him. "Well, ain't much here."

About that time, Old Charlie gets him a bite and pulls in a nice-size bass. He puts it on a chain and stakes it out in the water.

Then Old Charlie rebaits his hook and tosses it again. A bass twice the size of the first hits it immediately, and he adds it to his chain.

Wasn't five minutes later and he'd nabbed another.

Me, I hadn't caught doodlysquat. So I sort of forgot about the old boy and his odd smile and got to watching him haul them in. I bet he had nine fish on that chain when I finally said, "That rod and reel must be the way to go."

He looked at me and smiled again. "No, don't matter what you fish with, it's the bait that does it. Got the right bait, you can catch anything."

"What do you use?"

"I've tried many baits," he said smiling, "but there isn't a one that beats this one. Came by using it in an odd way, too. My wife gave me the idea. Course, that was a few years back. Not married now. You see, my wife was a young thing, about thirty-two years younger than me, and I married her when she was just a kid. Otherwise, she wouldn't have been fool enough to marry an old man like me. I knew I was robbing the cradle, impressing her with my worldly knowledge so I could have someone at home all the time, but I couldn't help myself.

"Her parents didn't mind much. They were river trash and were ready to get shed of her anyway. Just one more mouth to feed far as they were concerned. I guess that made it all the easier for me.

"Anyway, we got married. Things went right smart for the first few years. Then one day this Bible-thumper came by. He was something of a preacher and a Bible salesman, and I let him in to talk to us. Well, he talked a right nice sermon, and Amy, my wife, insisted that we invite him to dinner and buy one of his Bibles.

"I noticed right then and there that she and that Bible-thumper were exchanging looks, and not the sort to make you think of church and gospel reading.

"I was burned by it, but I'm a realistic old cuss, and I knew I was pretty old for Amy and that there wasn't any harm in her looking. Long as that was all she did. Guess by that time, she'd found out I wasn't nearly as worldly as she had thought. All I had to offer her was a hardscrabble farm and what I could catch off the river, and neither was exactly first-rate. Could hardly grow a cotton-pickin' thing on that place, the soil was so worked out, and I didn't have money for no store-bought fertilizer—and didn't have no animals to speak of that could supply me with any barnyard stuff, neither. Fishing had got plumb rotten. This was before the bait.

"Well, me not being about to catch much fish was hurtin' me the most. I didn't care much for plowing them old hot fields. Never had. But fishing . . . now that was my pride and joy. That and Amy.

"So, we're scraping by like usual, and I start to notice this change in Amy. It started taking place the day after that Bible-thumper's visit. She still fixed meals, ironed, and stuff, but she spent a lot of time looking out the windows, like she was expecting something. Half the time when I spoke to her, she didn't even hear me.

"And damned if that thumper didn't show up about a week later. We'd already bought a Bible, and since he didn't have no new product to sell us, he just preached at us. Told us about the ten commandments and about hellfire and damnation. But from the way he was looking at Amy, I figured there was at least one or two of them commandments he didn't take too serious, and I don't think he gave a hang about hellfire and damnation.

"I kept my temper, them being young and all. I figured the thumper would give it up pretty soon anyway, and when he was gone Amy would forget.

"But he didn't give it up. Got so he came around often, his suit all brushed up, his hair slicked back, and that Bible under his arm like it was some kind of key to any man's home. He even took to coming early in the day while I was working the fields, or in the barn sharpening my tools.

"He and Amy would sit on the front porch, and every once in a while I'd look up from my old mules and quit plowing and see them sitting there in the rocking chairs on the porch. Him with that Bible on his knee—closed—and her looking at him like he was the very one that hung the moon.

"They'd be there when I quit the fields and went down to the river in the cool of the afternoon, and though I didn't like the idea of them being alone like that, it never really occurred to me that anything would come of it—I mean, not really.

"Old men can be such fools.

"Well, I remember thinking that it had gone far enough. Even if they were young and all, I just couldn't go on with that open flirting right in front of my eyes. I figured they must have thought me pretty stupid, and maybe that bothered me even more.

"Anyway, I went down to the river that afternoon. Told myself that when I got back I'd have me a talk with Amy, or if that Bible-thumper was still there amoonin' on the porch, I'd pull him aside and tell him politely that if he came back again I was going to blow 'is head off.

"This day I'm down at the river there's not a thing biting. Not only do we need the food, but my pride is involved here. I'd been a fisherman all of life, and it was getting so I couldn't seine a minnow out of a washtub. I just couldn't have imagined at that time how fine that bait was going to work . . . But I'm getting ahead of myself.

"Disgusted, I decided to come back from the creek early, and what do I see but this Bible fella's car still parked in our yard, and it getting along toward sundown, too. I'll tell you, I hadn't caught a thing and I wasn't in any kind of friendly mood, and it just went all over me like a bad dose of wood ticks. When I got to the front porch I was even madder, because the rockers were empty. The Bible that thumper always toted was lying on the seat of one of them, but they weren't anywhere to be seen.

"Guess I was thinking it right then, but I was hoping that I wasn't going to find what I thought I was going to find. Wanted to think they had just went in to have a drink of water or a bite to eat, but my mind wouldn't rightly settle on that.

"Creeping, almost, I walked up on the porch and slipped inside. The noises I heard from the bedroom didn't sound anything like water-drinking, eating, or gospel-talking.

"Just went nuts. Got the butcher knife off the cabinet, and . . . I don't half remember.

"Later, when the police came out there looking for the thumper, they didn't find a thing. Turned out he was a real blabbermouth. Everyone in town knew about him and Amy before I did—I mean, you know, in that way. So they believed me when I said I figured they'd run off together. I'm sure glad they didn't seine the river, or they'd have found his car where I run it off in the deep water.

"Guess that wouldn't have mattered much though. Even if they'd found the car, they wouldn't have had no bodies. And without the bodies, they can't do a thing to you. You see, I'd cut them up real good and lean and laid me out about twenty lines. Fish hit that bait like it was made for them. Took me maybe three days to use it up—which is about when the police showed up. But by then the bait was gone and I'd sold most of the fish and turned myself a nice dollar. Hell, rest of the mess I cooked up and ate. Matter-of-fact, them officers were there when I was eating the last of it.

"I was a changed man after that. Got to smiling all the time. Just couldn't help myself. Loved catchin' them fish. Fishing is just dear to my heart, even more so now. You might say I owed it all to Amy.

"Got so I started making up more of the bait—you know, other folks I'd find on the river, kind of out by themselves. It got so I was making a living off fishing alone."

That's Old Charlie's story, fella . . . Hey, why are you looking at me like that?

Me, Old Charlie?

No sir, not me. This here on my right is Old Charlie.

What do you mean there's no one there? Sure there is . . . Oh yeah, I forgot. No one else seems to see Old Charlie but me. Can't understand that. Old Charlie tells me it used to be no one could see *me.* Can you believe that? Townsfolks used to say Old Charlie had gone crazy over his wife running off and all. Said he'd taken to talking to himself, calling the other self Ned.

Ain't so. I'm Ned. I work for Old Charlie now. Odd thing is, I can't remember ever doing anything else. Old Charlie has got to where he can't bring himself to kill folks for the bait anymore. Says it upsets him. So he has me do it. I mean, we've got to go on living, don't we? Fishing is all we know. You're a fisherman. You understand, don't you?

You sure are looking at me odd, fella. Is it the smile? Yeah, guess it is. You see, I got it, too. Once . . . Wait a minute. What's that, Charlie? . . . Yes, yes, I'm hurrying. Just a minute.

You see, once you get used to hauling in them fish, using that sort of bait, it's the only kind you want to use from then on. Just keeps me and Charlie smiling all the time.

So when we see someone like yourself sitting out here all alone, we just can't help ourselves. Just got to have the bait. That's another reason I keep the end of this cane pole so sharp.

Oldest Living Serial Killer Tells All

John R. Platt

THE PAIN in his knuckles was almost unbearable this morning. Throbbing, stabbing pains every time he flexed his hands. But Rockwell had stopped complaining about the arthritis years ago. He knew the guards would be unresponsive, uncaring, unflinching in their contempt for him.

Rockwell shoved his hands into his pockets and paced slowly back and forth in his cell. His knees and ankles also ached with each step, and his back was sore from the thin mattress, but those pains were minor compared to his hands, and he did his best to ignore them. Later, when the sun rose enough to burn the dampness out of the air, he would probably feel better. But for now he would have to keep moving, or else his joints would become so stiff he would be unable to move by late morning.

Rockwell wondered what day it was. He hoped it was Wednesday. He got to spend an hour outside every Wednesday, and the fresh air would no doubt make him feel better. Once, long ago, he had been able to keep track of the days and hours by his own internal clock, but gradually, he realized, he had lost that ability. Or maybe he had just given it up.

He pulled his hands out and massaged the middle joint on his right hand as he paced. That one was always the worst, thanks to a bar fight in 1936. Rockwell smiled at the memory.

He felt the air shift before he heard the cell door open behind him. It had been that way for him for a few years now, ever since a young gang member had boxed Rockwell's ears in the yard one wintry Wednesday afternoon. Rockwell smiled at that memory, too. He could still see the blood streaming down the Chicano youth's face, splattering on the concrete and hissing as it landed in a patch of snow. The little bastard never even saw it coming.

A memory like that was worth a little lost hearing.

Rockwell turned to face the guard. The light from the hallway was behind him, but Rockwell recognized the silhouette. Short, stocky, no neck and a barrel of a chest. It could only be Evans. That disappointed Rockwell. Evans didn't work on Wednesdays.

A pair of leg irons skidded across the floor and came to rest against Rockwell's left foot. "Put them on," said Evans. "You've got a visitor."

Rockwell looked into the thick yellowed glass and the cold, hard eyes that stared back at him. He took the face in bit by bit. Unkempt beard, gray and white but stained brown at the corners of the mouth. Sunken cheeks. Pale skin. A criss-cross of scars above and below the right eye. Lips thin and pressed together. And in the center, the cold, dead eyes.

God, it had been years since he'd seen his own reflection.

"-oday is?" Rockwell looked past his shadowy figure in the glass to the face on the other side. The kid couldn't have been much more than twenty. He was way too thin, but still had a small amount of baby-fat under his eyes. His face was clean-shaven, but Rockwell doubted the kid even had to shave very often. He seemed nervous, couldn't sit still, constantly tapping a pen on the table. In front of him was a long, thin pad of paper. Rockwell had seen the cover of the pad as he walked up to the visitor's booth. It said "Reporter's Notebook."

"I asked, do you know what day today is?" the kid repeated, voice cracking ever so slightly.

Rockwell rubbed his hands together, handcuffs clinking on his wrists like sadistic wind chimes. He didn't want to be here. "Graduation day?"

The kid twitched nervously in his seat. He tapped his pen several times to the notebook, then looked up again at Rockwell with his best steely gaze. "It's Monday, May 8. You've been here in prison for fifty years, as of today."

Now it was Rockwell's turn to look away. He swallowed slowly, mouth dry. Suddenly, he felt very tired. When he spoke, his voice was weak and raspy. "I . . . I would've thought that'd be a few years away, still."

The kid grinned and leaned in towards the glass. "How does it feel," he asked with newfound confidence, "to be the oldest living American serial killer?"

A sudden crash, and Rockwell was standing, his chair skidding backwards, his hands pressed up against the glass, face inches away from the young reporter's. The kid jumped back in his chair, and his pen snapped in his hand. Blue ink dribbled onto the Reporter's Notebook. Rockwell bared his yellowed teeth, the tip of his nose just barely touching the glass, and snarled quietly. "How does it feel," said Rockwell so softly his damaged ears could barely hear it, "to be the dinner for a hungry wolf?"

The guards pulled him away before he could see the kid's reaction, but as he was pushed into the hallway that led away from the visiting area, he was sure he smelled something sour, and he laughed inwardly to himself.

Back in his cell, the energy left Rockwell once again. He sat on his cot, arms crossed over his knees, and stared into the darkness of the deepening shadows. He felt weak and tired, like he did so often lately, whenever he was not provoked into explosive anger. When he was younger the anger was the only possession he had in the world. He wished he had more of it now.

His shoulder ached and throbbed. He had struck a door jam in the guards' haste to get him away from the boy-reporter. The guards had held little faith in Rockwell's complaints, and just shoved him along further until he was back in his cell and out of their hair.

Of course, the kid hadn't been entirely correct about the fifty years. Rockwell hadn't been here all of this time. He had been moved around from prison to prison, like so much baggage, every few years. No warden wanted the responsibility of holding on to him for very long. Each one was the same. They would shove him into solitary and try to forget about him. Then there would be an explosion of anger and violence during the few hours he was allowed out, and Rockwell would find himself on the way to another institution.

Rockwell imagined a group of wardens trading their prisoners around like kids with baseball cards. I'll give you two dope dealers and a rapist for your serial killer . . .

And the sad thing was, Rockwell was innocent.

"I don't believe you."

The kid was back on the other side of the glass, looking even more nervous than before. He also looked rather bitter and doubtful. Rockwell's performance of the day before had left quite an impression.

"Look, kid," said Rockwell, in a resigned tone. "I've done a lot of things in my life. I've hurt a lot of people, both before and after I went to prison. That jury fifty years ago knew what they had in their court room when they saw me sitting there. They were right to convict me of murder." His voice was rough and gravelly, bitter and angry. "They just convicted me of the wrong murders."

They sat in silence for a few moments. The kid held a pen above his pad of paper, as if he were about to write something but could not think of the words. Rockwell rubbed his knuckles and tried to ignore the growing pain in his shoulder.

At last the kid spoke, rather meekly. "So . . . so if you didn't kill that family . . . who did?"

Rockwell thought about that, thought about how to answer. The last time a reporter had come to see him was several years ago. A middle-aged black woman, beautiful and full of passionate anger, writing about the irony of a killer outliving the judge, jury and prosecutor that had convicted him. Rockwell had refused to talk to her. He never knew how her story had come out. But that was a different prison. Here, now, the warden was adamant that Rockwell would speak to this reporter. 'Public Relations.'

He ran his fingers through his beard. When the words came out, he was as surprised at what he heard as the kid was.

"The sheriff," he said.

"I don't know what the place is like now," Rockwell began, "but back then Willow Falls, Arkansas, could barely even be called a town. Poor homesteads spread out over fifty or sixty miles, orchards and farms sitting between everything, so no one's house was very close to anyone else's. Lots of migrant workers, coming to bring one crop in, then moving on to the next farm and the next crop down the road.

"I came into town one afternoon on a truck full of workers who were coming there to help harvest the latest batch of corn. I'd been working my way across the country. No ties. I made enough money to move on and then I did so.

"And there was no way for anyone to track me down when they found what I had left behind." The kid swallowed loudly. Somehow he knew what Rockwell meant.

"As I said, I rode into town, and one of the first people I saw as I got off the truck was the sheriff. I think I pretty much saw him at the same time he saw me. And we recognized each other."

"You knew the sheriff?" the kid interrupted, questioning.

"No," Rockwell sighed. "But we did recognize each other. More precisely, we recognized what we were. He knew I was a killer same as he was, and he didn't want me around."

"The sheriff was a serial killer, too?"

Rockwell sighed, coughed slightly. "I don't think of myself a 'serial killer', kid. I don't even know what that is. All I know is that I've killed a lot of people. Sometimes I was angry, sometimes I just needed a few bucks or a new pair of shoes." Rockwell paused and stared at the kid. "Sometimes I killed just because I enjoyed it."

The kid swallowed loudly again and looked down at his paper.

"I don't know if that makes me a serial killer," Rockwell continued, "but I think Sheriff Hutson must have been the same way. Neither of us thought the life of one man was worth all that much. Only I could tell from the first time I saw him that he had something I never really did, something that drove him: Hatred."

Rockwell took a sip of water from the plastic glass on the table. He wasn't used to talking this much. Hell, he wasn't used to talking about himself. A bead of sweat trickled down the side of his forehead. This wasn't easy for him.

"The family that was killed, they were black, weren't they?"

Rockwell looked back up at the kid. He was smarter than he'd given him credit for. "Yeah," he said, rubbing his shoulder. "Most of the people working the fields down there were black, Spanish, whatever. Not a lot of whites, at least, not usually.

"The feeling was that if a migrant died, another migrant had to have done it, and the culprit was already long down the road before they even discovered the crime. As long as it didn't affect the permanent residents of the town, no one worried about it much. I proved how that worked a few dozen times. All of those small towns were the same. They'd investigate a bit, but if the victim was black maybe they wouldn't even do that.

"Willow Falls didn't have more murders than any other of these farmer communities in the South, but I think the number committed by the same person was a lot higher than anywhere else."

"Sheriff Hutson was killing the workers and then blaming the murders on another worker, or just not investigating?"

"That's what I would have done, if I'd thought about it enough."

Pause. "S-so . . . what happened to you?"

Rockwell took another swallow of water. It was getting hotter in the room, and it made him feel even weaker. "The sheriff told me to keep moving the day I arrived there, to not stick around, but I couldn't go until I had at least a day's wages to get me to the next town. I worked harvesting corn for a day, got my pay, and fell asleep under a tree, ready to move on at first light.

"Hutson must have known that I hadn't left. And he must have really hated having that black family living so close to him. He . . . he went into their house, slaughtered them in their sleep, then got his deputies together and came looking for me."

Rockwell felt the anger seeping back into him, and gritted his teeth. "Hutson and I may have been the same in some ways, but he was a lot worse than me. I never killed no kids, didn't spread the bodies around like . . .

"They found me and jumped me while I was sleeping! I didn't even know who they were, but I fought back!" Rockwell's eyes were wild now, and the kid subconsciously pushed himself back a few inches from the table. "They pulled me up and started hitting me, but I kicked out, and I'm sure I felt someone's ribs crack! The next man who tried to hit me got his nose broke! I started to run . . ."

Rockwell coughed. "I started to run, but they . . ." More coughing, and a sudden dizzy sensation. "But they . . . oh, shit . . ." Rockwell reached for the water glass again, but his arm felt tired and heavy, and the glass slipped from between his fingers and the water spilled and spread out over the table, dripping down in slow motion. His vision was foggy; all he could seem to concentrate on was the dripping water. He was vaguely aware of the kid screaming for the guard, but the sound came from so far away, and then he felt rough hands on his shoulders and he screamed and everything came painfully into focus but he couldn't move, and then he saw his shirt ripped away to reveal the swollen, purple mess of his shoulder and he screamed again.

Two pairs of hands lifted him up out of his seat and he looked up to see the kid, standing on the opposite side of the glass, his face pale and his mouth hanging open. "Don't write the story, kid!" Rockwell yelled as they carried him out. "Hutson died years ago! It doesn't matter any more!"

As the door between them closed, Rockwell saw the kid still standing there, Reporter's Notebook in hand, but hanging forgotten at his side. He wasn't even sure if the kid had heard his last words to him. But if he did, he hoped the kid would ignore them.

By the time they carried him into the infirmary and placed him onto the operating table, the pain had subsided into a dull flame. Dr. Chandler looked at the shoulder and told Rockwell not to worry as he placed a plastic breathing tube over his mouth. "A few broken blood vessels," Chandler said. "Maybe some muscle damage." There was internal bleeding, but it wouldn't kill him. The guards left, and Chandler wheeled out a tray of surgical tools, then checked the anesthetic machinery and turned to prep himself at a nearby sink. It was just the two of them now.

"I'm just going to do enough now to stabilize you," said Chandler as he scrubbed his hands. "Then we'll get you to the hospital. I don't have the equipment or the staff here anymore to do much else."

"I'm not going to die?" asked Rockwell, his voice echoing inside the breathing apparatus.

"No," laughed Chandler. "But from what I understand, a couple of guards are going to wish *they* were dead after the warden gets through with them for messing up your shoulder."

Rockwell reached up with his good hand and pulled the anesthetic mask away from his face. This hiss of the gas could barely be heard over the running water. Painfully, he sat up, and reached over to the tray of stainless steel tools a few feet away.

His knuckles were stiff and they ached enormously as he closed his fingers around a shiny new scalpel. "You know, Doc," he said quietly, "I haven't had much fun in a very long time. I think I'm due."

"What was that?" Chandler asked over the running water.

Rockwell smiled, and headed to the door.

Omit Flowers

Morris Hershman

MY MEMORY isn't too bad," Rusty said. "I can even remember how many days I've been here."

"How many?"

"Seventy-three hundred, just about. Twenty years."

"How many more days have you got left to be here?"

"Maybe a million," Rusty said sourly. "It depends on my getting paroled next month when the board meets."

It was morning and he had dressed himself, as usual, with time to spare. The gray uniform fit nicely, because he'd bribed one of the boys in the tailor shop to make changes. The patch in one sock, just above the heel, hardly showed.

His cellmate, Harry Long, still fumbling with his shirt, yawned and said, "A man's got to play parole real careful."

"I'll say." Rusty rubbed his nostrils. "Now me, I always send out flowers for the grave of the guy I croaked. You know why?

'Cause when the parole board asks me if I'm sorry for what I did, I can always tell 'em about that.''

Harry Long opened his pants and let them down so as to tuck in the ends of his gray shirt. He was a short heavy man whose sloppy habits irritated Rusty.

"What do you mean you 'always' send out flowers?"

"Well, you know, the anniversary of the day I did it."

"Smart idea." Long gave an approving nod. "What day is it?"

He was curious, nothing more. All around them were noises of men getting up, shaving, cursing, yawning, arguing, talking, laughing. The morning smells of shaving cream and soap were pleasant.

"It's in November," Rusty said casually, then frowned. "Naw, that ain't right. December." He glared at the wall calendar. "At least I think so."

He was embarrassed, at first. It was wrong to forget a date that had been so important to him.

"Well, it's not too hard to find out," Harry Long said. "The cemetery that you send it in care of . . ."

"Good Hope, or something. I'm not sure about that, either."

"It'll come back," Long shrugged. "You know what the guy's name was, don't you? That makes it a cinch."

Suddenly Rusty struck his forehead. Long looked quickly at him. Rusty was holding his hands over his stomach as if in actual pain.

"God, no!" he muttered. "Jesus God, no! The name." His face was pale. "The guy I killed, the guy they sentenced me for killing. I forgot his name."

"How could you do a thing like that? I know I won't ever forget the stickup that landed me in here."

Rusty pleaded, "Lemme think." He sat with hands pressed to his temples. "It was a liquor store, a heist, see. I had to knock it off quick. Depression was on. Everybody needed money."

"Depression?" Harry Long frowned, then nodded. "Oh yeh, I remember reading about that in High School."

Rusty sighed. His mind was in the past. "He was a big guy, see, and making trouble. My gun jammed, see, so I had to choke him. I don't even remember what he looked like. Walter, maybe, his name was. Williams? Maybe it don't start with a W at all. How am I gonna find out before the next hearing of the parole board? And that's just a month away, a lousy month!"

Bells sounded and Rusty marched down with the others to the dining room. Breakfast would be eaten in fifteen minutes, the same as always. Rusty ate slowly, eyes half-closed, and his hand drummed remorselessly on the table.

"A blue suit," he muttered to himself. "Was wearing a dark blue suit, smoking a cigar when I came in. I'm pretty sure of that. But what was his goddam *name?*"

Next to him, Nat Norris said sharply, "Stop yammering, Rusty! Do I have to hear you yammering just after I wake up?"

The four other men at the table fell silent, except for chomping cereal heavily.

"Nat, I'm in a jam, a bad jam." A weak smile formed on Rusty's lips. "Maybe you—or one of the other guys—maybe you can all figure out something for me."

He talked slowly, stumbling over the words as he told them what had happened. ". . . so it's all wrong that I should forget the name," he finished. "On top of everything else, it's practically a sin."

Nat Norris pressed his lips to keep a grin within bounds. "Well, Rusty, it isn't going to look good to the parole board next month. You know that, don't you?"

"Oh God, yes! That's why I gotta remember the guy's name or the board won't think I'm sorry any more for choking him."

"If you ask me, that'd be a break for you," Nat Norris said, suddenly harsh. "You been here so long already, Rusty, you wouldn't know what to do if you got out. A week or so outside and you'd be back in again."

Whimpering noises rose in Rusty's throat. One of the men listening casually, looked up and began shaking his head at Nat Norris as if telling him to lay off. Norris glared back and the other con looked away.

Harry Long, facing Rusty at the table, said quickly, "The way it sounds to me, Rusty, you forgot on purpose. You don't really want to get out. You're scared of the outside after such a long time here, and this is an easy way you can blame . . . that's psychology!"

A con had made circular motions with a forefinger at right angles to his temples. Somebody laughed.

"If I don't get that guy's name," Rusty said tensely, "I'll go stir-bugs, I swear I will."

"That ain't very far for you to go," Nat Norris said, and looked to see if the men were smiling at his remark. "But maybe I'll think of something."

A con winked at Nat and started to talk, but Nat put a forefinger to his lips.

"Just you leave it to me," Nat added, "Rusty, old pal."

All the men stiffened as whistles sounded. Rusty marched down with some of them to the machine shop. He had disliked the place at first, with all its smells, but he was used to it by now. His morning's work was more listless than usual. When he could manage it, he looked out the window instead of throwing little glances over his shoulders to see if anybody was back of him, a major rule for all prisoners.

At the recreation hour after lunch, as the men milled in the yard, Nat Norris and Harry Long sought him out. Rusty was sitting in a corner, his head sunk in his hands.

"Can't remember the name, Rusty?" Nat Norris began, with a sideways glance at Harry Long. "I've got a hunch the last name starts with an S. Just a hunch."

"Maybe." Rusty lifted his head briefly, repeating the letter several times. Then he sank his head in his hands again.

"I'll never get it," he babbled. "I'll die in this place because I can't remember. All I want to do is send flowers for his grave so the parole board . . ."

"There he goes again!" Nat Norris grunted to Harry. "The same old crap!"

The sound of talk in the yard was a pleasant warm murmur. Men's faces looked more healthy than at any other time of day.

"It's not too hard," Harry Long said suddenly, sympathetically. "You write to people in your family, they'll tell you."

"I got nobody I can write to. No family any more."

"Close friends?"

"You mean, on the outside?" Rusty scratched his head. "You can't be close with any of them, you ain't seen 'em in twenty years. And why would *they* remember the name, anyhow?"

"What about writing to your lawyer? He'll know what happened."

"He's dead."

Harry scratched his chin thoughtfully. "What about the district attorney? Write to him."

"Some assistant sent me up," Rusty said hopelessly. "I don't remember his name, either. He might not be there any more. Might be dead, too, for all I know.''

"But the D.A.'s office is still there," Harry Long said very patiently. "They've got files, records.''

"You mean, I send a letter to the D.A.'s office?'' Rusty was confused. "But that'll get to the parole board, too, and they'll know I forgot and I'm not sorry for what I did.''

"Tell 'em you had amnesia or something.''

Nat Norris suddenly covered his lips with a big hand and slowly rubbed it across them, as if trying to hide a smile.

"Sure, Rusty, that's the answer," he said finally. "In fact, we'll write the letter for you. Turn around, Harry.''

Harry Long hesitated, then squatted and turned, presenting his broad back to them. Big Nat sank down to one knee and whipped out a piece of jagged-edged brown wrapping paper and a stubby pencil.

"Go ahead, Rusty, you say what you want and I'll write it.''

Rusty looked in dismay at the paper, at Harry's back and then at Nat's big arms.

"Every day counts, Rusty," Nat Norris warned. "For all you know, the anniversary could come tomorrow or the day after.'' He added heavily, "If you don't want me to help you, Rusty, I'll be offended. You know what I mean?''

He looked down at one of his huge muscled arms. Rusty, his eyes on the wrapping paper, tried to control the sudden rush of food to the area just below his throat, swallowed again and again.

"I haven't sent out a letter in ten years, maybe more.'' Rusty wiped sweat from his cheeks. "Okay, Nat, if you want it like that. Here's what you write. Dear Sir: Maybe you don't know who I am . . .''

Big Nat wrote unevenly and clumsily, Rusty was sure. But one of Nat's hands hid the sight of it from Rusty.

A couple of cons, attracted by what was happening, wandered over, shrugged or laughed and walked away to another group. On the far side of the yard, a con with a harmonica began playing folk songs and maybe a half dozen men sang along.

When Nat finished, he folded the letter over so that only the words, "Sincerely yours," could be seen, and offered the pencil to Rusty.

"Here, sign.''

Rusty took it, wet the tip with his tongue and slowly wrote his full name. When he finished, Nat put away the wrapping paper in a pocket and got to his feet.

"I'll address it and put it out to the censor for you, Rusty, old pal," he said again rubbing his lips with a hand. "And maybe I can figure out something else in the meantime."

"Thanks, Nat. It means a lot to me."

Harry Long, complaining that a foot was asleep, suddenly turned away. Rusty had fallen back on the ground, and looked up unseeingly at the heavy gray sky.

"I can remember how my gun jammed that time, and I threw it down and went for him and got his fat neck between my hands. I can remember how it felt."

He put out his hands and brought them more closely together without their touching. He shut his eyes tight till he saw pinpoints of fire, and pain back of his eyelids forced them open.

At the sound of the guards whistles, Rusty joined the other men in marching back to work and, later, in eating dinner. As he sat in his cell afterwards, a guard came along, carrying a heavy gray-bound book.

"Big Nat asked me to give you this," the guard said. "Don't ask me how he got it in the first place."

Bribery, probably. Rusty was surprised at kindness from a guard; probably a new man.

"Much obliged," he said sincerely.

It turned out to be a phone book. Harry Long, on the upper bed, stepped down the ladder and joined him, looking shamed, somehow.

"Nat shouldn't have," he mumbled. "It's not fair."

"He wants to help me," Rusty answered, "but all those names!"

He held the book unbelievingly, trying to weigh it in his hands, then rifled the pages and read aloud. "Armbruster—Daniels—Lowndes. So many names!"

"Nat doesn't want to help you," Long snarled. "He figures it for a gag, that the book will get you more mixed up." He held the book and glanced through it. "My girl friend's phone number's been changed . . . the place I used to work . . . goddam mean, to send you this crap!"

He threw the book to the floor and jumped angrily into his bed. Rusty stood dazed, his mouth open as he tried to speak.

He looked up suddenly as the young guard came back, a yellow key in one hand. At his orders, Rusty walked with him down two tiers of cells to the principal keeper's office. Leo Gant was scowling at the mess of papers on his small desk. He was a hard homely man with patient eyes.

"Rusty, what are you up to?" Gant picked up the jagged-edged brown wrapping paper that Nat Norris had used for the letter. "Did you write this yourself? Look at it."

Rusty stared at the words. When he looked up again, Gant was stuffing tobacco into the bowl of a death's-head pipe.

"Sure, I wrote it," Rusty said. He had been in prison long enough to know what would happen to him if he told the truth.

"You're saying that you wrote a letter addressed to the Warden of this prison and containing profanity in every word." Gant was being patient. "You were played for a sucker, somehow. A lot of the men here don't know right from wrong."

Rusty smiled weakly. The last was a personal joke between them. Gant had been here almost as long as Rusty. At Gant's nod of dismissal, Rusty left the room. The young guard walked with him to the auditorium. The men were sitting restlessly on hard wooden benches in the large stuffy room, and waiting for the projectionist to begin showing the week's movie. A whistle blew for quiet and a con stood up in front of the audience to make some announcements. Rusty, red-faced with suppressed anger, took a seat next to Nat Norris. It was the only empty seat he saw.

"Anything new?" At Rusty's silence, Nat Norris added slyly, "Y'know, I remember that you told me the name once. It just popped into my head all of a sudden."

"I don't believe it," Rusty said thinly. He hesitated, then burst out, "You've got to tell me."

"Maybe I will." Nat Norris laughed harshly, crossed his arms. "What'll you do for me if I tell you?"

In a nearby seat a con looked back at them and laughed. Nat smiled in return. The lights were put out. The projector whirred, coughed, then words blurred dizzily on the screen and slowly came into focus on view of New York City, and girls wearing strange-looking clothes. Rusty sighed. He had been sent here during President Roosevelt's second term.

"Nat, it means my parole, maybe." Rusty's mouth was hard. "I've got no dough. I'm wiped out, I've been here so long."

"No money, Rusty, you'll have to ask me real pretty. You can beg for the name, Rusty. Get down on your knees and beg."

In the backwash of light from the screen, their eyes locked. Nat turned to look at the picture. Rusty took a deep breath, and suddenly his hands moved as if by themselves, digging into Nat's neck.

"Liar!" Rusty screamed. "Goddam liar!" Nat, caught by surprise, couldn't bring up his arms. He gurgled briefly, the sounds rumbling between Rusty's fingers. Then he was very still.

Lights came on quickly. The movie's sound track boomed on for a minute, then faded out.

A strange gleam showed in Rusty's eyes. "I remember it now," he said slowly. "That time after I did it, the guy looked the same as Nat does now."

He surrendered without giving any trouble, and walked almost springily to Leo Gant's office. The principal keeper talked about a second murder, a new trial. Rusty hardly heard.

On the way to a solitary cell, he turned to one of the guards walking with him. He couldn't help being cheerful.

"Isn't it funny I remembered the name just then? I'll be able to send the flowers, too, 'cause I remembered the right day and the date and the name of the cemetery, and all. You know what'll happen at the next hearing of the parole board? They're a sure bet to say, 'We can see you're sorry for what you did, for killing a man, we can see that.' "

He laughed happily.

A care had rolled away from him.

The two guards taking him to solitary looked at each other and shook their heads slowly.

Ormond Always Pays His Bills

Harlan Ellison

IT WAS, perhaps, that Hervey Ormond had been a criminal for ten years. And when a man has been a criminal for that long—concealing it as well as Hervey Ormond—the first person to cry "Thief!" at him may well meet with misfortune.

Hervey Ormond shot his secretary three times.

Eleanor Lombarda was not a beautiful girl, a fact so obvious it had caused wonder among the more inquisitive residents of Chambersville. Wonder as to why Ormond—who was known to like his women full and fawning—had hired her. More, they wondered why he had kept her on for six years. Eleanor had been preceded by a string of comely girls, few of whom could actually take shorthand, or find the business end of a dictaphone. So it was with wonder that the residents of Chambersville saw the too-thin, too-nervous girl with the too-red face establish herself in the office of the Ormond Construction Company as Hervey Ormond's personal secretary—for six years.

They might have been surprised to know that the reason for her stranglehold on the position was simply that she did a marvelous job. She was industrious, interested in the work and kept things in top-drawer shape. She always knew what was going on, precisely.

That was another reason Hervey Ormond shot her three times.

"I found the reports," Eleanor said, her face white in the glare of the lone desk lamp. For the first time in her life her face was not florid but a pale and unhealthy white.

"Yes," Ormond said slowly, thoughtfully, closing the office door, "I know you did."

He had returned for the dossier left behind that afternoon. He had returned abruptly and without warning, at midnight, to find Eleanor leafing through his hidden file.

Eleanor's voice was nervously firm. "You aren't paying me enough, Mr. Ormond. I want a raise . . . a big raise."

Hervey Ormond was a fat little man. No more fitting description could be summoned up than that. He was a fat little man, almost the caricature of a butterball. Round of face and form, with rosy cheeks, little squinting eyes of gray paste, execrable taste in clothes and unsavory breath.

Luckily, it had not been his personal appearance that had made him his fortune. Perspicacity and a certain ruthlessness in business had done that.

That ruthlessness was now needed; much as he appreciated Eleanor's sterling qualities around the office, she was tinkering with a long prison term for him as she riffled the papers.

"How did you get the drawer open?" he asked quietly, ignoring her demand for more money.

"The lock sprung," she answered, a faint blush rising up from her long neck. It was this expanse of neck that had kept Ormond from making advances to her during the entire six years of their relationship. She had an exceedingly long neck and did not have the sense to wear necklaces or high-collared dresses to remove the exaggeration.

Ormond stared down at the desk drawer momentarily. It had been forced. The blade of her letter opener was bent.

"You were snooping," he said.

"I want that raise, Mr. Ormond," she said with persistence. "I don't see any reason to beat about the bush; I want three hundred dollars a week, and I only want to work three days each week."

She seemed uncomfortable making demands, but she was firm. They were outrageous demands, but she made them firmly and quickly, as though plunging through with an unpleasant duty.

Ormond continued to ignore her requests. "What made you think there was anything in that drawer, Eleanor?"

She fumbled for a second with one of the stacks of notated papers, sliding them back into a three-ring notebook, snapping the clasps shut.

She didn't answer.

"Why did you go snooping, Eleanor? Haven't we been friends for a long time? Haven't I paid you well?" His voice was one of confusion. His tones remained on one level, not angry and certainly not vindictive. Merely inquiring, as though trying to establish some pattern here.

Her head lifted, and she assumed a defiant tone. "There have been some large discrepancies in the material orders. I've been noticing it for some time.

"Why, you've been using inferior materials on *all* those state road constructions! You've been cutting requisition quality for ten years! They could put you in prison for twenty . . ."

It was at this point that Eleanor Lombarda received her three bullets.

Night surrounded the office building of the Ormond Construction Company. It stood two storeys high in a tract of carefully clipped lawn, on the highway outside Chambersville. As the night came down, the crickets of Chambersville tuned themselves raspingly and waited for their baritone accompanists, the frogs, to arrive.

In the office, Hervey Ormond sat slumped in his desk chair, turned away from the desk itself. He slumped over so he could watch the body on the floor. Remarkably enough, in spite of everything he had ever believed, there had been very little blood.

Eleanor Lombarda lay twisted in the dim yellow egg-shape of

light cast by the desk lamp. Her auburn hair had fanned out against the unpolished floorboards, and she seemed, in death, all the more unattractive.

"An unpleasant person," Ormond murmured to himself, lowering his perfectly round chin into his cupped hand. "Just perfectly unpleasant.

"You work with a person, you sweat with her, you give her good money and she turns against you.

"It just doesn't seem fair, that's all. Just doesn't seem fair." Then he added as a tentative afterthought, "She was a fine secretary, though. Just fine. But an unpleasant person."

Then his thoughts sank darkly. This was nothing circumspect like providing short shrift on building materials. This was not cutting the quality of goods so the kickback would be fatter. This was—and he hesitated to use the word in so close a juxtaposition to himself—murder.

Oh, my God, I've killed her! he thought, an agonized grimace briefly masking his loose features. *I've killed the girl. I never, oh I never would have wanted to do that. No one would believe me—if I told them I'd lost my head. They all say that, I imagine. Oh, good Lord, this is terrible! She's lying there in the middle of my floor, and I'm just sitting here, looking at her. I'll* "have to do something," he finished, aloud.

But what *could* he do? Ormond swung idly back and around in the swivel chair, as though seeking some direction that led out. When the big wall clock, donated by Prester's Jewelry Store at the office's opening, struck three o'clock, Hervey Ormond was no further than before.

It had been different, a different thing when the State Investigating Committee had come. They had gone over his books, found them satisfactory and been quite pleasant about everything.

The roads had buckled and warped, fallen apart at the shoulders and split at the points of most wear, but as Ormond had told Senator Frankenson and the other distinguished visitors, "There's been some pretty heavy and unusual weather in this state recently, gentlemen. You might not be aware of that in Washington, and it's certainly no slur against you or your attentiveness to the local situation—your place is at the seat of our great government, naturally—but it's something we're all too aware of, around here.

"With all that, and these new fuels they're using that eat into the very molecular structure of roadbeds these days, well . . ."

He had left it hanging as his hands hung outstretched. A man who had done his job despite the vagaries of Man and Environment.

The committee had left.

There had been a substantial amount deposited to Senator Frankenson's personal account—under the listing "campaign fund donations"—that next week.

Hervey Ormond always paid his bills promptly.

And this bill, too, had been paid. After six years it had been stamped, sealed and spindled—as Eleanor Lombarda lay silently on the floor of his office.

The clock had passed the 4:15 position, and suddenly, abruptly, as though the idea had been perching there on his knee, sucking ruminatively at his consciousness, Ormond knew how he would get rid of his ex-secretary.

It was the work of ten minutes to get the cement mixings from the shed behind the building, mix the gloppy mess and lay Eleanor in it.

He stood by, leaning against a tree, watching her harden into the mass. When it was sufficiently dry, he would take her out, dump her on the grass—he imagined it would be quite heavy so he stripped off his jacket, hanging it on a low branch—and let her finish hardening completely.

Then he would put her in the trunk of the car, cover her with a brick tarpaulin, and drive up to Round Schooner Lake.

He would tell everyone that Eleanor had been forced to visit sick relatives in Omaha. She had no one close here in town, and it was obvious a girl of her exceeding unattractiveness could not have a lover, so the ruse could very easily succeed.

With a little patience and a great deal of reserve, he was certain this bill would stay paid—and, happily, no rebates would be forthcoming.

He smiled, and listened to the crickets welcoming their baritone accompanists.

The drive to Round Schooner was quiet and pleasant.

The state troopers were, also; and they looked alike, of course. They were faceless and looked alike. Had one been two-headed with purple warty skin and wearing tie and tails, and the other a six-armed and gelatinous mass of mold, they would have looked alike to Hervey Ormond.

They were whipcord, impartial, disinterested Furies. They had come for him, and they meant to take him away. His State proscribed the electric chair; and though he had a great and abiding fear of personal extinction, he had an even greater fear of closed-in places. His State had its appeal for reinstatement of the death penalty in the courts. At the moment, his State proscribed *everything* but years in closed-in places.

"All right, Mr. Ormond, get your hat. Let's go."

They walked him down the steps of the building, while the entire office staff watched. They hustled him heavily into the patrol car, and tooled it out the winding drive, onto the highway.

They sped toward the state police station five miles away, and beside Ormond in the back seat, the faceless police officer had decided to be clever.

"She came to the surface this morning . . . spotted by some kids fishing, Ormond."

The fat little man clung to the car strap, silently watching the lines of houses and fir nurseries flit by.

And I've always been so good about paying my bills on time.

"Your big mistake," the trooper said, with a grin, "was using your own cement. You should know that much sand don't hold together."

The Pattern

Bill Pronzini

A T 11:23 P.M. on Saturday, the twenty-sixth of April, a small man wearing rimless glasses and a dark gray business suit walked into the detective squad room in San Francisco's Hall of Justice and confessed to the murders of three Bay Area housewives whose bodies had been found that afternoon and evening.

Inspector Glenn Rauxton, who first spoke to the small man, thought he might be a crank. Every major homicide in any large city draws its share of oddballs and mental cases, individuals who confess to crimes in order to attain public recognition in otherwise unsubstantial lives; or because of some secret desire for punishment; or for any number of reasons that can be found in the casebooks of police psychiatrists. But it wasn't up to Rauxton to make a decision either way. He left the small man in the company of his partner, Dan Tobias, and went in to talk to his immediate superior, Lieutenant Jack Sheffield.

"We've got a guy outside who says he's the killer of those three women today, Jack," Rauxton said. "Maybe a crank, maybe not."

Sheffield turned away from the portable typewriter at the side of his desk; he had been making out a report for the chief's office. "He come in his own volition?"

Rauxton nodded. "Not three minutes ago."

"What's his name?"

"He says it's Andrew Franzen."

"And his story?"

"So far, just that he killed them," Rauxton said. "I didn't press him. He seems pretty calm about the whole thing."

"Well, run his name through the weirdo file, and then put him in one of the interrogation cubicles," Sheffield said. "I'll look through the reports again before we question him."

"You want me to get a stenographer?"

"It would probably be a good idea."

"Right," Rauxton said, and went out.

Sheffield rubbed his face wearily. He was a lean, sinewy man in his late forties, with thick graying hair and a falconic nose. He had dark-brown eyes that had seen most everything there was to see, and been appalled by a good deal of it; they were tired, sad eyes. He wore a plain blue suit, and his shirt was open at the throat. The tie he had worn to work when his tour started at 4:00 P.M., which had been given to him by his wife and consisted of interlocking, psychedelic-colored concentric circles, was out of sight in the bottom drawer of his desk.

He picked up the folder with the preliminary information on the three slayings and opened it. Most of it was sketchy telephone communications from the involved police forces in the Bay Area, a precursory report from the local lab, a copy of the police Telex that he had sent out statewide as a matter of course following the discovery of the first body, and that had later alerted the other authorities in whose areas the two subsequent corpses had been found. There was also an Inspector's Report on that first and only death in San Francisco, filled out and signed by Rauxton. The last piece of information had come in less than a half-hour earlier, and he knew the facts of the case by memory; but Sheffield was a meticulous cop and he liked to have all the details fixed in his mind.

The first body was of a woman named Janet Flanders, who had been discovered by a neighbor at 4:15 that afternoon in her small duplex on 39th Avenue, near Golden Gate Park. She had been killed by several blows about the head with an as yet unidentified blunt instrument.

The second body, of one Viola Gordon, had also been found by a neighbor—shortly before 5:00 P.M.—in her neat, white frame cottage in South San Francisco. Cause of death: several blows about the head with an unidentified blunt instrument.

The third body, Elaine Dunhill, had been discovered at 6:37 P.M. by a casual acquaintance who had stopped by to return a borrowed book. Mrs. Dunhill lived in a modest cabin-style home clinging to the wooded hillside above Sausalito Harbor, just north of San Francisco. She, too, had died as a result of several blows about the head with an unidentified blunt instrument.

There were no witnesses, or apparent clues, in any of the killings. They would have, on the surface, appeared to be unrelated if it had not been for the facts that each of the three women had died on the same day, and in the same manner. But there were other cohesive factors as well—factors, that, taken in conjunction with the surface similarities, undeniably linked the murders.

Item: each of the three women had been between the ages of thirty and thirty-five, on the plump side, and blonde.

Item: each of them had been orphaned non-natives of California, having come to the San Francisco Bay Area from different parts of the Midwest within the past six years.

Item: each of them had been married to traveling salesmen who were home only short periods each month, and who were all—according to the information garnered by investigating officers from neighbors and friends—currently somewhere on the road.

Patterns, Sheffield thought as he studied the folder's contents. Most cases had one, and this case was no exception. All you had to do was fit the scattered pieces of its particular pattern together, and you would have your answer. Yet the pieces here did not seem to join logically, unless you concluded that the killer of the women was a psychopath who murdered blonde, thirtyish, orphaned wives of traveling salesmen for some perverted reason of his own.

That was the way the news media would see it, Sheffield knew, because that kind of slant always sold copies, and attracted viewers and listeners. They would try to make the case into another Zodiac thing. The radio newscast he had heard at the cafeteria across Bryant Street, when he had gone out for supper around nine, had presaged the discovery of still more bodies of Bay Area housewives and had advised all women whose husbands were away to remain behind locked doors. The announcer had repeatedly referred to the deaths as "the bludgeon slayings."

Sheffield had kept a strictly open mind. It was, for all practical purposes, his case—the first body had been found in San Francisco, during his tour, and that gave him jurisdiction in handling the investigation. The cops in the two other involved cities would be in constant touch with him, as they already had been. He would have been foolish to have made any premature speculations not based solely on fact, and Sheffield was anything but foolish. Anyway, psychopath or not, the case still promised a hell of a lot of not very pleasant work.

Now, however, there was Andrew Franzen.

Crank? Or multiple murderer? Was this going to be one of those blessed events—a simple case? Or was Franzen only the beginning of a long series of very large headaches?

Well, Sheffield thought, *we'll find out soon enough.* He closed the folder and got to his feet and crossed to the door of his office.

In the squad room, Rauxton was just finishing a computer check. He came over to Sheffield and said, "Nothing on Franzen in the weirdo file, Jack."

Sheffield inclined his head and looked off toward the row of glass-walled interrogation cubicles at the rear of the squad room. In the second one, he could see Dan Tobias propped on a corner of the bare metal desk inside; the man who had confessed, Andrew Franzen, was sitting with his back to the squad room, stiffly erect in his chair. Also waiting inside, stoically seated in the near corner, was one of the police stenographers.

Sheffield said, "Okay, Glenn, let's hear what he has to say."

He and Rauxton went over to the interrogation cubicle and stepped inside. Tobias stood, shook his head almost imperceptibly to let Sheffield and Rauxton know that Franzen hadn't said anything to him. Tobias was tall and muscular, with a slow smile and big hands and—like Rauxton—a strong dedication to the life's work he had chosen.

He moved to the right corner of the metal desk, and Rauxton to the left corner, assuming set positions like football halfbacks running a bread-and-butter play. Sheffield, the quarterback, walked behind the desk, cocked one hip against the edge and leaned forward slightly, so that he was looking down at the small man sitting with his hands flat on his thighs.

Franzen had a round, inoffensive pink face with tiny-shelled ears and a Cupid's-bow mouth. His hair was brown and wavy, immaculately cut and shaped, and it saved him from being non-descript; it gave him a certain boyish character, even though Sheffield placed his age at around forty. His eyes were brown and liquid, like those of a spaniel, behind his rimless glasses.

Sheffield got a ball-point pen out of his coat pocket and tapped it lightly against his front teeth; he liked to have something in his hands when he was conducting an interrogation. He broke the silence, finally, by saying, "My name is Sheffield. I'm the lieutenant in charge here. Now before you say anything, it's my duty to advise you of your rights."

He did so, quickly and tersely, concluding with, "You understand all of your rights as I've outlined them, Mr. Franzen?"

The small man sighed softly and nodded.

"Are you willing, then, to answer questions without the presence of counsel?"

"Yes, yes."

Sheffield continued to tap the ball-point pen against his front teeth. "All right," he said at length. "Let's have your full name."

"Andrew Leonard Franzen."

"Where do you live?"

"Here in San Francisco."

"At what address?"

"Nine-oh-six Greenwich."

"Is that a private residence?"

"No, it's an apartment building."

"Are you employed?"

"Yes."

"Where?"

"I'm an independent consultant."

"What sort of consultant?"

404

"I design languages between computers."

Rauxton said, "You want to explain that?"

"It's very simple, really," Franzen said tonelessly. "If two business firms have different types of computers, and would like to set up a communication between them so that the information stored in the memory banks of each computer can be utilized by the other, they call me. I design the linking electronic connections between the two computers, so that each can understand the other; in effect, so that they can converse."

"That sounds like a very specialized job," Sheffield said.

"Yes."

"What kind of salary do you make?"

"Around eighty thousand a year."

Two thin, horizontal lines appeared in Sheffield's forehead. Franzen had the kind of vocation that bespoke of intelligence and upper-class respectability; why would a man like that want to confess to the brutal murders of three simple-living housewives? Or an even more puzzling question: If his confession was genuine, what was his reason for the killings?

Sheffield said, "Why did you come here tonight, Mr. Franzen?"

"To confess." Franzen looked at Rauxton. "I told this man that when I walked in a few minutes ago."

"To confess to what?"

"The murders."

"What murders, specifically?"

Franzen sighed. "The three women in the Bay Area today."

"Just the three?"

"Yes."

"No others whose bodies maybe have not been discovered as yet?"

"No, no."

"Suppose you tell me why you decided to turn yourself in?"

"Why? Because I'm guilty. Because I killed them."

"And that's the only reason?"

Franzen was silent for a moment. Then slowly, he said, "No, I suppose not. I went walking in Aquatic Park when I came back to San Francisco this afternoon, just walking and thinking. The more I thought, the more I knew that it was hopeless. It was only a matter of time before you found out I was the one, a matter of a day or two. I guess I could have run, but I wouldn't know how to begin to do that. I've always done things on impulse, things I would never do if I stopped to think about them. That's how I killed them, on some insane impulse; if I had thought about it I never would have done it. It was so useless . . .''

Sheffield exchanged glances with the two inspectors. Then he said, ''You want to tell us how you did it, Mr. Franzen?''

''What?''

''How did you kill them?'' Sheffield asked. ''What kind of weapon did you use?''

''A tenderizing mallet. One of those big wooden things with serrated ends that women keep in the kitchen to tenderize a piece of steak.''

It was silent in the cubicle now. Sheffield looked at Rauxton, and then at Tobias; they were all thinking the same thing: the police had released no details to the news media as to the kind of weapon involved in the slayings, other than the general information that it was a blunt instrument. But the initial lab report on the first victim—and the preliminary observations on the other two—stated the wounds of each had been made by a roughly square-shaped instrument, which had sharp ''teeth'' capable of making a series of deep indentations as it bit into the flesh. A mallet such as Franzen had just described fitted those characteristics exactly.

Sheffield asked, ''What did you do with the mallet, Mr. Franzen?''

''I threw it away.''

''Where?''

''In Sausalito, into some bushes along the road.''

''Do you remember the location?''

''I think so.''

''Then you can lead us there later on?''

''I suppose so, yes.''

''Was Elaine Dunhill the last woman you killed?''

''Yes.''

''What room did you kill her in?''

''The bedroom.''

''Where in the bedroom?''

''Beside her vanity.''

''Who was your first victim?'' Rauxton asked.

''Janet Flanders.''

''You killed her in the bathroom, is that right?''

''No, no, in the kitchen . . .''

''What was she wearing?''

"A flowered housecoat."

"Why did you strip her body?"

"I didn't. Why would I—"

"Mrs. Gordon was the middle victim, right?" Tobias asked.

"Yes."

"Where did you kill *her?*"

"The kitchen."

"She was sewing, wasn't she?"

"No, she was canning," Franzen said. "She was canning plum preserves. She had mason jars and boxes of plums and three big pressure cookers all over the table and stove . . ."

There was wetness in Franzen's eyes now. He stopped talking and took his rimless glasses off and wiped at the tears with the back of his left hand. He seemed to be swaying slightly on the chair.

Sheffield, watching him, felt a curious mixture of relief and sadness. The relief was due to the fact that there was no doubt in his mind—nor in the minds of Rauxton and Tobias; he could read their eyes—that Andrew Franzen was the slayer of the three women. They had thrown detail and "trip-up" questions at him, one right after another, and he had had all the right answers; he knew particulars that had also not been given to the news media, that no crank could possibly have known, that only the murderer could have been aware of. The case had turned out to be one of the simple ones, after all, and it was all but wrapped up now; there would be no more "bludgeon slayings," no public hue and cry, no attacks on police inefficiency in the press, no pressure from the commissioners or the mayor. The sadness was the result of twenty-six years of police work, of living with death and crime every day, of looking at a man who seemed to be the essence of normalcy and yet who was a cold-blooded multiple murderer.

Why? Sheffield thought. That was the big question. *Why did he do it?*

He said, "You want to tell us the reason, Mr. Franzen? Why you killed them?"

The small man moistened his lips. "I was very happy, you see. My life had some meaning, some challenge. I was fulfilled—but they were going to destroy everything." He stared at his hands. "One of them had found out the truth—I don't know how—and tracked down the other two. I had come to Janet this morning, and she told me that they were going to expose me, and I just lost my head and picked up the mallet and killed her. Then I went to the others and killed them. I couldn't stop myself; it was as if I were moving in a nightmare.''

"What are you trying to say?'' Sheffield asked softly. "What was your relationship with those three women?''

The tears in Andrew Franzen's eyes shone like tiny diamonds in the light from the overhead fluorescents.

"They were my wives,'' he said.

The Phone Call

Roman A. Ranieri

T HE ROOM was dimly lit, and on first glance, appeared to be empty. A few moments later, the padded chair behind the desk moved, and the man seated there reached for the telephone. He tapped the buttons without looking at them, then waited patiently for his call to be answered.

"Hello?'' came the voice of an elderly woman.

"Mrs. Hannah Gelbman?'' asked the man in a low, soothing tone.

"Yes, this is Hannah Gelbman. Who am I speaking to?''

"It's time to rest, Hannah. You've lived a long, troubled life, overcoming countless hardships and disappointments. It's time for your suffering to end.''

"Who is this? What kind of stupid joke are you trying to play? I can have the police trace this call, you know that?''

"Please calm yourself, Hannah. I mean you no harm. I only wish to help you achieve peace. Haven't you endured more than your fair share of suffering? Isn't it time for something better?''

"Who are you? Are you a member of some parasitic religious group? If you're looking for a donation, you're wasting both your time and my time, because I'm not giving you a penny.''

"No. I don't represent any particular group. But all religions acknowledge me, and try their best to understand the cosmic logic of my work.''

"Who are you?'' the old woman asked again, her voice betraying her uncertainty. She had no idea what this man wanted from her, but she sensed that she *needed* to know his purpose.

"I am the Angel of Death. Haven't you recently prayed that I would come to release you from your suffering? Aren't you so very tired of the constant pain of old age, and the indifference of your relatives? If not for the change in the programs you watch on television, would you even know what day it was?"

"This is really a cruel and sick-minded joke to play on an elderly person. You're nothing but a filthy lunatic. I'm not going to tolerate this nonsense any longer. I'm going to hang up right this minute."

"You are Hannah Gelbman. You have lived at 421 Forest Lane for the last forty-five years. You had two sisters; Abigail, who moved to Florida in 1953, then remained there until her death in 1969; and Esther, who lived on the street directly behind you before she was tragically killed in an automobile accident in 1971. You were married to Asher Gelbman for sixty-three years until a stroke took him in 1993. Shall I continue? How much will it take to convice you of my identity?

There was a long pause before Hannah replied. "Everything you just told me is filed in various government records: birth certificates, tax bills, marriage licenses, and death certificates. A good con man could find out those things easily enough."

"That's sharp thinking, Hannah. I see the years haven't dulled your mind. But what about Sharon Dell, your husband's mistress? That whole affair was kept very discreet, wasn't it? You never even mentioned it to your sisters, did you? How could I, a complete stranger, know about her?"

"If such an affair ever took place, I suppose Miss Dell could be bribed into revealing a few details."

The voice on the phone chuckled. "I don't blame you for being skeptical. Nearly everyone I call doubts me at first, until they realize that I'm offering them the two things they most desperately want: freedom from pain, and eternal peace."

"Enough is enough," said Hannah angrily. "You're not even making any sense. Why would the Angel of Death need to use a telephone? Why couldn't you just appear here in my living room right now?"

"Why *not* the telephone? It's the most common means of communication, isn't it? Besides, I want you to welcome me when I come to you. I don't want to *scare* you to death by popping in on you out of thin air. My goal is to give you comfort, not pain."

"You're a nut, and you're full of crap. I'm hanging up."

"Don't make me angry, Hannah. If you hang up, I won't call

you again for at least ten years. Do you *really* want to endure this life for such a long time? Think of the inevitable pains of old age, not only physical, but emotional and intellectual as well. What point is there in going on? Haven't you completed nearly everything that truly mattered to you?"

"What do you want me to do?" she asked softly.

"Are you sitting in a comfortable chair?"

"Yes."

"Then just relax and listen to my voice. I'm going to guide you to a place of joy and tranquility. Lean back into the cushions and close your eyes. Let your body relax. You desperately need to rest. For your entire life, you've done everything that was asked of you. You've earned the right to think of yourself for a change."

"I'm frightened," said Hannah, her voice barely above a whisper. "What's going to happen to me?"

"Calm yourself. Everything will be just fine. A few minutes from now, you'll be joining your husband and your sisters in a better world. Try to set your mind adrift on a cool, gentle breeze as you listen to my voice. You can do that, can't you, Hannah?"

"Yes, I guess so."

"Fine. In a moment you'll begin to feel a numbness in your left arm. Don't be alarmed. I'm going to make this as painless as I can. Just relax and allow it to happen."

"My arm is starting to tingle. What should I do?"

"Remain calm, Hannah. Think of the tingling simply as the beginning of your new existence. Let the feeling flow up your arm to your shoulder. Release yourself from the prison of your aged body. You don't need it any longer."

"I'm starting to feel a tightening in my chest," said Hannah anxiously. "You said this wasn't going to hurt. Make it stop. I'm in pain."

"It's only a brief twinge, Hannah. Let go. Your soul already knows the way. Just let go."

"I—I can't breathe. Stop—stop the pain."

He heard the thump of something falling to the floor, then silence. He listened patiently for several minutes, but there were no other sounds. He glanced down at the open notebook on the desk, and dialed a new number.

"Hello?" answered a young man.

"Your Aunt Hannah just died of a heart attack, Mr. Fine."

"I understand. How did you know that she had a heart condition?"

"I endeavor to know *everything* about my clients, Mr. Fine. By noon tomorrow, you will place the balance of my fee in the same location as before."

"That's impossible. I'll need at least a week to get that much money without arousing suspicion."

"The money will be paid by noon tomorrow as we agreed, or your heirs will be inheriting *your* estate by the end of the week."

"Don't threaten me. I'm not some sickly little old lady. You can't induce *me* to have a heart attack."

"No, Mr. Fine. No heart attack. Your death doesn't need to appear natural. With you, I can be more *creative.*"

The man at the desk hung up. He wasn't concerned. He knew he would be paid. One way or another, he always got paid.

Posthumous

Joyce Carol Oates

THIS IS THE WAY it was, or will be.

In the distance as if emerging from the horizon as the earth rotates to dawn, a spiky-notched hammering, pounding. You imagine it in a building miles away, a building populated by strangers. But then it is closer. By leaps, by blocks, closer. And on the avenue twelve floors below your window there is an emergency siren. In fact two sirens, coils of sound like mad red ribbons, rushing and twining together from opposite directions: north, south. It's a familiar panic—*Is the alarm a fire? A fire in our building?*

The hammering noise, the pounding of men's fists, grows louder by quick degrees. There can be no mistaking it now: and the rude rattling of the doorknob: they are at the front door of your apartment. Voices, male voices. Heavy, booted steps. "Hello? Is anyone in there? This is the police, please open the door." A matter-of-fact declaration. Yet it fills you with terror. Lying in bed, you believe it is your bed, unless, so strangely, it is the floor, floorboards pressing through the carpet hard and solid seeming to push upward against

411

your back, buttocks, tender naked heels. You are only partly clothed and very cold. Why are you so cold, you can't comprehend, the light woollen blanket wrapped tightly about you as in a child's urgent embrace but your legs are exposed, calves, ankles, feet. So exposed, the soles of your feet. *Why are you here? Go away! No one has called the police!* You try to sit up but can't, nor even push yourself up from your reclining position onto an elbow. Your legs seem twisted beneath you as if you've fallen from a great height. Your body is limp, paralyzed, as if every nerve, muscle, joint has been severed.

"Open this door, please!"—and another, deeper voice, "Police! Open up!" You hear the unmistakable sound of a door being forced, broken inward, *Go away! Leave me alone! You have no right!* Though your eyes are fixed stark and staring at the ceiling indistinct in shadows above you you can see the straining doorframe, the flying splinters. This is impossible, this cannot be happening, yet it is happening, and where can you hide? Crawl beneath the bed, when you can't move? Crawl into the bathroom, on the farther side of the room? The thin blanket is inadequate to protect you, there is something shameful in your near-nakedness, *Please leave me alone, please go away, we don't need you!*

Where is your husband, why hasn't he awakened?—or is he away, has he gone and left you alone and how long have you been alone waiting for his return? Married thirty years, and you can't recall his face! But no one will know.

The policemen pay not the slightest heed to your protests. There is a stamping and a crashing in the foyer of the apartment and the very floor shakes. A two-way radio emits a squawk like a parrot's, a blinding light is switched on overhead. You try to wrap yourself tighter in the blanket. *Leave me alone, how dare you,* you are sobbing, pleading, *don't look at me, go away!* In the bedroom doorway are strangers' faces, fleshy blurred faces and rude staring eyes. One of them is young, with glinting wire-rimmed spectacles that reflect the glaring overhead light. *No no no don't look at me!*

You are desperate to hide in the blanket but there is something congealed in it, sticking to your hair. And you are so cold you can't move: skin the sickly color of curdled milk, fingernails and toenails bruised from within as plums. So ashamed, so exposed, what right have these strangers in their uniforms to break into your apartment into your privacy into your thirty years' marriage into your soul now approaching you slowly, long trousered legs, gleaming leather belts, metallic studs, buckles, pistols drawn. Three uniformed men unknown to you staring down at you with expressions of a kind you have never seen before. "Je-sus God!" one of them says, whistling thinly. Another says, swallowing, "What *is* it? Is—?" The third says grimly, yet with an air of satisfaction, "Huh! You know what that is."

Through the rainspecked window a dark blue phosphorescent sky shot with veins of orange like something rotting.

Don't touch me, don't lift this blanket, go away, I am all right, I am myself, I will always be myself, I am only sleeping and you are my nightmare, apart from me you don't exist, don't touch me!

Two of them are squatting close by you, staring. A long moment of silence. One wipes his mouth on the edge of his hand, the other is speaking in that brusque matter-of-fact voice over the two-way radio. In the doorway of the white-tiled bathroom light bounces off the eyeglasses of the youngest policeman. It's a laugh, or a nervous clearing of his throat. Saying, If you think that's bad, take a look in here.

The Price of the Devil

J. L. French

I T WAS A PLEASANT Spring day, the first real day of Spring after an all too hard Winter. On this day, in a quiet suburb of Harbor City, children were riding their bikes while their fathers watched and talked about the upcoming baseball season. The Harbor City Crabs had made some good trades during the off-season, and everyone was thinking pennant for the first time in the club's history.

While the children rode and the fathers talked, the mothers sat on the front porches and discussed vacation plans and traded gardening tips. Some looked forward to the ending of school while the others saw the beginning of their children's vacation as the end of theirs.

In the distance could be heard the roaring of two engines. As the noise got louder and closer, fathers pulled their children off the street and onto the sidewalk. The roaring got louder still and soon two cars came racing down the boulevard. Both were large black sedans. The lead car's back window was shattered and a man was leaning out of it firing a gun at the car behind. The occupants of the second car were firing back, heedless of where any stray bullets were flying. The driver of the first car, bent over his wheel, was desperately trying to elude his faster pursuer. Finally, a lucky shot struck the front tire of the fleeing auto. The driver lost control. With sparks flying from where the rim was meeting the pavement, the car swerved up onto the sidewalk, rode over a freshly cut lawn and crashed into the front porch where just minutes before housewives sat watching their children at play.

The second car sped off, leaving only spent shell casings on the pavement behind it. When the police finally arrived on Walker Boulevard, it was too late to do anything but count the dead.

"Table for one, please. I have a reservation."

"Yes, sir, and the name is. . . ?"

"Devlin, Frank Devlin."

If the maitre d' recognized the name of Harbor City's most notorious police detective he gave no indication of it. After all, was he not in charge of the dining room of the best restaurant in Harbor City's Little Italy, which made it the best restaurant in all of the city. He considered himself the equal, if not the better, of the man who stood before him, even if he had not killed ten men with the Police Commissioner's approval.

"Devlin, Devlin, ah yes, here it is, Devlin. Come with me, please."

The maitre d' escorted Devlin to a small table in the back of the restaurant. Unasked, a waiter brought Devlin a glass of wine. Devlin sipped it while pretending to study the menu. Within minutes, the maitre d' returned.

"Sergeant Devlin." There was a respect in the man's voice now, and Devlin noted the use of his rank.

"Yes?"

"Mr. Martinelli wishes to invite you to dine with him in his private dining room."

"And I would be happy to accept his invitation. Lead on."

Leaving his glass, Devlin followed the man through a door further in the back. There he found a smaller version of the outer restaurant, with only a few tables, one of which was set for dinner. The man at the table was the one Devlin had come to see.

Devlin nodded his thanks to the maitre d' and addressed his host. "Mr. Martinelli, it was nice of you to invite me to share your meal."

"Which you no doubt knew I would once I saw your name on the reservation list. I asked Nicholas to let me know as soon as you arrived."

To the waiting man, Martinelli said, "Thank you, Nicholas, you may tell them to start serving now.

"And now, Sergeant Devlin, what brings the Devil to my restaurant?"

To the crime lords and other gangsters of Harbor City, Frank Devlin was known as "the Devil." The Police Commissioner had given Devlin the assignment of cleaning up the crime-plagued city using any means necessary. When these means brought a sudden and violent end to a pair of these gangsters, he was tagged with the name. Devlin willingly adopted it, using the reputation that came with such a name as one more tool with which to fight crime.

"I think, Mr. Martinelli, that you know why I am here. It is because of this."

Devlin handed his host a newspaper clipping. The clipping detailed the chase which had ended in five deaths.

"A woman crushed by the car which smashed into her front porch, another crippled for life. Two children dead on the sidewalk, killed by stray bullets."

"And the driver and passenger of the car, let us not forget them, Sergeant Devlin."

"Their kind are always on my mind."

The conversation paused while waiters brought the food. After they were served and again left alone, Martinelli continued.

"You do not mind if we talk and eat at the same time? Or are you the noble type who refuses to eat with his enemy?"

"If you were my enemy you would not be still sitting at this table. No, I've come to ask you to deliver a message to your fellow mob bosses."

"Fellow mob bosses? Sergeant Devlin, surely you don't believe the lies they print about me in the papers?"

"Mr. Martinelli, let's not kid each other. You run Little Italy as your own small kingdom. Nothing happens inside its borders that you are not aware of. You control the gambling, loan sharking, and other rackets. Your companies supply the local businesses and they pay you to protect them. Anyone who opposes you is quickly dealt with."

"All this, and yet you are here to ask a favor of me? Why?"

Devlin smiled at his host. "As gang leaders go, you're not that bad. You seem to have no ambitions beyond Little Italy. You do protect your people, but you also look out for everyone in your area. You feather your nest, but you're not greedy. In short, you're a crook, but there are worse ones out there, and they are the ones I'm after."

"That's a strange sort of compliment, Sergeant, but how do the deaths of these people concern me?"

"There's a gang war in this city. Up until now, the Commissioner and I have not worried too much about it. The more of your kind that gets sent to hell the better for the city. And the gang murders give the boys in homicide something to do. Maybe one day they'll actually convict somebody of one of them."

"If there is a gang war in this city, Sergeant, you have only yourself to blame. Your killing of Alexander Tomas upset a delicate balance, and now the other bosses are each trying to seize as much of his territory as possible. There is bound to be some conflict, and with conflict, killing. Each death, of course, requires a response in kind. But I still do not see what you want of me."

"As I said, I'm not all that bothered by your kind killing each other off. It's when their war causes innocent deaths that I become involved. And that's what you're going to help me prevent."

"How?"

"Send a message to your fellow bosses. You've stayed out of this war, so they'll listen to you. If any more civilians are hurt or killed, I'm coming after the ones who did it, and, if I can prove it, the ones who ordered it done."

"And how would you find these men? Not many people are willing to talk to the police about such matters, not those who wish to stay healthy."

"We have a few leads on the ones involved in yesterday's killings, and most people are willing to talk if they're assured they won't be identified or have to testify. I'll be looking for information, not witnesses."

"And how will you bring them to trial without witnesses? How will that serve justice?"

"I never said that I'd bring them to trial."

"So they will face the Devil's Justice. Ah, Sergeant, what a price you are paying. To whom has the Devil sold his soul, and how may it be reclaimed. I will deliver your message, though I doubt any good will come of it."

The next day found Devlin at Police Headquarters. The car which had fled Walker Boulevard had been found abandoned several blocks away from the scene of the killings and had been towed to the City impound lot. It was registered to a Mr. Smith who lived at what proved to be an abandoned building. Devlin had asked that a crime lab man be sent to fingerprint it and recover any other evidence from the car. After reporting to the commissioner, Devlin went down to the Lab to see what progress had been made.

He left happy. Prints from the car had been matched to Alan Morgan, a member of the Jonas Lombardi gang. Lombardi controlled the waterfront and part of the west side. This put him in conflict with Harry Pratt, who had his tentacles wrapped around organized crime in the business district. The territories of both men had bordered those of the late Alexander Tomas, and, with his death, each saw a chance to expand his empire. Of course, other gang leaders and would be gang leaders also saw Tomas's death as their own opportunity for expansion. This lead to a war on all fronts, with each mob boss trying to grab as much as he could at the expense of the others.

Devlin did not think Morgan was one of the men responsible for the deaths on Walker Boulevard. Morgan was more of an errand boy than a gunman. If you needed a message delivered, a payoff picked up or a witness bribed, Morgan was your man. From what Devlin had heard, Morgan didn't have the heart for the rough stuff. Still, he was reliable, and could be trusted to do the jobs given him. Like getting a car to use in a gangland hit.

Alan Morgan was a happy man. He had left Lombardi's gambling den on Cheapside St. with money in his pocket. Lombardi had paid him his monthly wage, and he had stayed awhile and doubled it in just a few hands of cards and a couple rolls of the dice. He was feeling lucky, and now he was looking for some place with cheap liquor and cheaper women with the hope that his luck would continue. He was a very happy man.

So he was not expecting it when someone dragged him into a dark alley and threw him against the wall. His head struck the brick and, dazed, he slumped to the ground. Before he could fall, however, he was caught, lifted up and thrown again, deeper into the alley. He landed against some trash cans, just past the dim lamp that illuminated the end of the cul-de-sac. He laid there, waiting for his assailant to step into the light.

He heard his attacker before seeing him.

"A good place for garbage like you. I should leave you there, but I have questions and you have the answers." The figure approaching him finally stepped under the light.

"The Devil!"

"Very good, Morgan," said Frank Devlin. "Ready to pay for your sins?"

"I ain't done nothing, Devil. I'm just a gopher for Lombardi." Morgan desperately opened his coat. "Look. I ain't even carrying a gun. I never hurt nobody."

"Tell that to the dead from Walker Boulevard. You got the car used in the hit that killed those people." Devlin leaned down and picked Morgan up. Once he got the man standing a swift punch in the stomach doubled him over and Morgan again collapsed in the garbage.

"Honest, Devlin," said Morgan once he could breathe again, "I didn't know why that car was needed. Lombardi said get a car, I got a car. Nobody told me nothing past that."

"Which is why you're still alive." Devlin stood over the fallen man and dramatically drew his service revolver. "If you want to stay that way, you'll tell me who used the car that night."

"I can't tell you nothing. If it gets out I talked, Lombardi'll have me killed."

Devlin pointed the gun at Morgan. Slowly he thumbed back the hammer until it clicked. "Well, Morgan, somebody has to pay the Devil, and if you want the bill, that's fine with me."

"Wait. It was Frazier and Woods. I gave the keys to them."

That made sense. Eddie Frazier was one of Lombardi's best trigger men, and Tommy Woods one of his better drivers.

"And where are Tommy and Eddie tonight?"

"I just left them at Lombardi's place. They were losing. Eddie was drinking pretty good."

"Thank you, Morgan. That wasn't so bad, was it." Devlin gently released the hammer of his revolver and put the gun away. "Now go away."

"You're letting me go?"

"As long as you don't go back to Lombardi's, you can go anywhere you like, that is, until your boss catches up to you."

Devlin stepped aside and the scared little man ran off into the night. Devlin watched Morgan run until he was out of sight and then put him out of his mind. He had more important considerations.

Lombardi's place did not have a name. It was just "Lombardi's place." Nor did it have a permanent location. Gambling was illegal in Harbor City, and Lombardi kept his casino in one place just until his informants inside the police department told him that a raid was imminent. Then he would shut down for a time and reopen somewhere else.

Lombardi's place was currently on Cheapside St., on the second floor of a former cordage company. The owner of the business had had the chance to move to a better location, and had not yet sold the building. In the meantime, he rented the space to Lombardi's frontman.

Devlin knew about Lombardi's. He didn't care. People will gamble, and at least the gang boss ran a clean game. All Devlin cared about tonight was finding his prey.

There was no guard on the outside door. Having a guard standing outside a supposedly empty building was not a mistake Lombardi was apt to make. There were, however, two men standing in front of the freight elevator. Devlin walked past them and toward the stairs.

"Hey, you. You can't go up that way. Employees only."

"That's OK. Think of me as the building inspector." Devlin showed them his shield and at the same time pulled back his coat to display his revolver.

"So you're a cop. You still can't go up unless we get the OK."

Devlin reversed the wallet his shield was in to show his identification. The two men read it and turned pale.

"Now can I go up?"

"Go right up, Sergeant Devlin. We'll let the floor boss know you're here."

"That's not necessary. He'll find out soon enough."

As Devlin went up the back stairway, he wondered if he would not have been wiser to have waited for Frazier and Woods to leave the gambling hall. He could then have taken them without the risks he was about to run. No, he decided, better to have witnesses, both for what he would probably have to do and as a public announcement of what would happen to those who involve innocents and bystanders in their wars.

The stairway lead Devlin to a back room, which he could see was devoted to roulette. Devlin did not think his quarry were the roulette kind of gamblers, but he scanned the crowd anyway. The only ones he recognized were a few city officials, one or two judges and a police lieutenant who would be a patrolman tomorrow, once the commissioner got Devlin's report.

Devlin went through the other rooms. There was blackjack in one, slot machines in another, poker in a third. Finally, in the room set aside for the dice players, he found what he was looking for.

Woods was at the table, dice in hand. Frazier was watching him. Both seemed to have money riding on the throw. Woods threw an eight, picked up the dice, threw and made his point. As he picked up his winnings, Devlin stepped to the table.

Standing opposite the two men, Devlin said in a loud voice, "Thomas Woods, Edward Frazier, you are both under arrest for the murders on Walker Boulevard. Step away from the table and keep your hands in sight."

Devlin's announcement silenced the crowd. Half were looking at him, the others were watching Frazier and Woods to see what they were going to do. The smart ones were already backing away.

Both men recognized the Devil. Such was his reputation, neither believed that they would reach the station house alive. Woods made the first move.

Not wanting to start a gun battle in a crowded room, Devlin pushed the heavy craps table into Woods just as he was drawing his gun. The table slammed into the hood and hit the gun he had just pulled from his waistband. The impact caused Woods to pull the trigger and he shot himself in the chest. He was dead before he hit the floor.

Devlin still had not drawn his gun. "What about it, Eddie? Want to join your buddy in hell?"

"You got nothing on me, Devil."

"No? What Tommy just tried to do was as good as a confession," Devlin lied. "A witness puts you at the scene, and I'm betting you weren't even smart enough to get rid of the gun you used."

When Devlin said this, Frazier knew he was trapped. The Devil was right about his gun. He had not gotten rid of it. It was, in fact, on a holster on his belt.

To Frazier, it was die now or burn later. He stepped away from the table. As he did, his hand went to his weapon. It never got there. Devlin, seeing that the room behind Frazier was now clear, beat him to the draw and ended the career of Eddie Frazier.

Two days after the deaths of Frazier and Woods, Tony Chambers was gunned down while eating at his favorite restaurant. Three other diners were killed as well. Two days after that, Frank Devlin found the men responsible. Only Devlin walked away from the encounter. A week later, a man taking a casual stroll through the park was mistaken for the east side gang boss Anthony Peterson. His death was also avenged by the Devil. The next day, when a stray bullet went through a school window and wounded a substitute teacher, the gunman rushed to the local precinct and turned himself in. He always considered the ten-year sentence he received a good trade for his life.

The teacher was the last casualty in the Harbor City gang war. Faced with ever growing losses and rebellion among their troops, the mob bosses settled for an uneasy truce. The price of the Devil had proven too high.

The Queen of Corpses

Costa Carousso

THERE WAS SOMETHING very strange in the way he walked as he came toward me. His feet moved uncertainly, as though he couldn't control them. His head hung limply between his shoulders, wobbled grotesquely from side to side. His arms groped out in front of him as though he were afraid of smashing his face against some unseen object. He lurched heavily to one side, crashed against a tree, then stumbled onward.

As he came closer I could hear him moaning. It was a soft, whimpering moan. I had heard a puppy moan something like that once, just before it died. But there was no pain in this cry, no sorrow. It was as though the man had known the ultimate in pain and sorrow—and gone beyond them. Why had my thoughts tried to tell me that this man was not alive?

I lit a cigarette with shaking fingers and moved aside to let him pass. But he stopped in front of me. He made an effort to lift his head, but it lolled limply downward. I couldn't see his face. I saw his eyes for a moment, a terrible moment. His hands made vague, groping gestures.

Then he spoke. "Cigarette," he said. "Give me a cigarette."

His fingers groped blindly toward the pack I held out to him. They touched my wrist. They were cold as death. He found a cigarette, lifted it uncertainly toward his mouth, then his fingers relaxed and dropped it. He began to whimper again, then stumbled away.

I moved a few steps, but the cold hand of horror tightened around my body, pulling me to a stop, freezing my bowels with fear. Somewhere, in the deep recesses of my mind, stirred a dim memory of this man. It was as though at some time in the forgotten past of a previous incarnation, I had known him, spoken with him and been his friend.

That strange friendship called to me now—wouldn't let me go on and leave him to face his abysmal sorrow alone. I turned. And as I turned I saw him stagger and fall.

When I reached his side again, I saw his face fully for the first time. It was Kincaid Gordon! There was no pulse beating beneath the marble-cold flesh of his wrist. He was dead. But Kincaid Gordon had died two weeks ago . . . and I had carried his body to its final resting place.

I had known Kin from as far back as I could remember. He and Don Bruce and I had sworn a boyhood oath of eternal loyalty and undying friendship after Kin and I had both claimed guilt of a classroom crime committed by Don. It had involved only an unpleasant, freckled and bucktoothed little girl, and a spitball soaked in ink, but Don was already in mischief up to his scrawny neck, and this would have meant expulsion. So Kin and I both claimed we did it, but since two boys can't throw one spitball, a very confused principal had split Don's punishment into three small parts, and we all shared it. Then we drew up a document of our mutual fidelity and signed with drops of blood gingerly drawn with a hatpin.

We all went to the same prep school and college, and we all played football in the backfield. We came to be known as the Unholy Three. We weren't really unholy. We were three healthy young animals with a wild, almost savage hunger for living. Now Kin was dead. Dead, my God, for the second time!

Don Bruce's father had left him fifty thousand dollars, and

when we got our sheepskins Don insisted that as long as it lasted we would all share it. There was no reason, he pointed out with unshakable logic, why we should work when we didn't have to. When the time came . . . but why think of that when there were so many other things to do?

We started doing them right away. We bought a sixty-foot, three-masted schooner with a nice kicker, and we went whichever way the wind blew. We saw the places that had been exciting names in geography books, sweet as honey to the tongue, and a thorn of curiosity and longing to the mind. Borneo, Sumatra, Pondicherry, Ceylon. . . ! The things we saw, the people we met Hon-au-wali, the Buddist monk, and Kin saved his life.

Anyone would have done the same thing when he saw two drunken sailors beating an old man unmercifully, but old Hon-au-wali's gratitude was boundlessly deep—and troubling.

He looked long and steadily into Kin's grey eyes, and finally he spoke. "You are the son of my soul," he said in a voice that was soft and slow with wisdom. "In the ultimate depths of darkness that is the source of all light, it was ordained that in your splendid young body my soul would make one more link in the infinite chain that binds us to the One. I have been waiting long. Very long. Now that I have found you, I can die."

But before the old man died, he spent several days talking with Kin. Then the two of them went off together into the jungle. A week later Kin came back alone. There was a strange, distant look in his eyes that filled Don and me with a deep fear. No, not fear. Awe.

"He gave me this," said Kin, showing us a ragged piece of parchment traced with Sanskrit characters. "It tells of an ancient hiding place of rubies—rubies that will buy his people freedom from the bonds of ignorance. The old man wants me to get the money and use it for schools and hospitals and the enlightenment of his people. I want you to be with me—to help me."

There was something in the tone of Kin's words that made us feel as though we were being offered a chance to share in a sacred mission.

We returned to New York where Kin spent two tireless years of study to learn enough Sanskrit to interpret the document. Kin got married at the end of the first year. Elaine was beautiful, strangely, exotically beautiful, and we were all more or less in love with her.

But it caused no disturbances in our triumvirate when she married Kin. At the end of the second year we were once more ready to sail. Then Kin died.

Heart disease, the doctor had said. But there had never been anything the matter with Kin's heart. Somehow I still felt dissatisfied with the doctor's explanation. I found myself remembering something that Kin had told me: The Polynesians never commit suicide as we understand it. When life is no longer sweet to them, they can make their hearts cease beating—simply by willing to die.

Had Kin learned that control of life from the occult wisdom of the ancient holy man? But why would Kin will to die? Reckless, life-loving Kin, whose friends idolized him, and whose beautiful young bride adored him! Why would Kin, on the eve of an adventure he had anticipated for so long, take his own life?

The police now thought that I was mad. "Kincaid Gordon?" They laughed. "He died two weeks ago."

"Yes," I said. "I know. I was there."

A cop grabbed my arm impatiently. "Go on home, bud," he said. "Go on home and sleep it off."

"That's Kincaid Gordon," I said. "I've known him for twenty years."

The captain frowned worriedly. "He had a wife, didn't he?" She'll be able to clear it up."

Elaine stood in front of the marble morgue slab twenty minutes later. The attendant pulled back the sheet. She looked at the corpse. Her lips parted, then closed. Her hands clenched at her sides for a moment. She said nothing.

"Is this man your husband?" the captain asked.

"No," she said. "My husband is dead."

I couldn't sleep that night. A man who knows that he has gone mad doesn't dare sleep. For in the darkness, I knew, strange shapes would come; strange voices whisper. I was afraid of the darkness. Terribly afraid. The man I had seen fall dead in the street, the man that Elaine had looked at lying on a marble slab was Kincaid Gordon, Kincaid Gordon, who was dead!

I tried to remember the words that old Hon-au-wali had spoken: In your flesh, my soul will make one more link. . . . Could it be that Kin had chosen another body—picking one that had proven too weak to hold the wild spirit that was Kin? Was that the explanation for the dead man I had seen—the twice-dead Kin? No! such things couldn't be. Kin was dead. His flesh was rotting with decay; his life, his eagerness and his laughter were forever stilled. Kin was dead. Kin would never live again, had never lived to leave his coffin.

But that man? That other? Who was he? The body was Kin's. I knew that as certainly as I knew my own. But what had lived inside it? What was the thing that had died in Kin's body today? Could it be that somehow the spirit of old Hon-au-wali had come to claim once more the flesh that he had said would house his spirit? My God, no. The dead cannot walk again. Ever! From the beginning of God's time, and to all eternity, dead flesh would rot!

We had told that to each other, Kin, and Don, and I many years ago when we became aware, with the bitter awareness of twenty, that we were not immortal and would someday die. We believed that then, and we decided that we would live as fully as possible before dissolution and death came. I believed it then, but I couldn't believe it now. And I dared not believe anything else. I had to see. I had to see Kin's flesh crawling with decay before I could ever dare to sleep again!

I didn't stop to phone Don. I knew that my story of the dead thing that had been Kin had upset him as much as it had me, and I didn't want to let another human being face the terrors that I was facing now.

I drove to the cemetery like a madman, with wild eagerness to see the horrible sight that would bring some peace to my agonized mind. It was not hard to find the burial vault. I had walked the same path two weeks ago with the weight of Kin's coffin on my shoulder and the cold, leaden weight of sorrow in my heart. And now that weight was a freezing lump of ice. A hole was tunneled beneath the wall of the vault—a hole wide enough for a man to crawl through!

I stood looking at the hole. My body went numb and light and then seemed to float upward. Upward through the darkness and the cold. Darker and colder, to the spaces where the stars burn with a fierce, incandescent brilliance, but give no warmth and no light. Upward to darkness and silence—silence so still that it screamed for something to shelter its infinite, aching emptiness.

I felt my being ache to leave my body and merge with the infinite nothingness that was death; I heard my scream burst through my lips that were no longer able to hold back the imponderable thing that I had learned. With my scream the silence was shattered and the darkness melted into fire, and the stars exploded into a blinding kaleidoscope of light. I plunged downward with sickening speed, and once more I was standing on the earth. I was facing the vault that had held Kin Gordon's body. And I knew that Kin had come back from the dead. . . .

I had accepted this by the time that I crawled into the vault and, with flickering matches, looked at the empty coffin. The lid had been clawed and splintered and pried off from the inside. There was not one mark on the outside of the cover. Then I knew that something from the ultimate regions of heaven or hell had come into Kin's body and given it the strength to splinter wood and twist steel. And I had never believed in heaven. . . .

I got back to my room somehow, and I turned on all the lights. But where the walls should have been mellow squares of soft ivory, there was an unfathomable infinity of darkness. Cold darkness. Suddenly the darkness swayed, reeled softly, enveloped me. My body rose and fell. Rose and fell. Deeper and softer each time. . . .

It was the smell that awoke me—a strange, exotic perfume that no man can breathe for long without his body quivering, and his senses yearning with the pain of desire. It was soft and sultry like a woman's breath. It came closer and closer and I tensed and waited for it. Then I saw the knife. My fingers, that had been ready to grasp the softness of a woman's arm, closed around an iron wrist that was plunging a glittering Malay kris down to my chest. I twisted my body to the side and snapped the wrist downward; heard the cracking of bone. But there was no scream of pain. I had broken this thing's arm and there was no scream of pain! The thought went through me with an agony sharper than steel. A dead man had come to kill me!

My fist smashed out with that horrible fury of hatred that is born from the depths of fear. It crashed against flesh and bone and the body sagged to the floor with a dull thud. I turned on the lights and looked. It was Don Bruce. Don Bruce had come in the darkness with a dagger to murder me!

He stirred, opened his eyes and looked at me. But there was no recognition in his eyes. For a terrible moment I thought of the way Kin Gordon had looked when he asked me for a cigarette—a moment before he. . . .

There was no expression in Don's eyes. His features were slack. There was no life in his brain. He was . . . my God! I couldn't say it! The dead don't walk. The dead don't lie on your floor and look at

426

you with empty horror in their eyes. The dead don't whimper like sick dogs do before they die!

"Don!" I screamed. "Don. Speak to me!" But he lay there, staring. Staring like a corpse that has died and gone to heaven and hell. And has known the terrible meaning of nothingness.

His muscles convulsed when I screamed. Then he leaped to his feet and ran insanely from the room, making horrible whimpering sounds. I heard him pounding down the stairs. Then there was silence. Terrible silence.

My first thought was for Elaine. Don had gone mad and tried to murder me. Suppose he tried to kill Elaine, too?

I rushed down to my car. I had to get to Elaine's before that pitiful thing that had been my friend tried to murder her. But my car was not in front of the house. Then I remembered I had left it in the cemetery when I fled from that scene of unholy death. I ran. I ran as I had never run before—till my footsteps faltered and my lungs burned with agony.

I crashed into Elaine's house without knocking. "Elaine!" I called. "Elaine!" Was I already too late? A light flashed in the stairway, and I heard soft footsteps approach.

She was dressed in a black satin robe. Her black hair hung down about her shoulders, accenting the pallor of her face. Her eyes were shadowed with sorrow. Her lips parted tenderly when she saw me. "My dear," she murmured. "My dear."

I rushed to her and took her in my arms. She was life. She was warmth. She was peace. I had seen too much of death. I needed her nearness. I clung to her.

Her voice was soft, soothing. "It's been terrible," she said. "But it will be all right now. Everything will be all right." She caressed my arms, my face, softly as she spoke. I felt a soft peace flowing into me from the tenderness of her fingers.

"Lie down," she said, leading me to the sofa. "Lie down and I'll bring you a drink."

She returned with a glass a moment later, and as I drank I felt the liquid warmth spreading through my body. It soothed each aching, throbbing nerve and I felt contentment and drowsiness flood over me in soft, warm waves. I lay back quietly. Elaine sat beside me.

"Close your eyes and rest," she said in her low, soft voice. "Don't think of anything. Rest."

Her pale face above me was lambent, like that of a madonna.

Soft and beautiful with sorrow and tenderness. I smiled and closed my eyes.

"You will think of nothing," she whispered. "Nothing . . . nothing . . . nothing. . . ."

My mind became as empty and still as a limitless ocean in the gray hour before dawn.

"You will think of darkness," she said. "Of the soft darkness, where there is no motion, where there is no pain. Deep, quiet darkness—soft and deep—where nothing can disturb your slumbers."

Soft sleep came near me, covering me with a blanket soft as snow.

"Sleep," she said. "Sleep will come in the darkness. Soft sleep will come closer, and softer, and the darkness will become deep . . . deep . . . eternal sleep. . . . Sleep in the darkness forever . . . ever . . . sleep. . . ."

The darkness deepened and became softer, and I let my being sink into it—sink and expand, and fade into nothing. The nothingness from which there is no return. Then a fragrance came to me from the darkness—a perfume that no man can breathe for long without his body quivering, and his senses aching with the longing of desire. I let my eyelids fall apart. I wanted to see Elaine's deep, compassionate eyes once more. I wanted to see the sweetness of her parted lips. I wanted to. . . . And then I remembered where I had known that perfume before, and I knew instantly that it was she who had sent poor Don to murder me!

When she saw that I knew, her eyes were no longer soft. All the cruelty of a tiger was in them.

My fingers reached out and clamped into her throat. I squeezed till my fury spent itself.

"You killed Kin," I said. "It was you that made him will to die. But he didn't die. He lived long enough to break out of the coffin you put him in, and come back from death to try to find you. And it was you who sent Don to kill me, and when he failed you tried to will me to death the same as Kin!"

"You'll never prove it," she snarled contemptuously. "Who'd ever believe that suggestion can stop a heart beat; that hypnotism can make a man want to die?" She lifted herself from the floor. "But," she said, walking to the table and picking up a pack of matches. "They'd believe it when . . ." she paused and reached for the cigarette box. Then there was an automatic in her hand. ". . . when I say that I shot you in self-defense!"

The gun was centered steadily at my heart. I looked at it dispassionately. My mind had known too much horror.

"Don doesn't matter any more," she said. "His mind is completely gone. And I can use those rubies much better than a lot of ignorant savages."

Her lips curled back over her teeth as her finger tightened on the trigger. At that moment the door opened. "Look out!" I yelled.

She turned, fired twice as she saw the knife in Don's left hand. The bullets slammed into his chest with a dull thud, and before he began to sag, the blood fountained out. His upraised arm swept downward, and the kris hissed through the air. It caught Elaine in the throat.

When the police came I told them Don had run amok and Elaine had had to kill him in self-defense. That was the truth. But not the whole truth. They wouldn't have believed me if I had told them the whole truth.

Remains to Be Seen

Jack Ritchie

I AM A CITIZEN and a taxpayer," I said stiffly. "When you are through with this destructive invasion of my property, I demand that everything be restored to its exact and original condition."

"Now don't you worry about that, Mr. Warren," Detective-Sergeant Littler said. "The city will put everything in apple-pie order again." He smiled. "Whether we find anything or not."

He was, of course, referring to the body of my wife.

So far, they hadn't found it.

"You're going to have quite a job of repair, Sergeant. Your men have practically excavated the garden. The front lawn resembles a plowed field. You are apparently dismantling my house, piece by piece, and now I see that your men are carrying a jackhammer into the basement."

We were in the kitchen and Littler sipped coffee.

He still bathed in confidence. "The total area of the United States is 3,026,789 square miles, including water."

Littler had undoubtedly memorized the figure for just such occasions.

"Does that include the Hawaiian Islands and Alaska?" I asked acidly.

He was not ruffled. "I think we can exclude them. As I said, the total area of the United States is 3,026,789 square miles. This encompasses mountains and plains, cities and farm land, desert and water. And yet when a man kills his wife, he invariably buries her within the confines of his own property."

Certainly the safest place, I thought. If one buried one's wife in the woods, invariably some trespassing boy scout digging for arrowheads would uncover her.

Littler smiled again. "Just how big is your lot?"

"Sixty by one hundred and fifty feet. Do you realize that I worked for years to produce the loam in my garden? Your men have burrowed into the sub-soil and now I see yellow streaks of clay all about."

He had been here two hours and he was still certain of success. "I'm afraid that you'll have more than the tilth of your garden to worry about, Mr. Warren."

The kitchen window gave me a view of the backyard. Eight or ten city laborers, supervised by the police, were turning the area into a series of trenches.

Littler watched them. "We are very thorough. We will analyze the soot of your chimney; we will sift the ashes from your furnace."

"I have oil heating." I poured more coffee. "I did not kill my wife. I do not, in fact, know where she is."

Littler helped himself to sugar. "How do you account for her absence?"

"I do not account for her absence. Emily simply packed a suitcase during the night and left me. You did notice that some of her clothing is missing?"

"How do I know what she had?" Littler glanced at the photograph of my wife I had provided for him. "Meaning no offense, why did you marry her?"

"For love, of course."

But that was patently ridiculous and even the sergeant didn't believe it.

"Your wife was insured for ten thousand dollars, wasn't she? And you are the beneficiary?"

"Yes." The insurance had certainly been a factor for her demise, but it had not been my primary motive. I got rid of Emily for the honest reason that I couldn't stand her any more.

I will not say that when I married Emily, I was in the throes of flaming passion. My constitution is not shaped in that manner. I believe I entered into matrimony principally because I succumbed to the common herd-feeling of guilt at prolonged bachelorhood.

Emily and I had both been employed by the Marshall Paper Products Company—I as a senior accountant and Emily as a plodding typist without any prospect of matrimony in her future.

She was plain, quiet, subdued. She did not know how to dress properly, her conversation never soared beyond observations on the weather, and she exercised her intellect by reading the newspaper on alternate days.

In short, she was the ideal wife for a man who feels that marriage should be an arrangement, not a romance.

But it is utterly amazing how once the security of marriage is established, a plain, quiet, subdued woman can turn into a determined shrew.

The woman should at least have been grateful.

"How did you and your wife get along?"

Miserably. But I said, "We had our differences, but then doesn't everyone?"

The sergeant, however, was equipped with superior information. "According to your neighbors, you and your wife quarreled almost incessantly."

By neighbors, he was undoubtedly referring to Fred and Wilma Treeber. Since I have a corner lot, theirs is the only house directly next door. I doubt if Emily's voice carried over the garden and the alley to the Morrisons. Still, it was possible. As she gained weight, she gained volume.

"The Treebers could hear you and your wife arguing nearly every evening."

"Only when they stopped their own infernal shrieking to listen. And it is not true that they heard *both* of us. I never raise my voice."

"The last time your wife was seen alive was Friday evening at six-thirty as she entered this house."

Yes, she had returned from the supermarket with frozen dinners

431

and ice cream. They were almost her sole contribution to the art of cooking. I made my own breakfasts, I ate lunch at the company cafeteria, and in the evening I either made my own meal or ate something that required forty minutes of heating at 350°.

"That was the last time anyone *else* saw her," I said. "But I last saw her in the evening when we retired. And in the morning when I woke, I discovered that she had packed up and gone."

Downstairs, the jackhammer began breaking up the concrete floor. It made so much noise that I was forced to close the door to the rear entry leading to the basement. "Just who was it who saw Emily last? Besides myself, I mean."

"Mr. and Mrs. Fred Treeber."

There was a certain resemblance between Wilma Treeber and Emily. They had both become large women, Amazon in temper and dwarf in mind. Fred Treeber is a small man, watery-eyed by nature or by the abrasions of marriage. But he plays a credible game of chess and he rather admires me for possessing the inherent firmness that he lacks.

"At midnight that same evening," Sergeant Littler said, "Fred Treeber heard an unearthly scream coming from this house."

"Unearthly?"

"His exact word."

"Fred Treeber is a liar," I said flatly. "I suppose his wife heard it, too?"

"No. She's a heavy sleeper. But it woke him."

"Did this so-called unearthly scream wake up the Morrisons?"

"No. They were asleep, too, and they are also a considerable distance from this house. The Treeber place is only fifteen feet away." Littler filled his pipe. "Fred Treeber debated waking his wife, but decided against it. It seems she has a temper. But still he couldn't go back to sleep. And then at two in the morning, he heard a noise coming from your yard. He went to the window and there, in the moonlight, he saw you digging in your garden. He finally got up the nerve to wake his wife. They both watched you."

"The wretched spies. So that was how you knew?"

"Yes. Why did you use such a large box?"

"It was the only one I could find. But it was still not anywhere near the dimensions of a coffin."

"Mrs. Treeber thought about that all day Saturday. And when you informed her that your wife had 'taken a trip and wouldn't be back for some time,' she finally decided that you had . . . ah . . . organized your wife's body into a more compact package and buried her."

I poured more coffee for myself. "Well, and what did you find?"

He was still faintly embarrassed about that. "A dead cat."

I nodded. "And so I am guilty of burying a cat."

He smiled. "You were very evasive, Mr. Warren. First you denied that you had buried anything."

"I felt that it was none of your business."

"And when we found the cat, you claimed that it had died of natural causes."

"So it appeared to me at the time."

"The cat was your wife's and someone had crushed its skull. That was obvious."

"I am not in the habit of examining dead cats."

He puffed at his pipe. "It's my theory that after you killed your wife, you also killed the cat. Perhaps because its presence reminded you of your wife. Or perhaps because the cat had seen you dispose of your wife's body and just might lead us . . ."

"Oh, come now, Sergeant," I said.

He colored. "Well, animals *have* been known to dig at places where their masters or mistresses have been buried. Dogs, usually, I'll admit. But why not cats?"

I actually gave that some thought. Why not cats?

Littler listened to the jackhammer for a moment. "When we get a report that someone is missing, our routine procedure is to send out flyers through the Missing Persons' Bureau. And then we wait. Almost invariably after a week or two the missing person returns home. Usually, after his money runs out."

"And then why in heaven's name didn't you do that in this case? I'm sure that Emily will come back home within a few days. As far as I know she took only about a hundred dollars and I know that she is mortally frightened of self-support."

His teeth showed faintly. "When we have a missing wife, a person who hears a scream, and *two* witnesses to a mysterious moonlight burial in a garden, we recognize all the symptoms of a crime. We cannot afford to wait."

And neither could I. After all, Emily's body would not keep forever. That was why I had killed the cat and managed to be seen burying the box. But I spoke acidly. "And so you immediately grab your shovels and ruin a man's property? I warn you that I will sue if every stick, stone, brick, and scrap of humus isn't replaced exactly as it was."

Littler was unperturbed. "And then there was the blood stain on your living room rug."

"My own blood, I assure you. I accidently broke a glass and gashed my hand." I showed him the healing cut again.

He was not impressed. "A cover-up to account for the stain," he said. "Self-inflicted."

He was right, of course. But I wanted the spot on the rug in the event that the other circumstances were not enough to drive the police to their search.

I saw Fred Treeber leaning on the boundary fence watching Littler's men at their devastation.

I got to my feet. "I'm going to talk to that creature."

Littler followed me outside.

I made my way between mounds of earth to the fence. "Do you call this being a good neighbor?"

Fred Treeber swallowed. "Now, Albert, I didn't mean any harm. I don't think you really did it, but you know Wilma and her imagination."

I glared at him. "There will be no more chess games between us in the future." I turned to Littler. "What makes you so absolutely positive that I disposed of my wife here?"

Littler took the pipe out of his mouth. Your car. You took it to the Eagle Filling Station on Murray Street Friday afternoon at five-thirty. You had the car lubricated and the oil changed. The attendent placed the usual sticker inside the doorframe of your car, indicating when the work was done and the mileage on your speedometer at the time it was done. Since that time, the only additional mileage registered by your car has been eight-tenths of a mile. And that is the exact distance from the filling station to your garage."

He smiled. "In other words, you brought your car directly home. You do not work on Saturdays and today is Sunday. Your car hasn't moved since Friday."

I had been counting on the police to notice that sticker. If they hadn't, I would have had to call it to their attention in some manner. I smiled thinly. "Have you ever thought of the possibility that I might have carried her to an empty lot near here and buried her?"

Littler chuckled indulgently. "'The nearest empty lot is more

434

than four blocks away. It hardly seems conceivable that you would carry her body through the streets, even at night, for that distance."

Treeber took his eyes from the group of men at my flower patch. "Albert, as long as your dahlias are being dug up anyway, would you care to trade a few of your Gordon Pinks for some of my Amber Goliaths?"

I turned on my heel and stalked back to the house.

The afternoon wore on, and gradually, as he received reports from his men, the assurance drained from Littler's face.

The daylight faded and at six-thirty the jackhammer in the basement stopped.

A Sergeant Chilton came into the kitchen. He looked tired, hungry, and frustrated, and his trousers were streaked with clay. "Nothing down there. Absolutely nothing at all."

Littler clamped his teeth on his pipe stem. "You're positive? You've searched everywhere?"

"I'll stake my life on it," Chilton said. "If there's a body anywhere here we would have found it. The men outside are through, too."

Littler glared at me. "I *know* you killed your wife. I *feel* it."

There is something pitiful about a normally intelligent man retreating to instinct. However, in this case, he was right.

"I believe I'll make myself liver and onions tonight," I said cheerfully. "I haven't had that for ages."

A patrolman came into the kitchen from the backyard. "Sergeant, I was just talking to this Treeber character next door."

"Well?" Littler demanded impatiently.

"He says that Mr. Warren here has a summer cottage at a lake in Byron County."

I almost dropped the package of liver I was removing from the refrigerator. That idiot Treeber and his babbling!

Littler's eyes widened. His humor changed instantly and he chuckled. "That's it! They *always, always* bury them on their own property."

Perhaps my face was white. "Don't you dare touch one foot of that land. I put two thousand dollars worth of improvements on that property since I bought it and I will not have the place blitzed by your vandals."

Littler laughed. "Chilton, get some floodlights and have the men pack up." He turned to me. "And now just where is this little retreat of yours?"

435

"I absolutely refuse to tell you. You know I couldn't have gone there anyway. You forget that the speedometer reading of my car shows that it hasn't left the garage since Friday afternoon."

He hurdled that obstacle. "You could have set the speedometer back. Now where is that cottage located?"

I folded my arms. "I refuse to tell you."

Littler smiled. "There's no use stalling for time. Or do you plan to sneak out there yourself tonight, disinter her, and bury her someplace else?"

"I have no intentions of the kind. But I stand on my constitutional rights to say nothing."

Littler used my phone to route out officials in Byron county and within forty-five minutes, he had the exact location of my cottage.

"Now see here," I snapped as he put down the phone for the last time. "You can't make the same mess out of that place as you have of this one. I'm going to call the mayor right now and see that you're fired."

Littler was in good humor and practically rubbing his hands. "Chilton, see that a crew gets here tomorrow and puts everything back in place."

I followed Littler to the door. "Every flower, every blade of grass, or I'll see my lawyer."

I did not enjoy my liver and onions that night.

At eleven-thirty, there was a soft knock at my rear door and I opened it.

Fred Treeber looked contrite. "I'm sorry."

"What in heaven's name made you mention the cottage?"

"I was just making conversation and it slipped out."

I had difficulty controlling my rage. "They'll devastate the place. And just after I finally succeeded in producing a good lawn."

I could have gone on for more furious minutes, but I pulled myself together. "Is your wife asleep?"

Fred nodded. "She won't wake up until morning. She never does."

I got my hat and coat and we went next door to Fred's basement.

Emily's body was lying in a cool place under some canvas. I thought it had been a rather good temporary hiding place. Wilma never goes down there except on washdays.

Fred and I carried Emily back to my house and into the basement. The place looked like a battlefield.

We dropped Emily into one of the deepest pits and shoveled about a foot and a half of clay and dirt over her. That was sufficient for our purposes.

Fred looked a bit worried. "Are you sure they won't find her?"

"Of course not. The best place to hide anything is where somebody has already looked. Tomorrow the crew will be back here. The holes will be filled up and the floor refinished."

We went upstairs into the kitchen.

"Do I have to wait a whole year?" Fred asked me plaintively.

"Certainly. We can't flirt with suspicion. After twelve months or so, you may murder your wife and I will keep her in *my* basement until the search of your premises is over."

Fred sighed. "It's a long time to wait with Wilma. But we flipped the coin, fair and square, and you won." He cleared his throat. "You didn't really mean that, did you, Albert?"

"Mean what?"

"That you'd never play chess with me again?"

When I thought about what the police were at this very moment undoubtedly doing to my cottage and its grounds, I was tempted to tell him I had meant it.

But he did look pathetic and contrite, and so I sighed and said, "I suppose not."

Fred brightened. "I'll go get the board."

The Right Kind of a House

Henry Slesar

THE AUTOMOBILE that was stopping in front of Aaron Hacker's real estate office had a New York license plate. Aaron didn't need to see the yellow rectangle to know that its owner was new to the elm-shaded streets of Ivy Corners. It was a red convertible; there was nothing else like it in town.

The man got out of the car.

"Sally," he said, to the bored young lady at the only other desk. There was a paperbound book propped in her typewriter, and she was chewing something dreamily.

"Yes, Mr. Hacker?"

"Seems to be a customer. Think we oughta look busy?" He put the question mildly.

"Sure, Mr. Hacker!" She smiled brightly, removed the book, and slipped a blank sheet of paper into the machine. "What shall I type?"

"Anything, anything!" Aaron scowled.

It looked like a customer, all right. The man was heading straight for the glass door, and there was a folded newspaper in his right hand. Aaron described him later as heavy-set. Actually, he was fat. He wore a colorless suit of lightweight material, and the perspiration had soaked clean through the fabric to leave large, damp circles around his arms. He might have been fifty, but he had all his hair, and it was dark and curly. The skin of his face was flushed and hot, but the narrow eyes remained clear and frosty-cold.

He came through the doorway, glanced towards the rattling sound of the office typewriter, and then nodded at Aaron.

"Mr. Hacker?"

"Yes, sir," Aaron smiled. "What can I do for you?"

The fat man waved the newspaper. "I looked you up in the real-estate section."

"Yep. Take an ad every week. I use the *Times*, too, now and then. Lot of city people interested in a town like ours, Mr.—"

"Waterbury," the man said. He plucked a white cloth out of his pocket and mopped his face. "Hot today."

"Unusually hot," Aaron answered. "Doesn't often get so hot in our town. Mean temperature's around seventy-eight in the summer. We got the Lake, you know. Isn't that right, Marge?" The girl was too absorbed to hear him. "Well. Won't you sit down, Mr. Waterbury?"

"Thank you." The fat man took the proffered chair, and sighed. "I've been driving around. Thought I'd look the place over before I came here. Nice little town."

"Yes, we like it. Cigar?" He opened a box on his desk.

"No, thank you. I don't really have much time, Mr. Hacker. Suppose we get right down to business."

"Suits me, Mr. Waterbury." He looked towards the clacking noise and frowned. *"Sally!"*

"Yes, Mr. Hacker?"

"Cut out the darn racket."

438

"Yes, Mr. Hacker." She put her hands in her lap, and stared at the meaningless jumble of letters she had drummed on the paper.

"Now, then," Aaron said. "Was there any place in particular you were interested in, Mr. Waterbury?"

"As a matter of fact, yes. There was a house at the edge of town, across the way from an old building. Don't know what kind of building—deserted."

"Ice-house," Aaron said. "Was it a house with pillars?"

"Yes. That's the place. Do you have it listed? I thought I saw a 'for sale' sign, but I wasn't sure."

Aaron shook his head, and chuckled dryly. "Yep, we got it listed all right." He flipped over a loose-leaf book, and pointed to a typewritten sheet. "You won't be interested for long."

"Why not?"

He turned the book around. "Read it for yourself."

The fat man did so.

AUTHENTIC COLONIAL. 8 rooms, two baths, automatic oil furnace, large porches, trees and shrubbery. Near shopping, schools. $75,000.

"Still interested?"

The man stirred uncomfortably. "Why not? Something wrong with it?"

"Well," Aaron scratched his temple. "If you really like this town, Mr. Waterbury—I mean, if you really want to settle here, I got any number of places that'd suit you better."

"Now, just a minute!" The fat man looked indignant. "What do you call this? I'm asking you about this colonial house. You want to sell it, or don't you?"

"Do I?" Aaron chuckled. "Mister, I've had that property on my hands for five years. There's nothing I'd rather collect a commission on. Only my luck just ain't that good."

"What do you mean?"

"I mean, you won't buy. That's what I mean. I keep the listing on my books just for the sake of old Sadie Grimes. Otherwise, I wouldn't waste the space. Believe me."

"I don't get you."

"Then let me explain." He took out a cigar, but just to roll it in his fingers. "Old Mrs. Grimes put her place up for sale five years ago, when her son died. She gave me the job of selling it. I didn't want the job—no, sir. I told her that to her face. The old place just ain't worth the kind of money she's asking. I mean, heck! The old place ain't even worth *ten* thousand!''

The fat man swallowed. ''Ten? And she wants seventy-five?''

''That's right. Don't ask me why. It's a real old house. Oh, I don't mean one of those solid-as-a-rock old houses. I mean *old*. Never been de-termited. Some of the beams will be going in the next couple of years. Basement's full of water half the time. Upper floor leans to the right about nine inches. And the grounds are a mess.''

''Then why does she ask so much?''

Aaron shrugged. ''Don't ask me. Sentiment, maybe. Been in her family since the Revolution, something like that.''

The fat man studied the floor. ''That's too bad,'' he said. ''Too bad!'' He looked up at Aaron, and smiled sheepishly. ''And I kinda liked the place. It was—I don't know how to explain it. The *right* kind of house.''

''I know what you mean. It's a friendly old place. A good buy at ten thousand. But seventy-five?'' He laughed. ''I think I know Sadie's reasoning, though. You see, she doesn't have much money. Her son was supporting her, doing well in the city. Then he died, and she knew that it was sensible to sell. But she couldn't bring herself to part with the old place. So she put a price tag so big that *nobody* would come near it. That eased her conscience.'' He shook his head sadly. ''It's a strange world, ain't it?''

''Yes,'' Waterbury said distantly.

Then he stood up. ''Tell you what, Mr. Hacker. Suppose I drive out to see Mrs. Grimes? Suppose I talk to her about it, get her to change her price.''

''You're fooling yourself, Mr. Waterbury. I've been trying for five years.''

''Who knows? Maybe if somebody *else* tried—''

Aaron Hacker spread his palms. ''Who knows is right. It's a strange world, Mr. Waterbury. If you're willing to go to the trouble, I'll be only too happy to lend a hand.''

''Good. Then I'll leave now . . .''

''Fine! You just let me ring Sadie Grimes. I'll tell her you're on your way.''

Waterbury drove slowly through the quiet streets. The shade trees that lined the avenues cast peaceful dappled shadows on the hood of the convertible. The powerful motor beneath it operated in whispers, so he could hear the fitful chirpings of the birds overhead.

He reached the home of Sadie Grimes without once passing another moving vehicle. He parked his car beside the rotted picket fence that faced the house like a row of disorderly sentries.

The lawn was a jungle of weeds and crabgrass, and the columns that rose from the front porch were entwined with creepers.

There was a hand knocker on the door. He pumped it twice.

The woman who responded was short and plump. Her white hair was vaguely purple in spots, and the lines in her face descended downwards towards her small, stubborn chin. She wore a heavy wool cardigan, despite the heat.

"You must be Mr. Waterbury," she said. "Aaron Hacker said you were coming."

"Yes," the fat man smiled. "How do you do, Mrs. Grimes?"

"Well as I can expect. I suppose you want to come in?"

"Awfully hot out here." He chuckled.

"Mm. Well, come in then. I've put some lemonade in the icebox. Only don't expect me to bargain with you, Mr. Waterbury. I'm not that kind of person."

"Of course not," the man said winningly, and followed her inside.

It was dark and cool. The window shades were opaque, and they had been drawn. They entered a square parlor with heavy, baroque furniture shoved unimaginatively against every wall. The only color in the room was in the faded hues of the tassled rug that lay in the center of the bare floor.

The old woman headed straight for a rocker, and sat motionless, her wrinkled hands folded sternly.

"Well?" she said. "If you have anything to say, Mr. Waterbury, I suggest you say it."

The fat man cleared his throat. "Mrs. Grimes, I've just spoken with your real estate agent—"

"I know all that," she snapped. "Aaron's a fool. All the more for letting you come here with the notion of changing my mind. I'm too old for changing my mind, Mr. Waterbury."

"Er—well, I don't know if that was my intention, Mrs. Grimes. I thought we'd just—talk a little."

She leaned back, and the rocker groaned. "Talk's free. Say what you like."

"Yes." He mopped his face again, and shoved the handkerchief only halfway back into his pocket. "Well, let me put it this way, Mrs. Grimes. I'm a business man—a bachelor. I've worked for a long time, and I've made a fair amount of money. Now I'm ready to retire—preferably, somewhere quiet. I like Ivy Corners. I passed through here some years back, on my way to—er, Albany. I thought, one day, I might like to settle here."

"So?"

"So, when I drove through your town today, and saw this house—I was enthused. It just seemed—right for me."

"I like it too, Mr. Waterbury. That's why I'm asking a fair price for it."

Waterbury blinked. "Fair price? You'll have to admit, Mrs. Grimes, these days a house like this shouldn't cost more than—"

"That's enough!" the old woman cried. "I told you, Mr. Waterbury—I don't want to sit here all day and argue with you. If you won't pay my price, then we can forget all about it."

"But Mrs. Grimes—"

"Good *day*, Mr. Waterbury!"

She stood up, indicating that he was expected to do the same.

But he didn't. "Wait a moment, Mrs. Grimes," he said, "just a moment. I know it's crazy, but—all right. I'll pay what you want."

She looked at him for a long moment. "Are you sure, Mr. Waterbury?"

"Positive! I've enough money. If that's the only way you'll have it, that's the way it'll be."

She smiled thinly. "I think that lemonade'll be cold enough. I'll bring you some—and then I'll tell you something about this house."

He was mopping his brow when she returned with the tray. He gulped at the frosty yellow beverage greedily.

"This house," she said, easing back into her rocker, "has been in my family since eighteen hundred and two. It was built some fifteen years before that. Every member of the family, except my son, Michael, was born in the bedroom upstairs. I was the only rebel," she added raffishly. "I had new-fangled ideas about hospitals." Her eyes twinkled.

"I know it's not the most solid house in Ivy Corners. After I brought Michael home, there was a flood in the basement, and we never seemed to get it dry since. Aaron tells me that there are termites, too, but I've never seen the pesky things. I love the old place, though; you understand.''

"Of course,'' Waterbury said.

"Michael's father died when Michael was nine. It was hard times on us then. I did some needlework, and my own father had left me the small annuity which supports me today. Not in very grand style, but I manage. Michael missed his father, perhaps even more than I. He grew up to be—well, wild is the only word that comes to mind.''

The fat man clucked, sympathetically.

"When he graduated from high school, Michael left Ivy Corners and went to the city. Against my wishes, make no mistake. But he was like so many young men, full of ambition, undirected ambition. I don't know what he did in the city. But he must have been successful—he sent me money regularly.'' Her eyes clouded. "I didn't see him for nine years.''

"Ah,'' the man sighed, sadly.

"Yes, it wasn't easy for me. But it was even worse when Michael came home because, when he did, he was in trouble.''

"Oh?''

"I didn't know how bad the trouble was. He showed up in the middle of the night, looking thinner and older than I could have believed possible. He had no luggage with him, only a small black suitcase. When I tried to take it from him, he almost struck me. Struck *me*—his own mother!

"I put him to bed myself, as if he was a little boy again. I could hear him crying out during the night.

"The next day, he told me to leave the house. Just for a few hours—he wanted to do something, he said. He didn't explain what. But when I returned that evening, I noticed that the little suitcase was gone.''

The fat man's eyes widened over the lemonade glass.

"What did it mean?'' he asked.

"I didn't know then. But I found out soon—too terribly soon. That night, a man came to our house. I don't even know how he got in. I first knew when I heard voices in Michael's room. I went to the door, and tried to listen, tried to find out what sort of trouble my boy was in. But I heard only shouts and threats, and then . . .''

She paused, and her shoulders sagged.

"And a shot," she continued, "a gunshot. When I went into the room, I found the bedroom window open, and the stranger gone. And Michael—he was on the floor. He was dead."

The chair creaked.

"That was five years ago," she said. "Five long years. It was a while before I realized what had happened. The police told me the story. Michael and this other man had been involved in a crime, a serious crime. They had stolen many, many thousands of dollars.

"Michael had taken that money, and run off with it, wanting to keep it all for himself. He hid it somewhere in this house—to this very day I don't know where. Then the other man came looking for my son, came to collect his share. When he found the money gone, he—he killed my boy."

She looked up. "That's when I put the house up for sale, at seventy-five thousand dollars. I knew that, someday, my son's killer would return. Someday, he would want this house at any price. All I had to do was wait until I found the man willing to pay much too much for an old lady's house."

She rocked gently.

Waterbury put down the empty glass and licked his lips, his eyes no longer focusing, his head rolling loosely on his shoulders.

"*Ugh!*" he said. "This lemonade is bitter."

The Rod and the Staff

Donald Wandrei

T HE HEAT was on. Johnny the Tailor took a run-out powder. The G-men elevated him to the fatal title of public enemy number one. Johnny had been far down on the list, but the G-men went through the names above his like a cyclone through Kansas.

Johnny the Tailor was a free-lance artist, a professional killer. His prices ranged with the job. He killed because he liked to kill. He got a kick out of the way a body jerked when a slug hit it. The least he ever received was a C-note for a hood, but once he splurged thirty grand for rubbing out a labor union racketeer.

Sometimes he used a Tommy, but generally he used a rod. His

arms were short and he carried the automatic in a coat pocket where his hand always hung beside it. A revolver wasn't so likely to jam and it shot truer than an automatic, but it bulked larger. You couldn't get it out as fast or shoot as fast. You were one up on coppers and dicks with their heavy service revolvers.

Johnny the Tailor got his nickname for a lot of reasons. For one thing, his face was sallow. He had thin, nimble fingers. He stood about five feet nine, with a straight mouth, pale green eyes, and a perfectly blank expression. Originally, the grim humor of the underworld had labeled him Johnny the Cooler. That was because Johnny ventilated people. But Johnny had spent a little time in the cooler and he didn't like to be reminded of the fact.

Frank Marsuelo made the mistake of calling him Johnny the Cooler to his face one day. A couple of nights later, they took Frankie to the morgue. The underworld took the hint, gave him the new title because the undertakers had to do quite a lot of fancy sewing and stitching to make Frankie and Johnny's other victims recognizable.

Johnny hadn't been a big shot but the G-men went after him just the same. Johnny had known for some time that the heat was on. The past two weeks he had holed up in Myrt's apartment on Jane Street. He didn't go for molls as a rule, but Myrt was a recent tie-up, and he didn't think the G-men would be on to her yet.

One morning the papers pointed with pride to the fact that the G-men, seven slugs, and a one-way ticket to oblivion had simultaneously overtaken Nick Morani. That left Johnny at the top of the list and Johnny didn't want to be there. It scared him and it worried him.

He knew of other hideouts. You had to keep moving to keep ahead of the game. While Myrt was away, he took the runout powder. He reached the sidewalk and swept the street with a glance. Just the usual run of punks. He headed for a taxi.

But the street-cleaner said, "Just a minute, Johnny," and the street-cleaner's hand was coming out of his left armpit. It took the killer much less than a second to reach his rod. The gun surged up for a shot through the coat pocket.

The next thing Johnny knew, he lay on the pavement with a numb sensation in his right arm and shoulder, and a red stain spreading.

The G-man hadn't tried to erase the gunman. Information about a score of killings was locked up in Johnny's head. He lost a good deal of blood, however, and they took him to a hospital, operated, gave him a blood transfusion. Then they tucked him away in the psychopathic ward with a special guard.

When he could talk, he wouldn't. In three days, he was well enough to move. They planned on taking him away. Now and then, as the guard moved around, Johnny managed to talk to the interne. Internes are poorly paid. Johnny had a couple of aces in the hole. A grand lay between heel and sole of both his shoes. His clothing hung in a locker that the interne could reach.

If he crashed out, he was resolved never again to rely on a pocket gun. He remembered vividly the way the G-man had flicked his rod from a shoulder holster with a speed that would have beaten Johnny any time.

He crashed out that night. He could walk and the guard didn't object to his moving as far as the window. The window was cross-barred, and it didn't matter if Johnny stretched his hands through for the freedom he wished he had. Just above the window hung a rod tied to a string tied to a roof-support. When Johnny turned around, the rod was in his hands.

The guard's clothes didn't fit him but had to serve. He was seen, of course. The alarm went out before he reached the outside entrance. Surgeons on night duty are careless with their cars. They leave the ignition switch key in. A quick start sometimes means a life. Johnny beat the prowl cars by less than a minute as he disappeared in traffic.

They would be combing the cities where he had always laired. He avoided the cities. He grew a mustache. He had been a natty dresser, but he went rough. He had keen eyes, but now wore plain glasses. He hopped clear across the continent. There was a town in the foothills of the Sierras, back of San Francisco.

The natives of the place were a strange and clannish lot. They were suspicious of each other and would have none of the hotel people. The town had no sanitarium, but its healthy climate filled the hotels with invalids recovering from various ills of breathing.

It was a swell hideout. New faces passed unnoticed because strangers came and went so frequently. Johnny had just the sallow look that got him taken for what he pretended to be.

On trigger edge with the fear of the hunted, he holed up for a week. He practiced by the hour drawing from his shoulder holster, until he became more adept at flicking the rod out than he had ever been when he carried it in his pocket.

When he thought he'd go stir crazy, he took to cautious forays out. Two miles from town, he found abandoned hydraulic diggings. An immense crater a mile across had been washed down to bed lava. It was a lonely spot, and Johnny the Tailor did some target practice. He was satisfied that his skill would beat any G-man.

He kept an eye on the papers, but the D. I. clamped down with silence. It was impossible to find out how much they knew, where they were searching, or how close they had come to ferreting him out.

Then, one day, as Johnny was hiking down to the pit, a prospector he'd noticed there before and whom he'd spoken to once or twice, suddenly said, "Johnny the Tailor, you're under arrest—"

Johnny didn't hear any more. He didn't stop to think. He acted instinctively at the first word. He went for his gun. Then he went to the morgue, and somebody else was public enemy number one.

"What beats me," said the G-man, "is why he reached for his pocket when the gun was in a shoulder holster."

The Scent of Murder

Jack Byrne

REX MASTERS hated bees. True, they were about to make him a rich widower, but he hated them anyway.

He opened a small vial, sending a hefty dose of a chemical into his wife's perfume atomizer. *It won't be long now,* he thought as he slipped the vial into his shirt pocket. He smiled into the mirror as he smoothed his hair and straightened his tie.

Rex had a lot to smile about these days.

When he first met Traci—beautiful, young, sexy Traci—at the health club, his life was comfortable. His wife Margie's gourmet honey company was doing quite well and orders were pouring in from restaurants, caterers and the idle rich.

Then two months ago, right after he and Traci snuck off on a short trip together and he realized how expensive her tastes were. Margie's father died and she inherited the bulk of his fortune.

Last week, while Margie thought he was out trying to sell more of her damn honey, he and Traci spent the afternoon in her apartment discussing their future plans. They'd agreed on something important—Margie had to die.

Poor old Margie. She was so sweet, so trusting. It wasn't her fault the years had taken such a terrible toll on her looks. But she had to die because Rex and Traci wanted each other. And, most of all, they wanted her money.

And soon they'd have it, thanks to Margie's bees. Rex hated them, and if one dared fly near him while he was at the hives, he killed it without hesitation. He was a sensible man, and knowing they would soon make him a rich man made them easier to abide. But he still hated them.

The plan was simple . . . incredibly simple. An old drinking buddy who possessed both a degree in chemical engineering and an insatiable taste for high-stakes gambling gave Rex the answer.

"This stuff," the engineer had said, holding up the tiny vial of dark liquid, "makes bees go crazy. Just one whiff of this potion and they go into a stinging frenzy.

"They start attacking anything, or anyone, who comes near them and keep on stinging until the entire hive is dead. Only takes a drop or two, and it dissipates in less than ten minutes. It won't leave a trace."

His friend had huge gambling debts and Rex paid dearly for that vial, but it was worth every penny. Because of the prenuptial agreement he'd foolishly signed, he'd get nothing if he divorced Margie. But this way, soon, he and Traci would have each other . . . and all that wonderful money.

He'd already loosened the latch on the gate in the fence surrounding the hives so that it wouldn't open easily. Rex didn't want Margie to escape her little assassins. All he had to do was get her to go near the hives once she'd sprayed herself with the perfume he'd bought her as a no-special-reason present.

He smiled remembering how she'd hugged him and nearly cried, overcome with happiness and love for her dear, charming Rex. Little did the stupid fool realize what was really in store for her!

Rex rubbed his hands together and checked his watch one more time. Margie should be home soon. He'd tell her to get all dressed up for a night out on the town.

"Oh, and by the way, Margie, darling," Rex whispered into the mirror, practicing his betrayal, "use some of your new perfume.

Just for me." Maybe he'd even kiss her. He shook his head, appalled at the thought.

He had one more thing to do. Rex wanted to check the latch again to be sure that the hives were all full of the beastly little insects.

After all, it wouldn't be fair if they didn't *all* get to have some fun, now would it? He chuckled and made his way to the beehives.

The tiny killers were all there, ready and waiting for Margie. Most of them would be dead soon too, but that didn't bother him. He planned to sell the hives once his wife was . . . gone.

Rex turned to leave, sure that everything would go exactly as planned. He stopped and smiled, a dark, evil smile. Maybe he'd get the little buggers good and ready for her.

He laughed out loud as he poked and swatted the side of the hive nearest him, not hard enough to get the bees fighting mad, just enough to get them a little stirred up.

A few bees buzzed out sluggishly and hung nearly motionless in the early evening air. He could hear a low droning as the others rustled around inside the hive. Perfect.

Rex turned to go back inside when he noticed a bee, a single tiny bee, clinging to the front of his clean striped shirt.

Without hesitation, Rex slammed his hand into his own chest, crushing the bee. "I hate bees!" he mumbled angrily.

Then he heard something crunch and realized, too late, that he still had the small vial in his pocket. A tiny stain spread across the front of his shirt, and Rex gaped at it in horror.

In seconds, the still night air was filled with an angry black noise, the roar of thousands of frenzied bees swirling up and out of their hives, driven to kill. They swarmed all over Rex, covering his face and hands and arms.

And as he fell to the ground, one final thought flickered through the dying brain of Rex Masters: *I hate bees.*

The Shill

Stephen Marlowe

EDDIE GAWKED and gawked. The crowd came slowly but steadily. They didn't know they were watching Eddie gawk. That's what made a good shill, a professional shill.

He was, naturally, dressed like all the local thistle chins. He wore an old threadbare several years out of date glen plaid suit, double-breasted and rumpled-looking. He wore a dreary not quite white shirt open at the collar without a tie. And he gawked.

He had big round deep-set eyes set in patches of blue-black on either side of his long narrow bridged nose. His lower lip hung slack with innocent wonder. He had not shaved in twenty-four hours. He looked exactly as if he had just come, stiff and bone weary and in need of entertainment, off the assembly line of the tractor plant down the road at Twin Falls. He stared in big eyed open mouthed wonder at Bart Taylor, the talker for the sideshow, as Bart expostulated and cajoled, declaimed and promised the good-sized scuff of townsfolk who had been drawn consciously by Bart Taylor's talking and unconsciously by Eddie's gawking.

He was a magnificent shill and he knew it and Bart Taylor knew it and not only the people at the Worlds of Wonder sideshow knew it but all the folks from the other carnival tents as well, so that when business was slow they sometimes came over just to watch Eddie gawk and summon the crowd with his gawking and they knew, without having studied psychology, as Eddie knew, that there was something unscientifically magnetic about a splendid shill like Eddie.

They used to call Eddie the Judas Ram (cynically, because the thistle chins were being led to financial slaughter) and the Pied Piper (because the thistle chins followed like naive children the unheard music of his wondering eyes and gaping mouth). But all that was before Eddie fell in love with Alana the houri from Turkestan who did her dance of the veils at the Worlds of Wonder, Alana who was from Baltimore and whose real name was Maggie O'Hara and who, one fine night when she first joined the carnival at a small town outside of Houston, Texas, stole Eddie's heart completely and for all time. After that Eddie was so sad, his eyes so filled with longing, that they didn't call him anything and didn't talk to him much and just let him do his work, which was shilling.

From the beginning, Eddie didn't stand a chance. He was a shill. He was in love with Alana, who was pale, delicate and beautiful, and everyone knew at once he was in love with her. In a week, all the men in the carnival were interested in Alana, whom nobody called Maggie. In a month, they all loved Alana, each in his own way, and each not because Alana had dunned them but because Eddie was a shill. It was as simple as that. Alana, however, for her own reasons remained aloof from all their advances. And the worst smitten of all was Bart Taylor, the talker and owner of Worlds of Wonder.

Now Bart finished his dunning and Eddie stepped up to the stand, shy and uncertain looking, to buy the first ticket. Bart took off his straw hat and wiped the sweat from the sweat band and sold Eddie a ticket. A good part of the scuff of thistle chins formed a line behind Eddie and bought tickets too. They always did.

Inside, Eddie watched the show dutifully, watched Fawzia the Fat Lady parade her mountains of flesh, watched Herko the Strong Man who actually had been a weight lifter, watched the trick mirror Turtle Girl, who came from Brooklyn but had lost her freshness in Coney Island and now was on the road, and the others, the Leopard Man and the Flame Swallower who could also crunch and apparently swallow discarded light bulbs and razor blades, Dame Misteria who was on loan from the Mitt camp down the midway to read fortunes at Worlds of Wonder and Sligo, a sweating red-faced escape artist who used trick handcuffs to do what Houdini had done with real ones.

But there was no Alana. Eddie waited eagerly for her act of the dancing veils, which was the finale of the show, but instead, the evening's organized entertainment concluded with Sligo. After that, the booths and stalls inside the enormous tent would remain in operation although the central stage was dark. The thistle chins, wandering about listlessly under the sagging canvas both because it was hot and because they too sensed something was missing from the show, had left the expected debris, peanut bags and soft drink bottles and crumpled sandwich wrappers, in the narrow aisles among the wooden folding chairs in front of the stage.

Eddie found Bart Taylor outside in his trailer, spilling the contents of his chamois pouch on a table and counting the take. "Two and a half bills," Bart said. "Not bad."

"How come Alana didn't dance?" Eddie wanted to know.

"Maybe she's sick or something."

"Didn't she tell you?"

"I haven't seen her," Bart Taylor said, stacking the bills and change in neat piles on the table in front of him. He was wearing a lightweight loud plaid jacket with high wide peaked lapels of a thinner material. One of the lapels was torn, a small jagged piece missing from it right under the wilted red carnation Bart Taylor wore. The carnation looked as if it had lost half its petals too.

"Well, I'll go over to her trailer," Eddie said.

"I wouldn't."

Eddie looked at him in surprise. "Any reason why not?"

"No," Bart said quickly. "Maybe she's sick and sleeping or something. You wouldn't want to disturb her."

"Well, I'll go and see."

A shovel and a pick-ax were under the table in Bart Taylor's trailer. Eddie hadn't seen them before. "Don't," Bart said, and stood up. His heavy shoe made a loud scraping sound against the shovel. He was a big man, much bigger than Eddie and sometimes when the carnival was on a real bloomer with no money coming in they all would horse around some like in a muscle camp, and Bart could even throw Herko the Strong Man, who had been a weight-lifter.

"O.K.," Eddie said, but didn't mean it. He went outside and the air was very hot and laden with moisture. He looked up but couldn't see any stars. He wondered what was wrong with Bart Taylor, to act like that. He walked along the still crowded midway to the other group of trailers on the far side of the carnival, past the lead joint where the local puddle-jumpers were having a go at the ducks and candle flames and big swinging gong with .22 ammo, past the ball pitching stand where shelves of cheap slum were waiting for the winners, past the chandy who was fixing some of the wiring in the merry-go-round. For some reason, Eddie was frightened. He almost never sweated, no matter how hot it was. A shill looked too obviously enthusiastic if he sweated. But now he could feel the sweat beading his forehead and trickling down his sides from his armpits. He wasn't warm, though. He was very cold.

There was no light coming through the windows of Alana's trailer. The do not disturb sign was hanging from the door-knob. The noise from the midway was muted and far away, except for the explosive staccato from the lead joint. Eddie knocked on the aluminum door and called softly, "Alana? Alana, it's Eddie."

No answer. Eddie lit a cigaret, but it tasted like straw. His wet fingers discolored the paper. He threw the cigaret away and tried the door. It wasn't locked.

Inside, Eddie could see nothing in the darkness. His hand groped for the light switch. The generator was weak: the overhead light flickered pale yellow and made a faint sizzling sound.

Alana was there. Alana was sprawled on the floor, wearing her six filmy veils. In the yellow light, her long limbs were like gold under the veils. Eddie knelt by her side. He was crying softly before his knees touched the floor. Alana's eyes were opened but unseeing. Her face was bloated, the tongue protruding. From the neck down she was beautiful. From the neck up, it made Eddie sick to look at her.

She had been strangled.

He let his head fall on her breast. There was no heart beat. The body had not yet stiffened.

He stood up and lurched about the interior of the small trailer. He didn't know how long he remained there. He was sick on the floor of the trailer. He went back to the body finally. In her right hand Alana clutched a jagged strip of plaid cloth. Red carnation petals like drops of blood were strewn over the floor of the trailer.

"All right, Eddie," Bart Taylor said softly. "Don't move."

Eddie turned around slowly. He had not heard the door open. He looked at Bart Taylor, who held a gun in his hand, pointing it unwaveringly at Eddie.

"You killed her," Eddie said.

"*You* killed her," Bart Taylor said. "My word against yours. I own this show. Who are you, a nobody. A shill. My word against yours."

"Why did you do it?"

"She wouldn't look at me. I loved her. I said I would marry her, even. She hated me. I couldn't stand her hating me. But I didn't mean to kill her."

"What are you going to do?" Eddie said.

"Jeep's outside. Tools. We'll take her off a ways and bury her."

453

"Not me," Eddie said.

"I need help. You'll help me. A shill. A nobody. They all know how you were carrying a torch for her. You better help me."

"Your jacket," Eddie said. "The carnation. They'll know it was you."

"Not if we bury her."

"Not me," Eddie said again.

"It's late. There are maybe thirty, forty people left on the midway. We've got to chance it now. It looks like rain. Won't be able to do it in the rain. Let's get her out to the jeep now, Eddie."

"No," Eddie said. He wasn't crying now, but his eyes were red.

Bart came over to him. Eddie thought he was going to bend over the body, but instead he lashed out with the gun in his hand, raking the front sight across Eddie's cheek. Eddie fell down, just missing Alana's body.

"Get up," Bart said. "You'll do it. I swear I'll kill you if you don't."

Eddie sat there. Blood on his cheek. The light, yellow, buzzing. Bart towering over him, gigantic, menacing. Alana, dead. Dead.

"On your feet," Bart said. "Before it starts raining."

When Eddie stood up, Bart hit him again with the gun. Eddie would have fallen down again, but Bart held him under his arms. "You'll do it," Bart said. "I can't do it alone."

"O.K.," Eddie said. "I feel sick. I need some air."

"You'll get it in the jeep."

"No. Please. I couldn't help you. Like this. Air first. Outside. All right?"

Bart studied him, then nodded. "I'll be watching you," he said. "Don't try to run. I'll catch you. I have the gun. I'll kill you if I have to."

"I won't try to run," Eddie promised. He went outside slowly and stood in front of the trailer. He took long deep breaths and waited.

Eddie gawked at the trailer. It was like magic, they always said. It had nothing to do with seeing or smelling or any of the senses, not really. You didn't only gawk with your eyes. Not a professional shill. Not the best. You gawked with every straining minuteness of your body. And they came. The thistle chins. The townsfolk. Like iron filings and a magnet. They came slowly, not knowing why they had come, not knowing what power had summoned them. They

454

came to gawk with you. They came, all right. You've been doing this for years. They always came.

You could sense them coming, Eddie thought. You didn't have to look. In fact, you shouldn't. Just gawk, at the trailer. Shuffling of feet behind you. A stir. Whispering. What am I doing here? Who is this guy?

Presently there were half a dozen of them. Then an even dozen. Drawn by Eddie, the magnificent shill.

There were too many of them for Bart to use his gun. They crowded around the trailer's only entrance. They waited there with Eddie. Unafraid now, but lonely, infinitely lonely, Eddie led them inside.

They found Bart Taylor trying to stuff carnation petals down his throat.

Something for the Dark

John Lutz

I T BOTHERS ME," the lieutenant said.

"It didn't bother the jury," I told him. "They found me guilty."

The scent of fear wafted across the waxed wood table where I sat in the prison visiting room. I understood the lieutenant's fear, felt sorry for him, but nothing could be done about that. He was a conscience case and always would be.

"Your wife had many enemies," he said in a voice dulled by the resonance of the words in his memory. My lawyer had reminded the jury of Miriam's enemies over a dozen times during the trial.

Of course I had pleaded not guilty, claiming my confession had been made under duress. But I had little doubt as to the trial's outcome. The smoking gun, the locked room . . . Justice was as blind as I was.

I heard the lieutenant shift his weight uncomfortably in his chair, caught the scent of his lime after-shave lotion as it mingled with the doubt that would never loose its hold on his conscience. He'd been the arresting officer, the one who'd forced my confession and whose testimony at the trial had destroyed my case. He had reason to doubt, but doubt was all he could do.

The lieutenant's breathing leveled out as he relaxed somewhat. On the left side of my face, I felt a subtle coolness as someone quietly opened the door. A soft-soled shoe whispered abruptly on the cork floor. I heard the lieutenant turn in his chair, felt faint vibrations along the wide table as he strained to see the visitor. "You have about ten more minutes, Lieutenant," the voice of Graves the guard said evenly, "then I have orders to take him back to his cell." I felt the movement of air as Graves left, heard the click of the door latch, the turn of the key, the sigh of the lieutenant as he leaned on the table and made it live with the tenseness of his frustration.

Miriam had stood by me in my blindness. That says all I need to know about her, all I need to remember. It proved her love for me.

It's true about Miriam having had many enemies, but what gossip columnist doesn't? I can vouch that everything in the Miriam Moore Tells All columns was true. And more importantly, there was much that was true that Miriam kept out of her columns. Probably only I know that. Miriam was too concerned with her image of quintessential bitch ever to tell anyone of the dirt she didn't write. She knew that image gave her a certain credibility with her readers and meant an uninterrupted flow of money into the bank.

My medical expenses after the accident were astronomical.

I honestly believe that if it weren't for the accident, for me surviving after all those dark months in the hospital, Miriam would have given up her column. It bothered her more than anybody knew, some of the things that happened as a result of her stories. I tried to tell her she wasn't responsible for what other people did when confronted with the truth. The agonizing part is that neither of us really believed that.

"She was shot exactly in the temple from a range of less than fourteen inches," the lieutenant said. "That's what won't go down with me, that a blind man could fire a revolver with that much accuracy."

He'd never be able to let it go. "I can see my lawyer should have subpoenaed you," I said.

"You've been sentenced to die, Edwards. You'll be the first under the new state law. But you don't seem concerned, and that bothers me almost as much as the accuracy of the death wound."

I shrugged. "There are few successful blind fugitives. I was dead when Miriam died. I knew that would be the case and decided to kill her anyway. I'm not happy with my predicament, but it's not unexpected.''

''Suppose you told me the truth confidentially,'' the lieutenant suggested in a conspiratorial tone. ''There's no way you can get another trial now, and you could deny this conversation if you wanted.''

''The truth came out in court, the way it's supposed to happen.''

He sighed again. I felt sorry for him and wanted him to leave. There was no other direction for our conversation to take. I had been found sitting in a room locked from the inside, the gun in my hand, Miriam on the floor dead of a bullet wound in her head. How could the lieutenant blame the jury for finding me guilty? How could he blame himself? He should never have become a policeman; he was a creature of the heart, doomed to suffer.

I heard chair legs scrape, felt the caress of air on my face as the lieutenant stood. His defeat permeated the room, a tangible question that would never be answered, that would thrive in dark places.

''This is your last chance, Edwards,'' he told me, knowing it was his last chance. ''I'd like to know—I need to know—if you're really guilty.''

I wanted to tell him everything, but I couldn't risk it. He started to say something else, then abruptly left the room, his footsteps fading on the other side of the thick door he closed behind him. Leaving me alone.

I sat quietly with my hands on the smooth tabletop, thinking despite myself of that day of the unexpected thunder in the tiny bedroom, of my wrenching fear as I crawled over the coarse carpet toward the source of the great crash that still hovered in the charged air. My hands had sought like separate, desperate animals before me, exploring every contour of the deep-woven rug. Then the sticky wetness, the well-like, sucking edge of the wound, the gun, the still flesh.

The gun was in my hand as I made my way to the closed door and locked it. Already I could hear and feel approaching footsteps in the hall outside. For a long time I ignored the knocking. Then the door was forced.

I'll never let them know the truth—that the haughty and wise Miriam Moore committed suicide. I owe her that and more. They never found the note she had written, the note I'd folded into a narrow, tight strip and wedged between the molding and the wall near the floor.

They found me seated on the carpet, my back against the wall and the murder weapon in my hand. A guilty man in any impartial court of law.

So now the lieutenant has to wonder, and I feel sorry for him. And as long as I keep my silence, I have to wonder along with him. Was I actually guilty in a way the jury couldn't imagine? Was I responsible for Miriam's death? I know I'll have to live and die with a question even more haunting than the lieutenant's, a question I'll do anything rather than face:

What was in Miriam's note?

Something Like Murder

John Lutz

I WAS LEANING slightly from my fifteenth-floor window in the Norwood Arms, watering my geraniums, when Mrs. Vixton passed by wearing a pink flower-print kimono of shimmering silk. She passed by vertically, you understand, not horizontally, which would have been much more conducive to her health though not nearly so remarkable.

She saw me, I believe, though to her I was of only passing interest. Still, I'm sure I saw a slight inclination of her head in my direction. Whatever else might be said of Mrs. Vixton, she was never a snob. She was descending face down, her arms spread incredibly wide, a frozen, determined expression on her face, as if she might yet have time to catch the knack of flying. Startled, I over-watered the geraniums. I didn't look down; there was no doubt of the outcome.

My name, incidentally, is Cy Cryptic. Not my real name, of course. I'm a movie reviewer for one of the larger papers here in town, and Cy Cryptic sounds and looks more like show biz than Marvin Haupt.

I'd have forgotten completely about Mrs. Vixton's death, except that cinematically it might have been effective, when a week later in the lobby I overheard a chance remark between Mrs. Fattler of the third floor and Gates the doorman.

"... from her window ..." I heard Mrs. Fattler say, dragging out her vowels as women often do when discussing a tragedy.

I edged closer. "Mr. Cryptic," Mrs. Fattler said in greeting, and Gates gave his ridiculous little salute. I joined the conversation.

Mrs. Vixton had committed suicide, I was told, by leaping from the south window of her apartment while the horrified Mr. Vixton looked on. A typewritten signed note was found later, expressing Mrs. Vixton's despondency and her desire to leave this world. I did not mention that I had seen Mrs. Vixton resplendent in midair the morning of her death. I did not think it wise in light of the fact that the Vixtons lived on the fourteenth floor, in the apartment *below* mine.

The matter of Mrs. Vixton's gravity-assisted death kept creeping into my mind that afternoon as I sat through an advance showing of *Life's Slender Thread,* a French import about, believe it or not, a man who pushes his mistress from a high window rather than turn her over to a gangland czar. It was a happy-ending film of unlikely gimmickry, small consequence, and incoherent subtitles. Yet the movie did create a certain mood. When I left the theater I decided to call on Mr. Vixton before writing my copy.

Mr. Vixton was of medium-height, a pear-shaped man in his fifties, with a sleek set to his neck and shoulders that suggested that once he might have been lean and muscular. We shook hands and he invited me into his apartment, a twin to my own but for Vixton's tasteless and mismatched furniture on a riotous green-and-black carpet. The carpet alone might have driven Mrs. Vixton to suicide. But I knew that it wasn't suicide.

"Sit down, Cryptic," Mr. Vixton invited, waving a compact arm toward a low sofa with clear Lucite arms.

I sat, glancing at the south window. "I'm sorry about your wife," I said. "Are you?"

Vixton stood with his arms crossed; he cocked his head, then laughed. There was something froglike in his broad bespectacled features, his wide downturned mouth.

"I thought you might have seen me leaning out to water my geraniums," I said. "At any rate, I could never be sure you hadn't."

"And I could never be sure you didn't see my wife pass by you, Cryptic. Yours was the only window she had to pass above this fourteenth floor, after which it didn't matter. But as it happened, I did see your hand holding the watering can, some few seconds after Gloria's fall."

I leaned back in the gauche sofa and crossed my outstretched legs at the ankles. "I surmise that you pushed her from the roof."

"You surmise correctly. That way there would be no window frame for her to clamp onto, and no sign of a struggle in our apartment. I tricked her into signing the note I had typed, lured her onto the roof, then pushed her. None of it was difficult—certainly it was easier and more profitable for me than a divorce. What I'm curious about, Cryptic, is why you came down here and brought out in the open what both of us could only suspect—that you did see Gloria pass your window, and you knew that I was aware that you had."

"I could never be sure you wouldn't kill me," I said candidly, "and if I went to the police with my story, they might not have believed me and you might have killed me out of revenge or to protect yourself, or possibly even sued me for libel."

"Truthfully," Mr. Vixton said, "I was considering the first alternative—to kill you. It was that glimpse of the watering can . . ." He frowned slightly, a toadlike contraction of his features. "But how does this visit improve the situation?"

"The situation, as I see it, is that we can't trust one another. You'll always feel I might go to the authorities, and I'll always feel you might do something drastic to preclude that eventuality. Now, what needs to be done is for circumstances to be arranged so that we *can* trust one another. Suppose you had something on me?"

Vixton puffed his cheeks and seemed to deliberate. "Something like murder?"

"There is a young woman named Alicia whom I often escort."

"I've seen her," Vixton said. "A charmer."

"Suppose I do away with Alicia in your presence, even let you photograph the event? That would make us even, so to speak, and we could be confident of each other's silence."

"It would be a standoff," Vixton said slowly, brightening to the idea. "Better than a standoff, actually, as I'd have absolute proof of your guilt. But what do you have against Alicia?"

"Absolutely nothing. She's merely convenient for our purpose."

I watched Vixton consider this, then saw his eyes darken at the sudden thought behind them. "I'm even more convenient than Alicia, Cryptic. Wouldn't it solve your problem if you"—he laughed a flat croaking laugh—"murdered me?"

"You're *too* convenient," I told him. "One: you're in the apartment below me; the police are bound to question me and suspect. Two: however deeply buried, I do have a motive. On the other hand, I'm only one of Alicia's many escorts, and she and I get along splendidly and always have."

Vixton nodded slowly. "It's crazy but it makes sense—if that makes sense."

"It does," I assured him. "Alicia lives in a west-side penthouse apartment on the thirtieth floor. I'll arrange things so we can go there together tomorrow night, and she can meet the same fate as your late wife."

Vixton's broad face widened in a smile. He chuckled, then laughed aloud and went to the bar in the corner and poured us each a drink. We toasted tall buildings.

The next night Vixton and I took the elevator to the thirtieth floor of Alicia's building and walked down the deep-carpeted hall to the door labeled with her apartment number. She must have heard us coming, for as I raised my hand to knock, the door opened.

"Cryptic," she said, "how good to see you!"

But it was better to see her. She was slender and tan in a long pink dress, with honey-blond hair cascading in carefully arranged wildness to below her shoulders. She wanted to be in films, and on looks alone she had a chance.

"This is Mr. Vixton," I told her, as Vixton and I stepped inside. "He's a film producer from Los Angeles here to consider some outdoor locales for a movie."

Alicia's eyes took on a special, harder light. "Which of the studios are you from?"

"I'm an independent producer," Vixton said smoothly. He regarded Alicia with what passed for professional interest. "According to Mr. Cryptic, you're a talented young woman."

"All she needs," I said with a smile, "is a little push."

Vixton coughed as Alicia led us out onto the balcony for drinks.

The balcony was large, bounded by a low iron rail on the east side and a four-foot-high stone wall on the north and south. Along the base of the iron rail ran a trough of rich earth from which grew a dense wall of exotic green foliage, including two small trees. Like many cliff dwellers, Alicia was addicted to what green she could squeeze into her steel-and-cement-dominated existence.

Vixton had a martini, as did I. Alicia, as usual, drank a whiskey sour. I hastened to mix the drinks, my plan being to drop several capsules of a depressant into each of Alicia's whiskey sours. "Dangerous when mixed with alcohol," I had said to Vixton earlier, showing him a handful of the tiny capsules. "Downers in the true sense of the word."

In the thin cool air of the balcony I heard Vixton's harsh voice rasp. ". . . going to be a great movie . . ." He actually seemed to be enjoying himself. Alicia was on him like wet clothes.

After the third whiskey sour Alicia's eyelids seemed unable to make it more than halfway over her beautiful blue orbs, and I nodded to Vixton. While he watched, I held Alicia by the waist and guided her toward the iron railing.

"Don' wanna dance," she protested.

Vixton readied his pocket camera as I positioned Alicia just so before the lush green wall of foliage beyond which was the star-speckled night sky. "Cryptic!" she said, suddenly alarmed.

"Sorry, love," I said, and pushed with my right hand. There was a quick sharp flash.

Alicia disappeared between the dense branches, tumbling backward. One high-heeled shoe flew off as her tanned ankles flicked through the green leaves and disappeared. I heard a trailing scream, punctuated by Vixton's, "Got it!"

I glanced through the branches and quickly turned my head. "Let's go!" I said to Vixton, but he was already at the door that led inside the apartment. We took our martini glasses with us and hastily wiped our fingerprints from whatever else we might have touched.

There was no one in the hall as we walked quickly along the spongy carpet to the elevator and punched the button. Within a few minutes we were descending to street level. Perspiration had boiled to beads on Vixton's flat forehead.

We left by the building's side exit, got in my car, and quickly, but not too quickly, drove away. As we rounded the corner and passed the front of the building we saw a knot of people and a bare tanned foot protruding from a fold of pink material on the sidewalk. I drove faster.

Two days later I gave Vixton the details of Alicia's funeral.

And that's how we accomplished it—the perfect crime. I got the idea from *Life's Slender Thread,* that abominable French film. Only instead of a thin nylon rope, as was used in the movie, we used a net from which there was access to the open window of the vacant apartment below Alicia's. It's true that Alicia wants to break into movies, but as a stuntperson, as I suppose they're now called. As promised, I might be able to arrange something for her.

After being caught in the net, Alicia quickly climbed through the window below, then ran out into the hall where she took the service elevator to ground level with Vixton and me minutes behind her. She then faked a crowd-gathering fainting spell on the sidewalk directly below her balcony.

I no longer have anything to fear from Vixton, but just in case, I've moved out of the Norwood Arms and will be extremely difficult to locate. There was no way I could bear to kill Alicia, or even Vixton. Seeing that sort of thing done constantly on film is one thing, actually doing it another. I'm not a violent person; I like musicals.

My one concern is that Vixton will go to see *Life's Slender Thread.* But that isn't likely. Not after the review I gave it.

The Stocking

Ramsey Campbell

T HE PHONE RANG.
"Phone's ringing," Tom said.
"Yes, well?" Sheila countered.
"You get it, I'm too tired."
"Are you tired, Tompuss?" called Tina in mock sympathy.
"Let's toss for it."
"Go on, Tom, answer it," said Sheila. "You'll have Mr. Tubb telling us off again."

Wearily he lifted the receiver. A girl repeated: "Hello? Hello?" He brandished the receiver: "It's for you anyway."

"Bridget?" Sheila greeted, lowering her voice. "And where were *you* last night? . . . Now you know I don't like to go out on my own . . . Well, you'll never guess who I went out with! . . . Yes, that's right . . . Oh, fabulous, he took me to that club . . . Yes, he drove me home . . . Well, I wouldn't normally, but he's different . . . And how did *you* go on? . . ."

Tom fixed his eyes on his work; he always felt depressed by these conversations of Sheila's. But he was not to be left undisturbed. Tina was in a happy mood today; obviously she'd "had a good night", as she was fond of telling them. Now she called: "Why are you tired, Tompuss?"

"Lack of sleep, Mrs. McLaine."

"Hectic night?"

"Now, Tina, don't corrupt Sheila."

"No, but seriously, Tom, have you ever?" She raised an eyebrow.

"What?" He felt trapped.

"Do you often?"

"Often what?"

"Can you?"

"Can't you, Tom?" said Sheila in his ear, having finished her conversation.

"Now, don't be naughty." He spanked her and she squealed. Tina arched her eyebrows. "Kinky," she commented. "Yes," said Sheila with a long look at Tom, and went back to her desk.

When he left for home that night, Tom dawdled on the pavement near the entrance to an alley which he knew Sheila used as a short cut. He saw her leave the building, and ducked into the alley. Soon he heard her high heels on the cobbles, overtaking him. "Aren't you speaking to me?" he asked as she passed.

"Oh, hello, Tom, I didn't see you." They picked their way between the dustbins, crushed cartons and locked back doors of two main streets. One black door, half off its hinges, creaked in shadow. Sheila pressed close to Tom. "What's wrong?" he enquired.

"Oh, that door. It's always open when I come by. It frightens me. Silly, really."

"I didn't know you were the nervous type."

"I am, you know." They emerged into a square, bright as day between blazing store windows. Sheila's bus was swallowing its queue. "See you tomorrow," she said, and ran. Tom began to walk to the traffic lights where the bus might be halted. It was, and he waved, but Sheila did not see him.

Next morning she had made the coffee; a cup awaited Tom when he arrived. He sipped it down, his eyes on Sheila, then carried it round to her desk. "Thanks, kitten," he said.

"Ready for work?" Mr. Tubb called, striding past.

Tom and Sheila swapped grimaces. She stretched back in her chair, arm behind her head, closed her eyes, and yawned. He tickled her armpit. She squeaked and squirmed out of reach. His fingers followed.

"At it early, children?" Tina commented, sitting down to repair one eyebrow before her compact mirror.

"Never miss an opportunity," Tom replied. His fingertips continued. Sheila had worked herself almost into a knot, one leg hooked around the corner of her desk. "Oo—" she protested yet again. Then: *"Oh!"*—a genuine protest. She shoved back her chair and gazed at her leg. "Now look, my stocking's laddered."

"I'm sorry, Sheila," Tom apologised, trying to insinuate regret into his expression as he took in her legs. "Get some at dinnertime and I'll give you the money."

"It's all right, Tom, I had to buy a pair anyway."

"No, come on, I insist."

"Thanks, Tom, but I'd really rather you didn't."

"You're just finishing your break, are you?" suggested Mr. Tubb.

Sheila stretched the laddered stocking before her face and peeked at Tom. "Thanks," he said, holding out his hand. She hesitated. "Go on, Sheila, if he wants it," Tina urged. Shrugging, Sheila balled the stocking and tossed it to him. Smiling at her, he hung it from the corner of his desk. Mr. Tubb cleared his throat. Sheila's head went down. Now and then Tom fingered the stocking, glancing up at Sheila. Tina watched him.

"Make me some coffee, Tompuss," Tina said.

He was spooning the ingredients from jars on the window-ledge; blank morning fog walled them in. "I can only carry two cups," he explained.

"Well, I'm here, you're here, so make ours."

"No, I must look after Sheila," and he did so. She was at her desk when he returned, leafing through a women's magazine with Tina. Tom waited for her to turn to him, then handed her the cup. His fingers lingered among hers.

"Are you holding my hand, Tom?" she asked.

His hand, found out, retreated and was suspended for a moment in mid-air. Her neck showed between her cardigan and hair. Tom's fingers found the gap and stroked. They progressed upward, lifting her hair; it was a gesture such as he might have used to sweep up her skirt.

Tina's fingers closed around her cup as she rose. "I'm embarrassed," she told them. "It's like watching you courting."

"We were innocent until you came, Mrs. Libido," he replied.

"At least I brought you two together, then. When are you getting married?"

"Oh, sure!" said Sheila.

"You really killed that," Tom followed, and sat down with his coffee. Tina smiled mysteriously. At that moment Mr. Tubb entered through the door beneath the clock; his temper and his winter cold were suffering from fog. Tina sat down again.

Later, gusts of rain cleared away the fog and plastered newspapers against the pane. Nobody went out at lunchtime. Tom unpacked his sandwiches and ate, trying to conceal the sound of chewing. Sheila rustled pages in the silence; Tina stubbed out a cigarette and began to knit. Mr. Tubb coughed. Tom heard only the pages turning onward. The thought possessed him that both he and Sheila had scoffed at Tina's observation; could Sheila be concealing a desire as deep as his?

"That'll go stale," Sheila said beside him. He started; he could not remember how long he had been holding the half-eaten sandwich. He gnawed at it and she picked up the phone.

"Is that Bridget? . . . Look, I can't make it tomorrow . . . No, it's terrible, he's in hospital . . . Appendix . . . Yes, I'm going tonight . . . Of course, except Thursdays, because then visiting's in the afternoon . . . The hospital across the field . . . I *do* get frightened! . . . Yes, seriously! Thinking of what happened to that girl last week, and that was in the street . . . I'm still as frightened, but this is different, I've got to go . . ."

"Why don't you ask Sheila out?"

Tom went cold. Tina had whispered the question, and he could not be sure if Sheila had heard. He forced himself to look; she seemed intent on the receiver. Tina was watching for an answer. "Yes, why not?" he managed, and smiled and nodded violently. Then he picked up a sandwich and began to chew, keeping his eyes on the food, feeling mercilessly exposed to Tina's gaze. Sheila replaced the phone and left his side. Slowly his face cooled, but he could not think. He reached out and caressed the stocking.

That night he loitered at the mouth of Sheila's alley, but in vain.

Eventually he turned down the alley, walking slowly, letting the wall of fog precede him and reveal each remembered door and cobblestone. Silence isolated his footsteps. Suddenly he stopped; a black door had loomed up on his left, rustily ajar. The shifting obscure walls cut them off together. Tom hesitated; then he took out a box of matches and, dragging the door further open, squeezed inside.

"I hope you two enjoyed yourselves last night?" Tina smiled radiantly at Tom and Sheila as she combed the fog from her hair.

"Of course," Tom said.

"I went to the hospital," explained Sheila, "then back across the field. It was terribly creepy. Sort of thing you'd have liked, Tom. But I didn't really mind."

"How was he?" Tina asked.

Tom stirred his coffee, deliberately blotting out their conversation. When he put down the cup, Tina was remarking: "New perfume?"

"Yes, *L'Imprévu.*"

Later, Mr. Tubb coughed over next week's time-sheet and pinned it up. Tina rose to scrutinise it. Returning, she called: "Say, Sheila, you'll be working alone tomorrow night, did you realise? I can't work Thursdays."

"Oh, no," Sheila's eyes widened. "Tom, work tomorrow night."

"Well, I don't know." He did, but liked to be persuaded.

"Go on, Tom, keep Sheila company."

"All right, pussycat, I'll stay with you," he said, not minding Tina's knowing grin.

The moon grinned down mysteriously. Lying in the stripe of moonlight painted on his bed, Tom closed his eyes; behind his eyelids all was white, as if before a vision. He thought of Thursday night. Then he frowned. Why had Tina been unable to work? He could not recall that she had previously said so. He sorted throught the last few days, and, as he drowsed, a pattern seemed to form. Was Tina giving him a chance to ask Sheila out? Could Sheila herself have arranged for him to be alone with her? He had never never considered that she might want to go out with him. But as he searched—the way she let him touch her, the way she laughed off Tina's exaggerations of the relationship between them, the perfume she wore to the office (surely only for him, for Tina, married wore none when at work)—each incident yielded evidence. Tomorrow night. He must not let this opportunity pass. They would be alone, and he would ask her casually to meet him Friday night. He slept. The moon still grinned.

The morning chilled him. Last night's resolution seemed as distant as the sun behind the fog, visible when he squinted as a white-hot sixpence dulled by grey breaths. But at work, snug with Sheila while the fumes receded deceptively outside the windows, he began again to anticipate the evening. There was no call for Shiela, nor did she touch the phone; this seemed a favourable sign. The day drew on; the fog crept back, unnoticed. It was almost five o'clock. "Make some coffee, Tom," called Sheila, "to keep us awake."

"See you in the morning, children," said Tina, bundled up inside her coat, as she returned to collect her handbag. "Don't do anything I wouldn't do." She winked at them, then frowned at Mr. Tubb, and left.

"Want a sandwich, Sheila?"

"No thanks, got my own."

"Come here a minute." He pulled her down towards him. Surprised, she resisted briefly. "What about old Peeping Tom there," he hissed, "when's *he* going?"

Sheila glanced at Mr. Tubb, now carressing his nostrils with a handkerchief. "I thought you knew," she whispered back. "He's not. He'll be on 'til eight o'clock like us."

"*What?* But you said you'd—you said you'd be alone . . ."

"Well, I would be if I was alone with him! He's looking, I'd better get back." And she abandoned Tom to his thoughts. At first he felt tricked, and hated Sheila; he began to curse her under his breath as his nails scraped on the mesh of the stocking. Then Mr. Tubb coughed, recalling Tom; it wasn't Sheila's fault, she'd wanted to be with him, it was that swine Tubb's for staying. Surely he would leave the two of them together before eight o'clock. Tom settled down to wait.

He looked up. It was five to seven. Sheila's head was bent upon her writing; Mr. Tubb had disappeared. Tom watched Sheila's long blonde hair, brushed back, shining; out of the corner of his eye he sensed the lurking fog. Now was the time to ask. He would have to speak her name; would he be able to bring out the invitation when she looked up? Unsureness gagged him. But if he did not speak she might glance up and destroy the moment. "Sheila," he called; he tried to catch it, but too late. She met his gaze. He struggled. "I was wondering if you'd—"

"Spare me a minute, Sheila, will you?" Mr. Tubb rose from behind his desk, returned triumphant from a search for his Vick inhaler.

"Hang on, Tom." Tom's expression did not change as he watched her cross to Mr. Tubb, but out of sight his nails ground into his palms. He glared blindly at his desk. "All right, just as soon as I've finished what I'm doing," Sheila said. Then Mr. Tubb called after her: "Oh—if you're making coffee, would you get me a cup?"

My God, no, it's too ludicrous, thought Tom. "What were you saying?" Sheila asked, taking his cup.

The opportunity was past. "I forget," he said.

The first gulp of coffee burned his throat; he gritted his teeth and enjoyed the pain. Then he began to work obsessively, unable to dull his awareness of Sheila as she rustled papers, picked up her drink and after a dainty sip set it down with a clunk, dropped her pen and retrieved it, tripped away to the washroom. When she returned Tom reached for his coffee, found it stagnant, and was able to look up at her. Behind her Mr. Tubb was struggling into his overcoat. As he passed them he croaked: "Now, don't get into mischief." This effort proved too much; coughing, he exited beneath the clock, which showed a quarter to eight. The door caught his cough and muffled it.

"Well, if he's going, I'm off," Sheila said. With a lurch of the heart Tom realised that a quarter of an hour was left to him, which he must grasp. Sheila was stretching and yawning preparatory to getting up. Tom wrenched out the pin from which the stocking dangled and moved behind her, the nylon taut between his hands. "Are you going to strangle me, Tom?" she asked. He held open the top of the stocking and fitted it over her forehead.

"Don't, Tom you'll mess my hair."

"Come on, put your nightcap on."

"No, you wear it." She stood up, pushing him back, removed the stocking and lifted it over his head. Her arms were high, delicious with perfume; for a second her breasts touched him. His hands hung loosely at his sides. She pulled the stocking down over his eyes.

"You think I'm going to commit a crime or something?" The

nylon cramped the bridge of his nose, but he could not take off the stocking; Sheila had put it there. Instead, he began to draw it over his face.

"Now you can go out and frighten someone."

"Maybe I will." As she made for the cloakroom she glanced back to see him standing undirected, fingering the edge of the stocking.

She lifted her coat from the hook; her fingers brushed the cloth of Tom's. She waited to hear his footsteps approaching, but there was only silence. She was a little disappointed, for she had had the impression at least twice tonight that Tom was about to kiss her. In fact, just before she had tried to make it easy for him; she felt rather sorry for Tom—she was sure he had no girl-friend—and if he wanted to kiss her, she would let him now and then, while making it clear that she could not go out with him. As a matter of fact, she was rather excited by the idea of such a secret relationship; she and Tom would be secretly united against Tina's morning reports. Where *was* Tom? Perhaps she could take his arm as they left. She returned to the office; it was empty. She peeked under the desk; Tom might be planning to leap out at her. But he was nowhere to be found. Well, she could play games too; she turned off the light. He would scarcely have gone home without his coat.

But she reached the street without finding Tom. Momentarily, as she imagined him standing silently beyond the edge of the lurid fog beneath the sodium lights, she shivered. Then the blurred hands of a clock which hung above the alley across the road caught her eye; it was eight o'clock. If she hurried she could catch the early bus. She ran across the road, no car engines threatening in the fog, and into the alley.

Her heels slipped on the cobbles. The fog edged in front of her, darkening, drawing back along the walls, passing over drainpipes climbed by rusty barbed wire like vines; then something loomed behind it, blocking at least half the alleyway. Sheila stopped but almost falling, was carried forward, and the shape resolved into a door and the figure which held it wide open; a figure with a crushed face.

"Tom, what are you doing?"

Without speaking, he indicated the open doorway. The stocking, now pulled down to his chin, dragged his features out of shape. Sheila told herself that Tom was still there beneath the mask. Why should she hesitate? What could there be beyond the door to harm her? The mouth moved; the lower section of the nylon billowed out.

"Don't be frightened," he said, "Sheila."

She stepped forward to the doorway; the fog peered over her shoulder. In the dimness she made out the beginnings of what appeared to be an abandoned storage room, shattered beer-barrels, broken bottles, and misshapen lengths of wood and metal against the wall. She entered a few paces, and the door closed behind her.

She froze; her sense of direction had deserted her, and she no longer knew where she might step without falling on glass. Then she heard movement behind her, approaching. "Where are you?" asked Tom.

"I'm here, Tom." Her voice was in front of him. He advanced one foot; it kicked a piece of glass, which tinkled in the silence. If only there were some light! He searched for his matches, then remembered that they were in his overcoat pocket. He lifted his hands and shuffled forward. Her perfume reached him, almost suffocated by a stench of stale alcohol which had been shut in with them. Then his hands found her body.

No! Sheila screamed, her lips pressed tight in horror. This was not what she had meant. She tried to wrench his hands away, but he was already pulling her towards him. She forced her hands up between his arms and reached his face. She expected to encounter the stocking, but he had rolled it up to his forehead. Before she knew what she was doing, she had raked his cheeks.

Pain seared his face like trickles of acid. He backed away towards the wall, and tripped.

Sheila heard something fall, and a crack of glass. She whirled around, but no glimmer of light outlined the door. She bit her lip. "Tom, let me out," she called desperately, "or I'll scream." A piece of wood clattered, and again glass cracked. His silence terrified her; she thought she could hear him breathing painfully. Suddenly it occurred to her that she might have injured him. "Tom, I'm sorry," she said. Still there came no answer; another plank fell to the floor, and she thought she could glimpse a shape rising to its feet. A final intuition came to her. "Come on, Tom, I won't tell anyone," she called. The movement stopped; so did the breathing. At last feet shuffled towards her, and she heard a tight brushing followed by an elastic snap, as of a garment being pulled off; it was the stocking.

A Story on Page One

Richard L. Hobart

DETECTIVE SERGEANT FLYNN, idling at headquarters, thrust
out his hand and grabbed the jangling telephone.

Without moving from his comfortable position, he listened intently to the voice over the wire for nearly a minute. Then,
slamming the receiver back on its hook, he swung into action.

He walked swiftly from the Central Station and hopped into the
official car parked in the police lot across the street. Seven minutes
later, he was pulling up at the curb in front of the *Daily Post.*

As he stepped from the car, a man rushed out to the sidewalk
and grasped his arm. Flynn recognized him as Wilcox Barron, special feature writer for the *Post.*

"It's terrible, Sergeant. Malcolm Keith has been murdered!"

Flynn grunted. "Murdered, eh? When and how did it happen?"

As the two walked through the deserted front offices, Flynn
heard the story from Barron. It must have happened about nine
o'clock that night, he said. He (Barron) happened to meet Keith
down town and the editor asked the feature writer to accompany
him to the newspaper office. The "bulldog" edition of the *Post* went
on the press at ten each night. This edition was dated the following
day and was sent to those cities located too far away to receive a
newspaper on the date of publication.

It was the editor's custom to return to the office every night
around eight-thirty to see that this edition, amounting to nearly
twenty thousand copies, reached the mailing room in time for the
ten o'clock, eleven o'clock, and midnight trains. It was a habit of
long standing with the editor, a detail in the making of a newspaper
that probably accounted for the *Post*'s supremacy as a journal of
nation-wide renown.

Barron had lingered in the city room, looking over some late
wire reports still coming in on the automatic AP telegraph typewriter, relieving the night editor who went out for a cup of coffee.
Keith had gone to the stereotyping room to see that the plates for
the bulldog edition had been sent to the press room below. After
that, the editor had gone down into the press room. There, on the

paper-littered floor, the feature writer had found the body of Malcolm Keith, a welter of blood surrounding his head and shoulders. Then, after seeing that nothing could be done to aid the man, Barron had phoned the police.

The two men were in the press room now and joined a group of half a dozen pressmen and stereotypers standing about something, grim and still, on the cement floor. The body had been covered with a large sheet of white paper torn from a handy roll.

Detective Flynn examined the body of the dead man carefully.

The lethal wound had apparently been inflicted with a large spanner wrench that lay on the floor to one side. The blow had been struck with quite some force, for there was a deep indentation on the dead man's head just over the left ear.

"You found the body, Barron?" asked Flynn of the feature writer.

"Yes, Sergeant, just as I explained to you," answered Barron, somewhat nervously.

"And that was about nine o'clock to the best of your memory?"

"Yes. I would say that nine o'clock wouldn't miss it over five minutes either way."

"How do you explain the fact that the press room was apparently deserted at that time?"

The feature writer turned to the foreman of the press room.

"Jenkins, you boys don't get on the job until around nine-thirty. Right?"

The foreman nodded.

Barron turned back to the detective. "I do remember I had just discovered the body, when Jenkins and two of his men entered. I yelled at them and they rushed over. Of course, we were all pretty excited for a few minutes, but I knew headquarters should be notified at once."

The pressmen nodded in agreement.

"This stereotyping room," asked Flynn—"it's not located on this floor?"

Barron shook his head. "No, the stereotyping department of a newspaper is usually next to the composing room—where the type is set, you know. The press, being heavier, is usually on the solid floor of the basement in newspaper plants. The finished plates are cast in the room above, one for each page, you know, and then sent down here on that gravity chute over there in the corner."

The newspaper man pointed, and Sergeant Flynn noticed for the first time the gravity chute down which the finished plates slid. It was built in a half-round shape so that the plates from the casting machine, also half-round, would not be warped or bent on their speedy trip to the press room. Later, these plates were bolted onto the cylinders of the huge Goss printing press and the endless width of newsprint passing over them was imprinted and then folded into individual newspapers.

As he looked, there was a noise overhead and one of the heavy cast metal plates slid rapidly down the chute. It reached the lowest part of the track while moving at a very fast rate and then passed up an ever increasing incline, which retarded the speed until it came to a full stop.

Wilcox Barron saw the question in the detective's eyes as the heavy cast metal plate came to a stop.

"In this business, Sergeant, we have to keep on, no matter what happens or what our individual feelings might be. It may seem a terrible thing to you, but I am getting out an extra on the death of Malcolm Keith. I'm sure he'd want it that way. You see, a newspaper man's one obsession is to scoop the opposition. That's why—"

"I see," nodded Sergeant Flynn. Tearing off a piece of the white newsprint from a nearby roll, he picked up the spanner carefully, so as not to obliterate any fingerprints that might be on its oily surface. Carrying it over to a strong electric globe, he examined it minutely.

The spanner was coated with a thin covering of oil and dust, and the detective could see no fingerprints on the heavy tool. Stooping, he examined the floor around the spot where he had picked it up. He grunted soberly and stood erect, wiping his grimy hands on his handkerchief.

There was a clattering from the chute in the corner, and another cast metal plate dropped to the level of the press room floor. Sergeant Flynn turned his head and caught the feature writer eying him.

Wilcox Barron shook his head sadly. "A story on page one for the Chief! It's only something big that makes the first page, Sergeant. To a newspaper man that's the final test of public attention, the culmination of notoriety or fame. Yes, the Chief gets an eight-column streamer on page one."

Wilcox Barron motioned with his hand to the pressmen, and they began making the huge press ready for its run. Upstairs, Flynn could hear the shrill chatter of hastily assembled newsboys, eager for the ink-damp sheets that soon would come off the press by the thousands.

Sergeant Flynn walked over to the nearby wall where, in a small enclosure, were located the showers and wash basins for the press crew. The detective stayed in the washroom for nearly five minutes. Then he returned to the press room, but walked on past the limp form on the floor and stopped at the edge of the chute used for the cast metal plates.

"Jenkins!" The detective called the press room foreman over to him. "Get an old plate and put it right here on the lowest level of the chute. Then get another old plate, go upstairs and send it down."

Jenkins clearly wanted to ask questions, but without putting them into words, obeyed Flynn's instructions.

The foreman, in the stereotyping room above, shouted that the plate was coming. Sergeant Flynn answered, and the plate hurtled downward, striking the other one at the lowest level of the chute. It struck with considerable force—enough either to seriously injure or kill a man if it hit, say, above the ear or on the temple!

Meanwhile, the coroner and his physician had examined the dead editor and the wagon had called for the body.

Sergeant Flynn was leaning against a roll of newsprint in a deep study. The presses clicked into action with the pushing of the Cutler-Hammer control buttons and then roared into full speed.

The press room foreman handed Sergeant Flynn two copies of the *Post,* damp and smelly from the press. Without looking at them, Flynn folded them twice and stuffed both copies into his side coat pocket, nodding his thanks. Thirty minutes later, after a number of photographs had been taken by the police camera man, Sergeant Flynn shook hands with Wilcox Barron preparatory to leaving.

"Better come to the coroner's inquest tomorrow at ten o'clock," suggested the detective as he walked away.

"Certainly, Sergeant. Thanks a lot for helping out in this terrible affair." The feature writer shook hands abstractedly and watched the detective climb the stairs to the floor above.

At ten o'clock the following morning the coroner held his inquest. A number of officials, the crew of the press room, the stereotypers, Wilcox Barron, and Sergeant Flynn were those called for the official investigation.

At the end of a ten-minute session, the coroner pronounced that Malcolm Keith was "done to death by a lethal weapon, probably a press room spanner, in the hands of a party or parties unknown."

Gray faced, Wilcox Barron shook his head sadly. Apparently, the death of his chief was a hard blow. Sergeant Flynn sat off to one side, seemingly paying no attention to the questions asked unless directed to him.

The inquest was about over. Sergeant Flynn rose and stalked up to a position in front of the gathered men.

"Mr. Coroner, I'd like to ask some questions, if you please."

The official nodded and Flynn turned to face the assembled men.

Again Sergeant Flynn turned to the coroner. "Mr. Coroner, you don't mind if I smoke, do you?"

The coroner nodded his permission.

Sergeant Flynn extracted a cigarette from his case and placed it between his lips. With a muttered apology, he handed the case over to Wilcox Barron who accepted it.

"Can't take your last smoke, Sergeant," laughed the feature writer, seeing there was but one cigarette in the case.

"Go ahead and take it; I'll get some more," insisted Flynn, taking back the empty case. He turned to a uniformed policeman standing near the door. "Here, O'Flaherty, fill this case for me and bring it back in a hurry."

O'Flaherty nodded, took the case from the detective and walked from the room.

Sergeant Flynn smoked for a moment in silence, and then hit the yawning cuspidor unerringly with the flipped cigarette. He cleared his throat huskily.

"Gentlemen," he began, annoyingly deliberate, "I can't help thinking there are a number of points we haven't cleared up yet. I'd like to ask those questions now, with the coroner's permission."

Wilcox Barron shifted nervously in his chair. "Sergeant, I'd appreciate your getting through as quickly as possible, for I've got to get back on the job. I'm taking over Keith's work—temporarily, of course. I'm writing a special feature of his life that still needs some polishing up before I send it to the composing room. Poor fellow, he'd want the good work he's done to go on without a hitch."

Sergeant Flynn nodded.

"Sure, Barron, I'll make it snappy. But you're the one who'll have to answer the majority of the questions. First of all, you met your boss at about eight-thirty last night and accompanied him back to the newspaper office. He went downstairs, or to the stereotyping room, directly after arriving at the office. The stereotyping foreman said he was in his department not later than twenty minutes of nine. He stayed there not more than two or three minutes and then went on down into the press room while you, as you stated, stayed in the city room looking over night wire dispatches coming in over the AP automatic telegraph typewriter. That's correct, I believe?''

The newspaper feature writer nodded his head, puffing easily on his cigarette.

Sergeant Flynn eyed Barron keenly. ''That's a rather queer statement for you to make, Barron, when I've found out this morning that the AP wire service was out of commission for nearly forty minutes. The time given and *sworn to* by the night AP chief was 8:20 to 8:57. Therefore, it was impossible for you to watch that machine type reports when nothing was coming in at all. How do you account for the time between 8:40, when Keith left the stereotyping department for the press room, and around 9 o'clock, when you discovered his body?''

Wilcox Barron smiled indulgently. ''That's easy, Sergeant. Perhaps I should have said I was looking over the dispatches that *had* come in prior to the time the machine was out of order. I think Hull, the night man who wanted to be relieved for a time so as to get a cup of coffee, will bear me out in this.''

''I've already talked to Hull,'' snapped Flynn. ''He says *you* are the one who suggested he get a cup of coffee. He also stated he had already sent the AP flimsies back to the composing room after the service failed and that there was nothing to be looked over at all!''

Barron was still smiling. ''Oh, that could be just a difference of thinking. There were certainly some dispatches on the desk when I sent—er—when Hull said he wanted a cup of coffee.''

Flynn's face was harsh, cold.

''All right, Barron, have it your own way. But listen. You sent Hull away and then went to the press room and waited for Keith. You knew the men there wouldn't report for fifteen minutes. He came in and you hit him—with your fist, I believe—while he was looking at the newly cast plates on the chute. Just as you hit him, knocking him down, a stereotyper sent down a plate. That plate hit Malcolm Keith on the side of the head where he had fallen, face down, on the chute. It bashed in his skull.''

* * *

477

"That's quite a story you've concocted, Sergeant. But of course it's too ridiculously fantastic to have an iota of truth."

"Yeah? I *know* it's the truth, for the coroner's physician in his autopsy has proved that the head wound was made by the beveled edge of a cast metal plate. I proved to myself that it came down the chute with enough force to kill a man."

Wilcox Barron wet his lips and lighted another cigarette.

"Then," continued Sergeant Flynn, "you carried the body of Keith to the back of the press to where that spanner was on the floor, thinking it would be discovered as the weapon of death. You didn't touch that spanner, Barron, for fear of leaving fingerprints, but I saw that that spanner had been untouched for hours. After I picked it up, I saw its outline on the floor where dust had settled. I'll take oath it had been there for at least six hours, for its shape was outlined plainly in dust!"

"Regular Sherlock Holmes, aren't you, Sergeant?" smiled Barron.

"Now something else, Barron," went on Sergeant Flynn. "You got blood on your hands when you carried Keith over behind the press to that conveniently placed spanner. You arranged his body and went in the washroom. You washed your hands carefully, but you had sense enough not to use the towel. You used paper torn from a roll outside but, quite carelessly, threw it in that tall waste basket. I found the piece you had used and the chemist says there are blood stains on it. That set me to thinking—"

Suddenly the door opened and officer O'Flaherty entered the inquest room.

"Here's your cigarettes, Sergeant," said the officer.

"Oh, yes. Thanks." The detective was the only one in the room that caught the hint of a nod from O'Flaherty as he passed over the filled cigarette case.

"Barron," Flynn snapped the name as he leaned forward, eyes flashing, *"you killed Malcolm Keith!"*

"You're insane!" blazed the newspaper man, half rising from his chair.

"You killed him," Flynn continued, "because you hated him. You were jealous of his ability, of his position. I know it now. You heard that plate sliding down the chute and held Keith's head so it would be struck a bone-crushing blow. You got blood on your hands and washed it off just as I said. But first you carried Keith over to the feed end of the press, near that conveniently placed spanner on the floor. Then—" Sergeant Flynn paused dramatically, "—then, Barron, you wrote a front page confession of your deed!"

"What!" The scream welled from Wilcox Barron's white lips. His face was livid.

Sergeant Flynn laughed harshly.

"Yes, Barron," he said, "you wrote a front page confession of what you did and then signed it! You had blood on your hands and carried Keith over to where the paper is fed into the press. On a fresh roll of newsprint you steadied yourself for an instant with your right hand—the hand covered with the blood of Keith."

"It's a lie—a damnable lie!" screamed Barron, standing now, face contorted.

"No, Barron; the truth. I wanted your fingerprints, so I offered you a cigarette a while ago. There was just one left and I sent the case out to be filled by O'Flaherty after you had handled it. That was all arranged before we came in here. Your fingerprints were on that case, Barron, and—they tallied with this!"

With the last words, Sergeant Flynn whipped an extra edition copy of the *Post* of the night before into view. He unfolded it quickly, disclosing page one. Across the top was an eight-column banner line telling of the murder of the famous editor, Malcolm Keith.

In the center of the front page, dully red, was the imprint of a bloody right hand!

"Jenkins, your press room foreman," explained Detective Sergeant Flynn, "gave me two copies of the extra edition of last night fresh from the press. On the front page of one of them was the imprint of a hand, outlined in blood. It tallies with your fingerprints on the cigarette case, Barron. You put your hand on that roll of white newsprint which later went through the press and was printed into an extra. Your *signed* confession was on page one. You've made page one with your last feature story, Barron."

The Tennis Court

Brenda Melton Burnham

I SETTLE into the familiar contours of the wicker chair as the first sliver of sun appears over the eastern mountains. The screen door squeals its usual complaint, and Leah steps onto the porch, her entire concentration focused on the tray in her hands.

She arrives at the table and sets her burden down without spilling it, always a triumph to be savored, then pours my coffee and hands me the mug before dropping into the chair beside me. She reminds me of myself at twelve, all legs and eagerness; physically racing to catch up with her mind while emotionally still clinging to childhood.

"Gonna be another hot day," Leah says, using her grownup voice as she picks up her glass of milk.

"A scorcher," I agree.

We sip our refreshments in our best tea party manner. I can usually last longer than my granddaughter at this game of Let's Pretend; I've had years of adulthood in which to practice.

Sixty yards in front of us, across the slope of grass turning brown in the August heat, the men of the family bend their energies—and their backs—to the cause of tearing out the old tennis court. The noise of the heavy jackhammers echoes against the foothills.

"I was your age when my grandfather built this court," I say, even though I know I've said it many times before.

Nineteen forty-two saw countries at war and families in turmoil. Our family was no different. My father and Uncle Theo joined the army in the spring. When they left for training, my mother and my aunt packed up their children and returned here, to their father's farm.

I fell asleep to the sound of my mother and her three sisters as they laughed and talked among themselves. I woke in the morning to the same sounds—as though they had continued, unceasing, throughout the night. Bras and panties hung from the clothesline in the mud room. Lipsticks and powder lay atop the dresser scarves, next to the old inlaid brushes and tortoiseshell combs. Chinese checkers and dominoes decorated the side table in the living room, always ready and waiting for a quick game.

In the early mornings, before the sun reached the valley, my grandfather went fishing on the river at the back of the farm. Often one or more of his daughters accompanied him as they had done when they were young.

In the evenings, after dinner, we sat on the porch to catch the air and listen to Gabriel Heater on the radio. I helped turn the crank on the ice cream maker. We watched my seven-year-old sister and Aunt Marge's five-year-old twins chase fireflies.

Always, *always* my grandfather had dominated this house, these lives. Even when he wasn't present, his shadow was. But 1942, in the Krueger household, was to be the year of the women.

"C'mon, Sonia," they would call to me. "If you want to go with us you'd better hurry."

And of course I wanted to go with them. Every morning I examined my fat child's chest for signs of a bosom. I tried to brush my hair in a pageboy the way Aunt Trudy, the youngest of the sisters, did. Aunt Inga taught me to play cribbage and the strategy for winning at dominoes. Aunt Marge showed me how to use her nail polish. My mother let me stay up after the younger kids had been put to bed.

"I'm coming," I would call with one last glance in the mirror.

"Have you got the rackets, Inga?"

"Don't forget the balls this time, Liz."

Every afternoon we headed for the park in town where I watched my sister and the twins while the four women played tennis. I had never realized how beautiful they were with their blond hair and white teeth and strong, healthy bodies.

Soldiers and civilian personnel from the nearby military base realized it as well. There was always a contingent of them waiting to challenge the Krueger women. My mother, Marge, and Inga had no favorites and soundly defeated most comers, but Trudy was soft on a thin, dark, intense young man named Ira Glass.

It was a day like all other days as we headed home. Early June, perhaps, when the sun still promised a summer that would last forever. The car seats burned the backs of my legs, and my throat tasted of dust. The other women were teasing Trudy.

"You should've had the last point, Trudy. Don't give away the game just because you give away your heart."

"Tennis matches start with love. They don't always end that way."

"Oh, Ira, my wonderful one."

Trudy protested loudly and they all laughed.

When we got home, Grandfather waited on the porch. "Where have you been?" he shouted in German.

"Speak English, Poppa," Marge said.

"Playing tennis," Inga said. "At the park."

"Tramps! Strumpets! Parading yourselves in front of those men!"

I huddled back with the little kids, trying to be ignored.

"Was it hot that summer, Gram?" Leah asks.

"Hotter even than now," I reply.

The heavy pounding of the jackhammers ceases just as the sun pops over the ridge. My daughter comes out of the house with a pitcher of lemonade to refresh the laboring men before they begin the effort of removing the moss-stained chunks of concrete.

Trudy had worked as a druggist's assistant in town and Inga as a secretary. Within a week of each other they were fired from their jobs. I was shooed from the room both times and was forced to listen at the door.

". . . a sympathizer," Trudy sobbed.

"Silly man," my mother said.

"If only Poppa wouldn't insist on aggravating them."

"They're afraid," Marge scoffed. "That's all. It's the war."

"Besides," Inga said, "it gives us more time to be together."

And always the young men waited at the courts. More and more now Trudy and Ira were a pair. He gave her a pin, a gold tennis racket with a tiny ball of glittering stones. She gave him a silver ring she'd worn as a child; he wore it on a chain around his neck.

Some nights Trudy slipped out the side door after everyone had gone to bed, and I knew she went to meet Ira. I discovered this by accident one night when I got up to go to the bathroom. When I came out, my mother was waiting in the hall.

"What's wrong?" I whispered.

"Nothing. Go back to bed."

"But I saw Trudy . . ."

My mother focused a hard look on me. "Yes? What did you see?"

"Nothing."

My mother put her arm around my shoulder and kissed the top of my head. "It isn't easy growing up, *liebchen*," she murmured into my hair.

"Were you happy that summer?" my granddaughter asks.

"Oh yes," I reply. "Yes, I was happy."

Throughout the whole time my grandmother cooked. A short, round woman, she left the sanctuary of her kitchen only to feed her precious birds, calling to them in her native tongue. "Come, my pretty ones, come see what I have for you. Come, come."

July days melted one into the other. The temperature continued to soar. My grandfather seemed to shrivel with the heat while the women plumped out and grew taller and stronger. On the court their faces shone with perspiration. The tennis dresses whipped around their thighs. They were Valkyries . . . Amazons. I thought they were indomitable.

One day, as we walked to the car, a woman ran up and spat in Inga's face. "Nazi bitch!" she screamed, her face twisting with the ugly words.

Inga calmly wiped her cheek with the towel she had been carrying while my mother and Marge marched along beside her, their expressions closed and inscrutable. Trudy and I and the little kids stumbled alongside, silent with shock.

Another time, as we were driving past, a gang of boys threw rocks at us.

"You mustn't let it upset you, Sonia," Marge said to me. "They don't know who to take their anger out on."

"But we're Americans. Aren't we?"

"Of course we are."

"Even though some people forget it," Inga added.

"Were you surprised when your grandpa decided to build the tennis court?" Leah asks.

"You might say that," I acknowledge.

Out on the lawn the men finish their lemonade and bend to their labors once again. They tie handkerchiefs about their heads to keep the sweat out of their eyes. Their bodies glisten with moisture.

* * *

When we came down to breakfast that morning in early August, Grandfather was outside, astride his tractor. Behind him the huge discs chopped up the once-green lawn.

"What's he doing?"

"What in the world . . ."

"He's tearing up the whole yard."

"You want to play tennis, *ja?*" he called out to them. "Fine. I build you a tennis court."

The women looked at each other and said things with their eyes.

The next day the Gruener brothers arrived and agreed to pour a concrete slab when Grandfather had the ground ready.

"Does this mean we won't be going to town anymore?" I asked. The women glared at me.

"No need," Grandfather said.

Our outings took on a desperate air those last days.

"We can always invite people over to play," Inga suggested.

"Can't you see it?" Marge said. "Poppa standing at the gate, checking everyone as they come through?" She laughed.

"He'll never let Ira come," Trudy said. She nibbled at the corners of her stubby red fingertips.

Her sisters didn't answer.

"Oh god, what'll I do?" she cried out.

"Everyone must've been pretty excited," Leah remarks.

"It was a pretty exciting time."

Already the heat is building. In front of us, their muscles bulge as the younger men load the concrete pieces on the flatbed truck.

Every day Grandfather worked, harrowing, leveling, then building the forms for the concrete slabs. Every day the women's voices grew shriller.

"You really needn't tear up the yard like this for us," my mother, being the eldest, said at dinner. "Why don't you put in a flowerbed for Momma?"

"Momma has enough flowerbeds."

"We don't mind going into town."

"Even when someone spits on you?"

The women darted glances at one another. "We do have friends there," Marge said.

"Invite them here."

"Poppa," my mother said, "we *like* going to the park."

484

"I will not have my family spit on." Grandfather's fist crashed onto the table. Dishes rattle. One of the twins began to cry. Grandmother decided to make coffee cake so it would be ready for breakfast the next morning. "I will not have my daughters behaving like sluts. Do you hear me? You will play here or you will play nowhere."

Trudy jumped up and ran from the room.

In town the next day Trudy and Ira took the car while the others played tennis. Afterwards, as we were driving home, she said, "It's decided. We'll go tonight and be married over in Slocum County." Her eyes glittered, and she bit her lip nervously.

"Trudy, are you sure?"

"Of course I'm sure. I love him. He loves me."

"Then bring him home. Poppa will give in when he knows you're serious."

"No. He won't. And you know it. He still has one foot on German soil."

"But you can't sneak off . . ."

"If you don't want to help me, you don't have to. I'll do it by myself."

"We'll help you," Inga said.

"I'll bet you couldn't wait until the court was finished, right?" Leah prompts.

"It seemed to happen very fast." I close my eyes and let the heat seep into my bones.

"How do I look?" Trudy twirled, fluffing her hair, showing off her soft white dress. The little gold racket pin gleamed at her breast.

"You look beautiful," I said. The others nodded.

They all hugged each other, then my mother and Trudy slipped out the bedroom door and down the dark stairs. I rushed to the window and watched my youngest aunt disappear across the lawn.

And saw the other figure step out of the barn behind her.

"Someone else is out there," I whispered.

The others rushed over. "You're seeing things, *liebchen*," Inga said.

"No, no, I'm not!"

The door opened and my mother came in, her face pale. "Poppa was waiting by the barn. He's following her. He must've known about them all along."

"How could he know?"

"How did he know about the spitting? It's a small town. I tell you he knows."

"What'll we do?"

"What can we do?"

"Why didn't you go after her?"

"It was too late." My mother shrugged her shoulders and shook her head. "It was too late the minute Trudy stepped out the door."

We sat in the silent bedroom and waited, our ears straining to hear a strange noise among the night sounds, afraid to speak for fear of missing it.

There was no missing it when it came. Trudy raced back across the wet grass, slamming the screen door behind her, pounding up the stairs and into the room. Her hair hung in tangles. A huge red mark ran across her cheek. Dark stains covered her dress. The bodice was ripped and the tiny pin gone.

"Oh, Liz," she cried, "I'll never see him again," and fell into my mother's arms.

"Trudy, did you and Ira—" Inga paused. "You aren't pre—"

Marge turned to me, bumping Inga with her elbow. "Go to bed, Sonia."

"But I want . . ."

"Go to bed," my mother said.

"I still don't understand why you never played tennis, Gram," my granddaughter says.

One of the men—is it Max? or Charley? I can't tell—stops digging and kneels to work at the dirt with his hands.

I never heard Grandfather come back. I woke late the next morning. No air moved through the silent house. Dressing was an effort. My clothes felt heavy on my body as I walked down the stairs. Mother and Marge and Inga were down by the dock. My sister and the twins dug ditches in the mud, something they weren't normally allowed to do. The women talked of the heat and answered the little kids' questions about bugs and dirt and trees. From the front yard we could hear the sounds of the Gruener brothers pouring the concrete slab for the tennis court.

"I've always hated this court," I whisper. To Leah? To myself? To the past? "Always."

The kneeling man—it is Max; I can see the bright cloth tied

about his head—calls to the other men. They gather around him. I hear their exclamations but can't make out the words.

My mother discovered Trudy's body when she went upstairs to check on her. The coroner's report said "suicide while of an unsound mind." It was assumed she had gotten the sleeping pills when she was working at the drugstore.

Two MP's from the army base came to the house a week later. Ira Glass had gone AWOL, and they were trying to locate him.

"But I don't understand," Leah persists, her eyes full of the innocence of youth. "If you hated it so much, why did you wait until now to tear it out?"

All the men scrape at the earth with their hands.

"Pour me another cup of coffee, will you, dear?" I say.

The morning the heat wave broke, my mother and Inga went fishing with my grandfather. When the boat returned to the dock two hours later, only the women were aboard. They came ashore silently, their backs erect, their wet clothes dripping on the soft green grass.

"Poppa had a strike and had started to reel it in," they said, "when he dropped his pole and clutched at his chest."

"He must've had a heart attack," they said.

"He was overboard before we could catch him," they said.

"It was downstream where the current was strongest. That was where he always liked to fish, you remember," they said.

"We went in to help him, but he never came up," they said.

The police decided against dragging the river. His body surfaced four days later several miles away. He was buried in the family plot next to Trudy.

They're all gone now . . . Trudy . . . Mother . . . Marge. Inga, who never married, died a week ago. After the funeral I asked my son Karl and my son-in-law Max, Leah's father, both stalwart, upright men, to tear out the tennis court.

Now the men walk up to the porch in a group. They let Karl lead.

"We found—" he begins, then stops to take a deep breath. "There were bones under the concrete, Mother." He holds out something. "And this." A set of dog tags. And a tiny silver ring.

I take the small objects in my hands. They are still cool from the dark, damp soil. I am aware of so many things. The heat from the sun, the river singing in the distance. The contours of the old wicker chair. Of debts owed and the debts paid.

My granddaughter, unusual for her, sits silent beside me.

"Mother," Karl says softly, fearful of startling me. "We'd better call the police, don't you think?" He looks at me. Waits. A good son.

"Yes," I answer. "You're right. We must."

The Test

Maurice Level

NOT A MUSCLE quivered as the man stood with his gaze fixed on the dead woman. Through half-closed eyes he looked at the white form on the marble slab; milky-white it was, with a red gash between the breasts where the cruel knife had entered. In spite of its rigidity, the body had kept its rounded beauty and seemed alive. Only the hands, with their too transparent skin and violet finger-nails, and the face with its glazed, wide-open eyes and blackened mouth, a mouth that was set in a horrible grin, told of the eternal sleep.

An oppressive silence weighed on the dreary, stone-paved hall. Lying on the ground beside the dead woman was the sheet that had covered her: there were blood-stains on it. The magistrates were closely watching the accused man as he stood unmoved between the two warders, his head well up, a supercilious expression on his face, his hands crossed behind his back.

The examining magistrate opened the proceedings:

"Well, Gautet, do you recognize your victim?"

The man moved his head, looking first at the magistrate, then with reflective attention at the dead woman as if he were searching in the depths of his memory.

"I do not know this woman," he said at length in a low voice. "I have never seen her before."

"Yet there are witnesses who will state on oath that you were her lover . . ."

"The witnesses are mistaken. I never knew this woman."

"Think well before you answer," said the magistrate after a moment's silence. "What is the use of trying to mislead us? This confrontation is the merest formality, not at all necessary in your case. You are intelligent, and if you wish for any clemency from the jury, I advise you in your own interest to confess."

"Being innocent, I have nothing to confess."

"Once again, remember that these denials have no weight at all. I myself am prepared to believe that you gave way to a fit of passion, one of these sudden madnesses when a man sees red . . . Look again at your victim . . . Can you see her lying there like that and feel no emotion, no repentance? . . ."

"Repentance, you say? How can I repent of what I have not done? . . . As for emotion, if mine was not entirely deadened, it was at least considerably lessened by the simple fact that I knew what I was going to see when I came here. I feel no more emotion than you do yourself. Why should I? I might just as well accuse you of the crime because you stand there unmoved."

He spoke in an even voice, without gestures, as a man would who had complete control of himself. The overwhelming charge left him apparently undisturbed, and he confined his defense to calm, obstinate denials.

One of the minor officials said in an undertone:

"They will get nothing out of him . . . He will deny it even on the scaffold."

Without a trace of anger, Gautet replied:

"That is so, even on the scaffold."

The sultry atmosphere of an impending thunderstorm added to the feeling of exasperation caused by this struggle between accusers and accused, this obstinate "no" to every question in the face of all evidence.

Through the dirty window-pane the setting sun threw a vivid golden glare on the corpse.

"So be it," said the magistrate: "You do not know the victim. But what about this?"

He held out an ivory-handled knife, a large knife with clotted blood on its strong blade.

The man took the weapon into his hands, looked at it for a few seconds, then handed it to one of the warders and wiped his fingers.

"That? . . . I have never seen it before either."

"Systematic denial . . . that is your plan, is it?" sneered the magistrate. "This knife is yours. It used to hang in your study. Twenty people have seen it there."

The prisoner bowed.

"That proves nothing but that twenty people have made a mistake."

"Enough of this," said the magistrate. "Though there is not a shadow of doubt about your guilt, we will make one last decisive test. There are marks of strangulation on the neck of the victim. You can clearly see the traces of five fingers, particularly long fingers, the medical expert tells us. Show these gentlemen your hands. You see?"

The magistrate raised the chin of the dead woman.

There were violet marks on the white skin of the neck: at the end of every bruise the flesh was deeply pitted, as if nails had been dug in. It looked like the skeleton of a giant leaf.

"There is your handiwork. Whilst with your left hand you were trying to strangle this poor woman, with your free right hand you drove this knife into her heart. Come here and repeat the action of the night of the murder. Place your fingers on the bruises of the neck . . . Come along . . ."

Gautet hesitated for a second, then shrugged his shoulders and said in a sullen voice:

"You wish to see if my fingers correspond? . . . and suppose they do? . . . What will that prove? . . ."

He moved towards the slab: he was noticeably paler, his teeth were clenched, his eyes dilated. For a moment he stood very still, his gaze fixed on the rigid body, then with an automaton-like gesture, he stretched out his hand and laid it on the flesh.

The involuntary shudder that ran through him at the cold, clammy contact caused a sudden, sharp movement of his fingers which contracted as if to strangle.

Under this pressure the set muscles of the dead woman seemed to come to life. You could see them stretch obliquely from the collar-bone to the angle of the jaw: the mouth lost its horrible grin and opened as if in an atrocious yawn, the dry lips drew back to disclose teeth encrusted with thick, brown slime.

Every one started with horror.

There was something enigmatic and terrifying about this gaping mouth in this impassive face, this mouth open as if for a death-rattle from beyond the portals of the grave, the sound only held back by the swollen tongue that was doubled back in the throat.

Then, all at once, there came from that black hole a low, undefined noise, a sort of humming that suggested a hive, and an enormous blue-bottle with shining wings, one of these charnel-house flies that live on death, an unspeakable filthy beast, flew out, hissing as it circled round the cavern as if to guard the approach. Suddenly it paused . . . then made a straight course for the blue lips of Gautet.

With a motion of horror, he tried to drive it away: but the monstrous thing came back, clinging to his lips with all the strength of its poisonous claws.

With one bound the man leaped backwards, his eyes wild, his hair on end, his hands stretched out, his whole body quivering as he shrieked like a madman:

"I confess! . . . I did it! . . . Take me away! . . . Take me away! . . ."

The Tin Ear

Ron Goulart

I T WAS a bad day to be ransacked, a yellow, smoggy, eighty-five-degree morning. John Easy tossed his denim sport coat over his desk chair and scratched the place where his shoulder holster chafed him. Beyond his office windows he could see limp palm trees, and sports cars flickering. Easy hunched his wide shoulders and cracked his knuckles. "How about Ad?" he asked his secretary. It was after ten and his partner hadn't yet called in today.

"He's still down in San Amaro, I guess," said Naida Sim, fanning herself with an empty file folder. "On the Shubert case, I suppose."

Easy frowned and unstrapped his gun. "This damn thing," he said.

"I thought you and Mr. Faber were going to get a burglar alarm in?"

"We got you the electric typewriter instead." He wiped perspiration from his forehead and squatted down. Spilled all across the gray rug were file folders, letters, envelopes, tape spools. "Wonder what they took."

"Something pretty important, I suppose," said Naida. She was a pretty blonde girl, slender and freckled. Her hair had no curl today.

Easy sniffed. "What's that smell?"

"Cinders in the air. Another fire over in the valley."

"Why did I leave the San Francisco police and come down here to L.A.?" Easy complained.

"I guess because they busted you after you were supposed to have taken that bribe," said Naida, kneeling down beside him.

Unbuttoning his top shirt button, Easy said, "Well, let's get this stuff gathered up and try to figure who swiped what."

The phone rang and Naida popped up to answer it. "Faber and Easy, Detective Service." She blinked. "He's right here, I guess."

To Easy, she said, "It's a Lieutenant Disney of the San Amaro police."

The phone was damp. "Yeah?" said Easy.

"This is Lieutenant Bryan K. Disney. We found your partner down here."

"Found him how?" asked Easy, inhaling sharply. "And where?"

"Dead. Shot twice with a .38, it looks like. In a place down the beach called Retirement Cove."

"What is Retirement Cove?"

"New senior citizens' beach town being built. Not finished yet and nobody living there. Workman found the body about two hours ago, spread-eagled on a badminton court."

"Damn," said Easy, grimacing at their secretary.

"What was he working on?"

Easy answered, "Nothing. He was taking a few days off. Vacation. He was a latent beach bum and liked to get the sun." A silver sports car flashed by and the glare made Easy duck.

Naida had started to cry. "I guess Ad's hurt."

"He's dead," said Easy. "Do you want to see me for anything, Lieutenant Disney?"

"You might come down and talk to me today sometime, yeah," said the policeman. "Anything you can say now? Enemies, affairs, that kind of thing?"

"Ad led a blameless life," said Easy. "But I'll think about it."

"My office is across the street from the equestrian statue of General Grant. See you."

Easy cradled the phone and wiped his palms on his thighs. "Well," he said. He sat down in his swivel chair.

"Why didn't you tell them Mr. Faber had been watching Mrs. Shubert for a week and a half?"

"I don't know," said Easy. "I've got a habit of not confiding in the police. Anyway, I want to check some things out myself." He strapped his gun back on.

"Maybe he found out something big," suggested the girl.

"I doubt it," said Easy. "Ad had a tin ear most of the time. If he heard anything important he wouldn't have known it probably."

"He was your partner."

"That doesn't mean he was an exceptional operative. We were probably going to bust up this partnership in another few months anyway."

Naida wiped her eyes. "I hate to have anybody I know get killed."

Easy looked past her at the bright morning. "I'll go down to San Amaro now. Clean up the office and let me know what's gone."

"Does this rummaging here tie in with what happened to Mr. Faber?"

"Maybe," said Easy, shrugging into his coat. "If Ad's reports on the Shubert case are missing it might mean something."

"Shall I close the office?"

"Why?"

"I imagined we might go into mourning for a day."

"Nope. Ad didn't have any family. That means we have to see him buried. We can't afford to lose a day. A client might walk in any minute."

"I guess you're not very sentimental."

"No," said Easy, walking out into the hot morning.

The real estate cottage looked down on a white stretch of beach. The San Amaro afternoon was relatively mild. Easy rested his arms on the half open Dutch doors and called in, "Mr. Majors?"

There was a purple-haired secretary, old and wide, sitting at the nearest desk and a thin blond man of about forty at the further desk. "Yes," the man said, half rising.

A phone rang and the secretary caught it. "Mr. MacQuarrie for you, Mr. Majors."

"I'll call him later," said Majors, walking out of the shadows toward the unmoving Easy. "Did you want to come in?"

"Out here would be better," said Easy. "This is what they call a delicate situation."

Majors had on a golf sweater, tweed slacks. He had a nice outdoor tan. "Who are you?"

"John Easy. Until today my outfit was called Faber and Easy."

"You're trying to sell me something, Mr. Easy?"

"Maybe," said Easy. "Protection and security. It all depends. Right now I want to find out who killed my partner."

Majors smiled, his lips pursing. "This is a very cryptic sales pitch."

"I'll be direct," said Easy. "You're Norm Majors, aren't you?"

"Of course. So?"

"For the past three months, from what I've been able to put together from the reports and tapes my partner turned in, you've been having an affair with a Mrs. Nita Shubert. We've been on the case a couple of weeks. That is, Ad Faber was down here at the request of our client, Mr. Shubert. Okay?"

Majors opened his mouth and studied Easy. He reached back and felt for a low rustic bench that fronted the cottage. "I didn't know," he said, letting himself sit.

"Didn't know what?"

"That we were watched." He straightened. "Tapes, did you say? That's illegal, isn't it?"

"So's adultery. I'm not here to chat on ethics, Majors. I wanted to see you."

"Why?"

"To ask you," said Easy, "if you killed Ad Faber."

Majors coughed. "No, Easy, no. No. I didn't."

"Did you ever see him? Know about him?"

"I told you I didn't."

"You were with Mrs. Shubert yesterday."

"No," said Majors. "Not at all yesterday. Nita said she couldn't get free yesterday." He put his knuckles against his cheek. "Wait. Your partner must be the one who was found down at Retirement Cove. A friend of mine is selling that and called me."

"That's right," said Easy. "I drove by it a while ago. It's not too far from the beach house Mrs. Shubert is renting for your meetings."

Majors rose up. "Shubert is aware of us?"

"For a week."

"Then what did you mean about protection?"

"The police don't know about you as yet. You might mention that to Nita Shubert."

"This sounds like blackmail," said Majors.

Easy shrugged and headed back for his car.

Easy called his secretary from a phone booth in a drugstore near the San Amaro town square. A few seconds after he'd stepped into the booth a teenage singing group appeared on a platform next to the soda fountain. They were singing about surf riding now as the place filled up with a sun-bleached after-school crowd.

"Are you in a saloon?" Naida asked.

"A soda fountain. What's happening there?"

"Did you see Lieutenant Disney yet?"

"I'm en route." A silver blonde in an orange shift jumped up on the entertainment platform. A big sign over the fountain said Grand Opening. All the guitars were amplified. "What's missing?"

"Nothing at all," said Naida. "I double-checked. But listen . . ."

"Any new business?"

"A man called you a couple of times but wouldn't say who he was. But listen . . ."

"Okay, what?"

"A final report came in from Mr. Faber. Mailed late yesterday in San Amaro."

"Well, tell me what he said."

"I'm trying. No tape this time. He said that Mrs. Shubert met somebody new yesterday. He listened in and got the feeling this was somebody she hadn't seen for a while. No names. He couldn't catch any name for the man. But the man mentioned money, a lot of it. And he wanted Mrs. Shubert to leave with him but she said no."

"Leave with him?" He had the impression the phone booth was gently rocking.

"To Mexico."

"This new guy came to the beach place she uses to meet Majors?"

"Yes," said Naida. "Is there some kind of political rally going on where you are?"

"It's a musical event. How hot is it in L.A.?"

"I guess about 92," answered his secretary. "Are you going to Lieutenant Disney?"

"Soon," said Easy, and hung up. He worked his way out of the thick crowd of teenagers. Until now, thirty-four hadn't seemed that old. Suddenly he felt his years.

Lieutenant Disney was almost too short to be a cop. He smoked cigarette-sized cigars and kept his hat, an almost brimless checked thing, on indoors. The walls of his humid office were papered with what looked to be long out-of-date wanted posters. He didn't tell Easy much, and Easy didn't tell him anything. Their interview lasted twenty-five minutes.

Kevin Shubert, Easy's client, made his money in some way that allowed him to be home daytimes. He talked to Easy beside a glass-enclosed swimming pool. The grounds around the big low Moorish house were almost sufficient to let the place be called an estate.

"I'm in perfect health," Shubert said. He was tall and about fifty, with his balding head crewcut. "You'd think all this anguish Nita heaps on me would make me ill."

"Maybe you'll collapse unexpectedly," said Easy.

"Does the murder of your partner tie in with Nita and her lover?" Shubert asked him.

Easy was sitting at an awkward angle in a striped canvas chair. "Probably."

"Do the police know about us?"

"Not by way of me. But they could find out," said Easy. "You told me you'd been married how long?"

"Nearly two years. My second marriage. Nita's first."

"You met her where?"

"In San Francisco," said his client, making a flapping motion with his thin elbows. "Your old haunt."

"Something I'm trying to place. Something about the pictures of Mrs. Shubert you showed me. What was her name then?"

"Halpern. Nita Halpern."

"There was some bank scandal, wasn't there?"

The skin of Shubert's pale lips was dry. He moistened it with his tongue. "Well, yes. She was secretary to a bank official who vanished, a man named Robert L. Brasil. Three hundred thousand dollars vanished along with him. You may have seen Nita's photo in the press. Nothing was ever laid at her door, however. That was three years ago."

"I wonder," said Easy. "Is your wife around?"

"For a change, yes. She's in her studio. Nita paints a little."

"I'd like to talk to her."

"Listen, Easy," said Shubert, rising, "I'd like no more scandal to touch my wife. I appreciate your keeping things to yourself so far. What will it cost for you to continue silent?"

"You've already paid us," said Easy. "I'd like to see Mrs. Shubert alone," he added peremptorily.

"I assumed as much."

Large on the canvas was a faithfully rendered box of wheat cereal. Nita Shubert was rangy and dark, angular in yellow stretch pants and a shaggy yellow pullover. The small pitchfork wrinkles at her eyes indicated she was about thirty-five. "You've fouled things up, Mr. Easy," she said, putting a white-tipped brush aside. "You and your late partner. I don't even think it's legal to eavesdrop the way you apparently were."

"When did you first realize you were being watched?" Easy asked her.

"Kevin told me just a short time ago, when the death of your partner became known."

"Ad," said Easy. "That's Ad Faber, my partner, was given to being heavy-handed at times. I think he gave himself away yesterday somehow; yesterday, when you didn't see Majors at the beach house."

The woman didn't reply. She slowly squeezed earth-colored paint onto her palette.

"Ad had a tin ear," said Easy. "But sometimes he could tumble to what he was hearing. I think he heard something yesterday, and finally figured out what it might mean."

"I was with Norm Majors yesterday," said Nita Shubert. "No matter what you might believe."

"Ad must have gone back to your beach house last night, after he'd sent his last report off to me. Somebody spotted him and got worried."

"Yes?"

"Probably your ex-boss," said Easy. "Robert L. Brasil."

Her head gave a negative jerk. "He vanished three years ago."

"I want," said Easy, "to be clear on one thing. I haven't told the police any of this. For a consideration, nobody has to find out about Brasil."

"Nobody will find out anything," said the woman. "He's long gone."

"If he wants to stay vanished," said Easy, "he might think about as little as $20,000."

Nita Shubert turned her back on him.

"I noticed a motel down near your beach house, the Mermaid Terrace. I'll stay there tonight if anyone wants me." He studied the painting. "You spelled wheat wrong."

"Perhaps I wanted to," she said. Easy nodded and left.

Easy got the call at a little after nine. A muffled male voice told him to be at the #3 lifeguard station on the beach in a half hour.

The night was warm and overcast. The lifeguard station was down the silent empty beach, near a closed soft-drink stand. Easy found it early, but there was someone sitting up in the lifeguard chair.

The dark water glowed faintly, fluttering silently.

"Brasil?" Easy called to the figure on the tall-legged chair.

The shadow of the protecting beach umbrella hid the upper half of the man. He was wearing a dark coat, hands in the pockets. "I didn't know we were being watched and listened to," he said. His voice had a touch of chest cold in it. "I picked a bad time to come out of the woodwork."

"My partner bumped into you?"

"I had planned to spend the night in the beach house. He came poking around, not too covertly, and offered to keep quiet for a fee. He had figured out that I wasn't anxious to be found here in California."

"You shot him, huh?"

"Yes," said Brasil.

"Then drove up to L.A. to see if he'd turned in anything to the office."

"I'm cautious, and I don't like paying money out needlessly, Easy."

"I figured you didn't go in for payoffs," said Easy. He lunged and caught the man's legs, and jerked him from his perch. Brasil's head hit the lowest rung of the chair as he fell.

Brasil rolled and grabbed out a pistol from his coat pocket.

Easy dived sideways, got out his own .38.

Brasil's first shot went up and tore the umbrella into tatters.

Easy planted himself and fired twice. Brasil twisted up until he was almost standing and then fell. He died face down in the sand.

Easy put his gun away. He still didn't know what the man looked like.

* * *

His secretary said, "Iced tea," and put a paper cup on his desk.

The office was cleaned up now, and the sunlight on the street was not too glaring. Easy drank tea and leaned back in his chair. "You really weren't planning to blackmail anybody, were you?" Naida asked.

"Wasn't I?"

"No, you were just setting yourself up as a decoy to lure somebody out into the open, I guess."

"Run over to the delicatessen and get me a sandwich. No chicken."

"I think you really are sentimental," said the girl. "You actually do care about Mr. Faber and you wanted to avenge him. Right?"

"And don't take any of those dill pickles they give away."

"I guess you're not a bad person at all," said Naida, leaving the room.

Easy sighed and closed his eyes.

Today's Special

Dennis Etchison

"HOW ABOUT some nice bottom round steak?" asked Avratin the butcher. "Is today's special."

"No round steak."

"Ah. Well, Mrs. Teola—"

"Taylor."

"—Mrs. Taylor." Avratin the butcher tapped the trays behind the open glass, then thumbed back another display of cuts. "I got some nice, nice clods, can cut for Swiss steak if—"

"No Swiss steak."

Avratin started to sigh, pinched off his nose with his thick curving forefinger, which was getting cold. "Excuse me. I know what you want. For you, some nice, nice, very nice pot—"

"No pot roast, neither."

His hands began describing in the air. "Some lovely chuck, some darling rump, a little—" He squeezed the air. "—Tender, juicy flank steak, eh?" He saw her turn away, the gray bun at the back of her neck beginning to wag. "Some brisket for boiling!" He heard his wife's heavy heels in the sawdust and at that slapped his fore-head with both hands—*I give up*—for her to see.

"My, you're looking very well today," Avratin's wife cooed.

Muttering, Avratin slid the last tray back in place, grumbling to himself, sifting the red chunks of beef tenderloin through his fingers, which were now quite cold; the meat plopped back onto the paper liner and he slammed the glass, knocking the parsley loose from the top of the ground round.

"Yeah, you should hope you don't see my sister, Rose."

"Oh, Ro-sie. And how is her operation?"

"Don't ask."

"Well, Mrs. Teo—"

"Taylor. Taylor! My husband puts Teola in the book, nobody calls him." The gray bun wagged in growing impatience. "But now he's Manny Taylor. Manny Taylor! I want you tell me, would you call from the yellow pages a man with the name Manny Taylor?"

"Well," began Avratin's wife, standing closer to her husband, "what's good for your mister's business—"

"We should all live so long, I promise you. My God, my God." She shook her bun and hunched toward the door.

Avratin's wife cleared her throat. "Today special, we have some very nice fish, Mrs. Taylor," she called sweetly and waited for the woman to turn back under the creaking overhead fan.

"You got nothing I want," said the woman finally, only half-turning, shifting her brown carry-all to her other hand.

"Why, Mrs. Taylor," sang Avratin's wife. "You've been our faithful customer for thirteen years. Those years, they mean only that you should come to this? You're taking your business else-where now? God forbid that Lou and I should forget *our* friends so easy."

"You should talk, dearies. *You* should *talk!*" This she said directly to Avratin, sizing him up in his white apron as if he were an imposter. "You get Luttfisk back, then maybe we talk meat. That Luttfisk, he *knows* meat!" And she shuffled out the door.

A moment later, to no one in particular, to the passing cars, to the old man at the curb with the white beard and the stiff black hat, Avratin's wife called, "My Lou, he was owning this shop before that Luttfisk was starting in the business! Don't you forget that!"

But Avratin was shaking his head, reaching around to untie the strings, throwing his apron on the hook.

"Louie?"

He headed across the empty store to the back.

"Ask me why I'm closing an hour early. But ask me! Go ahead! You ask me about business, and I'll tell you. Business . . . is . . . lousy!"

Avratin's wife threw up her hands, imploring the ceiling fan to do something, anything.

In the tiny bedroom, by a single small lamp with the crisp, yellowed cellophane still clinging to the shade, with the sound turned down on the Johnny Carson Show, Avratin and his wife were having an argument.

". . . Twenty years in the retail meat business and you knife me in the back. Twenty years putting bread on your plate, only to have you—"

"Listen to this! He's too proud, too proud to admit a mistake . . . ."

"—Twist, twisting the knife!"

Reproach, recrimination, guilt, counter-accusation, self-deprecation. The old pattern.

And only to come to this: that at the end, the finish, before grumbling into bed, during the sermonette, Avratin raised his hurt face to the water-stained ceiling one last time to declare, before the gods and whatever other audience might be listening:

"All right, I take care of it, I take care of everything. No matter that Luttfisk tries to rob me, his own partner. I get a man can take care of the job. I promise you, the problem be fixed, once-for-all!"

At the Century-Cudahy Storage and Packing Co., the White Collar Butcher was a very important man. No one at the plant could say exactly why, though it had to do with the fact that he was the best butcher in the county, that he had the finest set of tools anyone had ever laid eyes on, and the obvious quiet pride he took in his work. It had to do with the way he picked his own shifts, coming in unpredictably and always with the attitude of a man who has already been at work for several hours. It had to do with the air of authority he carried with him into the walk-in, the indefinable look of knowing something that he would never tell on his thin, expressionless lips, his smooth, ageless face, his small steel-blue eyes that were perpetually set on a place somewhere beyond the carcasses and the warehouse.

Alone at night, the White Collar Butcher stood motionless before the freezer, his eyes on the temperature gauge. But they were not focused there. Then, slowly, surely, he turned his back on the hook beam scales and stood over his meat block. He moved his hand from the evenly beveled edges to the guard at the right of the block. His hand was heavy, a special tool itself, quite perfectly balanced, smooth and pink and tapered ideally to the handles which he now allowed his fingers to play over lightly: the meat saw, the cleaver, the steak knife, the boning knife, below them the small scale, the aluminum trays, the spool of twine and, to the left, the blackboard. Then, with smooth, automatic, practiced moves he took down his tools one by one and washed them, wiped them and rubbed the handles, proceeded to sharpen them on the slow grinding wheel and then the whetstone, touched up the edges with the steel and wrapped them individually in soft, protective leather.

He set the pouches out neatly and then, by reflex acquired through years of practice, slipped his hand into his trouser pocket and withdrew a folded square of white paper. With one hand he opened it and read the name and address printed there with a grease pencil in straight block letters. *The name and address.*

He refolded it and slid it back into his pocket under the apron. Another job.

Then, positioning in an easy, familiar stance, he reached for the wire brush and steel scraper and box of salt and began cleaning his cutting block, employing short, sure motions with his strong arms and shoulders, conserving his energy for the job to come. And as he worked on into the night, his tanned face and immaculately styled hair set off tastefully above the high, fashionable collar and wide hand-sewn tie that lay smoothly against his tailored shirt of imported silk, the whole effect suggesting a means far beyond his butcher's salary, was that perhaps the beginning of a narrow, bloodless smile that pinched the corners of his thin, efficient, professional lips?

For five nights Avratin hammered his pillow and spent more time than he should have in the cramped bathroom. Then the good news arrived.

Up went the noisy butcher paper painted with the proclamation he had kept rolled and hidden for three days now. He was nervous with anticipation as he tore off strips of masking tape and slapped it up across the plate glass windows. It covered the whole front of the store, right over the futile daily specials from the week past, as well it should have.

The first customers of the day were already waiting at the door when Avratin's wife finished dressing and joined her husband.

She stopped in the middle of the fresh sawdust floor, looking about as if by some transmogrification of sleep she had just walked into a strange, new life, or at least someone else's store. She smoothed her hair and gaped, turning around and around.

"This is a holiday? Or I'm sleeping still. Pinch me, Lou."

Avratin had pulled out all the trays in the meat case and was busy arranging his new, large display.

"Take it easy, take it easy, Rachel. You got your wish."

The last parking space in front filled up, and at last Avratin stood and leaned back and watched the women milling around on the sidewalk, pointing excitedly to the sign. He smiled a special smile that he had not used in years.

"Lou! Lou! Lou! You didn't do nothing too drastic, did you?" Then what he had said seemed to hit her.

She clipped to the door, shook the knob, apologized to the woman with the gray bun who was first in line, hurried back to get the keys, almost ran to the door and opened it.

Avratin watched her outside, shading her eyes, holding off their questions until she could get a good look at it herself.

She stood with one hand on her hip, one hand above her eyes, reading and rereading the banner with disbelief.

The women scrambled inside, heading for the meat case. He leaned back on his hands, watching them over the scales, a bright morning chill of anticipation tingling in his blood.

They stopped in front of the case, staring for long seconds.

Avratin wanted to speak to them, but held himself in check a moment longer.

His wife was the last to enter the store. She pushed her way through the inert bodies, ignoring the still, dulled faces on a few of which was beginning to dawn the first dim, uncomprehending light of recognition.

"Lou, I saw the sign," she beamed. "Is it true? Is it? Where is he?"

Avratin leaned forward. He spread his arms behind the transparent case in a gesture of supplication, palms out. His eyes rolled up to the creaking, slowly revolving fan and then returned to the display, newly arrived from the man in the high white collar, which he had just now finished arranging so carefully under the glass, the whole length of the counter, to the new cuts, strange cuts, so invitingly laid out, preserved by the cold, here something red, there something brown and almost recognizable, there a fine shank, there an opened ribcage, there a portion of a face you knew so well you almost expected it to greet you.

"Here," Avratin answered, in a voice he had not used in years. "Here! Can't you read the sign?

"LUTTFISK IS BACK!"

Very shortly thereafter the short, muffled cries began.

Triple Indemnity

Charles E. Fritch

THE THOUGHT OF KILLING her husband Jeffrey had never seriously crossed Helen Spindler's mind until the man in the gray flannel suit suggested it.

The man's name, he told her, was Jones, and he was a "kind of insurance agent."

"We already have a sufficient amount of life insurance," she told him, though she really wasn't sure just how much life insurance they had. Jeffrey had never confided that information to her, and she had no head for figures.

She started to shut the front door, considering the matter closed, but Mr. Jones placed his foot expertly in the way, efficiently blocking the door open.

"I'm not selling life insurance, Mrs. Spindler," he told her with a pleasant smile. "It's more like . . . *death* insurance. May I come in and discuss it with you?"

And before she could protest, he insinuated himself through the opening past her and was walking from the foyer into the living room.

Helen felt exasperation tug at her. She was supposed to meet Harvey at his apartment in a half-hour, to spend a blissful afternoon of carnal pleasure while Jeffrey labored at the advertising agency. Well, she'd get rid of this Mr. Jones in short order. What was he selling? *Death* insurance? That was strange. She'd never heard of that.

"Very nice place you have here, Mrs. Spindler," Mr. Jones said, gazing around the large living room at the expensive furniture, the tasteful paintings, the costly drapes.

"Thank you, Mr. Jones," Helen said. "Now about this insurance you're selling. Jeffrey—Mr. Spindler has quite enough—"

"One hundred thousand dollars," Mr. Jones said.

Helen stared at him. "What?"

"Your husband has one hundred thousand dollars on his life, Mrs. Spindler, with a triple indemnity clause."

"A triple . . ."

"—indemnity clause which will pay off three hundred thousand dollars in case of violent death."

Helen caught her breath. Jeffrey gave her a hundred dollars a week expense money, which had seemed like an awful lot to her. The notion of three thousand times that was mind-staggering.

Mr. Jones' smile broadened. "You and Harvey Brill could really have yourselves a time on that, couldn't you?"

Breathlessly, Helen nodded. "Harvey has always wanted lots of money. I give him what I can out of my hundred dollars a week, but—"

She stopped, the blood rushing to her cheeks as she realized what Mr. Jones had said—and what she was saying.

Mr. Jones laughed. "Don't worry, Mrs. Spindler, I'm not planning to tell anyone—including your husband—about your affair."

She watched him make himself comfortable on the couch, then she sat in a chair opposite him. She wet her lips uncertainly. The conversation had taken a strange turn. A stranger was sitting here in her home telling her he knew about her affair with a man who was not her husband, and she didn't know what to say to him.

"I'm also not going to blackmail you, Mrs. Spindler," Mr. Jones assured her, "in case that notion had entered your pretty head."

It hadn't. But now it did. Also, she felt a warm glow at his compliment. *Pretty head.* Yes, for a woman in her mid-thirties, she was quite attractive, not only in face but in figure as well. The admiring glances of Mr. Jones renewed her realization of this.

Mr. Jones leaned forward. "Perhaps, Mrs. Spindler, you're curious as to the purpose of my visit."

Helen nodded. "To sell me insurance, I suppose."

"Not at all," Mr. Jones said. "You have quite enough insurance. I am here, Mrs. Spindler, to see that you collect on the insurance already in existence."

Helen's eyes widened. "But the only way I could collect," she said, "would be if—"

"—if your husband Jeffrey died," Mr. Jones agreed.

It was Helen's turn to laugh.

"My husband is as healthy as a goat, Mr. Jones. He'll probably outlive us all."

"Not," Mr. Jones said, "if he has an accident."

"An accident, Mr. Jones?"

"An accident, Mrs. Spindler, in which case you stand to get from the insurance company not merely one hundred thousand dollars, but *three* hundred thousand dollars."

Helen Spindler caught her breath once more. There it was again, those large numbers. If she had that much money, she and Harvey could have a lot of fun together—even more, if that was possible, than they were having now.

Or would be having now, she corrected her thought and frowned, if she weren't sitting here talking to Mr. Jones. She stood up. "I really must ask you to leave," she told him. "I have an appointment—"

Mr. Jones raised a hand. "I fully understand. Harvey is waiting at his apartment for you." He rose. "I trust, however, you'll think over my offer."

"Offer? What offer?"

Mr. Jones sighed. Helen Spindler was a beautiful, a desirable, woman, but she was rather shallow in the brain department. He said, "Let me put it this way, Mrs. Spindler. I guarantee to arrange a violent accident for your husband in return for my fee, after you collect the money of course, of one-third of the insurance monies."

"One-third?"

"One hundred thousand dollars is my fee, but remember you have two hundred thousand dollars left over. And there's the bank accounts, the stocks and bonds, the personal property, this house and that land out in the desert."

Helen Spindler nodded thoughtfully. Two hundred thousand dollars didn't seem quite as much as three hundred thousand dollars. Still, it was a sizable amount. Besides, as Mr. Jones had pointed out, there were the other assets; she didn't know how much they were worth, but she was sure, now that she bothered to think about it, that it would amount to quite a bit all by themselves.

"You don't have to give me your answer right now," Mr. Jones told her. "Talk it over with Harvey. I'm sure he'll have some ideas on the subject. But don't wait *too* long. After all, I do have other customers, you know, and I operate on a first come, first served basis." He extended a white pasteboard. "My card."

Helen stared at the card, which contained the name *Mr. Jones* and a local address. There was no firm name, no telephone number. She followed Mr. Jones to the door.

"Good-bye, Mr. Jones," she said.

"Be seeing you, Mrs. Spindler," he corrected.

For a long moment after the man had gone, Helen stood by the door and wondered what she should do. Jeffrey was a good man, and she genuinely liked him. He was good to her, too. True, the fire had gone out of their marriage, and it had taken Harvey to rekindle the smoldering embers, but she didn't hate her husband enough to kill him.

On the other hand, she didn't love him enough to pass up the opportunity of getting a lot of money.

Perhaps it was a practical joke.

Yes, that was it—a practical joke. She smiled at the card and prepared to tear it into pieces—then changed her mind. She'd show it to Harvey. He'd get a good laugh out of it.

Harvey Brill didn't get a good laugh out of it. He stared thoughtfully at the business card and shook his head. "It's no joke. This man Jones knew all about your husband's insurance—and about us. What did he look like?"

"Mr. Jones?" Helen thought a moment. "Well, he was wearing a gray flannel suit, which I thought was kind of tacky and old-fashioned. He had dark hair with some specks of gray in it. Sort of ordinary-looking, otherwise, but kind of cute in a way."

Harvey stared at her incredulously. "Kind of cute?"

"Well, not as cute as you," she assured him, moving in to hug him.

But Harvey wasn't in the mood. He shrugged her off. "There's something funny about this," he said. "I don't like it."

She pouted. "But I've hugged you lots of times like that."

"No, no," Harvey said, trying in vain to keep the exasperation from his face and voice. There were times when Helen Spindler was so dumb he couldn't stand her. But she did give him money from her modest weekly stipend. His face softened and he held her close. "I'm sorry I snapped at you."

"That's okay," she told him, nibbling at his ear. "I didn't realize this would upset you or I wouldn't have mentioned it."

"I'm glad you did. It opens up an interesting possibility." He hesitated. "What do you think about—about having Jeffrey killed?"

She shrugged. "I hadn't thought much about it." She wasn't in the mood to think about it now, not with Harvey holding her close to his hard, young masculine body and with the masculine scent of him filling her nostrils and making her head swim.

"Without Jeffrey, it'd be you and me, baby," he reminded her, "all the time, and with two—hundred—thousand—dollars of our own to play with."

"Whatever you think best," she said. "But let's talk about it later, okay?"

Harvey Brill put it out of his conversation but not out of his mind. The thought of killing Jeffrey Spindler and marrying the rich widow had crossed his mind many times. But he knew that he was not a killer. He was too afraid of botching the job, or getting caught.

But if someone else did it, an expert, someone who could make it appear like an accident . . .

Two hundred thousand dollars plus in one lump sum was certainly better than the pittances doled out each week. A resourceful man could do a lot with all that money.

"I'm going to see Mr. Jones," he told Helen sometime later.

She struggled a rear zipper up the back of her dress. "Oh, that's nice. Are we going to have Jeffrey killed?"

Harvey smiled. Funny how easy, how casual, it seemed to talk about it. "Yes. We're going to have Jeffrey killed."

Helen left so she could be home when her husband arrived from work. She didn't offer to go with him to see Mr. Jones, but then Harvey didn't want her along. He was certain the "death insurance" man wouldn't mind talking to him. After all, he knew exactly what the relationship was between Harvey and Helen.

Harvey drove his ancient Plymouth to the address on the card, thinking how nice it would be to be driving a big shiny, expensive automobile when he had the money—but the address was that of a vacant lot.

"Damn!" He threw an annoyed punch at the steering wheel. So it was a practical joke after all!

He parked the car and got out, walked up and down the street for a few minutes, fuming. By the time he got back to his car a large black sedan was pulling up in back of it. A gray-flannel-suited man sat behind the wheel, motioning for him to get in.

Harvey opened the car door, slid into the front passenger seat, closed the door behind him. He indicated the empty lot. "I thought—"

"In my business, Mr. Brill," the man said, "It's better that I don't have a permanent address."

"You're Mr. Jones?"

"Of course. And you're here to negotiate a deal to have Jeffrey Spindler killed."

Harvey wet cottony lips. "You'll make it look like an accident, so the police won't suspect?"

"Believe me, Mr. Brill, I am an expert on these matters. I stage them very carefully, with the skill of a choreographer. The motives don't matter to me, but tell me, don't you feel a twinge of conscience in planning another person's death?"

Harvey shrugged. "Why should I? I've never met the man. And he's worth two hundred thousand dollars to me dead. So why not?"

"Why not, indeed," Mr. Jones agreed. "An admirable philosophy, Mr. Brill. I concur most heartily."

"I—uh—don't have to sign any papers, do I?" Harvey wanted to know.

"I think not, Mr. Brill. The fewer complications, the better."

Harvey breathed a sigh of relief. "Good. You trust us and we'll trust you." His eyes narrowed. "Hey, what's that?"

Mr. Jones had extracted a shiny thing from his jacket. "A hypodermic needle, Mr. Brill. This is how I render my victim immobile, so I can do what I want with him."

"Hey, wait a minute," Harvey said, backing away, "I don't want to know anything about it. Just do what you have to do, but don't tell me, okay?"

"I'm afraid I have to tell you, Mr. Brill."

Suddenly Mr. Jones plunged the needle in Harvey's neck and pushed the plunger.

Harvey yelped and slapped his neck where a drop of blood had appeared. "What'd you do that for?"

"Because you, Mr. Brill, are the victim," Mr. Jones said. "You were set up for this—oh, not by that dear, sweet, naive Mrs. Spindler, but by her husband Jeffrey."

Harvey knew he had to get out of the car—fast—but his whole body seemed to be growing numb and he couldn't move.

"Mr. Spindler doesn't show it, Mr. Brill, but he can be quite jealous, and lately the beautiful Helen has been getting indiscreet in her meetings with you. He decided to hire me to kill you—and make it look like an accident, of course."

"No," Harvey said thickly.

"Yes," Mr. Jones disagreed. "A pity I won't be getting much money for you—a mere ten thousand—but the method of death should be enjoyable. You've got an old car there, Mr. Brill. You'll have an accident in it, and you'll be trapped behind the wheel when the car catches fire. And you'll be fully awake during every agonizing second!"

"An excellent meal, my dear," Jeffrey Spindler complimented his wife across the dinner table. "You're really a marvelous cook."

Helen Spindler blushed modestly. "The automated microwave oven did all the work, my darling. Can I get you more apple pie and brandy sauce?"

"No, thanks, I'm stuffed. But tell me, how did your day go? Anything interesting?"

Helen thought about Mr. Jones' visit to her and her visit to Harvey Brill's apartment. "No. I just puttered about."

"A shame you don't find some outside interests," he said with a smile. "You know, go out and make new friends . . ."

"Oh there *was* something interesting that happened today," Helen said. "A Mr. Jones dropped by. Twice. Once when you sent him to me to set up poor Harvey for the killing, and later, after he'd killed Harvey, to offer me a proposition I couldn't resist."

The smile faded from Jeffrey Spindler's face. "What?"

Helen smiled and nodded. "Mr. Jones said he'd sell me a poison that was absolutely undetectable—for one hundred thousand dollars of the insurance money. He'll stop by later to arrange the accident."

Jeffrey Spindler half-rose from his chair, clutching his heart, then collapsed forward, his astonished face settling on the empty plate before him.

"That was a good idea you had, Jeffrey," his wife said. "Thanks. I never would have thought of it myself."

Twine

Edward D. Hoch

THE MAN BEHIND the hardware counter said, "Yes, twine. The old guy collects twine. Been doin' it for maybe twenty years now, ever since about the time his wife ran off with another man."

My eyes followed the progress of the tall man as he moved carefully between a display of power mowers and a stack of packaged fertilizer. From his left hand he trailed a loop of thick brown twine that he'd just recovered from the store's trash. I would have guessed his age at close to seventy, though it was difficult to tell with any degree of accuracy.

"Do you know him well?" I asked the man behind the counter.

"Just as one of the neighborhood characters. Name's Sentin Brock. He's retired from a civil service job. They claim he's got a ball of twine that fills a whole room in his apartment."

I found it hard to believe. "A whole room?"

The counter man shrugged. "So they say. Why don't you do a story on him for your paper? It ought to make a feature."

It was a possibility. We ran a weekly feature on unusual hobbies, and certainly a man who'd collected twine for twenty years would seem to qualify. I thanked him and asked if he knew Sentin Brock's address.

"That big old apartment house on the corner of the next block. I don't know the number but that's where he lives."

I went outside and walked down the block. It was a mixed neighborhood of older apartment buildings and specialty shops, hovering on the edge of lower middle class. I generally stopped here on the way from work, when I needed something at the hardware store. Today, with the temperature hovering near ninety and no rain in sight, I'd remembered we needed a new sprinkler for the yard.

I put the sprinkler in the trunk of the car and stood for a moment deciding what to do. I could phone Brock the following day from the office and request an interview, or I could go up there right now and try for one.

I decided there was no time like the present.

The building where Sentin Brock resided was one of the oldest in the neighborhood, but the landlord had kept it in good repair. The entrance was brightly painted and well lit, and I had no trouble finding Brock's name on the directory. I climbed the stairs to the third floor and knocked on his door.

"Who is it?" he called without opening it.

"Sam Garner. I'm with the *Daily Telegraph,* Mr. Brock. I'd like to speak to you about an interview."

The door came open a crack, but I noticed that the chain lock stayed on. "What d'you want to interview me for?" the old man asked.

"You're Sentin Brock?" I asked him.

"Yeah," he answered suspiciously.

"We run a hobby feature every week in the paper, Mr. Brock. Maybe you've seen it on Saturday mornings."

"Maybe," Brock conceded.

"They tell me you have a twine collection that's quite spectacular."

"Who tells you?" he snapped.

"I think I heard it at the hardware store."

The door closed momentarily and I heard the chain being removed. "I guess you can come in."

The apartment was clean and well-furnished in the style of twenty years ago. I saw nothing in the place that looked more recent. Even the television set was a model long since consigned to the junk pile by most families. "Nice place you have here, Mr. Brock."

"It's home," Brock replied. "Sittin' room, kitchen, two bedrooms and a bath. All I really need. Don't entertain very much any more."

"About this twine . . ." I nudged.

"I have it in a large ball. Twenty years' worth, in here."

I followed him into the nearest of the bedrooms. The ball of twine did not fill the room, as I'd been led to expect, but it was still a considerable sight. I guessed it to be better than five feet in diameter, tightly wound and knotted with care.

I ran my hand over its surface in admiration. "It's a beauty," I conceded.

"I got enough twine there to stretch around this whole city."

"That'll be handy if it starts to come apart."

"Huh?" he said, densely.

"Tell me how you started collecting it."

" 'Twas after my wife left me." He gestured toward the bureau where a framed picture stood. He was tall and handsome. She was a head shorter and maybe ten years younger. It was an old story. "I needed something to occupy me at night, something to keep my hands busy."

"I see." I'd taken out a pad and was making a few notes as he talked. "What would your wife think if she came back now and found this big ball of twine in the bedroom?"

"She won't be back," he answered firmly.

"Do you ever hear from her?" I asked.

"No. Not since the day she ran away with my partner. And I won't, now. She probably thinks I'm dead by this time." He patted the ball of twine as if it were his child, smoothing the ends, preparing to tie on the day's acquisitions.

"Mr. Brock, if I came back tomorrow with a photographer, do you think we could get a picture of you with your ball of twine?"

"I guess so."

"Fine. Then I'll be back." I held out my hand and was surprised by the firmness with which he shook it. In that instant I had my first real look into his deep gray eyes. He was an aging eccentric, yes—but I thought I saw something more there too.

Something I couldn't quite put a name to.

As I pulled into the driveway I saw that Vera was out in the rose garden, digging weeds. She looked up and brushed the dirt from her hands. "You missed dinner," she said simply. "The kids and I ate without you."

"Sorry I didn't call. I stopped at the hardware store and then decided to interview someone for a story."

Vera looked up, smiling without humor. "Was her name Angela?"

"God, Vera, I haven't seen Angela in months! You know that!"

"You haven't been late for dinner in months either."

"Let's not start all that again," I pleaded. "Angela is over! I was late and I'm sorry!"

Vera followed me into the house and fixed me a sandwich while I played with the kids. For a long time she didn't talk, but finally she asked, "Who did you interview?"

"Guy with a big ball of twine. Thought it might go as a Saturday hobby feature."

"A ball of twine?" she stared at me incredulously.

"But big! Takes up most of a room and it's growing all the time. He's been doing it for twenty years, since his wife left him." I told her in detail about my visit to Sentin Brock.

"The man's mad, Sam. You're not going to publicize that, are you?"

"So he's mad. Aren't most hobbyists?"

"Not like that! Not with a ball of twine filling a room!"

"It's taking the place of his wife," I said. "For all I know, maybe he kisses it every night."

We watched television for a while and went to bed a little after eleven. The heat of the day had tired me, but sleep would not come easily. I stretched out in bed and stared at the dark ceiling.

"Vera?"

"Hmmm?" she murmured.

"You awake?"

"I am now," she said resignedly.

"I was thinking about Sentin Brock."

"Who?"

"The man with the ball of twine," I explained.

"Oh." She didn't sound too enthusiastic.

"Vera, what if his wife never left him? What if she's still there?"

"Where?"

"Inside that ball of twine. What if he killed her and—"

"My God, Sam! That's horrible!" she was awake now. She sat up.

"I didn't say it was true. But what if—"

"Go to sleep, for God's sake! You're giving me nightmares!"

"It might be, Vera. He looked crazy enough. His eyes . . ."

She stopped me short. "I won't talk about it! Go to sleep!"

"There'd have been the odor at first, of course. But maybe if he wrapped the twine tight enough, and thick enough, it would be like the Egyptians wrapping a mummy. She was a small woman, at least on that picture."

"Go to sleep!"

But the vision didn't fade with the coming of the dawn. I wakened with the image of that big ball of twine still before me. Vera didn't mention it at breakfast, and neither did I, but I knew it was on both our minds.

I spent the morning in the newspaper morgue, looking through old clippings. The only thing we had on Sentin Brock was an item in the business column from twenty-six years back, announcing the formation of a small printing company under the name of Brock & Winner, Incorporated.

I checked our file of local phone books and discovered that the company had been listed for seven years, disappearing just nineteen years ago. Next I checked the current book for a phone in the name of Winner. There were three, and I started calling them.

The first number went unanswered, but on the second I found what I wanted. "Is your husband there?" I asked the woman who answered. "This is the *Daily Telegraph* calling."

"He's at work."

"Would he be the Winner who owned a print shop some years back?"

"That was his brother, Claude."

"Oh. Is he still in town?" I asked.

"Moved to California. Long time ago. Maybe twenty years now."

"I'm especially interested in his wife," I pressed on.

"Claude never married."

"A woman named Brock?" I prompted.

"That was a long time ago! So long ago I'd just about forgotten it."

"Didn't she go to California with him?"

"Say, what's this for? You're not goin' to publish this in the paper, are you?" The voice was almost hostile now.

"No, no—it's just background material. We're running a feature on Mr. Brock, and he happened to mention that his wife ran off with Winner."

"Well, she did no such thing! We always suspected Claude went out to California to meet her, but if that was the case, he was disappointed. She never showed up."

I thanked Mrs. Winner for the information and hung up. Nothing she'd told me had discouraged my bizarre notion of Mrs. Brock's fate.

After lunch I put in a request for a photographic assignment and drew a young bearded cameraman I knew slightly. "What is it this time?" he asked. "More politicians congratulating each other?"

"A man with a big ball of twine."

"You're kidding!"

"Wait and see."

* * *

Sentin Brock welcomed us to his apartment, and stood proudly by his creation while the photographer snapped away. "I'd told the neighbors I'll be in the paper," he said. "Will it be this week, do you think?"

"More likely a week from Saturday," I replied. "I haven't finished the story yet."

The bearded photographer went off to his next assignment, but I lingered at Brock's apartment. "More questions?" he asked.

"Maybe." I went into the bedroom and put both arms around the ball of twine. "You know what would make a great story? If we could roll this down to the street and unwind—"

"Get your hands off that!" he shouted, lunging at me.

"Hold on, hold on! Why so excited?"

"Just—Look, you've got your story. Now get out!"

"Just one more question, Mr. Brock." I edged past him toward the door. "What really happened to your wife?"

"Get out of here!" He almost shouted it.

"Is she in there, Mr. Brock? Is that where she is? I found out she never went to California with your partner. She just disappeared twenty years ago, didn't she?"

"Get out or I'll call the police!" His voice was edged with panic.

"All right," I said, going out the door. "But I'll be back."

On the way home that evening I tried to decide what to do. I could write the story as I had it and forget about what might be inside that big ball of twine. Or I could fill the story with my speculations and end up with a nice fat libel suit against me and the paper. Neither of those possibilities seemed satisfactory, and that only left one alternative—to tell the police what I knew, or suspected.

Vera was awaiting me at the door. "She called just now, Sam. You were late and you missed her."

"Called? Who called?"

"Angela, of course. Who else? Or is there more than one now?"

"Oh, for God's sake, Vera! Cut it out!" I snarled.

"When I answered she pretended she had the wrong number. But I recognized the voice!" Vera's voice was shrill.

"I don't even know if Angela is still in town." I tried to placate her.

"Don't lie to me, Sam."

I walked past Vera into the house. There was no sense talking to her when she was in these moods. And I had more important things on my mind.

I phoned police headquarters and asked for Sergeant Matthews, a detective I knew who trusted my judgement.

"How are you, Sam?" he said as he came on the line. "I was just goin' home."

I carefully explained what was on my mind. He listened, grunting from time to time, and said finally, "What do you want me to do, Sam? I can't ask a judge for a search warrant to unroll a ball of twine—not on the basis of what you've given me. It's all too speculative."

"I know it is, Sergeant. But I have a hunch about this one." I told him.

He was silent for a few seconds. Then he said. "Your hunches have been pretty good in the past, Sam. I'll go out tomorrow and talk to Brock. That's the best I can do."

"Thanks, Sergeant."

That night I dreamed of a giant ball of twine, rolling after me down a hill. Like those snowballs in cartoons, it kept getting bigger as it rolled. When I woke up I didn't mention the dream to Vera. She already thought I was a bit wild on this whole Brock business.

I went down to the office and started getting together some items for my weekly column on city life. It was nearly noon when Sergeant Matthews phoned.

"I checked out that Brock, Sam. The guy with the ball of twine. Nothing to it."

"What do you mean?"

"I mean the missing wife is back. I talked to her," he added.

"Back!" I exclaimed.

"That's right."

"Back, after twenty years?" I asked.

"Yep. She was in California, and she decided to come home."

I was never one to believe in coincidences, and I wasn't buying this one. "What did she look like, Sergeant?"

"Tall woman, elderly. Husky voice."

"I see," I said. I thought I did, too.

"She seemed quite pleasant."

"Was Sentin Brock in the apartment at the time?" I enquired.

"She said he'd gone off to the store. I waited around, but he didn't get back before I left."

"Sergeant, I saw a picture of Mrs. Brock. She was a short woman, and quite a bit younger than her husband."

"Then who—?"

"That was Brock himself, masquerading as his missing wife!"

"Could be," the detective admitted. "If it was, he sure took me in!"

"I told him I'd be back. He must have guessed I might call the police."

"Yeah," Sergeant Matthews grunted.

"Do you need any more proof, Sergeant?"

"That's no proof, Sam," he insisted.

"Get a search warrant for that ball of twine."

"Sam . . ."

"We've got to move today, Sergeant, before he can get rid of it somehow."

Suddenly the detective reached a decision. "All right, Sam— meet me there in an hour."

Sentin Brock opened the door when we knocked. He smiled at me and turned to Matthews without thinking. "How good to see you again, Sergeant."

That was all Matthews needed. "You didn't see me the first time, Brock. That was your wife—remember?"

The old man let out a cry of rage and tried to run past us to the door. Matthews grappled with him and managed to get the handcuffs onto his bony wrists.

Then we set to work unwinding the ball of twine.

The kids were playing in the driveway when I got home. I'd written my story and turned it in for the morning edition, along with the picture of Brock and his ball of twine that we'd taken the day before. It wasn't exactly the hobby story I'd planned to write.

"Did you finally finish with that business?" Vera asked me.

"All done. You'll read about it in the morning paper, if it doesn't make the evening news."

"You mean she was there?"

I nodded, washing my hands at the sink. "She was in there. And a pet dog too."

"How horrible!"

I shrugged and didn't say much. It hadn't been pleasant.

After dinner, while Vera was putting the kids to bed, I glanced

down the cellar stairs and noticed the light was on in my workroom. I went downstairs to turn it off.

I had no reason to look in Vera's laundry room. I hardly ever
did. But this night something made me open the door.

I didn't know what it was at first, spread out in lengths across
the floor, looking a bit like a giant spider's web. Then I realized that
it was twine. She'd bought a dozen rolls or more, and unwound
them in the basement floor.

I closed the door and went back upstairs.

"Vera?"

"Yes, dear?"

Then I saw her eyes, and I knew I didn't have to ask the
question.

Two Inches in Tomorrow's Column

Harlan Ellison

BENNY KICKED the electric blanket off his naked feet, patted
Bonnie on her naked stomach, and placed the telephone receiver to his naked ear. Three chuckles of ringing and
abruptly, on the other end, a cricket was rubbing its hind legs together. It was Candy, Orson Heller's right-hand boy.

"Mistuh Helluh's office," the cricket chirruped.

"Candy baby!" Benny was not smiling. "Like to talk to Mr.
Heller. This is Benny." Bonnie had lit a filter; now she handed it
across, and Benny puffed deeply.

"Jus'a'minnit, Mr. Mogelson. Mr. Helluh'll be right whichah."
There was the soggy sound of a hand coming across the mouth-
piece, a faraway voice, and the phone changed owners.

Orson Heller—who, for seventeen years, had been in charge of
the Combine's hit system, i.e., its assassination branch—cleared his
throat. As befitted the new owner of the Sunset Strip's poshest dining club. "Benny. How's my PR man?"

"Orson, I'm a hero."

"That so?"

The public relations man straightened in Bonnie's bed, and

flicked ashes unceremoniously onto the white pile rug. "So. Very much so. Remember I told you I'd make you a star? Well, by this time tomorrow, The Barbary Coast and its new owner—the celebrated Mr. Orson Heller—will be the hottest properties in Hollywood."

"You talk a lot, Benny."

Heller had not quite lost the thug tones he had employed for seventeen years. Or perhaps the weight of sixty-four men's souls—shot, stabbed, doused with acid, embedded in concrete, and fed to the fishes—rested heavily on the vocal cords as well as the spirit.

"What I'm trying to build you up for, Orson sweetie, is—"

"Don't call me those names, Benny."

"—uh, yessir, yessir, well, what I'm trying to tell you is that you get two inches in tomorrow's paper. And are you sitting down? Are you planted firmly? Are you ready for this? Ta-ra-ta-*taaaa!* You, oh employer of mine, will be two inches in *Bonnie Prentiss'* column."

The smirk came unbidden to Benny Mogelson's publicly related face.

The gasp was tiny, but audible, at the other end. "Bonnie Prentiss? Saaaaaay . . ." Heller drew the word out with awe and pleasure. "Benny boy, you are a winner. An authentic winner. How did you manage *that?*"

Benny's hand strayed absently to Bonnie's full breasts. Firm and still warm from the recent encounter. "Oh, just a little *schmachling*—a little butter—Orson. Miss Prentiss and I are old friends."

Heller was delighted. "Great, Benny, just great. I knew when I hired you on as PR for the club, I just knew, you were going to pan out. Glad to see it. See you tomorrow after the column hits the newsstands. A little bonus perhaps."

"Fine, Orson. Just fine. Talk to you tomorrow."

He racked the receiver and turned to Bonnie. She was really getting long in the tooth, he mentally noted for the thousandth time. The little crow's tracks were becoming more prominent, even with her heavy tan, evenly laid on by metal reflectors, poolside. And the sooty puddles of dissipation under the eyes were daily becoming a little harder to disguise with heavier and heavier layers of pancake makeup. Too many oversweet daiquiris, and too many overplayed young boys. Too many rocks in the rack with hustlers like Benny Mogelson, PR man supreme.

"That hood!" Bonnie Prentiss snorted viciously. "All the French cuffs, big studs and white-on-white ties will never make him anything more than a hood. Why do you associate with such filth, Benny?"

"Because," Benny replied nastily, snubbing the butt in the onyx ashtray, "this is a town full of teeth, Bonnie baby, and I have this thing about fang marks in my neck. Heller pays me a nice fee for getting him promo coverage. If I don't do it, some other *schlep*'ll do it instead."

"He's a dangerous clown," Bonnie said, rubbing herself up against Benny.

As he turned toward her again, feeling her body heat rise, Benny murmured softly, "Hey, baby, that, uh, that column already went to bed, didn't it? Tomorrow's items?"

"Mmm-hmm," Bonnie hummed, reaching her half-open mouth up to his. "Time for *everybody* to go to bed . . ."

Benny closed his eyes and moved in next to her. He had to close his eyes; he couldn't stomach making love to Bonnie with them open . . . the aging harridan . . . and with his eyes closed he could dwell in silence and darkness on the exquisite pleasure of the letter she would receive in her mail that day. The letter that would tell her it was all over between them; that he had been using her lust and his cunning against her for three months; bedding her in exchange for favorable items about his clients in her column. The letter that wished her hail and farewell, since he now had a happy and contented list of big-name clients who would stick with him despite the anger he knew she would direct against him.

". . . but it gets to be time for me to remember that I'm a human being, not a rutting machine," the letter concluded, "and there are other columnists I don't have to wallow in scum with, to get a mention. Bye bye baby. Stay well, and say hello to the next young patsy you sucker into your sack."

With eyes closed, and hands mechanically busy, Benny could dwell on the fact that he had outsmarted Hollywood, that the town had not gotten to him, that he had come out on top.

Yes, this time he was on top.

And after a while, she was.

Benny's tailor was fitting the new hopsacking sport jacket in the office (very Palm Springs: double-breasted, royal blue, military crest buttons), when the phone call came. It was a full day since he had last seen Bonnie, and he had been expecting this call. She had gotten the letter.

"Mr. Mogelson," said the switchboard girl, "Miss Prentiss on 45, sir." He pressed the button and Bonnie's voice came floating out at him.

"Benny darling, I got your letter."

He took a deep breath. What threats would she offer? "Sorry, Bonnie. But it's been a hard three months." He tapped his right cuff, holding the phone with his shoulder, indicating to the kneeling tailor that he wanted more length at the wrist.

"I understand perfectly, darling. Perfectly." Bonnie almost purred. Benny's eyes narrowed. She didn't sound angry.

"It was fun while it lasted, Bonnie, that's it." He tried to goad her into frenzy, trying to extract from her a tiny measure of anguish for the degradation she had heaped on him for the blackmailing hours in her bed of pain.

But Bonnie was soft as one of Dali's watches. "Benny, my sweet, I understand completely. I'm sorry I misused you. Well, I'll just sign off now, darling."

There was a golden pause.

"Oh, yes," Bonnie added, almost as an afterthought, "you know my friend Theo, at the Amusement Center? He also sends his hellos and goodbyes. Night-night, darling." And she was gone.

He was still holding the phone as the switchboard girl came back on. "Mr. Mogelson? Today's papers are here, sir. Do you want me to send them in with Diane?"

Benny answered yes, absently, and hung up the phone, still perplexed by Bonnie's call. No fury? No threats? There was something wrong. That woman had ruined better men than Benny Mogelson for less than what he had done to her. She was infamous in Hollywood; the most vindictive shrike going. And that comment about Theo, at the penny arcade. Now what the hell did she mean by that . . . ?

The office door opened and Diane came in, depositing a stack of daily papers on Benny's desk. "I'm leaving now, Mr. Mogelson," she said. "My afternoon with the dentist." She smiled at him with her almost complete set of capped teeth. Benny nodded absently; he was still thinking about Bonnie.

"Oh, there's a paper there from Miss Prentiss's office, Mr. Mogelson," she added, hand on doorknob. "It came over by special messenger a few minutes ago."

Benny had hurriedly rummaged through the paper seeking Bonnie's column before the office door had closed behind the secretary. He found it and scanned down the column till he found the item:

For T-Men curious about phony restaurateur Orson Heller's income tax, a reliable tipster informs this columnist that a careful study of safety deposit boxes in the Farmers' Trust, the Surety National and the Seaforth Savings & Loan under the respective names Seymour Sunson, Walter Moon and Kenneth Starzl will reveal interesting results. Mr. Heller's current enterprise, the shabbily renovated Barbary Coast boîte, fails to purchase for this gentleman the respectability denied him by a career as checkered as his tablecloths.

Benny's mouth was dry as chalk-dust. It was impossible. He had read the item before she had sent it to the newspaper. She couldn't *possibly* have changed it. The edition had gone to bed a day ahead of time, standard procedure for syndicated columnists, and there was no way of calling it back. He grabbed up a newsstand copy of the paper from the desk, and turned to the column. He'd been right. It was as she had sent it in.

Then what was this other, deadly, item?

He had no more time to wonder about it; the door to the office opened, and Orson Heller and Candy came into the room softly. "Leave!" Candy jabbed a finger at the tailor.

The tailor took one look at Candy, at the set of his yellow teeth against his lower lip, and nearly swallowed the pins in his mouth. He looked up at Benny Mogelson. "I said: leave," Candy repeated. The tailor left, hurriedly.

Benny found himself staring at the blued-steel bulk of a .38 Police Special, the cumbersome cylinder of a silencer marring its smooth muzzle length. "Orson, baby, I—"

"I got this by a special messenger, fifteen minutes ago, Benny buddy," Orson said gently, handing across the folded edition of Bonnie's newspaper.

One glance told Benny it was the bogus edition, and all at once, clearly and quickly, he knew what Bonnie had done. Theo, at the penny arcade, printed up dummy newspapers. The kind hick tourists bought, with jazzy headlines like HARRY SMITH HITS HOLLYWOOD, GIRLS TAKE TO THE HILLS!

And before Heller could get to Bonnie, she would somehow let him know it had been a gag, and get the real, the street, edition to him, saying Benny had thought it would be a funny bit, for his eyes only . . . or some-such drivel. But it would work; Heller would think ten times before giving Bonnie—as big as she was on the scene—a hard time.

But that wouldn't save Benny.

It would be too late, then.

"Orson, baby, sweetie, listen, I—"

"I've told you, Benny, don't call me those names," Heller said companionably.

The silencer chugged once, asthmatically.

Benny was spun backward, against the desk, and as he hit the floor, as the light began to flicker and dim, he realized they would never find his body. He would be gone, like most of the other men Heller had hit. Bonnie had fouled him good. Very good.

Today, Orson Heller had gotten his two inches in the daily edition.

And by tomorrow, Benny Mogelson would have gotten six feet, or possibly full fathom five.

And as the light went farther and farther away, finally fading out entirely, he contemplated the ultimate irony of his career; that Benny Mogelson would never, never even get his two inches in tomorrow's column. The obituary column.

Tyrannosaurus

Norman Partridge

S HE SAT in the back of the police car. The deputy sat up front, his face too white in the harsh glow of fire engine headlights. Her ex-husband's car stood in stark silhouette between the two county vehicles. With its trunk sprung open, the scorched Honda reminded her of a dinosaur skull.

Jaws open wide, ready to snap.

Tyrannosaurus, the killer dinosaur. That was the one it resembled.

"Can't we do this in the house?" she asked. "It was self-defense.

You have to believe that. If I hadn't ended it tonight, he would have come back again."

"We have to get your story, Mrs. Rose."

"I changed my name after the divorce. It's Janet Perkins."

"Okay, Ms. Perkins."

"Can't we do this inside? I want to see my son."

"It won't take long. Really. Just a few questions. And it has to be done."

"Okay . . . Okay. Let's get it over with.

"The man in the Honda is your ex-husband?"

"Right. I told your boss that the bastard would come after us. Parole. What a stupid idea. After what he did to Sean in that motel room, and the threats he made—"

"Sean? That's your boy's name?"

She nodded. "And I hate to admit it, but Jack Rose was Sean's father."

"You say that Rose made threats—"

"Not recently. A tabloid reporter got under his skin before the trial. Jack exploded—just verbally, but an explosion nevertheless. He wised up after that, especially when he went in front of the parole board. But how they could look at the pictures of Sean in the burn ward and let Jack out of jail, especially when he'd made those threats . . . It just doesn't make sense."

"Yeah. I remember the story. I followed it in the papers. How brave your boy was, undergoing all those skin graft operations. I want to tell you, that's real bravery."

"Thanks. He's a tough kid."

The deputy nodded. "Why don't you take me through what happened tonight, step by step, and then we'll see where we go from there."

She looked through the window. A light mounted on the fire engine scanned the gravel driveway. The tire still lay to one side of the charred Honda, half hidden by the tall weeds that bordered the driveway. The jack lay next to it. So did the empty gas can. Firemen scurried around, their faces masked against thick black smoke.

"I'm glad the windows are up," she said. "The smell must be—"

"Let's talk about tonight."

"Okay." She took a deep breath. "I finished work at seven. I'm a bartender at the Iron Horse, and the boss takes over for the night shift."

"That's a long commute. Why don't you live in town?"

"Part of the plan. First I changed my name, then I went rural. I figured it would be tougher for Jack to find us out here in the boonies. Besides, I like it here. We've got a few neighbors, and they watch out for us."

"But what about Sean? Didn't you worry about leaving him alone?"

"Sean's independent. I'm not raising him to hide like a bug under a rock. He doesn't want to live that way and neither do I, though sometimes I get so scared that I want to start running again." She sighed. "I just can't give in to that fear, though. It's hard enough on Sean—getting around in a wheelchair, looking the way he does—without me trying to mother-hen him."

"Yeah. I see what you mean."

"Anyway, it was almost dark by the time I got home. I saw Jack from the road. I blocked the driveway with my truck. Then I got my .38 out of the glove box and headed after him. I've got a permit for the gun."

"Where was he?"

"Let's see—I heard the Honda's trunk slam as I got out of the truck . . . Yeah. Jack was behind the Honda. He'd parked it on the far side of the barn so Sean couldn't see him from the house. I guess he'd just finished changing the tire, because I saw the flat lying in the weeds near the driveway. The jack was there, too. There was a gas can in between, with the lid still on it. It was just dumb luck. If Jack hadn't had the flat, he would have torched the house with Sean in it and been out of here before I showed up."

"Did Jack see you coming?"

"Yes, but I shot him before he could do anything. In the shoulder." She smiled. "I'm a good shot."

"Just wounded him?"

"Right. He got in the car and started the engine. That's when I shot the front tires. I hope I got the one he'd changed." She sighed. "Then I walked up to him, keeping the gun aimed at his head the whole time."

"How did he react?"

"He laughed. Called me Sigourney Weaver. Said that I might as well go call the cops. Then he started making promises again."

"More threats?"

She nodded. "He said that he'd be back, that they probably

wouldn't even lock him up this time because he hadn't done anything but violate the restraining order. Then he got back to the old stuff. How he'd burn down the house some night while we were asleep. Look, I just couldn't take it anymore."

"That's when you shot him the second time?"

"Right. I'd rather not say where."

"We don't have to go into that right now."

"Good. Anyhow, I turned away, and when I saw that gas can lying there I really lost it. I grabbed it. Jack saw me coming and tried to get out of the car, but I shot through the door. Hit him again. I don't know where, but it hurt him bad, because he started to cough up blood." She shrugged. "That's when I heard the sirens—I guess someone reported the gunshots—but they didn't stop me. I opened the can and poured gas all over him. He just sat there, grinning that crazy grin of his. Look, I don't have to describe the rest of it, do I?"

"No." The deputy stared at the Honda.

She looked at it, too, but saw only tyrannosaurus jaws. "It was self-defense. He really would have come back."

The deputy nodded.

"Can we go inside now?"

"In a minute," the deputy said.

Outside, the night was alive with the sound of machinery. She watched as a fireman opened the dinosaur's brainpan with some kind of gas-powered saw. Her ex-husband was inside, burnt and shriveled. A man took photos of the corpse, then of the gas can and the tire. A van drifted by, long and white, silent and slow.

"Your ex-husband lied to you," the deputy said. "About not doing anything tonight, I mean."

She swallowed, her throat suddenly dry.

The deputy sighed. "The other time, the first time, Rose took Sean somewhere before he hurt him. A motel, you said. Right?"

She didn't answer.

"Those Japanese cars have awfully small trunks. The tire you saw—it wasn't flat. And the jack and the gas can—Rose wasn't using them. He had to get everything out of the trunk. He had to make room . . . for the wheelchair . . . for . . ."

The deputy's voice cracked.

Sean's mother started to cry.

"Near as we can tell, Sean was gagged. He couldn't cry out."

The deputy couldn't look at her. "Rose lied to you, Ms. Perkins. Remember that. You couldn't have known."

Long and white, silent and slow, the coroner's van rolled past the police car.

But the monster's skull remained.

Unwinding

William Fryer Harvey

L IKE MANY other bachelors of forty, I have a horror of parlour games.

My worst nightmare—for I have unfortunately a whole dream stable full of them, is to be pursued down endless corridors by a maiden lady who wishes me to join herself and two elder sisters at Halma.

After Halma, and a game I played one evening fifteen years ago, called 'Ludo,' my pet aversion is 'Unwinding.'

What are the rules? Why simplicity itself! Someone thinks of ham and eggs; that reminds me of my landlady, and she in return reminds my neighbour of Sarah Gamp; and so you proceed until you arrive at the north pole or some other equally remote point, when you unwind, going through all the nonsense again backwards way.

The game, however, has one advantage; you see the curious way in which some people's memories work.

And with this as an introduction I will tell you the only story I know about a parlour game.

If you are a naturalist you may be acquainted with the name of Charles Thorneycroft, the author of the three-volume treatise on British spiders; his name also figures in the clergy list as vicar of Willeston Parva, but it is to the former fact that he owes the five lines in last year's edition of *Who's Who*.

Though he is almost an old man now, his friends hardly notice the change, for he has always had an old man's characteristics, a certain garrulity in anecdote, great mismanagement in business affairs, coupled with an extreme degree of absentmindedness.

For twenty years the Reverend Charles Thorneycroft has held

the living of Willeston Parva, declining all offers of preferment; for Willeston Fen lies in the borders of his parish, and Willeston Fen is one of the few remaining breeding grounds of two species of butterfly that are rapidly becoming extinct.

Besides his spiders and his library, the vicarage is large enough to give shelter to Mrs. Thorneycroft and her three daughters, charming girls in spite of the atmosphere of mixed hockey and parish small talk in which they live.

Last year my customary visit to Willeston coincided with Millicent's second birthday party. By that I do not mean that Millicent, in clerical parlance, was standing upon the threshold of her second year, for she was fifteen, and very proud of the fact.

But it was her overflow party, when her grown-up friends were called in to eat of the fragments that remained.

The arrangement was excellent, for the guests on the first occasion, with girlish indiscretion, devoured everything that was indigestible, leaving to their elders on the following day a safe if uninteresting repast.

On this occasion the party consisted entirely of men. There was Dr. Philpots, an old-fashioned homoeopath; Mr. Greatorex, who farmed a couple of thousand acres Fenchurch way, and who drove tandem to the delight of all Fenchurch children; and Captain Dawson.

These three were old friends and had come to Millicent's second birthday party for years in succession. It was this that made her two sisters object to the proposal to ask Mr. Cholmondley of Oldbarn-house.

As Madge said, Mr. Cholmondley was a newcomer. He never came to church; their father and he had never met.

According to Laura, the upholder of propriety, who went with her mother to pay calls, he was a mere nobody, in spite of his aristocratic name. She, for one, thought him uneducated, but as it was not her birthday party, she forbore to interfere.

And so Millicent, actuated a little by pity for the lonely gentleman, and largely by obstinacy, invited Mr. Cholmondley.

At the last moment she almost hoped he would refuse, but to her own and every one else's surprise, he accepted, and his present won her heart at once.

The guests assembled late in the afternoon, and as the evening was warm we were on the lawn playing croquet until within half an hour of supper; but when the captain twice in succession sent black spinning into a clump of geraniums under the impression that it was his partner's ball, we had to admit that it was too dark to continue.

'Let's fill up the time by playing at Unwinding,' said Millicent. 'It's perfectly simple; we can wind until supper's ready, and unwind afterwards.'

Laura said the game was silly, Madge that it was quite nice, and as no other suggestions were forthcoming, we began to wind. I forget most of the string of nonsense we concocted, but I remember that from Irving we went to Hamlet, from Hamlet to Champainbury, a little village on the other side of the parish, then to champagne and from champagne to luxury.

Dr. Philpots, who, when not fully absorbed in homoeopathy, was apt to fall back on Socialism, declared that luxury reminded him of first-class railway carriages.

The vicar, deep in an article in *Nature,* had not been listening.

'What is it?' he said. 'Oh, first-class railway carriages! First-class railway carriages remind me of murder! An admirable criticism of the whole question,' he went on, 'I only hope Fortescue will have sufficient sense of decency to read it.'

Needless to say, we passed over Fortescue's shortcomings, to inquire how he had got the idea of murder into his head. There was really no connection between the two things at all.

But the vicar's opinion was not to be shaken. 'Whenever I see a first-class railway carriage I think of murder. I'll tell you why when we go into supper.'

'It's like this,' he said as soon as we were seated. 'About ten years ago I had to travel down from London by the last train on Saturday night. The day had been tiring, and as the Sunday's sermon was still unprepared, I departed from my usual habit, and took my seat in an empty first-class compartment.

'I wrote undisturbed for an hour and a half, until the sudden grinding of brakes, and the flash of red and green signal lamps, informed me of the fact that we had reached Marshley junction.

'One or two people got out, but it seemed as if I were to have the carriage to myself again. The guard had blown his whistle, and we had begun to move, when the train from Saunchester drew up. I put my head out of the window to see if there was any one who had been rash enough to risk the connection. Yes, almost before the train had stopped, a door was thrown open, and a man rushed across the platform.

'The carriage I was in was the last in my train. He had just time to open the door of my compartment, when the guard shouted to him to stand clear. He flung himself down in the corner, panting. "That was touch and go," I said. "It was lucky for you the door was not locked." He assented, and I went on with my work, only noting that the man looked very pale. When I had finished the page I was writing, I chanced to look on the floor. "If you don't mind," I said to my companion, "we will have the window raised. The rain seems to be getting in." It was trickling across the floor, making its way along a crack in the oilcloth. But though I had closed the window, the little stream still ran on. I am short-sighted, and it took me twice as long as it would have done another to realize that it was not water but blood. It was dripping from a wound in the hand of the man who sat opposite me.

'"It's a nasty cut," he said, as his eyes caught mine. "Could you bind it up for me? You will find a handkerchief in my coat pocket. There was a drunken man in my carriage. He filled himself with whisky, and then smashed the bottle, and when it came to a free fight, I fell and cut myself. There's something to be said for the teetotaller's point of view after all.

'"That's better," he said, as I finished tying the bandage. "It's exceedingly kind of you to have put yourself to so much trouble. I'm afraid I shall have ruined this suit, and as bad luck would have it, it's new to-day."

'We were silent some time, while the stranger wiped the mist from the pane with the window sash.

'"Yes," ' he said, "drunkenness is a horrible thing, but I doubt very much whether prohibition would have the effect so many people think." He went on to talk of America which he seemed to know. I turned the conversation on to the question of mob law and its relation to crime.

'"It's useless," I remember him saying, "to think that violence can suppress violence. In most cases I think that even the compulsory detention of criminals in prisons and reformatories defeats its own object. A man's conscience, though it may permit a crime, may be trusted to cause him more discomfort than all your dark cells and strait waistcoats. But, of course, I may be prejudiced."

'He kept me busily engaged in talk, until we reached the next station. Lowering the window before the train stopped he looked out upon the platform. "My brother ought to be here to meet me," he said, "but I don't see him anywhere. Good night, sir!"

'My first feeling, after he had gone, was one of curiosity as to his profession. In spite of his talk, he seemed hardly a gentleman. I finally docketed him as a newspaper reporter. I went on with my writing, but broke off a minute later. "What a curiously disagreeable fellow his brother must be," I said to myself. "He seemed actually relieved to find that he was not on the platform to meet him."

'Next morning the papers were full of an awful murder committed on the line. The body of an old gentleman horribly mutilated had been found in a compartment on the 10.30 train from Saunchester. There was every sign of a desperate struggle, and a hand-bag and pocket-book found under the seat had evidently been rifled. No clue to the identity of the murderer had been observed.

'I thought little of the matter at the time. It was not till late in the day that I realized that it was the 10.30 from Saunchester that had steamed into Marshley station just as we were leaving. Immediately following this, came the thought that the stranger who had entered my carriage was the murderer. I dismissed the idea as preposterous, as unjust to a man of whom I knew no ill, but try as I would, it came back again and again until finally I had to receive it, and to fashion some sort of lurid story around my fellow-traveller.

'As the months went by, I felt at times that I ought to communicate my suspicions to the police, but I comforted myself with the belief that they would probably know as much as I did. I agreed with the stranger's theory that conscience is the best of sleuth-hounds, and so I let the matter rest. But whenever I think of first-class railway carriages, I think of murder. The two things are linked together in my brain as closely as two things can be.'

Supper finished, we separated, some of the men strolling on to the veranda for a smoke, while the rest of us went back to the drawing-room.

The vicar showed us some spiders he had received that morning from a friend in Brazil. He was all enthusiasm, but we were relieved when he left us at last to hunt some reference in his paper-backed German books.

'Let's unwind!' said Millicent. 'Never mind father and the others. They can join in later' So we began. We started with three lives each, which when exhausted, were liable to be extended, after the merciful manner of old ladies and children. After we had been unwinding for five minutes, the vicar came in with his book, his five fingers marking the places of the references.

'The tower of London,' said Laura, 'reminds me of Richard the Third.' 'Richard the Third,' said Millicent, 'reminds me of murder.' 'Murder,' said her mother, 'reminds me of first-class railway carriages.'

It was the vicar's turn, but he was deep in his book.

'Wake up, father!' said Madge. 'What do first-class railway carriages remind you of?'

'Mr. Cholmondley,' said the vicar, and went on with his reading.

Madge shook the old gentleman, and took his book away. 'Now, father,' she said, 'do play properly! You've lost five lives already. What do first-class railway carriages remind you of? You can have till we count ten.'

The vicar took off his spectacles, and wiped them carefully. Then with a little nervous smile he had when he thought that his daughters were not treating him with respect that was his due before company, he said: 'Murder.'

'Oh, dear! I'm afraid he's hopeless,' said Millicent to the gentlemen who just then came in from their smoke. 'Here's papa saying that first-class railway carriages remind him of Mr. Cholmondley, and then that they remind him of murder.' 'Yes, Mr. Cholmondley,' said her mother, 'you will have to defend yourself. Why he isn't here! Hasn't he finished his cigar?' she asked of Greatorex.

'We thought he was in here with you,' he replied. 'I haven't seen him since supper.'

There was silence for a minute, broken by a knocking at the door. The maid came in with a note. It was from Cholmondley, apologizing for running off without saying goodbye. He had had a telegram from his mother, who was dying in the south of France, and had been obliged to catch the earliest train.

'Poor man!' said the vicar's wife, 'I remember now how silent he was during supper. Our careless talk must indeed have been a trial to him!' and she began to discuss with Greatorex the insanitary conditions of all continental hotels.

But the vicar sat in his arm-chair, his book on spiders had dropped unheeded to the floor. He was gazing into the fire with an expression of utter incredulity.

The Vital Element

Talmage Powell

I WOULD NEVER again love the warm water of Lake Boniface . . . never find beauty in its blue-green color . . . never hear music in its rustling surf . . .

The dead girl had been hurriedly buried in the lake. She was anchored in about thirty feet of water with a hempen rope that linked her lashed ankles to a pair of cement blocks.

I'd stirred the water, swimming down to her depth. Her body bobbed and swayed, with her bare toes about three feet off the clean, sandy bottom. It was almost as if a strange, macabre new life had come to her. Her long blonde hair swirled about her lovely gamine face with every tremor of the water. A living ballerina might have enjoyed her grace of motion, but not her state of being. I wept silently behind my face mask.

A single stroke sent me drifting, with my shoulder stirring silt from the bottom. I touched the rope where it passed into the holes in the cement blocks and out again. A natural process of wear and tear had set in. The sharp, ragged edges of the blocks were cutting the rope. In a matter of time, the rope would part. Her buoyancy would drift her toward the sunlight, to the surface, to discovery.

I eeled about, careful not to look at her again, and plunged up toward the shadow of the skiff. My flippers fired me into open air with a shower of spray and a small, quick explosion in my ears.

I rolled over the side of the skiff and lay a moment with my stomach churning with reaction. Sun, blue sky, the primitive shore-line of mangrove and palmetto, everything around me was weirdly unreal. It was as if all the clocks in the world had gone *tick*, then forgot to *tock*.

"You're a too-sensitive, chicken-hearted fink," I said aloud. I forced myself to peel out of my diving gear, picked up the oars, and put my back into the job of rowing in.

I docked and tied the skiff, then walked to the cottage with my gear slung across my shoulder. Sheltered by scraggly pines, the lonely cottage creaked tiredly in the heat.

I stood on the sagging front porch. For a moment I didn't have the strength or nerve to go inside.

The Alabama heat was a cloying shroud lined with a film of ice. Make sense? Perhaps not. It was such a day, insects humming, birds singing joyously, life seething, in the black-hole emptiness of death.

Movement came to me with a twitch. I turned and went inside. The cottage was its usual mess, a hodgepodge of broken down furniture, dirty dishes, empty beer bottles and bean cans, none of which bothered me. But *she* was strewn all over the place, the dead girl out there in the water. She was portrayed in oil, sketched in charcoal, delicately impressed in pink and tan watercolors. She was half finished on the easel in the center of the room, like a naked skull.

Shivering and dry-throated, I slipped dingy ducks over my damp swim trunks, wriggled into a tattered T-shirt, and slid my feet into strap sandals. The greasy feeling was working again in the pit of my stomach as I half-ran from the cottage.

Palmetto City lay like a humid landscape done with dirty brushes as my eight-year-old station wagon nosed into DeSota Street. Off the beaten tourist paths, the town was an unpainted clapboard mecca for lantern-jawed farmers, fishermen, swamp muckers.

I looked at the street scene, trying to make some reality take shape in the day. Black man in laborer's jeans coming out of Jack's Eatery picking his teeth . . . same front door his daddy had not dared to enter . . . same pinpoint on a map of muggy lowland where a long-deceased fellow had located a cotton gin and mule-powered wagons had hauled the bales to the port of Mobile, and a few tradesmen had optimistically called their burgeoning village a city.

Echo from the miasma of the past. You are not quite real, Palmetto City. Alabama is the science of Huntsville, the steel of Birmingham, a Crimson Tide and ghost of Bear Bryant. It's a George Wallace today unrecognizable by the young governor reared in defiance. It's blacks in high elective offices putting the memories behind of police dogs and cattle prods in Selma.

But you must be real, like all the other Palmetto Citys lurking in the concrete, glass, and steel hustle of the New South. You are as real as the covert lingering KKK whispers in decent, Bible-reading country. You are as real as death. . . .

I angled the steaming wagon beside a dusty pickup at the curb and got out. On the sidewalk, I glimpsed myself in the murky window of the hardware store: six feet of bone and cartilage without enough meat; thatch of unkempt sandy hair; a lean face that wished for character; huge sockets holding eyes that looked as if they hadn't slept for a week.

Inside the store, Braley Sawyer came toward me, a flabby, sloppy man in his rumpled tropical weight suit. "Well, if it ain't Tazewell Eversham, Palmetto City's own Gauguin!" He flashed a wet, gold-toothed smile. "Hear you stopped in Willy Morrow's filling station yestiddy and gassed up for a trip to Mobile. Going up to see them fancy art dealers, I guess."

I nodded. "Got back early this morning."

"You going to remember us country hoogers when you're famous, Gauguin?" The thought brought fat laughter from him. I let his little joke pass and in due time he waddled behind the counter and asked, "You here to buy something?"

"Chain." The word formed in my parched throat but didn't make itself heard. I cleared my throat, tried again, "I want to buy about a dozen feet of medium weight chain."

He blinked. "Chain?"

"Sure," I said. I had better control of my voice now. "I'd like to put in a garden, but I have stump problems. Thought I'd dig and cut around the roots and snake the stumps out with the station wagon."

He shrugged, his eyes hanging onto me as he moved toward the rear of the store. "I guess it would work—if that bucket of bolts holds together."

I turned and stared at a vacant point in space as the chain rattled from its reel. "Easier to carry if I put it in a gunny sack, Gauguin," Sawyer yelled at me.

"That's fine." I heard the chain clank into the sack.

Seconds later Sawyer dropped the chain at my feet. I paid him, carried the gunny sack out, and loaded it in the station wagon. Then I walked down the street to the general store and bought a few things—canned goods, coffee, flour, and two quarts of the cheapest booze available, which turned out to be a low-grade rum.

I'd stowed the stuff beside the gunny sack, closed the tailgate, and was walking around the wagon to get in when a man called to me from across the street. "Hey, Taze."

The man who barged toward me looked like the crudest breed of piney woods sheriff, which is what Jack Tully was. Big-bellied, slope-shouldered, fleshy faced with whisky veins on cheeks and nose, his protruding eyes searched with a sadistic hunger. His presence reminded me that not all Neanderthals had died out ten thousand years ago.

He thumbed back his hat, spat, guffawed. "Kinda left you high and dry, didn't she, bub?"

An arctic wind blew across my neck. "What are you talking about, Sheriff?"

He elbowed me in the ribs; I recoiled, from his touch, not the force behind it. "Bub, I ain't so dumb. I know Melody Grant's been sneaking out to your shack."

"Any law against it?"

"Not as long as the neighbors don't complain." He gave an obscene wink. "And you got no neighbors, have you, bub?"

His filthy thoughts were written in his smirking, ignorant face. No explanation could change his mind, not in a million years. Might as well try to explain a painting to him.

"Maybe she ain't told you yet, bub?"

"Told me what?"

"About young Perry Tomlin, son of the richest man in the county. She's been seeing him, too, now that he's home with his university degree. Going to marry him, I hear, honeymoon in Europe. Big come-up for a shanty cracker girl, even one as pretty as Melody. I reckon that shack'll be mighty lonesome, knowing you'll never see her again."

"Maybe it will, Sheriff, maybe it will."

"But . . ." We were suddenly conspirators. He gloated. ". . . there's one thing you can waller around in your mind."

"What's that, Sheriff?"

"Son of the county's richest man is just getting the leavings of a rag-tag artist who's got hardly a bean in the pot." Laughter began to well inside of him. "Bub, I got to hand you that! Man, it would bust their blood vessels, Perry's and the old man's both, if they knew the truth."

Raucous laughter rolled out of him, to the point of strangulation. When I got in the station wagon and drove off he was standing there wiping his eyes and quaking with mirth over the huge joke.

Back at the cottage, I opened a bottle of the rum, picked up a brush, and stood before the easel. I swigged from the bottle in my left hand and made brush strokes on the unfinished canvas with my right. By the time her face was emerging from the skull-like pattern, the rum had begun its work. I knew I wasn't cut to fit a situation like this one, but the rum made up a part of the deficit.

I dropped the brush and suddenly turned from the canvas. "Why did she have to leave me? Why?"

She was, of course, still out there when the gunny sack dragged me down through thirty feet of water. Her thin cotton dress clung to her as she wavered closer. Behind and beyond her a watery forest of weed dipped and swayed, a green and slimy floral offering.

I felt as if my air tanks were forcing raw acid into my lungs as I spilled the chain from the gunny sack. My trembling hands made one . . . two . . . three efforts . . . and the chain was looped about her cold, slender ankles.

I passed the chain through the holes in the cement blocks, and it no longer mattered whether the hempen rope held. The job was done. No risk of floating away.

In the cottage, I picked up the rum jug and let it kick me. Then I put on a clean shirt and pants and combed my hair nice and neat.

I went to the porch and took a final look at the bloodstains on the rough planking. My eyes followed the dripping trail those blood droplets had made down to the rickety pier and the flatbottom skiff. Before my stomach started acting up again, I dropped from the porch, ran across the sandy yard, and fell into the station wagon.

I pulled myself upright behind the wheel, started the crate. Through the nonreality of the day, the wagon coughed its way over the rutted, crushed seashell road to the highway. Trucks swooshed past and passenger cars swirled about me.

On the outskirts of Palmetto City, I turned the wagon onto the private road that snaked its way across landscaped acreage. The road wound up a slight rise to a colonial mansion that overlooked half the county, the low skyline of the town, the glitter of the Gulf in the far distance. A pair of horse-sized Great Danes were chasing, tumbling, rolling like a couple of puppies on the vast manicured lawn.

A lean, trim old man had heard the car's approach and stood watching from the veranda as I got out. I walked up the short, wide steps, the shadow of the house falling over me. The man watched me narrowly. He had a crop of silver hair and his hawkish face was wrinkled. These were the only clues to his age. His gray eyes were bright, quick, hard, as cold as a snake's. His mouth was an arrogant slit. Clothed in lime slacks and riotously colored sport shirt thirty years too young for him, his poised body exuded an aura of merciless, wiry power. In my distraught and wracked imagination he was as pleasant as a fierce, deadly lizard.

"Mr. Tomlin?"

He nodded. "And you're the tramp artist who's become a local character. Didn't you see those no trespassing signs when you turned off the highway?"

"I've got some business with your son, Mr. Tomlin."

"Perry's in Washington, tending to a matter for me. He flew up yesterday and won't be back for another couple days. You call, and make a proper appointment. And get that crate out of here—unless you want me to interrupt the dogs in their play."

My stomach felt as if it were caving in, but I gave him a steady look and said in an icy voice, "If Perry's away, you must be the man I want to talk to. Sure. Perry wouldn't have killed her, but you didn't share your son's feeling for her, did you?"

"I don't believe I know what you're talking about." He knew, all right. The first glint of caution and animal cunning showed in his eyes.

"Then I'll explain, Mr. Tomlin. Yesterday I went to Mobile to interest an art dealer in a one-man show. When I got back this morning I found some bloodstains. They led me to the water. I spent the morning diving, searching. I found her in about thirty feet of water."

I expected him to say something, but he didn't. He just stood there looking at me with those small, agate eyes.

"It wasn't hard to figure out," I said. "She'd come to the cottage to tell me it was all over between us. The shanty cracker girl was marrying the richest son in the county. But you didn't cotton to that idea, did you?"

"Go on," he said quietly.

"There's little more. It's all very simple. You sent Perry out of town to give you a chance to break it up between him and the cracker girl. Not much escapes your notice. You'd heard the gossip about her and the tramp artist. When you couldn't find her in town, you decided to try my place. I guess you tried to talk her off, buy her off, threaten her off. When none of it worked, you struck her in a rage. You killed her."

The old man stared blindly at the happy Great Danes.

"Realizing what you'd done," I said, "you scrounged a rope, couple of cement blocks, and planted her in thirty feet of water." I shook my head. "Not good. Not good at all. When the blocks sawed the rope in two, a nosy cop might find evidence you'd been around the place; a tire track, footprint, or maybe some fingerprints you'd left sticking around."

He studied the frolicking dogs as if planning their butchery. "You haven't named the vital element, artist; proof of guilt, proof that I did anything more than talk to her."

"Maybe so," I nodded, "but could a man in your position afford the questions, the scandal, the doubts that would arise and remain in your son's mind until the day you die? I think not. So I helped you."

His eyes flashed to me.

"I substituted a chain for the rope," I said. "The cement blocks will not cut that in two." I drew a breath. "And of course I want something in return. A thousand dollars. I'm sure you've that much handy, in a wall safe if not on your person. It's bargain day, Mr. Tomlin."

He thought it over for several long minutes. The sinking sun put a golden glitter in his eyes.

"And how about the future, artist? What if you decided you needed another thousand dollars one of these days?"

I shook my head. "I'm not that stupid. Right now I've caught you flat-footed. It's my moment. Everything is going for me. You haven't time to make a choice, think, plan. But it would be different in the future. Would I be stupid enough to try to continue black-mailing the most powerful man in the county after he's had a chance to get his forces and resources together?"

"Your question contains a most healthy logic, artist."

"One thousand bucks," I said, "and I hightail it down the drive-way in the wagon. Otherwise, I'll throw the fat in the fire, all of it, including the chain about her ankles and my reason for putting it there. And we'll see which one of us has most to lose."

Without taking his eyes off my face, he reached for his wallet. He counted out a thousand dollars without turning a hair; chicken feed, pocket change to him.

I folded the sheaf of fifties and hundreds, some of them new bills, and slipped it into my pocket with care. We parted then, the old man and I, without another word being spoken.

The station wagon seemed to run with new life when I reached the highway. I felt the pressure of the money—the vital element—against my thigh.

The chain on her ankles had lured Tomlin, convinced him that he was dealing with a tramp interested only in a thousand bucks, so he had signed his confession of guilt by putting his fingerprints all over the money.

I didn't trust the gross sheriff in Palmetto City. I thought it far better to take the vital element and every detail of the nightmare directly to the state's attorney in Montgomery.

I was pretty sure the battered old station wagon would get me there.

Walks

Joe R. Lansdale

(For Dan Lowry)

MY SON WORRIES ME. He only leaves his room for long walks, and he treats me like the hired help. I ought to throw him out, but I cannot. He is my son and I love him and I share his pain, though I am uncertain what that pain is.

Even as a little boy he was strange. Always strange. After his mama died he only got stranger. He was eighteen then, and of course it was a bad thing for him, but I thought he would have coped better at that age. It was not as if he were ten.

He certainly misses his mama.

He goes into the attic and digs through the trunk that holds her keepsakes. Perhaps I should have destroyed it long ago, but it never occured to me. I am one of those people who hangs onto everything.

These days he sits in his room at his desk and cuts things out of the newspaper. He does not think I've seen him, but I have. I walk quietly. I learned that when I was a boy. You did not walk quietly, my old man would fly off the handle. He hated a heavy walk. Me and my sisters got a lot of beltings because of the way we walked. My old man taught me to walk softly. When he was not drinking he

541

would take me hunting and he would teach me how to walk like an Indian. When he was drinking, that was the way he wanted us to walk around the house. He never taught my sisters how to walk, he just expected it. He used to say girls ought to walk like girls, not water buffalo. My old man was a horrible, cruel drunk, and I am thankful that I managed to be a better father to my son.

But now the boy has pushed me out, will not let me in. I wish he respected me. I never did to him what my father did to me. I never made him walk quietly. I even let him come back home and take his old room when he lost his job.

When he was a child, we used to talk about everything. Even the weird things he was interested in like horror movies and comic books and pyramid power. I did not like any of it, but I talked to him just the same, tried to understand his interests.

After his mother's death, he became quieter, more withdrawn. He will not accept she stepped out in front of a car and was killed and will not be back. I think he keeps expecting to look up and see her walk through the door.

I am sorry for him, even if his mother and I never got along. It happens that way sometime.

And these clippings of his, they worry me. Why is he cutting them out and saving them? That makes me very nervous. He thinks I do not know about them. Thinks I have not seen him cutting them out and pondering them, gluing them in his scrapbook, putting them in the bottom desk drawer under the family photo album.

And these long walks. Where does he go and what does he do? I wonder all the time, then feel guilty for wondering. He's a grown man and can take walks if he wants to. He probably walks and worries about not having a job, though he has not yet pushed hard enough to find one if you ask me. But I am sure it worries him. The walks probably help him get his mind off things. Then he comes back here and collects his clippings as a sort of hobby.

I hope that's it. Hope that explains his fascination with the clippings. I hate it when I think there is more to it than that.

One time, when he went on one of his walks, I snuck in and opened the desk drawer and got his scrapbook and looked to see what he was cutting out.

It was articles about the Choker murders snipped from a dozen newspapers. Local papers, out of state papers. Just about everything the newsstand sells in the way of papers. He cut out the pictures of the whores who had been strangled and glued them all in a row and underlined their names in red.

That worries me. And he has a scrapbook full of articles about the Choker from a half dozen different papers.

And the way he acts around me. Strange. Nervous. Sullen.

Today I asked him if he wanted some soup and he glared at me and would not answer. He turned his back and stared at the window and watched the rain gather on the glass, then he got up and got his raincoat and umbrella and went for a walk.

It was like when he was a little boy and he got mad about something and started being obstinate for no real reason, or sometimes because you disappointed him.

That is always the worse thing, disappointing your son. Him knowing you are not the man you want him to be.

After he was gone, I went to the window to see which way he was going, then I went to the desk drawer and took out the scrapbook and looked at them.

He had a lot more clippings. He had his mother's picture in the scrapbook. The photo used to have me in it too, but he had cut me out.

Guilt or not. Grown man or not. I had to know where he went on those walks.

I put on my raincoat and pulled up the hood and went in the direction he took. I am getting old, but I am not getting slow or weak. In fact, I am probably in better condition than my boy. I do exercises. I can still walk fast and I can still walk quietly. My old man's legacy, walking quietly.

After a short time I saw him way ahead of me, walking over toward The District, where the poorer people live. It is a very bad place.

It was very dark because of the rain and it was getting darker because it was closer to nightfall.

He went into a bar and I crossed the street and stood under an old hotel awning and looked across the street at the bar and watched him through the glass. He ordered a drink and sat and took his time with it. I started to feel cold.

I waited, though, and after a bit he had yet another drink, then another.

Now I knew where the money I give him goes.

I was about to give up waiting, when out he came and started up the street, not wobbling or anything. He can hold his liquor, I guess, though where he got a taste for drink I'll never know. I do not allow it around the house.

I followed him and he walked deeper into the bad part of town, where the Choker murders take place.

It grew dark and the sun went down and the neon came out and so did the hookers. They called to me from the protection of doorways, but I ignored them.

I thought of my son. They had to be calling to him too, and up ahead I saw him stop and go to a doorway, and though I could not see the girl, I knew she was there and that he was talking to her.

I felt very nervous suddenly. It hurt to know that my son was frequenting the bad parts of town, the way his mother had. Perhaps he knew about her. Perhaps he was trying to understand what she saw in places like this. And perhaps he was very much like her. God forbid.

I stopped and leaned against a building and waited, pulled the hood tight around my face to keep out the rain.

Then I saw my son go into the doorway and out of sight.

So now I knew where he went when he took his walks. He liked this part of town like his mother liked this part of town. Maybe, if he had a job, less to worry about, he would not need it anymore. I hoped that was it. Whores and whisky were a sad way for a man to live.

A girl called to me from across the way. Something about old man do you want to feel younger. It bothered me she could tell I was old from that far away. I had a raincoat and hood on for Christ sake.

Guess it is the way I hold myself, even though I try to keep my back straight and try to walk like a younger man.

But I guess there is no hiding it. Even though I am strong and healthy, I have always looked old, even when I was young. My wife used to say I was born fifty years old. She used to tell me in bed that I acted eighty.

I do not miss her at all. If she were alive, I wonder what she would think if she knew her son was seeing whores. Would she feel proud he liked this part of town the way she had? Or would she feel ashamed?

No, I doubt she would feel ashamed. She loved the boy, but she was a bad influence. When I thought of her I always thought of her coming home with whisky on her breath, her skin smelling of some man's cologne.

I crossed the street and the girl smiled at me and talked about what she could do for me. She reminded me of my wife standing there. They all do.

I smiled at her. I thought of my son and what he was doing and I felt so sad. I thought of his mother again, and how she had been, and I was glad I had done what I did. A woman like her did not deserve to live. Just a little push at a dark intersection at the right moment and it was all over. It was not as good as getting my hands on her throat, which is what I would have liked to do, but it was easier to explain. More efficient. The police believed it was an accident.

And now, when I am with the others, I pretend each of them is her and that it is her throat I am squeezing.

But my boy, does he know what I do? Is that why he collects my press? Maybe he takes his walks not only for the whisky and the whores, but because he suspects me and does not want to be around me, thinks what I do is wrong.

I hope that is not it.

God, I hope he does not get a disease from that slut. Can he not find a nice girl?

I smiled at the whore again, got under the doorway with her, peeked out and looked both ways.

No one was coming.

I grabbed her and it only took a moment before I let her fall. I am old, but I am strong.

God, I hope my son does not get a disease.

As I went away, walking my quick but quiet walk, I told myself I would talk to him when he came in. Try to decide what he knows without giving myself away. Maybe he does not know it is me. He might collect the articles because he likes what he reads. Sympathizes with the Choker.

If so, if he would talk to me and try to understand, I think we could have the relationship I have always wanted. One like we had when he was little and we talked about the weird things that interested him, anything and everything under the sun.

I certainly hope it can be that way.

I do not want to have to choke him too.

Why I Didn't Murder My Wife

Arthur Lawson

WELL, PARSON, if it'll make you any happier, I might just as
well go ahead and confess to you before they come to take
me away to the chair. I don't believe in any of those
things you been telling me about God and the Hereafter and the
rest of that, but I can see that you are a pretty decent sort of a
gent and that you aren't trying to pin something on me like the
judge and the reporters and all those rats. So I'll confess to you,
Parson, and give you something to think about. Maybe it will rest
my soul like you suggest—but I'm ready to bet it won't rest yours.

There isn't a chance in the world I'll miss that chair. But even if
I was sitting in it I'd tell you the same. I didn't murder my wife.
They got the wrong man.

I didn't murder her, and this is the reason why. I didn't murder
her because I knew I'd get caught if I did, and I didn't want to get
caught and brought up here to the death house. And where did you
ever hear a better reason than that for not murdering your wife?

I had other reasons for not murdering her, but that was the main
reason. I didn't want to be electrocuted for it; I didn't want to sit in
that chair with my hair shaved off and wait for the juice to hit me.
And I knew all along that if I did murder her the chances were a
million to one of my getting the jolt for it. In fact I was being shadowed even before I thought of murdering her. We hadn't been back
from our honeymoon for more than a couple of days when this
flatfoot from the 65th precinct began shadowing me. His name was
John Keenan, and one day when I came in from walking around the
reservoir in Central Park there he was sprawled out on the divan
with his big feet taking up all the floor in front of him. When my
wife saw me she said, "This is John, Leo. You heard about him."

"Sure," I said, "I been hearing a lot about you, John."

John shook hands with me and almost broke my fingers. He was
a big cop with a red face and muscles like iron, and I wasn't anybody but an author of detective stories that I couldn't very often
sell. When he looked down at me his eyes squinted, and I knew he
was trying to hide something behind them.

But I didn't say anything about it and we sat down and ate the meal that Florence had cooked, and I could hardly hold my fork because of what he had done to my hand. I just sat there and let them go ahead and talk until afterwards when John was drunk and began riding me.

"Leo," he said, "I guess you could go to your typewriter and solve the Gedeon case just like that." He snapped his fingers.

"I guess I could," I said. "But what's the sense? You flatfoots got it all solved—by blaming a gent you can't catch. That's a hot solution."

"I guess you got a better one!" John leaned up close to me and scowled.

"I guess I couldn't of made up a worse one," I said.

Then Florence came in and yelled, "Now don't you two begin fighting right when you just met!"

John piped down and Floss got us into a game of rummy. He beat me because I was thinking out a plot and couldn't get my mind on the game which I don't like anyway. So when he got up to go he laughed.

"Just shows," he said, "how a real cop can beat a paper dick any time."

He was still laughing when he kissed Florence good night.

Well, he came to supper pretty often after that, and it was always the same way. He'd ride me about my detective stories. He'd read them when I wasn't around and would tell Floss that any hick cop could solve the cases I thought up. It got to be so that when I came home at times like that the two of them would pull apart the last story I'd written. He'd laugh at it and Floss would look at me with disappointment in her eyes. She had thought that marrying an author was something romantic. But one night after the flatfoot had gone home she said to me:

"Leo, why don't you go out and get a job instead of writing these things?"

And I knew the time had come when I'd have to do something big to shut them up. I was still thinking it out when two things happened at once. I sold a story for two hundred dollars, and a life insurance agent that John knew came up to see us. I was sore at John and Florence for the way they talked about my stories so I didn't tell them I'd sold one and I kept the cash. I still had most of it when that agent came up and told us how accidents were happening everywhere, how people were dying like flies, and how wonderful it would be if we were insured, especially how wonderful it would be if I had some insurance. John was there too that night and between them they talked us into it. Floss passed the physical test but I failed. She also pretty near got run over crossing the street because she never did think to look where she was going, so with the cash from that story I went out and bought her a policy for ten thousand dollars. You see, I'd gotten to believing that something might happen to her just as that agent said, and besides I'd figured that ten thousand bucks was just about what I'd need to live on while I got myself established selling to the big magazines.

And right there is the first reason why I didn't murder my wife. I had sense enough to know that if Floss died under mysterious circumstances they might hold that policy against me. But everybody laughs at me when I tell them about it now.

The second reason why I didn't murder her was this: I came home one night and there John was with Floss, both dolled up in their best clothes. They were laughing and had been drinking some. I tried to skip it but John shook hands with me and I felt the pain all the way up to my shoulder. Then they told me they were going out to a party to celebrate John's birthday and that I had to go along. We went down to the French Follies and had some more to drink, and just like it had always happened before when John got a couple under his belt he began to ride me.

"The Ace Sleuth!" he said. "Or King of the Underworld! Which is it?"

"Shut up!" I said.

"Now, boys—" Floss began.

"I guess you could think up the perfect crime and then solve it?" John said.

I got mad then and started yelling. "I can think it up. But you couldn't solve it. You couldn't solve it even if I committed it right under your nose!"

"Now, boys," Floss said again.

The waiter ran up saying, "Was somebody at this table calling me?"

And I realized that I had already gone too far, that I should not have said as much as I had. John was a detective, in the 65th precinct as I told you before, and he might begin suspecting me. In fact, if my wife should happen to die accidentally and there were no witnesses and I didn't have an alibi, he'd remember that statement in the French Follies and hold it against me. Between the insurance and what I'd said I wouldn't have a chance in the world.

So there's the second reason why I didn't murder my wife.

There were plenty of more reasons, but I won't tell them all to you. I was walking in Central Park one day and happened to meet a red-headed girl I knew who had a dog and wrote stories for the confession magazines. I hadn't seen her since I'd gotten married, so we got to talking about things and I invited her over to a hotel to have a couple of drinks. Pretty soon I was telling her about Floss and how John was always cadging meals and making cracks about my stories until even Floss lost faith in me and tried to get me to find an "honest job" as she called it these days. I could see that the red-headed girl sympathized with me and suddenly I realized what a sap I'd been all along and how she was the kind of girl I should have married instead of Floss.

She even said: "Think how difficult this is in real life and how easy we make it in our stories. In one of your stories you'd figure out some way of murdering a man. But of course the murderer always has to get caught in the end and sent to the chair in a story. That wouldn't be so good. But how dramatic!"

"Dramatic," I said, "but not healthy. But in real life you don't have to worry about the editor. Cops are dumber than editors. You could figure a way of murdering your wife and never get caught."

She screamed, not very loud, and said, "You're not really thinking of murdering your own wife, are you?"

I tried to shut her up, but already the bartender and a couple of other people had heard her, and I knew right then that if Floss was murdered all those people would get up and testify against me.

And that's the third reason why I didn't murder my wife.

Don't you see, Parson, I would have been a fool to murder the woman, the way things were shaping up. And I would have been a big fool to murder her after I bought that old World War bayonet. I was walking down Second Avenue after a date with this red-head when I saw the bayonet in a hock shop window. It looked like a good weapon to kill somebody with, so I bought it for a quarter and brought it home. As usual John was there with a big grin on his Irish pan when I arrived and he said, "What have you got there in that funny looking package, Leo?"

I didn't want to tell him, but Floss came in and asked the same thing, so I had to unwrap it and show it to them. They asked me what I wanted with such a thing and I had to tell them something so I said, "Just wanted it for a decoration. An inspiration, sort of. Was thinking how easy it would be to kill somebody with a thing like that." They were looking at me in a kind of funny way so I added, "In a story, I mean. A story where the murderer was in the war, maybe, and had a thing like this around. It got to working on his mind, and—"

"Maybe we better have supper," Floss said, "before it gets too cold. You got home kinda late tonight, Leo. Meet somebody?"

I didn't feel like talking to them so I shoved the bayonet into a drawer and went out to eat and then went to the little room where I did my writing and left them doing the dishes and chattering. And right there, Parson, is the fourth reason why I didn't murder my wife. The hock shop keeper and John would both swear I'd bought that knife. The insurance and the things I'd said at the Follies and that crack the red-head had made would be bad enough. But the bayonet, the D.A. would say, showed premeditated murder. That is, if my wife was killed with that bayonet.

But here is the biggest reason of all. You see, when anybody murders somebody, he's always got to have a motive, and what happened next provided a motive, in fact the motive that always causes a man to murder his wife. And knowing that, wouldn't I have been a sap, Parson, to murder my wife?

I was seeing pretty much of that red-headed girl and knew more and more what a big mistake I'd made in marrying Floss. She took no interest in my work, and she was always feeding John Keenan, who constantly rode me about my stories and convinced her I should go and get a job. The red-head was beginning to feel the same way about it, so after talking it all over with her one afternoon while drinking rye in her apartment I went home to tell Floss I was through with her.

John, like the carpet on the floor that I hadn't paid for yet, was there. But he wasn't being walked on. I was the one who was walked on, especially after supper when I was getting ready to tell them what I had on my mind. I was working up my nerve when Floss said:

"John and I have been talking about you, Leo, and John has fixed it for a job for you down at—"

"Floss," I said, "I don't care what John did. John may be a good cop, but he isn't a literary critic and I'm tired of hearing him pan my stories all the time. I'm also tired of having you and John fix up my life for me. That's what I'm mostly tired of, having you always side with him. I'm sick of it. I'm sick and tired. I'm through. You got to divorce me!"

I'd had a lot of drinks to get to the place where I could even tell Floss that much, and those drinks got me plenty excited. I yelled at John: "You done this, Kennan! I would've got along okay with Floss if you hadn't stuck your nose in. Don't you know a wife is supposed to stick to her husband after she marries him? I'll be glad to get rid of you, Floss!"

They were staring at me, startled and silent, and it calmed me down some and I said, "Besides, I got another girl. She'd appreciate me. A writer like I am. And she wouldn't have the house full of some dumb cop's big feet all the time."

Floss began to cry. John was patting her on the shoulder. Then she suddenly screamed at him to get out. He didn't look so big as he had as he crept to the door. When the latch clicked Floss got up from the table and edged over to me.

"Leo," she whispered, "we'll make out. We've got to make out. I still love you, Leo. You'll forget that red-headed woman. We'll be all right after we get over our growing pains."

We were in the sitting room then, and the drawer was open where I kept the bayonet. I had a drink of rye in my hand that I'd just mixed. But my mind was very clear, and my eyes were clear. I could see the little drawer in the desk that held the insurance policy, just above the big drawer with the bayonet in it.

And over the desk was the crucifix that Floss had hung ther when we were first married almost a year ago.

"I can't give you a divorce, Leo," she whispered, and her head jerked just a little bit, I thought, toward the crucifix. I knew what she meant, all right. She was a very religious girl. She and John had always gone to church together on Sundays.

"John won't . . ."

And my mind was very clear just then before it went blank. I remembered the last talk I'd had with the red-headed girl. She had been very understanding. And we'd made plans of what we'd do when I was free.

Then Floss said, "John won't . . ." and my mind whirled and went blank.

* * *

When I came to again it was morning and Floss was sprawled out in the middle of the living room floor right beside me. The bayonet had gone clear through her and its point was stuck in the floorboard under her. I poured a drink for myself and called the cops.

In another couple of hours I'll go to the chair.

But I didn't kill my wife, Parson. I'd have been a sap to have killed her. That's what I've been telling everybody and they only laugh and say I was a sap, all right. I tell them that the insurance policy was reason enough for not killing her. That would make me a suspect right at the start without anything at all to support it. And how about what I said in the Follies and the red-head's crack and my buying that bayonet? All those people got up to testify, even the girl who wrote confession stories who I thought was so understanding. "How dramatic," I heard her tell a reporter. "What material for a yarn! Sure, I'd like a Scotch and soda, big boy." Why, Parson, I would have been a sap to murder my wife especially with that divorce as motive and my wife not giving it to me because it was against her religion.

Yes, sir, they all say I'm a sap, all right, and they won't even listen when I tell them who really murdered my wife, the only person who had a real motive and no alibi and something to get out of it. I don't have any relatives. When I go to the chair no relative of mine will get that ten thousand dollars if the company pays up. A relative of Floss' will get it. And she has only one living relative— her brother, who says he spent the whole night during which she was murdered walking around in Central Park kicking himself for ruining his sister's married life.

Can you imagine a smart detective making a lame excuse like that? But nobody even listens to me. Tomorrow I go to the chair although I had every reason in the world for not murdering Floss. And Floss' brother John will probably get a promotion for breaking the case whether he gets that ten thousand dollars or not.

So I've confessed, Parson, like you asked. And I'm going to the chair. But like I said, I don't suppose it's going to rest your soul very well to think about it.

Whodunit

Michael A. Black

L AURA'S DARK EYES narrowed under her profusion of brown curls as she looked at me across the table in the dining car. I felt her long fingers squeeze my hand.

"What's the matter, darling?" she said.

I didn't answer. I just finished off the last bit of my drink and watched the progress of the head waiter as he nervously made his way through the aisle toward our table. I set the glass down and nodded slightly.

"Here comes trouble," I said.

She glanced over her shoulder, then turned back to me.

"Now how do you know that?" she asked.

"Believe me, I can tell."

Seconds later the waiter stopped and leaned over toward me.

"Mr. Pope, I'm so sorry to disturb you, sir," he whispered. "But Mr. Ambrose was wondering if you were the same Vincent Pope who is the very famous detective?"

"Some people would say 'infamous,' " Laura said, smiling mischievously. She picked up her glass and took a dainty sip, leaving a red smear on the rim.

"If you would be so kind, sir," the waiter said, "to speak to Mr. Ambrose? He's waiting over to your left." He cocked his head fractionally.

I glanced over and saw Francis P. Ambrose, all two hundred and sixty pounds of him, wedged between the accordian-like separation between the cars. He was the rich guy who'd set up this interactive-mystery-play-on-a-train. I looked over at Laura and watched her lips curl into an exaggerated pout.

"I won't be long," I said, rising. "I promise."

"You'd better not be," she said. "The show's set to begin in a little over fifteen minutes, and I want to figure out whodunit before you do."

I smiled, winked, and walked down the aisle following the waiter, compensating ever-so-slightly for the rhythmic sway of the moving train. Ambrose was white as a ghost as I looked down at him. He was holding a smoldering cigar in his left hand and a small shot glass in his right. Even the gray patches around his temples seemed to appear more ashen.

"Looks like you've been having a rough night," I said.

He nodded and brought the glass to his lips. The drink brought a flush of color to his flaccid cheeks, but the rest of him still looked chalky. He made a dismissive gesture with his hand and the waiter disappeared, leaving the two of us crammed in the small area, the sound of straining, buckling metal masking our conversation.

"Clancy, the conductor, told me you're a detective," Ambrose said. "That you've done work for the railroad before."

"From time to time," I said. "Why?"

"Reginald Pearson," Ambrose said. "He's been murdered."

"What?"

"Can you come take a look?" he said, puffing nervously on his cigar. "He was found in his compartment, shot in the back of the head. I need some expert advice on handling this properly."

"Sure thing," I said, glancing back at Laura. "Just let me tell the missis."

"Are you sure that's wise?" he said, his hand suddenly gripping my arm. He withdrew it as soon as he saw my stare.

When I got back to the table she'd lit up a cigarette and was staring out the window at the blackness.

"Hey, Mrs. Pope," I said. "Want to solve a crime?"

Her head swiveled toward me. "Oh, you know I love a good mystery. Now hurry up and sit down. They're already collecting the plates," she said, her impatient gestures pointing to my seat.

"Un-un," I said, bending over to whisper in her ear. I filled her in and told her to wait two minutes, and then get up, like she was going out to the ladies' room, but to make her way up through the two playing room cars. The actor's car was in front of them, and right behind the engine. Her eyes widened expectantly as she nodded. I straightened up and walked as nonchalantly as I could back toward the front of the dining car. The rest of the diners appeared oblivious to me, huddled in muted conversations as the waiters cleared off the tables. Ambrose stood in a cloud of smoke in the separation, watching me.

As we made our way through the first playing, or stage car, several stage hands and bit part actors were busy setting up the set for the first act. The play was sort of a parody of an old Sherlock Holmes movie called "Terror by Night." It involved Holmes, Watson, and Moriarty and the theft of some jewel. Reginald Pearson, a rather well-known English actor, was playing Holmes, and the part of Watson was played by Andrew Georger. Pearson had once been something of a force at the box office, but that had been twenty-five years ago. He and Georger had played the famous duo before in several movies and a British television series. The fact that they were both now doing dinner theater on a train-to-nowhere in the Midwest probably said something about their waning appeal. The novelty of this train-show was purported to be one of selecting a few members of the audience to assist in the unraveling of the plot, once the play got going. The play was written so that some of the would-be actors could read a few lines to assist the great detective in his deductions.

We went through the second stage car, which was only slightly less busy than the first. Since the setting of the play was a train, they didn't have a lot to do. I tugged on Ambrose's sleeve as we got into the final separation before the actor's car.

"Who all knows about this?" I asked.

He paused and dropped the stub of his cigar, grinding it under his shoe.

"Me, you, and Clancy," he said. "Unless you told your wife."

"That makes four then," I said, grinning. "Or maybe five, counting the murderer."

Ambrose seemed to pale visibly, as if all the blood was draining out of his face. I slapped him on the shoulder, not wanting to risk a hernia if he fainted and I had to pick him up. We went through the separation and entered a car with a long aisle. Solid looking walls and sturdy doors on each side, forming several compartments. The first one held about twelve of the lesser known players. Pearson, Georger, and Vivian Lake all had their own rooms. Lake had been Pearson's leading lady in a number of films dating back a few years and was rumored to be involved with him romantically. But then again, according to the tabloids, Pearson had always been something of a Lothario. I followed Ambrose up toward the end compartment where the uniformed conductor, Clancy, stood leaning against the wall. As soon as he saw me his big block face cracked into a wide smile and he extended his hand.

"Mr. Pope," he said, pumping my hand. "It's a pleasure to meet ya, sir. You probably don't remember me, but I was one of the trainmen you interviewed a few years back when you cracked that big Amtrak robbery."

He was right, I didn't remember him, but I said, "I thought you looked familiar."

This made him smile even more, and after he finally released my hand, I told him to keep an eye out for the missis, who was going to be coming forward to assist me in a very discreet fashion. Clancy nodded and winked conspiratorially.

"Oh, Clancy, by the way," I said. "How many railroad staff do you have on board?"

He licked his lips, then said, "Two cooks, three waiters, the engineer, and me. All regulars, and trustworthy."

"Thanks," I said, and twisted the knob to open Reginald Pearson's compartment, but it was locked. Clancy took out a huge ring of keys and sorted through them. He shoved a thin silver key into the lock, pushed open the door, then stepped aside. I went in, followed by Ambrose, who took out another cigar and started peeling back the wrapper. The compartment was fairly small. About 8 × 12.

"I'd rather you didn't do that," I said, pointing to the cigar. "The state police boys are gonna want to go over this place, and they don't appreciate spare ashes."

Ambrose nodded and put the cigar back in his pocket. I looked over at Pearson, who was seated in front of his make-up table with a circular hole in the back of his head. He'd been losing his hair at the crown, so the bullet made a neat little hole. Small caliber round, I surmised, from the size of the entry wound, which showed noticeable starring and powder burns. Pearson's face had been contorted from the internal impact, and he'd apparently slumped forward onto the table top. The mirror in front of him reflected the top of his head. A glass lay on the floor beside his left foot, its contents spilled into the tile floor. I touched his neck, feeling for a pulse. Nothing, but he was still warm and soft.

"He's dead, isn't he?" Ambrose asked. The loud clickety-clack of the wheels nearly covered the sound of his voice.

"Yeah, but I'm from Missouri. Now who found him, and when?"

"It was Clancy," Ambrose said. "The director was trying to prepare for the section where we use members of the audience, and Pearson had the amended script in his compartment. They sent Clancy to see if he was ready yet. He found him, and then got me."

"So you came to check him out?" I asked, looking around.

"No, I told Clancy to guard the door," he said.

"When was the last time anybody saw Pearson?"

Ambrose pondered this, then said, "We had an early dinner in the dining car. Afterward he went to put on his make-up and prepare. Maybe fifteen minutes."

A quick three raps on the door, and Clancy popped his head inside. "Mr. Pope, your missis is here."

"Fine," I said, nudging Ambrose. "We're done in here." As we stepped toward the door something crinkled under the sole of my shoe. I looked down to see what it was, then, as we stepped out, I told Clancy to lock the door again.

"Is he really dead?" Laura asked, leaning close to me.

"Extremely," I said. I turned to Clancy. "How fast is this train going?"

"We average anywheres from thirty-five to forty miles per hour."

"Any stops?"

He shook his head. "Nope. This section of rails is not even used anymore, except for us. Used to be a regular route back when the steel mills was running. But now we just start out at the main station downtown, travel on this line to the old Glenberry Station, then reverse the engine and go back. Timed for two hours and twenty-five minutes, round trip." He pulled a big watch out of his vest pocket and glanced at it. "Just about half-way now."

"Can anybody get off when we make the stop?" I asked.

"Not unless they pop one of the emergency exits," he said. "Then the buzzer'll go off. But they'd be in the middle of nowhere."

"Okay, Clancy. This is what we'll do. Let's assume that unless the killer's got a death wish, he ain't gonna jump off a train that's traveling at this rate of speed. Nor is he gonna jump off when we get to our half-way stop, unless he wants to be marooned in some remote location. So we'll operate under the assumption that he's still on board."

"Or she is," Laura said, smiling handily. "One mustn't jump to conclusions, must one?"

I paused and rubbed my fingers over my chin. "Right. So have the engineer keep moving as fast as he can, and you go radio the cops to meet us at the station when we get back. Got it?"

"Got it," he said with a grin. He ambled up toward the engine.

"What's next, darling?" Laura asked. Her face was flushed with excitement.

"We round up the usual suspects," I said.

"So you want me to have everyone move to the dining car?" Ambrose said.

"On the contrary," I said. "This had to be somebody that Pearson knew, otherwise he woulda seen 'em sneaking up on him in his mirror and turned around. Likewise, it most likely was somebody with a grudge against him. I suppose that eliminates most of the guests, myself and the missis here included."

Laura giggled. Ambrose's brow furrowed, and he asked what I wanted him to do.

"Let me speak to the other actors, starting with Georger and Miss Lake." I squinted sternly at both of them, adding, "And let me do all the talking."

We went down and knocked on Andrew Georger's room first. After a moment it swung inward and Georger appeared. He was a short, heavyset man of around fifty, with some sort of white bib tied under his chin. His fingers were pressing against a thick mustache, and his face was powdered with make-up. Two stiff-looking wings of hair flared out from a part down the center of his head.

"Yes?" he said.

"Mind if we come in?" I said, stepping past him. Laura and Ambrose filed in behind me. His compartment was slightly smaller than Pearson's. "There's been a new development. Reggie won't be able to perform tonight."

I'd wanted to watch his reaction as I'd said it. His thick eyebrows seemed to jut out over his eyes.

"What?" he said. "Don't tell me he's drunk again?"

"Let's just say that he's . . . indisposed," I said.

"Oh, damn it all," Georger said. He immediately went to his mirror and sat down. "Well, I can modify the performance, playing the Holmes role myself." He ran the comb through his hair, eliminating the center part in favor of one on the left side. "Lord knows, I've done it before. But you can tell him that this is positively the last time I will bail him out." He threw the comb onto the top of the table. "And you can tell him that I'm doing this in spite of his leaving me high wide and handsome." He slowly peeled off his gray handlebar mustache and began tracing descending lines on either side of his lips with an eyebrow pencil.

"High wide and handsome?" I said, thinking his face suddenly looked leaner somehow.

"Yes." Georger turned. "He signed for another twelve episodes of 'The New Adventures of Sherlock Holmes.' But they're hiring another actor for the part of Watson." His lips pursed sourly. "More money to pay his already inflated salary. Fidelity means nothing to the man, but I've known that for years."

"Sounds like you had reason to be bitter," I said. "Bitter enough to blow his brains out?" I grinned and watched, but Georger's expression didn't change.

"Don't think I haven't thought about it," he said, turning back to his mirror. He quickly glanced at his clock.

"Where'd you go after you ate?" I asked.

"I came here to put on my make-up," he said.

"Alone?"

"Of course. Why?"

"When's the last time you saw Pearson?" I said.

"I can't remember," he said, tossing down the pencil in favor of a brush. "At dinner, I suppose."

I cocked my head toward the door and said we'd be looking forward to his solo performance. Outside I looked at Laura.

"Well, whaddya think?" I said.

"I don't know," she said. "But it sounds like he despised Pearson. I guess he had reason to bump him off."

Ambrose nodded.

"Let's go see the lady," I said, moving over to Miss Lake's compartment. I knocked gently and heard a soft voice say, "Come in." I opened the door and saw the bare shoulders of Vivian Lake extending out of a white lace slip. She sat with her back to us, carefully etching the dark line of her left eyelid. "Yes, what is it?" she said, not looking away from the mirror.

"Hello, Miss Lake," I said. "My name's Pope. There's a slight problem with Mr. Pearson."

"Oh, really," she said, still tracing the dark liner over her eyelid. "Don't tell me that little blond number he'd been seeing on this rumbling heap showed up and tired him out too much?"

"Little blond number?" I said.

"Oh yeah," she said. "He didn't know that I knew, but after all this time, the only thing that surprised me was that he went to such uncharacteristic lengths to be so secretive. It wasn't like Reggie. Usually he flaunted each new conquest."

"I take it you weren't too upset then?" I said.

"No, why should I be?" she said.

"Well, I heard you and him were an item," I said.

She giggled as she stared intently at her reflection.

"The only item on Reggie's agenda was going to bed with as many women as he possibly could," she said. "Everything in a skirt was fair game to him. Your sister, your wife, your daughter. . . . They were all just potential notches on his bedpost."

I glanced over at Laura, who stood there wide-eyed. Ambrose's face seemed to darken, and he snorted as he went out into the hall. I nodded to Laura, and we left the lovely Miss Lake to the task of making herself even more lovely.

"Well, whaddya think now?" I asked Laura, pausing to take out my cigarettes. I held the pack toward her, then to Ambrose, who shook his head. He pulled the cigar out of his pocket, unwrapped it absently, and let the clear plastic wrapper fall to the floor.

"She didn't seem very upset that he'd been seeing someone else," Laura said. I held out my lighter for her, lit my own cigarette, then held the flame for Ambrose. "But she's an actress. The question is, how good of a one is she?"

"Pope, this is getting us nowhere," Ambrose said, exhaling a cloud of smoke. "I'm going order Clancy to herd everyone into the dining car, and we'll wait for the police there."

"Now why do you want to do that?" I said. "Let the show go on. Things might work out."

He snorted and stormed away. I let my gaze follow after his squat frame. The door separating this car from the engine slid open and Clancy came in.

"Okay, Mr. Pope," he said. "I got the state cops on the horn. They said nobody gets on or off till we get back to the station."

I turned to face him and felt something crackle under my shoe again. This time I stooped down to pick it up. It was the cellophane wrapper from Ambrose's cigar.

"Hey, Clancy," I said. "You smoke?"

"No, sir."

"Tell me again about how you found the body," I said.

"Well," he said. "The director said he needed the script to go over any changes that Mr. Pearson had wanted, so I went to his compartment to fetch it. I knocked on the door a couple of times, and when there was no answer, I opened it with my pass key. I seen him, and checked for a pulse, just like they do on TV. Then I locked the room back up and went and found Mr. Ambrose."

"Where'd you find him?" I asked.

"He was standing between the two stage cars smoking his cigar," Clancy said. "He asked what should we do, and that's when I told him about you being on board. He went to get you, and I guarded Mr. Pearson's compartment."

"Anybody go in before I got there?" I said.

"Nope," Clancy said, shaking his head emphatically.

I crumpled the cellophane in my hand, and took a final drag on my cigarette. "Clancy, this is real important." He nodded attentively. "Can you recall your exact words to Ambrose?"

Clancy's tongue traced over his lips before he answered. "Well," he said slowly. "I said, 'Mr. Pearson's dead. Somebody musta shot him or something.' "

"Is that all you said?" I asked quickly. He nodded. "Are you sure?"

"Yeah." He nodded again.

"And you didn't tell Ambrose that Pearson had been shot in the head?" I asked.

"No," he said slowly. "All I said was what I told ya."

"And Ambrose didn't go in till I got here?"

"Nope. I didn't let nobody in," he said. "Why?"

"How well you know Ambrose?" I asked.

"Pretty well," Clancy said. "We been doing this theater run with Mr. Pearson, Mr. Georger, and Miss Lake for the past seven months."

"Ambrose has been at it that long?" I said. "Any problems between him and Pearson?"

Clancy considered this for a moment, then shook his head.

"None that I ever seen," he said. "Mr. Ambrose seemed to like it. He never missed a trip till the tragedy with his daughter."

"What tragedy?" I said.

"His daughter, well, his step-daughter actually. Pretty little thing. Only seventeen. She used to ride this route with us all the time."

"What happened to her?" Laura asked.

He let out a slow breath before he answered. "She hung herself. Three weeks ago. Heard some guy knocked her—" He paused and glanced at Laura, who smiled coyly. "Got her in trouble. She didn't want to face her parents, I guess. They was crushed. Mrs. Ambrose took it real hard. I was kinda surprised that he came back to work so soon. But like I said, I guess this theater run was real important to him."

I fondled the cellophane wrapper in my hand, thinking about the last time I'd stepped on one. Then asked, "Ambrose's daughter . . . Was she a blond?" Laura was following my every word.

"Yeah," Clancy said slowly. "How'd you know?"

"Come on," I said, moving down the aisle in the direction that Ambrose had gone. "We gotta go grab your boss and hope that he was as careless about dropping the gun, as he was about dropping that other cigar wrapper inside Pearson's compartment. After he killed him."

"Holy mackerel," Clancy said. "Are you kiddin' me?"

"My husband never kids about murder," Laura said, falling into step beside me with a broad smile. "And somehow he always manages to figure out whodunit before I do."

Will Lunch Be Ready on Time?

Elizabeth Engstrom

SISSY STEPPED aside to let the policemen enter. The hot feeling in her tummy sank down low and rumbled in there like gas. Even though she'd been expecting them, she didn't expect they'd be so—so—powerful, or something.

The big policeman sat down on the edge of the secondhand sofa. His huge belly hung over his wide black belt and he looked uncomfortable and out of place. He set his hat on the threadbare cushion next to him and seemed careful not to touch the sofa arm, which was dirty, and had stuffing pulled out and worried into little balls by children's idle fingers. The thin policeman removed his hat, showing an amazing amount of bright red hair, then he turned a kitchen table chair around and sat on it. Sissy couldn't see them both at the same time, and that made her nervous. She smoothed her dress and buttoned the only two buttons left on her brown cardigan.

"Now," the big policeman said. "Why don't you tell us about the party you had here last night?"

"It was no party," Sissy said. "Those people came and tried to bully us around."

"They said you served them liquor."

"Papa had a jug. They took it."

"Where is your papa, Sissy?" The question came from over at the kitchen table, and it threw Sissy off balance.

"I'm not sure, but he'll be back soon. He always is."

"Your daddy drink a lot, Sissy?" It was the big policeman on the couch again.

"Yeah. He goes off on 'toots,' Ma used to call them."

"Where's your Ma?"

Sissy whipped around to face the redhead. "Ma died during last year's thaw."

"And your papa leaves you kids all alone?" It was the fat one again.

"We're not alone," Sissy said, "we're together. I'm fourteen, and I keep a good house, can't you see? I'm the one sent Jane to call you police when those people came, ain't that bein' responsible? And there's—Meg, she's older . . ." Sissy's voice trailed off as she pointed at Meg, who stood, looking more retarded than ever, leaning against the kitchen wall. "And besides. Papa will come back pretty soon. He's just out hunting."

"His shotgun is leanin' up against the kitchen door, Sissy," the thin policeman said.

The feeling in her stomach was giving way to anger. "He got hisself a new one."

The big policeman stood up. "Okay, Sissy. The house looks—it looks like you're doing a fine job here. We're not here to hassle you. But if you need help, you just give a shout, okay?"

"Long as those people don't come back, we'll be fine."

"You're sure they didn't hurt any of you?"

"Nah. They didn't hurt nobody."

"I don't think they'll be back here. We had a nice long talk with them, if you know what I mean."

Sissy looked at her dirty toes and wished she had some socks or something. She hadn't done a very good job being a grown-up in front of these big policemen and their uniforms. "Okay," she said.

"I'm going to send Miss Ruthie over to check on you, maybe tomorrow, just in case there's anything you need."

"We won't need nothing."

"You got food for all of you?"

The feeling in her bowels gave a lurch. "We got food," she said, and her face grew hot.

"Well, I'll have her come by, just in case, Sissy. And when your pa shows up, have him give us a call, okay? I'd like to talk to him." The policeman bent over and picked up the baby that was crawling over his shoes.

"That's Bucky," Sissy said. "He's always into mischief."

The big policeman held Bucky at arm's length and the baby and the fat man smiled at each other for a minute, then he handed him over to Sissy. "So there's Bucky here, and Meg, and Jane, and you—that's four. Any others?"

"Willie." Sissy looked at her feet again, brushed some dust around with her toes.

"Where's Willie?"

"Out back. Chopping wood for the cookstove."

The policeman put on his hat. "Have your pa come see me, Sissy."

"Yes, sir, I will." Sissy saw them to the door and held the screen so it didn't slam behind them. The baby squirmed in her arms at the blast of frigid air, but all she felt was relief that the intruders were gone and she was back in her home with just her family.

She closed the wood door, giving it an extra shove with her shoulder, then she felt Bucky's full diaper, so she took him over to Meg. "Change him, Meg," she said, "then you better get started on washing them diapers. I'll have Willie bring in some wood for hot water." Sissy waited to make sure her big sister understood, then she pulled on Ma's brown cloth coat, wrapped the plaid scarf around her neck, shoved her feet into Pa's big old gumboots and went out back where Willie was working.

Her little brother, already muscular, shirt off and thrown into the snow, steamed sweat from his skin as he split another chunk of wood and threw the pieces onto the pile. Sissy picked up an armload and smiled at Willie, who looked like a man before he'd seen her and now looked like a little boy about to whine. "Doin' fine, Willie," she said, then went back into the house and dropped the wood into a cardboard box next to the stove. She wrapped the end of her scarf around the handle of the stove and opened it, threw in three pieces of wood, then closed it again, and adjusted the damper. Then she filled two white enamel pots with water from the pump at the sink and set them on the stove to heat. One for washing diapers, one for cooking lunch.

She wet down a rag and folded it, then lay it on the stove between the pots. It sizzled, and she took off the coat and scarf while she waited for it to warm through. Then she turned it over and sizzled it on the other side while she took off Pa's boots and stood them next to the kitchen door. Then she picked up the hot rag, and tossing it lightly between her hands, took it into Ma's bedroom where Jane was in bed with her frostbitten feet wrapped up.

"How ya feelin', Janey?" Sissy asked.

"Fine."

Sissy unwrapped the cool rags and checked the toes. They looked about the same. Bloodless, and pruny from being wrapped up in warm, wet cloths. She rewrapped them, including the fresh, hot rag, then took a look at the picture Jane was drawing on her chunk of chalkboard.

"That was a brave thing you did last night, Janey," Sissy said, smoothing the hair away from Jane's forehead. "It musta hurt like holy hell to run to the Parkers' on them feet."

"Wasn't so bad."

Sissy kissed her little sister's forehead.

"Will lunch be ready on time?" Jane asked.

"Sure will, won't be long. Soon as Willie's finished chopping wood, I'll send him in to tell you a story, okay? Helps to pass the time."

"You're a good mom, Sissy," Jane said, and Sissy felt warm and proud.

"We gotta be a family, Jane," she said. "A family's the most important thing in the world, remember Ma used to say? We gotta stick together, and if we do," she touched her sister's freckled nose, "ain't nothing going to hurt us."

"If those people don't come back."

"They won't. The policeman said—"

"I heard the policemen. I heard you tell them Papa was out hunting."

"I'm going to take care of us, Janey. You've got nothing to worry about."

"What if they come back?"

"You heard—"

"I *mean* the policemen."

Sissy fingered the worn quilt that had been on Ma's bed ever since Sissy was born—before, even.

"You just work on them feet, Janey. You get life back in them feet, and that's all you need to do. Everything else will work out just fine. You just get them feet well."

Sissy patted her little sister on the head, then returned to the kitchen, doubts and worries heavy on her shoulders. People were all the time interfering. Those bad people could come back, Miss Ruthie was coming tomorrow, the police would eventually get nosy . . . With five mouths to feed, now that Meg wouldn't nurse the baby anymore, they'd need a lot of food.

That feeling in her stomach began to burn. Maybe somebody *should* interfere. Maybe somebody *should* come and take over.

No, Sissy said to herself, pushing the feeling away. We can do it on our own. I can shoot a rabbit. I can hunt a pheasant. So can Willie. We can do it. We don't need Pa breathing booze all over us. We don't need no more babies. We can take care of our own.

The kitchen was warming up around the stove. Sissy stood close to it, soaking up the warmth, feeling the tops of her feet warming, even though the bottoms, with their thick crust of callus, were perpetually cold. She tested the diaper water with her finger, and called to Meg to come get it. The frozen pile of dirty diapers out the back door was an eyesore, and Bucky had only a couple of clean ones left. When Meg came into the kitchen, Sissy showed her which pot was for diapers, then took a freshly changed Bucky into the bedroom to entertain Jane. Then she rummaged around in the dusty boxes underneath the sink and came up with a misshapen potato and two runty onions. She fetched the half carrot she'd put on the cold windowsill to keep, and cut them all up into the water.

"See, Ma?" Sissy looked at the ceiling. "You teached us good, and we'll get along just fine. We're a good family, now. A real good one."

She sprinkled salt into the water and threw in a handful of dried beans from the burlap sack Willie had refilled at the church the first of every month.

She stirred the water around with the wooden spoon and looked into the pot. The vegetables and beans floated on top of the water. Children need meat every day, Ma used to say. The hot feeling rose from her stomach and lodged under her heart. We can always afford to eat meat, she said, even if it's just the broth cooked off a chicken leg. Sissy swirled the water around again. Five children can't grow on this—it needs meat.

Sissy put the spoon down and got back into Ma's coat. She wrapped the scarf around her neck and pulled a kitchen chair over to the tall cabinet. She stepped up on the chair and opened the cabinet, then reached way into the back. Ma had taught her good about safety with little children around the house. Sissy took extra care, now that she had taken Ma's place.

Her hand closed on the wood handle and she brought Grandma's heavy cleaver forward, with care and reverence. Carefully, she stepped down from the chair, and without setting the cleaver down again for fear she'd forget it just long enough for Bucky to hurt himself, she put her feet into Pa's gumboots and opened the door.

She stopped for a moment, and listened. Jane was talking to Bucky in the bedroom, and the baby was giggling. Meg was sloshing the diapers in the screened room. Willie brought the axe down and split another piece of wood.

Sissy hid the cleaver inside the big coat and closed the door behind her. The hot feeling wrapped itself around her heart and gave a squeeze.

She stopped to watch Willie for a moment. He'd made quite a pile of firewood.

"Four more pieces, okay, Willie?"

He looked up and she saw he was crying. Tears made streaks in the dirt on his cold-reddened face, and his nose was running.

"Just four more pieces, okay, Willie? Then maybe we'll have enough to last us through tomorrow, too."

Without comment, Willie set another hunk of log on the stump and picked up the axe. He was beginning to move like an old man, Sissy thought, and the feeling eased up its grip.

Sissy hurried beyond him, her feet crunching in the snow. She had to hurry if she was going to beat Willie inside. It wouldn't take him long to finish up.

She unhooked the door in the chicken-wire deer fence that housed the vegetable garden in the summer, slipped inside and closed it behind her. It was a good fence; it kept out the deer in the summer and kept out the dogs in the winter. Sissy shivered, feeling the cold on her bare knees. Her eyes moved to the corner of the garden, next to the shed, where Jane had hidden, huddled in the dark, afraid. The snow in the corner was all stomped down, and Sissy could see the bare footprints with the little toe marks. That snow had frozen those little toes and they might never recover. Poor Janey. Poor, brave little Janey.

Willie's axe came down and split a chunk.

Sissy returned to the task at hand.

The snow covered Pa so thick he looked like a grave mound, which was the right kind of thing for him to look like, Sissy thought. She set the cleaver down and dug through the snow until she found his foot.

She started on it with the cleaver, thinking about Janey, shivering there in the dark. "Get out!" Sissy had yelled as soon as she'd been able to pull Pa off her, and Janey had run out the door, had run here to the garden, barefoot, in just her little nightie, while Pa raged and finally Willie had got the axe and put Pa down.

She chopped on the frozen flesh, and as she did, she thought of how they'd had to deal with Pa ever since Ma died. The feeling in her heart turned to anger. How could he have treated Ma the way he did? It was no wonder Ma died, and after she did, then he started going after Meg, only Meg never put up a fuss, so Sissy and Willie and Janey kind of never minded, but then when Meg got so big with Bucky, he began eyeing Janey, and Sissy wouldn't stand for that.

The foot suddenly came free, and Sissy gasped at what she'd done, then noticed that she, too, was crying. And the hot feeling was gone.

She wiped the tears off her cheeks with her hands, then wiped her nose on the sleeve of Ma's coat. That foot's no good, she thought. They'll all recognize it. She sliced through Pa's trousers with the sharp edged cleaver, then began again, midshin. She worked quickly, without emotion. When it came free, she covered up the rest with snow, then tucked the meat inside her coat with the cleaver and left the garden, wiring the door shut carefully behind her. Willie was on his last piece of wood. She saw that he wasn't crying anymore, either. Sissy ran to the house, letting the screen door slam behind her. She pulled the meat from under her coat, wondered for a second if it should be peeled, then slipped it into the boiling soup.

She smiled to herself. There'll be a nice bone for the hound, too, she thought, then got up on the chair to put the cleaver away.

Win Some, Lose Some

Jack Ritchie

I RUBBED my hands. "Ah, what have we here?"

"A body," Ralph said.

We did indeed. It was that of Paula Washburn, age 36, weight possibly a bit over 130.

She lay prone on the carpeted floor of the walk-in vault-safe. Just beyond her right hand lay a pearl necklace and two diamond rings. Her body had been discovered at 4:30 P.M. by her stepdaughter, Marianne, when she had opened the vault to take another admiring look at her law diploma.

The vault was perhaps eight feet deep, seven wide, and seven high. I supposed that, if it became necessary, I could resort to mathematics and determine just how long a person would survive locked in a room of that size; in this case, however, I did not think that would be necessary. There were other things to consider.

On the far wall of the vault ranged a bank of various-sized safety-deposit boxes. To one side stood three four-door filing cabinets.

"Ralph," I said, "we are here faced with three possibilities."

"All I see are two. Either she got accidentally locked inside or somebody did the locking on purpose."

I chuckled good-naturedly. "Have you considered suicide?"

"Not lately, Henry. Who's going to commit suicide by locking herself in a vault? It isn't a neat way to go."

"Ralph, you, as others, are guilty of a common misconception on the question of asphyxiation in vaults. You seem to think that the ending would entail a desperate gasping for air. *Au contraire.* As the percentage of oxygen in the air decreased, one would simply become drowsy, lapse into unconsciousness, and then glide into death."

"You think she might have committed suicide?"

"By no means, Ralph. I was merely touching all bases. If she came down here with the intention of committing suicide, would she just stand there clutching her jewelry—possibly for hours—until she keeled over? No, it would be the normal thing to at least put them down somewhere. On the filing cabinets, for example. Or in the pocket of her dressing gown." I shook my head. "No, Ralph, she did not commit suicide."

I went to the bank of safety-deposit boxes and tested them once again. They were all locked. So were the filing cabinets.

Ralph watched me. "All right, Henry, so maybe she came down here to put away her jewels for the night and the door swung shut behind her and trapped her inside?"

"No, Ralph. As we have seen and tested, the vault door is quite heavy and not at all free-swinging. It requires at least some continuous effort either to open or to shut it. In short, it cannot accidentally drift shut."

Ralph agreed. "Which leaves us with murder. Let's talk to the suspects." There were three of those and they waited out of earshot at the farther end of the rather large drawing room.

James Washburn, husband of the deceased, age in the early fifties: tall, distinguished, open-countenanced, and deep in thought. Marianne, his daughter: small, raven-haired, wary eyes behind shell glasses. And Ronald Goodcart, a distant cousin of the deceased and a weekend guest at the house. Ronald was in his early forties, had black hair, a thin black mustache, and the general mien of a cad.

All three were quite solemn, none of them exhibiting undue grief at the death of Paula Washburn. They had, of course, undergone some preliminary questioning by the uniformed officers who arrived first at the scene. Ralph and I now moved in for in-depth interrogation.

I introduced Ralph and then myself. "Detective Sergeant Henry H. Turnbuckle, MPD." I waited for signs of recognition, but they withheld them.

I regarded James Washburn. "How long were you and the deceased married?"

"Three years. About that."

"When and where did you last see your wife alive?"

"In our bedroom last night at about eleven thirty. She suddenly remembered her jewelry and told me she was going back downstairs to put it into the vault for the night."

I nodded judiciously. "It is now five thirty in the afternoon of the following day and the body was discovered less than one hour ago. How can you explain that?"

"Nobody opened the vault until then."

"I mean you hadn't seen your wife for approximately eighteen hours and yet you never thought to sound some kind of an alarm?"

"I didn't know she was locked in the vault."

I smiled thinly. "Your wife leaves your bedroom, telling you that she is going to put her jewelry into the vault, and she doesn't return? Didn't that make you wonder just a smidgen where she might be?"

"Not really. We sleep in twin beds. After she left the room, I closed my eyes and immediately fell asleep. I didn't wake until nine this morning."

"But surely when you glanced at her bed this morning and found it unoccupied, didn't you begin to wonder where she was?"

"No. I thought she'd just gotten up early and gone downstairs. Paula usually has no more than a cup of coffee for breakfast and then is off. She led a rather independent life and usually didn't bother to let people know where she was going or for how long. I've gone entire weekends without ever seeing her."

"Who discovered the body?"

Marianne Washburn now spoke. "I did. At about four thirty this afternoon when I opened the vault to take another look at my sheepskin. Paula lay there on the floor inside, quite dead."

"Your sheepskin?"

"My law degree. *Magna cum laude,* and stuff. I'm going to have it framed when I open my office, but for now I keep it in the vault and peek at it every now and then. The vault is our storage place for valuable things that are smaller than a bread box. Jewelry, cash, papers, records, mementoes, and new diplomas."

"Isn't there any way to open the vault from the inside? Or at least an alarm button which a person could press if he were imprisoned inside?"

"I'm afraid not. The vault was built into the house nearly fifty years ago. Today I suppose a vault must incorporate all kinds of safety features, but in those days they weren't so particular."

"The vault is opened by a combination lock?"

"Yes."

"Who has the combination? Besides you?"

"Dad does. Paula did." She looked at Ronald Goodcart.

He shook his head. "No. Why should I?"

I spoke to Marianne. "When you found Mrs. Washburn, did you touch her, move or take anything?"

"No." Marianne sighed. "Poor Paula. It's obvious that when she went downstairs to put away her jewelry the door of the vault accidentally shut behind her, trapping her inside."

I smiled. "My dear young lady, I have inspected and tested the vault door thoroughly. No vagrant breath of air could set it in motion."

She considered that, then sighed again. "I was just trying to protect Paula's memory. She was so depressed lately. Her health, you know. She had this bad heart. Everybody knows it. Morose and downhearted. Brooding all the time. She must have decided to take her own life."

"Nonsense," Ronald Goodcart said. "Paula was quite cheerful. Vibrant. Besides, she would have left a note."

Marianne regarded him with disdain. "Suicides do not necessarily leave notes. Besides, it could have been a sudden impulse and she discovered too late that she didn't have a pencil and paper with her."

"Ah, yes," I said. "Actually the most interesting aspect of this entire case is the fact that the victim did not leave a note or any *other* communication behind. It is the very crux of this matter."

Ralph was impressed. "You've gotten to the crux already, Henry?"

I nodded. "The body of Paula Washburn was examined by us, was it not, Ralph? And what did we find in the pocket of her dressing gown?"

"Just a small handkerchief."

"Exactly." I turned back to the suspects. "Let us suppose that Paula Washburn came downstairs to put away her jewelry. She opened the vault door by dialing the combination. And *then* what? *Where,* inside the vault, did she intend to put this jewelry?"

Washburn volunteered. "She stored her jewelry in one of the safety-deposit boxes."

I nodded encouragement. "And how did she intend to get *into* that safety-deposit box?"

"With her key, of course."

"Ah, but we found *no* key on her person, or on the floor, or anywhere else in the vault. And all the safety-deposit boxes *and* the filing cabinets are locked. So where did she intend to put this jewelry if she had no key with her?"

Marianne was still trying to sell suicide. "It's obvious, isn't it? She simply forgot the key. It was the last straw, so to speak. Everything had been going wrong all day and she had a headache too. So in one mad moment of frustration and despair, she pulled the vault door shut after her and said goodbye to the world."

I did not buy. "No, Paula Washburn did *not* forget her key. Someone *else* did. And that was the person who closed the vault door behind her."

I had been expecting a gasp or two, but they restrained themselves.

"Ralph," I said, "were there any marks of violence on the victim's body? Anything to suggest that she had been shot, stabbed, bludgeoned, strangled? Any discoloration or suspicious odor which might suggest poisoning?"

"Nothing. The coroner won't get around to the autopsy until after he's had supper, but he says that asphyxiation is a good bet."

I agreed. "And now we come to the poser, the conundrum, the puzzle. Why did Paula Washburn leave no note, no message, no communication of any kind?"

I smiled about. "Suppose that you had just been locked in a vault and knew it had been no accident. Wouldn't you at least have tried to tell the world who locked you in there?"

"Maybe she didn't know," Ralph said.

"A possibility, Ralph. However, even if she *didn't* know who had locked her in, wouldn't she at least have left some kind of information behind indicating that she *had* been locked in and that it hadn't been accidental?"

"She lost her head and panicked," Ralph said. "And it just didn't come to her mind."

"No, Ralph. While panic might be the first and natural reaction, I find it impossible to believe that she could have sustained that panic for three, four, five, or whatever hours it would have taken her to collapse. At some point during that time she would surely have recovered enough aplomb to at least leave a message about her suspicions or certainties. And yet she left none. Why not?"

Ralph speculated. "Maybe she *did* leave a message, Henry. A note. But the murderer waited a few hours until he was certain she was dead. And then he opened the vault, pocketed the note, and closed the vault again."

"Possible, Ralph. However, that flimsy theory depends on the victim just happening to have a writing implement and paper in her pocket. Hardly likely, I should think."

573

I allowed a pause. *"However,* in such an emergency couldn't she have found some other instrument to write with or a surface to put it on?"

I smiled. "The *diamond* rings. Surely it would have occurred to her to use her diamond rings as writing implements and she could have used any plain surface—the sides or the tops of the filing cabinets, for instance—as her slate? She could very easily have scratched the name of her murderer, or simply indicated that someone unknown had locked her in there. And yet she didn't do this. Why not?"

There was silence.

Ralph frowned. "She was unconscious? The murderer knocked her out before he put her in there?"

"But we found no cranial bruises or injury sufficient to produce such unconsciousness. Besides, even if she were unconscious before being put in there, what guarantee did the murderer have that she would *remain* unconscious until she died by asphyxiation."

Ralph tried again. "She was drugged. That would have held her until she suffocated."

"But surely the murderer must have known that, under the mysterious circumstances of her death, an autopsy would be performed and the presence of drugs discovered in her body." I shook my head. "No, Ralph, the murderer was not the least bit worried about her leaving a message or drugs being found in her system because Paula Washburn was *already dead* when she was locked in the vault."

There were moments of awed silence at my relentless reasoning and then Ralph said, "She didn't die of asphyxiation?"

"Ah, Ralph, but she *did* die of asphyxiation. That was the whole point in putting her body into the vault."

I assumed a grim expression. "She was asphyxiated, but *not* in the vault. And she was put into the vault to cover up the fact that she *was* asphyxiated, but somewhere else. And considering what she was wearing at the time of her death—that is, pajamas and a dressing gown—would not that lead us back to one particular room in the house?"

I turned to stare at James Washburn. "Perhaps a plastic bag slipped over her head? But more likely the old-fashioned pillow?"

James Washburn sighed heavily, looked utterly resigned, and opened his mouth to speak.

Marianne spoke first. "I see it all so clearly now. At eleven thirty last night Paula left father's bedroom, telling him she was going downstairs to put away her jewelry. But instead she slipped down the hall to Ronald's bedroom for a tryst, an assignation, a rendezvous."

Goodcart blinked. "She did *not*."

Marianne ignored him. "The two of them had a lover's quarrel. Harsh, bitter words were exchanged. She told him their affair was finished."

Ronald protested. "It never began."

Marianne swept on. "In his moment of rage he seized a pillow and smothered Paula. Then, realizing he had to cover up the crime, he carried her body down to the vault, hoping to make it appear that she had died there accidentally."

Ronald had begun to perspire. "But I don't even know the combination of the vault."

She smiled insincerely in his direction. "We have only your untrustworthy word for that. *Everybody* knows that Paula was a complete witch—if I pronounced that word correctly. She continually flittered from hither to yon and last night you were the nearest hither."

I shook my head. "A noble effort, Miss Washburn, but sheer logic indicates that a woman would not blatantly tell her husband she was going to put her jewelry into the vault and then instead sashay down the hall to an assignation. Her husband might not innocently fall asleep at her departure. After a time he might even come looking for her. No, it is much more logical to assume that if she intended any such action, she would *first* wait until she was certain her husband had fallen asleep before she ventured out of the bedroom."

I took my celluloid card out of my breast coat pocket.

Ralph stopped me. "What are you doing, Henry?"

"I'm about to read Mr. Washburn his rights."

"Why?"

"The Supreme Court insists on it."

Ralph took me aside. "Henry, you know and I know that Washburn killed his wife. Everybody in this room does. But what *solid* proof do we have? I'm talking about things that people can see and touch. People like district attorneys who have to get the indictments or the judges who have to issue them."

"Ralph, the man seems almost eager to confess."

"Henry, I doubt that his daughter, the brand-new lawyer, will allow him to confess to anything."

Marianne had edged close enough to hear us. She nodded and smiled sweetly.

I experienced moral indignation. "Ralph, we have here a cold-blooded murder. This man held a pillow over the face of his wife until she was asphyxiated. Seven or eight minutes, assuming that there was no leakage of air. But probably longer."

James Washburn had joined us. "Seven or eight minutes? But it wasn't anywhere near—"

Marianne quickly put her hand over his mouth. "Suppose," she said, "suppose this somebody who wielded the pillow merely wanted to stop the victim's vituperation and hysteria. He had no intention at all of murdering her. He just wanted to shut her up for a while. He held the pillow over her head for perhaps one minute."

Washburn freed his mouth. "Maybe not even that long."

"Maybe less," Marianne said swiftly. "And when Paula ceased to struggle, he removed the pillow from her face and was utterly astounded to discover she was dead."

Washburn nodded eagerly.

Marianne glared at him for a moment, then continued, "And suppose that since he had no conception at all as to the amount of time it takes to asphyxiate anyone with a pillow, he merely *assumed* he had killed her? Actually she had died of a heart attack, not of asphyxiation. And so, succumbing to perfectly understandable panic, he carried her body down to the vault and tried to make it appear as though she had accidentally locked herself inside."

I folded my arms. "Even assuming that is what occurred, in this state if a person dies as the result of stress during a hostile act, it would be considered at least manslaughter."

Marianne smiled. "But can you *prove* even manslaughter? And there will be *no* confession. And if this person were somehow convicted—which is highly unlikely since thirty-seven character witnesses will testify in his behalf—he will probably—considering his unblemished past and his standing in the community—be put on probation for six months. Would you cause all that trouble just to stick some poor unfortunate soul with a six-months' probation?"

There was respectful silence while I stared out of a window.

Finally I put my celluloid card back into my pocket. "Ralph, my mother cried for three days when she discovered that I had joined the Milwaukee Police Department. She was right."

"Now, now, Henry," Ralph said. "We win some and we lose some." He turned to the others. "Does anyone have a glass of sherry?"

"Not here, Ralph," I said firmly.

Ralph embarrassed me further by explaining. "Whenever one of Henry's cases doesn't go just right, he finds that a glass or two of sherry helps to buck him up."

Ronald Goodcart folded his arms. "I'll bet he drinks a lot."

That remark was entirely uncalled for. I consume perhaps one bottle of sherry a year. Well, maybe two.

I declined their sherry and we left.

At eight that evening the coroner phoned me at my apartment to let me know that the autopsy had shown that Paula Washburn had died of a heart attack, not of asphyxiation.

At nine my door buzzer sounded.

It was Marianne. "Do you realize that you are the only Turnbuckle in the telephone directory?"

I sighed. "I am the only Turnbuckle who ever left Sheboygan for more than a weekend."

She held up what looked like a bottle in a paper bag. "I thought I'd drop in and see if it's possible to cheer you up."

It was.

The Woman at the Pond

Hugh B. Cave

THE POND WAS Eric Carlson's creation, so cleverly done that I thought at first it was natural. He smiled when he told me it was not. Willows lined its gently sloping banks, dipping their branches among lily pads. Sunfish fed with little popping sounds on an evening hatch of insects. A slender, attractive woman, all in black, sat on a stone bench under an ancient white oak, gazing at the water.

I glanced at Eric in surprise. When inviting me to his Connecticut estate for the weekend, he hadn't told me there would be another guest.

"Ruth's sister, Myra Cartwright," he said. "Did I tell you about her in Greece?"

"Not that I remember."

"I'd better, then, or you'll think us a bit queer. Suppose we go back to the house."

The woman on the bench did not even look up as we turned to depart.

In his study Eric gazed at me in silence for a moment before he spoke. We were good friends by this time: moments of silence between us were a natural thing. I had met him and his attractive wife, Ruth, while on a holiday in the Mediterranean a couple of months before. We had knocked about Italy and Greece together. He was an architect, one of the best and most expensive. Ruth painted.

"The woman you saw out there is Ruth's twin," he said at last. "I don't suppose you noticed the resemblance. The light wasn't too good."

I shook my head. "Sometimes even a close resemblance has to be pointed out before you actually notice it," I said.

Eric nodded understandingly. "She's been with us more than two years now. Ever since her husband died. I think I may have to fill in the pond because of her. You're a doctor, George. Perhaps you can advise me."

I waited.

"Just over two years ago," Eric went on, "Myra married a man she hardly knew. We were not really surprised. She had been ready for marriage for a long time—ever since changing from a spoiled, unhappy girl to a lovely and loving young woman. The change began when her mother remarried, letting her live her own life. Her father had died years before.

"The man Myra married was six years older than she, and she met him in Florida where he was considering the purchase of a hotel. For three weeks—she assures me they were the happiest weeks she had ever known—they swam, danced, dined, and talked. Then they returned to New York together and were married.

"Alan Blanchard had a home here in Connecticut, not more than an hour's drive from this place. He was a widower. His money—he told Myra this quite frankly—had come from his former wife. She had been exceedingly well off, there had been no children, she had left everything to him. He was investing it in hotels. He knew a good deal about hotels, and had managed a big one in the West Indies.

"Myra knew nothing much else about him except that he was seemingly devoted to her. They spent three wonderful months at his Connecticut house and then, in June, Alan suggested a week at a fishing camp he owned in Maine.

" 'Just the two of us,' he told her. 'No friends dropping in. No phone. Almost no road.'

"When Myra protested that she didn't know the first thing about fishing, he promised to teach her.

"She had been writing some letters, and when he drove to the village that evening to buy some paperback novels at the drug store she gave them to him to drop at the post office. 'Now don't forget,' she cautioned him. 'This long one is those papers Ted wanted me to sign.' Ted Ashenheim was her lawyer. She was having him re-arrange her will and insurance policies.

"In the morning they got off a bit later than they had planned. In fact, the mailman was coming up the walk as they left. But it was a perfect day. They stopped at intimate little places for lunch and dinner, and darkness found them on a dirt road, deep in the Maine woods, miles beyond the last drowsy hamlet.

" 'You know something, Mrs. Blanchard?' Alan said. 'I love you.'

" 'You'd better,' Myra told him. 'I can't very well walk out from here.'

"It was true: she never could have walked out from that place. The lodge was on a wilderness lake at the end of an abandoned, eighteen-mile-long logging road. But it was a heavenly spot, serene and beautiful.

"While Alan was building a fire in the big stone fireplace, Myra went out to the car for the mail they had taken from the postman that morning. There were two letters, both for her. One was unimportant. The other was from her mother."

Interrupting his story, Eric unlocked a drawer of his study desk and silently handed me a letter. It was on expensive paper, and the handwriting was such that, right or wrong, my mind immediately saw a grim, sharp-faced woman triumphantly scratching out the words.

As you know, the letter said, *I was suspicious from the beginning. Now I am certain. Do you know how his first wife died? Has he ever told you? At last I have found out. She 'fell overboard' one night from a cruise ship in the Caribbean. Can you imagine a perfectly normal, healthy girl, who didn't even drink, falling over a ship's rail? I'm sure I can't. But she was his wife long enough to name him her sole beneficiary. Think of that before you commit the same fatal mistake.*

Eric took the letter from me and returned it to the desk.

"Myra read that ghastly thing," he went on, "and thrust it back into its envelope as Alan, a heavy poker in his hand, turned from the fire to face her. 'Tomorrow we'll go fishing,' he was saying, 'and have a picnic lunch on the island.'

"She had become a statue, of course, staring at him.

" 'What's the matter, darling?' he said, apparently startled. 'Is something wrong?'

"She could only shake her head. Her tongue, like the rest of her, was frozen. With a frown of concern he put the poker down and reached for her hands. 'Why, you're cold,' he said. 'You're like ice. Darling, you're all in. It was that eighteen miles of bad road.'

"She nodded helplessly.

" 'You need sleep,' he said, lifting her to her feet. 'You go on up to bed while I unload the car.'

"She pretended to sleep, but it was near dawn before she stopped being aware of the vast loneliness of that place. The wind sighed in the pines. Waves slapped against the lake's rocky shore. An owl kept up a mournful complaint just outside the bedroom window. When she did fall asleep at last, she did not wake until noon.

"Alan was in the kitchen, making coffee, and her carefully applied makeup fooled him. 'Now you look more like it,' he said, embracing her. 'Hungry?'

" 'A little,' she replied.

" 'Good. Sit and talk to me while I scramble some eggs. You didn't know I could cook, did you?'

"You can imagine what thoughts must have been passing through her mind. There were so many things she did not know about him.

" 'After lunch I'll row you around the lake,' he said. 'We have both a rowboat and a canoe, in case you haven't noticed. The fish won't be biting this time of day, but we can go for a cruise.'

Cruise, she told herself. *A cruise ship in the Caribbean. And I don't swim. And he knows it.*

"She shook her head at him. 'This place needs a good cleaning. You go, while I put things straight here.'

"But he would not leave her. All afternoon he helped her about the lodge, and in the evening, with a fire again blazing in the fireplace, he read one of his paperbacks. It was a mystery story, she noticed. They all were. And she began to think—why had he refused to leave her alone? To make sure she would not take the car and escape? But to prevent that he could simply have put the ignition key in his pocket.

"Perhaps he had, to make doubly sure.

"In the morning she was downstairs before him, and when she heard him in the bathroom she ran out to the car. The keys were not in it. He *had* taken them. But had he done so deliberately, or merely from habit?

" 'Today we *are* going fishing,' he told her. 'No excuses now. I won't listen.'

"Panic seized her for a moment, but she had prepared for it and the moment passed before he could be suspicious. 'It's going to rain,' she protested. 'Look outside.'

" 'Nonsense.'

" 'No, really. Go look.'

"The sky *was* dark; he could not deny it. But he knew the patterns of weather here, he insisted. After a light shower the sun would shine. 'Come on,' he begged. 'We didn't drive all this way just to sit around the house.'

" 'I don't want to get wet. If I do, I'll catch cold and be useless.'

"For an hour he pleaded with her, keeping his disappointment under control until the very end. Then, showing some annoyance, he said, 'Well, I'll go out alone then, just to the island.' And with rod and tackle box he marched down to the shore.

"He took the canoe. From a window she watched him paddle it expertly away from the pier. When he was half way there, she ran upstairs and snatched the clothes he had worn on the drive from Connecticut.

"The car keys were in a pocket of his trousers. He had been so eager to get her out on the lake that he had forgotten to take them when he changed.

"She watched him now through binoculars. He was going to the island, he had said. She would let him get there before she fled; then, if he heard the car and raced back to stop her, it would be impossible for him to get back in time. She saw him ease the canoe against a rocky ledge and tie it to an overhanging branch. With rod and tackle box he disappeared into some trees.

"Now.

"She threw some of her things into a suitcase and ran downstairs, through the kitchen, into the yard. She was desperately afraid, even now. What if the car refused to start? What if she came to grief on that eighteen-mile stretch of wilderness road? He would find some way to overtake her, she was certain. He was resourceful. Look how patiently, how cunningly, he had tried to lure her into going out on the lake with him.

"Opening the car door, she turned for a last panicky look at the island, and saw him. He was high up on the ledge of rock, gazing down at the canoe. And the canoe was moving.

"She saw at once what had happened. A gust of wind, darkening the surface of the water as it raced across the lake, had plucked the craft from its flimsy mooring. It was already thirty feet from shore.

"She saw Alan drop his rod and tackle box and hurl himself down the promontory. Saw him leap a chasm, miss his footing, and fall. He struggled to get up and fell back again, seemingly unable to rise. Aghast at the suddenness of it, she stood by the car and watched him, while the wind swept the empty canoe toward the far end of the lake.

"He must have seen her in the yard then. Seemingly with great effort he struggled to one knee and waved to her. Probably he was calling to her as well, but with the rushing sound of the wind in the pines, and now a clatter of pelting rain, she could not hear him. Suddenly she saw that he was waving something white—it must be his shirt—in an apparently desperate effort to attract her attention.

"Myra hesitated. She was a deeply loving woman, and she adored this man. And in spite of her mother's letter she could not be *sure*. But if this were a trick—and it could be a trick—her life hung in the balance.

"He could easily have only pretended to tie the canoe, leaving it so it would drift away with the first puff of wind. Why, in the first place, had he carried both the canoe and the rowboat from the boathouse? And why, if he had gone to the island to fish, had he climbed to the top of the ledge where she would be sure to see him when he fell?

"It had to be a trick. Wrenching her gaze from the fluttering white shirt, Myra flung herself into the car and drove wildly down the road.

"She had to walk the last eleven miles of that nightmare road, for in her panic she lost control of the car and wrecked it against a stump. When she reached the village she was exhausted and hysterical, and night had fallen. Alan was close behind her, she was certain. She *must* find a place to hide.

"She hired a fellow in the village to drive her to the nearest good-sized town, where she took a room at a small hotel and phoned us. Ruth and I arrived just at daybreak, after driving all night.

"We had to know, of course, whether or not Alan was really marooned on the island, hurt by his fall. That was my job. Leaving Ruth with Myra at the hotel, I picked up the local police chief and we drove in there. We were more than an hour moving Myra's wrecked car off the logging road, so we could get past it.

"There was no one at the lodge. We rowed out to the island and there we found him, face down on the ledge, with his shirt still clutched in one hand. He was alive then, though unconscious. He died in my car, on the way out. Internal bleeding, they told us at the hospital. Had Myra brought him ashore when he signalled her, and driven him to a hospital then, he would have survived.

"So you see," Eric Carlson concluded, frowning across his study at me, "the big question remains unanswered. Did he mean to murder her or didn't he? Obviously he didn't mean the business to end as it did, but up to the point of the accident what were his intentions?"

"Poor girl," I said. "She did so many things wrong, didn't she?"

"Reason flees in the face of terror, George."

"Yes, of course. Is it true that his first wife fell overboard from a cruise ship?"

"It's true, but there's a question in that, too. She didn't drink—dear Mrs. Cartwright was correct in that—but she *was* a chronic sleepwalker and she *did* suffer from dizzy spells. And there's another thing. When we finally got Myra's car out of that place, we found some letters in the glove compartment. They were the letters she had given him to mail, including the all-important one to her lawyer. He hadn't posted them. Of course, he might have intended to, but forgotten."

"So she will never know."

"She will never know. And she loved him. She loved him dearly. George, tell me—you're a doctor—should I get rid of the pond? If she sits there day after day staring at it, as she does, will she some day decide to—make use of it?"

"Fill it in," I advised. "The sooner the better."

Woodland Burial

Frank Belknap Long

S OME SMALL ANIMAL of the night was making a rustling sound out on the front porch. Will Gage arose from the dinner table and crossed to the window, to see whether or not the squirrel he'd given some nuts to at sundown had come back for more. It had looked thin and bedraggled and he'd felt sorry for it, if only because it had reminded him so much of the woman he'd covered with freshly turned earth and raked-over leaves eight weeks previously.

He'd felt sorry for her, too, right up to the time she'd taken the last sip—quite possibly the fatal one—of the arsenic-laced tea.

It was the same squirrel and he had to admit that it reminded him a little of himself as well, particularly when his face stared back at him in the bathroom mirror upstairs, the shaving cream making his cheeks seem more puffed out than they actually were.

He wasn't cut out to be a lean man, he told himself, whether from worrying about Molly Tanner's extravagance and his fear of losing her, or just from not getting enough expensive steaks and good table wine to make every moment when Molly wasn't coiled up in bed at his side seem worth paying the toll.

She's late, he thought, and this separate cottage business has got to stop. Who's going to give a hoot now whether she stays here night and day? Not Sheriff Merril. Everyone knows he's keeping two women in separate cottages down at the Point, and he's been re-elected three times.

Do your job and do it well, and people look the other way. Nowadays, with the Bomb and the rising crime rate, it's twice as true as ever before. It's on everybody's mind that maybe tomorrow or the next day you won't be around to mind your neighbor's business—or your own. Higgety pop and whoosh—you're gone.

He suddenly became irritated with the squirrel for wanting two helpings of nuts in less than three hours. Going out on the porch, he picked up a rock and hurled it at the scrawny little beast, the stone smashing into it as it made a dive for the nearest tree.

He saw her then, emerging from the double row of pines on the opposite side of the clearing, the moonlight glimmering on the silver-textured scarf she had wrapped around her shoulders, more out of vanity, he was quite sure, than as a protection against the October night's increasing chilliness.

There had been times in the past when great vanity in a woman had not been entirely to his liking. But it mattered not at all with Molly, for she was shaped to perfection and had that certain added something—

Twenty years fell from Gage's shoulders, coiled up at his feet and died. He was a boy of twenty again and Molly was seventeen. Except that no seventeen-year-old Molly could have pleased him quite as much as the Molly he'd come to know.

A moment later she was in his arms. "Well . . ." he murmured. "Well . . ."

"I bet if we were together all day you wouldn't grab hold of me like that," she said. "Do you still love me? How much?"

"What kind of question is that?" he asked.

"The kind a woman always asks."

"Sure, I know. And the guy spreads his arms wide and gets off some spiel about how big the ocean is, and that's how it is with him. But not me. I'm not that kind of sentimental kook."

"Couldn't you be that kind of a kook . . . just once."

"Come off it, Molly. You know damn well that every time I wrap my arms around you, tight like this, I can't think of anything to say. Maybe later . . ."

"You never say anything later either. You're such a strange, silent man."

"Who'd want to do any talking when—"

"You'd be surprised."

"What's that supposed to mean? I'm not a jealous man, but you'd better be careful. Don't run the number up too high."

"Have I ever?"

"I wouldn't put talking about it beyond you. But you're sensible enough to know it doesn't take more than a carelessly dropped hint or two in that direction to set a man off."

"How do *you* know I wouldn't *like* you to rough me up a little?"

"Stop talking nonsense. I've never struck a woman in my life."

Gage was amused, despite himself, by how true that was. Basically he was a kind and gentle man. He'd even wanted to go down on his knees, stroke his wife's hair and beg her to forgive him for putting a little too much arsenic in her tea.

"Let's go inside," Molly said. "It's getting chillier by the minute out here."

"I'll mix you a bourbon and soda," Gage said. "I went into town today and bought some new blankets. The soft, baby-wool kind— nice to cuddle under. You'll like them."

"What color are they?"

"Did you ever see a robin's egg?"

"Oh, that *is* nice," she said. "Robin's egg blue. That's my favorite color."

They went inside, and Gage hummed a few lines from the Little Sonata in C Minor while he mixed her a drink and carried it to her on a tray, jarring it a little to make the ice cubes clink, a sound he always enjoyed.

"I don't like to drink even the first one alone," Molly said. "You forget so many little things a woman treasures. But I'll forgive you this time if you fix yourself a stiff one quick and bring it over here before the chill settles into my very bones."

"That was my idea," Gage said, grinning. "You said it was cold outside. Why don't you gulp that down and let it warm you. Then we'll have the rest together and go on from there."

"You're not such a silent man after all," Molly said, patting his cheek. "Get one for yourself. I'll wait."

They had several drinks together as the evening wore on and the grandfather clock said it was ten minutes to eleven.

"I'm getting sleepy," Gage said, at last.

"So am I," Molly said. "There seems to be a strong bond of empathy between us."

A half hour later Gage was telling himself that if there were nights to remember this was certainly one of them. Molly knew how to please a man in so many different ways that he had the feeling at times that he was holding in his arms some phantom woman who might at any moment vanish in the night, if it had not been impossible for him to doubt her flesh-and-blood reality. There were delights in lovemaking which Molly alone had mastered to perfection, and there were times when her kisses seemed to burn their way through his lips into his brain. She moved away from him at last with a still rapturous sigh, and he was content to let her physical closeness recede, since no man could remain forever raised high above the earth amid revolving beams of loin-dissolving fire.

How long he slept he had no way of knowing. He could only be sure that the night had passed and that the darkness had been replaced by the first bright flush of dawn.

He had never been a light sleeper and few men were more beholden to sleep for long hours of blissful forgetfulness, untroubled by dreams of any kind. But he was also quick to awaken, with little of the drowsy feeling of unreality that can make familiar objects seem to blur and run together for a considerable period of time.

His hand had gone out for an instant to feel around under the sheets until it encountered a motionless form that was ice-cold to his touch. But a full realization of what that coldness could have implied occurred almost simultaneously with so acute a sharpening of his faculties that his head jerked backward and he sat bolt upright, tossing the sheets aside. The robin's-egg blue blanket went as well, it being as crumpled as the sheets and just as dark with stains, as if it had been carried outside and trampled in rain-splashed earth before being returned to the bed. Strangulation, if it has been slowly and not too violently applied, does not always distort the human countenance into a hideously grimacing mask. But Molly Tanner's face had been spared nothing in that respect. Her eyes bulged from their sockets and stared sightlessly up at him and her mouth was so twisted and convulsed that it was impossible to think of it as having been normally formed at any time in the past.

The long, matted strands of ash-blond hair that had been used as a noose had been drawn so tightly about Molly Tanner's throat that most of them were embedded in her flesh. But enough remained visible to make it impossible for Gage to doubt that it was the exact shade of the hair that he had gone on admiring in his wife when the rest of her attractiveness had dwindled to the vanishing point.

There are horrors too ghastly to be sanely endured, or, at the very least, as sanity-endangering as a cobra poised to strike with all avenues of escape blocked off, the great head with its swollen, pulsating hood weaving back and forth. Gage knew that there were only two courses open to him. He could leap from the bed and stagger about, his terror finding vent in shriek after shriek. Or he could hold the horror at bay just long enough to escape from the cottage and go plunging through the woods, to seek immediate confirmation—absolute proof—that his mind and the evidence of his eyes had conspired to betray him in some way. It was precisely that latter course he chose.

Despite a violent trembling he managed to get dressed, struggling into the dungarees and flannel shirt he'd thrown across a chair in his haste to get undressed when there had still been a living Molly to make haste meaningful. In another moment he was crossing to the porch in the heavy boots he'd dragged out from under the bed, turning back just once to glance again at her lifeless form in the wildly irrational way some people have of inflicting needless torment on themselves.

Outside the cottage the dawnlight could hardly have been brighter, but it had rained during the night and he had to slosh through a wide pool of water to get to the tool shed at the edge of the forest, and the heavy shovel and small trowel he felt he might be needing. The trowel he thrust into the hip pocket of his dungarees as he might have done with a pistol, but he had in mind a far more sinister use for it than merely killing someone. Prepared now, he headed off. He knew exactly where to go, even though a gloom enveloped the forest against the brightness of the dawn, and that no visible path remained from his journey of eight weeks ago with his limp and not-very-heavy burden. It angered him still, despite the black horror that continued to clutch at his throat, that his wife had allowed herself to become so thin and unattractive in the months following their marriage. It was almost as if she had done it to spite him because of their numerous quarrels and her ungovernable temper. It was no way to treat a man who was by nature thoughtful and tender-minded.

It took him less than five minutes to traverse the distance from the cottage to where he had deposited her. The instant the site came into view all of the horror he'd experienced on awakening swept over him again.

The site itself looked very much as he'd thought it might. Eight weeks can bring about many changes. Carefully raked over leaves and branches are certain to be displaced to some extent by the scampering feet of small forest animals. Small mounds of earth may be born as a result of torrential rains and subsequent channels carrying off the water. These small modifications, though, were not what made him stand transfixed at the far end of the site. His momentary paralysis came from the immediate recognition of an object that protruded from a small mound of dirt. It was twisted and mud-spattered and had lost all of the silver-textured beauty which it had possessed last night when it had been wrapped around Molly Tanner's shoulders. Still, it was the same scarf, beyond any possibility of doubt.

He thought he knew why an attempt had been made to carry it down into the charnel darkness of the pit where what had once been a woman lay mouldering. It had been to her a token, a trophy, a symbol of triumph over a rival and of retribution against the man who had once been her beloved husband. For a moment longer Gage remained transfixed, unable to move or cry out in protest at the monstrous injustice that had been done to him. Then he stepped back, raised the shovel, and started digging.

He was still digging furiously, throwing up great clods of earth when Sheriff Merril stepped out from between the trees where the shadows clustered thickly. He was accompanied by Lou Evans, who acted as his deputy when he wasn't clerking at Tilman's hardware store.

"What are you doing here, Will?" Merril asked, advancing swiftly. "It's quite a surprise, I must say, although we were about to pay you a visit before we got sidetracked."

Gage straightened, letting the shovel remain buried in the earth and looking at the sheriff in so wildly distraught a way that Merril seemed to feel it might be wiser to go right on talking.

"We were on our way just now to ask you a few more questions about your wife's disappearance when something rather astounding happened."

"Something—" Gage seemed almost unaware that he had spoken, for his gaze was riveted on the sheriff's face with a close to manic intensity.

"Astounding, yes. There was a persistent chattering sound overhead, almost a calling to us. When Evans looked up he saw that a squirrel was moving swiftly about on one of the lower branches. It almost purposefully dropped something to us that it had been gnawing on. Let Will see it, Lou. I'm sure it will be of interest to him."

Evans spoke then, for the first time. "After the squirrel dropped its burden, it ran to this clearing. And once you see what it dropped, you'll know why we postponed our call and started searching in the woods for the stop it must have come from. Funny thing, though. If Mr. Gage has to dig so deeply to unearth what's buried here, it's hard to see how a squirrel could have gotten to it. Maybe that squirrel found it somewhere else . . . but that's crazy—"

"You can say that again," Merril grunted. "Just show him what the squirrel dropped."

Gage's hand went out automatically to receive the object Evans placed on his palm.

It was an almost fleshless human finger, one with just enough sinew left to hold it together. On it, just below the bony knuckle joint, was a golden wedding ring Gage knew well.

The trembling of *his* hand was the last and only motion Gage made before he crashed to the ground in a dead faint.

Merril shook his head, and his hand darted to his hip. "I never saw a wife killer look quite so peaceful," he said, after a moment of tight-lipped silence. "But I guess I'd better put the cuffs on him, just to be on the safe side."

Acknowledgments

"40 Detectives Later" by Henry Slesar. Copyright © 1986 by Henry Slesar. Reprinted by permission of the author.

"600 W" by Basil Wells. Copyright © 1945 by Basil Wells. Reprinted by permission of the author.

"Action" by David J. Schow. Copyright © 1990 by David J. Schow. All Rights Reserved. Reprinted by permission of the author.

"All the Angles" by Basil Wells. Copyright © 1954 by Basil Wells. Reprinted by permission of the author.

"All-Star Team" by Jon L. Breen. Copyright © 1987 by Jon L. Breen. Reprinted by permission of the author.

"Art Is Anything You Can Get Away With" by Stefan Jackson. Copyright © 1990 by Stefan Jackson. Reprinted by permission of the author.

"Aunt Dolly" by Ardath Mayhar. Copyright © 1992 by Ardath Mayhar. Reprinted by permission of the author.

"Blank . . ." by Harlan Ellison. Copyright © 1957, 1985 by Harlan Ellison. Reprinted by arrangement with, and permission of, the Author and the Author's agent, Richard Curtis Associates, Inc., New York, USA. All Rights Reserved.

"Bless Us O Lord" by Ed Gorman. Copyright © 1992 by Ed Gorman. Reprinted by permission of the author.

"Boomerang" by Hugh B. Cave. Copyright © 1939 by the Frank A. Munsey Company. Reprinted by permission of the author.

"Close Calls" by John T. Lutz. Copyright © 1978 by Davis Publications, Inc. Reprinted by permission of the author.

"The Cobblestones of Saratoga Street" by Avram Davidson. Copyright © 1964 by Avram Davidson. Reprinted by permission of the Executrix for the author's Estate, Grania Davis.

"Come Clean" by Donald Wandrei. Copyright © 1938 by Pro-Distributors Publishing Co., Inc. Reprinted by permission of Harold Hughesdon.

"Counterplot" by Francis M. Nevins, Jr. Copyright © 1980 by Francis M. Nevins, Jr. Reprinted by permission of the author.

"The Creek, It Done Riz" by Ardath Mayhar. Copyright © 1991 by Ardath Mayhar. Reprinted by permission of the author.

"Crime Wave In Pinhole" by Julie Smith. Copyright © 1980 by Julie Smith. Reprinted by permission of the author.

"Crowbait" by Everett Webber. Copyright © 1948 by Popular Publications, Inc. All Rights Reserved. Reprinted by arrangement with Argosy Communications, Inc.

"The Dark Hour" by Morris Hershman. Copyright © 1996 by Renown Publications, Inc. Reprinted by permission of the author.

"The Dead Woman" by David Keller. Copyright © 1932 by David Keller. Reprinted by permission of the Executor for the author's Estate, John P. Trevaskis.

"Deadhead Coming Down" by Margaret B. Maron. Copyright © 1978 by Margaret Maron. Reprinted by permission of the author.

"Death Double" by William F. Nolan. Copyright © 1963, 1991 by William F. Nolan. Reprinted by permission of the author.

"Desert Pickup" by Richard Laymon. Copyright © 1970 by Richard Laymon. Reprinted by permission of the author.

"Dramatic Touch" by Donald Wandrei. Copyright © 1934 by Street and Smith Publications, Inc. Reprinted by permission of Harold Hughesdon.

"The Encyclopedia Daniel" by Fred Chappell. Copyright © 1996 by Fred Chappell. Reprinted by permission of the author.

"Eyewitness" by Wilbur S. Peacock. Copyright © 1945 by Popular Publications, Inc. All Rights Reserved. Reprinted by arrangement with Argosy Communications, Inc.

"Fin de Siècle" by Joyce Carol Oates. Copyright © 1988 by the Ontario Review, Inc. Reprinted by permission of the author.

"Fixing Mr. Foucher's Fence" by Todd Mecklem. Copyright © 1994 by Todd Mecklem. Reprinted by permission of the author.

"Four-in-Hand" by William Relling Jr. Copyright © 1989 by William Relling Jr. Reprinted by permission of the author.

"Fresh Thuringer Today" by Leo R. Ellis. Copyright © 1964 by H. S. D. Publications. Reprinted by permission of Larry Sterning/Jack Byrne Agency.

"Hi, Mom!" by William F. Nolan. Copyright © 1992 by William F. Nolan. Reprinted by permission of the author.

"Hiding Place" by Basil Wells. Copyright © 1956 by Basil Wells. Reprinted by permission of the author.

"High Heels in the Headliner" by Wendy Hornsby. Copyright © 1994 by Wendy Hornsby. Reprinted by permission of the author.

"His Beard Was Long and Very Black" by Stewart Toland. Copyright © 1944 by Popular Publications, Inc. All Rights Reserved. Reprinted by arrangement with Argosy Communications, Inc.

"Homesick" by Richard T. Chizmar. Copyright © 1997 by Richard T. Chizmar. Reprinted by permission of the author.

"Hound of Justice" by Thomas A. Hoge. Copyright © 1939 by Popular Publications, Inc. All Rights Reserved. Reprinted by arrangement with Argosy Communications, Inc.

"I Could Kill You" by Judith Merril. Copyright © 1952, 1980 by Judith Merril. Reprinted by permission of the author's Estate and the Estate's agent, Virginia Kidd.

"Johnny Halloween" by Norman Partridge. Copyright © 1992 by Norman Partridge. Reprinted by permission of the author.

"Killer Cop" by Morris Hershman. Copyright © 1958 by Morris Hershman. Reprinted by permission of the author.

"Last of Kin" by Jo Bannister. Copyright © 1994 by Jo Bannister. Reprinted by permission of the author.

"The Last Pin" by Howard Wandrei. Copyright © 1940 by Pro-Distributors Publishing Company, Inc. Reprinted by permission of the Harold Hughesdon.

"Like Father, Like Son" by Richard T. Chizmar. Copyright © 1997 by Richard T. Chizmar. Reprinted by permission of the author.

"Listen" by Joe R. Lansdale. Copyright © 1983 by Joe R. Lansdale. Reprinted by permission of the author.

"A Little More Research" by Joan Hess. Copyright © 1990 by Davis Publications, Inc. Reprinted by permission of the author.

"Locking Up" by John Maclay. Copyright © 1986 by John Maclay. Reprinted by permission of the author.

"The Longest Pleasure" by C. J. Henderson. Copyright © 1998 by C. J. Henderson. Reprinted by permission of the author.

"The Man Who Was Everywhere" by Edward D. Hoch. Copyright © 1957, 1985 by Edward D. Hoch. Reprinted by permission of the author.

"The Marrow of Justice" by Hal Ellson. Copyright © 1963 by Renown Publications, Inc. Reprinted by permission of the agent for the author's Estate, Scott Meredith Literary Agency.

"Mercy Killing" by Dale Clark. Copyright © 1939 by Popular Publications, Inc. All Rights Reserved. Reprinted by arrangement with Argosy Communications, Inc.

"Murder" by Joyce Carol Oates. Copyright © 1992 by The Ontario Review, Inc. Reprinted by permission of the author.

"Murder Blooms" by Charles R. Fritch. Copyright © 1979 by Charles R. Fritch. Reprinted by permission of the author's agent, Forrest Ackerman, The Ackerman Agency, 2495 Glendower Avenue, Hollywood, CA 90027-1110.

"Murder in the Fourth Dimension" by Clark Ashton Smith. Copyright © 1930 by Clark Ashton Smith. Reprinted by permission of the author and the author's agents, JABberwocky Literary Agency, P.O. Box 4558, Sunnyside, NY 11104-0558.

"Murder on My Mind" by Charles Beckman Jr. Copyright © 1949 by Popular Publications, Inc. All Rights Reserved. Reprinted by arrangement with Argosy Communications, Inc.

"A Nice Save" by Edward Wellen. Copyright © 1993 by Edward Wellen. Reprinted by permission of the author.

"The Night the Rat Danced" by George William Rae. Copyright © 1947 by Popular Publications, Inc. All Rights Reserved. Reprinted by arrangement with Argosy Communications, Inc.

"Old Charlie" by Joe R. Lansdale. Copyright © 1984 by Joe R. Lansdale. Reprinted by permission of the author.

"Oldest Living Serial Killer Tells All" by John R. Platt. Copyright © 1995 by John R. Platt. Reprinted by permission of the author.

"Omit Flowers" by Morris Hershman. Copyright © 1957 by Morris Hershman. Reprinted by permission of the author.

"Ormond Always Pays His Bills" by Harlan Ellison. Copyright © 1957, renewed 1985 by Harlan Ellison. Reprinted by arrangement with, and permission of, the Author and the Author's agent, Richard Curtis Associates, Inc., New York, USA. All Rights Reserved.

"The Pattern" by Bill Pronzini. Copyright © 1971 by HSD Publications. Reprinted by permission of the author.

"The Phone Call" by Roman A. Ranieri. Copyright © 1996 by Roman A. Ranieri. Reprinted by permission of the author.

"Posthumous" by Joyce Carol Oates. Copyright © 1995 by The Ontario Review, Inc. Reprinted by permission of the author.

"The Price of the Devil" by J. L. French. Copyright © 1997 by John L. French. Reprinted by permission of the author.

"The Queen of Corpses" by Costa Carousso. Copyright © 1940 by Popular Publications, Inc. All Rights Reserved. Reprinted by arrangement with Argosy Communications, Inc.

"Remains to Be Seen" by Jack Ritchie. Copyright © 1961 by HSD Publications. Reprinted by permission of the agent for the author's Estate, the Larry Sternig/Jack Byrne Agency.

"The Right Kind of a House" by Henry Slesar. Copyright © 1984 by Henry Slesar. Reprinted by permission of the author.

"The Rod and the Staff" by Donald Wandrei. Copyright © 1937 by Pro-Distributors Publishing Company, Inc. Reprinted by permission of the Harold Hughesdon.

"The Scent of Murder" by Jack Byrne. Copyright © 1992 by Heinrich Bauer North America. Reprinted by permission of the author and his agent, the Larry Sternig/Jack Byrne Agency.

"The Shill" by Stephen Marlowe. Copyright © 1955 by Stephen Marlowe. Reprinted by permission of the author.

"Something for the Dark" by John Lutz. Copyright © 1977 by Davis Publications, Inc. Reprinted by permission of the author.

"Something Like Murder" by John Lutz. Copyright © 1977 John Lutz. Reprinted by permission of the author.

"The Stocking" by Ramsey Campbell. Copyright © 1968 by Ramsey Campbell. Reprinted by permission of the author.

"The Tennis Court" by Brenda Melton Burnham. Copyright © 1994 by Brenda Melton Burnham. Reprinted by permission of the author.

"The Tin Ear" by Ron Goulart. Copyright © 1966 by HSD Publications, Inc. Reprinted by permission of the author.

"Today's Special" by Dennis Etchison. Copyright © 1972 by Dugent Publications Corp., renewed 1982 by Dennis Etchison. Reprinted by permission of the author.

"Triple Indemnity" by Charles E. Fritch. Copyright © 1979 by Charles E. Fritch. Reprinted by permission of the author's agent, Forrest Ackerman, The Ackerman Agency, 2495 Glendower Avenue, Hollywood, CA 90027-1110.

"Twine" by Edward D. Hoch. Copyright © 1975 by Edward D. Hoch. Reprinted by permission of the author.

"Two Inches in Tomorrow's Column" by Harlan Ellison. Copyright © 1965, renewed 1993 by Harlan Ellison. Reprinted by arrangement with, and permission of, the Author and the Author's agent, Richard Curtis Associates, Inc., New York, USA. All Rights Reserved.

"Tyrannosaurus" by Norman Partridge. Copyright © 1994 by Norman Partridge. Reprinted by permission of the author.

"The Vital Element" by Talmage Powell. Copyright © 1967 by Davis Publications, Inc. Reprinted by permission of the author.

"Walks" by Joe R. Lansdale. Copyright © 1997 by Joe R. Lansdale. Reprinted by permission of the author.

"Whodunit" by Michael A. Black. Copyright © 1997 by Michael A. Black. Reprinted by permission of the author.

"Will Lunch Be Ready on Time?" by Elizabeth Engstrom. Copyright © 1992 by Elizabeth Engstrom. Reprinted by permission of the author.

"Win Some, Lose Some" by Jack Ritchie. Copyright © 1991 by Davis Publications. Reprinted by permission of agents for the author's Estate, Larry Sternig/Jack Byrne Agency.

"The Woman at the Pond" by Hugh B. Cave. Copyright © 1964 by Renown Publications, Inc. for Mike Shayne Mystery Magazine, January 1964.

"Woodland Burial" by Frank Belknap Long. Copyright © 1981 by Frank Belknap Long. Reprinted by permission of the agent for the author's Estate, Kirby McCauley.